My One
and NEVER
Done

A Honeysuckle Creek Novel

Macee McNeill

ISBN 978-1-66783-357-6
eBook ISBN 978-1-66783-358-3

Books
by
Macee McNeill

<u>Finch Family Series</u>

Once and Forever

Unmasking the Heart

My One and Never Done

DEDICATION

To Spencer, my younger son,

I'm blessed to be your mom!

Love you to the moon!

ACKNOWLEDGEMENTS

Thanks to:

My hilarious husband, for his oh-so-helpful suggestions for my books even though he has no idea what I'm writing about.

My ever-supportive family, even though they like pie better than cake.

Tess, for staying up late "to find out what happens next" even though her three-year-old has a no-daytime-naps policy.

Jann, for her endless encouragement and for not hanging up the phone when I've had too much caffeine.

Christina—always a joy—and the rest of Bookbaby's fabulous staff.

God, for loving me anyway.

I cannot fix on the hour, or the spot, or the look,
or the words, which laid the foundation.
It is too long ago.
I was in the middle before I knew that I had begun.
—Pride and Prejudice by Jane Austen

Contents

PROLOGUE

Newport, Rhode Island
May 2018

"*M*allory is going to kill me."

Diana Merritt spoke the words aloud. She had never...*never*...been this late for work. *Drat.* She felt like smacking her head against the steering wheel in frustration, a far less painful activity than listening to Mallory rant. Sighing heavily, she forced herself from the sanctuary of her car.

To Diana's credit, she *had* left the meeting as soon as good manners allowed. It wasn't *her* fault that her publisher was the most loquacious woman ever to walk the face of the earth. That pertinent fact, however, meant nothing to Mallory as it implied that *she* was less important than, well...than anyone. The complete self-absorption of Diana's difficult employer was nothing new. She often found herself on the receiving end of Mallory's caustic tongue. The familiar nasally voice echoed through her mind: *Why am I—the* very important *wife of the* very important *head of the legal department of McCallum Industries—forced to employ a clearly inferior nanny like you, Diana?*

Mallory was as fond of asking that question as she was of answering it. She positively loved reminding Diana that the *only* reason Diana still had a job was because Mallory and Devin felt sorry for her. Diana was Devin's first cousin, after all, and *someone* had to take care of her. Blah, blah, blah…

Diana was used to Mallory's disdain. Well, she liked to pretend she was used to it. Did anyone ever grow accustomed to hateful and malicious words? No matter, she decided. She would deal with much worse for the sake of a blond, blue-eyed imp named Amalie.

Barely glancing at Mallory's Porsche, Diana hurried up the sidewalk, suddenly anxious to make sure the little girl was safe. Mallory's supervision was the same as no supervision at all. And Diana knew from experience just how much mischief one five-year-old could create while her nanny was away. She felt a twinge of unease as she walked up the steps to the *very elegant* portico of the *very impressive, waterfront* townhouse on the *very exclusive* end of Harrison Avenue.

Diana punched in the code to unlock the door. Bracing herself for Mallory's explosive displeasure, she turned the knob and pushed.

The foyer was empty.

"Mallory, I'm finally here," she called. "Sorry I'm late. I had no idea that my meeting would run so long."

Without waiting for a reply, Diana shut the front door. After a brief search, she found her phone on the bottom of her overly large tote bag. Why, she wondered absently, was her phone always so hard to find? She crossed the foyer and opened the door to the coat closet. She hung the heavy tote bag on the hook beside Mallory's newest obsession…a black leather Galleria handbag by Prada.

Phone in hand, Diana stepped into the foyer expecting the worst. But Mallory was not there waiting to gleefully castigate her errant nanny. She was not in the hallway, either. Nor did she swoop out of her sitting room like a demon bent on vengeance.

"Mallory," Diana called, raising her voice slightly this time. She stepped back to close the door to the coat closet then continued down the hallway toward the den at the back of the townhouse. "Mallory, I'm here. I'm sorry I'm so late."

Silence.

"Mallory?" Diana stepped into the den. Hmm. This was strange. "Amalie," she called, changing tactics. "Nanny Di's here. Where are you, sweetie?"

But no little girl giggles echoed from behind the curtains. And no nasty innuendos flew from the mouth of her mother.

Nothing but complete and utter silence.

Diana frowned, racking her brain. Wasn't she supposed to take care of Amalie today? Had *she* forgotten something important? Where was everybody? She checked the French doors that led onto the patio, just to make sure nobody had stepped outside. As usual, the doors were locked. Her eyes took in the vista in front of her. The puffy clouds and peaceful expanse of Newport Harbor—currently dotted with sailboats—offered no answers.

She retraced her steps to the foyer. Mallory's heinous friends must have picked her up for another expensive shopping expedition. And, Diana surmised, she had to take Amalie along because *her nanny* was late. *Drat.* That's why Mallory's car was still in the parking lot.

Two seconds later, Diana discarded her theory. *No way* would Mallory go anywhere without showing off her brand-new—and ridiculously expensive—Prada bag. The one currently hanging in the coat closet.

Diana sighed, slumping down onto the plush loveseat across from Mallory's *by-invitation-only* sitting room. She checked her phone again to be sure she hadn't missed a reply to the *I'm-sorry-but-I'm-going-to-be-late* text she sent the minute her meeting had ended. Mallory—whose phone could well be counted as another appendage—usually texted back immediately, whether she was angry or not. Not so, this time.

Diana blew out a little breath of frustration. What was a nanny to do? She had no idea whether she was supposed to wait for Amalie or return to her own apartment. She didn't even feel guilty about arriving late for work anymore. Well, maybe a little.

She wasn't supposed to call Mallory unless—in her employer's own words—*someone important dies*. So, she would just have to call Devin. She hated to bother him at work, but…

Diana sat straight up as her brain finally kicked in. How could she have forgotten? Devin had flown to Virginia earlier that morning. He was headed to the family law firm in Alexandria for a meeting with Diana's brother to discuss some unexpected business. And, knowing Devin, he probably took Amalie with him. *Awww…how sweet.* Diana couldn't help but smile. Devin was such a good dad. And, of course, that would leave Mallory free to go out with her friends. Diana breathed a sigh of relief. Everything made sense now.

Or did it? She couldn't seem to shake the feeling that something wasn't quite right. Devin hadn't once mentioned taking Amalie with him when he texted his plans for the day. And there was the matter of the Prada bag….

That handbag made her decision for her. Diana called Devin. But the call went straight to Devin's voicemail, something that rarely happened. *It figures.* Diana groaned, knowing she was out of options. *Drat.* She was going to have to call Mallory.

As she waited for the little-used number to ring, she tried to prepare herself for the ugly outburst that was sure to follow. She was not prepared, however, for what happened next.

Mallory's phone rang.

Across the hall.

In her sitting room.

Diana nearly jumped out of her skin at the sound. Mallory's phone was *not* ringing in her perfectly manicured hand at a fancy restaurant. It was *not* even ringing in her new Prada bag in the coat closet. It was ringing in her sitting room.

Her. Sitting. Room.

And if Mallory's phone was ringing in Mallory's sitting room, then that meant that Mallory was…

Diana's eyes flew across the hall, noticing for the first time that the habitually locked door stood slightly ajar. Before she had time to reconsider, her hand was on the forbidden room's doorknob.

"Mallory," she said, softly. "Are you in there? Is everything all right?"

The phone stopped ringing as Diana's unanswered call headed to Mallory's voicemail. There was no sound at all except for the pounding of Diana's heart. Which was loud enough to wake the dead. She opened the door.

The phone was lying on Mallory's desk against the west wall. A still sweating champagne bottle—a little less than half full—stood beside it. Diana frowned in confusion. Mallory was so obsessed with her antique desk that she would never...*never*...place a sweating bottle of champagne on its pristine surface. Something was very, very wrong. Diana shivered, involuntarily

She turned, slowly, letting her gaze sweep over the room. When her eyes reached the sofa on the east wall, she let out a soft gasp of surprise.

Mallory was stretched out on the lavish brocade cushions. She was wearing a low-cut black blouse and a pair of tight—and ridiculously expensive—designer jeans. Her feet were bare, devoid of the tiny sandals she usually wore to show off her perfectly manicured toes. She was also wearing a diamond necklace Diana had never seen before, likely another of the purchases Mallory seemed incapable of resisting.

Diana took a hesitant step toward her employer. Mallory's slender arm dangled over the side of the sofa. An empty champagne glass lay on the costly oriental rug as if she had carelessly dropped it when she dozed off. Or passed out. Diana felt fear rising in her throat. Mallory wasn't a big drinker. What could possibly have happened to make her drink half a bottle of champagne in the middle of the day?

As she came closer, Diana noticed an unlabeled pill bottle, half-hidden by the fancy flounce of the sofa. The bottle was open; some of the pills were scattered haphazardly on the carpet. The lid of the bottle was nowhere to be seen.

Pills? Diana's already pounding heart kicked into overdrive. Why would Mallory have pills when she regularly complained about her inability to swallow them? Even the tiny ones. Diana reached the sofa and touched Mallory's shoulder.

"Mallory," she said, urgently. "Wake up."

But Mallory didn't move, not even to flutter her long, fake eyelashes. Diana shook her employer's shoulder harder.

"Mallory!" her voice rose frantically. "Wake up, Mallory!"

No response.

Dropping her phone, Diana fell to her knees beside the still figure on the couch. She put her fingers on Mallory's dangling wrist to check for a pulse. She couldn't find one. She tried her neck. Still no pulse. She checked to see if Mallory was breathing. She wasn't. Diana sat back on her heels, paralyzed by the horrific reality.

Mallory. Was. Dead.

"*Amalie!*" Diana gasped. An image of the little girl, frightened and alone—or worse—thawed Diana's frozen limbs. She leapt to her feet, praying that Amalie was upstairs. And safe.

She flew into the hallway, slamming into a brick wall. No, not a wall. A man's chest. Even the shock of the collision couldn't deter Diana's single-minded quest to find the innocent child. She shoved the man, her mind refusing to acknowledge the threat. At that moment, he was nothing but an obstacle standing between her and Amalie.

The man grabbed her and spun her around so her back was to his front. He moved effortlessly and efficiently, placing one arm around her waist and one around her neck. He easily immobilized her, as if he did this sort of thing every day. The crook of his elbow pressed against her throat.

Diana panicked. She struggled, flailing against the man's hold. She tried to use her feet. Her legs. Anything she could think of. She had to get to Amalie. But her efforts did nothing to loosen the unbreakable embrace of the stranger.

No. Of the *murderer.*

He killed Mallory, she thought, hysterically. *And now he's going to kill me.* She opened her mouth to scream, but a little upward pressure from the man's arm stopped her from making a sound.

"You are quite a fighter," the man said, sounding almost pleased with her struggles.

That voice. Diana knew that voice. She had heard it before. She stopped struggling.

He twisted her a little, so they were facing the huge mirror beside the open door that led to Mallory's corpse. She stared at his face in the mirror in disbelief, unable to process exactly what was happening. Her mind whirled, trying to make sense of a familiar face in the wrong setting. He was talking, but she couldn't understand what he was trying to say. The roaring in her ears had taken the place of conversation.

The man unexpectedly released his hold on her. She stumbled to the wall, which she pressed against gratefully. Her tongue felt numb. Her whole face, actually. She was well on the way to passing out at the feet of the man who wasn't supposed to be there.

Diana forced herself to concentrate. She knew this man. And he wasn't a murderer at all. Bill Watkins was a friend. Although, she admitted to herself, maybe she didn't know him well enough to call him a friend. An acquaintance, then. Yes, she decided, that was a better fit. Bill Watkins was an acquaintance. Someone she saw occasionally at Aquidneck Park. In fact, she had *never* seen Bill anywhere but Aquidneck Park. Still, she acknowledged with some relief, he was an acquaintance who *wasn't* going to kill her. But even as her terror receded, questions remained. She had *never* given him her work address. How did he find her and…why now?

With a great effort, Diana forced herself to speak: "What are you doing here?" She heard the strain in her own voice.

"It was a coincidence," he explained, watching her. "I was training for a half-marathon and I heard screaming. The door was wide open. So, I came in to check it out. You know, to see if I could help."

Who was screaming? Diana's mind latched onto his words. *Was I screaming? I don't remember screaming.*

But before she could pursue that thought…

"Where's your phone?" Bill asked, still watching her face.

"What?" Mallory was dead on the sofa and *Mr.-I'm-Not-Where-I'm-Supposed-To-Be* wanted to borrow her phone?

"Where. Is. Your. Phone?" he enunciated slowly, as if she was too stupid to understand him.

Maybe she was.

"In there." She managed to push the words through her numb lips, pointing weakly in the direction of Mallory's body.

He walked quickly into the sitting room, returning with her phone. He thrust it into her hands and waited.

She gazed at her phone uncomprehendingly.

He snatched it from her hands, impatiently. He placed the phone back in her hand a few seconds later, closing her fingers around it.

"Talk," he demanded. "It's 9-1-1. Tell them what you found."

She tried to focus. She heard the woman on the phone asking what was wrong. But she couldn't seem to answer.

"Tell them that someone is dead," Bill urged, glancing at the wide-open front door.

"Someone is dead," Diana repeated.

Bill nodded, looking pleased.

The operator's calm response to Diana's initial statement, and her subsequent questions, loosened her paralyzed brain. She even managed to give the correct address of the townhouse to the patient woman. When the call ended, she realized that Bill was still looking at her as if she was a moron.

"Where's the little girl?" he finally snapped.

"What?" Diana looked at him with dawning comprehension. "Amalie…" she whispered in horror as her eyes filled with tears. How could she have forgotten the sweet child in her care? Suddenly, finding Amalie was more important than breathing. Leaving Bill in the foyer, she took the stairs two at a time, racing down the hall, only to discover that the door to Amalie's bedroom was locked…from the inside. The little girl had, apparently, locked herself in her room.

Diana almost panicked before she remembered the key Devin had set on top of the door frame for just such a purpose. She lifted her hand, thanking God she was tall enough to reach the door frame, and felt around until she found the key. Her hands were shaking so badly that it took several tries before she managed to insert the key into the lock. She opened the door and nearly wept with relief. The tail of Amalie's stuffed iguana was poking out from under the bed.

"Amalie," she whispered. "Amalie, are you under the bed?" *Please, please, please, Lord,* Diana prayed. *Please let my baby girl be under there.*

At the sound of Diana's voice, Amalie promptly burst into tears. But the little girl remained under the bed. Diana got down on her hands and knees. "Amalie. It's going to be all right. You can come out now." She forced herself to speak in a calm voice, even though she herself was anything but calm. Tears of relief were rolling down her cheeks unheeded.

The normally verbose child didn't speak a word. She flatly refused to move. The same could not be said, however, for the stuffed iguana, who appeared eager to come out from under the bed. Diana almost smiled as she watched Iggy's tail inch its way toward her. Soon his whole body was visible, although his traumatized owner was nowhere in sight.

"Oh, Iggy," Diana crooned, pulling him the rest of the way out. She sat back on her heels, hugging the iguana. "I'm so glad that you're all right. I was *so* worried about you. Thank you for taking care of Amalie."

Because little eyes were probably watching, Diana continued to address the iguana. "Do you think Amalie's ready to come out from under the bed?" Iggy stared back at her, serene as always, in spite of the unknown terrors he may have witnessed during the last few hours.

Diana held the iguana's mouth close to her ear for a few seconds. "What's that, Iggy? You want me to tell Amalie something? I'll be happy to." Out of the corner of her eye, she caught sight of one eye and a blond curl near the bottom edge of Amalie's pink Disney Princess comforter. Diana placed Iggy on the carpet then leaned over on her elbows so that she could look under the bed. Wide, blue eyes looked back at her.

"Amalie," Diana said, holding out her hand, "Iggy says 'be brave.' Can you do what Iggy says?" The familiar words from Diana's books managed to coax the child from under the bed and into her nanny's waiting arms.

They sat together on the floor of Amalie's bedroom—the now motherless five-year-old, her nanny, and a stuffed iguana named Iggy—until the police knocked on the door of the townhouse.

Diana never had a chance to thank Bill Watkins for helping her call 911.

By the time she came downstairs, he was gone.

CHAPTER ONE

Providence, Rhode Island
August 2018

*I*f Diana had to deal with one more overprotective male, she was going to scream. "It's a boat ride, Devin, not a trip to Vegas. I am going on a boat ride. Around the bay. With a friend. That's all."

"No," said Devin, adamantly. "I've never met this guy. And I don't think it's a good idea." He leaned back in his chair as if that settled everything.

He should have known better. Diana was seated right beside him, close enough for him to see the determination glowing in her eyes.

"You can't tell me what to do, Devin. You're not my boss." As soon as the words were out of her mouth, Diana wished them back.

Devin smiled cheekily. "Oh, but technically, I *am* your boss, Diana. At least, I think I am. Somebody gets an automatic deposit every two weeks from my bank account. The last time I checked that somebody was *you*."

Diana made a sound of frustration. "Honestly, Dev, you know exactly what I mean."

Devin continued as if she hadn't spoken: "And as your boss, I have to think of the welfare of *my* employee, not to mention what's best for *my* child." He paused, pretending to ponder the point. "I think it's in Amalie's best interest that you do *not* go to Newport today."

"What does Amalie have to do with this?" Diana asked, throwing up her hands.

Devin stopped grinning, suddenly serious. "All right. Forget I mentioned the little girl who adores her Nanny Di. Let's talk about *me*, then, Diana. Let's make it all about *me*. *I* don't want you to go."

Diana was irate at his high-handedness. "*You* don't want me to go? *You* are not my *dad* or my *brother*, Devin, and if I don't let *them* tell me what to do—"

"No, but I am your boss *and* your cousin," Devin interrupted.

"That is completely irrelevant," Diana objected, regarding her boss/cousin with narrowed eyes. "I already have an overprotective father *and* brother. I don't need an overprotective cousin, too."

Blane McCallum, CEO of McCallum Industries, chose that moment to join the conversation. Moving away from the arched windows that overlooked the flower beds in front of McCallum's North American headquarters, he casually walked to his enormous black desk.

Ignoring her infuriating cousin, Diana smiled at Blane across the desk's shiny surface. His office was large and impressive, she decided, rather like its commanding occupant. Far from being intimidated by the powerful man, she considered Blane something of an ally. He often took her side when Devin was being unreasonably overprotective. This time, however, his words made her frown.

"Devin is also your brother's best friend," Blane added, sinking into his enormous black desk chair. "I think that is very relevant."

Devin agreed with his boss immediately. "And, as Blane just reminded us, Diana, I'm Roman's best friend. In other words, I'm supposed to look out for you in his place. And that, my dear cousin, is very relevant." He turned to address his friend. "Thank you, Blane."

Blane nodded. "You're welcome."

They both regarded Diana hopefully.

Diana closed her eyes, striving for patience. The friends' concern wasn't completely unwarranted. Nearly three months had passed since she had discovered Mallory's lifeless body. According to the Newport authorities, an accidental drug overdose was the cause of death. The circumstances surrounding Mallory's death, however, didn't make sense to those who knew her well, leaving them with the disturbing suspicion that her death was *not* an accident.

Diana was aware her family expected her to be extra careful until all the questions were answered. Especially when dealing with strangers. So, she tried a different tactic. "I met my friend last fall in Aquidneck Park," she explained, calmly. "I remember because it was a couple of weeks after your wedding, Blane." She directed that bit of information to the man across the desk before turning toward her scowling cousin. "My friend and I have chatted—very casually, Devin—for months now. The guy's been nice to me. And he has a boat. Since I'm moving, this is the last time I'll see him. The. Last. Time." Since Devin's expression hadn't changed, Diana returned to Blane for the grand finale. "And I found out two days ago that my friend works at McCallum Industries. That means he works for *you*, Blane, so he can't be that much of a loser." She smiled, hoping they would appreciate her attempt at humor.

They didn't.

"What's your friend's name, Diana?" Blane asked. "Rafe can run a background check while Devin and I go to our meeting."

Rafe Montgomery—heretofore a silent presence—raised his eyebrows inquiringly. He was Blane's personal assistant, an expert in security issues. Blane's request pulled him away from his laptop—and his comfortable chair by the windows—forcing him to join the conversation.

"Bill Watkins," Diana said, hoping that would be the end of it. *A background check*, she fumed to herself. *Ridiculous*.

She stood up, hoisting her heavy tote bag onto her shoulder. She paused to admire her brand-new Apple Watch for a moment. According to the device, she still had plenty of time to make the thirty-minute drive to Newport. When she looked up, she was surprised to see Blane and Rafe regarding her intensely. Devin looked from one man to the other, as confused by their reaction as Diana.

Rafe spoke first. "You said your friend's name is Bill," he confirmed. "Do you know if Bill is the short form of something else? William, perhaps? Or Billix?"

Diana frowned. "I don't know," she said. "Maybe William?"

"Why would anyone name a child *Billix*?" Devin mused to no one in particular. "Sounds like some sketchy payday lending company to me."

"Are you sure he said Watkins and not Watson?" Blane asked, ignoring Devin. "You're sure he didn't say Billix Watson?"

"Bill Watkins," Diana reiterated. "I'm positive."

Rafe's tone was polite but brooked no argument. "Sit down, please, Diana. We need to ask you some questions."

Diana sighed as she sat down. Again. An exploding bomb would have garnered less of a reaction than the casual mention of her friend's name.

"Who is Billix Watson, anyway?" Devin couldn't seem to resist asking.

Blane sighed. "He was a student at the same boarding school I attended. He was something of a bully."

Rafe fixed Blane with a disapproving glare. "Billix Watson was the *psychotic thug* who nearly beat you to death, Blane," Rafe corrected.

Blane didn't deny Rafe's words.

Rafe switched his gaze to Diana's horrified expression. "And Blane was only twelve years old, Diana," he said softly.

"That's terrible," Diana gasped, instantly sympathetic.

Devin's eye gleamed with a militant light. "Whatever happened to Billix Watson, the psychotic thug?" he demanded, obviously ready to do battle for his friend. "Was he ever punished?"

Rafe easily evaded the question. "I haven't given him much thought since he was expelled from the school."

"Until now," Devin added, under his breath.

Diana saw her cousin raise his eyebrows at Blane in a silent question, but Blane merely shrugged. Apparently neither man believed Rafe's offhand reply, but neither was inclined to question the motives of the enigmatic man.

"One can never be too careful, Devin," Rafe stated, effectively ending that part of the discussion. Then, much to Diana's annoyance, he focused his complete attention on her.

"And now, Diana," he said, pleasantly. "About your friend..."

His inquisition was, in Diana's opinion, a pointless endeavor. She knew less than nothing about Bill Watkins, so she couldn't answer the majority of Rafe's very specific questions. She was willing to admit, at least to herself, that Bill was a little, well...odd. Yes, Diana decided, that was a good way to describe him. He was odd, but she certainly wouldn't call him a "psychotic thug." Besides, there had to be plenty of Bill Watkins—or Bill Watsons—in the world. And she was certain that every single one of them did not go around beating up twelve-year-old boys.

In the name of self-preservation, she chose to omit the fact that Bill Watkins helped her call 911 after she found Mallory's body. Diana wasn't ready to deal with the questions *that* would bring. Talk about an explosion. She had no doubt Blane and Rafe would freak out. Not to mention how Devin—her boss/cousin/brother's best friend—would react. She simply couldn't handle it. She didn't even like to *think* about finding Mallory's body, much less *talk* about that terrifying day. She just wanted the whole thing to go away. In fact, she tried very hard to pretend it had happened to someone else.

She telegraphed a silent plea for intervention to Devin. Her cousin took the hint and stood up. "The meeting just started, Blane. Since it's *our* meeting, we probably ought to be there."

Blane nodded, his expression troubled. "Diana, until we can do a thorough background check on this Bill Watkins, I'd feel better if you didn't keep your date."

"It's not a date," Diana said emphatically.

"Your appointment, then," Blane amended, with a slight smile.

Rafe glared at Blane before addressing Diana. "It's just a precaution, Diana. We are *not* telling you what to do."

"Rafe's right, Di." Devin got the point. "I apologize. I shouldn't have acted like your boss," he admitted.

"Thank you," Diana said, slightly mollified.

"Even though I am." Devin grinned as an expression of supreme irritation returned to Diana's face. He had never been able to resist teasing his cousin. "We are *asking* you to be careful. That's all."

Diana relaxed. "I know." She looked at her three well-meaning watchdogs. "Don't worry," she promised. "I'll be careful."

CHAPTER TWO

Newport, Rhode Island
Two hours later

*D*iana paused when she reached Bowen's Wharf, impressed, as always, by the variety of boats in Newport Harbor. Beyond the harbor area lay gorgeous Narragansett Bay. In the past five years she had certainly taken advantage of all that Newport had to offer. She would carry with her memories of afternoons on the Cliff Walk with its lovely view of the Atlantic Ocean, the impressive mansions on neighboring Bellevue Avenue, the shops, restaurants, and historic architecture on Thames Street, and the lovely bay. There was no doubt: she would miss this city.

She was, however, ready for a change. Moving to North Carolina would give her a fresh start *and* allow her to continue as Amalie's nanny. Life was funny like that, she mused. Just when it felt like everything was falling apart, it suddenly came back together. Better than before.

Her present vocation was still something of a surprise. Even to herself. If anyone had told her that five years after graduating from the University of Virginia she would be working as a nanny, she would have applauded his (or her) creativity. If anyone else had added that she would also be the author of a best-selling series of children's books loosely based on her experiences as a nanny, she would have laughed her head off.

She wasn't laughing now. She was incredibly blessed. And thankful. So very thankful. Because for several very long weeks after Mallory's funeral, she thought her time caring for the little girl she loved so much had come to an end. She remembered every word of the life-changing conversation she accidently overheard between her cousin, Devin, and Darcie Finch, the woman he intended to marry.

"There you are, you nosy iguana." Diana said. "I thought I'd find you hiding back there behind the curtains. Shame on you, Iggy." She automatically delivered her reprimand aloud, so ingrained was her habit of speaking for the benefit of Amalie. She sat down on the window seat, picking up the errant iguana. "I've missed hunting for you, Iggy."

The iguana's plastic eyes were full of sympathy.

Diana sighed, impatiently swiping away a tear. She hugged the iguana to her chest. "Oh, Iggy, I wish..."

She paused, listening as the sound of voices came closer. Drat. She didn't want to be found holding a stuffed iguana and crying in her father's office. Her life was already pathetic enough. She glanced at Iggy in alarm.

"Hide," he seemed to say.

Diana pulled up her feet to rest on the window seat. Now she was hiding behind the curtains on the advice of a stuffed iguana. Pathetic was an understatement.

"I can't believe Diana turned you down." Darcie's rich tones invaded the quiet office. "I am so disappointed. I was almost positive she would come with us."

The genuine bewilderment in Darcie's voice ignited a spark of hope in Diana. She listened, barely breathing.

Darcie continued: "Amalie is going to be devastated when we tell her. She's been so excited about seeing Diana again. What exactly did she say when you asked her, Devin?" Darcie seemed determined to get to the bottom of things. "What were Diana's reasons for not moving to Honeysuckle Creek with us?"

Devin let out a breath of frustration. "She didn't say anything, Darcie, because I didn't ask her."

"What?" Darcie asked in disbelief. "You didn't ask her? But, why, Dev? I don't understand. You said Diana was the best thing that ever happened to Amalie. And to you. Don't you want her to come with us?"

Diana's heart turned over. Darcie's words were the loveliest imaginable. But if that was the way Devin really felt, why hadn't he asked her to continue as Amalie's nanny?

"I didn't ask her because it isn't right, Darcie," Devin admitted, regret in his voice. "Asking her to come with us just isn't fair. She's given up five years of her life for Amalie and me. She—more than anyone else—took the brunt of Mallory's criticism and anger every day. She never complained and she never quit. Diana deserves the chance to have a life of her own."

Diana didn't try to stop the tears that were running down her cheeks. That was Devin…generous and unselfish to a fault. Didn't he know that being Amalie's nanny wasn't just a job? It was part of her heart. A very large part.

"Oh, Dev," Darcie sighed. "Your intentions are good, but Diana deserves the chance to make her own decisions." She raised her voice slightly. "Don't you, Diana?"

Diana froze, but it was no use. How had Darcie known she was behind the curtains? Diana glared at Iggy as if blame for the entire incident rested on the iguana's soft, fake fur-covered shoulders.

"Diana?" Devin said. "Are you back there?"

She heard his footsteps approaching across the wood floor. Without warning, he pulled the curtain back to reveal her not-so-clever hiding spot. She managed a wobbly smile as she unfolded herself from the window seat.

"Diana?" Devin asked. "Why are you hiding behind—"

She thrust the iguana into his hands as she stood up. "It was Iggy's idea," she said, calmly. If it worked for Amalie…

Devin looked at his cousin, a tiny smile tugging at the side of his mouth. "Now I see where Amalie gets it," he quipped.

Darcie, however, was more observant. "Diana, honey. Are you crying?" She closed the distance between them, peering at her friend's pale face.

"Not anymore." Diana smiled. "I obviously couldn't help but overhear, and…oh, Devin, Darcie, I would love to continue as Amalie's nanny, as long as you need me."

"Oh, thank God," Darcie squealed, throwing her arms around Diana. "You don't know how much we need you. There's no way Devin and I could possibly do this without you."

"Thank you, Di," was all that Devin said, but his eye was shiny as he, too, embraced his cousin.

Looking back Diana realized, once again, just how much she owed to Darcie Finch. She already loved Devin's almost-fiancée like a sister and would always be grateful for her timely intervention. Because of Darcie, Diana had so much to look forward to. She couldn't wait to put the past behind her, where it belonged.

That's why she stood on Bowen's Wharf, getting ready to tidy up the last of her loose ends before embarking on her new chapter. The accidental literary analogy caught her off guard. What did she expect? she asked herself with a chuckle. She was an author, after all.

A woman in a yellow sundress brushed by Diana, leaving behind the lovely aroma of the drink in her hand. *Mmm*, Diana thought, enviously. Coffee and caramel. Was there a better combination? She glanced at her Apple Watch, wondering whether she had enough time to run around the corner and duck into her favorite coffee shop. Their caramel iced latte was to die for. One *last* coffee on her *last* day in Newport to get her through her *last* meeting with Bill Watkins. It was a day for lasts, apparently. As usual, her busy writer's mind turned to potential titles for stories.

Nanny Di and the Last Goodbye.

She discarded that title quickly. It sounded too much like Nanny Di was headed straight for the funeral home. She tried again.

Nanny Di and the Last Latte.

That one had promise, she decided, as did an iced cup of caramel deliciousness. Now Diana *really* wanted that latte. She had a strong feeling she was going to need the extra jolt of caffeine. But before she could act on her impulse, she spotted Bill's boat, still some distance away. *Drat.* She might be able to get her latte and make it back in time, but she didn't want to take a chance. She couldn't quite bring herself to be rude, even though she was more than ready for Bill Watkins to become a long-forgotten memory.

As she watched his boat approach, Diana pondered their odd relationship. Her path had crossed frequently with his since the first day he jogged past her favorite park bench. That was last November. She and Amalie visited Aquidneck Park several times a week, and so, apparently, did Bill. But—except for one ill-advised meeting at a coffee shop—Diana had made sure their paths crossed *only* in the park.

It seemed harmless, at the time, to acknowledge an unknown runner when she was safely surrounded by children and adults of all ages. Diana always returned his silent greeting with a smile. One day, however, he joined her, awkwardly attempting to strike up a conversation. Diana took pity on him, volunteering a bit of harmless chatter to make him feel more comfortable. He was attentive. She was flattered. He appeared often after that or, at least, often enough to keep her from chalking up their run-ins to coincidence. Diana sighed. She should have discouraged Bill's interest early on; she knew that now. But his presence had always been a brief respite from the stress of working for the narcissistic and disparaging Mallory.

Bill's looks were unremarkable, in Diana's opinion. He wasn't unattractive, but he didn't have any defining features to make him stand out. In fact, there wasn't a single thing about him she would consider memorable. Even his clothes were nondescript. He wore dark hoodies when the weather turned cold and dark T-shirts when the cold retreated. He was the kind of person who could blend into the background and—if he wished to—disappear.

The lack of movie-star good looks wasn't a deal-breaker to Diana. She—of the unruly red hair and gray eyes—was certainly no movie star. Besides, looks weren't important when a guy had a good personality. Or wit. Or a kind and gentle nature. But…

Bill had none of these qualities. He wasn't a great conversationalist. He never expressed an opinion about anything. Politics. Sports. His favorite food. Bill had yet to reveal a single preference. Instead, he seemed content to ask *her* questions, listening patiently to *her* answers. He knew more about the cruel way Mallory treated her daughter's nanny than anyone else. But Diana soon realized there was absolutely nothing about Bill that made her heart quicken. She had experienced the effervescent thrill of romantic attraction once before. And she refused to settle for less.

Today, Bill was wearing black—she could see that much as his boat drew closer. No surprises there, she thought. His preference for black coupled with his long and wiry frame, pale skin, and dark hair gave him the appearance of a wraith…as if he might vanish right before her eyes. Diana assumed that Bill's life must be as devoid of color as his wardrobe. And his nonexistent personality. It was one more reason to feel sorry for him.

But trying to be extra nice because she felt sorry for Bill was how she had gotten herself into this situation in the first place. He had, unfortunately, confused kindness with something else. The signs of his romantic interest were right in front of her, but she hadn't noticed them until two weeks before Mallory's death, when Bill invited her for coffee. She didn't want to hurt his feelings, so she agreed. But she didn't meet him alone. She brought her cousin, Lydia—Devin's sister—as a subtle reminder that getting coffee wasn't a date. She hoped he would understand her unspoken message.

He didn't.

Diana was determined to correct that mistake. She was going to tell him she was leaving Newport. Today. After all, she thought, it was the considerate thing to do, especially after he helped her call 911. She was here for the express purpose of thanking him for his help. And letting him down as easily as possible.

As Bill's boat moved closer, Diana considered the forgotten details of that supremely awkward day at the coffee shop. Her first mistake, she realized, was agreeing to go at all. Her second was dragging Lydia along. Her cousin's general distrust of men was an unfortunate by-product of a violent ex-husband. Diana was surprised—and a little unnerved—by Lydia's genuine fear of the man who was buying their coffee. Lydia excused herself, almost immediately, with the flimsiest of excuses. After a few minutes of uncomfortable conversation with Bill, Diana followed her cousin outside. She hadn't thought much about Lydia's negative reaction that day. Until now. Suddenly, Diana wished she had paid more attention to her cousin's objections.

The closer Bill drew his boat to the dock the more Diana began to second guess herself. Maybe talking to him alone—*on a boat*—wasn't the best idea. What if he didn't take her goodbye well? What would she do if he got upset in the middle of Narragansett Bay? Maybe she should have arranged to meet him in the park, as always. Or at a coffee shop surrounded by people. *Lots* of people. Or, she thought regretfully, maybe not at all. *Drat*. It was too late to change her mind now.

Or was it? At present, there were three boats in front of Bill. A crowd of passengers waiting to board their respective crafts—two wearing enormous hats—blocked her from his view: he was so focused on navigating the busy port that he hadn't looked for her yet. Diana realized she did *not* have to get on that boat. She could turn around and walk away. She could avoid the whole scenario....

She thought about her conversation with Rafe, Blane, and Devin—*The Suspicious Three*. Diana frowned. The name didn't quite fit. She mulled it over in her head.

The Catastrophic Triad?

The Triumvirate of Trouble?

The Trio of Doom?

Yes, that sounded about right. Maybe she should listen to the Trio of Doom. She *had* promised them to be careful. She could always send Bill a letter, explaining that while she appreciated his friendship, it was time to move on and blah, blah, blah.

Great idea, Diana, she told herself sarcastically. But where would she send the letter? She almost groaned in frustration. She couldn't exactly have it delivered to "Bill Watkins, c/o the park bench near the playground equipment." That was the only address she knew. No, she decided, she had to say goodbye in person. She wasn't usually skittish, so she blamed her atypical uncertainty on the most logical source...the Trio of Doom. They had planted and watered the seeds of doubt in her mind. And now those seeds were starting to sprout.

Bill pulled into the dock with the ease of an expert. She watched as he jumped off the boat, tied a line to a cleat on the dock, and motioned for her to join him. He regarded her with a goofy-looking grin as she walked toward him.

"You look so pretty today."

"Um...thanks," Diana mumbled. She hadn't meant to look pretty. In fact, she had tried to dress casually, throwing on a skirt, a T-shirt, and a comfortable pair of sandals like she did on any other summer day. Easiest outfit ever. Her unruly, auburn hair was pulled back in a loose ponytail. And she was wearing her favorite wide-brimmed hat. She didn't want Bill to think she had gone to a lot of trouble. That would only exacerbate the problem.

She should have looked in the mirror. The light-colored material of her long, flowing skirt caught the breeze like butterfly wings. The hat was the perfect finishing touch. Lydia always complained that Diana would look stylishly put-together wearing a pillowcase. From the admiring look in Bill's eyes, it seemed that today, Lydia was right. Bill's expression reminded Diana of a puppy. Too eager and slightly pathetic.

Nanny Di and the Lovesick Puppy.

Drat. If the way the puppy was looking at her was any indication, the sooner she said goodbye, the better. She could only hope that when she did, the puppy didn't bite. She felt a new wariness in Bill's presence, as if she couldn't trust him. Who was Bill Watkins, anyway? She really didn't know anything about him. And now that she thought about it, he had never contributed anything to their conversations.

Not. One. Thing.

The Trusting Nanny and the Man They Warned Her About.

Bill stepped back on the boat, holding out his hand to help her aboard. But Diana hesitated. The sight of his arm—or maybe it was his elbow—triggered a memory she had successfully buried. Until now. She remembered all too clearly how he had grabbed her in Devin and Mallory's foyer. She knew exactly what that arm felt like…wrapped around her neck. Why, oh, why hadn't she thought of this before now?

Too many unanswered questions.

Too many inconsistencies.

Abort.

Abort.

She would later attribute her vacillation to an instinctive sense of self-preservation. "I'm dying for an iced latte," she said, smiling brightly. "Can we get one *before* we take the boat out?" She was suddenly eager to avoid the water.

Bill frowned. "Of course not," he said, in a clipped, impatient tone she had never heard him use before. "This is a transient dock and there are plenty of people waiting. We have to leave now."

Before she could react, he grabbed her hand, pulling her forward onto the boat.

CHAPTER THREE

*D*iana stumbled, but Bill caught her before she could fall. Something about the feel of Bill's long fingers on her waist caused her to step back quickly, recoiling from his touch.

I do not like this, she thought, racking her brain for an excuse to get off the boat.

"I don't think I should go out in a boat today," she heard herself saying. "I'm not feeling very well." She sounded a little desperate even to herself.

Bill ignored her protests. With his hand on the small of her back, he quickly propelled her to the boat's leaning post. But as soon as he went to the bow to untie the boat, Diana scooted to the opposite side. She wanted to sit as far away from Bill Watkins as possible.

When he returned to the leaning post, he frowned at her decision, but didn't say anything as he seated himself. Bill started the motor and the boat moved forward. Two seconds later he was grinning again. She had never noticed his lightning-fast changes of emotion before. He had bounced from goofy to impatient to goofy again in a matter of seconds. Was that normal? she wondered. Maybe, but not for him. She had never seen *any* emotion from him before. No emotion at all.

Calm down, she instructed herself. It was a harmless little boat ride in a very crowded bay. Nothing bad was going to happen. She blamed the Trio of Doom for her inability to take a deep breath. If not for their prior conversation, she would be enjoying herself.

Maybe.

Well, probably not.

No, she finally admitted, she would *not* be enjoying herself. Even a little.

"This is a nice boat," she said, desperate for innocuous conversation.

"I thought you would like it," Bill replied, a hint of pride in his voice. "It's a Sea Fox Traveler 226. The guy I rented it from said it was one of the best."

"Oh," said Diana faintly as Bill launched into a detailed description of the vessel.

Fifteen minutes later, Diana wished she had never asked. The one-sided conversation cemented her belief that she had zero in common with Bill Watkins. *Zero.* Diana knew next to nothing about boats. Nor was she particularly interested in learning more. The boat appeared to be seaworthy. That was all she really cared about.

"My dad has lots of boats that are better than this one." Bill paused, distracted by the fancy yacht that was trying to pull ahead of them. After exchanging several rude remarks with the captain of the other boat—and one unfortunate hand gesture—Bill passed the yacht and headed toward nearby Goat Island.

Unnerved by the ugly exchange, Diana tried to resume the subject that Bill had seemed to enjoy. "So, your dad has lots of boats?" Diana inquired, pleasantly.

"Oh, yeah." Bill's face twisted into an ugly snarl. "And you know what? Dad promised to give me one of his boats, but that *bastard* lied." His hands gripped the steering wheel until his knuckles were white.

Diana moved a little closer to the edge of her seat, surprised by Bill's intense display of anger. Another unexpected emotional swing. She hoped he wasn't having some sort of bipolar episode.

Oblivious to her distress, Bill continued: "He didn't give me a boat. He *never* gives me anything. He *never* lets me take one of his fancy boats out, either." Bill's voice grew louder and louder with each word. "Dad has boats that are a lot newer than this one *and* a lot better. He won't let me touch any of them. He won't even let me ride in them with him. Not since I was a kid." His hands clenched and unclenched on the steering wheel.

Horrified, Diana studied the man in the driver's seat as he navigated the heavy boat traffic close to the island. She watched Bill's hands. Unbidden, her mind formed a picture of those hands clasped around some innocent person's neck. Bill's face was flushed with anger. His foot tapped the gas pedal impatiently. He looked like a spoiled child who had gotten one scoop of ice cream instead of two.

The Nervous Nanny and the Bitter—But Harmless—Child.

Harmless? Diana fervently hoped that was the case. Especially since she found herself alone with him on a boat. Yet she couldn't quite shake the feeling that Bill's anger was of the dangerous variety. Maybe Lydia's first impression of him wasn't too far off the mark. Her cousin had sensed Bill's anger. Diana's supposition was confirmed by Bill's next words.

"Yeah," he sneered. "Dear Old Dad. He treats me like crap most of the time. You know, disrespects me."

He looked at Diana. The coldness in his gaze chilled her soul.

Bill gazed out across the water. "But all of that is going to change. Old Dad's going to figure it out real soon, and if he doesn't…" Bill shrugged his shoulders. "Well, he'll just have to disappear."

"Excuse me?" asked Diana in alarm, for surely she must have misunderstood him. He couldn't be saying that he was going to—

"Disappear," Bill said, matter-of-factly, as if he was talking about the weather. "I said he would disappear." His bland expression lacked either compassion or remorse. "There are a lot of ways to make people disappear, Diana. Did you know that?" He grinned, glancing at her shocked face. "It's very, very easy. It only takes a few minutes. I could snap his neck…" Bill snapped his fingers in front of her horrified nose.

Diana jumped. Her reaction seemed to amuse him.

"I could snap his neck," he said again. "Just like that. Easy. Then, all I would have to do is get rid of the body. That part's easy, too. There's a lot of water out here." The smile he turned on her was full of anticipation and genuine pleasure.

Diana forced herself not to react to his words, but her heart was pounding. Bill increased the boat's speed as they reached an expanse of open water. He was quickly taking them around the far side of Goat Island.

The Terrified Nanny and the Bipolar Man Who Wants to Kill His Father.

She looked around, frantic for some means of escape. *What are you looking for,* she asked herself. *The exit?* At this moment, the only exit available was the water. She quickly decided the boat was moving too fast for that.

Diana tried to think. She tried to be rational. She tried to be calm. But the fog of fear was stealing what little problem-solving ability her brain had left. She could only stare as they passed the Marriott Hotel on the end of Goat Island. The lawn was crowded with people—travelers and tourists, she presumed—enjoying a lobster bake. Or maybe they were a group from some conference. To her surprise, Bill waved, cheerfully, as they passed the end of the island. Several people waved back. All of those people, she thought…and they had no idea she was trapped on a boat with a man who wanted to snap his father's neck.

She pinned her eyes to Goat Island Lighthouse. It was so very small compared to the lighthouses she had visited in the Carolinas. Diana felt very small, too. And helpless. And trapped. She looked down at her hands, clasped tightly together against her stomach. That's when she had the first glimmer of an idea.

"I'm sick," she blurted out, holding her stomach with both hands. She leaned over as if in tremendous pain.

Bill slowed down a little, looking mildly concerned. "What's wrong with you?" he asked, suspiciously. "You felt fine a few minutes ago."

Diana clutched her stomach. "No," she dared to disagree. "I told you I wasn't feeling well when I got onto the boat." *Think, think, think.* "I'm lactose intolerant. Did you know that? There must have been milk in my eggs this morning. I need to go to the bathroom. We'll have to go back to the wharf or stop at Goat Island or something."

Diana, she congratulated herself, *you are a genius. How can he say no to that?*

"I'll anchor the boat and you can go in the water," Bill said, looking rather pleased at his solution.

No, no, no. "But, Bill, I don't have a bathing suit," Diana hedged, looking truly horrified.

Bill seemed to like his idea, gazing at her with undisguised lust. "Don't worry, Diana. I won't look."

For the first time in her life, Diana's skin actually crawled. Bill's unexpected response rendered her speechless for a moment.

The Desperate Nanny and the Disturbingly Creepy, Bipolar Man Who Wants to Kill His Father.

"Well, okay," she said reluctantly, apparently falling in with his plan. If he could snap his father's neck, he could certainly snap hers. One of the people on the boat was clearly insane and, well…

Her watch vibrated. She nearly jumped out of her skin. How had she forgotten her Apple Watch? She purchased it three days ago to celebrate the bonus she received from her publisher for completing her new *Nanny Di* holiday series. She felt a surge of hope. Maybe, just maybe, she would be able to call for help without alerting Bill. So far, she didn't think he'd noticed her Apple Watch. She would have to keep it that way.

Diana felt better now that she had a plan…until she looked up to find Bill regarding her suspiciously.

"What's wrong now?" he demanded. His cold eyes bored into hers.

A spark of pure unadulterated fear caused the words to fall right out of her mouth. "Text on my Apple Watch. I'm not used to wearing it yet."

Way to go, Diana, she berated herself. *Why don't you tell him to call 911 for you, too? I'm sure he would be happy to help.* Fear had, apparently, dissolved her filter. Her brain was turning to mush.

The Terrified Nanny with Mush for Brains and the Helpful Psychopath.

She almost laughed out loud at that one. Hysterically, of course. The book titles were not helping, but she couldn't seem to stop making them up.

"Well?" demanded Bill, killing the motor.

"Well, what?" Diana asked, in the same loud voice she had been using since the boat sped up. Without the sound of the motor, she sounded like an idiot.

Bill grinned. "Aren't you going to read your text?" he asked, in a teasing voice.

Just like that, his threatening persona was gone. Also gone was Diana's earlier opinion that the man who was driving the boat was odd. Unfortunately for her, he was far beyond odd. In fact, she was absolutely certain that there was something very, very wrong with Bill Watkins.

So, she did as Bill asked. She read her text. Then, she read her text again. It was from Devin.

The only Bill Watkins in the McCallum Industries' international database is 68-year-old William (Bill) Wallace Watkins from Aberdeen, Scotland. He retired three years ago. Please don't go near your "friend" until we can figure out who he really is and what he wants. Mom's making one of her Charleston specialties for dinner in honor of your last night in Rhode Island. If you're late, I'll eat all your shrimp.

Before Diana could do more than stare at Devin's words, Bill's hand came down, pinning her wrist to the seat. Hard. She looked up into his snarling visage. He was, she realized, coming unhinged right before her eyes. Diana struggled to remain calm. And to free her wrist. Her efforts at both endeavors were, sadly, unsuccessful.

"What's your text say?" His face was flushed with anger.

"Nothing important."

Bill increased the pressure on her wrist. Clearly, her answer wasn't good enough. He had no intention of letting go. "Why don't you read it to *me*?" He almost growled.

"Let go of my wrist and I will." Diana tried to laugh, but the sound was shaky and pitiful, even to her own ears. To her relief, Bill accepted her bargain. He released his hold on her throbbing wrist. She would surely see bruises tomorrow morning...*if* she was still alive tomorrow morning. Diana battled a wave of fear that nearly swallowed her. Somehow—maybe from sheer desperation—a familiar passage from her books popped into her mind.

"Be brave, Nanny Di," Mara Lee whispered. "Iggy says, 'Be brave.' "

Nanny Di nodded, giving Mara Lee's hand a gentle squeeze. "Then, we must do what Iggy says."

How would Nanny Di handle this situation? Diana asked herself. That spirited lady wouldn't let some psychotic father-hating lunatic tell her what to do. And neither would Diana. As her panic receded, she calmly touched her Apple Watch. She read the text she had received yesterday morning in a loud, clear voice: " 'Miss Merritt, we are sorry to inform you that your comforter was ruined by a machinery malfunction. Hadley's Dry Cleaning will be delighted to reimburse you for your inconvenience. Remember, a Hadley's customer is a happy customer.' "

She met Bill's eyes as she continued: "The text goes on to tell me that I have to have the original receipt to prove the purchase price of the comforter or they'll just pro-rate it themselves." Diana shook her head in what, she hoped, was a convincing display of angst. "I'm so upset. I love that comforter. I swear, it's so hard to find a good dry-cleaner these days. Why..."

"Give me your watch," Bill demanded. "I want to read your message from Hadley's myself."

Righteous anger overwhelmed Diana's fear. "No," she said. "I won't." Who did he think he was, anyway, telling her what to do like that? Before Bill could react, she darted to the stern. She waved her arms over her head. There weren't any boats close by, but perhaps she could get someone's attention on the shore.

"Bitch," Bill growled, moving faster than Diana could have imagined. He grabbed her from behind, immobilizing her arm between her back and his own wiry frame. He unclasped the watch with the ease of a seasoned pickpocket. She managed to scream before he shoved her down onto the back seat.

To Diana's relief, several people at the lobster bake were looking her way. She opened her mouth, but the second scream never made it past the lump in her throat.

"Shut up, bitch." Bill stood directly over her, clenching and unclenching his hands.

Diana did as she was told as another paralyzing wave of fear rushed through her. She glanced, desperately, at the shore. The rough way that Bill treated her—or maybe it was her scream—had attracted the attention of several people at the lobster bake. A few were pointing and shouting. One looked as though he was trying to flag down an approaching boat.

Diana's relief that someone knew she was in trouble disappeared as a sobering thought took its place: Bill could strangle her right in front of her would-be rescuers. Not one of them would be able to reach her in time. Although...

Was she dreaming or did the distance between the boat and the island seem a little shorter than it was before? No, she thought, excitedly, she was *not* dreaming. And, yes, every swell was taking them closer to Goat Island. Their boat was drifting of its own accord because Bill, the nosy psychopath, cut the motor to ask about her text. And, so far, the watch-stealing fiend was completely unaware. Diana latched onto that fact like a drowning woman grabbing a life preserver.

As Bill read her text, something like surprise appeared on his face. The rage vanished. "I'm sorry about your comforter," he said, cheerfully. "I hate it when my stuff gets messed up. Maybe we can go buy another one. I'm so glad you're not a nanny anymore. You'll have a lot more time to..."

His face changed again, going nearly purple with rage. "*Yesterday?*" Apparently, he had only just now seen the message's time stamp. "*You got this text message yesterday?"* He searched until he found the most recent message. The one from Devin.

His face changed, again, as he read the text. The look he gave her was full of hurt and confusion. Almost childlike. "You told me a lie?" he asked, crouching down in front of her. "Why did you tell me a lie?"

Diana remained where she was, afraid to breathe. His emotional instability was terrifying. At the moment, he didn't look very dangerous. Only sad. And a little lost.

"Why does it say tonight is your 'last night' in Rhode Island?" he asked, in a whisper.

Diana took a deep breath. Maybe she could reason with him. At this point, she had nothing to lose.

"I'm sorry you had to find out this way, Bill." She spoke calmly, making her voice soft and soothing. "I'm moving to North Carolina so that I can still be Amalie's nanny. Isn't that wonderful news? I've been so upset about being far away from her."

Bill tilted his head sideways, listening intently.

"I came to thank you for being so kind to me, Bill, and to tell you my plans." Diana smiled, hopefully. "I knew that you would be happy for me." *And not want to kill me.* She added that last part in her head.

"I like your watch," Bill said, holding it up and swinging it back and forth. His eyes were glued, almost hypnotically, to the device.

"Why don't you keep it?" Diana suggested, carefully. She would happily trade that watch for her life any day.

The Watch-Obsessed Psychotic, Bipolar Man Who Wants to Kill His Father...But NOT the Nanny.

Bill looked at the watch for a few seconds longer. Without warning he leapt to his feet. Diana could only stare as he lobbed her watch across the water in the direction of the Claiborne Pell Bridge. When he turned around, he spoke calmly, but she could see the madness glowing in his eyes.

"I've decided that I'm going to keep *you* instead."

Diana's heart sank as quickly as her Apple Watch. The stunned expression on his captive's face seemed to please Bill. He left her where she was as he hurried back to the leaning post. He seated himself and attempted to start the motor. But instead of roaring to life, the engine sputtered and died. A string of vile curses burst from Bill's lips as he fiddled with the key.

Diana's mind worked furiously. She glanced at the island again, noting that it was even closer than before. She stood up, waving her arms at the small crowd gathered on the shore. She tried to estimate the distance and the way the wind was blowing. It was a long shot, but she thought she could make it. She never imagined that holding her high school's record for the best time in the 500-meter swim might one day save her life. She, silently, thanked God—and Coach Zabrowski—for making her a distance swimmer.

After kicking off her sandals, she stepped up onto the seat. She put one foot on the side of the boat, wasting a few precious seconds getting her balance. Timing would be everything…but starts were her specialty. When Bill sped up, she would dive as far away from the side of the boat as possible. Then, she would stay underwater as long as she could before beginning her stroke. That should get her far enough away to keep the boat's wake from slowing her down.

Of course, another boat could come by and chop her up into little pieces. At present, that was preferable to being kidnapped by a psychopath. *But wait,* Diana thought frantically, *what if the psychopath decided to turn his boat around?* What if *he* decided to run over her? Fear threatened to envelope her again. Diana swayed a little, her stance precarious at best. She knew she couldn't afford to hesitate.

"Be brave, Nanny Di."

The encouraging words of a fictional iguana made up her mind.

Diana never had a problem acknowledging her own mistakes. Nor was she adverse to admitting when she was wrong. The recently deceased Mallory would have substantiated the fact that Diana was wrong nearly all the time. And although that wasn't quite the case, Diana knew she was far from perfect. She did have a problem, however, with ceding anyone the right to say "I told you so."

That all changed the minute she dove into Narragansett Bay. At that moment, she was wholeheartedly willing to admit that the Trio of Doom was right, and that she—Diana I-Thought-I-Knew-What-I-Was-Doing-But-Obviously-I-Was-Mistaken Merritt—was wrong. Oh, yes, she had been very, very wrong about her "friend" Bill. And there was no doubt that meeting him in Newport was a very, very bad decision. When this was all over, she was going to let the Trio of Doom say "I told you so" to their hearts' content. And her cousin, Lydia, too. She would even agree with them, she promised herself. She would agree with them, that is, if she ever saw them again. If she survived.

Bill sped away from Goat Island, oblivious to everything except his desire to reach the open water beyond the bridge. He never saw the beautiful dive Diana executed from the side of the boat. When he finally glanced back to gloat at his prisoner, she was gone.

CHAPTER FOUR

Newport, Rhode Island
Later that day

*T*he phone rang in the cottage at the shore's edge. Douglas McCallum's longtime lover checked the clock on the wall. *How interesting,* Calli thought with a pleased smile. Douglas' plane couldn't have landed more than an hour ago. He usually waited until he was comfortably ensconced in his Bellevue mansion before calling. Or—more often than not—he didn't call at all. He came straight to the cottage. And Calli's bed.

Not so, this time. Apparently, Douglas couldn't wait. Was that because he had already heard about Bill's latest debacle? Calli hoped so because the cocky son of a bitch had finally done it this time. Bill had finally gone too far. If Douglas listened to reason, the world was going to become a much better place. Calli let the phone ring a couple of times before answering, just to heighten the drama. Besides, it wouldn't do to appear too eager.

"Welcome home, Douglas." Calli said in a husky voice.

Douglas McCallum ignored his lover's greeting. "I'm sending Bill to Mexico for a couple of months," he said instead. "Carlos can find him something productive to do."

"*Bill*?" Calli jumped on his words with more than a little sarcasm. "Are you talking about *Billix Watson*, who—using the terribly creative alias *Bill Watkins*—tried to kidnap some poor woman this morning? In a boat? A well-connected woman, I would surmise, whose name was conveniently left out of the media reports?"

The man on the other end of the line was silent. Fortunately for Douglas, his detested nephew—Blane McCallum—had enough clout to keep Diana Merritt's name out of the media. Blane, Douglas knew, was only trying to protect the innocent Miss Merritt. He had no idea that his actions were protecting his uncle, too. And Douglas had no intention of enlightening him.

Calli gleefully continued: "Are you talking about the same *Billix Watson* who rented a boat under the name of failed blackmailer—and very dead—Kenneth Wade?" Calli had played an integral part in making the death of Wade look like a zip-lining accident. Having the man's name floating around again wasn't good for anybody. And who knew how many times Bill had used Wade's name before now?

Douglas maintained a strained silence.

Calli happily filled it. "Are you talking about the same *Billix Watson* who can't follow instructions? Who makes his own rules? Who has been a liability to our whole operation since the day he—"

"Shut the hell up," Douglas roared, at the limits of his patience. He had been confronted with Billix's latest screwup almost before he stepped off the plane. The news of today's attempted kidnapping on Narragansett Bay was everywhere. Douglas—who recognized Billix's pathetic attempt at an alias—was still trying to wrap his head around the far-reaching implications of the whole mess. He had no idea of the identity of the woman Bill tried to kidnap until he stopped by McCallum Industries headquarters for a rare in-person appearance. Since the unfortunate discovery of his embezzling scheme, Douglas had forced himself into the hated guise of an exemplary employee. His pretense was, for once, rewarded when an irate Devin inadvertently shared that his nanny—and first cousin—was the kidnapper's intended victim.

If the little moron had to kidnap someone, why couldn't he have picked some nameless woman without connections? Leave it to Billix to make the worst possible choice. Douglas rubbed the tense muscles in the back of his neck with one hand. Diana Merritt was the beloved daughter of Barrett Merritt, one of the brothers of Merritt Brothers Law, a powerful and influential firm well-known for their unconditional familial loyalty. Douglas sighed. He was getting a headache.

Seriously, he asked himself, how much incompetence could one man deal with in a mere seven days? Hadn't he spent the last week in hell—what some people referred to as Scotland—playing the dutiful son to his pathetically gullible father, Fergus McCallum? And hadn't he tolerated the Bastard—Douglas' preferred name for his despised half brother, Ian—who was too shrewd by half? Sitting through meeting after endless meeting at McCallum Industries' worldwide headquarters while trying to act like he gave a damn was exhausting. Not to mention the effort it took not to act on the lascivious impulses called forth by Ian's unbearably sultry wife, Alina.

For a few seconds, Douglas gave in to erotic visions of subduing the exquisite brunette. An unhappy sound from Calli forced such dark pleasures from his mind. Hell, he admitted to himself, his lethal sister-in-law would probably kill him before he had time to enjoy himself. There was no doubt: Douglas needed an outlet for the almost unbearable sexual tension in which he was mired. He needed Calli.

"Sorry, love." Douglas forced himself to apologize, knowing he would reap the rewards later. "My week was hell. And coming home to this—"

"Dereliction of duty?" Calli suggested pleasantly. "Epic disaster? Catastrophic failure?"

Douglas grimaced. He was tired. He did *not* want to have this conversation right now. "Just tell Billix he's going to Mexico the next time he checks in." There. That should be the end of it.

Calli huffed out a frustrated breath.

Damn it. Douglas wanted to groan aloud. How could his instructions be any simpler? "What's wrong now?" he asked brusquely. His lover was pouting. He could tell.

"Billix doesn't listen to me anymore," Calli whined.

Douglas did groan then. "Then why don't you just tell him *I'm* sending him to Mexico, Calli? Quit acting like you've never done this before." He was getting damn tired of dealing with the working relationship between Calli—who wouldn't stand up to Bill—and Bill—who refused to listen to Calli, Douglas' second-in-command. Their animosity made everything more difficult. "When does Billix check in again?"

"Three days *ago*." Calli's voice oozed with satisfaction.

"Three days ago," Douglas repeated, an edge in his voice.

Calli relished the signs that Douglas was getting angry. "That's right. It appears our boy has gone rogue. AWOL. M-I-A. Just like he did last year when he hit Devin Merritt with that car."

"Find him."

It was not a request. It was a necessity: Douglas *had* to get Billix out of the country. And he had to do it fast. For a variety of reasons, not the least of which was that Billix knew too much. And he was too cocky. And too careless. The impulsive idiot had taken matters into his own hands last year, nearly killing Devin Merritt in the process. Fortunately for Bill, Merritt survived. Unfortunately for the world, Merritt's handsome visage was forever scarred and disfigured. Even Douglas felt a rare twinge of guilt about that one. Occasionally.

Since the hit-and-run, Calli had been on a mission to get rid of Billix Watson. The situation had deteriorated to the point that Douglas had become the unwilling liaison between the two. And he was damn tired of it. And damn tired of Billix being a brainless fool. It appeared he was damn tired of a lot of things.

Or perhaps he was simply *too* damn tired to express himself creatively. Douglas agreed with Calli that Bill's decision to rent a boat using the name of a man who died under questionable circumstances was incredibly stupid. And dangerous. Prior to Bill's latest screwup no discernable link existed between Kenneth Wade's death and Devin Merritt's hit-and-run "accident." The attempted kidnapping of *Merritt's* nanny in a boat rented under *Wade's* name was a solid—and possibly damning—connection.

Calli had no idea that Devin Merritt's nanny was Bill's intended victim. And Douglas intended to keep it that way. Discovering that dangerous bit of information would make Calli wonder why Bill would target Merritt's nanny in the first place. Questions such as these were better left unasked. And unanswered.

Douglas certainly didn't want Calli to discover that, while Bill was keeping tabs on Devin's *nanny*, Douglas had been conducting a torrid affair with Devin's *wife*. Devin's recently deceased wife, he reminded himself. The fact that Mallory was dead still irritated Douglas. He had enjoyed her a great deal. But, he rationalized, she forced his hand. What else was he supposed to do? Billix knew that Douglas murdered Mallory. And Billix knew about Sheila, another lover who died shortly after she, too, became a liability.

Calli wouldn't have a problem with the murders. Douglas was certain of that. But discovering that he had conducted *two* lengthy liaisons with *two* different women would send his longtime lover over the edge. And what man knew to what lengths a thwarted lover might go for revenge? Douglas wasn't willing to find out. So Billix had to go to Mexico. Immediately. Short of killing him, too—which Douglas flatly refused to do—there was no other option.

At present, Douglas was confident of Bill's loyalty. But, he asked himself, was he too confident? If given a choice, would Bill sacrifice himself on the altar of Douglas McCallum? Maybe he would. Or maybe he wouldn't. Either way, Douglas wasn't willing to risk it. When push came to shove, it was every man for himself.

"Find Billix," Douglas intoned. Then, he waited. He knew it was only a matter of time until his predictable lover reminded him that several of their former "unreliable" employees had disappeared. Permanently. And for far less than what Billix Watson had done.

He didn't have to wait long. "Hmm...You know *I* can't find Billix unless *he* wants to be found." Calli paused before making a suggestion Douglas had rejected several times before. "We could put out a hit on him. Someone would find him immediately for the right price. Then we wouldn't have to worry...."

"No," Douglas snarled.

"But, Douglas…" Calli took a deep breath, prepared to argue.

"I said no, Calli. And if you mention this again, then *you*—not Billix—are the one who's going to be sorry." Douglas' tone was as cold and remorseless as his words.

Calli knew there was no recourse. Billix had won. Again. Insisting would only make Douglas angry, and making Douglas angry could be extremely painful. *Unless you are Billix Watson,* Calli thought bitterly. *Then the only punishment you receive for a colossal screwup is a free trip to Mexico.*

Clearly, Douglas' refusal to rid the world of the despicable thug was some kind of strange insanity. But Calli was realistic. There was no other choice but to accept Douglas' particular brand of insanity. Understanding it, however, was another story entirely. Still, bowing to Douglas' will did have its rewards….

"I'll tell Billix he's going to Mexico when he checks in," Calli said, placatingly. "He'll check in eventually, Douglas. He always does."

For the first time since hearing about the kidnapping attempt, Douglas relaxed. "I'll be there in half an hour, love," he purred. "I'm coming straight to the cottage. And I can't wait to show you how glad I am to be back…." With Calli's capitulation, he could move on to more pleasurable activities…like his lover's capitulation in other, more enjoyable arenas.

CHAPTER FIVE

A week had passed since Diana was pulled from Narragansett Bay by a vacationing family from New Jersey. On the positive side, her desperate gamble paid off. She was soggy and exhausted by the time they managed to drag her into their boat. But she was—thankfully—alive.

On the negative side…Diana sighed. The list just kept getting longer. As expected, she had lost count of the number of times someone said *"I told you so"* or *"You should have known better."* She tried to remind herself that all the scolding and fussing was done out of love and concern for her safety. Heaven knew that, as a nanny, she had used those same phrases often enough with Amalie, and for the same reasons. Besides, her critics had a point. She *should* have known better. Still, a person could only swallow her pride so many times without choking on it.

Diana had been staying in Providence with Devin's parents since her narrow escape. It was a perfect solution. She adored her aunt Allana and her uncle Rob. They, in turn, had always treated her like a second daughter. And, conveniently enough—for the overprotective souls who thought Diana needed a babysitter—Devin was already living with his parents. He had moved back home two weeks earlier after selling the Newport townhouse he had once shared with Mallory. If not, Diana grumbled to herself, he would surely have invented some ridiculously transparent reason to be there now.

Since the *incident*—as it had come to be called—Devin had stayed home to keep an eye on Diana. Of course, *he* called it "working from home," but Diana wasn't buying it. Rob and Allana lived about fifteen minutes from McCallum Industries' North American headquarters. The too-convenient scenario also gave Blane and Rafe the perfect excuse to stop by several times a day to confer with Devin about "business." In other words, to check on Diana and to make sure she was behaving herself.

In addition to the loss of her new Apple Watch, her sandals, and her favorite hat—all casualties of her ill-fated boat ride—Diana had lost her freedom. Well, maybe her *privacy* was a better way to phrase it. She was twenty-eight years old and she hadn't had a waking moment alone since Bill Watkins—or whatever his real name was—tried to keep her.

She couldn't blame her family for being upset. She couldn't even blame the Trio of Doom. (Even though she really, really wanted to blame the annoying threesome for *something*.) After all, it wasn't every day that she was almost abducted by a psycho. Her narrow escape was—to put it mildly—terrifying. Diana was in a desperate hurry to put the *incident* behind her.

After all, she reasoned, the whole unpleasant…no, she decided, it was a bit worse than that. How about *unfortunate*? She dismissed that description, too. Okay, she conceded, *nightmarish*. Yes, what had happened to her was definitely the stuff of which nightmares were made.

The whole nightmarish incident could have been avoided if she had never gone to meet "Bill" in the first place. And, if not for the unhappy accident of running into him at McCallum Industries, she would never have made any attempt to see him again. *Ever.* She would be in North Carolina right now taking care of Amalie as planned.

But no, Diana thought. She ran into Bill coming out of an elevator. And she agreed to go on a boat ride with him because she was grateful for his help the day Mallory died. Although…In retrospect, she still couldn't figure out why he had appeared in the foyer of Devin and Mallory's townhouse just in time to call 911. She felt confident that she had closed and locked the front door even though he said it was open. And she was almost positive she didn't scream at all after finding the body although he said her screams brought him to the open—but not-really-open-because-she-had-already-closed-it—door. And…

Each time Diana reached this exact part of her retrospection, her brain flatly refused to continue. Her heart pounded. Her hands shook. Her knees felt weak. And, once or twice, she became physically ill. Was it any wonder that an extended question and answer session with the Trio of Doom—perhaps *debriefing* was the better word—brought out the worst in her? In response, she refuted every theory the helpful trio suggested. In other words, she would not listen to anything they said.

Diana refused to consider the possibility that running into "Bill"— who *did not* work at McCallum Industries after all—was, in fact, a deliberate act on his part. She argued that it was nothing but bad timing sprinkled with bad luck.

She simply could not be convinced that her kidnapping attempt was premeditated. Diana decided, instead, that "Bill's" inability to handle her move to North Carolina was the trigger that caused his unstable mind to snap. She attributed the entire episode to her uncanny ability to make friends with crazy people.

But, most of all, she emphatically rejected the frightening idea that "Bill" had been stalking her for months. Every single thing that had to do with "Bill" was, she stated to herself adamantly, a coincidence. An unfortunate. And disturbing. But above all not-to-be-repeated. Coincidence. And Diana simply *would not* acknowledge the possibility that she was being pursued by a stalker.

Nor discuss it.

Nor think about it.

Nor think about discussing it. With anyone.

Did she want to help the police identify "Bill" so they could find him and get him off the streets? Of course she did. Hadn't she volunteered to work on a facial composite with a police sketch artist? Of course she had.

People with mental illnesses needed medical treatment. She hoped they would find "Bill" and get him the help he obviously needed.

Did she want to have anything else to do with him if they found him? Absolutely not. The idea made her skin crawl. As a matter of fact, every time she thought about seeing him again, her skin crawled. She wanted to stop thinking—and talking—about the whole mess. She wanted her skin to stop crawling. It was over.

Or was it?

According to Rafe, the name Bill Watkins was an alias. That was disturbing enough. But in a bizarre twist that no one could explain, "Bill" used another alias to rent the boat: Kenneth Wade. Even Diana couldn't ignore the small, irrefutable fact that this alias belonged to a dead man.

The previous summer, Wade—an employee of McCallum Industries—skipped the meeting *he* had scheduled with Devin, opting, instead, for an impromptu cruise. In a freak zip-lining accident in Belize, Wade plunged to his death. His reason for scheduling the meeting with Devin remained a mystery, as was the suspicious way in which Wade had died.

Equally troubling was the vehicular attack, several days later, that nearly killed Devin. Neither Rafe nor McCallum Industries' security specialists had been able to find any evidence linking Wade's death to Devin's "accident." Still, questions remained.

When Diana's family and friends learned about the connection between "Bill" and the dead man, the Trio of Doom swelled its numbers.

The Quartet of Quandaries.

The Quintet of Quagmires...Q was such a difficult letter.

The Sextet of Suffering. And so on and so forth.

At present, Diana was calling the nosy group *The Chorus of Extreme Caution*. Hence, her irritating lack of privacy.

Diana would *not* allow herself to consider the possibility that they were right. She could *not* permit herself to believe she was still in danger. If she did, she might let the fear that was hovering around her—howling like a hungry pack of wolves—devour her. That she flatly refused to do. Diana

chose, instead, to concentrate on the unwanted and very exasperating surveillance that was slowly suffocating her.

Apparently, Diana surmised, her driving privileges had been revoked
by the Chorus of Extreme Caution while she slept. That was the only possible explanation for the sight that met her eyes when she walked out of
Robert and Allana's residence the next day. Her brother, Roman, was firmly
ensconced behind the wheel of her Mustang convertible and she—the
rightful owner of the car—was riding shotgun.

Roman let his sister fume for the first half hour; then her uncharacteristic silence finally got the better of him. "Can't get enough of my
dashing good looks, little sister? You've been staring a hole through me for
the last thirty miles," he teased. When Diana still didn't answer he continued: "I know. I know. Once you see this profile, it's hard to look away." He
grinned as his sister glared at him in response.

Diana very deliberately turned her head to look out the passenger
window. *Traitor.* The fact that her own brother was in on the scheme did
not sit well with her. He was usually on her side.

Roman regrouped and tried again. He was nearly always able to
make his sister smile, even under extenuating circumstances. "What kind
of book are you writing over there? *Nanny Di and Her Unbelievably Good-
Looking Brother*? Sounds like a great idea. I'll bet it'll be a bestseller."

Diana refused to smile back, even though it was hard to resist
Roman's good-natured humor. "I was thinking of calling it *Nanny Di and
the Family Conspiracy.*" She huffed out an exasperated breath. "Did *Dad* tell
you not to let me drive?"

"Nope," Roman said, shaking his head. "It was Mom."

"Mom?" Diana was surprised. Lucinda Merritt was usually the one who talked Diana's slightly overprotective father out of his slightly overprotective tendencies. Diana sat back in her seat. "Oh."

"Now you understand, don't you?" Roman nodded in satisfaction. "Aunt Allana was on the phone with Mom last night after you went to bed. Mom is still ripped up that she and Dad couldn't come home from Charleston immediately after your..."

Roman hesitated slightly. He couldn't bring himself to say the words *kidnapping attempt*. Try as he might, he couldn't seem to rid his mind of the idea that something terrible had almost happened to his little sister. His inability to banish the disturbing thoughts was one of the reasons he had volunteered to see Diana safely from Providence to their parents' home an hour outside of Alexandria, Virginia.

Of course, he couldn't tell his sister that. Emotional stuff between siblings was strictly off the table. Diana didn't understand how deeply her narrow escape was affecting her family. She just looked annoyed, so Roman continued his explanation.

"Anyway, Mom's still upset. So, when Aunt Allana handed the phone to *me* I got an earful. Mom *never* asks me to do stuff like drive my little sister somewhere. No way I was going to tell her, 'No.' If it had been *Dad*, well...Mom would have talked him out of it. Then, *I* might have had a chance to take a nice nap on the way. But since it was *Mom*..."

Diana sighed. Roman was right. They had both learned early in life that when their Southern mother made a rare show of force, acquiescence was the best option. Diana couldn't help but grumble. "So, now, *I'm* not allowed to drive my own car, because my mommy said so."

"Yep," Roman said, agreeably. "Glad you understand."

Diana crossed her arms as she continued to fume. "You know Aunt Allana probably called Mom to report the minute we pulled out of the driveway. Those two tell each other everything."

Roman spoke in an unusually sober tone. "It's hard for us to let you out of our sight after what almost happened, Diana. I hope you know that."

Diana was a little taken aback by the seriousness in her brother's voice. He had dropped everything to make the trip to Providence, tasked with instructions to bring Diana safely home. Other than an overlong hug, he hadn't mentioned her "almost" kidnapping. His silent support, however, meant the world to her. It always had.

"I'm just glad they didn't make us drive The Terminator." Roman's reference to their grandfather's ancient—and practically bulletproof—pickup truck drew a giggle from his annoyed little sister. Roman relaxed. Diana was used to her independence. Even a little thing like not being allowed to drive her own car was likely to grate. He had expected some degree of resistance. Now, he was relieved by the return of his sister's sunny smile.

"Remember that Christmas parade when we got to ride in The Terminator with Granddad?" She chuckled. "I thought he was going to kill Connor and Lance when he found out all of the candy was gone."

"Yeah, they begged to ride in the truck bed and not up front with us, 'little kids,' " Roman added. "Then they threw out all the candy they didn't like in the first five minutes and ate the rest."

"They thought they were *so* smart," Diana added, gleefully. "Until Granddad made them wash and wax that nasty, old truck. I still remember the looks on their faces." It was one of Diana's first lessons of what justice felt like.

Roman laughed, too, satisfied that he had won. His cheerful sister had returned.

After a rocky start, their trip took a rather enjoyable turn. Diana was reminded of the first time their parents let Roman drive his own car to Charleston for their summer vacation. He was seventeen, then, and, at fourteen, Diana was his happy sidekick. They spent the drive singing along with the radio and eating the treats packed by their mother. The moment they joined the slew of cousins with whom they would spend the summer,

Roman once again turned into her too cool older brother. But for a few precious hours in the car, it was almost like they were friends.

Today, the siblings talked nonstop as the hours flew by before they finally lapsed into a comfortable silence. One-on-one time with her beloved brother happened all too infrequently, Diana mused, especially since they had become adults. For the first time in days, she was able to relax a bit. Whether her improved state of mind could be attributed to time spent with Roman or the fact that every mile took her farther and farther from the scene of the crime was irrelevant. The important thing, she decided, was that she was feeling better.

Roman's phone rang, effectively interrupting Diana's self-analysis. She glanced at the screen. "It's Dad. Maybe he wants to know where we want to go for dinner," she suggested, hopefully. Their parents had gotten home from Charleston the day before. They were expecting Roman and Diana to arrive in time for the evening meal. "Tell him we want to go to The Pumphouse." The most popular restaurant in their hometown seemed like the perfect place for a family reunion.

"The Pumphouse will be too crowded on Friday night," Roman said, before answering with his hands-free device: "Hi, Dad. What's up?"

"How close are you to Alexandria, Roman?"

The siblings exchanged a look of surprise at Barry Merritt's unusually terse question.

Roman checked the GPS. "About ninety miles, but traffic is pretty heavy. I figure we'll get there around six o'clock." He glanced at Diana. "What's up, Dad? And, um, Dad..." he added carefully. "Diana is, um... right here."

"In other words, Dad," Diana announced loudly, "don't forget that I'm in the car listening to every word."

"Hush," Roman admonished her, frowning slightly.

Diana scrunched up her nose and frowned back. But she stopped talking.

Barry Merritt got straight to the point. "Roman. Diana. The trial is over."

"What?" Roman couldn't believe it. "There should have been days and days of testimony remaining. How could the trial be over?"

"What happened?" Diana couldn't hide the surprise in her voice.

"Vanessa confessed," Barry said, in a grim voice "And, then—according to Joey Finch—all hell broke loose."

"Confessed?" Roman couldn't believe it. He glanced at Diana. She looked just as shocked as he felt.

Barry continued in a subdued tone: "Yes. The defendant confessed. Apparently, her housekeeper was the only witness to the murder. Vanessa called I-N-S and reported the woman as an illegal to keep her from talking. Since the housekeeper had an outstanding warrant for shoplifting or something, it was easy to get her out of the way. The prosecuting attorney located the housekeeper while she was waiting to be deported. I have to give him credit for his tenacity. It must have been hell to work out the deal that put that housekeeper on the stand. Anyway...hold on. I'm getting a call from Gary. I have to take it." Barry unceremoniously dropped their call.

"Bye, Dad," Roman said into the silence. He and Diana exchanged a sober glance.

"Poor Lance," Diana said, softly. "He has to be devastated."

"Hellfire and damnation," Roman swore, smacking his hand on the steering wheel. It was his favorite of all their grandfather's colorful curses. "I never saw that coming."

CHAPTER SIX

*N*o one saw it coming. The defendant had fooled them all. Vanessa Kiplinger's murder trial ended with her jaw-dropping, headline-grabbing, completely unexpected admission of guilt. When she boldly confessed to the poisoning death of her husband, Senator Ian Kiplinger, the courtroom erupted into chaos. It was a spectacular defeat for Lance Merritt, defense attorney. The expression on Lance's face changed from disbelief to betrayal to genuine pain in a matter of seconds before he covered it with a professional mask.

Joey Finch vowed then and there that he would *never* put himself in such a vulnerable position. As one of the firm's associates, Joey—along with a core group—had contributed countless hours of work over the past two years to this particular case. But it was Lance Merritt who would bear the burden of defeat. Lance was passionate in his defense of Mrs. Kiplinger, absolutely convinced of her innocence. The fallout was gut-wrenching. Any lingering doubts Joey harbored about the wisdom of leaving his position in the offices of Merritt Brothers Law Firm vanished without a trace.

Joey stood beside his colleague and friend as Lance calmly fielded questions at the packed press conference. He listened as Lance congratulated the prosecuting attorney for his dedication to justice. He watched Lance thank the jury for their conduct during the high-profile and lengthy trial. He listened to the prosecuting attorney expound on the merits of the

American judicial system. He shook hands with the opposing counsel, then he followed Lance from the courthouse.

They exited in silence, waving away the barrage of microphones that were thrust in their faces. The other members of Lance's team scattered like ants, but not Joey. He wasn't leaving his friend to his own devices. Besides, he wasn't sure that Lance was in any condition to drive. His assumption was confirmed when they reached the sleek black Mercedes.

Lance tossed the keys to Joey. "You drive," was all he said.

Joey slid behind the wheel of Lance's car and plunged headfirst into the mess that was late afternoon traffic in Washington, DC. He glanced at his passenger several times, as concerned by the increasingly wan pallor of his friend's skin as he was by his uncharacteristic silence.

"You all right, man?" Joey asked softly.

Lance merely nodded as he continued to stare out the window.

Joey didn't know what to say, so he turned on the radio, hoping a little music would help. Miranda Lambert's "Gunpowder and Lead" blared through the speakers.

Joey grimaced. It wasn't the most opportune song. The last thing Lance needed to hear was a song about a woman planning to kill a man.

The song was half over before Lance spoke. "Change the station, please," he requested politely.

Joey pressed a random button on the console. "Cell Block Tango" from *Chicago* was not the most fortuitous choice, either. Multiple women in prison for killing multiple men. Joey sighed. The irony was almost painful.

Lance turned off the radio himself. The ensuing silence surrounded the two men like a smothering blanket, but Joey had no intention of breaking it. Instead, he concentrated on navigating the heavy rush hour traffic.

By the time they reached the outskirts of Alexandria, Joey was growing more and more concerned. Lance's skin had taken on a greenish hue. His face was shiny with sweat. Joey hesitated a few seconds before asking, "Lance, are you sure you're..."

"Pull over." Lance was holding onto the car door with a death grip.

Joey pulled off onto the side of the road. He stayed where he was, watching Lance stagger from the car and into the bushes. A few minutes later, he was back. Joey tossed him a bottle of water, glad to see that Lance's complexion was, once more, a normal color. The worst was over. Or so Joey thought. Before he could breathe a sigh of relief, however, Lance's self-flagellation began.

Lance berated himself in the harshest language for his "blind stupidity and inexcusable gullibility." He also described the verdict using such sublime phrases as "career-ending" and "reputation-destroying." Lance was most concerned, however, with the damage his failure would do to the— heretofore—sterling reputation of the family firm. Merritt Brothers didn't lose high-profile cases, he moaned. And they were never, ever, blindsided by a defendant's admission of guilt on the witness stand.

Joey wanted to argue that Merritt Brothers *had* lost big cases before. It happened to every law firm. He wanted to point out that Lance's perception of the fallout was much worse than the reality. And he wanted to remind Lance that his family would never blame him for Vanessa's confession. But Lance never stopped talking long enough to give his friend the chance.

By the time Joey pulled into a rare open parking spot in front of Chutley's Bar and Grille—the favorite watering hole of the Merritt Brothers crowd—he was more than ready to hand Lance over to someone with the insight and experience to help the poor man. Lance's brother, Connor, was the perfect choice…loud, brash, and unfazed by pretty much everything. With a great deal of relief, Joey turned off the motor.

"I need a drink," Lance mumbled, climbing out of the car.

"I'm right behind you," Joey said. He watched until his friend was safely inside before checking his own messages.

Well, hell, he thought after reading Connor's brief text. Lance's brother was, unfortunately, still at the courthouse and would be for some time. In addition, Lance's cousin, Roman, was still an hour away, stuck in heavy traffic. Joey sighed. No way was he going to leave Lance to his own devices. The longest day in living memory was about to get even longer.

With no reinforcements in sight, he reluctantly followed his friend into Chutley's.

"Wait your turn, you moron," Roman snapped, as a beat-up, blue Toyota tried to force its way into the line of traffic in front of them. He didn't know what irritated him more: drivers who didn't merge when they were supposed to or the strangled, wheezing noise Diana made when she thought said drivers were going to slam into the side of *her* car. Or maybe it was the way she kept putting on imaginary brakes.

Roman soberly faced the facts. He and Diana were at least an hour away from their destination and his little sister was slowly driving him crazy. He didn't blame her for being a nervous wreck. She had been through a lot. Plus, he was driving *her* car...paid for and insured by *her*. Under the circumstances, Roman decided he would try his best to give Diana the benefit of the doubt. And he did.

For five whole minutes.

Roman knew it was five minutes because he timed it, out of sheer curiosity to see how long he could last. But when the driver in front of him slowed down rather abruptly in response to the driver in front of him slowing down rather abruptly...well, Roman had no choice but to slow down equally abruptly. And when Diana gave a breathless little squeal before smashing both feet firmly into the floorboard while bracing one hand against the car door and the other against the dashboard, Roman couldn't hold back any longer. Enough was enough.

"*My dear sister,*" he began, innocuously. "Are you, perhaps, under some delusion that this is a Driver's Education car?"

She released her imaginary brake, regarding him blankly. "What?"

Roman heaved an overly exaggerated sigh. "This..." he repeated—pronouncing every syllable of every word in an excruciatingly slow manner—"...is *not* a Dri-ver's E-du-ca-tion car."

Not to be outdone, Diana responded in kind. "What are you talk-ing a-bout, Ro-man?"

Roman tightened his grip on the steering wheel ever so slightly. "There are no brakes on the passenger side of this car. No brakes at all. Therefore, slamming your feet into the floorboard every thirty seconds has no effect whatsoever on decreasing the speed of this vehicle. And while I appreciate your determined assistance in that area, I can assure you that it is not necessary."

"Really?" Diana asked. "How *kind* of you to point out the fact that you don't need *my* help driving *my* car. What you do, apparently, need, *my dear brother*, is assistance in determining the proper distance to maintain between *my* car and the car in front of you."

"Oh, really, sister dear?"

"Yes, really, brother dear."

Roman knew he should not be enjoying the outrage on his sister's face quite so much. He really should leave well enough alone. He couldn't, however, resist one parting shot. "And, by the way, *sister dear*, using your hands to whack the dashboard and the passenger door doesn't have any effect on the brakes on *my* side of *your* car, either, just in case you were wondering."

Diana narrowed her eyes in response. She opened her mouth to say who knew what, but closed it again, almost immediately. Crossing her arms in front of her (probably to keep from slapping the dashboard again, Roman thought) she gazed silently out the window. Although she chose not to comment on Roman's words, her opinion of those words—and of her big brother—was quite clear.

When Roman glanced at his sister a few imaginary brake-less miles later, he was surprised to see that she was staring out the window, completely oblivious to merging traffic. A soft smile danced on her lips. He didn't know what that smile was about, but his irritation dissolved in a wave of fierce, familial love. By God, anyone who messed with Roman Merritt's little sister better watch his back.

Concentrating on the heavy traffic—along with Roman's penchant for driving too close to the car in front of him—hadn't helped. Nor had verbally sparring with her know-it-all big brother. It was a useless battle anyway. Diana had learned that years ago. So, she finally gave in to the urge to think about the one man she couldn't forget.

Joseph Ezekiel Finch, Jr.

Joey or Joe, to his friends.

Little Joe, if his father was around.

Diana's pulse sped up a little bit every time she heard his name. She just couldn't help it. She tried her best to keep the thoughts from coming, but it was no use. She would go for weeks—sometimes, months—without thinking about *him*. Then someone would say his name and her pulse skipped a beat. It was ridiculous. To make matters worse, she knew better. *He* wasn't for *her*. But, try as she might, she just couldn't make her heart believe it.

Diana would never forget how she felt the first time she ever saw Joey Finch. Nine years ago. Joey was in the middle of an internship at Merritt Brothers the summer after his junior year of college. She was home from Charlottesville for the week of July Fourth, on break from her job at a children's summer music camp. She was filling in on her week off so Connor's admin could have a much-needed vacation. She remembered how grown-up she felt that day, having just finished her freshman year at the University of Virginia. Until she saw *him*. Funny how a rising senior seemed so much more mature back then than a rising sophomore....

Connor Merritt, Diana's thirty-one-year-old cousin, had become a junior partner at the firm two months earlier. To say that he was pleased with himself was the understatement of the year. Connor thoroughly enjoyed lording over the younger members of his family, especially his brother, Lance. He took particular pleasure in being the first to choose his summer intern. His choice, of course, was none other than Joseph Ezekiel Finch, Jr.

Diana was minding her own business at her desk when the intern of whom she had heard so much walked out of the corridor that housed Connor's new office. Diana almost gasped aloud in surprise. If she had known there existed even the slightest possibility that Joey Finch was going to appear out of thin air, she would have…what? What would she have done?

Well, she informed herself, somewhat adamantly, she would have been ready. She would have fluffed her hair. Or applied more lipstick. Or…something. Now she was caught off guard, completely unprepared for a face-to-face encounter.

Diana knew with one glance that Joey Finch was out of her league. He was so far out of her league that she didn't even make her usual effort to introduce herself; something which was, for her, completely out of character. She just couldn't bring herself to do it. Diana had never had such a feeling of inadequacy in her life.

It wasn't Joey's good looks. She knew lots of handsome men. Tons. Bucketfuls. Her own family was full of them. Her high school boyfriend was very attractive, and the handful of guys she had gone out with her freshman year certainly weren't ugly. Handsome was nothing new to her. But she had never encountered handsome like this. Never found it hard to take a deep breath after only a glimpse. Never felt like her heart was going to beat right out of her chest.

She looked down at her desk so she wouldn't have to meet his eyes. She opened her desk drawer, feigning a sudden interest in the colorful assortment of paperclips lurking there. Joey must have gone into Connor's office, she *surmised, when she had run downstairs earlier to check the mail.* Drat. Drat. Drat. *She counted to five before allowing herself to peek. By then, the object of her fascination was bent over the water fountain directly across from her desk. Diana stared. She couldn't help but enjoy the view.*

Joey Finch certainly knew how to wear a suit. Maybe that was it, she reasoned. Maybe it was the suit. She had always been partial to navy blue. It was a well-known fact that even average-looking guys looked good in a navy blue suit. She tried to remind herself of that, but she was pretty sure Joey Finch would look exactly the same in casual attire. Gorgeous. There was no doubt about it.

When Diana realized that she was staring, she glanced around quickly to make sure no one else had noticed. The outer office was, thankfully, still empty. That was good. There would be hell to pay if any one of her overprotective family members thought she was staring at Joey Finch.

The object of her perusal finished up at the water fountain. Before he could turn around, Diana attacked her computer as if her life depended upon it. As Joey crossed to the workroom, she noticed—out of the corner of her eye—that he was studying the folder he held in his hand. He didn't even notice she was sitting at the admin's desk. Right across from the water fountain. In plain sight. In the center of the room.

Great, *Diana thought.* Now I'm invisible. *She tried to follow him with her eyes, but even though she was leaning forward in her chair as far as possible, she couldn't quite see what he was doing. So, she pushed a thick folder off the desk, forcing herself to get down on her hands and knees to pick it up. From there she was able to continue her study of him—surreptitiously, of course—from her new vantage point.*

Joey Finch's dark hair was short and perfectly styled. It probably never moved from the time he got out of bed in the morning until his head hit the pillow at night. His eyes were so dark she couldn't tell what color they were, but she could see they were alert and full of life. He was probably someone who didn't miss much, an excellent trait for a future lawyer. He was blessed with good bone structure in his face. Good Lord, *she exclaimed to herself,* even his ears are attractive and perfectly proportional. He was of average height for a man—not much taller than her own unfortunate stature—yet he managed to fill the room with the energy and vitality of a giant. As for the rest of him...Diana shook her head. It was no good to dwell on that. Absolutely pointless. Suffice to say that Joey Finch looked good. That is, he obviously took care of himself. Oh, who was she kidding? The man was devastatingly handsome in every way.

But it wasn't just that. It was the whole aura that surrounded him. Mysterious. And unattainable. With a charming smile. She had never met someone who had an aura, but Joey Finch did. She had a feeling if she got too close to him, she would be reduced to a complete imbecile, babbling incoherently about nothing at all.

Diana sat back on her heels, pondering the enigma that was mere steps away. The stories her cousins had told her—and the ones she had "accidently" overheard—had led her to a rather unfortunate conclusion. Suffice it to say that the, seemingly, perfect fellow in the workroom was F-L-A-W-E-D. Yes, she sighed, the beautiful man—presently struggling to use the copy machine right down the hall—had a flaw. And it was a big one.

According to every member of her family and—well, everybody who knew him, apparently—Joey was something of a player. In plain English: he never dated the same girl twice. To use the vernacular: he never dated the same girl twice. For that reason, alone, Diana should have made up her mind to stay as far away from Mr. Joseph E. Finch, Jr. as she possibly could.

But, she rationalized, there was always the possibility that every single member of her family—and every single person who knew him—was wrong. What if Joey was just waiting for the right girl to come along? What if he walked up to her this very minute and told her she was the one? What would that be like? Diana closed her eyes and imagined the scene. She was sitting at her desk. Her curly hair was contained, for once. Her makeup was perfection. Joey walked up to the desk. Their eyes met. Sparks flew. He gazed at her for a moment in abject adoration. He opened his beautifully sculpted lips to speak...

"Excuse me," he said, politely. "Do you need help?"

Outwardly, Diana didn't move, but inwardly, her heart dropped all the way down to her feet. She opened her eyes and looked straight at the navy blue creases of the pants belonging to the object of her daydream. Those *creases were so close, she could reach right out and touch them. She couldn't say anything. She remained frozen right where she was. On the floor. On her knees. At the feet of...*

Oh drat. *She nearly groaned aloud.* Maybe if I close my eyes again, he'll go away. He'll think I'm meditating or something. *She tried. But she couldn't do it. So, after a few long, drawn-out seconds, she opened one eye. He was still there. She gathered her courage and raised both eyes to his... wicked ones.*

Wicked was the precise term for his dark brown eyes. There were mahogany specks around his pupils, and they seemed to be dancing. He had wicked eyes and a knowing smile to go along with them. He knew exactly what she was doing there on the floor. He was obviously enjoying her discomfort. "Do you need help?" *he asked again.*

She could hear the amusement in his voice. "No, thank you," *Diana said, with great dignity. She might also have managed to stand with great dignity, too, if she hadn't planted her foot on the hem of her long skirt. Instead of standing up, she sat back down on the floor. Hard.*

To his credit, Joey didn't laugh out loud. He simply extended his hand to help her up. And if his grin grew downright devilish, well...Diana couldn't blame him.

She could, however, blame him for the spark of electricity that shot up her arm at his touch. She could also blame him for the way that tingling feeling ran down her spine, settling somewhere in the pit of her stomach.

The answering flash of awareness—of her!—faded from his gaze as quickly as it had appeared, making her certain that she must have imagined it. He released her hand quickly, almost as if he had been burned. All signs of the easygoing Mr. Finch vanished as he studied her soberly.

Desperate for normalcy, she rested one hand on the desk, motioning to the floor with the other. The folder was still lying there, its contents spilling onto the Oriental rug. "I was just straightening up my desk." *Her words sounded pathetically lame, even to herself.*

Joey chuckled easily as he nodded his head in agreement. "You're doing a great job," *he said, the smile reappearing on his well-formed lips.*

She nodded her head once, regally accepting his false praise. "I'm..."

"Diana. Roman's sister. Yeah, I know," Joey said, with a slightly less wicked smile this time. "I'm Joey Finch, Connor's intern. It's nice to meet you."

Much to Diana's surprise, he held out his hand. As she shook hands with Joey Finch, she tried to ignore the little tingles that ran up her arm. Again. She concentrated instead on the pleasing fact that he had manners. Most players didn't. At least she assumed they didn't. She really hadn't met that many actual players to know for sure. Still...

Joey released her hand, which was probably a good decision on his part as she was temporarily incapable of letting go. He studied her again, running his finger around his shirt collar as if it was a little too tight.

"Listen, Diana. You're filling in for the admin, right?" At her nod, he continued: "I'm supposed to print something for Connor, but the machine isn't cooperating and, well..." He grinned, looking like a mischievous, little boy. "I can't figure out how to fix it."

Diana found herself grinning back. She couldn't help it. He was adorable. "Maybe you should add paper," she suggested, coming out from behind the desk and moving toward the workroom.

Joey shoved both of his hands in his pockets and shrugged. "Now, why didn't I think of that?" He followed her into the workroom and leaned against the wall, watching as she efficiently loaded the copy machine with paper.

She shut the panel and pressed the "Copy" button. "It's ready to go," she announced, feeling like the queen of efficiency. Her earlier embarrassment was a distant memory. Diana knew Joey should have been able to fix the paper on his own, but, in his defense, it was a complicated machine.

"Thank you, Diana," he said, simply, looking ridiculously pleased as his copies rolled out of the machine.

"You're welcome," she replied, proud of her professional poise.

"FINCH!" Connor's voice boomed from somewhere down the hall, "Get your ass in my office now!"

Joey shrugged his shoulders again, good-naturedly. But, as he grabbed his copies and turned to go, he paused in the doorway. "Say, Diana," he said, "if you're still having trouble picking up that folder beside your desk, I'll be happy to help you with it later." He gave her a wicked wink to go along with his wicked smile and dashed down the hallway.

It took Diana a little longer to regain her composure. She had straightened up her desk—including the recalcitrant folder—taken six messages and shown two clients to Connor's office before she realized something that seemed significant. She hadn't needed to introduce herself earlier because, for some incomprehensible reason, Joey Finch already knew her name.

"What do you want?" Roman asked, dragging Diana back to the present.

She looked up, surprised to find that she and her brother were waiting in line at a Dunkin' Donuts drive-through just off the interstate. She quickly pretended to be thinking hard about her choices, although there was zero chance Roman would guess what...or who...she was really thinking about. "Ummmm...I think I'll have a medium caramel iced coffee with almond milk."

"What a surprise," Roman chuckled as he gave her order.

"What are you laughing at?" Diana asked suspiciously.

"I'm laughing at you," Roman said, simply. "I can't believe you took so long to decide. You always get the same thing at Dunkin'."

In response, Diana wrinkled her nose at her know-it-all brother.

It took only a few minutes before they were on their way again, armed with a welcome jolt of caffeine. Roman pulled out of the parking lot and headed for the ramp that would take them back to the interstate.

As Diana sipped her coffee, her mind quickly returned to another cup of coffee and Joseph Ezekiel Finch....

Diana checked her watch. They should be getting back from lunch any time now. She had been waiting for the elevator doors to open for the past ten minutes. The moment they did she was ready to pretend she hadn't been waiting at all, of course. Her eyes were still firmly fixed on their target when a voice spoke right into her ear.

"Waiting for someone?"

So intent was her concentration that she screamed, nearly jumping out of her chair in shock. She felt ridiculous when she realized who had spoken.

"Easy, now," Joey Finch said, thoroughly enjoying her reaction.

Her surprised eyes met his knowing ones. He leaned one leg against the desk, basking in the confidence that the person for whom she was waiting was him.

Diana went hot and cold and hot again. Drat. Double drat...oh, to hell with it. *"What are you trying to do, sneaking up on me like that?" The words burst from her lips before she could stop them. "You almost made me have a heart attack."*

Joey raised his eyebrows and actually took a step back from the desk. "I...um...well..." he stammered, warily.

"Seriously," she continued. "What's your problem? How did you get up here, anyway?"

Joey moved his head to indicate the door to the left under the big "Exit" sign. "I took the stairs," he said, innocently, trying and failing to keep his lips from turning up at the corners.

Diana's eyes widened in horror then closed in defeat. "Of course you did." She sighed. And I am an idiot.

"I wanted to bring you this." Joey placed a large, iced coffee on Diana's desk.

Diana looked at the coffee. Then she looked at Joey, a question in her eyes. "You brought me iced coffee?" Genuine surprise replaced her wounded dignity.

"Uh-huh." Joey nodded smugly, leaning against the desk again, ready to bask in the glory of her gratitude.

Diana narrowed her eyes, looking at him with deep suspicion. "Why?"

"Why?" Joey was puzzled. "Why what?"

"Why did you bring iced coffee...to me?" Diana elaborated, crossing one arm on top of the other on the desk.

Joey shrugged easily. "Because my sister fills in at Dad's office when she's on break and she likes it. So, I figured you would, too."

Diana's frostiness melted immediately. "Oh, that's so sweet," she said, adding rather loudly: "Your sister is so lucky to have such a thoughtful brother. Isn't that right, Roman?"

Joey looked puzzled for a minute before he realized that the elevator doors had finally opened. His confusion turned to amusement at the familiar sibling interaction.

"Whatever you say, Di," Roman murmured as he walked by, his eyes never leaving the screen of his phone. He put his coffee on the edge of the desk and disappeared into the Men's Room.

Connor and Lance were involved in an intense discussion as they left the elevator. Neither of them even looked up as they passed Diana's desk and headed down the corridor.

Diana propped her chin on her hand. "It's kind of like working for the Three Bears," she said, philosophically. "Connor is like Papa Bear. He growls and fusses and tries to act all tough..."

Connor stomped back into the outer office as if on cue. "Diana, where in the hell is the file that I asked you to find before I left for lunch?" His big voice boomed, echoing through the ample space.

"It's on your desk, Connor. Right in the middle...of...your...desk." Diana enunciated each word carefully.

Connor's bravado disappeared instantly. "Oh, yeah, well, thanks, Di." He glanced at Joey and hesitated before adding, "Did I mention what a great job you're doing? You're doing a great job." He turned around to return to his office, almost running into Lance, who had followed him out.

"And Lance is like Mama Bear," Diana resumed. "Always defending the innocent and trying to take care of his people."

True to her words, Joey could hear Lance berating Connor all the way back to his office. "Damn it, Connor. You're such an asshole. She didn't even take a lunch break, and you're barely paying her enough to buy lunch anyway...." The door slammed on his words.

Joey wasn't trying to hide his grin, now. He looked like he was thoroughly enjoying himself. "What about Roman?" he asked. "Baby Bear?"

"Uh-huh," Diana said, nodding. She was smiling, now, too. It seemed so easy to smile with Joey Finch. "Roman always picks up on the little things. He's quality control."

Roman came out of the Men's Room still glued to his phone. He paused at the desk, picked up Diana's coffee, and took a big swallow. He made a frustrated face. "Coffee's cold," he said, to no one in particular. "I hate it when that happens." He grimaced. "There should be a few things in life a man can depend on, one of those being a hot cup of coffee...."

Diana interrupted him before he could really get wound up. "Roman, you're drinking my coffee. Your coffee is right there." She pointed to his cup on the edge of the desk.

Roman looked at the cup in his hand and laughed, good-naturedly, at his own mistake. His eyes filled with mischief as he pondered his options. "I don't know, sis, this cold stuff is pretty good." He took another big swallow and held it up, just out of her reach. "Maybe I'll switch with you."

"Not a chance, dude. That coffee is a special order."

Joey came to the rescue, whisking the coffee out of Lance's hand and giving it to Diana, much to her delight.

Roman picked up his own coffee and headed toward the corridor that led to Connor's office, pausing in the doorway. "C'mon, Finch. Can't keep the junior partner waiting."

Joey winked at Diana before following Roman down the corridor. She watched them disappear into Connor's office.

They were still there when five o'clock rolled around. And even though she spent an inordinate amount of time getting ready to leave, she didn't see Joey again.

Staring out the window as Roman navigated the heavy traffic near the Alexandria exit, Diana still remembered her disappointment the next morning upon discovering that Joey Finch had taken the rest of the week off to visit his family in North Carolina. She had never—before or since—felt such an immediate and irresistible attraction to any other man. And she was starting to wonder if she ever would.

CHAPTER SEVEN

"*Y*ou thought she was innocent, didn't you?" Lance asked, for what seemed like the fiftieth time in the last two hours, his voice slurring his words.

Joey tried unsuccessfully to slide what remained of Lance's Scotch out of his reach.

"No, you don't, Finch," Lance said, making a last-second grab for the glass. He raised it triumphantly into the air, sloshing what remained of the contents onto himself and the floor. With a smile of victory, he brought the now empty glass to his lips. "All gone," he said, sadly, turning the glass upside down and staring into it. He motioned for the bartender. "I believe I'll have another."

Joey shook his head imperceptibly, and the bartender nodded. There would be no more Scotch for Lance Merritt that day.

Lance folded his arms on the bar then rested his head on them. He was so still that Joey assumed he had fallen asleep or finally passed out. He was still breathing, regardless. A good thing.

"Tough day in court, huh?" Sid, the bar manager, strolled over. He casually propped his elbows on the bar. The big man obviously held Lance in high esteem. There was genuine sympathy in his tone.

"Yeah," Joey agreed. "It didn't end quite the way we thought it would."

"The Senator would probably agree with you," Sid said, wryly, referring to the deceased victim of the crime. He gestured to the still motionless Lance. "I've never seen him have more than two drinks in one night, and he usually spaces 'em apart. If you need any help getting him home, let me know. Thought the rest of The Boys would be here by now." He referred to the second generation of the law firm.

"I'm expecting them any minute," Joey responded, checking his phone again, "Last I heard, Connor was finishing up at the courthouse and Roman was on his way. It shouldn't be too much longer before—" Joey stopped speaking at the renewed signs of life emerging from the man beside him.

Lance's head popped up. He looked around as if surprised to find himself seated on a barstool at Chutley's Bar and Grille. His eyes fixed on the television behind the bar. He watched the video clip of himself shaking hands with the district attorney before dropping his head onto his arms in defeat. "Damn it." His muffled voice drifted up from the bar. "I thought it was a dream." He raised his head, peering at Joey as if he had all the answers. "You thought she was innocent, didn't you?" he asked again.

Joey wanted to pound his fist on the bar in frustration. He understood Lance's desire to drown his sorrows, but if Connor and Roman didn't get there soon, Joey was going to start drinking, too. There was no doubt that his first—and most assuredly last—foray into the high-profile world of sensational murder trials had been an eye-opening experience. He held the drunken man seated beside him—and his family—in the highest esteem; otherwise, he would have been tempted to have left Lance Merritt in the capable hands of the bartender an hour ago.

Joey's respect for Lance's integrity and the way he handled himself and his clients had made a lasting impression. Joey could only hope to emulate that degree of professionalism in the years to come. He did not, however, want to deal with the constant scrutiny and pressure of doing his job while being put under the Washington, DC, microscope. Lance could barely go out to dinner without being subjected to a barrage of questions from various members of the media. He dealt with all of it admirably, as just another part of his job, but Joey hated it. He couldn't wait for the trial to end so he could wrap up his time with Merritt Brothers and return to his North Carolina roots. Taking an associate position with his father's law firm might be perceived, by some, as moving down a couple of rungs on the ladder of success. But to a small-town boy from Honeysuckle Creek, it felt exactly right. It was time for Joey Finch to go home.

Diana and Roman felt as if they were never going to get home. Scarcely a mile after exiting the interstate the stop-and-go traffic had become more stop than go. Any attempt at adultlike behavior had dissolved into adolescent silliness, their usual response to abject boredom.

"Stop it, Roman," Diana gasped. "I can't breathe." She had collapsed in the passenger seat, giggling hysterically at Roman's impression of a walrus. It wasn't the first time she had experienced her brother's spot-on imitations of wildlife—or creativity with drinking straws—but it had been a while. It was a shame, she thought, that the lady at the Dunkin' Doughnuts drive-thru would never know how much Diana and Roman had enjoyed the four extra straws she included with their coffee. The sound of Roman's phone put an end to their fun.

"It's Uncle Gary this time," said Diana. The serious expression on her face told Roman she was as worried about Lance as he was. She raised her eyebrows in silent question.

Roman took the plastic straws out of his nose and sighed before answering. "Hi, Uncle Gary. What's going on?"

"Roman, I need a favor." Gary's big voice seemed to echo in the enclosed space.

"I'll do what I can," Roman agreed. "I'm assuming this has to do with Lance. How's he handling the fallout?"

"According to Finch, Lance is in no condition to find his way back to his apartment or to do anything else by himself. Your Aunt Naomi and I are already at home and we want him to stay with us tonight."

"Sounds like the best plan, but…" Roman hesitated. "What exactly do you need me to do?"

"Simple, Roman," Gary confidently explained. "I…what?" They could tell he was talking to someone else, probably their feisty aunt. "Oh, yeah, sorry…*we* want you and Connor to go to Chutley's, retrieve Lance, and bring him here, to our house. We could do it, but your aunt says that Lance would never forgive us if anyone saw his mommy and daddy picking him up at a bar. That's on the outside chance he even remembers any of this tomorrow morning."

Roman glanced at Diana before he spoke. His own instructions involved taking her straight to their parents' house. In addition, he wasn't supposed to let her out of his sight. "I have Diana with me, Gary, and I'm supposed to take her straight to Mom and Dad's and—" He winced at the disgruntled expression on Diana's face. *Oh great,* Roman thought, *not that again.*

Gary interrupted: "Well, hello there, Diana."

"Hello, Uncle Gary," Diana said, sweetly.

"You wouldn't mind making a little pitstop before going home, now, would you?"

Diana was quick to reply. "Of course not, Uncle Gary. You know I'd do anything for Lance." She smiled triumphantly at her brother, batting her long eyelashes.

Roman thought fast. He was out of options…almost. "I'll meet Connor at Chutley's, then. Probably going to be about half an hour, though."

"Thanks, Roman. I knew I could count on you. And you, too, Diana. Wait a minute…What?" He was, apparently, receiving more instructions from Aunt Naomi. "Oh, yeah, right…And be sure to thank Finch for his loyalty. The other associates disappeared right after the trial ended, but

Finch stuck with Lance through the press conference *and* drove him back to Chutley's. Said he tried to talk Lance into going back to his apartment, but Lance wouldn't hear of it. He's been babysitting our boy for the past couple of hours and I'm sure he needs a break. He's leaving tomorrow, anyway, and probably still has packing to do. Joe and Juli raised a good one. I hate to lose him." Gary said, regretfully.

"Yeah," Roman agreed. "I like having him around."

Gary mumbled his agreement before adding, "Well, thanks, you two, and…what? Oh, yeah… Aunt Naomi says to drive safely." He hung up before they could reply.

Roman drove in silence for a few seconds before noticing Diana's catlike grin. "What?" he asked.

She regarded him with a superior air. "Hmm?"

"Why do you look so smug?"

She ticked the reasons off her fingers. "Stood by Lance. Drove him back to Alexandria. Babysitting him in a bar. You can't ask for anyone to be more loyal than that. And loyalty is an admirable trait. You've said so yourself, many times. Uncle Gary is all ripped up that Joey's leaving—and so are you. You just admitted it and…"

"Oh, now I get it. This is about Finch," Roman shook his head in disgust. "Listen, Diana, I've told you a thousand times that Joey Finch is a great guy. He's all the things Gary said and more. I'm going to miss him a lot and I'll always consider him a friend, but…"

"But…" Diana mimicked his warning, crossing her arms in frustration.

"But he's *not for you*. He's *not* a one-woman man. And you, my dear, little sister, are a one-man woman. Nothing will come of it but hurt feelings on your part and awkwardness on his. Don't go there. Well, hell…" Roman swore as traffic once again slowed to a crawl.

"Oh, lighten up, Roman. Here. Have another gummy bear," Diana said, handing him the bag that was more than half empty. Certain items were non-negotiables for long trips. Diana had packed every single one.

Roman took a handful of the gummy bears out of the bag before popping three or four into his mouth. "I thought you gave up on Finch a long time ago," he said, though his words were a bit off because of the sticky bears. "You're not still thinking about him, are you? You haven't seen him in years. Except for Mallory's funeral, and you didn't even talk to him then, did you?"

"I talked to him at Blane and Grace's wedding, Roman," Diana said, tartly.

"Yeah, but that was, like, a year ago." Roman regarded her with brotherly pity.

"It was ten months ago, thank you very much," Diana snapped, leaning her head against the passenger side window as her thoughts drifted back to last October.

"And who do we have here?"

The genuine astonishment on Joey Finch's face when Diana turned around mirrored her own. One minute she was inspecting the paintings hanging in the grand foyer of Heart's Ease, Blane McCallum's beautiful home, and the next…well, she was inspecting her idea of masculine perfection. She knew she would see him—it was his sister's wedding, after all—but she certainly hadn't expected him to seek her out. She hadn't even realized he was in the room until he tapped her on the shoulder.

She was equally flattered, and a bit disconcerted, that even though he hadn't recognized her, he apparently found her attractive enough to pursue. At least he found her back attractive enough. Or something. She watched as he quickly recovered his usual composure, hoping that her own expression looked equally bland. She wasn't a wide-eyed, nineteen-year-old anymore. She had, over the years, learned a thing or two about hiding her true feelings.

"*Diana Merritt.*" *His expression changed almost immediately to one of pure masculine admiration. "I should have recognized those red curls," he continued, smoothly, hooking a finger in one long spiral. He pulled it gently, watching as it sprung back in place.*

Diana tried to hide the shiver he invoked.

"How does it feel to be a famous author?" He was teasing her, his dark eyes sparkling mischievously.

"Well," she joked, following his lead. "I'm quite popular on the show-and-tell circuit. And I do get invited to all the best birthday parties. For eight-year-olds. So, I would say it feels pretty good."

It was her automatic response when someone mentioned her so-called "fame." In her own head, she was just Diana, and she always would be. She was blessed to be paid for doing something she loved. That was all.

Joey grinned, clearly pleased by her answer. "Seriously, I think you do great work." He casually leaned his shoulder against the wall beside the painting.

She studied him for a minute, not quite sure if he was still teasing or just being polite. "And you've read my work?" she asked, striving for nonchalance, even though she could feel the heat creeping into her cheeks.

"Of course," Joey said. "Hasn't everybody?"

Diana didn't reveal by even a flicker of an eyelash that his answer disappointed her. His casual dismissal stung a little, but only for a few seconds. His next words more than made up for her initial reaction.

"So, how did you ever come up with the ending of Nanny Di and the Perfect Harmony? *The idea that singing backwards* and *in a minor key would open the frozen door was genius. Pure genius." Joey's words were completely sincere. "I like the fact that you always surprise me, the way there's some development in the story that I don't see coming. You're extremely talented, Diana."*

Diana's wayward heart skipped a beat as another wave of heat flashed through her body. She couldn't quite believe it, but Joey Finch knew what he was talking about. He really had read her books. She relaxed under his genuine interest, flashing him a grin. It was a heady feeling to know that she had captured the attention of the most attractive man in the room.

"And..." he continued, obviously warming to his subject, "...I also liked the tap-dancing penguins in Nanny Di and the South American Surprise. *They really were." He hesitated a split second before continuing. "A surprise. The penguins, I mean. The penguins were, um...a surprise."*

Was Diana imagining things or was a faint flush creeping up Joey's cheeks? She watched as his expression went from confident to chagrined. He stumbled with his words. "I mean, I like all of your books. They're all good... um...every single one."

The amused voice of one of the groomsmen Diana had met earlier explained Joey's suddenly pained expression. "What's up, Joe?" the groomsman asked. "Is it possible you're trying to convince this lovely lady to put you *in one of her books? Something like...*Nanny Di and the Awestruck Attorney?*"*

The two groomsmen who accompanied Joey's interrogator grinned good naturedly, obviously enjoying their companion's little joke.

Joey recovered quickly. "I was actually thinking of the word awesome, *Roger.* Nanny Di and the Awesome Attorney. *Now that sounds, well...awesome." He winked at Diana, once again in control.*

"Naw, Joey." The youngest groomsman in the little group—Diana thought his name was Zack—quickly disagreed. "Not awesome. *There are lots of better words that rhyme with* attorney." *He turned to Diana, raising his hand to shield his mouth as if telling a secret, but speaking loudly enough for half the room to hear. "You could use* Awful. Arrogant. Aggravating. Annoying...*"*

"How about Aging? *Or even* Ancient?*" The other groomsman—the one who looked like Denzel Washington—interrupted, his eyes twinkling merrily. "*Nanny Di and the Ancient Attorney. *That's a great book title if I ever heard one."*

Diana couldn't help but giggle a little at the irritated expression on Joey's face.

"First of all, Evander, you are *older than I am," Joey reminded the grinning giant before turning on the teenager. "And, for your information, Zack, none of the words you suggested in any way rhyme with* attorney." *He turned*

to Diana, who couldn't stop giggling at their exchange. "And I don't know why you're giggling. You're supposed to be on my side." Joey raised his eyebrows in mock disapproval.

"How about the word lawyer?" Diana asked, feigning innocence. "I'll bet you could come up with all kinds of words to use with lawyer."

"I can, as a matter of fact," Joey began. Nanny Di and the Loveable Lawyer, Nanny Di and the Laughing Lawyer, Nanny Di and the—"

"Lousy Lawyer," Zack piped up, happily.

"How about Lazy?" Evander asked, "Nanny Di and the Lazy Lawyer."

"Loser?" Roger's contribution was accompanied by a wicked grin.

"Wait a minute. I've got it," Zack announced proudly. He paused for effect as Joey sighed loudly, pantomiming a bored yawn. "Nanny Di and the Love 'Em and Leave 'Em Lawyer."

A laughing blonde joined the group just in time to hear Zack's words. Diana had met Lou Ann—she preferred to be called Lou—earlier. The lovely woman was a bridesmaid and the designer of the wedding dress.

"Almost, Zack," said Lou with a mischievous wink in Joey's direction. "But you need to rearrange it a little. Nanny Di and the Lawyer Who Loved Them and Left Them. Perfect."

Joey laughed along with their good-natured heckling. After dramatically running his finger around the front of his collar, he delivered the appropriate exit line, "Guess that's my cue. Time to leave 'em." He walked away with a salute and a sheepish grin, to the delight of his friends.

Diana hadn't talked with Joey much after that, except for a few memorable moments when he stood toe-to-toe against Mallory on her behalf. She had, however, been able to observe him—surreptitiously, of course. And, in spite of what she had previously been told, she was willing to attest that Joey Finch was exactly what she had always thought him to be. A nice guy.

Diana frowned. Unfortunately, there was just one thing wrong with that assessment. He was a nice guy with zero interest in her. Because even though Joey asked her to dance at the reception, she knew he had done so only because he didn't want to dance with Mallory. That didn't count, she reminded herself. And what did they talk about while they were dancing? Diana sighed. They spent the entire song talking about Mallory and Devin's mess of a marriage. While she had been happy to lend Joey some insight into the man who was destined to become his brother-in-law, she couldn't help but wish that Joey had danced with her because he wanted to. Was that too much to ask? Apparently so.

Since then, she had tried to convince herself that a relationship with Joey Finch was never going to happen. Every time she heard someone mention his name, she reminded herself it was never going to happen. On the few occasions when their paths crossed in Alexandria, she purposely avoided him, because it was never going to happen. Except for a token "Hi, how are you?" she hadn't spoken to him since the wedding. What was the point?

It was never going to happen.

But Mallory's death in June and Diana's own close call just a week ago were making her reconsider her deep-rooted assumptions. Life was fleeting. There were no guarantees and, definitely, no do-overs. Maybe, just maybe, it was time to take a few more chances. And, since it appeared fate was giving her another chance with Joey Finch, she intended to take it.

CHAPTER EIGHT

*J*oey casually glanced toward the large front window of Chutley's. The woman was still there. He could feel her eyes boring into his back. So far, he had managed to avoid meeting the pouty gaze of the hot brunette, but he had a feeling his luck was running out. *Well, hell.* He really didn't have time for meaningless frivolity tonight. And, to be brutally honest, he just wasn't interested in what she had to offer. He was pretty sure they had gone on a date a couple of years ago. Her name was Carley. Or, possibly, Carrie. Or was it Shirley? Hell, he couldn't remember. She remembered him, though, if her increasingly obvious efforts to get his attention were any indication.

Joey grimaced. That was the trouble with his *one and done* dating policy. While he was extremely careful to steer clear of false expectations, a few women always refused to believe he was immune to their charms. He was, though. He was completely immune. And because of that blessed immunity, his life was his own. He remained blissfully free from the romantic angst, complications, and heartaches he had witnessed so many times in the lives of his family and friends. He was free. And he liked it that way. At the ripe old age of thirty, Joey Finch was a confirmed bachelor with no plans to change that status. He had tried to explain his thoughts on the subject to his marriage-obsessed sisters the last time he was at home. Without success.

"But, Joey, if you don't get married and have children, they'll have to change the name of the firm to Parker and Merritt after you retire instead of Parker, Finch, and Merritt. Did you think about that?" Joey's little sister, Darcie looked ridiculously pleased by her observation.

His other sister, Grace, nodded encouragingly. "That was a good one, Darcie."

Ouch. Joey hadn't thought of that. As a matter of fact, Darcie's observation hit a little too close to home. He refused to let his sisters know that, of course. "How long have you been waiting to use that one, Princess?" he asked, casually.

"I just thought of it," Darcie admitted proudly, pleased to have scored another point in their eternal game of sibling one-upmanship.

Joey gave a long, suffering sigh. "If the good Lord wants me to get married, He'll send me a sign," he said, hoping such a definitive statement would be enough to end the current version of their ongoing conversation.

But Darcie was a fledgling attorney. She never sugarcoated the truth as she saw it. "The good Lord could send a text straight to your phone, Joey, and you wouldn't read it," she complained. "He would have to drop a ton of bricks on your head to get your attention."

Grace frowned. "Do you think it would take a ton of bricks?" She was the middle child and tended to be the peacemaker of the trio. "Couldn't it be just one brick?"

"It would have to be a really big brick," Darcie said, "to get through that thick skull of his." She was supremely irritated with her brother if her glare was any indication.

"Well, what if it was just big enough to get his attention, but not big enough to do any permanent damage?" Grace asked, biting her lip.

Darcie paused to consider the suggestion. "One brick would work but it would need to be big enough to permanently un-damage his damaged brain."

Joey looked from one sister to the other in amazement. He couldn't believe they had nothing better to talk about. "Seriously, you two are going to waste time debating the dimensions of an imaginary brick?"

He glanced at Grace's husband, Blane—who was also his best friend— expecting sympathy. "See why I don't want to get married? Give me a hand here."

Blane tightened his arm around Grace's shoulders, basking in the glow of her bright smile. "Sorry, Joe, I can't help you out this time. You've got it all wrong. Marriage is an adventure."

"An adventure I choose to avoid," Joey added.

Grace studied her brother, thoughtfully, before nodding in satisfaction. "I understand completely, Joey."

"Thank you, Brat." Joey was surprised by Grace's unexpected support. "You always were more reasonable than the Princess." As their brother, it was his duty to invoke his sisters' childhood nicknames whenever possible. He would have done it regardless, for the sheer joy of watching their annoyed reactions.

Grace, however, ignored his comment. "I understand that you don't want a brick to fall on your head. You want God to send you a sign that's a little less painful." She smiled at the expression of pure exasperation on her brother's face.

Blane grinned at that. "I don't know, Green Eyes, a brick might actually be less painful than…say…getting mowed down by a wheelbarrow." His eyes were full of satisfaction. His first encounter with his future bride had been a comedy of errors.

Grace glared at her grinning spouse. "Seriously, Blane, do you have to describe it like that? Can't you just say 'run into by a wheelbarrow'? Honestly, I barely tapped you. Is it my fault you have terrible balance?" But she was laughing, too, along with everyone else.

"At least you weren't verbally attacked," Devin said, joining the group. He shook his head sorrowfully. "There I was…a poor, helpless invalid. Lying in my bed. And all of a sudden…POW!" He watched with glee as Darcie's dark eyes narrowed into slits.

"*You have never been a poor, helpless anything in your life, Devin Merritt. You know you started it. And you know you deserved it. Case closed.*" She crossed her arms and stuck her nose into the air.

The conversation dissolved into a melee of exaggerated versions of each story until Joey relaxed, assuming he was off the hook.

It was Devin who determined he wasn't getting off so easily. "*How about a bat?*" he asked, bringing the conversation back to its original focus.

Pain. Specifically, Joey's pain.

"*What are you talking about, Merritt?*" Joey regarded the man warily.

Devin's scarred visage and stark, black eye patch would have been intimidating if not for the mischief glowing in his single eye. Darcie's amused approval of her significant other's suggestion wasn't making the situation any better for her brother.

Devin, however, was glad to clarify his statement. "*Maybe you need to be hit in the head with a baseball bat,*" he said, matter-of-factly. Truth be told, he still owed Joey for giving him a hard time at the beginning of his relationship with Darcie. Devin grinned, glad to be on the other side this time.

"*A bat would be just the thing,*" Darcie agreed enthusiastically. "*Even Joey couldn't possibly ignore getting hit in the head with a bat.*"

"*Why does everything you two suggest involve a head injury?*" Joey asked. "*And why are you talking about me as if I'm not sitting right here?*"

"*Did you hear something...?*" Devin asked, causing the whole group to dissolve into laughter.

Joey shook his head in mock defeat. "*Devin, my unofficially-official future brother-in-law, I can believe you sold me out like that. I deserve it from you. But Blane...I never thought my oldest friend would desert me. See what happens to your brain when you're in a relationship? You two are living proof of why I need to stay single.*"

Devin glanced at his watch. "*Suit yourself, Finch. You're the one who's missing out.*" Leaning over, he planted a brief kiss on Darcie's lips. "*C'mon, Darce. It's time to go home.*"

Joey stared at the happy couple. The look in his sister's eyes for the man she loved was enough to make even an old bachelor like Joey Finch change his mind about marriage.

Almost.

"All right," Joey said, quickly, so he wouldn't have to think about Darcie going home with Devin. Darcie was his baby sister, after all. "All right," he said again. "If I get hit on the head with a brick…"

"A ton of bricks," chimed Darcie, smiling broadly.

"One brick," Joey continued.

"One really big, heavy brick," Darcie added.

"DAR-CIE," Grace, Blane, and Devin all said at once, causing Darcie to stick out her tongue at them.

"If I get hit in the head with a brick…" Joey repeated, because at this point, he would have agreed with anything to shut them up on the subject. "…then, and only then, will I know that the brick is a sign from God that it's time for me to get married. But, my sisters," Joey said, slyly. He had found the chink in their armor. "What if I'm with more than one woman when this prophetic brick falls on my head? What then? How do I know which one I'm supposed to marry?"

Blane and Devin grinned at his logic. Even Grace couldn't hold back a smile, although it was accompanied by an overly dramatic sigh.

Only Darcie refused to bend. "You just wait, Joey Finch, you're going to fall in love with some poor, unsuspecting woman eventually. It's only a matter of time. And when that momentous day comes, I hope with all my heart that the lady of your dreams doesn't give you the time of day."

"No chance of that, little sister," Joey said, smugly. He was born with the ability to charm the opposite sex, effortlessly. It was a well-known fact.

"Hmph." Darcie chose to end that particular conversation the way she usually did when Joey was right, much to his everlasting satisfaction.

"Joe. Hey, Joe."

Lance's overly loud whisper pulled Joey's focus squarely back to his current predicament. He studied the man in front of him. Lance was leaning a bit too far to the left, precariously close to toppling from his bar stool. Joey reached over to prevent just that, shaking his head sadly. Lance—one of the finest lawyers Joey had ever known—had made the fatal mistake of putting his trust in the wrong woman. Joey shuddered. Although Lance had many outstanding qualities that Joey would be glad to emulate, putting himself at the mercy of a woman was not one of them.

"How do you feel, Lance?" Joey asked. He didn't like the pallor of Lance's skin. Watching over a drunken man was one thing but cleaning up after him was a different thing entirely.

"You thought she was innocent, didn't you, Joe?" Lance lowered his head to the bar before Joey could answer.

"I'm sure one of The Boys will get here soon," the bar manager said, sympathetically.

Joey nodded, wordlessly. He had no choice but to continue his vigil.

CHAPTER NINE

"*H*ere we are," Roman announced, shaking Diana's shoulder gently.

She blinked, sleepily. "What?" she mumbled, arching her back to relieve the stiffness of her uncomfortable position. She had been napping just long enough to make her a little disoriented. She looked around in confusion. "Why did you park here, Roman?"

Her sleepy gaze roamed the sidewalk. Chutley's was nowhere in sight. For some reason, Roman had pulled into an open parking space on a side street several blocks from his apartment building. That was strange, her sleep-logged brain thought. Roman hadn't said anything about stopping by his apartment first. Unless…She studied her brother's shuttered expression, suddenly wide awake.

He refused to meet her gaze as he announced his decision. "Look, Di, I've been thinking, and…"

"And?" She was fairly certain she wasn't going to like whatever it was her overprotective brother had been thinking.

"I want you to take my key, go up to my apartment, and wait for me to come back. You'll be safe there."

"No," she said, stubbornly, crossing her arms.

Roman sighed. "Look, Diana, we don't know what kind of shape Lance is in. You know him as well as I do. He's always careful to hold himself to a certain standard. He'll be mad as hell if he finds out that you've seen him at his worst. And he'll be embarrassed and...damn it, Di, it's a guy thing. Okay? He's in a bad place and having you there is only going to make him feel worse." Roman waited, eyeing the mutinous expression on his sister's face.

Everything Roman said was true. Diana had been Lance's "little buddy" since she was able to toddle along behind him. *Drat.* He would be more than a little upset if she tried to tag along now. Diana's shoulders slumped in disappointment. Familial loyalty won out as she regretfully set aside the oh-so-tempting idea of "accidentally" running into Joey Finch at Chutley's. She was headed to Honeysuckle Creek, she reminded herself. And so was the attractive Mr. Finch. She would have plenty of opportunities for "accidental"—or not-so-accidental—encounters in the very near future.

"All right," she grumbled. "I'll wait for you. But I hope you have something to eat in your apartment. Otherwise, I'll probably starve to death before you get back." She scuffed the floormat with the toe of her shoe, trying to look pitiful. "We'll get home too late for Mom and Dad to take us to the Pumphouse, now."

"We were never going to go to the Pumphouse, anyway," Roman reiterated. "It's Friday night. No way we were going to walk in without a reservation on Friday night. But maybe we can go tomorrow. How does that sound?"

Diana wanted to laugh at the relief on her brother's face at her unexpected acquiescence, but she nodded instead. He had obviously expected her to put up a bit more resistance to being left behind. It was sweet that Roman had taken time to explain his decision. He had actually parked the car for a discussion as opposed to just dumping her out in front of his building like he would have done a couple of years ago.

"That sounds like a good plan, Roman," she agreed, enjoying the fact that, for once, he was treating her like an adult. "We can call first thing in the morning."

Roman grinned. "*You* can call, Di. You know how much I hate making reservations."

Diana wrinkled her nose at her self-satisfied sibling.

Roman started the car, checking his mirrors at the same time the driver in the car behind him switched on his bright lights. "Damn it," Roman swore, momentarily blinded. "That guy was just parked behind me thirty seconds ago. He needs to make up his freakin' mind."

"Maybe he's lost," Diana said, rustling through the pitiful remains of the bag of snacks she had packed earlier. "How do you know it's a man, anyway?"

"He's been behind us since we turned onto Washington Street. I checked him out at one of the stoplights," Roman said, as matter-of-factly as possible. "If it *is* a woman, she has a really impressive beard." He didn't want to alarm his sister, but he was taking his role as protector very seriously. This particular car had been behind them since they turned off the interstate. Roman had relaxed his guard only when he got a good look at the man's beard. And the "Hook 'em Horns" plate on the front bumper. No way Diana's almost-kidnapper had grown a beard in a week's time. Or moved to Texas.

Diana continued to dig in the snack bag, thoroughly vexed to realize that nothing remained. "Seriously, Roman. How could you possibly have eaten *everything* that was left? I wasn't asleep that long."

"Well," Roman admitted, sheepishly, "I was hungry. And after Uncle Gary called, I figured I wasn't going to get any dinner."

His sister's eyes filled with outrage. "You even ate both packs of 'nabs,'" she accused, using their childhood name for the orange crackers filled with peanut butter.

Roman fidgeted uncomfortably. "You were asleep," he hedged. It was the best excuse he could come up with.

"I'll starve," Diana said, mournfully, crumpling the bag and tossing it to the floorboard. She changed her mind a few seconds later, deciding instead to put the bag in the small trash bag she had brought with them. No need to dirty her own car to make a point.

"You will not starve," Roman said, defensively. "You're going to my apartment."

"What do you have to eat in your apartment?" she asked suspiciously.

Roman thought for a minute. "There's some cereal. And maybe a couple of protein bars."

"Cereal and protein bars? Oh, that sounds delicious," she said sarcastically. "Maybe I'll just make an omelet."

"Um…" Roman shrugged noncommittedly.

Diana's exasperation grew. "Eggs, Roman? You *do* have eggs?"

"Um, no eggs, but…"

"I'll starve." Diana leaned her head back against the headrest in a convincing display of despair.

Roman stopped the car under his building's awning. With a grimace, he dug into his pocket to take out his wallet. "Here. Take my key. *And* my American Express card. Order whatever you want."

Diana smiled happily. If she couldn't have Joey Finch, as least she could have teriyaki chicken with broccoli. And udon noodles. At least she could have udon noodles. She leaned over to kiss her brother on the cheek before glancing expectantly toward the building. Her favorite doorman usually rushed right outside to help her from the car. But at the moment, he was nowhere in sight.

"Where's Louie?" she asked as she opened the car door herself.

"Probably has the night off," Roman said, with a grimace. "I'm sure he'll be devastated that he missed you." Roman was convinced that Louie had a crush on his sister. And he didn't like it one little bit.

Diana grinned at her brother's caustic tone. "Bye, Roman. Call me when you get Lance settled."

Her brother's voice stopped her before she could put her foot on the pavement. "Hey, sis, aren't you forgetting something?"

"What?" She slid back into her seat, a puzzled expression on her face. "I have your key and your credit card in my pocket."

Roman grinned at her confusion. "What about that enormous excuse for a tote bag that you carry? You know, the one that weighs more than a small child." Greatly exaggerating his effort, Roman hoisted her heavy bag from behind the console onto the passenger seat. "Wow, Di, I'm exhausted." He fell back into his seat as if overcome by exertion. "My sister is a beast."

"A beast." Diana wrinkled her nose in distaste. "Thanks, Roman," she said. "That's exactly what every woman wants to be called." She hooked the offending tote bag over her shoulder. "Be careful, brother dear, and give my love to Lance." *And to Joey Finch.* She added the last part in her head as she closed the car door.

She blew her brother a kiss, watching his car until he drove out of sight. The thought of Roman's credit card in her pocket and her soon-to-be-ordered dinner softened any remaining animosity she may have harbored at being left behind. Poor Roman, she thought. She was pretty sure that dealing with a drunken, defeated Lance was going to make her brother wish he was still stuck in a car with his nervous wreck of a sister. Imaginary brakes and all. Maybe she should order him some Kung Pao chicken so he would have something to eat when he got home. Roman loved Kung Pao chicken. Mind made up, Diana walked briskly toward the double doors of her brother's apartment building.

Diana's attempt to walk into the building was halted by the frenzied efforts of a pair of senior citizens. The agitated ladies flatly refused to enter the building at the same time. And neither would yield to the other. Diana became increasingly irritated as she stood behind them, waiting for the two to sort it out. The doorman—oblivious to his responsibilities—stood watching from inside the lobby. Diana finally managed to get his attention by waving at him through the window. She pointed to the women impatiently. The doorman didn't move. He merely laughed, shrugging his shoulders.

Diana had almost decided to jump into the fray as impromptu mediator when she felt a tremendous shove from behind. The push propelled Diana forward, into the warring ladies and through the doors of the lobby, effectively ending the disagreement. The two ladies, their shopping bags, and one large cup of some unknown beverage sprawled in various directions on the lobby floor.

Diana, who managed to stay on her feet initially, gravely miscalculated her efforts to jump over the spill. She slipped on the edge of the mess but, thankfully, caught herself before her face hit the floor. She ended up in what looked like a very awkward yoga position. She also became intimately acquainted with the unknown beverage. It was Dr. Pepper.

The man who pushed her from behind never paused. He unceremoniously stepped right over her, narrowly missing her head with his fancy cowboy boots. He threw some remark over his shoulder to the doorman and kept right on walking. Diana couldn't hear what he said, but she was almost certain that it had been directed at her. The unhelpful doorman rewarded the cowboy with a loud guffaw.

The doorman's unprofessional laughter died a quick death under Diana's disbelieving glare, however. The two arguing ladies, united by mutual hardship, scurried to pick up their various bags. As Diana tried to stand, her foot slipped out from under her, caught on the far-flung remnants of the sticky spill. Regaining her balance was no easy feat, thanks to the awkward weight of her heavy tote bag. She wavered back and forth—arms flapping in the air like some deranged chicken—until she finally regained her footing. She tensed when she heard someone clapping behind her. A glance at the useless doorman confirmed that he was laughing again, obviously enjoying her discomfort. What a jerk!

"Thanks so much for your help." She didn't even try to keep the sarcasm from her voice. She detested those who gained joy from the misfortune of others. It was one of her pet peeves. "Don't you think you ought to get a mop or something?" she asked, gingerly putting some distance between herself and the worst of the spill. "This floor is dangerous."

The arrogant doorman was unimpressed. "Sorry, lady. I don't do mops," he said in a voice dripping with disdain.

"Well, maybe you need to call the person who does do mops," Diana suggested, politely. "Someone is going to get hurt."

The patronizing man pointed to his nametag. "Look, lady, I'm the doorman. See? It says so right here. There's the door and I'm the man."

Diana was tired, hungry, and very, very annoyed. There was absolutely no way she was going to let this *do-nothing* doorman have the last word. She gasped dramatically. "Thanks so much for telling me that you're the doorman. I would *never* have guessed, all by myself, since I have yet to see you touch the door." At his surprised expression, she launched into full-nanny mode. "You ought to be ashamed of yourself. You're here to keep the residents of this apartment safe, and—"

He interrupted smugly: "You don't even live here, do you, lady?" He looked her up and down, making her quite conscious of her bedraggled state. His lips curled into a superior smile.

Diana hesitated. "Well, no, but my brother—"

"Isn't here right now, is he?" The doorman looked from side to side as if searching for someone before addressing her in a tone dripping with condescension. "*You* probably need to move on, lady, before I call security."

Diana turned her back on the aggravating man, struggling to swallow her outrage. And the sudden urge to find a mop and whack him over the head.

The Dr. Pepper-Stained Nanny and the Dazed, Disconcerted Doorman.

She immediately reprimanded herself for her vengeful—and out-of-character—vocabulary, even though the title made her feel slightly better. She paused for a second to check on her skirt, hoping the stain would come out with a little extra stain remover. After readjusting her heavy bag, she glanced over her shoulder.

The cowboy had joined the doorman by the window. They were having quite a discussion, if their laughing camaraderie was any indication. The doorman was watching her, but the cowboy was studying his fancy pointed-toe boots. Eager to leave the obnoxious pair behind, she stomped across the lobby and headed toward the elevator. In reality, she stepped carefully across the floor to avoid giving the doorman the satisfaction of watching her fall. Again. But in her mind, she was stomping. By the time she made it to the elevator, the doors were just starting to close.

"Hurry, dear." The lady who had dropped her Dr. Pepper waved her hands frantically. The other lady—the one with the largest shopping bags—held the door until Diana was safely aboard.

But before she could thank the helpful woman, Tall Tex (as Diana had come to call the cowboy) shoved past Diana, knocking the strap of her heavy tote bag off her shoulder. The pushy cowboy must have sprinted across the lobby at the last minute. *He has a lot of nerve,* she fumed, readjusting her bag. As if the small space wasn't crowded enough. She tried to glare at him, but he had moved behind her and his head was down. All she could see was his cowboy hat and his bushy beard peeking out beneath it.

"What floor, dear?" Big Bags, the shopping-bag lady, asked.

"Four, please," Diana responded, resolving to maintain her distance from Tall Tex. She tried to limit herself to one angry confrontation per day, she remembered sarcastically. Sarcasm wasn't her specialty, but it had been a rather trying afternoon.

"I'm headed that way, too, dear," Dr. Pepper said, patting Diana's arm. Her gray hair was tinted a pale shade of purple. She leaned closer, adding, "We're so glad that somebody finally stood up to that doorman."

"I'm afraid it didn't do much good," Diana said. "And the wet floor made it really difficult to stand up at all." She tried to make light of the situation in an effort to avoid a pointless conversation. The ladies looked at each other, blankly, as her joke sailed right over their heads.

Big Bags patted her on the other arm. "Don't be so hard on yourself, dear. You made your point."

"Otherwise, he wouldn't have threatened to call security," Dr. Pepper added. "He's the rudest man. He's nothing like Louie. Why just the other day, he…"

Diana listened politely, amused that the former antagonists from the lobby, were, now, apparently, the best of friends. The ladies kept up a lively conversation about their mistreatment at the hands of the callous doorman.

Diana responded with a few nods and commiserating "Uh-huhs" at what she hoped were the appropriate intervals, but her mind wandered.

She had been so distracted by the doorman that she hadn't spent much time thinking about the tall cowboy. It was obvious that he was ill-mannered, too...a sorry excuse for a human being now that she thought about it. What kind of a man went around pushing women down, anyway? And, as if that wasn't bad enough, he tried to kick her in the head. He probably kicked babies, too. She'd like to give him a swift kick somewhere else with those pointed-toe boots....

Those fancy, pointed-toe boots, she fumed. They looked brand-new, as if they had never been worn. And so did his hat...She wouldn't be surprised if there was still a price tag hanging on it somewhere. He wasn't a real cowboy, she decided. He was a fake. A pretender. A Wyatt Earp wannabe. She was certain it was all for show.

She was also certain Tall Tex was watching her. She felt a cold chill run down her spine. He made her skin crawl. He really did. There was only one other person who had ever made her feel that way and...Her eyes flew wide open. *Drat, drat, and...oh, damn it.* The twisted scenario suddenly made perfect sense. Pinpricks as cold as ice swept through her body, nearly making her gasp aloud as the facts aligned themselves in her brain.

The man with the beard had followed them from the highway to Roman's apartment building. He had shoved her. Tried to kick her. Followed her into the elevator. He was, currently, standing somewhere behind her dressed like a cowboy. Sporting a fake beard. *And* making her skin crawl. As the reality sank in, Diana's heart began to pound.

Bill Watkins.

She stood perfectly still. She didn't even blink. It was every writer's worst nightmare. She was trapped in the sequel of a book she never wanted to write in the first place.

Nanny Di and the Psychotic Stalker: Part II—The Elevator.

Diana hated sequels, but—*oh well*—here she was. She tried to breathe in and out. She tried desperately to remain calm. She tried to access the situation logically, no easy trick under the circumstances. Her heart was beating so hard she was afraid it might just beat right out of her chest. Or explode. Yes, her heart just might explode. Or maybe she was going to hyperventilate. Or quite possibly both. Yes, that was it, she decided. She was going to hyperventilate immediately *before* her heart exploded. But, she pondered, would her heart still explode if she was lying prostrate on the floor of the elevator *after* hyperventilating? She quickly dismissed either option. With her luck, Bill would probably claim to be a doctor so he could "take her to the hospital."

Yeah. Right.

Diana forced herself to concentrate. She was in an elevator. With a psycho. A psycho was with *her* in an elevator. *She* was in an elevator with a psycho. She paused, but nothing was forthcoming. Her brain refused to function.

Psycho. Elevator...Elevator. Psycho.

As she glanced around in desperation, she saw the top of the book nestled in her giant bag. *Nanny Di and the South American Surprise.* The book with the tap-dancing penguins. Joey Finch liked that book. And she liked Joey Finch. She would like to get out of this elevator so she could continue liking Joey Finch...even if she had to like him from a distance.

Diana's brain was working again. If *she* was writing a book about being trapped in an elevator with a psycho, what would she write? In other words...what would Nanny Di do?

"Be brave, Nanny Di. Iggy says, 'Be brave.' "

Nanny Di would be brave, Diana told herself. She wouldn't stay in the elevator waiting to be the victim of a psycho. She would get out of the elevator.

GET. OUT. OF. THE. ELEVATOR.

As if on cue, the door to the third floor opened. Diana leapt into the corridor like a frightened fox pursued by a pack of hounds. There was only one hound, however, dressed in pointed-toe boots and a cowboy hat. Bill let loose with a completely inappropriate string of profanity as he pushed his way out of the elevator to continue the hunt.

"You need to clean up your mouth, young man!" Big Bags yelled.

"I thought she said she wanted the fourth floor," Dr. Pepper remarked as the elevator doors closed.

The only thing Diana wanted was to make it to the lobby. With that end in mind, she ran toward the *"Exit"* sign at the end of the deserted hallway. Her feet made no sound on the carpet. She didn't even consider yelling for help. Or knocking on any of the doors. Bill was a runner. He was fast. If she stopped for any reason…well, she refused to think about what would happen. And she refused to look behind her. She had no doubt that he was there. She heard the explosion of profanity that followed her flight; looking back would only slow her down. Every competitive swimmer knew that.

Instead, she concentrated on the door beneath the *"Exit"* sign. She braced herself for another sharp push from behind. Or a long-fingered hand closing around her arm. Instead, she almost paused in surprise when she reached the door, still ahead of her stalker. She barely fumbled with the handle as she shoved the heavy door open. She flew down the stairs, thankful she wasn't wearing heels. She had almost reached the landing that led to the second floor when she heard him enter the stairwell. The door slammed against the wall.

"Di-a-na…" he called. His voice echoed eerily off the walls. *"Di-a-na…"*

She forced herself to keep running. Her breath was coming in heavy gasps now. She felt lightheaded, a little dizzy. Probably from lack of oxygen. Or pure horror. She turned the corner of the first-floor landing as Bill—or Kenneth Wade, or whomever he was pretending to be today—easily scaled the railing. Diana might have been impressed with his athleticism if she wasn't completely terrified of his intentions. One more move like that on his part and the hunt would be over.

Unfortunately, he made that move, lunging down the last few stairs to catch her at the bottom. He shoved her back against the hard, metal railing, his arm against her throat. As Diana looked into his cold, trium-phant eyes, her survival instinct finally got the upper hand over her fear. She might be his prey, but she wouldn't be his victim. She was a Merritt, wasn't she? Her father. Her uncles. Her brother. Her cousins. At one time or another, they had all tried to prepare her for just such a situation.

Diana glared at him defiantly. She was not going down without a fight. Bill's legs were braced apart, one foot on the bottom step and one about two steps up. As he leaned his upper body into hers, he increased the pressure of his arm against her throat. He grinned cruelly, obviously enjoy-ing the opportunity to punish her a little bit more for trying to get away. He paid for it, though, because he unwittingly gave her the perfect target. Her knee came up—hard—to find its mark. Her attack was totally unexpected, sending her assailant to his knees. She swung her heavy tote bag at the back of his head. He sprawled on the steps, groaning and cursing.

Diana ran to the door, finding her voice as she rushed into the lobby. "Help!" she yelled. "I need help! I need..."

The lobby was completely empty, with the exception of the world's worst doorman. That useless excuse for humanity was lounging against the front window. Diana was momentarily flummoxed.

The cocky man didn't move. "What seems to be the problem, lady?" he asked in a bored voice.

Diana looked around in disbelief, still breathing hard from her exer-tions. How had the crowded lobby emptied so quickly? "Where...where is everybody?"

The doorman's arrogant gaze raked her form brazenly. He was, she realized, making no attempt to help her. If anything, he seemed to be stall-ing. "It's Friday night, lady." He shrugged, finally stepping away from the window. "Everybody is somewhere better than this. Except for me. And, well, looks like you're here, too." His gaze was suddenly alert as his lips tried to form a conciliatory smile.

He looked like a puffed-up toad. Diana experienced a strong feel-ing of wariness at his sudden friendliness. She attempted to speak calmly, hoping he wouldn't notice how her voice was trembling. "I need you to call

9-1-1. There is a man who has been following me. He attacked me in the stairwell. This has happened before and…"

"Where is this *man* who attacked you?" the doorman asked. "I don't see anyone but you."

Diana glanced at the stairwell, relieved that the door remained closed. "Um…he's…well, sort of incapacitated. That's why we need to call 9-1-1. Don't you have a security guard around here or something?"

"Sure, lady," the doorman nodded, talking to her as if she wasn't quite right in the head. "Don't you see the security guard? He's over there. By the elevator. He's an *imaginary* security guard. You know, just like your *imaginary* attacker." He let out a loud guffaw as if he was enjoying her distress.

"Seriously?" Diana let out a little huff of disbelief. And frustration. "Never mind." She started digging in her bag, searching for her phone. "I'll do it myself."

"Do what, Diana?"

She let out a squeak of surprise as Bill—slightly hunched over—limped into the lobby. He paused as the door to the stairwell shut behind him. His eyes glittered ominously, promising retribution, though he made no move to come closer.

Maybe he was playing with her like a cat with a mouse, Diana thought. Or, maybe, he was still a bit indisposed by his unexpected encounter with her knee. And with her giant tote bag. The part of her brain not overcome with fear—a very, tiny, small part—preened at the evidence of her small victory. The same detached brain cells also noted that her attacker's face was even more colorless than usual. Or maybe his extreme pallor was due to the stark contrast of his dark beard. His dark *fake* beard.

The doorman grabbed Diana's arm, pulling her closer.

"There he is," Diana said, desperately. "Now do you believe me?" She tried to pull her arm from the doorman's grasp, but he held on.

"She's a tricky one, Tex. Just like you told me," the doorman said, looking at Bill. "I almost believed her for a minute." He chuckled as Diana struggled to free her arm.

She looked at the doorman in amazement. " 'Believed me'? What are you talking about? What did he tell you?"

"She gets like this sometimes when she stops taking her meds," Bill said, with a respectable imitation of a Texas accent. "Then I've got to hunt her down and dose her up. Other than that, though, she's a decent little filly to have around. Ain't that right, honey?" Bill grinned, starting toward her.

Diana's shock gave way to panic. Panic gave way to the need for flight. She stomped on the doorman's foot. Caught off guard, he let go of her arm. She kicked him in the shin while swinging her heavy bag at his face. He lost his balance, landing in the large puddle of Dr. Pepper still on the floor. Diana didn't have time to enjoy the delicious irony of the doorman's self-induced misfortune. She ran through the front doors of the building, down the drive, and onto the crowded sidewalk. Logical thinking and sensible ideas—using her phone or telling someone else she needed help—disappeared. Only her adrenaline pushed her forward to the one location where she was certain to find help: Chutley's Bar and Grille.

CHAPTER TEN

A flurry of movement at the corner of the bar heralded Roman's arrival. To Joey's everlasting relief, the cavalry had finally shown up. Roman was a great favorite with the patrons of Chutley's. He paused to speak to several regulars before catching Joey's eye. He approached quickly, stopping beside Lance, who, once again, had his head buried in his crossed arms on the bar.

Roman raised his eyebrows. "Is he...?"

"Dead?" Joey asked, his lips tipping up at the corners. "No, not yet. But he'll probably wish he was when he wakes up tomorrow morning."

Lance's head popped up before his cousin could respond. "Roman," he slurred. "You thought she was innocent, didn't you?"

"Of course, Lance, we all thought she was innocent." Roman glanced at Joey, grimacing as Lance's head fell back onto his arms.

Joey shook his head in commiseration. Lance had left *beaten*, *defeated*, and *vanquished* behind hours ago. He had, it seemed, just crossed over to *pathetic*.

"Hellfire and damnation," hissed Roman, under his breath. "So, what am I supposed to do with this?" he asked Joey, indicating Lance's prone body. "I've never seen him like this before."

Their decision was put on hold by the appearance of the oldest of The Boys. There was nothing subtle about Connor Merritt. His red hair was as loud as his voice and exuberant personality. Nothing was sacred with Connor, either. Every word that came out of his mouth was the truth—at least as he saw it. Furthermore, he made no apologies for his—sometimes brutal—form of honesty. He was completely transparent and easy to read. Except in court. His uncanny ability to pull information out of an unwilling witness revealed his surprisingly hidden depths. His bluff and bluster disguised his savvy and intricate thought processes.

His hooded glance took in everything at once. Joey wasn't surprised by his immediate reaction.

"What the hell have you done to my teetotaling brother, Finch?"

Roman took a respectful step backward as his cousin advanced on Joey.

Connor's booming voice attracted the attention of at least half the patrons in the bar. "Lance hasn't been three sheets to the wind since law school," he said. "Unless you count that little episode two years ago with the DA's daughter." He shook his head in mock disappointment before holding out his hand to enfold Joey's in an almost painful grasp. "Thanks for handling him, Joe. I figured he'd fall apart after the verdict. Guess you got the worst of it, since this clown and I weren't available." He punched Roman in the shoulder before turning his intense perusal to his seemingly unconscious brother.

Joey was unable to hide her grin as Roman rubbed his shoulder the minute Connor's head was turned. Connor put a surprisingly gentle hand on Lance's arm. He shook him, showing not a hint of surprise when his brother's head popped up instantly.

Lance's face broke into a sideways grin. "Connie! What're you doin' here?"

"Thought I'd stop by to see how things were going with my *favorite* brother," Connor said, with a sigh.

"Aww...that's nice, Connie. I always knew I was your favorite... *Hey, wait a minute!* I'm your *only* brother." Lance leaned so far to the left, Connor had to catch him before he fell off the stool.

Connor put his arm around Lance, hooking his arm around his only sibling's shoulder. "Upsy-daisy, Lance," he urged. After helping his brother to stand, he watched Lance sway back and forth as his feet renewed their acquaintance with the floor.

Roman came up on the other side and smoothly slid his arm around his cousin's waist. "Whoa, now, Lance," he said, encouragingly.

"Roman," Lance said, happily...before his eyes were drawn to the unfortunate words—*Special Report*—flashing on the screen of the television on the wall. The media couldn't get enough of the trial footage. They continued to run the same clips over and over. Lance stopped dead in his tracks. For the first time in several hours, he appeared completely sober.

Connor, Roman, and Joey stood with him, watching another recap of Lance's part in the press conference. Joey cursed his carelessness in his head. He should have changed the channel on all the televisions in Chutley's...not just the one closest to Lance. Of course, if he had gotten up to do that, Lance would have fallen off his barstool. Still...

Lance's eyes went to his brother's face. "Connie, you thought she was innocent, didn't you?" he asked, hopefully.

Typical of the red-haired giant, he said the last thing anyone expected. "Hell, no, Lance. I thought she was guilty as sin the first time I met her. That's why I told you not to take the case, remember?" Connor regarded his brother with grudging amusement. "You, brother, were taken in by those big eyes and that pretty smile. No woman alive is that damn helpless. Now, let's get your drunken ass out of this bar."

Connor let go of Lance long enough to give Joey's hand another firm shake. "Thanks, again, Finch. And good luck in North Carolina. I'll miss seeing you around."

"Me, too," Roman added, struggling to hold up his sagging cousin. "Don't be a stranger."

Connor took up his share of the burden that was his little brother, turning their group in the direction of the door. "And, Finch," Connor added over his shoulder. "Check on Diana for us from time to time."

Joey's reaction was immediate. "Diana? What's going on with Diana? Nothing else has happened, has it?" The tension in his voice was obvious, as was his inability to hide his concern. "She's all right now, isn't she? After the kidnapping attempt, I mean." *Well, hell,* Joey berated himself. *Smooth, Finch, really smooth.*

Connor and Roman turned around at Joey's words, Lance a limp body between them.

"Relax, man." Connor regarded Joey curiously. "Diana's fine, now. And, so far, the kidnapper doesn't seem to have the balls to try again. Good news all around."

Joey's logical mind rushed to make sense of his reaction. He liked the Merritt family, he told himself. Therefore, he was always interested in hearing what they were up to. What *all* of them were up to, which, naturally, included Diana. And what was wrong with that, anyway? Why shouldn't he be interested?

But this time, Joey's rationale failed him. Just as it had consistently failed him since someone tried to kidnap Diana Merritt a week ago. The burning desire to see for himself that she was safe was unnerving to a confirmed bachelor like Joey Finch. His anxiety was sharp and specific, defined by something other than casual concern. And, obviously, very close to the surface.

Joey studied the two men in front of him, trying to assess their response to his outburst. Connor was eyeing him with amused speculation, while Diana's brother appeared downright offended.

Roman's frown deepened as Connor spoke. "Diana's moving down your way in a couple of days to take care of Amalie. Didn't Darcie tell you?"

In the presence of their obvious suspicion, Joey took the only way out.

He lied.

"I've been pretty busy lately with the trial and all." Joey's effort to sound casual ended up sounding incredibly shallow...even to his own ears. Unfortunately, however, it wasn't enough to shut him up. With his next words, he descended from shallow to complete jerk. "Darcie must have mentioned something about Diana moving to Honeysuckle Creek. I probably just forgot." *Sorry, Darcie.* Joey apologized to his sister in his head. In truth, he remembered every detail of their conversation about Diana's move.

Connor's eyes were full of humor. "Well, take care of her for us," the big man said. If his expression was any indication, he didn't believe a word of Joey's little speech.

Neither, apparently, did Diana's big brother. Roman was not amused. "Stay away from my sister, Finch."

Joey searched his friend's face, sure that Roman must be joking.

He wasn't.

No, Joey realized, somewhat disheartened. Roman wasn't joking at all.

Connor, however, seemed to think his cousin's warning was hilarious. He broke into loud laughter that, unfortunately, woke Lance from the nap he was enjoying.

"You thought she was innocent, didn't you?" Lance mumbled before dropping his head again.

And just like that, Joey Finch was forgotten. The look Connor and Roman exchanged was one of empathetic camaraderie.

The oldest of the Merritt Boys sighed, heavily. "C'mon, cuz, let's get our boy out of here."

As Joey watched them go, Connor glanced at Roman over his brother's bowed head. "Guilty as hell," he mouthed.

Joey wanted to chuckle despite the nature of the situation. He was going to miss the Merritt Boys.

Some part of Diana's brain finally reengaged midway through her flight, but in a detached, third-person sort of way. She could almost see herself running through the happy, Friday night crowds roaming downtown Alexandria. Dodging in and out of groups. Passing anyone who wasn't sufficiently inspired to excessive speed. Red curls flying. Giant tote bag swinging back and forth.

She must look like a lunatic. Roman was right. Her bag was ridiculously heavy. It might as well be full of rocks. Cowboy Bill and the doorman would attest to that fact, she thought, with satisfaction. In addition to a killer purse, she had one more advantage acting in her favor. She was wearing real shoes, not flimsy sandals. Cowboy Bill was wearing brand-new pointed-toe boots. Diana knew, from experience, that new boots were a speed killer, at least until the outsoles got roughened up. A few years ago, she had almost broken her ankle in a pair of new boots.

Really, Diana? she asked herself. *How fascinating.* A rational person with a fully functioning brain would be thinking about fleeing her kidnapper. But, sadly, Diana was not rational. Not at the moment, anyway. And her brain was barely functioning at all. She turned sideways to slide between a couple who were obviously in the middle of a disagreement. Both were unwilling to move on, it seemed, until their conflict was resolved.

"Excuse me," Diana managed to toss over her shoulder as she passed. She couldn't afford to slow down enough to be polite. She was struck by the difference between herself and the couple on the street. Fight or flight? Well, there was no doubt which option she had chosen.

Iggy says, "Be brave," she thought. *And I say, "Shut up, Iggy. You're not running from a psychotic cowboy."*

Nanny Di and the Overly Confident, Know-it-All Iguana Who Thought He was So Smart.

The title popped into her mind unbidden, followed by a high-pitched, slightly hysterical giggle. She was a bit surprised to realize the giggle belonged to her.

I'm sorry, Iggy, Diana apologized in her head. *I promise I will happily exhibit great bravery just as soon as I get to Chutley's.*

She was having an imaginary conversation with an imaginary iguana in her head. Nothing crazy about that. Nope, she decided, not a thing. Her sense of humor had suddenly reappeared. And her brain was working again. Perhaps the last few minutes of extreme cardio had done the trick or, maybe, it was the increased likelihood of reaching her sanctuary.

Facing the enemy with Roman or Connor—or, even, a drunken and defeated Lance—at her back was an appealing prospect. Any of those three would relish the chance to deal with Cowboy Bill. She hoped it would be Connor, though. He had enormous fists and used to play football when he was in college. Now, he worked out in a boxing gym.

She was close now. Chutley's was right across the street. So safe. And so very crowded. Customers were spilling out onto the sidewalk—relaxed and happy customers—celebrating the end of the work week. They were also innocent people, with no idea Diana was leading a psychopath into their midst. Guilt nearly gave her pause, but Diana forced herself to keep moving forward. She had exhausted all other options. Now, all she had to do was reach the crosswalk before the light turned green and traffic blocked her way.

She was going to make it.

The light turned green.

She was *not* going to make it.

"Be brave," said Iggy.

Diana squared her shoulders, willing the advice of the troublesome iguana out of her brain. That damn iguana was going to get a one-way ticket to some far away South American country, she decided. A country with active volcanoes. Yes, *lots* of active volcanoes....

Going against every safety rule ever advised by both the fictional and the factual Nanny Di—or perhaps the word was *actual*—Diana said a quick prayer. Taking a deep breath, she *ran*.

"What the hell...?" Joey's attention was drawn to the window. The honking horns and squealing brakes were the direct result of one woman's mad dash across the street. Against the light.

"What's happening?" the pretty brunette asked, peering over his shoulder.

Shirley had stepped in front of him as he attempted to follow the Merritts out the front door. At least he thought her name was Shirley. He had been addressing her as "honey" or "hon" ever since she had finally made her move in case he was wrong. To be honest, he didn't care what her name was. As soon as politeness allowed—maybe even before—he was going straight to his apartment. And straight to bed. Alone.

Shirley pressed closer to Joey, making him hyperaware of the difference in their height. "That woman has a death wish," she murmured into his ear.

Another strike against the attractive brunette, Joey mused. He added "extreme height" to the ever-growing list he was busily creating in his head. Shirley stood a full two inches taller than him in her flats. It made him nervous.

"Poor thing. She must be some kind of lunatic," Shirley added. "Or maybe she's late for an appointment."

"Or terrified," Joey said, under his breath. In his opinion, a person in full possession of her faculties would never put herself in mortal danger for something as mundane as a dinner date. His eyes swept the opposite side of the street, looking for...well, something that would explain her flight. The crowd of people on the corner looked completely innocuous. Some of them were even pointing at the random woman's suicide attempt to cross the street. No matter. Joey's intuition was undeterred. *Something* had caused the woman to run, and if he kept watching, he would figure out what that something was. He was used to working backwards to solve a puzzle. Every problem had a beginning, and sometimes...

"Wait a minute," he said aloud, his senses focused on the woman. Long skirt. Long legs. And those unforgettable red curls. He knew *exactly* who was risking her life right in front of his horrified eyes.

Diana Merritt.

He hadn't been able to get her out of his mind for days. And if he couldn't stop *thinking* about Diana, there was no way in hell he was turning his back on Diana-In-Trouble. What was it about the striking redhead that called to the primitive urges inside him? Whatever it was, his protective instincts were screaming. Without conscious thought, Joey shook off Shirley's clinging hands and moved toward the door.

CHAPTER ELEVEN

*V*ictory had never felt sweeter than it did the moment Diana reached the curb. She paused to glance across the lanes of traffic, spotting Bill's cowboy hat in the group of people still waiting to cross the street. She would have sighed with relief if she could breathe. Instead, she stood on the curb, gasping for air. She might be too far away to see Bill's eyes, but she was certain she could feel his anger. She wasn't safe yet. Not by a long shot.

As if to emphasize that point, the light turned yellow. Diana turned, plunging into the crowd outside Chutley's. She made it to the door just in time to collide with the broad chest of Joey Finch.

Joey Finch?

Her knees nearly gave way as her mind struggled to make sense of his presence.

Joey gently grabbed her upper arms to steady her. "Diana? Are you all right?"

His warm grip and compassionate voice were almost her undoing. He pulled her into Chutley's dimly lit interior, closing the door behind him.

Diana could barely squeak out a syllable. "Is…Roman…still…here?" she gasped.

Joey shook his head. "You just missed him. He and Connor are taking Lance—"

She nodded her head, her terrified eyes saying what she couldn't. She stood there shaking, looking unsure of her next move. Totally vulnerable. And very much alone.

Joey's heart couldn't stand it. "Hush, now. You're safe." He pulled her into a fierce hug.

More than anything, Diana wanted to burrow into Joey Finch's arms and stay there forever. His words, however, snapped her back to reality. She pulled away a little, her dark gray eyes meeting his. "No, I'm *not* safe. He's out there." She glanced out the window, catching a glimpse of the cowboy hat about halfway across the intersection. The light had finally turned red.

"Who?" Joey asked, urgently. "Your kidnapper?" When Diana nodded, he somehow managed to hide the surge of pure fury that rushed through him. It was the same way he had felt when he heard about the kidnapping attempt. Anger followed by an intense desire to protect. "What does he look like?" He could feel her tremble as she struggled to respond.

"Cowboy hat. Texas T-shirt. Beard. Boots. Pointed toes." She shook her head impatiently. "I mean…his boots have pointed toes." Her words were brief and choppy as she fought to catch her breath.

Joey nodded grimly. He released her from the haven of his arms. "You stay here." But as he turned toward the door, she grabbed his arm.

"No, Joey. You can't go out there," she said, a little desperately. "He's dangerous. He might have a weapon. There are too many people around."

"Damn it," Joey said, realizing the truth in her warning. He ran a hand through his hair, searching the area around him for an idea. His eyes lit on the massive bar that curled around the front of the room. The cramped space in front of it was currently unoccupied. He grabbed Diana's hand, tugging her around the corner of the bar.

"Get down," he said, pointing to the area behind the bar, under the counter. He put his finger to his lips. "Not a sound, Diana. And don't move until I tell you."

Diana nodded obediently, tucking herself into the small space. After a few seconds, Joey took off his jacket, tossing it down to her. She wrapped it around her shoulders, realizing for the first time that she was cold despite the warm August night. She watched Joey grab a hand towel from the bar. He tossed it over his shoulder and rolled up his sleeves, looking for all the world like a bartender just starting his shift. He appeared completely relaxed and competent behind that bar.

Diana was thankful for Chutley's typically heavy Friday night crowd. The other bartenders, she quickly realized, were too busy at the other end of the bar to notice Joey's masquerade. Sid, the bar manager—part bartender, part bouncer—had apparently stepped out to deal with a rowdy patron, the only reason he ever left the bar. Diana could only hope that when Sid did return, he wouldn't reveal her hiding place. Or use Joey as a punching bag.

"What'll it be, Texas?" she heard Joey ask, a few moments later.

"Nothing for me, thanks."

Hearing that voice made Diana tremble violently. Even with a Texas accent, she was certain. It was Cowboy Bill's voice. Oh, how she loathed the sound!

"Say, pardner," Cowboy Bill continued, "how about a little information?"

"Sure thing," Joey answered, in friendly invitation.

"My wife and I had a little misunderstanding, see, and…well, she got a little ahead of me and ran in here. She's about your height. Red hair. Gray eyes. And legs up to…well, let's just say they're memorable."

Out of the corner of his eye, Joey saw Diana flinch at the word *wife*. He saw her rest her forehead on her drawn-up knees, shrinking into a tight, little ball. She looked miserable. Joey had never wanted to punch anyone as badly as he wanted to punch the lying son of a bitch standing in front of him. Despite his intemperate wish, however, he managed to keep his voice light and cheerful.

"Sorry, Texas. I just got here. And I haven't seen anyone like that. I would have noticed, too." He grinned, in perfect understanding. "I'm partial to redheads. But I'll keep my eyes open. Sure you don't want something to drink?"

"No, thanks," Cowboy Bill mumbled. Without another word, he headed toward the tables in the center of the room.

Joey picked up a cocktail shaker. After filling it with ice, he began to shake the container in a relentless rhythm. He paused, forcing himself to take calming breaths. Allowing the cowboy—the one who dared threaten Diana Merritt—to walk away unimpaired had taken every bit of self-restraint Joey possessed. He tried to keep his body relaxed, an easy smile on his face, but he was pretty sure he couldn't hide the anger burning in his eyes. His grip on the shaker tightened as he started shaking it again. Hard. He couldn't beat the hell out of the cowboy at present, so the shaker would have to do. He was not, however, ruling out the beating idea completely. That depended entirely on the cowboy's next move.

Joey stopped rattling the cocktail shaker when he had regained a firm grip on his self-control. After a few seconds of silence, he reached down to squeeze Diana's shoulder. She looked up, squeezing his hand in return to let him know she understood. Her nemesis had moved on.

Joey put down the shaker. He picked up a glass from the counter, wiping it with the towel. His eyes followed the kidnapper's offhand perusal of the room. The cowboy was thorough, but casual. He moved leisurely between the tables. Talking to some of the patrons. Touching the tip of his hat. Nodding his head in greeting. In other words, painting the exact portrait of a Texas cowboy. The portrait they all expected to see.

Joey knew he had to involve the police. He was torn, however, between the desire to create a scene and the necessity for subtlety. Rushing from behind the bar to attack the scum was appealing on a deeply personal level. As was the potential pleasure of rearranging the cowboy's smug face.

Quietly summoning the law was probably the best choice, although not nearly as satisfying. Diana was right, he reminded himself. They didn't know if her attacker was armed or not. Hell, he could be some kind of psychotic serial killer cowboy.

Joey sighed, regretfully. For the safety of all concerned, he was going to have to contact the police. And he was going to have to do it quietly. Mind made up, he finally took his eyes off the cowboy long enough to search the long bar for someone who could be discreet.

When Joey's eyes met those of the bar manager—*How long had Sid been standing there?*—Joey realized that the man was studying him. Sid's casual stance—one ankle thrown over the other as he leaned against the rear counter behind the long bar—belied his intense scrutiny. He raised his eyebrows in response to Joey's subtle nod. Shoving away from his perch, he strolled over to Joey's end of the counter.

Sid clapped one enormous hand on the pretend bartender's shoulder, looking to all interested parties as if he was delighted to join his favorite employee. "What's going on, Finch?" he demanded in his gravelly voice. "Friday is our busiest night. You picked one hell of a time to be playing games." His tone was menacing. "I don't know who your friend is, but both of you need to—"

He stopped speaking as Diana poked her head out from her sanctuary, a wobbly little smile on her face. She waved her hand weakly.

"Miss Merritt?" Sid's grip on Joey's shoulder became a little painful. He had known Diana since she was a little girl. "Wait a minute...what's going on here?" Sudden understanding dawned in his eyes. He crouched down to Diana, letting go of Joey—and his stinging shoulder—in the process. "Miss Merritt?" Sid again asked in a gentle voice. "Does this have anything to do with what happened last week?" In response to Diana's surprised expression, he hastily explained, "Roman told me. I hope that's all right. He wanted to kill the bastard. They all did."

He looked up at Joey. "Still do," he amended.

"It's fine," Diana whispered. It was something of a relief that she didn't have to explain the situation. "But, Sid," she continued in a small voice, "He's here. In the bar. Right now. And...he's looking for me."

"Where the hell—"

Sid started to stand up, but it was Joey's turn to put his hand on the bartender's shoulder. "No sudden moves, Sid. He's dressed like a cowboy.

And he's wandering around from table to table. Says he's looking for his *wife*. We need to call 9-1-1 without calling attention to ourselves."

"Done," Sid said, rising to his feet. He casually grabbed a rack of glasses on the way up. He hadn't taken two steps when he paused. "Finch," he said, turning slightly so he could see Joey's face.

"What?" Joey asked.

"Don't poison anybody, okay?"

Diana couldn't help but smile at the irritation on Joey's face. She was still terrified. Completely terrified. But mixed in with that terror was the comforting knowledge that she wasn't alone.

Diana watched Joey pick up another towel so he could wipe the surface of the bar in front of him. She wondered what he would do if he actually had to mix a drink. He looked like he belonged in his impromptu role. His performance was so convincing that Diana was certain no one would ever guess he wasn't an employee of Chutley's.

"You're not a bartender."

Diana strained to hear the mysterious woman's voice over the noise of Chutley's on a busy night. Maybe Joey wasn't as convincing as she thought.

"Go away, Shirley," Joey said, in a low voice. "I'm busy."

The persistent brunette leaned in a little closer to whisper, "I know you're not a bartender, Joey Finch. You're a lawyer."

From her position under the bar, Diana was surprised to see amusement light Joey's face. He liked Shirley. She could tell. Shirley was probably petite. And blond. And sexy. All the things Diana wasn't. She probably had high heels and a little, tiny purse, too. Diana regarded her own stained skirt, dirty shoes, and giant bag ruefully. *Go away, Shirley.*

Joey flipped the cocktail shaker into the air, catching it behind his back. "Now, Shirley," he said, evenly. "What makes you think I'm not a bartender?"

"You're a lawyer, Joey." Her voice held a teasing quality that was getting on Diana's last nerve. "Everybody knows that." Diana pictured the elegantly petite Shirley raising her elegantly petite shoulders in an elegantly petite shrug.

"Suit yourself, Shirley," Joey said, in a businesslike manner. "It's really been great seeing you again, but the show's over. You can run along now."

Diana couldn't help the pleasure she felt in Joey's brief dismissal of the woman. *Bye-bye, Shirley.*

Shirley narrowed her eyes and continued in a low voice: "You're helping *her*."

"Helping *who*, Shirley?" Joey's bland expression gave nothing away. He cut his eyes briefly to Diana under the bar. Diana's wide gray eyes spoke volumes. She was afraid Shirley was going to reveal her hiding place. He scowled at the nosy brunette across the bar.

"You're helping the girl who crossed the street against the light," Shirley said, completely undeterred by his frown. "I know you are because I saw you hide her behind the bar." At Joey's continued blank look, she blew out a breath of annoyance. "She's one of the Merritts, isn't she?"

"Yes, she's one of the Merritts," Joey admitted.

"And she's in trouble," Shirley persisted.

Joey sighed. "That's right, Shirley. She's in trouble." Maybe if he was honest, the annoying woman would go away on her own.

"I'm in, then," Shirley said, with a decisive nod of her head.

"Excuse me?" Joey looked so confused that Diana would have been amused if the situation wasn't so dire.

"I'm in," Shirley said, again. "I'm going to help her, too. Lance is her cousin, isn't he?" At Joey's affirmative nod, she continued: "He took me home once. One night when I was...um...not feeling very well." Shirley met Joey's gaze honestly and shrugged. "Lance called an Uber for me, but he didn't just put me in it. He came with me *and* waited until I went into my apartment and locked the door. He's a nice guy. I want to repay the favor. So, tell me what to do."

Joey opened his mouth to argue but changed his mind at the stubborn determination he glimpsed in Shirley's eyes. Maybe he wasn't giving her enough credit. He could tell she had no intention of leaving, so she might as well make herself useful. "First of all, do you think anyone else noticed that Diana is hiding back here?"

Shirley relaxed against the bar. "I don't think so. Everything happened pretty fast. It's so crowded and loud in here that everybody is concentrating on their own conversations." She glanced around nonchalantly. "No one is paying us any attention at this moment, so I think we're good." She paused, regarding Joey expectantly. "What now?"

The crowd continued to grow as they talked. Several people were edging ever so slightly toward them. "Stand there and pretend you're having trouble deciding which drink to get. Slow service will keep people from hanging around."

The words had scarcely left his mouth when a man approached. He slid into the space between Shirley and the first barstool to her left.

"Hi there," he said, smoothly. "Can I buy you a drink?"

Joey looked down at Diana again. When their eyes met, he raised his eyebrows. *How original,* he seemed to say, pleased at the way her lips curved up slightly. At this point, the hint of a smile was better than nothing.

Shirley fiddled in her purse for a minute, stalling. "I don't think so," she said to her prospective drink buyer. "It's taking for-ev-er for me to decide on my *first* drink." She smiled, playfully batting her eyelashes. "I don't want to make you wait. But"—without giving the man the chance to object, Shirley smiled coyly—"if you save me a seat, you can buy me my *second* drink."

The man's grin widened in anticipation. "Sounds like a great idea. See you in a few." He moved back down the bar to place his order.

"Well played, Shirley." Joey nodded, approval in his voice. "Very smooth. I like your style."

"Didn't work on you, though, did it?" Shirley asked, a bit sarcastically.

Joey put his hand over his chest, seemingly astonished at her comment. "Now, Shirley," he said. "You know I'm not that kind of guy." He laughed at whatever nonverbal gesture she made in response.

Diana couldn't have been happier at how their conversation was turning out.

"Make me a drink, then, bartender," Shirley demanded, laughter in her voice.

"What'll it be?" Joey asked, waggling his eyebrows. He glanced at Diana, glad to see that she looked much better. The color was back in her face and she wasn't shivering anymore. She seemed to be enjoying his banter with Shirley.

"How about a gin and tonic?" Shirley asked, hopefully.

"Awww...c'mon, Shirley," Joey said, sadly, shaking his head. "Gin and tonic is for amateurs. You can do better than that."

Silence.

A jolt of anxiety rushed through Diana as she waited—in vain—for Shirley's sarcastic reply. She could see the indecision on Joey's face. She was certain the sudden halt to their banter spelled trouble. Unfortunately, she had guessed correctly.

"Stall him," Joey said. "The police have to be close."

"Got it," Shirley replied with confidence.

The continued silence filled Diana with foreboding. "What's going on?" she hissed, from her hiding place.

"Hush." Joey's lips barely moved.

The next moment, Shirley's voice cooed, "Hello, Cowboy."

Diana cringed. She tucked in closer to the wooden bar, making herself as small as she possibly could. Her psychotic cowboy stalker was right there on the other side of the bar. Barely two feet away...through wood, of course. Very thick, heavy wood. The wood she was currently crammed up against. She closed her eyes for a few long seconds, refusing to give in to a wave of nausea that came out of nowhere. *You can't get sick!* she told herself firmly. She absolutely *would not* get sick, because that would give her away.

Joey sensed her distress. He gave the cowboy a look of pure masculine irritation. Gesturing to Shirley with his towel, he lodged his complaint. "This pretty lady is having a lot of trouble deciding what to order. Maybe *you* could give her a little help."

He hoped his appeal resonated with the cowboy on a condescendingly masculine level. *Help me out, fellow Neanderthal, with the inferior female being who can't make a decision.* Or something like that. Chauvinistic male wasn't at all Joey's style. In fact, he detested sexist attitudes and the demeaning actions that usually accompanied them. If the cowboy's cold eyes were any indication, such behavior was the bastard's middle name.

Following Joey's lead, Shirley fell right into the character of overly chatty, empty-headed female. She launched into a detailed description of every alcoholic beverage she had ever tasted, pausing now and then to ask one ridiculous question after another.

Joey kept one eye on the front door—where Sid was waiting for the police—and one on the man in front of him. He recorded as many details as he could, cataloguing them in his mind for later, all while interjecting appropriately jaded comments about Shirley's inability to make up her mind.

The cowboy eventually ran out of patience. The next time Shirley drew breath, he interrupted. "You haven't seen my wife try to leave, have you?" At Joey's puzzled expression, he continued: "You know…my runaway wife? The redhead with the legs? The one that I told you about earlier?"

"Yeah, yeah," Joey said. "I remember, but I haven't seen her. Coming or going."

"Maybe she's in the bathroom," Shirley suggested, sweetly. "I can look while you wait here and—"

"No, don't worry about it," the cowboy mumbled, turning his back to the helpful pair.

Joey and Shirley watched him drift back into the crowd. Joey wondered if the cowboy's sudden departure was caused by Shirley's idea to check the ladies' room. More than likely it was an attempt to avoid the very conspicuous pair of police officers that had just walked in the front door.

"He has a gun," Shirley announced in a low voice.

"What?" Joey asked as Sid pointed the officers in their direction.

"The. Cowboy. Has. A. *Gun*," she enunciated, in a tense whisper.

"Damn it," Joey hissed, deliberately dropping his towel. He bent down to retrieve it, bringing his head level with Diana's. "You were right. He has a gun. Good call." He smiled then, searching her eyes. "Cops just got here. It's almost over."

Even though Diana managed to move her lips, her smile was a bit strained. Joey reached out to squeeze her hand. "You doing okay down here?"

Diana nodded, strangely heartened by the genuine concern in his dark eyes and the comforting feel of his warm hand closing over her cold one. He straightened again, flipping the towel back over his shoulder.

"Haven't you made up your mind yet, lady?" The voice belonged to a large man wearing a Virginia Tech hat. He was waiting, impatiently, a few feet down the bar.

Aware that a growing number of customers were eyeing them with interest, Joey realized he was finally going to have to make a drink. "What'll it be, lady?" he asked, grinning confidently.

"How about a Tequila Sunset?" Shirley asked. She smiled flirtatiously at Virginia Tech whose impatience vanished as quickly as it had appeared. The bedazzled fellow took a few steps in her direction before the exasperated woman behind him grabbed his arm. She proceeded to give him an earful. Sufficiently cowed, Virginia Tech reluctantly returned to his place in line. He still eyed Shirley with interest, despite his glowering companion.

"Can you make a Tequila Sunset?" Shirley whispered to Joey. "It was the first thing I could think of."

"Of course."

Joey flashed Shirley a confident grin. He knew exactly what he was doing thanks to his father's best friend, Will Parker, to whom he owed his bartending expertise. Joey had spent most of the weekend after his twenty-first birthday with Will, learning the finer points of tending bar. Such useful knowledge made the budding bartender much sought after at college parties. And being *behind* the bar provided Joey something of a buffer from overly ambitious females.

He grabbed a glass and got to work. "Keep an eye on the cowboy," he said to Shirley, under his breath.

"Got it." Shirley dug in her purse to find her lipstick. She turned sideways, leaning back against the bar. She carefully reapplied her lipstick while watching the cowboy.

Shirley would make a fine spy, Joey thought with approval. Leaving surveillance in her capable hands for a minute, he grabbed a tall glass. He easily located the first two ingredients but had to look a little harder for the blackberry brandy. When he found the stuff, he filled the glass with ice, tequila, and orange juice. After giving the concoction a stir, he placed the glass on the bar in front of Shirley. She had finished with her lipstick and was watching the concoction take shape with great interest. Then, he poured in the brandy. Several of the other patrons watched, approvingly, as the brandy filtered through the orange juice. It settled at the bottom of the glass, creating two distinctive layers. Joey placed an orange slice on the side of the glass, dropped in a cherry, and added a tiny yellow umbrella.

"Tequila Sunset," he announced, surprised at the number of positive responses he received for the pretty drink.

Shirley clapped her hands. "This is beautiful!" she squealed, reaching for the glass. Her eyes met Joey's as she took an appreciative sip. "The cowboy just went into the men's room."

As soon as the words were out of her mouth, one of the officers who had been speaking with Sid casually strolled toward their end of the bar. "Good evening, folks."

At the sound of his voice, the fear that had controlled Diana since she ran out of the elevator began to ebb. Help had finally arrived. Her ordeal was coming to an end.

The officer continued, but his friendly, relaxed demeanor didn't match his words. "Sid says our assailant is wanted in Newport for attempted kidnapping."

"That's right," Joey said, nodding. "He's presently disguised as a cowboy, complete with hat and boots."

"What? No spurs?" quipped the second officer as he approached, placing his arm casually on the counter.

"No," Joey said, shaking his head, a ghost of a smile on his lips. "No spurs."

"And no horse, either," added Shirley, helpfully.

The officers laughed but quickly stopped when they realized that she was serious. They both looked to Joey for confirmation.

He shrugged his shoulders. "The lady is correct. He does not have a horse."

The second officer nodded. "And no horse. Where is the assailant at present?"

"He just went into the men's room," Shirley said.

As if on cue, an outburst of angry voices erupted from the area around the men's restroom. The rest of the patrons fell silent at the unexpected ruckus. For Chutley's Bar and Grille—an establishment that enjoyed an excellent reputation as a safe and comfortable venue—such an occurrence was completely out of the ordinary.

"He's crazy," one customer yelled. He had stumbled out of the bathroom and was struggling to zip his pants. "He threw me out of the bathroom."

"Stay where you are," the first officer advised Joey and Shirley. "We'll need both of you to identify the assailant."

Joey nodded as the officers moved toward the melee. Shirley's desperate grip on his arm forced his attention back to her.

"The gun," she gasped. "We didn't tell them about the gun."

"Damn it," Joey hissed, taking a step to the corner of the bar. "I'll tell—"

"No, Joey!" Diana yelled, grabbing onto his ankle with a death grip. "Wait! Please wait! Tell me what's happening." She was halfway out of her hiding place, kneeling on the scuffed floor. She gazed up at him with gray eyes full of unshed tears. "Please," she begged. "Please, don't leave me here all by myself."

The tears were his undoing. He gave her shoulder a comforting squeeze. "I won't leave you, Diana," he said. "I'll stay right here with you until this is over."

She nodded, obviously relieved. With the ghost of a smile, she tucked herself back under the bar.

Stunned by his own sudden about-face, Joey resumed his position behind the bar. The realization that nothing—*nothing*—could compel him to walk away from Diana Merritt at that moment was a bit startling. He worked quickly to amend the thought in his head before it stuck. Nothing, he rephrased, could compel him to walk away from *anyone* in a similar situation. Yes. That sounded much better. He wouldn't leave *anyone* in her position. It had nothing to do with the fact that the person hiding behind the bar was Diana Merritt. Nothing at all, he continued to inform himself. Yeah, right. His brilliant defense sounded weak even in his own head.

"Joey!" yelled Shirley, frantically. "We have to tell them he has a *gun*."

He focused on her urgent words. The gun! *Of course, you brainless moron,* he berated himself. Telling the officers about the gun was what he intended to do in the first place. But he was too late, now. They were out of time. His eyes met Shirley's in mutual agreement.

"Do it," he said.

Shirley walked farther down the bar until she reached the middle of the room. "HE HAS A GUN!" she screamed at the top of her lungs. "HE HAS A GUN!" Her shrill voice seemed to echo off the walls of Chutley's.

For a split second, nobody moved.

Then all hell broke loose.

From his place behind the bar, Joey watched in horror as total panic ensued. The employees of Chutley's didn't even try to control the stream of people fleeing to the exit. They were, in fact, leading the way. It was every man for himself. *And every woman for herself,* Joey added, hearing the voice of his sister, Darcie, in his head. He felt oddly detached from the mob on the other side of the bar.

"Get Shirley!" Diana screeched from underneath the bar. She grabbed Joey's leg again, pulling on it to get his attention. When he looked down, she could tell he was struggling to get his bearings. "Get Shirley!" she said, urgently.

Her shrill command snapped him back into action. "Shirley!" Joey yelled above the din, trying to get her attention before she was completely swallowed by the crowd.

She looked over when she heard her name, eyes wide with fright. She was pinned against the bar, at the mercy of the frantic crowd.

He rushed toward her precarious position. "Up here." Joey held out his hands across the bar as Shirley tried, in vain, to climb onto a barstool.

A man in a black shirt stopped himself just in time to keep from plowing into her. He put his hands around her waist to help her up onto the bar. Before letting go, he whispered something in her ear. Joey couldn't hear what the man said, but whatever it was caused Shirley to freeze on her knees on top of the bar. She stared at the man's back, with a puzzled expression on her face, until he disappeared through the open door.

"Hurry up," Joey yelled, relieved when the tall brunette swung her legs over to his side of the bar. She carefully jumped to the floor.

Diana couldn't believe her eyes when Shirley sank down beside her. Except for her bright red lipstick, the young woman didn't look anything like the petite blonde wearing a low-cut dress and stiletto heels of Diana's imagination. The real Shirley had shoulder-length brown hair and brown eyes. She wore a pair of flowing black pants and a sheer red shirt over an embellished tank top. *And* black flats. She appeared perfectly respectable. She was tall, too. Taller than Diana. And, probably, taller than Joey Finch. For some reason, that obscure fact pleased Diana immensely.

"Hi, Diana," the pretty brunette said with a friendly smile. She seemed oblivious to the chaos erupting on the other side of the bar. "I'm Chrissy. It's nice to finally meet you."

"Chrissy?" Diana asked, in surprise. "I thought your name was Shirley."

Chrissy laughed. "Only for today," she explained. "You see, this is the first time I've talked to Joey in ages. We went out once about a year ago. He doesn't remember my name. He thinks it's *Shirley*."

"I'm sorry," Diana said, softly. "Guys can be jerks." She couldn't help but be a little disappointed by Joey's faulty memory, even as she mentally reprimanded herself for caring. *Try to stay focused, Diana. You're hiding from a psycho who wants to kidnap you. A psycho with a* gun. Now was not the ideal time to ponder how Joey Finch treated women.

"Don't be sorry." Chrissy grinned good-naturedly. "I should have expected it. He let me know he wasn't interested in anything when he asked me out. But the date was really fun. I have to admit that I expected him to call me again." Chrissy shrugged, philosophically. "He didn't. Don't get me wrong, though. He *is* a nice guy, just not the relationship kind."

Joey glanced down, just then, to check on the pair under the bar. He was more than a little unsettled to find himself the object of their intense scrutiny. He narrowed his eyes. "What are you two talking about?" he asked.

"Nothing," Diana said, hastily.

"Just this and that," Chrissy added at the same time.

They continued to look at him with bright eyes and innocent smiles until he returned his gaze to the nearly empty room. *Well, hell.* There was no doubt. They had been talking about him. His own sisters frequently wore the same expressions. And the good Lord knew that hashing over every miniscule detail of the life and times of Joey Finch was one of their favorite pastimes.

Get over it, Finch, he rebuked himself. *So, they're talking about you... so what?* There was an armed man in the men's room, he reminded himself. That's what he needed to worry about. Not the fact that Shirley was probably telling Diana...who knew what? He had a lot of respect for Diana Merritt. He would hate for Shirley to paint him as some kind of jerk...even if he occasionally was.

122

He watched several more officers enter the front door of Chutley's and make their way to the back. If the reflection of their police cars' blinking lights bouncing off the mirrors was any indication, half of the Alexandria police force was waiting outside. As the officers prepared to break through the locked bathroom door, Joey ducked down behind the bar to wait. He exchanged tense glances with Diana and Shirley. There was no way around it. This was going to get ugly.

The standoff was over in an instant. They heard the sharp explosion of splintering wood, followed by the sound of someone begging for mercy. The three under the bar exchanged surprised glances as the pitiful noises came closer.

Someone knocked on the top of the bar. "Everything's under control, folks," a confident voice announced.

Joey stood up first, motioning for the women to wait. The faces that greeted him belonged to the officers with whom he had spoken earlier. Joey's feeling of relief turned to disgust, however, at the sight of the blubbering, slightly inebriated prisoner slumped between two additional officers. The scruffy-looking man was wearing the same orange "Hook 'em Horns" T-shirt and cowboy hat that Joey had seen earlier. And the same pointed-toe cowboy boots. There was, however, no evidence of facial hair on any part of the man's face.

Joey motioned to his own chin. "What happened to his—"

"It was a fake," the first officer said. "A very well-done fake, but a fake all the same."

The second officer held out his hand to reveal the offending facial hair.

"That isn't mine," whined the prisoner. "I told you. The cowboy attacked me. And threatened my life. He made me change shirts with him. And he took my Birkenstocks. Then, he made me wear these." He raised his foot, turning it side to side for all to see. With a tragic sigh, he stomped his foot—encased in the offending boot—on the floor. He looked at Joey, desperately. "Don't you understand? He took my *Birkenstocks*."

Joey studied the man's eyes with a sinking feeling in his stomach. This was not the same man who had calmly asked Joey to look out for his errant, red-haired wife. The eyes of that man—Diana's would-be kidnapper—were disturbingly cold. Spine-chillingly cold, if Joey had to put a description to them. Soulless. The Birkenstock-obsessed man across from him had the watery, bloodshot eyes of a heavy drinker. That was all. Even though Joey was certain that this was the wrong man, the final decision was up to Diana. Before he could address the lady in question, however, Shirley popped up from behind the counter.

She didn't waste any time. "Is his face messed up?" she asked, studying the man carefully. "No, it isn't," she answered her own question. "His face isn't irritated or anything."

"What do you mean?" asked the first officer.

"If he was wearing a fake beard for any length of time, his face would show it. Especially if he had to remove the beard quickly. The glue, you understand." Shirley nodded her head, confidently.

"May I ask how you know so much about fake beards, miss?" the second officer inquired politely.

"I'm a makeup artist," Chrissy said, matter-of-factly. "But that's not all I noticed. He doesn't seem tall enough to me either. He—"

"The glue," the prisoner interrupted. "The glue would definitely make a difference. Look at my face," he said, turning his head from side to side the way he had earlier turned his boot. "My face looks great."

The *I've-had-a-lot-to-drink-in-a-short-amount-of-time* tint of the man's skin did not look great, in Joey's opinion. For obvious reasons. But, according to Shirley, the makeup artist, the condition of the man's skin did *not* show evidence of his having worn a fake beard. She enthusiastically launched into an explanation. "If you look closely at the surface area of his left cheek, you can see that—"

The first officer briskly intervened before Shirley could take over the conversation completely. "Is the young woman behind the bar ready to identify her attempted kidnapper now?"

Joey glanced down at Diana, who looked back steadily. "It's time," Joey said, holding out his hand. Diana took it, reluctantly, allowing him to pull her to her feet. She appeared as calm and composed as anyone who had spent the past half hour fleeing from a kidnapper and hiding under a bar. Joey could feel her trembling beside him. He didn't think she was aware that she was still clinging to his hand even after she was firmly on her feet. Her eyes never left his face.

She took a deep breath while Joey nodded encouragingly. He seemed to understand that she had no wish to see her attacker again. Ever. It took every ounce of courage she possessed to raise her eyes to the prisoner's face. When she did, she gasped. The sight that greeted her was *not* the one she was expecting.

"I've never seen this man before in my life," Diana said, torn between relief that she didn't have to face Cowboy Bill and disappointment that...

"He got away?" she asked, incredulously, looking one by one at the faces of her stunned audience. "How did he get away?" She glanced toward the open door. "You mean he's still out there?"

She slumped against the bar, her legs suddenly too weak to support her. But Joey was right beside her, holding her up. He regarded her steadily.

"It's all right, Diana," he said. "You're safe. And that's the *only* thing that matters right now. You. Are. Safe." *And I swear that you're going to stay that way.*

Diana seemed to understand his unspoken vow. She straightened her shoulders, took a deep breath, and directed her question to the officers in front of her. "What do I do now?" she asked in a calm, controlled voice.

The admiration that Joey had always felt for Diana Merritt grew enormously in that moment. She was one strong lady. Unfortunately, he couldn't say the same for the man swaying drunkenly on his feet between the two officers.

"What about me?" whined the man currently in custody. "The cowboy pointed a gun at me. *And* he took my Birkenstocks."

"Sir, we are going to let you go, but not before you answer a few additional questions," the first officer informed him. "What was the suspect wearing when he left you in the restroom?"

"My black shirt. And my *Birkenstocks*. Haven't you people been listening to anything I said?" He nearly fell over, knocked off-kilter by the passion of his own response.

"Oh my God," Shirley intoned, solemnly. "It was him." She turned to Joey frantically. "It was him."

"Who?" asked Joey, chilled by her serious expression. He and Diana exchanged worried glances. "Who are you talking about?"

"The man," Chrissy said, her eyes full of fear. "The tall man who helped me onto the bar. It had to be him. He was wearing a black shirt," she said. "And Birkenstocks." She nodded toward the man in custody. "They must have been *his* Birkenstocks."

The officers released their hold on the indignant man. "Thank you," the man said to Shirley. The man's condescending attitude, however, was ruined by the way he staggered to the nearest barstool. He tried to sit on the stool but couldn't manage to find his balance. He ended up slumped over the stool, his eyes staring at the floor.

"What did he say to you?" Joey asked the horrified brunette. "I saw him say something to you."

"He said 'thank you.' That was all he said." Chrissy shivered in revulsion. "Why would he thank me?"

"He was thanking you for providing him with a diversion," the second officer replied. At Chrissy's look of confusion, he tried to explain: "When you warned us that he had a gun, everyone ran for the exit. That made it easier for him to blend in and get away."

"You mean I helped him escape?" Chrissy's eyes filled with tears. She turned to Diana. "Oh, Diana, I'm so sorry," she said. She turned back to the officers. "I was just trying to warn you. We forgot to tell you about the gun and—"

"Don't worry, miss," the first officer said. "You did the right thing. Our cowboy is obviously a professional."

"And crazy. Don't forget that he's crazy." The man, swaying drunkenly on the barstool, was determined to contribute to the conversation. "And he stole my—"

"Birkenstocks." Both officers—and Chrissy—finished the man's sentence at the same time, sharing a smile afterward.

Joey was glad to see that at least one member of their trio was feeling better. He turned to check on Diana. Her gaze was fixed on the front doors of Chutley's, now closed and guarded by the Alexandria Police Department. She was leaning on the bar, deep in thought.

"Diana," Joey said, touching her hand to get her attention. "Diana."

Her eyes were haunted when she turned to face him. "He's still out there," she said.

"I know," Joey replied, covering her hand in a firm grasp. "I know."

CHAPTER TWELVE

*D*iana was still holding Joey's hand when they walked to the police cruiser. Because Joey didn't have his own car, two of the officers volunteered to take him and Diana to Joey's apartment. Diana thanked both men for their courtesy and got each man's name so she could write a note to their supervisor. The second officer, however, was a bit too solicitous, to Joey's way of thinking. And, perhaps, just a bit too interested in the lovely Miss Merritt. The officer gave Diana his name, email address, *and* phone number.

"In case she needs anything," he told Joey while gazing at Diana with obvious admiration. Joey didn't like it. In fact, he surprised himself by just how much he didn't like it. And by how quickly he set out to fix it. Maybe it was his unsmiling glare the moment before they got into the car. Or maybe it was the low growl he made in the back of his throat when the officer touched Diana's arm. No matter, he thought. His efforts had the desired effect. The "helpful" officer immediately backed off. Joey was glad Diana's admirer got the message, even though he, himself, wasn't quite sure what the message was.

Protectiveness?

Possessiveness?

How about…friendship?

Yeah, Joey decided, better go with that one. His emotions were all mixed up in the aftermath of extreme anxiety. Under the circumstances, he didn't have the energy to sort them out. Or the courage. Instead, he studied the pleasing profile of the redhead seated beside him until her gray eyes met his. "You holding up okay?" he asked, squeezing her hand gently.

She gave him a tight, little smile. "I've never ridden in a police car before."

He gave a surprised laugh. "That's a good thing, isn't it?"

She shrugged her shoulders. Her smile relaxed as some of the worry left her eyes.

He waited for more, but nothing came. A comfortable silence settled between them. He marveled at that. She didn't have the compulsion—shared by nearly every female of his acquaintance—to fill the silence with some kind of inane chatter. The good Lord knew Joey's sisters never stopped talking, especially Darcie. Even his beloved mother always seemed to have something to say. Their innate ability for small talk was charming. Really, it was. He loved the female contingent of his family to distraction. He wouldn't change a thing about any of them. But after the night he and Diana had shared, it was a relief to discover that she could appreciate quiet.

Diana had courage, too, Joey decided. More courage than most of the people he knew. Male or female. He was impressed with the way she handled herself. She answered the officers' numerous questions without flinching. No tears. No complaints. And—*Thank you, God*—no self-pity.

Instead, she was poised, calm, and gracious. Joey was glad she wasn't fragile. Or helpless. He wasn't very good at dealing with those particular traits. He was also more than relieved to find she didn't have any interest in throwing herself a pity party. Had he received an invitation to such an event he would most certainly have declined. His sideways glance found Diana deep in thought. *Brave girl.* She was probably pondering her second close call with danger in seven days.

Joey was only partially right. Diana *was* deep in thought. But what she was pondering had *nothing* to do with another close call with a kidnapper.

And *everything* to do with the man sitting beside her in the back of the police car.

Joseph Ezekiel Finch, Jr.

Joey had not let go of her hand since they left the bar. His warm fingers were still loosely entwined with hers. Not grasping. Or demanding. They were...comforting. She wondered if he was enjoying holding her hand. She wondered if her hand felt soft in his. Maybe he was just holding her hand because he was afraid she would fall apart if he let go. That was probably the reason, she decided regretfully. He was probably afraid she would cry if he released her hand. Maybe he was one of those guys who didn't know what to do with tears. Like the men of the Merritt family.

Roman couldn't stand it when she cried. Her brother invariably did something stupid—like pretending to be a walrus—to make her laugh instead. Her cousins were worse. Connor disappeared at the sound of the first sniff. And Devin was always able to find something else he needed to do. In another room. Diana sighed at the ineptitude of the male contingent of her family. Helpless—all of them—when faced with any display of emotion.

Lance was the exception, she decided. But he went too far the other way. Lance was a sucker for tears. Poor baby. He would do anything to make them stop. That's probably what made him agree to defend the Senator's guilty wife in the first place, Diana realized. Vanessa Kiplinger cried all the time. At least, she was crying every time Diana had ever seen her. Funny how the weepy Senator's widow didn't look like a murderer. But Cowboy Bill didn't look like a psycho, either, now did he? Guess the old saying was true, she decided. You really can't judge a book by its cover.

She glanced quickly at her companion. He seemed lost in thought. Was she judging Joey Finch by his cover? She pondered that important question for a second. No, she decided, she didn't think so. Diana glanced at him again. Joey had such a nice cover. But there was so much more to the man than good looks. She thought about everything he had done from the moment she ran into his arms at the front door of Chutley's until now. She couldn't help the small smile that tugged at her lips. Joey stepped behind that bar like he was supposed to be there. Nothing seemed to faze him. He was a rock. Always thinking on his feet. No wonder he was such a good lawyer. And a good hand-holder, too, she couldn't help but add. Joey Finch was an *excellent* hand-holder.

Joey reluctantly let go of Diana's hand when the police cruiser stopped in front of his apartment building a few minutes later. He chalked up his hesitation to his innate protectiveness rather than the fact that he liked holding her soft, smooth hand. Protectiveness was a lot easier to justify.

Joey got out first, as he was closest to the curb. He paused on the sidewalk to wait for Diana. He couldn't help but grin as she struggled to slide across the seat. Her heavy tote bag, apparently, had other plans. She stopped halfway to the door to thank the officers again for their help before sliding to the edge of the seat. Joey held out his hand, surprised at the way his pulse jumped when she put her hand in his. The brief jolt was obviously a kind of static electricity, he reasoned, while wondering—at the same time—if she felt the small spark, too.

Diana felt the tingling down to her toes. Her efforts to gracefully exit the police car, however, ended abruptly: her tote bag steadfastly refused to accompany her. Her squeak of surprise was the only sound she made as she all but tumbled backwards onto the seat. Her bag was stuck on the seatbelt. Of course it was, she thought, as warmth rushed into her cheeks.

Joey didn't know what had happened. One minute Diana was holding his hand, the next minute she was falling backwards. The hem of her stained skirt flew up, giving him a look at the pitiful state of her shoes. He was filled with a sudden desire to find the cowboy and beat the hell out of him. Quite a strong reaction for a peace-loving guy.

Instead, he stuck his head into the car to glare at the officers, who were watching Diana's fight with her giant tote bag. They seemed vastly entertained. "Diana, are you all right?"

"I'm stuck," she said, in a choked voice. "I mean, my bag is stuck. Hang on." She bent over, tugging on the stubborn strap with both hands.

Joey leaned in to help just as the strap pulled free, sending Diana tumbling backwards toward him. He caught her before she could fall out of the car. One hand on either side of her waist. Her head tipped back to rest on his shoulder. Gray eyes—wide with surprise—met eyes so dark they were almost black. Diana felt the impact of that penetrating gaze all the way to her toes.

The connection was strong.

The attraction was real.

At least, she thought wistfully, it was real for *her*. With regard to Mr. Finch...?

Joey was smiling, benignly, as they stepped into the elevator a few minutes later. He seemed completely unaffected by the moment that was still giving Diana heart palpitations. *Drat.* When she thought of the way his hands felt around her waist, she couldn't help but shiver. Her reaction to his touch was telling, but not obvious. To him. It was obvious to her, but not to him. Well, she *hoped* her reaction wasn't obvious to him. If he noticed, he was polite enough not to say anything.

In fact, Joey had, thus far, behaved like a perfect gentleman. Quite an impressive feat, Diana thought, especially since he had inadvertently become immersed in her very own personal day from hell. And he was being so nice about it, too. But then, Joey was always nice. And polite. And cheerful. At least to her. How, she asked herself, could he possibly be some-one that she should avoid?

Diana had been warned about getting involved with guys *like* Joey Finch—specifically, she had been warned about getting involved *with* Joey Finch—for years. Over and over. Blah, blah, blah. Was she involved?

No, she didn't think so. Not involved, but…connected. Yes, that was it. They were connected. They now had a permanent connection through shared trauma.

She, Joey, and…Chrissy. *Drat.*

Diana appreciated Chrissy's bravery. She really did. Chrissy had been wonderful. Kind. Concerned. Willing to put her own safety on the line for a stranger. Diana was very thankful for her help. She really was. Before saying their goodbyes, she and Chrissy had even exchanged numbers so Diana could take her new friend to lunch the next time she was in Alexandria. Taking Chrissy to lunch was the least she could do.

But…Diana didn't like thinking about the lovely brunette and Joey on a "really fun date." No, she didn't like thinking about that date at all. Thinking about Chrissy and Joey's "really fun date" made her think about Joey's dating habits. Or Joey's dating *habit.* He had only one: he *never* went out with the same girl twice. According to her brother and her cousins, Joey Finch was a "one and done". *After one date,* they reiterated, *he's done.* Diana must have heard that comment a thousand times. Only now, she realized with a sinking feeling, she had met actual proof. So, where did that leave her?

Nanny Di and the Player.

No, she decided, that wasn't quite fair. What had Chrissy said? Diana tried again.

Nanny Di and the Player Who Was a Really Nice Guy, Just Not the Relationship Kind.

Yes, she thought, that was better. Because somewhere in that unnecessarily wordy title lay a tiny glimmer of hope that a nice guy would eventually want a nice girl. And if that was the case…

Diana forced herself to stop thinking. She was clearly in danger of losing her mind.

Despite his outward serenity, Joey was far from unaffected by his close encounter with Diana. He was, in fact, struggling—quite unsuccessfully thus far—to free himself from acute sensory overload. Every tiny detail of the moment that Diana fell into his arms—literally—was ingrained in his brain. The warmth of her gaze. The feel of her small waist in his hands. The way her light scent made him think of the beach. It was unsettling in a way he rarely experienced.

As a result, he turned the key in the lock and opened the door to his apartment, feeling unaccountably nervous. What the hell was wrong with him? He was as jumpy as a sixteen-year-old whose parents were out of town for the weekend. Of course, Joey's own parents had always been too smart to leave him alone for the weekend when he was sixteen. And this was probably why.

"Well, it's not much…but it's home. I mean…it was home. Until today. It was home until today." Joey stumbled all over the words as he spoke. He actually stumbled. He had always prided himself on knowing exactly what to say in any situation. Hell, he had even been accused of being extremely articulate. Frequently. *Yeah, right.*

Diana stopped for a second as if to study her surroundings. Her quiet perusal made Joey even more nervous. *He* was usually the one waiting for someone else to fill the silence. Now, *he* was the one babbling like an idiot.

"This really is my last day at this address," he babbled. "My lease ends on the last day of this month. After that, I was planning on getting a hotel room in DC until the trial ended. But, now…well, I guess I don't have to worry about that. So, I'm headed home in the morning. For good. Well, I mean, I'll have to come back to move my furniture and the other stuff."

"Nice," Diana said, nodding her head absently. She walked across the living room to the window.

Joey waited for her to speak.

She didn't.

She stood at the window, gazing into the night.

Joey couldn't stand the suspense of her cryptic word. "What's nice?" he burst out a few long seconds later. He had to know. "My apartment?

That I'm going home tomorrow? The timing of the end of the trial and the end of my lease?" He no longer felt like a babbling idiot. He was the living, breathing personification of one.

"Hmm?" Diana murmured. Her eyes, however, remained fixed on the street below.

Joey cringed at the look of confusion on her face. Confusion caused by him. "Never mind," he said.

What the hell was wrong with him? She was probably wondering the same thing. *It's stress*, he thought. Unnatural amounts of stress in his brain. He had once heard that extreme stress could cause irreparable brain damage. He had scoffed at the idea. He wasn't scoffing now. He was, sadly, the perfect example of such a situation.

Diana's mind had zoned in on the fact that Cowboy Bill could be looking *in* the window while she was looking *out*. She closed the blinds before turning around. "I'm sorry." She took a deep breath. "I guess I wasn't paying attention," she admitted politely. "What were you saying?"

But Joey flatly refused to wade through that painfully awkward— at least on his part—conversation again. What they needed was a change of subject.

"I called your family while you were answering questions with the police," he told her. "I'm not sure who's coming, but somebody is on the way."

"Thanks," Diana said, without enthusiasm. "That'll be great." She assumed some combination of family members would show up eventually. But not yet. She needed a little more time. She just wasn't quite ready to face a full-scale interrogation.

Joey almost smiled at her disgruntled expression. "How about some tea?" He led the way to the kitchen area, motioning to one of the stools.

After she placed her gigantic bag on the floor, Diana obediently sat down. She propped her elbows on the counter. Then, she watched as Joey turned on the Keurig coffeemaker, opened the top, took out the used K-cup, and tossed it into the trashcan under the sink.

"Hot tea?" she asked. "You drink something besides *sweetened* iced tea?" She was intrigued at yet another unexpected side of the man in front of her.

"Yeah." Joey shrugged. "Sometimes I want something hot that isn't coffee."

"And you call yourself a Southern boy?" Diana scolded, shaking her finger at him as if he was Amalie.

He grinned as he got out several boxes of tea bags and placed them on the counter in front of her. "Take your pick."

"I can't believe you're making hot tea for me," she said.

"Don't be too impressed. I'm just heating the water. The tea bags will be doing most of the work." Joey grinned as Diana's lips tipped up into a tiny smile. This was better, he thought. Much better. He was feeling much more in control now. Apparently, most of his brain cells were still present and accounted for.

While the Keurig was heating up, Joey opened the cabinet, grabbed two mugs and a small dish, and placed them on the counter. One mug sported a blue sailboat with the words *"Lake Life"* printed over the top of the boat and *"Lake Norman, North Carolina"* underneath. The other mug featured a bear wearing a Santa hat. The inscription read, *"Have Yourself a 'Beary,' Merry Christmas."* Diana couldn't help but be amused by the sheer randomness of the two. Joey produced two spoons from a side drawer and placed them on the counter beside the boxes of tea.

Diana studied the selection in front of her—chamomile, herbal peach, Earl Grey, English Breakfast, Irish Breakfast. Obviously, Joey Finch was not a casual tea drinker. For some reason, she found that tidbit of information quite charming. "Which one has the most caffeine?" she asked, not because she didn't know, but from a strong desire to test his knowledge.

"Irish Breakfast is the strongest," Joey answered correctly. He slid the boxes of chamomile and herbal peach toward her, assuming she wanted something soothing. "If you don't want the chamomile, try the peach. It's Darcie's favorite."

Very deliberately, she reached across both of Joey's recommendations and picked up the box of Irish Breakfast tea. She was almost certain her nosy brother was going to show up soon. Then she would need all the caffeine she could get. She opened the box and took out a teabag.

"Joey," she asked, "would you call yourself an overprotective brother?"

Suddenly, he understood her choice of teabags. "Is there any other kind?" he asked, ruefully. He took a teabag for himself from the box of Irish Breakfast tea. The threat of the impending Merritt invasion inspired his need for something bracing. He put the teabag in the mug decorated with the sailboat.

"You're having tea, too?" Diana asked. Really, this was becoming more interesting by the minute.

"Of course," Joey replied, holding out his hand for her mug.

Diana dropped her teabag into the other mug and handed it over. She watched as he filled each mug with hot water from the Keurig. He set her mug on the counter and slid a box of sugar cubes and a container of honey—shaped like a little bear—in front of her.

Diana picked up the honey and studied it. "Cute," she said, unable to imagine the urbane and sophisticated Mr. Finch buying the whimsical bear himself. She knew Joey's sister had lived with him during her summer internship the previous year. "Did Darcie buy this?" She somehow managed to keep a straight face.

"No," Joey said, a little defensively.

"Or this?" she asked, holding up her "Beary Christmas" mug. She tried, but failed this time, to hide her smile.

"No, Darcie did not buy either one. I did." He tried to look as dignified as possible. "I happen to like bears."

Diana laughed at that. "Obviously." She reached for the little tag on her teabag, becoming thoughtful again as she swirled the teabag around in her mug. She propped her chin on her hand and sighed, staring into her teacup as if it held the answers to the mysteries of life.

"My sisters think the words *overprotective brother* are repetitive," Joey offered, easily following her unspoken thoughts.

She glanced up at him, surprised at the understanding in his gaze. She was, also, quite pleased that he didn't jump to her brother's defense. Diana sighed. "I just wish Roman wasn't so bossy about it. He acts like I'm a little girl who isn't very smart. Then he lays down the brotherly law and tries to smother me. All for my own good, you understand."

She picked up the spoon Joey had given her and pressed it against her teabag for a second. Then she removed the teabag and placed it on the dish between them. She opened the lid of the honey, tipped the little bear over her mug, squeezed, and stirred. She tasted her tea and repeated the process. Squeeze. Stir. Taste. Squeeze. Stir. Taste. It seemed to Joey that Diana was going to end up with more honey than tea, but, finally, she set the honey bear on the counter.

As he watched her sip her tea, he realized he knew exactly what was going on in her head. She dreaded the arrival of her own overprotective brother. Joey had a sudden flash of insight. An epiphany, really. He loved his sisters to distraction and always had their best interests at heart. But, he realized with a good deal of chagrin, this was how they felt when he tried to tell them what to do.

Oh, his intentions were good. Exemplary even. Everything he said or did was, inevitably, for their own good. Funny how he had always pictured himself as something of a knight in shining armor riding to the rescue of his poor, helpless sisters. In reality, they were anything but. They, like the woman in front of him, were strong, capable, and smart. Was it any wonder they seemed so annoyed by—and ungrateful for—his oh-so-helpful advice?

"Do you make cookies, too, or just tea?" Diana asked, a teasing note in her voice.

"No cookies," Joey said. "But there are some Jolly Gems cakes in the cabinet."

"Chocolate twirls?" Diana asked, sitting up straight on her stool. Her hopeful gaze flew to the cabinets.

"Just honey buns."

"Oh." She returned her chin to her hand, her disappointment evident.

At that moment, Joey would have paid a hundred dollars for a box of chocolate twirls. He searched his mind for something to lift her spirits. "So, why are you so surprised that I drink hot tea?"

"Oh, I don't know." Diana thought about it for a few seconds. "I guess it just doesn't seem quite your style."

Joey was intrigued by the playful way she said "style." Flirting, perhaps? He hoped so. "My style?" he asked. "Hmm…So, what did you think I would drink?"

"Hmm…" she mimicked, fluttering her long eyelashes. "Maybe something like a Tequila Sunset?" She grinned at him impishly, her gray eyes sparkling and full of mischief.

There was no doubt about it, Joey thought. Diana Merritt was adorable. Everything about her was adorable, from her laughing gray eyes and her glorious red curls to the way she teased him about his choice of mugs. And those eyelashes.

Thinking about the adorable Miss Merritt caused a funny feeling in Joey's chest. Actually, the center of the disturbance was closer to his stomach, but it was funny all the same. Joey found himself completely captivated and struggling, in those few moments, to remember why that was such a bad thing.

Someone knocked on the door.

Oh yeah, he remembered. *That's why.*

The knock startled Diana just as her teacup touched her lovely, peach-colored lips. Joey had given up trying to ignore the unconscious lure of those lips several sips ago. He could only watch, helplessly, as she struggled to hold onto the Beary Christmas mug. After several very impressive contortions, she managed to save the bear. Unfortunately, the hot tea sloshed out of her teacup, staining the left side of the neckline of her blouse and leaving little spots of tea all the way to her waist.

"Drat!" she yelled, annoyed as much by the abrupt end to—what had been, in her opinion—a lovely interlude, as by the sorry state of her attire. Her gaze fell on the forgotten Dr. Pepper stain along the right seam of her skirt, from mid-thigh to her hemline. She might be able to get the Dr. Pepper out, but not the tea stain. Definitely not the tea. She was a fashion disaster.

She heard a snort of what might have been laughter coming from the direction of Mr. Joey *I-Love-Bears* Finch. "What is so funny?" she asked.

"You said, 'drat.' " Joey tried his best to wipe the humor from his face, but to no avail. Not once, in all his life, had he ever heard anyone legitimately use the word *drat*.

She put her hands on her hips and glared. "So?"

"After what you've been through in the last couple of hours, I would think you could come up with a better word than *drat*." He paused, enjoying the way her eyes narrowed in annoyance. It was so much better than the fear he had seen earlier. "Seriously, Diana, is that the best you can do?" She looked so adorably befuddled that he burst out laughing.

Diana crossed her arms in front of her. "As you are well aware, Mr. Finch, I am a *nanny*," Diana intoned. "I can't go around swearing like a sailor in front of a five-year-old. Amalie's a very *smart* five-year-old. And let me tell you, that little girl hears *everything*. Then, she *repeats* everything that she hears. And she has a terrible habit of hiding behind—"

The knocking at the door turned into pounding, cutting her off midsentence.

Diana grimaced. "If you're interested in getting your deposit back you better let them in before they destroy your door."

"Are you ready for me to let them in?" Joey asked, suddenly serious. He was unsure of what he would do if she said no, but he was willing to risk it.

She braced herself for the onslaught. "Let them in."

As he walked to the door, Joey was pretty sure he could hear a quiet chorus of *drat, drat, drat* coming from somewhere behind him.

CHAPTER THIRTEEN

"*D*amn it, sis." Roman couldn't seem to stop pacing in front of Joey's sofa. "I told you to go straight to my apartment. How could this have happened?" He ran both of his hands through his hair in obvious agitation.

Diana sighed, glancing over at Connor. He was comfortably ensconced in Joey's recliner, eating roasted peanuts out of a jar, while he watched Roman make tracks in the carpet. His entire greeting had consisted of a single comment: "You should have kicked him in the balls." Diana could always depend on Connor to come straight to the point. Her attempt to inform him that she had done just that was lost in his all-encompassing bear hug.

Roman, on the other hand, seemed unable to understand how his clear instructions had been so completely misconstrued.

After several attempts to explain, Diana gave up. She settled herself on Joey's couch, crossed her arms, and resigned herself to the inevitable. When Roman's tirade came to an end, he sank down on the sofa beside his sister.

Diana raised her eyebrows at her brother. "Are you finished?" At his nod of acquiescence, she continued: "And now, do you want to know what *really* happened?"

"What do you mean?" asked Roman, genuinely puzzled by the lack of remorse she was exhibiting for her dismal failure to follow his instructions.

"For your information, brother dear, I *did* go straight to your apartment. Or at least, I tried to. 'Bill'—or whatever his name is—followed me into the elevator." She paused to savor the look of shock on Roman's face.

"But, how? I watched you walk inside. How did—"

"It was the man with the beard, Roman. The one who was behind us when we got off the highway." At Roman's uncomprehending look, she sighed. "Hook'em Horns."

"What? But you said your kidnapper didn't have a beard." Roman was horrified as it slowly dawned on him that *he* was the one who sent his sister into danger. He practically insisted on it.

"His beard was a fake," Diana explained.

"A very convincing fake," Joey added helpfully. He was proud of the way Diana was handling the situation.

Roman's face was a mask of concern. "But, Diana, how did you get away?"

Even Connor was leaning forward in his chair, his chewing substantially slower.

"I kicked him in the balls," Diana said, cheerfully.

"That's my girl," Connor bellowed, with great satisfaction. Snorting with laughter, he poured more peanuts into his palm.

Roman was on his feet again. "Hellfire and damnation, sis. I'm sorry. I'm so sorry. I should have…damn it." His pacing resumed.

Diana and Joey exchanged a commiserating glance. The scene he had just witnessed had been eye opening, to say the least. Then Joey winced, as he saw himself in Roman. The epitome of extreme overprotectiveness. Well-intentioned, but totally unnecessary. And unappreciated.

Roman stopped pacing. He held out his hand to Joey, who had taken Diana's stool at the kitchen counter. "Thank you, Joey. Connor and I can't thank you enough for taking care of Diana."

Joey shook his friend's hand but couldn't keep from adding, "I'm glad I was there, Roman, but I think Diana did a damn fine job of taking care of herself."

Connor snorted again, in approval. "Well said, Finch."

The smile Diana gave him for coming to her defense made him feel like a hero. It was the least he could do, he decided. Her ability to fend for herself under extreme duress was nothing short of amazing.

Connor cleared his throat, an amused glint in his eye.

That's when Joey realized he was staring at Diana. Staring into those long-lashed gray eyes like a lovesick teenager. He glanced at Roman to find that he—Joey Finch—was now under that worthy fellow's intense scrutiny. *Well, hell.*

Diana knew from experience that when the muscle in Roman Merritt's jaw twitched, a hasty retreat was in order. "I'm going to go freshen up," she announced, practically leaping to her feet. She grabbed her tote bag but paused in her flight, raising her eyebrows at Joey in quiet desperation. She had absolutely no idea which way to go.

"That way," Joey said, pointing toward the guest bedroom and wishing he could go with her.

"Thanks," Diana said, disappearing through the door.

Joey envied her timely exit. Uncomfortable was the best description for the silence that followed. He leaned back, casually propping both of his elbows on the counter. He tried to look like a man who *hadn't* been caught staring into the lovely eyes of Diana Merritt only seconds before. From the amused look on Connor's face, Joey wasn't doing a very good job. The big man stood and wandered into the kitchen. Roman stood up to pace the room again. His glare intensified every time he came close to the one who was now—in his opinion—the guilty party. Joey wouldn't have been at all surprised to see flames shoot out of Roman's eyes.

"Hey, Finch, you got any more peanuts?" Connor asked, bringing a brief halt to the standoff. He opened a cabinet and poked around, reminding Joey of a giant grizzly bear foraging for food.

"No more peanuts," Joey replied. "But there may be a box of Wheat Thins in the cabinet, and there are some Jolly Gems cakes."

"Chocolate twirls?" Connor asked, eagerly, sticking his head around the corner of the cabinet.

"No," Joey said, in exasperation. "Just honeybuns." He looked at Roman, who was trying to appear stern even though his lips twitched with suppressed laughter. "What is this weird obsession your family has with Chocolate twirls?"

"The credit for the twirls fixation falls squarely on our great-aunt Jeri."

"The one with the beard," Connor piped in from the kitchen.

Roman nodded in agreement, more amused than not at Joey's incredulous expression. "She really does have a beard. She's obsessed with chocolate twirls. She carries boxes with her wherever she goes. To church. To the beach. To the movies."

"To her therapy group," Connor added.

Roman didn't say a word. He simply glared at his overly informative cousin.

Connor didn't mind at all. "She's supposed to be in therapy on account of the twirls, but I think it's because of the beard," he added apologetically.

Roman grimaced. From the expression on his face, chocolate twirls weren't the only quirky thing about Great-Aunt Jeri. He made a concerted effort to change the subject. "I apologize on behalf of Connor," he began diplomatically, as the hungry giant continued to open drawers in the kitchen. "He's a bottomless pit. Unfortunately for you, we missed dinner and my chronically insatiable cousin will eat everything in your apartment if left unattended."

Nobody said anything for a few seconds. Connor's diligence had been rewarded, but he was having trouble opening the resealable tab on the box of honeybuns. Roman and Joey watched him struggle with the box in silent fascination, momentarily in accord. Finally losing patience, Connor ripped the offending box in half. Roman sighed heavily before turning his attention to the other man in the room.

Joey braced himself. He had a feeling he knew exactly what was coming.

"Look, Finch..." Roman began, but before he could say more, his phone rang. "Hello," he said, listening for a few seconds before informing the other men of the caller's identity. "It's Devin," he announced, walking over to the window to confer with their other cousin. He raised the blinds that Diana had lowered a few minutes earlier, peering out into the street.

Connor returned to the recliner, a honey bun in each hand. He settled himself comfortably, appearing completely focused on each delectable bite. Joey wasn't the least bit fooled by his distracted demeanor. He was certain Connor was listening to every word of Roman's phone call with Devin. They could hear enough of the one-sided conversation to surmise that Devin was giving Roman instructions regarding how to precede. From what Joey was able to infer, the plan made perfect sense. He was happy to play his assigned role. It was obvious that Roman would have preferred that a family member take the place of the esteemed Mr. Finch, but, apparently, Devin refused to budge. Roman's unsuccessful efforts to hide his irritation would have been amusing if the situation wasn't so deadly serious.

When the call ended, Roman turned from the window, suddenly all business. "Gentlemen, we have a plan," he announced.

Joey almost groaned at the determined look in his eyes. Roman may have resigned himself to Joey's involvement, but it appeared he was determined to have the last word.

"Look, Finch," he began, launching into *The Brother Speech: Part One—The Friendly Warning.* This would be followed by *Part Two—The Word of Advice.* If either of those were well-received, the ordeal would end. If not, *The Word of Advice* would be followed by *Part Three—The Threat of Bodily Harm.*

Yeah, Joey knew this drill. Since he had delivered the same speech himself—multiple times—he opted not to listen. Instead, he pondered his sudden change of status with his "good friend" Roman Merritt. Funny how Roman called him *Joey* or *Joe* most of the time. Only when discussing his sister did Roman default to *Finch*.

Joey knew from experience that when a sister was involved, a friend could quickly become a foe. He remembered wanting to punch Blane squarely in the mouth more than once during his courtship of Grace. And Blane was—and always would be—Joey's very best friend. Then, too, Joey experienced a similar desire to involve his fists when he discovered Darcie's involvement with Devin Merritt. Now, Devin was a trusted friend.

On one hand, he understood Roman's brotherly concern, but on the other hand…well, Roman and Connor had known Joey for nine years. They were smart. They were savvy. So, why hadn't they figured out that he wasn't *that guy*? Was Joey really that good of an actor? Apparently, he was. His performance, it seemed, was downright Oscar worthy. "And the Academy Award for *Best Performance as a Player on the Bar Circuit* goes to…" Joey sighed. What kind of a lecherous jerk did they take him for anyway?

The worst part was that the whole player persona—all of it, every damning little nuance—was Joey's own fault…the result of his desire to fit in during the summer of his first internship at Merritt Brothers. How to be accepted as one of the guys? The answer was easy, at least it had been easy for Joey…Go out with a different girl every night. The morning after every date the other interns at the law firm plied him with questions. And if Joey occasionally allowed them to believe what they wanted, well, then, what was the harm? He had no interest in a relationship and it was all in good fun. Wasn't it?

His friends would have been so disappointed if he told them he was home before eleven most nights. He was certain they wouldn't have believed he was more likely to take a book to bed than a woman. After he earned his law degree and joined the firm, he easily slipped back into his player persona. His colleagues seemed to expect it, and by then he had become something of a legend. A certain camaraderie was to be found in sharing the singles scene. And he had enjoyed being a part of that scene. But, lately, well…lately, he was just plain bored.

The way Joey figured it, his popularity with the ladies was twofold. First, he didn't drink too much, smoke, or do drugs. He wasn't demanding, disrespectful, or manipulative. He let every girl know *upfront* that he wasn't interested in a relationship. If he asked a girl out for drinks, they had drinks. If he asked her to dinner, they had dinner. He never, once, invited a girl back to his apartment, and—on the *rare* occasions when he accepted an invitation to go back to hers—he *never* spent the night. He also made sure his date understood the meaning of *"this is a one-time thing."* In Joey's opinion, his straight-up honesty made him attractive to women, especially those used to the alternative—a large majority, he had discovered—much to the detriment of his kind. So, in Joey's estimation, honesty was the first part of his appeal.

The second part was having zero interest in a relationship. He didn't want a girlfriend. Or—heaven forbid—a wife. He didn't even want a "friend with benefits." And, unlike most guys his age, he made his wants—or lack thereof—perfectly clear. Sheer honesty coupled with his refusal to commit made him surprisingly irresistible to women. Or, at least to the women he met on a regular basis.

Some women, unfortunately, took his reluctance to commit as a challenge. His elusive eligibility compelled them to try to be the one...*The Girl Joey Finch Asked Out Twice.* The failure of each woman to be *that girl* only added to his popularity. And Joey would be the first to admit he had enjoyed that popularity. He was *Joey Finch, One and Done.*

But right now, Joey had to admit he was irritated—maybe even a little hurt—that, after all these years, Roman and Connor still saw what they wanted to see. He tried to justify their assumptions in his mind. The situation really wasn't that surprising, he admitted, albeit reluctantly. He had done nothing to dispel their thinking. Joey suspected that Lance, with whom he was the closest, was aware he was something of a fraud. That helped a little. Funny, that what the Merritts thought of his personal life hadn't really mattered that much. Until today.

But today it *did* matter. It mattered a lot. Because Joey had just made an earth-shaking—potentially life-changing—discovery. Well, life-changing for him, anyway. He didn't want to be warned away from Diana Merritt. And he couldn't, for the life of him, understand why. Nothing had changed. He was still a confirmed bachelor. He wasn't looking for a relationship.

Or was he?

Joey nearly fell off his stool. Now, where the hell had that thought come from? He made a concerted effort to calm his racing heart. Breathing deeply seemed to help.

In and out....

In and out....

He had good, solid reasons for remaining a bachelor, he reminded himself, not the least of which was plain, old self-preservation. He did *not* want to consider the implications of his formerly obedient brain's bizarre thoughts. As a matter of fact, he refused to do so. He forced himself to focus on Roman's next words, hoping to find a way out of his lecture.

"Diana's had some sort of crush on you, Finch—or something like that—since she was nineteen. If there's any way you can discourage her *before* you get to Honeysuckle Creek, it would probably be for the best. We would appreciate—"

What was left of Joey's patience vanished like a waft of smoke. "What the hell is so wrong with me?" he burst out.

Connor dropped the last bite of his first honeybun. His lips turned up and he regarded Joey with something like approval.

Roman, however, looked at Joey as if he was an idiot. "Haven't you been listening to anything I've said, Finch? Diana is a *relationship* kind of girl. *Re-la-tion-ship.* She *wants* to get married someday. And she *wants* to have a family. She wants everything you don't. You..." he hesitated, choosing his words carefully. Joey was his friend, after all. "You like to have a good time. No strings attached. No obligations. No future. You are everything she *doesn't* want."

Connor opened his second honeybun. He peeled back the plastic. "Maybe *Diana* should decide what *Diana* wants and doesn't want, Roman," Connor observed. "She *is* twenty-eight years old. She's been taking care of Amalie for the past five years. Maybe a few laughs with Finch, here, are just what she needs."

Roman looked at his cousin like he had lost his mind. "Whose side are you on anyway?"

"Diana's," Connor said, taking a big bite of honeybun to emphasize the point.

What a pair of buffoons they were, Joey thought. The arrogantly overprotective brother and his unintentionally hilarious cousin. They were like some bizarre comedy team from an ancient sitcom. Joey tried to keep the frustration out of his voice. "What exactly is it that you want from me, Roman?"

"Simple." Roman crossed his arms in satisfaction. "Before you leave this room, I want you to admit that Diana is not your type."

Connor shook his head in disgust as he wandered back into the kitchen. But it was the easiest request imaginable for a bachelor like Joey Finch. Any marriage-minded female was certainly not his type. Simple. Except that it wasn't simple. Not this time. Because, suddenly, he, Joey Finch, couldn't say it. He *wouldn't* say it. He had purposely avoided contact with Diana Merritt for the past nine years out of respect for his position with Merritt Brothers. But now that fate—in the guise of a psychotic cowboy with a fake beard—had opened a door, Joey found himself reluctant to close it. *Yet,* he informed himself. He was reluctant to close it *yet*…for some unexplored reason. Joey was confident, however, that, in time he, himself, would slam that door shut.

Eventually.

Well, he was pretty confident.

Or, at least, sort of confident.

Or…well, hell. He had no idea what he was doing. Still, he crafted his reply carefully, to keep his options open.

"All right, Roman, I admit it," Joey confessed. "If marriage is your sister's only goal in life, then she is definitely not for me." He congratulated himself for his clever syntax. It was obvious—at least to him—that Diana's sole focus in life was *not* marriage. He heard Connor's snort of laughter from the kitchen.

Roman wrinkled his brow as he pondered the nuances of Joey's words. His glare intensified. He would clearly not be satisfied until he heard the words he was waiting for.

Joey wished he didn't see so much of himself in the man in front of him. "All right, Roman." The quickest way to end this conversation was to give in. "I'll clarify it for you. If Diana's *sole focus in life* is getting married, then there is no doubt." He tried his best to enunciate each word clearly. "Diana. Merritt. Is. Not. My. Type."

Connor froze, his hand on the last unexplored cabinet in Joey's kitchen. He looked concerned. "Um…Joe…"

"Damn it, Connor. How many times do I have to tell you that I don't have any chocolate twirls?" Joey turned back to Diana's brother, unable to decipher the strange expression on his face. All of Roman's posturing had disappeared. Now he just looked confused, as if he didn't quite know what to do.

"Diana. Merritt. Is. Not. My. Type."

Diana stopped at the edge of the room. Even though Joey's back was to her, she heard every word. Every single hurtful word. But it was his deliberately exaggerated delivery of those words that was still ringing in her ears. She wished she could turn around and walk right back into the bedroom, but it was too late to pretend she hadn't heard anything. The identical expressions on the faces of her brother and her cousin told her that. She didn't know whether to laugh or to cry. Her assumption that she and Joey Finch had formed some sort of a *connection* in the past few hours was nothing but wishful thinking. And to make matters worse, he didn't even consider her attractive enough to be his *type*. She could feel her face flush as the heat of complete and utter humiliation swept through her body.

"Do you want me to say it again for you, Roman?" Joey was determined to make his point so they could finish this conversation before Diana walked back into the room and got the wrong idea. That would be a disaster. "A woman like that will *never* be my type."

Joey paused. Connor seemed to have developed some sort of twitch. The big man kept jerking his head in the direction of the hallway that led to the guest room. Joey glanced at Roman who, for the first time since walking into the apartment, had nothing to say.

Suddenly reality crashed down on Joey. Hard. "Diana's standing right behind me, isn't she?" he asked, with a defeated sigh. His worst-case scenario had come to pass. So much for avoiding a misunderstanding.

Diana was indeed standing behind him and, unfortunately for Joey, was fresh out of self-control. Even worse, she found herself firmly in the grip of the uncharacteristic urge to lash out. She tried to keep her voice steady, but her words came out uneven and choppy. "In light of what I know about *you*, Joey Finch, I'm finding your last statement difficult to believe."

Joey didn't move. He simply couldn't bring himself to look at her. Connor stuck his hand in the box he had pulled out of the cabinet and began to methodically polish off Joey's Wheat Thins. One by one. Roman remained speechless.

Diana squared her shoulders, facing the three hapless males with her chin in the air. Well, facing two of them, anyway. Joey had yet to turn around. "Do you know why I find it difficult to believe that I'm not your type, Joey?"

Joey didn't know. And, more than that, he was pretty sure he didn't want to find out. But there was no way he could continue to ignore the telltale catch in her voice. Wishing himself to perdition, he turned to face her.

"Take a good look at me, Joey," she demanded, waving her hand to encompass her whole body.

He couldn't have looked away if his life depended on it. She had changed into a sleeveless linen shirt, in a pale shade of blue, and a pair of long, flowing trousers...the kind his sisters complained couldn't be worn by women who were under five foot eight. From what he could see, they probably had a point. The material emphasized her small waist and accentuated her lovely, long legs. She had pulled her red curls back into a ponytail on her neck and tied it with a coordinating scarf. Her delicate complexion was tinged with peach, making it easy to see the dainty freckles that graced her cheeks. Her gray eyes were full of righteous anger. She was like a flame come to life. In other words, irresistible.

"Take a good look at me," she repeated. "I'm female. *And* I have a pulse." She paused for effect before delivering the death blow. "From what I've been led to believe about *your type*, those are the *only two requirements*." Her voice was sharp, but her eyes were tinged with hurt.

"*Di-a-na!*" Roman said, sharply.

Connor sucked in a quick breath, nearly choking on his Wheat Thins.

Well, hell. Joey closed his eyes. He didn't know how long Diana had been standing behind him. Or how much of the conversation she had heard. The one thing he *did* know was that he had never felt like such an ass in his life.

The fire went out of Diana as quickly as it appeared. She walked toward the door that led out of the apartment—and, most importantly, away from Joey Finch. "I'm ready to go home now, Roman," she said, with as much dignity as she could manage. At that moment, she wanted as much distance as possible between herself and Joey's hurtful words. *Diana. Merritt. Is. Not. My. Type.*

Her hand was on the doorknob before she realized nobody had moved. She turned around, studying the faces in front of her. Connor was leaning on the counter. Roman's feet were firmly planted on the carpet. Joey was still on the stool, a resigned expression on his face.

Diana frowned. *Drat and double drat,* she thought. Was she even to be denied a dignified exit? She studied the trio suspiciously. "What's going on?"

"*You*...aren't going home, Diana." Roman sat on the sofa with his elbows on his knees. He leaned slightly forward, his hands in a loose grip that belied the tension on his face. One look at the belligerent expression in his sister's eyes, however, and he lost his nerve. "And, um...Connor is going to explain." Roman leaned back against the sofa as if he had just avoided a firing squad.

Diana wished she had a picture of the look on Connor's face when Roman threw him under the bus. The big man was still coughing a little, from the Wheat Thins. He looked as if he wanted to break his cousin in half. Connor went along with Roman, however, walking out of the kitchen to return to Joey's favorite chair. He sat down, folding his hands together, the way he did when he was delivering closing arguments. "You, see, Diana, we"—he indicated himself and Roman—"have a plan. And it's a good plan. It will keep you safe. And it will also keep your kidnapper from knowing where you are going."

"He already knows I'm going to North Carolina," Diana said, leaning back against the door. She toyed with the idea of opening the door and throwing herself into the hallway, so desperately did she want to escape.

"How the hell..." Connor reined himself in with difficulty under the full force of Roman's evil glare. "I mean, how could he possibly know that?"

"I told him," Diana said, wearily. "When we were on the boat."

"Why the hell did you tell him that?" Connor exploded. "Did you give him the address, too, so he could Google it?"

Diana clutched her tote bag in her arms like a shield. "It was before," she said, defensively.

"Before what?" Connor asked.

"Before I figured out that he was a psychotic kidnapper." Diana glanced at Joey as if looking for support. It was the first time she had met his eyes since she destroyed his ego. He felt a tiny bit better. At least she still acknowledged that he was alive.

"He's definitely a psycho," Joey agreed, helpfully.

Connor returned to his courtroom persona. "Regardless of what the kidnapper already knows, Diana, this plan will keep *you* as safe as possible. We have decided—"

"*You* have decided?" Diana asked, raising her eyebrows at Joey, who held up both hands to let her know he had nothing to do with this. He knew she understood when she turned her full indignation upon her relatives. "The *two of you* have decided?"

Connor nodded, confidently, happy she understood. Roman, however, looked a little wary.

Joey couldn't believe what he was seeing. It was a low blow to discover that two of the smartest men he knew were complete idiots when dealing with women. He recognized the expression on Diana's face. He had seen it on his sisters' faces too many times. Hell, Joey had seen his dad back down from that same look on the face of his sweet mother. More than once. Connor and Roman better start backpedaling, he thought, or they were in big trouble. *Never tell an independent woman what to do* was the first—and, undoubtedly, the most important—lesson of *Surviving an Encounter with an Irate Female 101*. Apparently, Connor and Roman had failed that particular course. And failed miserably.

Diana continued: "So this is *your* plan, Connor? Yours and Roman's?" Her voice oozed with skepticism.

Connor shifted in his seat. "Well…more or less."

"Connor," Roman hissed.

"I mean, we agree with it. That is…" Connor popped another Wheat Thin into his mouth and chewed, thereby ending his contribution.

"Oh, stop it." Diana straightened to her full height, challenge in her gaze as she looked from her bossy brother to her crumb-covered cousin. "The two of you are pathetic."

Joey was pleased to be excluded from her incendiary glare. He didn't know where the conversation was going, but he had a feeling it was about more than her unwillingness to hear the details of their plan.

"Give me a little credit." Diana's eyes continued to bore into each one of her dictatorial relations. "The least you can do is to be honest with me. You know as well as I do that you didn't come up with any plan by yourselves. I would be willing to bet that you two are the messengers, nothing more than the lowly minions of the Trio of Doom."

One glance at the subdued, slightly chagrined expressions on the faces of the dynamic duo was all Joey needed. He couldn't resist asking, "The Trio of Doom. And who might they be?" He was amused despite the situation. It sounded like something from a movie.

"*My* cousin, Devin; *your* best friend, Blane; and Rafe Montgomery. They—in addition to every other male in my family—seem to think I'm completely helpless and incapable of making a decision by myself." Diana's flash of righteous anger visibly ebbed as she slumped back against the door.

Although Joey's first instinct was to leap to her defense, he made a concerted effort to remain on his stool. He understood Diana well enough, now, to know that she would *not* appreciate his interference. Joey supposed he had his sisters to thank for that insight. He refused to ponder the reason why it was suddenly imperative that Diana didn't see him as just another member of the *Diana-Is-So-Helpless Club.*

Roman, however, appeared to have no such awareness. "Now don't overreact, Diana," he admonished, impatiently. "You know that Rafe was special forces or a spy or something. He's the best. If he tells you to do something, then you're going to do it."

Don't overreact? Joey shook his head in amazement. He was really going to have to have a talk with Roman when all of this was over. Now, he felt compelled to help because the hole that the clueless man was digging was getting deeper and deeper. If Roman continued, it was going to swallow him completely. Even from across the room it was easy to see the tears of frustration filling Diana's eyes...tears that she stubbornly refused to shed. Joey slid off the stool, determined to diffuse the situation.

He cleared his throat. "Roman, it seems that the three of you have come to something of an impasse. Would you mind if I try to explain the situation as I see it?"

"Go ahead, Finch," Roman stated wearily, leaning against the back of the couch. "Maybe she'll listen to you."

"Diana," Joey began.

The eyes that met his were wary.

"Diana," he repeated, "The Trio of..." He hesitated, raising his eyebrows. "What did you call them?"

"The Trio of Doom."

"Yes, the Trio of Doom." He couldn't help the tiny twitch at the corner of his lips. Wouldn't Blane and Devin hate to be lumped under that moniker? Joey was pretty sure Rafe wouldn't be bothered at all. The wily old man had probably been called worse. Joey cleared his throat again as

Diana regarded him dispassionately. "The Trio of Doom has a *suggestion* for getting you safely out of Alexandria. Connor would like to explain it to you."

Connor withdrew his hand—and part of his arm—from the bottom of the box of Wheat Thins. He straightened rather abruptly, nodding in agreement.

Before he could open his mouth, however, Joey continued: "Remember, Diana, you don't have to like or agree with the Trio of Doom's plan. If *you* have a better idea, *we* will listen to you. If not, and you want another plan, then *we*—all four of us—will come up with something else *together*. But I think we all need to remember that, ultimately, it is *your* decision. Right, Roman?" Joey cut his eyes to Diana's overbearing brother, who nodded, reluctantly.

Diana studied each man in turn, trying to tamp down an overwhelming wave of gratitude for Joey's consideration. Gratitude or not, she promised herself, she was determined to have nothing else to do with Joey Finch after this ordeal was over. She wasn't *his type*, after all. Diana sighed. "All right, Connor, what is this marvelous plan?"

CHAPTER FOURTEEN

*J*oey glanced at the woman sitting beside him. She looked right at home in the front seat of his truck. She would probably look right at home in a Jeep, too. Or a limousine. Or a damn Rolls Royce. Joey considered himself quite accomplished at appearing at ease regardless of where he was or with whom. If he was an expert, however, then Diana was a master.

Despite the awkwardness that now existed between them, she appeared completely relaxed. Her slender fingers flew across the keys of her pink MacBook, which she had quietly slipped out of her enormous tote bag. Her long legs were crossed under her and she was utterly engrossed in whatever it was she was writing. She hadn't looked up once since she opened that MacBook and put in her earbuds, nearly two hours ago. Well, except to respond to his feeble attempts at conversation. Her total absorption with her project and obliviousness to his presence made Joey's obsessive awareness of her even more pathetic than it already was.

He was riveted to her every move. He noticed the way she tilted her head slightly to one side when she was thinking. He couldn't help but respond to her breathy little sigh of irritation when she made a mistake. His heart beat faster every time she moved even a fraction of an inch. And his whole body tightened when she raised her arms over her head to stretch. What was wrong with him, anyway?

So far, she had responded to his inane attempts at conversation with polite disinterest. She may as well be an unknown passenger and he the random Uber driver, Joey thought, disgustedly. Even though it frustrated him, he couldn't help but be impressed with her unruffled aplomb. She looked nothing like a woman who had spent her day fleeing from a kidnapper, hiding behind a bar, and enduring a family interrogation. He didn't know how she did it. She wore her aura of calm control like armor.

His inability to find the chink in her armor weighed heavily on his conscience. It was all his fault that she was wearing her armor, anyway. He had gone from ally to antagonist in an instant, just by opening his mouth. The fact that the insult he had delivered so adamantly was unintentional was a moot point. Whatever she overheard—and subsequently misconstrued—in the unfortunate conversation between himself and her overprotective brother had been left to stand as fact. By him. That was the worst part. He hadn't made any effort to explain or even to discover what she had heard. He just stood there, watching her eyes flash with anger and unconcealed hurt as she threw the façade of his reputation back in his face.

He still couldn't stop thinking about it. With her red hair streaming around her shoulders and her gray eyes shooting sparks, Diana was a force to be reckoned with. Maybe that was what had caused his usually glib tongue to remain silent. He was blown away by the strength of her response. He had seen that side of her only once before, but he had never forgotten it.

He let his mind drift back nine years ago to the summer of his internship with Merritt Brothers. Joey was honest enough, and more than a little embarrassed, to admit that his popularity that summer had gone straight to his head. If he had to describe his twenty-one-year-old self, he would say that he was too cocky and far too sure of himself. Looking back, he could see that the self-confidence he seemed to have been born with had ratcheted up a notch during those three months, turning into something that, unflatteringly, bordered on arrogance. It didn't last long, however.

Thank God for family, Joey thought. When he returned home at the end of that summer, his overblown self-importance lasted less than twenty-four hours. It took only a sniff of disgust from his great-grandmother, a disappointed look from his mother, and a "Get over yourself, brother" followed by an eyeroll from his sister, Darcie, to burst the bubble of his overinflated ego. Without that reality check, he might have turned into a real jerk.

There was no doubt in his mind that at this very moment, Diana thought he was exactly that kind of jerk. And she probably hated him. *Damn.* Joey cleared his throat uncomfortably. The sound evoked not a single pause in the whisper-soft *tap, tap, tap* of Diana's hands on her keyboard.

She might wish him to the farthest reaches of the earth right now, but she hadn't felt that way nine years ago. No, she hadn't felt that way at all. Of that he was absolutely certain. The memories of the day Diana became more than just another faceless member of the prolific family Merritt were firmly planted in his mind.

"How in the darkest part of the outermost reaches of the pit of hell did this happen, Marlo?" Connor's voice grew louder and louder until he was nearly yelling into the phone. He gave Joey a look of complete disbelief and flopped back into his chair.

Joey hid a smile, having grown accustomed to Connor's creative speech and bluster during the first few weeks of his internship. He felt a little sorry for Marlo, though. So far, Joey had managed to stay on Connor's good side.

"Yeah, I'll hold," Connor said impatiently, covering the receiver with the palm of his hand. "She put me on hold," he said, unnecessarily, shaking his head in disgust. "Finch, go print the paperwork for the Huntley case. At least we know where that is." Connor indicated an empty manila folder labeled "Huntley" that was lying on his desk.

Joey nodded, saving his own project for the second time in five minutes; he wasn't taking any chances. He left his laptop open in case Connor needed to see his work before he got back. He picked up the folder and headed for the door.

"Hey, Finch, wait a minute." Connor put the phone on his desk.

Joey paused in the doorway and turned around. He was used to one errand turning into twenty. It was all part of working for Connor. It was fascinating, really, how the man's mind worked. Joey raised his eyebrows as Connor seemed at a loss for words. For once.

"Is there anything else I can get for you?" Joey asked politely.

Connor folded his hands together on his desk. "Um, Finch, Roman's sister is filling in for the admin today and, well..." his voice trailed off.

"Diana?" Joey asked.

"How do you know Diana?" Connor asked, eyeing him suspiciously. He leaned forward, waiting for an answer.

Joey shook his head. "No, Connor. I don't know her. I've never met her. But..." He paused for a second, having no idea where this conversation was going. His sense of self-preservation was on strong alert. "I've heard you mention her. We talk about our families a lot." Joey shrugged in an off-handed manner.

Connor relaxed back into his chair, apparently satisfied with his response. "Anyway, Diana is filling in for Delia today and...well, Finch, I know you like to play the field. But our Diana is..." He paused for effect, his eyes boring into Joey's. "Diana is hands off."

Joey had not seen that coming. He was taken aback by Connor's words, slightly offended, and more than a little hurt.

Connor must have seen something of what Joey was feeling in his face, because his expression softened. He raised both palms in the air and shrugged. "What did you expect, Finch? Diana's family. You have sisters. Would you want one of them to date a guy like me?" He grinned.

"Hell, no," Joey said, but he was smiling again.

He pondered Connor's words on his way to the workroom. Would he want one of his sisters to date a guy like Connor? The big man was a nice guy, for sure, but one with zero interest in anything beyond having a little fun. Joey's automatic response to Connor's question was spot-on. Hell. No. He liked Connor, admired him even. He was an excellent lawyer and *an all-around good guy, but Joey would not—absolutely would not—want Connor anywhere near his sisters.*

Joey stopped at the water fountain, still deep in thought. After a few sips, he continued to the workroom. The interesting question was this: Would he want Grace or Darcie to go out with a guy like their brother, like Joey Finch—Mr. One and Done? He thought about it for exactly two seconds before he knew the answer: Hell. No. He didn't know whether to be amused or disturbed that his answers to both questions were exactly the same. What did that say about Joey Finch at twenty-one? Would he be just like Connor Merritt in ten years? Did he want to be?

Once he reached the copier, Joey punched in Connor's copy code, pressed the "Copy" button, and waited. Nothing happened. He pressed the "Copy" button again. Twice, this time, for good measure. Nothing. He punched in Connor's code again. Nothing. Hmmm. Not good. He didn't want to be the intern who broke the copy machine. Maybe there was a checklist somewhere, something he could look at to figure things out. He glanced around the counter near the door. That's when he saw her, *out of the corner of his eye.*

She was on the floor beside the desk, on her hands and knees, pretending to pick up some papers that had apparently fallen out of the folder in her hand. He knew she was pretending because she had yet to pick up a single thing. He turned his head slightly as if he was studying the poster on the wall—the one from the Health Department about covering your mouth when you cough. She ducked her head, picked up a piece of paper, and placed it in the folder. Her behavior was strange, almost as if...

She was spying on him. He was sure of it. She was charming, sitting there on the floor peeking at him whenever he turned his head. She looked sweet and shy and very, very unsure. So, this was Diana, Roman's sister. Connor had wasted his breath. They didn't need to worry about a thing. She was definitely not his type. Still, he needed help with the copier, and he couldn't resist having a little harmless fun.

What a conceited jerk I was, Joey thought. A quick glance at Diana confirmed her continuing indifference to his presence. At this point, it was no less than he deserved. He sighed, heavily. "Well, hell." He didn't mean to say it out loud, but there it was. It took a few seconds to register that Diana was looking at him inquiringly.

She pulled out her left earbud. "Did you say something?" she asked, politely.

He opened his mouth and stupid fell out. "I like your pink laptop." He smiled broadly...like some kind of idiot.

She paused before answering. "It's rose gold." No smile. No change of expression. No encouragement.

"Oh." *And I am a moron,* he added to himself. But he couldn't stop. Stupid had him in its grip, along with Clumsy and Awkward. The words just kept falling out of his mouth. Pointless and Pathetic joined in. "Your case is pink."

Diana nodded slightly. "Yes, I suppose it is." She waited another second with raised eyebrows. "Is there something else?" she asked.

"No," he said, nonchalantly, forcing himself to focus on the road. He tried to look cool and relaxed, as if he had important discussions every single day about the color of laptops. He thought about making some other asinine comment about the color of her cellphone case—also pink—but he decided to save that little gem for later.

Out of the corner of his eye, he saw her shrug her shoulders and reinsert the earbud. She shifted so that one leg was tucked under her with the other dangling over it. She started typing furiously.

Joey quickly filed their little exchange in his brain under the ongoing column *Failed Conversation Starters.* He thought it was *Number Ten,* but it could be *Number Eleven.* There had been so many, he had honestly lost track. What a difference nine years made. The first time he met Diana he was an overconfident hotshot and now, well...now he was just lame. And a loser. And he realized, with a great deal of regret, that she was never going to look at him again the way she had then.

Diana sat behind the desk, eyes glued to the unopened elevator doors with the studied concentration of a cat at a mouse hole. Joey saw her glance at her watch once before resuming her vigil. He smiled, secure in the knowledge that she was waiting for him to step out of that elevator. Thank goodness he had decided at the last minute to take the stairs. He crept up behind her slowly, his steps muffled by the thick Oriental rug that covered most of the shiny wood floor. He was right behind her before he spoke.

"Waiting for someone?" he asked, close to her ear.

To his surprise, she screamed, nearly jumping out of her chair in shock. She put her hand on her heart when she realized who had spoken.

"Easy, now," he said, thoroughly enjoying her reaction.

Her surprised eyes met his knowing gaze. He leaned one leg against the desk, thoroughly pleased with himself. Until she spoke.

"What are you trying to do, sneaking up on me like that? You almost made me have a heart attack." Gone was the sweet, shy girl he had talked with earlier. In her place was a woman. An angry woman.

Joey raised his eyebrows and took a step back from the desk, intrigued, in spite of himself. She was still sitting down, but with her hands on her hips and fire shooting out of her gray eyes. She had...presence. She reminded him of a spitting kitten, all outraged dignity and pride. And completely captivating. He preferred this show of spirit to the schoolgirl admiration she had tried to hide during their first encounter.

He felt the connection that day, even if he was too self-absorbed at the time to realize it. That instant connection was the reason he had studiously avoided her whenever she visited Merritt Brothers during the past nine years. It was also the reason he had a copy of every book in the *Nanny Di* series. He was ridiculously proud of her success, even though it had absolutely nothing to do with him. He tried to write these feelings off as trivialities related to the fact that he worked in her family's law firm. He wasn't nearly as interested, however, in hearing what the rest of the Merritt family was up to; he never really paid that much attention. But, when he heard Diana's name, he tuned into every word. Still, somehow, he had managed to ignore his reaction to her until Grace and Blane's wedding. Even the lawyer in him could not explain away how he felt that day.

Joey's eyes scanned the grand foyer in search of new arrivals. He was acting as an unofficial host since he was one of the few who was acquainted with every person in the wedding party. That was when he saw her gazing at the painting that was hanging on the far wall. He couldn't see her face, but the rest of her was stunning. The sight stopped him in his tracks. He felt as if he'd been kicked in the stomach. He didn't like the feeling very much. No. He didn't like that feeling at all. He was off-balance and more than a little rattled. If his reaction was this intense, what would happen when she turned around?

Her dress was a pale sea-foam green, some kind of flowy material that was longer in the back than in the front. It emphasized her small waist and gave him a tantalizing peek at her long, lovely legs. Her elegant hands were loosely clasped behind her back, but it was her hair that held his gaze. Long red hair. No, red was too ordinary a word for the spectacular combination of scarlet, crimson, carmine, and every other reddish hue rising from the distant memory of his seventh-grade art class. All that glorious color swirled around her head in a cascade of riotous curls spilling down her back. Part of the crown was held back in a jeweled clip, but even that failed to tame the deliciously unruly mass. It was the kind of hair that gave a man all kinds of carnal ideas—mostly involving silk sheets and moonlight.

In Joey's experience, all redheads were trouble, plain and simple. They should be avoided at all costs. But…he studied the vision before him. Maybe this one would be worth a bit of trouble. With her flaming locks, porcelain skin, and tempting body, she exuded sex appeal. His feet made the decision for him, moving of their own accord. Who was she? And why was he compelled to find out?

"And who do we have here?" he asked smoothly.

When she turned around, he was certain that the shock on her face mirrored his own. He nearly laughed at his own folly. Diana Merritt. Of course, it was. She and she alone could call to him across a crowded room. He acquitted himself well, maintaining his casual façade for the duration of their subsequent conversation. He even managed an appropriately memorable exit. But he was shaken. Gone was the charming college girl he remembered. In her place stood a woman. Alluring. Stunning. Desirable. His siren.

He had danced with Diana at the reception. Once. He hadn't planned to dance with her at all. But when he saw his friend, Roger Carrington, heading straight for her, no force on earth could have kept Joey from getting there first. The dance had been a huge miscalculation on his part. The impact of touching her, of pulling her into his arms, well….He wasn't sure what they talked about during that dance because his brain had ceased to function. He made the decision then and there that he wasn't going to dance with her again. Ever.

Dancing with Diana confirmed what Joey had known all along. Further association with her was a threat to his position at Merritt Brothers. Her relatives would fire him in a heartbeat. They would also cheerfully kill him and hide the body if they thought he was messing around with their sister. Their daughter. Their cousin. In addition to that problematic scenario, it was quite clear that Diana was a threat to Joey's peace of mind, his sanity, and, ultimately, his heart.

Still, he couldn't explain away the invisible pull he felt whenever he was in her general vicinity. He didn't know if she felt it, too. He had decided a long time ago that he really didn't want to know. What he did know, however, was that every time he saw her, the strength of their connection grew stronger. Almost as if it had taken on a life of its own, like being caught in a particularly strong current. No matter how hard he tried, he couldn't break free. She drew him to her, effortlessly, and, apparently, unconsciously. He couldn't get away. He couldn't escape. And part of him was starting to wonder if he really wanted to. One dance had shown him that he would do well to avoid contact with Diana Merritt. And he had. Until today.

Fate, it seemed, had other ideas.

CHAPTER FIFTEEN

*D*iana studied herself in the ladies' room mirror as she washed her hands, trying hard to be objective. The woman who looked back at her had messy red hair, dark gray eyes, and a smattering of freckles across the bridge of her nose. She wasn't drop-dead gorgeous or anything close to that, but her appearance wasn't enough to send a man screaming into the night. She was, she reluctantly decided, pleasant looking. Comfortable. Average. And definitely not someone who would attract the attention of Joey Finch. Diana sighed as she shook the water off her hands. Why her realization was suddenly so depressing was a mystery. She had known he was out of her league the first time she laid eyes on him. Her brain had known, but apparently not her heart.

What was her problem, anyway? A person with normal thought processes would probably be concerned that the man who called himself Bill—the man who had tried to kidnap her not once, but *twice*—was still at-large. He was still out there, doing who knew what? Yes, she thought, any rational person would be worried, maybe even terrified. But not Diana Merritt. Oh, no. She was obsessing over the declaration enunciated by one unattainable man: *"A woman like that will never be my type."*

She held her hands under the hand dryer attached to the wall. Even though air dryers saved paper, she hated them. She never had enough patience to stand there long enough to actually dry her hands. Amalie, however, loved them. Whenever she used them, Diana practically had to drag the little girl out of the restroom. Thinking of her small charge made Diana smile. The little girl had a firm hold on her nanny's heart...Diana couldn't wait to see her. Maybe, she realized, Amalie was her light at the end of the tunnel.

Diana pushed the button on the hand dryer again. She knew it was cowardly to stall, but she needed a few more seconds to get her thoughts in order before she talked to Joey Finch. Since leaving Alexandria, Diana had created a detailed account of everything she could remember about her day. Every sight. Every sound. Every word. She had employed the same strategy after finding Mallory's body and after Bill's first failed kidnapping attempt. The process was cathartic somehow. Maybe writing it all down gave her the illusion that it had happened to someone else. To some poor, nameless character in a novel. Maybe it helped her look at everything objectively. She wasn't sure. She only knew that after typing the last word, she had been able to breathe again. That was enough.

After reading over the finished product, however, Diana realized she had made a grave error. She had no business being upset with Joey Finch. No business at all. He had done everything right. His actions were nothing short of heroic. His quick-thinking quite possibly saved her life and the lives of the patrons and staff at Chutley's. Who knew what would have happened if *Bill* started shooting? Just thinking about it made her slightly sick.

She should be thanking Joey, not pouting because he didn't find her attractive. *Time to look at the big picture,* she instructed herself. Joey Finch had taken her to his own apartment. Stood up for her in the face of her overbearing family. And now, he was driving her to Honeysuckle Creek. The poor man had to be exhausted. He had scarcely finished dealing with Lance before getting embroiled in Diana's own horrifying situation. He probably wanted nothing more than to go back to his own apartment, go to bed, and forget he had ever met anybody named Merritt. Yet here he was...driving her to safety.

The hand dryer cut off. Again. Diana took a deep breath. It was time to do the right thing. She was going to apologize to Joey Finch, even if she had to do it with slightly damp hands.

He was standing by the food pick-up counter when she came out of the restroom. And he was waiting for her. *Such a nice guy,* she thought. But why did he have to be such a nice guy? The genuine worry on his face made her heart clinch.

"Everything okay?" he asked anxiously when she reached him.

"Yes," she said. "Everything's okay."

His expression cleared. "I thought for a minute that I was going to have to come in there after you."

Diana raised her eyebrows, a trace of amusement in her gray eyes.

It was the first sign that she might be thawing out a little, and Joey ran with it. "Not that I make it a habit of going into women's restrooms, mind you," he said with a grin. "But I just wanted you to know that I could do it if I had to. For you, I mean." The slight twitching of her lips encouraged Joey to continue with his nonsense. "I've only actually been in the ladies' room once—and that was because of Darcie. We were playing hide-and-seek at the public library. I was *it* and she wouldn't come out of the bathroom so I could tag her, so..." Joey shrugged, charmingly.

"You went in," Diana finished for him.

Joey waggled his eyebrows up and down. "How did you know?" he asked, with a wicked grin.

"Just a hunch," Diana said. She waited a second, but when he didn't add anything else, she couldn't resist asking, "Well, did you?"

Joey looked puzzled. "Did I what?"

"Did you tag her?"

"No, I'm afraid not." Joey shook his head sadly. "She stood on the seat in the *first* stall, but I started by looking in the *last* stall. She ran out as soon as she heard me open the door to the empty stall and say, 'Gotcha!'"

"And you chased her?" Diana asked.

"Of course," Joey said, gravely. "I *had* to chase her. You know the rules of the game as well as I do. I *had* to do it."

Diana cocked her head to one side as if pondering the situation. "Because you were *it?*"

"Exactly." Joey nodded in mock approval.

"So..." Diana encouraged.

"So what?"

"So, did you ever tag Darcie?"

"Sadly, no. Unfortunately for me, the librarian was coming *into* the ladies' room when I was going *out* and we sort of...well, you know..." He took both of his hands and clapped them together. "Collided."

"Collided," Diana echoed. "How tragic."

"Yeah. It was."

Diana was thoroughly enjoying herself for the first time in hours. "I bet that made you super-popular with the librarian."

"Oh, yeah," Joey agreed. "She loved us. Still does."

Their banter was rewarded by a snort of laughter from the lady behind the counter. "Order number twenty-six," she said, setting two cups on the counter at Joey's elbow.

"Thank you, ma'am," he said with a smile before deliberately slipping his hand through the handle of a plastic bag that was lying on the counter. He picked up the cups while the bag dangled from his wrist. He handed one of the cups to Diana. "For you."

"Oh," she said. "Thank you." She took a sip and smiled in genuine delight.

Joey breathed a sigh of relief. That's what he had been waiting for. Her smile shone like the sun. He couldn't help but bask in its warmth.

"Caramel iced coffee. How did you—" Diana stopped short as understanding slowly dawned. "You remembered, didn't you? I can't believe you still remember what kind of coffee I like."

"Of course." Joey shrugged it off as unimportant.

But it was important to Diana. It was *very* important. If he still remembered, that must mean...*something*. It had to mean...*something*. Didn't it? *Of course not,* she reprimanded herself. *You're not his type. Remember?* Her next sip of coffee tasted a little bitter.

He watched her smile fade like the sun dipping behind a cloud. He resolved to do something about that cloud. "Ready to go?" Joey asked.

Diana nodded.

"You two have a good night," the lady behind the counter said, regarding Joey and Diana with grandmotherly approval.

"Yes, ma'am," Joey responded, giving Grandma a mischievous wink that brought a faint blush to her cheeks.

Diana barely refrained from rolling her eyes. Joey Finch was effortlessly charming. And the more time she spent with him, the more convinced she was that he couldn't help it. Charm came as naturally to him as breathing; she wished with all her heart that she could muster some kind of immunity to it. Unfortunately, she was as susceptible as everybody else. It just wasn't fair, she thought as they made their way back to his truck. She had to admit that the truck was something of a surprise. She didn't know what she had expected him to drive...a Lamborghini? A Ferrari? A BMW M-series? Granted, his Ford F-150 was equipped with all the bells and whistles, but it was still a truck.

He opened the passenger door of that truck for her *and* held her coffee—her *caramel iced coffee*—while she scrambled up into her seat. He handed her both coffees and carefully shut her door. *Drat.* Why did he have to be so appealing anyway? Diana asked herself.

She placed the coffees in the holder in the console and fastened her seatbelt, all the while pondering her obsession. Babysitting inebriated lawyers. Charming convenience store clerks. Hiding women from psychotic kidnappers. All in a day's work for Joey Finch. The man seemed blessed with the innate ability to do exactly the right thing at exactly the right time. Add to that his boyish charm and the promise of devilment dancing in his wicked eyes, and he was practically irresistible. To her. He was irresistible to Diana Merritt, the woman—she reminded herself *again*—who was *Not.*

His. Type. Diana sighed. Be that as it may, she was also the woman who owed him a very big apology.

Unaware of the thoughts running through his passenger's mind, Joey jumped up into the driver's seat and closed the door. Then he handed Diana the bag he had picked up from the convenience store counter.

He grinned at her puzzled expression. "Go ahead," he said. "Open it."

Diana peeped inside, unable to contain a squeal of girlish delight. "Chocolate twirls! A whole box, too! Connor would be *so* jealous!"

And just like that, the sun came out again.

But that smile disappeared while Joey was still congratulating himself. He watched in horror as her pretty, gray eyes filled with tears. "Diana," he said, in alarm. "What is it?" He couldn't help but reach out to take hold of her hand. "Should I have gotten the banana cream rolls, instead?"

Diana gave a watery chuckle.

"Or maybe the oatmeal cookies?" he asked, squeezing her cold, little hand in his warm one.

"Of course not." She shook her head, failing to dislodge those crocodile tears pooling in her eyes. "The chocolate twirls are perfect. But Joey..." She ducked her head, dabbing at her eyes with the back of the hand he wasn't holding. "I owe you an apology."

Joey was completely at a loss. "What do you mean, Diana? You don't owe me an apology for anything...oh." Suddenly, it all made sense. And he knew exactly what she was talking about. She didn't owe him an apology. He owed her an explanation. It was time to come clean. "Don't worry about it, Diana..." he began.

"No," she said, squeezing his hand. "Just listen. You've been wonderful today. First, with Lance, and then, everything you've done for me. You probably saved my life *and* the lives of so many people at Chutley's." Diana took a deep breath. "And you don't deserve the things that I said...."

"Diana, you don't have to—" Joey tried to make her stop.

"Please, let me finish," she interrupted. "I'm so grateful. So very grateful for your courage and your kindness. And, well...I should never have said those things. I *know* that I'm not your type; anyone who looks at me knows I'm not your type. That isn't news." She tugged her hand from his grasp, placing it back in her lap. That deliberate gesture, and her little shrug, spoke volumes.

Joey didn't know what to say. The fact that she felt less, somehow—because of him—was ridiculous. It made him feel small. Petty. Like a cowardly jerk.

She continued, her eyes on the hand in her lap: "I just, well…I guess I wasn't ready to hear it from you. So, what I'm trying to say is that I'm sorry." She took a deep breath and looked him in the eye. "I'm sorry, Joey."

She studied his face. He didn't seem upset with her. He didn't seem the type to hold a grudge, anyway. She gave him a hopeful smile. "Do you think you might be able to have a little amnesia where *that* conversation is concerned?"

"What conversation?" he asked. He couldn't help but return her smile even though it made him feel worse. She had given him an out. He could graciously accept her apology and that would be the end of it. He would never have to admit just how attracted to her he really was.

Not his type? Seriously? The man who wasn't attracted to Diana Merritt would have to be bereft of all five of his senses and…dead. Of that Joey was certain. Any man who wasn't attracted to her would have to be dead. There was no other way to explain it. And Joey Finch wasn't dead. In fact, he had never wanted to reach across the console of his truck—iced coffee be damned—and kiss any woman the way he wanted to kiss Diana Merritt at that exact moment.

Completely oblivious to his struggle, she picked up the box of chocolate twirls, put her peach-colored nails under the flap of the box top, and tugged. His eyes couldn't help but follow those hands. Every move she made was lovely. How was it possible to open a box gracefully? Joey didn't know. It was just another piece of a very attractive puzzle he wouldn't allow himself to put together.

Not only that, but he admired her. She didn't back down from anything. She stood up to the kidnapping cowboy, her brother, her cousin, and even, it appeared, the fabled Trio of Doom. Making that apology to him wasn't comfortable or pleasant for her, especially since it carried with it the unspoken admission that she wished she *was* his type. But she had apologized. *And* she had looked him in the eye. So, he would be exactly the kind of cad her family thought him to be if he didn't make his own admission. The very least he could do was to clarify what she thought she had heard him say to Roman. *But how?* Joey wondered. It wasn't the easiest subject matter to bring up. He was enjoying her smile too much to make it disappear.

Unlike her guilt-ridden companion, Diana felt much better after her apology. Joey didn't seem to be the least bit troubled about it. Relief filled her luminous gray eyes as she pulled one of the twin packs of chocolate twirls out of the box. With a tremulous smile, she opened the package and took one of the chocolate-covered, cream-filled twirls for herself. Solemnly, she offered the other one to Joey. "Truce?" she asked, hopefully.

Joey reached for the chocolate twirl instead of reaching for her. It was a poor substitute. He removed the little cake from the package. "Truce," he said, taking a big bite—nearly half the twirl.

Diana giggled before taking her own much smaller bite. "You're worse than Connor," she said, happily.

"Now, wait a minute," Joey objected, trying hard not to notice the tiny bit of white cream at the corner of Diana's peach-colored lips. "If we stayed at my apartment much longer, Connor would have started eating the furniture. I credit myself with a little more control than that."

Diana's tongue peeked out, delicately, to lick that delicious cream from the corner of her mouth. Joey fastened his seatbelt, trying to ignore the way his whole body tightened in response.

She finished her twirl, blessedly unaware of Joey's discomfort. "Did you hear what Connor said when we were leaving?" She laughed again.

"I did not," Joey said, as he backed out of the parking space.

"He said, 'Thank God this is over. I'm starving.' Can you believe him?" Diana shook her head as she hauled her tote bag into her lap and dug into it.

Joey couldn't help but chuckle. "Starving. After he already finished a container of peanuts, two honeybuns, and half a box of Wheat Thins." Thinking of Connor with crumbs on his face and his hand in a box of family-size Wheat Thins went a long way toward reestablishing Joey's tenuous hold on his libido.

He was firmly in control of himself until Diana pulled lipstick out of her enormous purse and carefully applied peach tint to her already peach-colored—and very delectable—lips. Why, he asked himself, had he never before realized how delectable her lips were? It was certainly an extreme oversight on his part. That Diana would be in possession of a pair of delectable lips made perfect sense now that he thought about it. Her delectable lips went along with the rest of her very delectable self.

And *she* thought she wasn't his type. Ha. His hands tightened on the steering wheel in self-disgust. It was time to face the music. Diana deserved nothing less than complete and total honesty.

CHAPTER SIXTEEN

*J*oey checked the time. Again. He was thoroughly disgusted with himself. He had allowed an entire hour to go by without making any attempt to begin—what he assumed would be—a difficult conversation. He had, instead, wasted time trying to imagine how Diana would respond when he attempted to clear up their little misunderstanding. At least, that was what he called it in his own little mind. *Their little misunderstanding.* The only thing he managed to establish was that—contrary to the oft-given opinion of his *delightful* sisters—he had quite an imagination. His moment of reckoning was further postponed when Diana received a phone call from her mother. Quite a fortuitous phone call, in Joey's opinion. At least for him. After all, he couldn't let Diana down gently (again, his own little mind's personal phrasing) while she was on the phone, now, could he?

But after thirty minutes his desire to be done with the unpleasant business, coupled with his guilt, had him glancing impatiently at Diana. She was *still* chatting with her mother. Well, maybe *chatting* wasn't the right word. She seemed to be doing most of the listening and her mother most of the talking. She rolled her eyes at him as she switched ears for the third time. Joey grimaced in sympathy. Apparently, Lucinda Merritt had a lot to say.

Since the phone conversation was currently—but not wholly—to blame for preventing him from confessing all, Joey allowed his stress-filled, overactive imagination to take over....

Joey took a deep breath. *"I'm attracted to you, Diana, but I don't want a relationship," he stated, carefully. "Can you understand that?"*

Diana's gray eyes glowed with an unholy light. "Understand?" she shrieked. "The only thing I understand is that I can't live without you."

Slowly, she unfastened her seatbelt.

"Diana, what are you doing?" Joey yelled, reaching out his hand in a desperate attempt to stop her.

But he was too late.

"Goodbye, my love."

With those final words, Diana opened the door and jumped from Joey's moving truck.

Now, wait just one damn minute, Joey thought. He nearly said it aloud, so adamantly opposed was he to the unexpectedly horrific ending. He cut his eyes to Diana, but she appeared not to notice his agitation. Breathing easier, he quickly added an addendum to that unacceptable scenario.

...And jumped from Joey's moving truck to land safely on the soft, cushiony blanket of deep snow piled on the roadside.

Yes, he decided, that was much better. What was the matter with him anyway? Whoever dreamed up that highly unlikely scenario must have one hell of an ego. *Oh*, he thought, dispiritedly, *that would be me*. He decided to try again....

Joey took a deep breath. "I'm attracted to you, Diana, but I don't want a relationship," he stated, carefully. "Can you understand that?"

Diana's serene gray eyes glowed with a holy light. "Of course," she replied. "I understand perfectly. And that's why I've decided to join a convent and become a nun."

Slowly, she pulled a string of rosary beads from her gigantic bag.

"Diana, what are you doing?" Joey yelled, reaching out his hand in a desperate attempt to stop her.

But he was too late.

"Goodbye, my love."

With those final words, Sister Diana put the beads around her neck and began to pray.

Hmm, Joey thought. *Diana as a nun*. He rejected the idea immediately. The whole scenario put her too far out of his reach somehow. *His reach? Now, wait just a minute*, Joey argued with himself. He did not like the direction of his thoughts. He decided to rephrase his statement. Not out of *his* reach, exactly. More like out of *anyone's* reach. He frowned. He didn't like that, either. The thought of anyone else reaching for Diana was completely unacceptable. It was...well, hell.

Joey took a deep breath. "I'm attracted to you, Diana, but I don't want a relationship," he stated, carefully. "Can you understand that?"

Diana's gray eyes glowed with vengeance. "Of course," she hissed. "I understand perfectly, Joey. And now, you need to understand something…If I can't have you, then no one will."

Slowly, she pulled a 57 Magnum from her gigantic bag.

"Diana, what are you doing?" Joey yelled, reaching out his hand in a desperate attempt to stop her.

But he was too late.

"Goodbye, my love."

With those final words, Diana calmly pulled the trigger.

Seriously? Joey shook his head at his own nonsense. He certainly thought a lot of himself, didn't he? But—and it was a big *but*…enormous, actually—what if *he* thought more of himself than Diana did? What if her reaction to his words at the apartment had more to do with stress than with him? What if she really didn't care at all? What if she thought he was an idiot for bringing up those unpleasant moments again?

Joey took a deep breath "I'm attracted to you, Diana, but I don't want a relationship," he stated, carefully. "Can you understand that?"

Diana's gray eyes filled with pity. "Of course," Diana said. "Nobody in her right mind would want a relationship with you. You're an idiot."

Ouch. But Diana wouldn't say *that.* Would she? Of course she wouldn't, he tried to reassure himself. That would never happen. Or would it? He glanced at the redhead riding shotgun. She was listening patiently to whatever her mother was telling her. Joey fixed his eyes on the car in front of him. The sad reality was he had no idea what Diana Merritt would say when he informed her that he was attracted to her but didn't want a relationship. Maybe she would simply tell him to go straight to hell, he thought, dejectedly. And maybe that was just what he deserved.

"Goodbye, Mom," Diana finally said. "Love you, too." She blew out a breath of relief. There was nothing like the maternal third degree. Diana's mom had missed her calling. She should have worked for the FBI. No min-iscule bit of information escaped her detail-oriented mind. Cowboy Bill better hope he never came face-to-face with Lucinda Merritt. With one glance Diana's mother would incinerate the imposter on the spot. Diana dropped her phone into her bag and rubbed her sore ear.

"Diana."

The urgent tone in Joey's voice made her jump. She straightened in her seat, suddenly tense. "What is it? What's wrong?"

Joey shook his head. "No, no. Nothing's wrong. Nothing like that, anyway." But he was frowning.

Diana didn't know if she had ever seen him frown before. His stern countenance made him even *more* attractive. *Drat.* She relaxed back into the seat. "Okay. Good. You scared me for a minute."

"What did you hear me say to Roman?" Joey asked. It came out brusquely, but he couldn't help it. He had to clear the matter up before his imagination killed him.

"What do you mean?" Diana hesitated, as understanding dawned. "Oh...*that.*" She blew out a disheartened breath. "Joey, I'd rather not rehash all that again."

Joey shook his head, a determined expression on his face. "Just hear me out, Diana. Please." He tried to make his voice soothing and gentle. He managed instead to produce a hoarse-sounding croak. He *was* an idiot. "When you walked out of the guest bedroom, what did you hear me say to Roman?"

Diana searched his face for a minute before coming to a decision. Reaching into her bag, she pulled out her computer case. The pink one, Joey noted absently. Very deliberately, she unzipped the case and took out her computer. *The rose gold one,* he added to himself, unnecessarily. She opened her rose gold computer and scrolled for a few seconds before finding the section she wanted. She read aloud in an expressionless voice:

" *'Diana. Merritt. Is. Not. My. Type.'*

" *'Damn it, Connor. How many times do I have to tell you that I don't have any chocolate twirls?'*

" *'Do you want me to say it again for you, Roman? A woman like that will* never *be my type.'*

"*'She's standing right behind me, isn't she?'* "

Joey cringed at the coldness in his own words. He was lucky Diana hadn't slapped him.

Diana very deliberately closed her rose gold computer and put it back in its pink case. She zipped the pink case and carefully placed it somewhere in the depths of her enormous bag. Only then did she raise her eyes to his.

He could almost feel the change of temperature as she surveyed him with the disdainful gaze of an ice queen. She crossed her arms and raised her eyebrows, hoping she looked calm and cool on the outside. On the inside she felt a little sick. "Anything else?"

"Yes," he said. "There is something else. Something very important."

"And what would that be?" Diana asked, politely.

"The part you *didn't* hear."

"What do you mean the part that I *didn't* hear?" She regarded him with an understandable degree of skepticism.

Joey tried to explain. "What I said to Roman *before* you walked in."

"Oh, great. You mean there's more?" She tried to be offhand about it, failing entirely. "Well, go ahead and tell me, Joey. What did you say *before* I walked into the room?"

"I said—and I quote—*'If marriage is your sister's only goal in life, then she is definitely not for me.'*" He paused to let the import of the words sink in.

"Oh," breathed Diana, in surprise. "Oh."

"Yes, '*Oh*,'" said Joey. "I also said, *'If her sole focus in life is getting married, then there is no doubt. Diana. Merritt. Is. Not. My. Type.'*"

"But my sole focus in life *isn't* getting married, so that would mean…" Diana stopped, unable to complete the sentence aloud.

Thank God, Joey thought with relief. The coldness had left her eyes and she was listening intently. "It means exactly what it sounds like it means. I *am* attracted to you, Diana. I've been attracted to you since I saw you sitting at that admin's desk at Merritt Brothers nine years ago. And every time I've seen you since, I'm more and more attracted to you."

"To me?" Diana asked, shock written all over her face. "But why?" Diana's heart was fluttering in her chest like some hyperactive butterfly.

Joey grinned, pleased with her reaction. "Have you looked in the mirror, Diana? How could I help it? You. Are. Exactly. My. Type. But…" Joey paused, hesitant to continue. How could he wipe away the expression of delighted surprise on her face? How could he not? She deserved the whole truth. He had to tell her the rest before she got the wrong idea. He steeled himself to deliver the bad news.

Diana was in a state of ecstatic disbelief. The hyperactive butterfly was going to fly right out of her chest. She was going to expire in the front seat of Joey's F-150.

She *was* Joey's type.

She was *exactly* his type.

He said so. He felt the attraction. He *actually* felt it.

She was not insane, delusional, or otherwise, mentally impaired. And she wasn't alone. Not anymore. They shared the same feelings; had shared them for nine years. But, despite the elation running through her veins, Diana was a realist. She forced herself to focus on the implications of Joey's last word:

But…

But, Diana reminded herself, because she knew a lot about the man driving the truck. In addition—thanks in part to Chrissy—she knew beyond a shadow of a doubt exactly where this conversation was heading. This time, however, the female was one step ahead of Joey Finch. And in honor of every girl that had come before her, Diana was going to say the words first.

"You're not a relationship kind of guy." She almost smiled at the astonished expression on Joey's face.

"That's right," he said, in surprise. He paused for a moment to take it in. *Well*, he thought, *this is new*. He had *never* had a girl tell him he wasn't a relationship kind of guy *before* he could tell her. "What gave me away?" he asked, trying to appear unaffected by her surprising words.

"Chrissy told me," Diana answered honestly. "She said you're a really nice guy, but not the relationship kind."

"She's right." Joey was a little nonplused. "Well, at least, I hope I'm a nice guy. I try to be a nice guy and…wait a minute. Who's Chrissy?"

"Shirley," Diana said. "I'm talking about Shirley."

Joey felt a little off balance, as if the universe had tilted ever so slightly. "If you're talking about Shirley," he asked, patiently, "then why did you call her Chrissy?"

"Because, Joey..." Diana explained, "...her name is Chrissy."

The whole conversation, in Joey's opinion, had taken a very weird turn. "Shirley's name is Chrissy?"

Diana regarded him with something like pity. Her expression rankled his already over-stretched nerves.

"Well," he responded, hoping for...something. "If her name is Chrissy, then why did she let me call her Shirley the whole night?"

Diana tried to make him understand. "Because you went out once and she knew you didn't remember her name."

Joey blanched, saying nothing. He was back to feeling like a jerk.

His stricken expression made Diana feel a little sorry for him. "Don't worry, Joey. Chrissy wasn't upset that you didn't remember her name. She seemed perfectly happy being *Shirley* for the night." Diana watched the play of emotions on his face, pleased that he was concerned about Chrissy's feelings.

"Damn it," he said, almost to himself. "I did remember her. Sort of. I remember that we went out once a couple of years ago."

"She said she had a really good time and she expected you to call her back...."

Joey was quick to interrupt. "But I'm sure that I told her from the beginning I was only asking her out for one—"

"I'm sure that you did." Diana could interrupt, too, *thank you very much*. "As a matter of fact, Chrissy said you told her the date was a one-time thing. But she really thought you would change your mind. You don't need to feel badly about it," Diana reiterated. "Chrissy didn't hold a grudge. She wasn't mad or anything. She even said you were a really nice guy. Just *not* the relationship kind. Chrissy's really nice, too. I'm going to take her to lunch the next time I'm in Alexandria."

"Chrissy, huh?" Joey pondered Diana's words for a few seconds before it dawned on him that Diana was smiling. No, he decided, she wasn't just smiling. She was beaming. Beaming with joy or…something. He could barely keep his eyes on the road. The woman's smile was lethal. He could tell she was relieved by his admission. He should be relieved, too. Their whole exchange had gone better than he expected. A lot better.

But, contrary to his own expectations, Joey was *not* relieved. Their conversation had gone well all right. Entirely *too* well. Diana's reaction was a revelation— so far from the one he was expecting that he was momentarily flummoxed. The longer he thought about Diana's beaming smile, the more irritated he became.

Apparently, he realized, she—Diana Merritt—was blissfully happy that he—Joey Finch—*wasn't* interested in a relationship. At the very least, he had expected a little disappointment on her part. She seemed to like him well enough, so he had just assumed that…*well, hell.* This kind of rejection had *never* happened to him before. He pondered the concept for a few seconds. At least he didn't *remember* it happening before now. He couldn't decide how he felt about another painful blow to his already bruised ego.

And what did that say about Joey Finch as a person? Was he really so shallow that he assumed every woman would fall at his feet, weeping with despair upon discovering he wasn't interested in a relationship? Apparently, he was, he surmised, uncomfortably. And where was the relief he had expected to feel? The relief of having avoided becoming embroiled in a relationship? Of having narrowly escaped a fate worse than death, in other words? He waited a few seconds more, but that relief still didn't come. Instead, a feeling of confusion, coupled with a little bit of insecurity, settled in its place. He wasn't sure that he liked this new feeling, but he tried to find the bright side. At least Diana hadn't pulled out a gun and shot him.

Diana continued to beam like some overly excited ray of sunshine. "I'm glad we got that straightened out," she said.

Her smile was blinding. If it continued, he might require sunglasses. Her good mood was grating on his last nerve.

"Now we can enjoy being friends," she announced, happily, already pulling her computer from her ridiculously large tote bag.

The size of her bag was beginning to annoy him, too. Joey didn't even try to keep the sarcasm from his voice when he responded. "Yeah, you can *never* have too many friends."

CHAPTER SEVENTEEN

*J*oey knew he was being childish. And surly. And very, very shallow. But, for once, he didn't really care. Why did Diana have to be so damn happy? he wondered, churlishly. He cut his eyes toward his passenger. She was, once again, typing away at her computer. Her *rose gold* computer, he added to himself. Why couldn't she have a computer that was a normal color like every-body else? Why did it have to be *rose gold*?

Rose. Gold.

What a stupid name for a color, he thought. Roses weren't gold... *golden*, he added, for the sake of grammar. His mother and sister were both English teachers, after all. As a matter of fact, he had never seen a golden rose in his whole life. The closest thing would probably be a yellow rose, covered with Charlie Ray's signature glitter, from Honeysuckle Creek Flower and Gift.

Golden roses. *Hmph.*

He was certain they didn't exist. If this God-forsaken road trip through End of the Earth, Virginia, ever came to an end, he would look it up. That's exactly what he would do, he promised himself. He couldn't wait to tell Little Miss Rose-Gold-Computer sitting over there that golden roses were a figment of her imagination.

Rose-gold. Ridiculous.

Joey tapped his fingers on the steering wheel. Diana had her ear-buds in again. Probably, he decided, so she wouldn't have to listen to Joey Finch—the man who *didn't* want a relationship. Joey scowled. He clearly wasn't the only one who *didn't* want a relationship. He gave her another quick sideways glance. Diana Merritt didn't want a relationship, either. If she did, she wouldn't be so damn happy.

She was industrious, though. He had to give her that. She wasn't wasting a single minute in idle conversation with the man who had admitted he was attracted to her. The one who was sitting beside her. Fighting said attraction. Lusting after her like a hormone-challenged teenage boy. Joey wanted to find a wall and punch it.

What could she possibly be working on, anyway? He found himself genuinely curious. She could have written a dozen *Nanny Di* books by now. Joey thought back to the moment she pulled up her transcript of his conversation with Roman. He had to hand it to her. She had one hell of a memory. Everything she quoted back to him was spot on. Every word was…Joey froze. What if she was writing about him right now? What if she was writing down every word that he said earlier so that she could use them in a book? What was the title Zack had suggested?

Nanny Di and the Love 'Em and Leave 'Em Lawyer.

Good Lord. Joey imagined what she might be writing about him at this very minute. It wasn't at all flattering:

The spoiled and shallow lawyer pouted behind the steering wheel of his well-equipped truck….

And the worst part was that it was true.

Determined to save what was left of his dignity, Joey pasted a charming smile on his face. "Diana," he said. "Hey, Diana."

"Hmm?" she asked, removing her left earbud. She regarded him with curiosity.

"What are you writing over there?" Joey asked.

She ducked her head shyly, as if she couldn't decide how she wanted to answer his question.

Joey thought her indecision was charming. "C'mon," he urged. "You can tell me. I'm completely trustworthy." He waggled his eyebrows up and down and grinned his sinful grin. "I'm a *lawyer*, you know."

Diana laughed. She couldn't help it. Joey Finch's ability to poke fun at himself was one of his most endearing qualities. One of many, she decided. Although, if the last half hour was any indication, he did seem prone to mood swings. Either that or he wasn't handling her response to his big *no relationship* reveal.

Or was it her *lack* of response? Hmm, she thought, tucking that interesting theory away to ponder later. At this point, she was so overjoyed and relieved that her feelings were reciprocated, the relationship issue was irrelevant. He was attracted to her, that was what mattered. For the time being.

Joey couldn't resist teasing her. Hearing her laughter restored his good mood. Somewhat. A niggling doubt remained, but he shoved it to the very back of his consciousness. "I know!" he announced. "You're writing your new bestseller...*Nanny Di and the Loveable Lawyer.*"

Diana's smile turned mischievous as she removed her other earbud. "Of course not," she denied, stealing a peek at Joey's handsome profile. She tried not to giggle. "Nobody would read *that.*"

He sat up very straight, pretending to be offended. Then he gave a very exaggerated version of a sigh as his grin returned. "You're probably right," he said ruefully. "What are you *really* working on?"

She took a deep breath. "I'm writing a romance novel." She braced herself for the typical comments about scantily clad heroines and lust-crazed heroes. But the comments didn't come.

"Contemporary or historical?" he asked.

"Historical," she said, surprised at his response.

"And the setting?"

He was completely serious, as if he actually wanted to hear her answers. Diana's surprise grew. "England, in the early 1800s."

"That's a good time period. You know, the war with France and Napoleon and all," Joey continued. "Are there any spies in your..." He suddenly became aware that she was watching him with a puzzled expression on her face. "What?" he asked.

She tried to explain. "You didn't make fun of me or volunteer to pose for the cover without your shirt or—"

He was quick to interrupt. "What kind of a jerk would do that?"

Diana couldn't help but laugh. "Dad, Roman, Uncle Gary, Uncle Rob, Connor, Devin..." She ticked them off on her fingers as Joey's lips quirked up a bit at the corners.

"Ah, the joys of family. But, what about Lance?" He couldn't help but notice his friend's absence from the list.

"Lance just pats me on the shoulder and promises to buy anything I write," she admitted.

How typical of Lance. "Good old Lance," Joey said.

"He doesn't promise to *read* it," Diana admonished. "Just to *buy* it."

"Sort of good old Lance," Joey corrected himself with a smile. "Well, I promise to read it. And I have no desire to grace the cover without my shirt." Joey's smile became a wicked grin. "Not that I wouldn't look good, mind you." He let go of the steering wheel with one hand to flex the muscles in his arm.

Diana's mouth went dry. Joey certainly had muscles. Oh, did he ever. She could easily imagine him on the cover of a book. She would depict him as a Scottish laird. A *shirtless* Scottish laird, she corrected herself. The sculpted muscles of his upper body standing in stark contrast to the rugged mountains in the background. The muscles of his thighs just visible under the edge of his kilt. His dark hair flowing past his shoulders. His eyes gleaming wickedly as his hot gaze focused on the woman in his arms. She, of course, had a waterfall of loose red curls....

"So, are there any spies in your book?" Joey asked, hopefully.

Diana tried to focus on his question without fanning herself. She was very warm all of a sudden. Drat her vivid imagination. At least Joey's arm, with its distracting muscles, was once again steering the truck.

She dove into her plot points in a deliberate attempt to find her missing equilibrium. "The hero is an ex-spy," she explained. "Wounded in the war with Napoleon. He retreats to his ancestral castle with his two wards. They're the sons of his best friend, who died during the war."

Joey nodded in perfect understanding. "His friend asked him to take care of his sons with his dying breath."

"What makes you think that?" she asked, suspiciously.

"I have two sisters who read romance novels," he replied, matter-of-factly.

"Oh." Diana pondered that for a moment. *Interesting*. She never talked to Roman about romance novels. He had absolutely no idea what she was reading. "So, you read romance novels with your sisters?" she asked.

Uh-oh. How to answer that? Joey was a voracious reader. He read *everything*, including an occasional romance novel. He had never read a historical romance, but he had learned a lot from the contemporary ones. Quite a lot. And some of it was rather…steamy. There was one contemporary romance in particular that stuck out in his mind. The heroine, coincidentally, had long, red hair like Diana and she…

Joey suddenly realized he felt a bit warm. Something must be wrong with the air conditioning in his truck. He turned down the temperature a few degrees while he considered the best way to answer Diana's question. He couldn't tell her that he read romance novels for educational purposes. Too awkward.

"Of course I don't read romance novels *with* my sisters," he finally said. And that was true enough. "I just listen when they talk about them." And, he added to himself, he did learn useful things from listening to his sisters' conversations. Occasionally. "Tell me more about your main characters," he said, to distract Diana before she could pursue that particular topic.

Diana was charmed by his genuine interest. "The hero is an earl, but he isn't supposed to be an earl. He inherited the title after his older brother died."

"That's tragic," Joey said.

Diana shook her head. "Not really."

"Why is that?"

"His older brother was an abusive ass," Diana confided. "I modeled him after Lydia's ex-husband."

Joey grimaced. While working at Merritt Brothers, he had heard all about Lydia Merritt's horrible marriage to Kyle Follansbee. Diana was right. Kyle was an abusive ass. Since Joey could think of nothing else to add, he moved on. "Does the earl have a countess?"

Diana was impressed that he didn't say wife. He actually knew that an earl's married counterpart was a countess. "The earl isn't married," she informed him.

"Yet," Joey added, waggling his eyebrows. "Remember, I know stuff."

Diana grinned. She was thoroughly enjoying their conversation. "Yet," she agreed. "He's not married yet. He was engaged before the war, but his fiancée jilted him."

"Too bad for the earl," Joey added.

"Not really," Diana disagreed.

"Why not?"

"Our earl didn't want a fiancée in the first place," Diana explained. "Judith was a greedy manipulative woman who set him up. She lured him into the library during a ball—knowing they would be discovered—and threw herself into his arms. He tried to disengage himself, but it was too late. They were caught, she was ruined, and they *had* to get engaged. But, while our earl was spying for the Crown during the war, she jilted him to marry his older brother."

"The former earl, now deceased?"

"That's right." She nodded, approvingly.

"So, after *our* earl returns to his ancestral castle…"

"With his wards," Diana added.

"With his wards," Joey repeated. "After *our* earl returns to his ancestral castle with his wards, he falls in love with his neighbor? Housekeeper? Stablemaster's sister…?"

"Governess," Diana said, decisively. "He has to hire a governess, you see, on account of the wards. And he falls in love with her."

"She's not *really* a governess, though, is she?" Joey asked.

Diana narrowed her eyes. "How did you know that?"

"I, my dear Diana, know lots of important things," Joey admitted, with a pleased smile. His dear Diana's lips turned up at the corners. She liked it when he said her name, especially with *my dear* in front of it. She liked it a lot. "Lady Genevieve is *pretending* to be a governess to avoid an arranged marriage."

"That's sad," Joey said. "Not sad that her name is Genevieve, but sad that she had to run away from home."

"Not really," Diana supplied. "Her father was going to force her to marry his best friend—a nasty, lecherous marquess—who is nearly sixty years old. She's better off at the castle with the wards."

"And with our earl, who is very much alive."

"Absolutely. But"—Diana hesitated—"there's a problem—and it's a big one."

Joey gasped in exaggerated shock. "What kind of problem, Diana? The suspense is killing me!" He grinned so she would know he was only teasing. He realized, with a bit of surprise, that he really wanted to know. He was thoroughly enjoying their conversation.

Diana placed the back of her hand on her forehead dramatically. "I know you're not going to believe this, Joey, but Genevieve doesn't like our earl." She tried not to giggle at Joey's disgruntled expression.

"How could Genevieve not like a poor, wounded ex-spy like the earl?" Joey asked. "His friend asked him to take care of his sons with his dying breath. The earl sounds like a great guy to me."

"Lady Genevieve doesn't trust him," Diana said, decisively.

"Why not?" Joey asked, a little put out. "Our earl is infinitely trust-worthy; otherwise, he wouldn't have wards."

"Because *before* the war..." Diana paused for effect, "...our earl was a rake."

"A rake, huh? Hmm."

To Diana's delight, Joey pondered this revelation for a few seconds before asking, "And you're sure about this rake business?"

"Yes," she said, decisively. "He was a rake."

"Does that make Genevieve a hoe?" Joey asked, enjoying the startled look on Diana's face.

"Joey Finch," she gasped. "Shame on you. Lady Genevieve most cer-tainly is *not* a 'ho.' She's not that kind of girl."

Joey laughed with delight at her outrage. "H-O-E. Like a garden hoe. I'm not insulting Lady Genevieve. I just figured if he was a rake then she might be a—"

Diana's eyes widened with understanding. "Oh, ha ha. I get it. Garden humor." She grimaced at his silly joke. "Anyway, our earl was a rake *before* he became a spy. You can use the word *rogue*, if you like," Diana said, sar-castically, albeit politely.

"In other words, the earl was a player," Joey said, drily. Diana's book was starting to hit a little too close to home. "Only now, he's a wounded, embittered player."

"Only until he meets Lady Genevieve," Diana confided. "Meeting her changes *everything*. He knows immediately that she is the only woman he will ever love."

"That's nice."

"Not really," Diana said, shaking her head sadly. "Genevieve doesn't believe that our earl has reformed. She thinks he'll always be a rake."

"Poor guy," Joey said, sympathetically. "So how does our earl win the heart of Lady Genevieve?"

Diana shrugged. "I don't know yet. That's as far as I've managed to get."

"What?" Joey gasped dramatically. "You're a cruel, cruel woman, Diana, to leave me hanging like that. I may lose sleep."

Diana smiled, studying him for a minute. "You know, Joey..." Her smile broadened. "...If you lived back then, I think you would have been considered something of a rake."

He laughed, more at the amused expression on her face than at her words. Those stung a little. "Not embittered or wounded, though?"

"Oh, definitely, not!" Diana giggled.

"You know," Joey said, thoughtfully, "my great-grandmother always tells me that I'm a rascal."

"Oh, I like that," Diana said, cheerfully. "You are definitely more rascal than rake."

Well, that's something of an improvement, Joey thought, feeling slightly better. For some reason, he didn't want Diana to think of him as a rake. Or a player. But a rascal? Yes, he could live with that. Grandma Sofi had certainly approved of Diana when she met her at Grace's wedding, he mused. Diana had no idea what an achievement that was. His great-grandmother wasn't easily impressed.

"McDonald's!"

Diana's excited squeal put an end to Joey's meandering thoughts. In fact, it almost made him jump out of his skin.

"Can we please, please, please stop?" she begged. "I'm starving!"

"Now who sounds like Connor?" Joey asked, chuckling, but he pulled off at the exit. He hadn't had anything to eat since the lunch recess of the ill-fated trial. As far as he was concerned, a handful of pretzels at Chutley's and a pack and a half of chocolate twirls didn't count.

"Oh, no!" Diana said, mournfully. "They're closed."

Joey saw the scaffold covering the area where the drive-thru was supposed to be, too, but as they drew closer, he also saw something else. "They're not closed. Look at all these cars. The place is packed."

Diana inspected the crowded parking lot. "You're right. And there's a huge line inside, too." She looked at him doubtfully. "Do you mind if we go in? I don't think I can eat another twirl."

"No problem," Joey said. "We're probably due for a stop. Help me find a parking space."

They made a full circle of the parking lot before Diana spoke up. "Somebody's backing out," she said, hopefully, pointing to a spot near the construction area.

Joey pulled in across from the scaffold.

Diana jumped out of the truck before Joey's feet could hit the ground. He smiled at her eagerness. *Poor girl must be starving*, he thought, resolving to wait in line as long as it took.

She hurried around to his side of the truck just as a bus filled with high school football players drove by. "Oh, no!" Diana screeched. "We've got to hurry! If they get in line in front of us, we'll *never* get any food."

"Let's go." Joey grabbed her hand and tugged her toward the scaffold.

"What are you doing?" Diana asked, planting her feet firmly in the parking lot at the edge of the scaffold. She refused to budge. "The sign says, 'DANGER. CONSTRUCTION AREA. KEEP OUT.' Did you suddenly forget how to read?" She regarded him as if every one of his brain cells had disappeared.

"Do you want to beat those hungry football players or not?" Joey teased, enjoying her outrage.

Diana blew out a breath of indecision. Caution and hunger were battling it out in her brain—and hunger was winning. She took a hesitant step toward Joey.

"C'mon, Diana," Joey said. "It's completely safe." He was standing under the scaffold now, flashing his most disarming smile. To demonstrate, he raised his arms up and down. "See? Perfectly safe."

Diana took another hesitant step forward. Then, she stopped. *What would Nanny Di do?* The thought seemed to pop into her head at the most inopportune times. Diana's better judgment jumped into the fray. She might not be sure what her fictional counterpart would do, but she knew what the real Nanny Di *wouldn't* do. She wouldn't disobey a warning sign and allow Amalie to walk under a scaffold simply because it was the quickest route to the door. "I'm going around," she said, her mind made up. "I'll meet you in line."

Joey's smile widened. "You think I'll let you break in front of me in line, huh? Shame on you, Nanny Di. Where's your spirit of adventure? Iggy says, 'Be brave.' "

"Be brave," Diana said, gifting him with her best nanny glare. "Not stupid."

"Ouch," Joey said, unable to hide his goofy grin.

She looked so appealing standing there with her hands on her slim hips. Her lovely eyes were shooting sparks of annoyance in his direction. He couldn't resist teasing her some more.

He spun in a circle, taking a little glide step at the end like a dancer on Broadway.

"Joey," she scolded, with a worried frown. "Be careful."

He turned smoothly to the side. "My dear Diana," he soothed. "*Careful* is my middle name." Giving a little jerk—a move reminiscent of Michael Jackson—he started walking backwards, one foot behind the other.

Diana couldn't help but giggle. "Joey *Careful* Finch? I thought your middle name was Ezekiel."

"I'm just full of surprises, aren't I?" he asked. He paused, waggling his eyebrows up and down. "Are you ready for the big finish?" Showing off for his lovely companion was the most fun he'd had in ages.

"Jo-ey," Diana said, worriedly. She couldn't help but notice that his back was getting awfully close to the edge of the scaffold. "Be. Careful."

Joey's spin didn't work out quite as well this time. His little glide step sent him straight into one of the legs holding up the scaffold. He lost his balance and tripped on a random piece of concrete lying on the ground. He made a desperate grab for the back corner of the scaffold, regaining his balance at the last minute. He took a step to the side. "See, Diana," he said, smiling victoriously. "*Careful* is my middle name."

"Joey! Look out!" Diana yelled. Her eyes were glued to a spot directly above his head. Joey looked up just in time to see the brick—teetering on the edge of the scaffold—lose its battle with gravity.

Diana watched helplessly as Joey Careful-Is-My-Middle-Name Finch fell backwards into the nearest bush. By the time she reached him, he was struggling to extract himself from the prickly leaves.

"Diana," he gasped, stretching out both hands. The offending brick was now lying harmlessly in the grass.

"Oh, Joey, let me help you." She clasped his hands in both of hers, braced her feet, and pulled. It took three tries to get him on his feet.

He felt a little woozy and his head hurt like hell.

"Sit down," Diana said, urgently. "Joey, please sit down." She had one hand on his shoulder; she was tugging on the scarf that tied back her hair with the other.

He ignored her instructions, taking a step forward. She wadded the scarf in her hand and pressed it to the side of his forehead. It hurt. Quite a lot. He brushed her hand aside, taking the scarf with it. It fluttered to the ground at his feet. He leaned over to pick it up. The sudden movement was a bad idea. A *very* bad idea. He straightened again—an equally bad idea.

"Joey Finch. Sit. Down," Diana said, urgently. She placed both hands on his shoulders and gently pressed. Joey complied until he was sitting on the curb in front of the bush. During his next failed attempt to reach the scarf, Diana didn't stop him. She wasn't paying attention anymore. She was talking to someone, but her hand was still firmly on his shoulder.

Diana was lovely, Joey thought, mulling it over in his fuzzy mind. She really was. And—despite his wavy vision—he could see that Diana had already made a new friend. Diana seemed to make friends wherever she went, he decided approvingly. Oddly enough, Diana's new friend looked exactly like Diana. She was standing quite close to Diana, too. And her movements mirrored Diana's exactly. What a crazy coincidence!

Joey grinned, happily for a few seconds before switching his attention back to the scarf. Or was it scarves? He couldn't quite make up his mind. One scarf? He blinked his eyes. No, two scarves. He blinked his eyes again. One scarf, he told himself decisively. Diana's scarf. If he leaned a little farther to the left, he could pick up the scarf without bending over. Bending over was a bad idea. Joey had already discovered that. Bending over made the ground tilt sideways. He stretched out his hand, encouraging himself all the while.

Left. And left. And just a little farther left and…Got it!

His fingers closed over the soft material. Joey picked up the scarf, bringing it close to his face so he could study it. The scarf was pretty. Blues and greens in a swirling pattern. It was soft, too. Like Diana, he thought dreamily. Soft and delicate and pretty. Beautiful, actually. And strong. He couldn't forget strong, he admonished himself. Diana was tough *and* strong. And soft. And delicate. And pretty. Beautiful, actually. Had he already said that? Damn, his head hurt.

He turned the scarf over to see if it was pretty on the other side. Diana was pretty on the other side. She had quite a nice other side. He had looked, he admitted to himself. More than once. Diana…she was trying to press something against his head again. He pushed her hand away as he examined the other side of the scarf. It was blue and green and…red.

Red? Why was the scarf red? He didn't remember red. It must be a stain, he decided. Poor Diana. Now her pretty scarf was stained. He focused on that stain. What was it anyway?

Paint? He didn't think so.

Lipstick? No. Her lipstick was peach-colored to match her lovely peach-colored lips.

It looked like...*blood*!

Joey panicked. Diana was bleeding. He had to help her. He tried to stand, but Diana and her new friend pushed him back down onto the curb. He studied Diana carefully, from the top of her red head to her pretty feet. What a relief, he thought. She wasn't bleeding after all, although she was wavering back and forth. Or was that because the ground was moving? Joey wasn't sure. What a relief, he thought again. He studied Diana's new friend. She wasn't bleeding, either. Joey was confused. Someone was bleeding. He was sure of it although for the life of him he couldn't quite remember why. He shrugged his shoulders. Who was it? Who was bleeding?

"Joey. Hold still," Diana's voice said, as she pressed something against his forehead again.

Something wet rolled down the side of his face. A red droplet plopped onto the back of his hand. He stared at it, mystified. Blood. Where had that blood come from? If Diana wasn't bleeding and her new friend wasn't bleeding that could only mean that the blood belonged to...

And that was the moment Diana discovered a well-kept secret. Joey Careful-Is-My-Middle-Name Finch fainted at the sight of his own blood.

CHAPTER EIGHTEEN

"*G*irlfriend?" asked Dr. Ravenwood.

Joey cleared his throat. "Um…not exactly," he hedged. That question should have been a no-brainer. So, why did he hesitate? Diana wasn't his girlfriend. As a matter of fact, he reminded himself, she was thrilled that he *didn't* want a relationship. The knowledge of that fact still rankled. "She's, um…just a friend."

The doctor looked up from his clipboard, eyeing Joey skeptically.

Joey returned his gaze, bracing himself. He didn't know what to expect. He had learned, during their brief acquaintance, that—in addition to being young, good-looking, and entirely too sure of himself—Dr. Ravenwood was quite a character.

"Not your girlfriend, huh? She's very attractive," the doctor continued. "Would it bother you if I asked her for her number?"

"As a matter of fact, it would," Joey answered without thinking. "It would bother me very much." *Where did that come from?* he asked himself. His mouth was now working independently of his brain. That brick must have hit him harder than he thought.

Dr. Ravenwood's lips twitched in amusement as he wrote "girlfriend" on the line beside Diana's name. She was the "responsible party."

Before Joey could comment, the nurse walked into the room, followed by Joey's very attractive *non*-girlfriend. He felt a pang of remorse. Poor Diana. She had been through so much on what was surely the longest day in human memory. Or at least, in his memory. And now, here they were at a tiny medical center in some godforsaken spot in Virginia courtesy the adolescent tendencies of Joseph Ezekiel Finch. If Diana Merritt wasn't already convinced he was an idiot, he was sure his most recent incident had erased all doubt.

But, as she came toward him, Diana's gray eyes were filled with concern, not contempt. Joey felt a small ray of hope. Until she opened her mouth.

"Well, doctor," Diana said, a wry smile on her peach-colored lips. "Will he live?"

Dr. Ravenwood nodded his head gravely. "I'm afraid so."

"I see." Diana nodded, equally grave. She gave a long-suffering sigh.

"I'm sorry," Dr. Ravenwood added. "Looks like you're stuck with him."

They shared a warm smile of complete understanding.

It was a little too warm, in Joey's opinion. He cleared his throat. "Excuse me," he said, politely. "*He's* right here."

Diana crossed her arms and gave him a look meant to silence a recalcitrant child.

Uh-oh. Joey almost groaned. He was in for it.

"Any suggestions, doctor, for his care and feeding?" Diana's voice held the slightest hint of sarcasm.

The doctor laughed at that, giving Joey an almost overwhelming desire to punch him right in the mouth.

"I don't think he has a concussion. Nothing points to that. If he does, it's a very mild one. His vitals are excellent. He never lost consciousness—well, except when he got a look at all that blood." The doctor turned to Joey then. "I'm assuming that wasn't the first time you've passed out at the sight of your own blood?"

Joey shook his head, fairly bristling with irritation. No, it was definitely not the first time.

Dr. Ravenwood picked up a card from a small stack on the counter and handed it to Diana. "Here's my number. You can call me if anything changes or if you have any questions. Or if you need anything…anything at all." The doctor grinned, enjoying Joey's obvious annoyance. "I don't anticipate any more problems for you two tonight. Your patient can take Ibuprofen for the pain, and it might be a good idea to wake him up a couple of times during the night just to make sure."

Diana raised her eyebrows. "To make sure…?"

"That he wakes up," the doctor said, matter-of-factly.

"What if he doesn't wake up?" Diana asked, pertly, cocking her head at her patient.

The doctor shrugged his shoulders philosophically. "Then I guess I was wrong," he said.

Joey's desire to punch Dr. Hilarious was back again.

The doctor opened the door, pausing to add, "Oh, and no driving for twenty-four hours."

That was too much. "How are we supposed to get home if I can't drive?" Joey asked, indignantly.

Diana was looking at him again as if he was an idiot.

"What?" he asked, in confusion.

"How do you think *I* got here, Joey?" she asked. "When you were enjoying your little ride in the ambulance? Hmm?"

"I…well…" He really hadn't thought about it. And he had *not* enjoyed his ride in the ambulance.

"I drove your truck," Diana said, calmly.

"*You* drove my truck?" Joey asked in disbelief. "*You?*"

Diana was clearly irritated. "Yes, me. What's wrong with that, anyway? Girls can drive trucks. I've been driving trucks like yours since I was fourteen."

Dr. Ravenwood swallowed a snort of laughter.

Diana glanced at the doctor standing in the doorway, suddenly aware of her slip. "Um…sixteen. I meant sixteen…when I got my license. My *driver's* license. So, it was all very legal." Diana nodded her head a couple of times to emphasize her point. She was charmingly guilty.

The doctor grinned. Joey could tell he thought Diana was charming, too. *Back off, doc,* Joey thought. He decided he was finished watching the suave doctor's subtle flirtation with his non-girlfriend. He jumped off the table, trying to ignore the way his head pounded when his feet hit the floor. Diana was at his side in an instant, holding onto his arm. He held out his hand to the doctor—the one attached to the arm Diana wasn't holding.

"Thanks for everything, doctor," he said, as they shook hands. And if Joey's smile was a little smug, well…Diana was leaving with *him*, wasn't she?

"Take care, you two," Dr. Ravenwood said, pleased with the results of his matchmaking.

Joey silently studied Diana as they walked down the short hallway that led to the waiting room. She looked tired, he realized with a sharp pang of guilt. The peaches were missing from her usual complexion, leaving only the cream. In other words, she was pale. He could also see faint purple shadows under her eyes. Despite what she must be feeling, her grip on his arm was strong, her momentary concern all for him. His heart twisted a little in his chest. He certainly didn't deserve her compassion. Their current situation was one hundred percent his fault. But here she was, still determined to take care of him. There was no way she could keep going. Driving much farther was not an option.

"Diana, you're exhausted," he began, pleased that she was still holding his arm.

"We're both exhausted," she agreed, as they walked out of the medical center and into the emergency room parking lot. Night had set in while they had been in the emergency room, and the parking lot was practically deserted.

"We'll have to find a hotel or something. Surely there's one around here…" His voice trailed off as he looked around. From where they stood, he saw nothing but trees. No houses. No lights. No hotels. It appeared the medical center was in the middle of nowhere. "Where are we, anyway?" he asked. At this stage of his life, he was not excited by the prospect of sleeping in the bed of his truck.

Diana removed the keys from her bag and unlocked the doors. "We are in Acorn Knob, Virginia," she announced. "Approximately twenty miles from the road we were on when we stopped at McDonald's."

Joey was stunned. The alternate route they had taken—per Rafe's meticulous instructions—was isolated enough. But now, it seemed they were in the *middle* of the middle of nowhere. "Twenty miles?"

"Uh-huh. They put you in the ambulance and I followed them here," Diana said, shrugging her shoulders. She walked with him to the passenger side. "Do you need help?"

"No," Joey said, confidently. "I've got it." He then proceeded to trip on the running board. He ended up, basically, crawling into his seat. *Smooth, Finch. Really smooth.*

Diana managed to hide her smile as she shut the door and walked around to the driver's side. He was such a contradiction of terms. Cool under pressure and sophisticated one minute, endearingly boyish the next. In short, Joey Finch was human. She would have to remember that.

Joey watched as Diana climbed effortlessly into the driver's seat. She fastened her seatbelt and started the truck. She looked completely at home, as if she drove a Ford F-150 every single day. *Why am I not surprised?* Joey asked himself. It was a rhetorical question.

He pulled his phone out of his pocket. The screen was cracked. *Great. How the hell did that happen?* He realized Diana was regarding him with something like pity. Her expression made the dull ache in his head a little worse. "Did I say that out loud?" he asked.

"Sort of," Diana said, apologetically. "It was kind of a cross between a mumble and a groan." His small attempt at a smile tugged at her heart. "Don't worry about it. We're both too tired to make much sense. I don't know if I'm coming or going, either."

"That's why I pulled out my phone—to see if there are any hotels or motels around here, but now..." He grimaced, putting his damaged property back in his pocket. "Maybe you can look for something."

"There isn't any cell service anyway," Diana said, gently.

Joey made a weak attempt at humor. "You don't happen to have a Holiday Inn Express in that giant tote bag of yours, do you?"

Diana narrowed her eyes in reply.

"Didn't think so," he said, dispiritedly. "There's always the bed of my truck."

That brought a tiny smile to Diana's face. "We're not that desperate yet, Joey. An opportunity has presented itself if you're willing to take a chance." She backed the truck out of the parking spot and headed to the exit.

"What kind of chance?" he asked suspiciously. If it had anything to do with Dr. Ravenwood, it was out of the question. The good doctor would probably smother Joey in his sleep.

"While you were getting your stitches, I had an interesting conversation with a really nice lady in the waiting room. Her son was the one they took straight in ahead of you. The one with the broken arm."

Joey nodded. "Yeah. I felt bad for that kid. It's tough to get hurt in a scrimmage before football season even starts. It was a bad break, too. He's probably looking at surgery and rehab, but what does that have to do with us?"

"His family owns the Acorn Knob Inn; Mrs. Maren said they had a cancellation this afternoon. We can have the room if we want it."

"Sounds great," Joey said, wearily. "Where is the Acorn Knob Inn?"

"There." Diana pointed straight ahead.

The headlights revealed a gravel driveway, of sorts, surrounded by dense foliage. The trees on either side grew very close together. Joey surmised that walking through the woods without a hatchet would be a problem. Not only that, but the branches met overhead, blocking out the small amount of light provided by the cloudy night. He doubted the tiny road was wide enough for two cars to pass each other, let alone a car and an F-150. Not only that, there wasn't anywhere to pull over on the side of the road. Hell, there *wasn't* a "side of the road." What would they do if they met another car? Would Diana be able to back down the curvy road? Would Joey's sore head explode?

Diana took his silence for assent. She crossed the paved road and started up the gravel drive. The road curved steeply up through the thick canopy of trees, disappearing into the darkness.

"What are you doing?" Joey bellowed. The skin around his stitches pulled painfully tight.

"I'm taking us to the inn." She drove up the winding road without batting an eye. "We *have* to get some sleep."

"There is no way this is the road to a decent inn," Joey argued, crossing his arms, stubbornly. "There's not even a sign."

The headlights flashed on something nestled in a sharp curve of the road.

"See," Diana said, indignantly. "A sign."

The faded wooden sign hung drunkenly from a pair of disreputable posts, one of which was barely vertical. The equally faded letters spelled the words, *"Acorn Knob Inn."* It was a sign, all right, Joey thought. A sign that they needed to turn around.

Diana refused to acknowledge Joey's snort of disapproval as she continued up the gravel road. The farther they went, the denser the foliage around them became. The denser the foliage, the darker the night grew— an exact mirror of Joey's thoughts.

He couldn't keep quiet for one more minute. "Have you ever seen *Deliverance*?"

"I don't see the relevance of that comment," Diana replied with great dignity.

"Does that mean you've seen it or not?" Joey was like a dog with a bone.

Diana sighed. "No, I haven't seen *Deliverance*, but I remember when Roman saw it. He must have been about thirteen. It scared him to death. He had nightmares for weeks. He got into trouble with Mom for telling me about it."

"And...?" Joey waited for her to figure out that driving up a deserted road at one o'clock in the morning in search of an imaginary inn was probably a bad idea.

Diana was thinking about what he said. He could tell. He could almost hear the banjo music that must be rolling around in her head. So, he waited. And he waited. And he waited some more. His mind wandered. It might not be so bad sleeping in the truck, he decided. It wasn't cold and it wasn't raining. He imagined Diana, stretched out in his truck bed, her flaming hair spread on a blanket, her long legs...

"They were going down a river in *Deliverance*," Diana pointed out triumphantly. "We are *not* going down a river."

The carnal nature of Joey's thoughts had him wishing for a river...a very cold river. He forced himself to focus on the current crisis. Oh, yes... *Deliverance*. His carnal thoughts disappeared instantly. "Well, I, for one, have no desire to be eaten by a bunch of strangers with banjos." Joey nodded for emphasis. His head pounded like a drum.

He was so adamant that Diana wanted to giggle. "You have your movies confused, Joey. That's not what happened at all. In *Deliverance*..."

"Don't say it." Joey shivered involuntarily. "Just don't say it."

Diana didn't. She said something else instead. "You, Joey Finch, have a very vivid imagination," she observed.

"Said the woman who takes advice from a talking iguana," Joey quipped.

Diana pursed her lips. "Let's leave Iggy out of this."

"Iggy says, 'Be brave,' " Joey replied in a sing-song voice, throwing her earlier statement back at her. "Not *stupid*."

"If you remember correctly, Mr. Finch, your *refusal* to take Iggy's advice is what got us into this situation in the first place."

"No, it was not," Joey said with absolute conviction. "We are in this situation because someone keeps trying to kidnap you. And that would never have happened if you weren't so damn irresistible." He knew he had gone too far the minute it was out of his mouth. Diana's soft gasp confirmed it.

"Oh, Joey. Look!"

He needn't have worried. The reason for her gasp was right in front of them. And it had nothing whatsoever to do with Joey Finch.

Spectacular.

Joey could think of no other word to describe the Acorn Knob Inn. And that was the view of the back. He couldn't imagine how grand it would be when they saw it from the front. The gorgeous mountain inn was meticulously maintained and beautifully landscaped. And, best of all, there wasn't a banjo in sight.

A wide porch stretched across the back of the inn. Gas lanterns—genuine gas lanterns—were strung up by every window and door, and between the posts of the porch. Comfortable-looking rocking chairs and wicker sofas sat in groups of twos and threes. Cheerful red and gold floral cushions begged weary travelers to stop and rest awhile. Joey would have been thrilled with these accommodations alone, happy to lie down on a sofa and rest his aching head.

As soon as Diana stopped the truck, several teenagers trudged down the steps and surrounded them. The tallest boy helped her out of the truck and politely asked for the keys.

Valet parking? Joey couldn't believe his eyes as he slowly and carefully climbed out of his truck. He leaned against the passenger door; his throbbing head was starting to make him feel a little nauseous. *Maybe I'm dreaming,* he mused. Maybe the brick had knocked him unconscious. Maybe he was still lying on the ground at McDonald's. It made sense in an odd sort of way and explained a lot, especially the happy accident of finding themselves in this mountain paradise. The only problem with his brilliant theory was his headache—because dreams didn't hurt. At least, *his* dreams didn't hurt. And at that moment, it was all he could do to ignore the pain in his head enough to put one foot in front of the other.

Diana noticed that Joey was fading fast. She was in complete sympathy, certain she would have fallen out an hour ago if not for the medical center's unusually strong coffee. Thank goodness she had three cups. Taking care of Joey was the least she could do after all he had done for her. She owed him. So…*she* dealt with their bags. *She* made charming small talk with the owners of the beautiful inn. *She* paid for the night. And *she* navigated the way to their assigned room on the third floor, all while keeping one eye on her rapidly deteriorating patient.

Diana unlocked the door of their room, pausing in the doorway to admire the décor. Windows covered most of the north wall. Light-filtering shades were currently drawn from floor to ceiling. The sheer curtains were pale gray with a delicate floral pattern in a lighter shade. Diana imagined the view would be breathtaking in the morning.

An enormous king-sized bed took up most of the south wall. Its huge, white fabric headboard stood higher than Diana's head. A dark gray quilt with billowing ruffles covered the bed, and a plethora of white and gray pillows added just the right touch of chic. The wood floors shone in the warm light of two white lamps sitting on identical nightstands on either side of the bed; each was adorned with delicate porcelain flowers. An Oriental rug in lovely shades of gray and cream covered about two thirds of the floor.

A fireplace, with an intricately carved, wooden mantel, held pride of place on the east wall. Though obsolete in the heat of summer, the fireplace was surely a welcome sight on a snowy, winter's night. Two overstuffed, black leather recliners created a small sitting area in the corner of the room, close enough to enjoy the fire's warmth. A white, wooden floor lamp with a pale gray shade lit that corner of the room. An enormous black armoire covered part of the west wall. Diana could see the edge of a claw-foot tub through the open door of the bathroom.

The room's cozy, understated elegance was a balm to Diana's exhausted spirit. She said a little prayer of thanks as she swiped at the tears that unexpectedly filled her eyes.

One glance in Joey's direction, however—he was plastered to the door frame—had her setting her emotions aside. The poor man looked pitiful. His stitches stood out starkly against his chalky white complexion. They stretched upward from the corner of his forehead, disappearing into his hairline. His hair was standing up in several places and he had dark shadows under his eyes. The devastating effect created by the sexy shadow of stubble on his jaw was spoiled by the tight lines of pain around his mouth. Diana automatically switched into efficient-nanny mode.

"Joey," she said as she gently propelled him toward the bed. "You need to lie down. And it's past time for some Ibuprofen."

He sank down on the bed and fell back onto the pillows. "That would be great." He tried to grin, failing miserably.

She handed him a bottle of water from the bedside table and dug the Ibuprofen out of her bag. Joey swallowed the pills, draining half of the water before handing it back to Diana. "Thanks," he said, gratefully.

She leaned over and brushed a bit of hair off the uninjured side of his forehead. "Tomorrow will be better," she said, softly.

"I know," he mumbled.

The unspoken words hung in the air. How could it possibly be worse?

CHAPTER NINETEEN

*W*hen Joey opened his eyes half an hour later, he was amazed by how much better he felt after lying down, even for a few minutes. He attributed his improved condition to the ridiculously comfortable bed, although the Ibuprofen Diana gave him probably deserved a little of the credit. His head no longer throbbed like the percussion section of a very large marching band. No, he decided, now it was more like the gentle pounding of a single small bass drum. A welcome improvement.

His favorable first impression of the Acorn Knob Inn had ratcheted up a notch thanks to the inn's brochure. Diana picked up the one lying on Joey's bedside table before his nap. After flipping through the brochure, she triumphantly informed him that their access road was *not* the only way to the inn. The real entrance was, apparently, quite picturesque, completely devoid of banjo-playing, man-eating strangers. Traveling the rarely used access road, she was quick to add, had saved them forty-five minutes. Her obvious relief at making the right decision was adorable. Joey would have enjoyed teasing her further if his head wasn't threatening to split open at the time.

He glanced around, taking a quick inventory of the room. Nice, he thought…just like Diana was nice. His inability to function had placed quite a burden on her slim shoulders, but she had come through in spectacular fashion. After living through the longest day in human memory, finding himself in this gem of an inn—with his unexpected roommate—was almost worth getting bashed in the head with a brick. And speaking of Diana...

His eyes focused on the bathroom door. *Diana is in that bathroom,* he informed himself as if he didn't already know the whereabouts of the lovely Miss Merritt. *In the shower,* he added unnecessarily. *The S-H-O-W-E-R.* He tried his best not to wrap his mind around the very pertinent fact that she probably wasn't wearing any clothes. *Of course, she isn't wearing any clothes, you idiot. Nobody wears clothes in the shower.* Joey sighed. He was pathetic. He really was. He tried to ignore the wet, soapy sounds coming from the bathroom by counting to a hundred. In Spanish.

It didn't work.

Joey sighed again. Maybe a shower would be a good idea. *No, not with Diana, you moron.* His sharp reprimand quashed that idea before it could *completely* take over his brain. His head throbbed in tandem with other, less intellectual parts of his body. *Well, hell.* His inner voice was getting completely out of hand. He made himself start over. Maybe a shower *of his own* would be a good idea. And, maybe, if the water was cold enough, it would erase the pleasing images of a wet, soapy Diana from his fevered imagination.

The sound of a hair dryer ended his erotic daydream as effectively as getting hit in the head with a brick had ended their plans for dinner. *That damn brick,* he thought. His injury had temporarily derailed their road trip *and* placed him in close proximity to Diana for the night. Too close. Now he was lusting after the captivating redhead...the same woman who, incidentally, had almost been kidnapped by a psycho a few hours earlier.

Classy, Finch. Real classy.

Maybe he *should* get out of bed. Of course, his head might explode if he moved. But at least that would give him something else to think about. Wait a minute. Would he still be able to think if his head exploded? After careful consideration, he decided to risk it.

He sat up slowly, pleased he didn't feel as dizzy as he had earlier. He was still a little wobbly, though. Maybe a shower wasn't such a good idea, he decided. Passing out in the shower wasn't very dignified. But if a clean and sweet-smelling Diana was going to be stuck in a room with this currently not-so-sweet-smelling, rumpled, sorry-excuse-for-his-usually-well-kept-self version of Joey Finch, the least he could do was to change his clothes.

He eased himself out of the bed and stood up. So far, so good. He focused on his bag in the corner beside the armoire while keeping his head very still. The floor remained solid and unmoving beneath his feet. Excellent. Since standing was going so well, his confidence grew. He pulled his T-shirt over his head and trudged across the room to open his bag.

He studied his blood-stained T-shirt before tossing it onto the floor beside his bag. Funny, how he could deal with the sight of his own dried blood on that T-shirt. He didn't even flinch. But one drop of the fresh stuff and—*pow!*—his lights went out. He mulled that annoying fact over while he successfully changed his clothes. As he padded back across the floor, he didn't allow himself even a glance at the bathroom door. He would *not* allow his overactive libido to imagine what Diana must look like behind that closed door. Wearing nothing but a towel. Drying her long, silky, luxurious red hair. Creamy skin. Luscious peach-colored lips....

Joey sighed. He seemed to be sighing a lot lately. He decided he was not very proud of himself. He carefully made his way back to the bed. When he was, once again, resting on the soft, white linen pillowcase, he took inventory. He was rather pleased that he had managed to replace his dirty, blood-stained clothes with a pair of Nike shorts and a clean T-shirt. It was an improvement. Not a significant improvement, but an improvement all the same.

By the time Diana emerged from the bathroom, he was drowsing under the covers. In spite of his relaxed state, all five of his senses roared to life the minute she opened the door. The rest of him pretended to be asleep. Through half-closed eyes, he watched her move around to the other side of the bed—her side—to turn off the lovely porcelain lamp on the bedside table.

She was clad in a long T-shirt with a big bouquet of bright pink flowers in the center. He assumed she was wearing shorts even though he couldn't see them. It was a logical assumption. Parading around the room

214

in a T-shirt without shorts wouldn't be very Diana-like, he decided. She had too much class for that. He didn't have to assume anything about her hair, though. It was breathtaking, hanging down her back in a riot of waves and curls. He could look at that hair all day. Or all night. Yes, he thought, his senses were definitely in overdrive.

He took a deep breath when she walked around to switch off the lamp on his bedside table. Her delicate scent reminded him of crashing waves and coconuts. When she bent to pick up the pillows strewn haphazardly on the floor, he got his answer about the shorts. Yes, she was wearing them, he noted with satisfaction. And they were hot pink.

Those shorts hugged her shapely derriere and accentuated her spectacular legs. Diana had long legs. Long, long legs. She really did. He realized he should probably apologize for making the mess with the pillows. And he would have, too, if he wasn't so busy reaping the rewards. He listened raptly to the melody she hummed as she worked. It was vaguely familiar. Something classical? From an opera? Whatever it was, the melody was very soothing....

Although sight, smell, and hearing were living it up, Joey's remaining senses—touch and taste—were destined for disappointment. Touching the creamy skin revealed by Diana's T-shirt and tasting the peach-colored lips he had been fantasizing about all day were obviously not an option. But try as he might, Joey couldn't seem to think of anything else. He attributed the lack of his usual control to that damn brick. It had scrambled his brain. That brick was significant somehow. He was sure of it, but at that moment he had no idea why. Figuring it out would have to wait, he thought, as a wave of exhaustion engulfed his lust-filled mind. He closed his eyes.

He had almost drifted off when he heard a loud *thunk* followed by a squeak of what had to be an expression of pain. Joey's eyes popped open. The only light that remained in the room was the tiny glow from the bathroom nightlight.

"Drat, drat, drat..." Diana's pet phrase echoed through the darkened room.

"Diana?" he asked, trying to locate the source of her distress. "Are you all right?"

"*I'm* all right," she said, disgustedly. "Just don't ask my big toe."

Joey smiled in the darkness. "What are you doing over there anyway? Why haven't you come to bed yet?" When she didn't reply, Joey pushed himself up onto his elbows. He had a sneaking suspicion that he knew exactly what she was trying to do. And he didn't like it. "Di-a-na," he said. "You're not planning on sleeping in a chair, are you?"

Diana almost groaned aloud, and not because of her sore toe. Talk about awkward. What was she supposed to do now? She *had* planned on spending the night in one of the black leather chairs. It was the easiest option. The only option, really...until Joey had to go and open his mouth. She had *never* expected to hear the words *"why haven't you come to bed yet?"* in the voice of Joey Finch. Well, she might have *hoped* to hear them, if she was honest, but she hadn't really expected them. And certainly not now. Still, she couldn't stop the delicious shiver that ran down her spine. *Seriously pathetic, Diana,* she reprimanded herself the next moment. *The poor man has a head injury.*

Diana struggled to explain. "Well," she began. "I thought that since there was only one bed..." *that I would show you how lame and unsophisticated I really am,* she finished in her head.

Joey was intrigued by her hesitation. It was refreshing. And endearing. And, yes, pretty damn sexy. Until he thought about it. *Hmm.* Finding out that the woman he had been attracted to for nine years didn't want to use their current position as an excuse to fall into his bed was...what? Surprising? Humbling? Or just plain exasperating? On one hand his already high degree of respect for her grew even more. On the other hand, he wondered why he wasn't as irresistible to her as she was to him. On the third hand—oops! That was the brick talking for him again.

He started over. His most worrisome observation so far led him to a disturbing question: Was Diana afraid of him? He hoped not, but he couldn't be sure. What the hell kind of ideas had Roman, Connor, and Devin planted in her head about him anyway? He certainly couldn't ask Diana, he decided. And now that he thought about it, did he really want to know? Probably not. He did know one thing, however: whatever misconceptions she was under were about to be ripped out by the roots. He was determined to prove to Diana that she could trust him.

"Diana," he said in his most soothing voice. "I appreciate the fact that there is only one bed, but you have to drive in a few hours; you need some sleep. You'll sleep better in a bed than in a chair."

"I know, but..." She was thankful the dark hid her blush. She knew she was blushing because her face was on fire. Her cheeks were probably glowing like a Christmas tree.

Joey was on a mission now. "This bed is huge. It might be the biggest bed I've ever seen. The other side of this bed is in another zip code. Maybe even another state."

Diana giggled. She couldn't help it. Joey Finch was trying to talk her into joining him in bed. The whole scenario was ridiculous. And, for some reason, completely hilarious.

Joey smiled. He was winning the battle. He was pondering his next words when a brilliant idea burst into his head. "Remember, Diana, I'm not a rake like the earl. I'm a rascal. The worst thing a rascal might do is snore. Or tickle you. Or something like that."

Oops. Joey wanted to recant his unintentionally suggestive words the minute they were out of his mouth. *Way to go, Joe,* he taunted himself. *Two steps backwards.* He tried to ignore the image of tickling Diana in the giant bed. No use. It was now firmly entrenched along with his other delightful imaginings. *Think, Finch, think,* he encouraged himself. *With your brain, this time.* He cleared his throat. "Diana, I was just joking about the tickling. You know I would never..." His voice trailed away. *Oh, yes, I would,* Joey admitted in his head, *if you wanted me to.* He didn't know what he was trying to say. He was grasping at straws until he latched onto a glimmer of a possible way out. "What would the earl do if he was in this situation, Diana? You know, being a reformed rake and all." This was even better than a glimmer. In Joey's fuzzy brain it was pure brilliance.

"Since the earl is a *reformed* rake," Diana said, trying to stop giggling, "I'm certain he would offer Genevieve the other side of the bed.

Platonically, of course." She waited breathlessly for his reply. This was, by far, their most bizarre conversation yet.

Good for the earl, Joey thought, feeling a strong empathy with the noble fellow.

"But…" Diana added, "…if the earl had to spend the night in the same room as Genevieve, well…he would let Genevieve decide if she wanted to go to bed with him or not." Diana stopped talking, shocked at the lusty phrasing of her own comments. She was drowning in a sea of embarrassment. *Where did those words come from?* she asked her panicked self. Why, oh, why, did she say "*go to bed with him*"? *Sharing the bed with him* would have sounded so much better. So very innocent. But, no, Diana Merritt couldn't *share the bed.* She had to *go to bed.* With Joey Finch, who— by the way—was going to think she was propositioning him. Or trying to seduce him. Or both.

Diana's use of the words *go to bed* was enthusiastically received by the parts of Joey's body that had nothing to do with intellect. As he wrestled his unruly libido into submission, he realized that he and the lovely lady standing in the dark seemed to have reached an impasse. He wracked his pitiful, exhausted excuse for a brain to think of something acceptable to say.

"Remember, Diana," Joey intoned, "Iggy says, 'Be brave.' " The childish phrase was the only thing he could come up with. "Not *stupid*," he added as an afterthought. And finally—maybe for the first time since Diana ran into him at Chutley's—Joey Finch had said exactly the right thing.

She laughed then. Really laughed. And she couldn't seem to stop. Her uncontrollable giggles were contagious, and soon, he was laughing, too. The tension disappeared like a wisp of smoke.

"All right," she gasped. "You win." She successfully navigated her way to the bed. No easy task in the darkened room. After a minute or so of wriggling about, she settled herself under the covers. On her side. Facing away from him. Then, she gave a contented little sigh.

That sigh was the most enticing sound Joey had ever heard.

"Good night, Joey," she whispered. She could only pray that the thick bedding and plush mattress muffled the pounding of her heart and absorbed the trembling of her limbs.

"Good night, Diana." He closed his eyes for about two seconds. That was exactly how long it took for her tantalizing scent to reach his nostrils. He opened his eyes again to stare at the ceiling. So much for sleep, he thought. The ridiculous irony of the situation was quite amusing.

Or it would be amusing later.

Maybe.

For now, it looked like the longest day in human memory was about to turn into the longest night. Back to Spanish, he decided—and this time, he was going to try counting backwards.

CHAPTER TWENTY

*D*iana had to keep moving. She knew who was chasing her and she knew what he wanted. The pathway was narrow and dark. Its unexpected twists and turns coupled with the threat of falling bricks made it impossible to move quickly. Even though she could barely keep her balance on the slippery gravel, she couldn't afford to slow down.

Everyone was counting on her.

The dense foliage tried to smother her. Individual tree limbs dipped and swayed, grabbing at her long, Dr. Pepper-colored skirt. Branches reached out, trying to pluck her giant bag from her hands. She could hear the roar of the river. The swift current was getting louder. So was the banjo music.

Suddenly she saw lights flashing through the trees. She knew those lights.

Chutley's.

If she could just get to Chutley's everything would be all right. But could she make it? Every muscle in her body was screaming. The banjo music was getting closer. She recognized the tune. It was the only song Roman had managed to learn in weeks and weeks of ill-fated banjo lessons. Cripple Creek. It was etched in her brain. He must have played it a thousand times. Badly.

She felt a hot, burning pain on her wrist. Looking down, she discovered that her brand-new Apple Watch was glowing. With a flash of insight, she *realized she was being tracked by the man-eating strangers. She should never have bought the watch when she stopped at that convenience store for a caramel iced latte. She grasped the watch band with one hand and ripped it off her wrist, throwing it into the woods as far as she could. She watched the glow fly away then fade into the darkness.*

She could hear the man-eating strangers crashing through the bushes in search of the watch. The sound of their footfalls grew fainter and fainter until they disappeared entirely. She had to get away before they figured out what she had done. She dodged another brick as she rounded the next sharp turn on the path. Finally, she stepped out of the forest. Her destination was only a few feet away. Chutley's! She had done it. She was free.

The neon sign blinked merrily. Her spirits lifted. Diana could see Roman, Connor, and Lance through the window. She saw Joey Finch, talking to Chrissy. They were all there, waiting for her. She was safe.

She was almost to the door when someone stepped in front of her.

"You don't live here, lady," the man said, smugly.

She looked up into the smirking face of the doorman from Roman's apartment building. Every muscle in her body froze under his mocking gaze. She couldn't move anything but her eyes. They blinked frantically.

The doorman grabbed the shoulder straps of her giant tote bag and slid it down her nerveless arm. "I'm taking all of your chocolate twirls," he announced. "Your husband said I could have them."

Suddenly, a shadowy figure stepped out of the darkness. "Hello, Diana," he growled in a voice she had hoped never to hear again. A voice that belonged to...

...Bill Watkins, Psychotic Cowboy Kidnapper!

He was wearing a brand-new cowboy hat and carrying a banjo.

Bill had found her. Again.

She was terrified. She tried to struggle, but to no avail. She couldn't move. She might as well be made of wood. She tried to scream, but no sound emerged from her paralyzed vocal cords. Her psycho kidnapper handed his banjo to the doorman. He picked her up and slung her stiff form over his shoulder. She dangled there. Unable to fight. Unable to scream. He carried her towards the forest, drawing quickly away from Chutley's.

"You're mine, now," he said. "You'll never escape. Never, never, never...!"

Diana sat straight up in bed, gasping for breath. Her heart was pounding; her body was shaking uncontrollably. She was completely disoriented.

"Diana?" Joey raised himself up on one elbow, peering into the darkness. He could barely make out her silhouette. His heart contracted when he heard a small sob. She must have had one heck of a crazy nightmare.

Joey was protective by nature; he always had been. But this, well... this was different. The fierce feeling that rose in his chest—when the person in need of protection was Diana—eclipsed anything he had ever felt before. He was compelled to comfort. To soothe. To...move.

He closed the space between them carefully. He wasn't sure if she was completely awake or not; he didn't want to make her nightmare any worse.

"Diana," he said, softly.

She didn't move her head. She didn't in any way acknowledge his presence.

"Diana, honey, it's all right. You're safe." Very slowly, he reached out his hand, placing it gently on her arm. Her skin was cold to the touch. Joey could feel her trembling. Worse than that, he could see the tears streaming unheeded down her cheeks.

She let out a frightened shriek when he touched her, jerking her arm out of his reach. She turned onto her side, facing away from him, wrapping her arms around herself protectively.

"Diana," Joey said, using his most reasonable tone. "It's Joey. Joey Finch."

She was quiet for so long that Joey thought she had fallen back to sleep. He was getting ready to do the same when she rolled over toward him. She blinked several times as she tried to make sense of her surroundings. Her eyes were glued to the quilt lying darkly between them.

Joey started talking again in the same calm tone. "It's all right, Diana. We're at the Acorn Knob Inn. We're sharing this bed because it has two zip codes. It's dark because it's the middle of the night. I danced into a scaffold and..."

"The brick," Diana said, tracing the pattern of the quilt with one finger.

"That's right," he encouraged her. "There was a brick. It hit me in the head."

"*He* was there," she said without looking up. "*He* took me with him. I couldn't move or scream or fight back or anything. I couldn't stop him. You were inside Chutley's with Roman and Connor and Lance and Chrissy. I could see all of you through the window. And I couldn't even yell for help." She looked up then, her eyes filled with tears and...terror. "Oh, Joey, he took me."

He reached for her then. No force on earth could have prevented it. He pulled her into his lap and let her cry until the shoulder of his Nike T-shirt was wet with her tears. At first, her muscles were so rigid he feared she would shatter, but after a few minutes she began to relax. He cradled her in his arms, rubbing her back with small, soothing motions until her sobs began to ebb.

"Hush, honey. You're safe now, and safe is how you're going to stay," he promised in a gentle whisper. "Just think, Diana. If Verizon doesn't know where we are, Cowboy Bill doesn't stand a chance."

His mouth continued to speak light, comforting, somewhat silly words. His brain, however, was fairly screaming a litany of actions he would take if, and when, he finally came face to face with the kidnapping cowboy. It wasn't going to be gentle. And it wasn't going to be pretty.

Diana gave a little hiccup and relaxed against Joey's shoulder, finally out of tears.

"This is the first time you've cried since he tried to take you in Newport, isn't it?" Joey asked into the silence.

She took a wobbly breath and pulled herself upright, marveling at his perception. "This is the first time I've cried since Mallory's funeral," she admitted. After a slight hesitation, she continued, "I've never told anybody that, except the therapist they made me talk to. She would be thrilled right now." She grabbed a tissue from the box on the bedside table.

Joey was profoundly touched by the easy way she confided in him. He was incredibly glad to be sitting in the middle of a giant king-sized bed at four-thirty in the morning in Acorn Knob, Virginia, listening to Diana Merritt. And if being with her at this moment meant that he had a wet T-shirt and a permanent scar on his forehead, well…so be it. It was a price he would gladly pay.

"I have to admit that I really do feel better," she sighed, mopping at her eyes with the tissue. "Maybe that therapist was right. Nothing like a good cry, I guess." She shrugged her shoulders and reached for another tissue. After multiple tissues, she gave up. "I must look like something out of a nightmare right now," she said with a self-deprecating, little smile. "I think I need a washcloth." She climbed out of bed and headed to the bathroom.

While she was gone, Joey got out of bed to change his tear-stained T-shirt. He replaced it with an old Carolina Law School shirt he had thrown into his bag at the last minute. Who knew he would need so many T-shirts for their unexpected road trip? He also straightened the sheets, exchanging Diana's slightly damp pillow for a dry one. The discovery that she was crying *during* the nightmare filled him with overwhelming anger. That dirty bastard kidnapper had no right to show up in Diana's dreams, he fumed. She didn't deserve to be haunted like that. Diana should dream about sunshine and flowers and rose gold Mac books and rakish—but reformed— earls. And chocolate twirls.

Joey was willing to admit he was slightly mollified by the knowledge that he had been present in the dream. Although it sounded as if he— like the Merritt men and Shirley—had been completely useless. What the hell had he been doing in that dream, anyway, while Diana was struggling with her kidnapper? Drinking a beer? Watching the game? Flirting with Shirley? Playing it cool? *Probably all of the above,* he thought in disgust.

But, no more. If a rake like the earl could reform his ways, so could a rascal like Joey Finch.

When Diana returned, Joey was comfortably propped up in the middle of the bed, leaning back on pillows stacked against the headboard. He patted the space beside him. "Will you tell me more about your nightmare?" He paused to give her a minute to consider his request. "I mean, if you want to," he added, carefully. He didn't know how she would react to his question. Or how much tissue was left in that box.

She plopped down on the bed beside him, completely unaware of her own appeal. She looked like something out of a man's most secret dream. Sleep-tousled red curls falling around her shoulders. Luscious peach-colored lips. The long T-shirt was, somehow, tantalizing as it embraced her long, lithe frame. And, he marveled, she had absolutely no idea how she affected him. She seemed equally unconscious that the glimpse of her in the doorway the split second before she turned off the bathroom light had done quite a number on his pulse. Joey was employing every bit of restraint he possessed to keep his reactions to his rascally self.

Diana, he noted ruefully, seemed to be settling in for a pajama party. Her trust in him was doing funny things to his heart. It would be a lot easier to objectively analyze his strange feelings when he wasn't sharing pillows with her in the dark. For now, it was enough to know that she trusted him. And, he vowed, he would never do anything to jeopardize that trust, no matter how many cold showers he had to take.

Diana leaned back against the pillows. Anybody else would have been snoring by now, but not Joey Finch. He was right beside her, wide awake, waiting for her to tell him about her ridiculous dream. Joey was sweet, she realized. She couldn't help but smile at this unexpected revelation. She would never say it aloud because she knew it would embarrass him, but it was true. And—best of all—it was her little secret.

"In retrospect, my nightmare seems a little silly," she admitted. "Like a whole lot of random details wrapped up into one bizarre scenario. Until the end. The end was scary."

Joey put his arm around her—all he would allow himself to do—and squeezed her shoulders. "Well, I'm here now so the end will *not* be scary."

His confident assurance brought an amused grin to Diana's face. "You *were* in the dream, Joey..."—she couldn't resist contradicting him—"...and it was still very scary." Diana laughed at his do-not-question-my-masculinity face. "All right, Joey Finch. You asked for it." She cleared her throat. "I was walking on a gravel path exactly like the one we took to get here..."

For the next few minutes, she spilled every detail to her rapt audience of one. By the time she finished, Diana was giggling hysterically. Dreams weren't nearly as scary when she was cuddled up to Joey Finch.

"Dodging bricks *and* trying to evade man-eating strangers who are tracking you with your Apple Watch?" he asked, gasping for air. "Now who has a vivid imagination?"

"Don't forget the chocolate twirls. And the banjos," Diana reminded him. "They're quite pivotal to the plot." She fanned her flushed face with her hand.

Joey, wiping tears of hilarity from his eyes, rejoiced in her laughter. Part of his brain, however, was working overtime. He was making plans in his head. Joey was determined to give the doorman of Roman's apartment building a little lesson in manners the next time he was in Alexandria. As for Bill...Joey would love to meet the psychotic, kidnapping cowboy on a dark gravel path. Yes, he would love that.

Diana slid down on the pillows, blowing out a tired little breath. Joey followed suit, pleased that she remained in the middle of the bed, close beside him. She truly trusted him, it seemed, despite the warnings she had received from her well-meaning relations. That warmed his heart. Having her soft form beside him was warming other parts of him, too. Again.

He racked his brain to think of a distraction. "So, what's the earl's name, anyway? I feel kind of bad that he doesn't have a name unless his name really is Earl." Joey pretended to ponder this weighty issue. "Is that it, Diana? Is his name Earl? The Earl of Earl?"

Diana huffed out a little breath of disbelief. "The Earl of Earl? That's ridiculous."

"Well, then, what's his name?"

"His name..." she said, solemnly, "...is Horatio."

Joey's face looked like he had tasted something awful. "Horatio?"

"What's wrong with Horatio?" Diana asked, indignantly. "I think Horatio is a perfectly lovely name."

"It sounds too old," Joey said. "Like he's somebody's grandfather or some old ship's captain. Not a young and handsome rake."

"A *reformed* rake," Diana added.

"Young, handsome, and *reformed* rake," Joey echoed.

"Well, what do you suggest?" She was curious now. His interest in her characters was flattering. " Edward?"

"Edward?" Joey said. "Is that the best you can do?"

She glared at him. "Well, Mr. Romance Novel Expert, what fabulous name would *you* give to our young, handsome, *reformed* rake?"

"Ezekiel." He liked the way she said *our rake*, but he didn't say so. Instead, he nodded his head definitively as if Ezekiel was the name she'd been waiting for all her life.

"Ezekiel?" She studied the man on the pillow beside her, mischief dancing in her eyes. "I don't know..." she hedged.

"What's wrong with Ezekiel?" Joey asked.

"*You* have an ulterior motive," she accused, pointing her finger at his very attractive chest.

His eyes widened innocently. "Ulterior motive? Me? Why Diana, whatever are you talking about?"

"Ezekiel is *your* middle name," she accused, still pointing at his chest.

"Is it?" he asked, pleased that she remembered his middle name. "Why, yes, it is. Ezekiel is a classic name. An outstanding name. A name that will stand the test of time." He put one hand over his heart in silent tribute.

Diana raised her eyebrows. "You mean, a name that will live in infamy." She smirked.

Undaunted, Joey continued: "Just think about it, Diana. Ezekiel and Genevieve. It's perfect. Like Romeo and Juliet."

Diana was trying not to laugh. "Romeo and Juliet died, genius."

Joey shrugged his shoulders. "Oh, yeah," he said, apologetically, but not very convincingly.

Diana considered his suggestion, her eyes sparkling. "All right, then, Mr. Finch. Ezekiel it is. But…" she added, "…no tragedy for Ezekiel and Genevieve. They *will* have a happily ever after."

Joey narrowed his eyes. Convincing her was entirely too easy. That and the sly little smile flitting around her mouth. Very suspicious. He could see that smile, even in the dark. What, he wondered, was she up to?

"The earl's first name is Ezekiel," she announced. "And his middle name is Horatio."

"I like it so far," Joey said, politely. He, however, remained unconvinced that her motives were pure.

Smiling innocently, Diana continued: "And the earl's last name is Edwards." She paused a few seconds before declaring, triumphantly, "The Earl of Ravenwood."

"*Ravenwood?*" Joey almost choked. "The Earl of *Ravenwood*?" He was not at all pleased that the good-looking—and oh-so-cocky—emergency room doctor had suddenly joined them in bed.

Diana, however, was completely undeterred by his reaction. "Say it all at once," she instructed, nanny-style.

Joey, sighing heavily, complied. "Ezekiel Horatio Edwards, the Earl of Ravenwood." He considered the name for a minute. It was, he decided, impressive. Diana was right. She had chosen the perfect name. He chuckled. "I like it."

"Me, too," she said, happily. "Thanks, Joey. For everything." She regarded him a moment in the dark before snuggling down into the covers.

"Awww...anything for the sake of literature, Diana." He enjoyed her soft giggle as much as the fact that she hadn't moved all the way back to her side of the giant bed.

"Goodnight, Joey."

"Good night, Diana." Joey closed his eyes, too. If he lived to be a hundred, he would never have another day like this one. The trial. The kidnapper. The brick...

The. Brick.

Joey's eyes flew open as the memory of the prophetic conversation jumped to the forefront of his mind: *"If I get hit in the head with a brick, then, and only then, will I know that the brick is a sign from God that it's time for me to get married."*

How was he supposed to know that his own cavalier statement would come back to haunt him? *Well, hell.* He gazed up at the ceiling. He had the suspicious feeling that God was laughing at him. Joey sighed deeply. He had always figured God had a sense of humor, and he was glad of it...even if he was, currently, the butt of the joke. Really, he thought, it was no more than he deserved.

He focused his attention on the attractive woman in his bed, listening to her deep, even breathing. He was glad to find Diana had finally fallen asleep. He hoped her sleep would be free of man-eating strangers, banjos, and kidnappers. But if it wasn't, he would be close beside her. And, he realized soberly, he was ready to fight anyone—real or imagined—to protect this woman. He heard her sigh just then, a sweet, alluring sound. Was she dreaming about him?

Joey's heartbeat kicked up a notch. Now, where did *that* thought come from? he asked himself. What was happening to him? Was he imagining things? Or was it possible that Diana was more important to him than he had ever imagined? The brick seemed to think so. He waited for the strong feeling of aversion that usually accompanied the mere mention of relationships, love, and marriage...but it didn't come. Strange, he thought, sleepily, but then, why should he be surprised? The whole day had been nothing but strange from beginning to end.

He would go to sleep, he decided, and when he woke up, everything would feel normal again. Diana was *glad* he didn't want a relationship, he reminded himself. And so was he. He really was. Sort of. Because something else had just occurred to him, something Darcie had said at the end of the cursed conversation about the brick:

"You just wait, Joey Finch, you're going to fall in love with some poor, unsuspecting woman eventually. It's only a matter of time. And when that momentous day comes, I hope with all my heart that the lady of your dreams doesn't give you the time of day."

Joey winced, because he remembered his smug response: *"No chance of that, little sister."*

Now, lying here in the dark beside the sweetly fragrant and—at present—unattainable redhead, he wasn't so sure.

CHAPTER TWENTY-ONE

"*W*ake up, Sleepyhead!" Diana said cheerfully.

Joey groaned, throwing one arm across his eyes. Diana must have opened the blinds. It was the only explanation for the bright light threatening to burst through his eyelids. "Did you see it?" he mumbled into the pillow.

Diana sat down on the side of the bed. At least, that's what it felt like. He still refused to look.

"See what?" she asked, barely pausing in her enthusiasm. "Oh, you mean the view? I see it right now, and it's gorgeous. Mountains that go on forever. Blue skies. No clouds. It's going to be a beautiful day!"

Joey was not impressed. "I was talking about the bus."

"What bus?" The confusion was evident in her voice.

"The bus that hit me while I was asleep," he replied, humorlessly. Joey was not a morning person. Not before breakfast, anyway.

Diana giggled with delight. "I'm guessing you're not a morning person," she said, conversationally.

"Whatever gave you that idea?" he grumbled, trying to ignore the delicious cinnamon aroma wafting from her body. Funny, he thought. He could have sworn she smelled like coconuts last night.

She stood up. At least that's what it felt like.

"Don't worry, Joey," she said, but his ears picked up at the teasing note in her voice. "You can go back to sleep. I won't bother you anymore. I guess I'll just have to eat this yummy, gooey, homemade cinnamon roll all by myself."

Diana didn't have to wait very long before her gamble paid off. Joey rolled onto his back and cracked open one eye. She was standing by the bed, grinning at him. In her hand was a plate, and on that plate was a yummy, gooey, homemade cinnamon roll, as advertised. Joey pushed himself into a sitting position. He eyed Diana with respect. "Well done, General Merritt. Your tactics look delicious." He reached for the cinnamon roll.

"Oh no. Not yet." Diana put the plate on the bedside table, just out of his reach. "How's your head?"

He placed one hand on either side of his head. "Still there," he said, wryly.

She raised her eyebrows. And waited.

Joey sighed, feeling a good deal of empathy for five-year-old Amalie. Nanny Di was tough. He moved his neck back and forth. "Actually, it feels pretty good. Just a slight headache. I'm sure it's nothing a cinnamon roll won't cure," he added, hopefully.

Diana picked up the glass of water that was still on the bedside table and handed it to him along with the bottle of Ibuprofen. As Joey opened the bottle and swallowed the pills, Diana added, "This cinnamon roll is only a tease. The breakfast buffet ends in an hour—and, trust me, it is spectacular. If you're not ready in ten minutes, Private Finch, this general is leaving without you."

Joey sat on the side of the bed, both feet on the floor. "What happened to the rule about no man left behind?"

She crossed her arms over her chest. "Doesn't apply to breakfast."

Joey grimaced and reached for the cinnamon roll. He pulled off the gooey edge and put it into his mouth, closing his eyes in ecstasy.

"You now have nine minutes and forty-seven seconds," Diana announced. She laughed as Joey headed for the bathroom, taking the plate with him.

Diana was right. The breakfast buffet was amazing. He was feeling better already. Joey slathered butter on his fluffy buttermilk biscuit. Diana was amazing, too, he decided. He watched her chattering with the small group at the coffee station. She was probably on a first-name basis with all of them by now. Diana's genuine warmth made anyone—friend or stranger—instantly at ease. It was a quality Joey admired immensely.

He took a bite of bacon as he pondered the woman who had shared his bed. How she managed to look so fresh and lovely after only a few hours of sleep was a mystery. Her eyes were sparkling as brightly as her dangling, silver earrings. Her skin fairly glowed with health. Her glorious hair was pulled up into a high ponytail. A few tendrils escaped to caress the soft skin of the shoulder that peeked out of the wide neck of her white peasant top. Her jean shorts showcased her legs—her long, lovely legs. If Joey leaned forward, he could just glimpse her peach-colored toenails in the open toes of her rhinestone-encrusted sandals. He had never before realized that a woman's feet could be sexy, but Diana's were. He wasn't sure why they were, but they were. She had soft skin, too, and she smelled good. And she was, well…cuddly.

He had arrived at that conclusion several hours ago after waking up to find her snuggled against his side, sound asleep. The Merritt Brothers' crowd would be astounded to learn that last night was the first time Joey the Player had spent an entire night in bed with a female since the Blizzard of 1996. But sharing a pallet with his sisters in front of the living room fireplace had not been eight-year-old Joey's idea of a good time. He still remembered how happy he was when the power came back on. Come to think of it, he had been pretty happy waking up with Diana, too.

As Joey picked up his juice glass, a firm hand patted him on the back before moving to rest on his shoulder. He looked up into the wise eyes of an older gentleman, probably in his early eighties. He was wearing a fishing shirt and a floppy hat.

"I don't blame you for staring, son," he said, grinning from ear to ear. "I felt the same way about my Esther when I was your age, and we've been together over sixty years." He winked at Joey's shocked expression. "Let me give you a word of advice from one lovesick fool to another: Don't let the grass grow under your feet."

Joey nodded, warily, raising his juice glass to his lips. His mouth was suddenly very dry. His fishing buddy's grin widened as he gave Joey's shoulder a firm squeeze before releasing it. "If you like her that much, you better put a ring on her finger," he said with another wink.

Joey choked on his juice.

The man walked away chuckling.

"What are you looking for?" Diana asked, sliding into the chair across from him. She glanced up at the ceiling, then regarded Joey questioningly.

"Falling bricks," Joey replied, popping the last bite of biscuit into his mouth.

Diana laughed, reaching across the table to pat his arm. "I don't think you have to worry about bricks here, Joey," she said cheerfully. "But the buffet closes in fifteen minutes and they're almost out of biscuits. That's what you *really* need to worry about."

Maybe she's right, he thought. Maybe concentrating on food would force the worrisome words of the older gentleman out of his mind.

He headed to the buffet, falling in line behind a mother with two elementary-age children. Joey couldn't help but feel a kindred spirit with the big brother. The mischievous boy was amusing himself by taking food off his sister's plate every time she turned her head. The perplexed expression on the little girl's face when she looked back at her plate was priceless. The third time it happened, the little girl looked up at Joey in frustration. He winked, putting a finger to his lips. He waited until the boy was distracted by the pancakes—plain or blueberry? He reached over the boy's shoulder to snatch a large piece of watermelon from the unsuspecting youngster's plate. He popped it in his mouth and waggled his eyebrows at the little girl. She burst into a peal of giggles.

Her giggles attracted the attention of her big brother, who looked at his plate in surprise. "Hey," he said indignantly. "Where's my watermelon?"

The child's mother calmly turned around. "All right, you two. What's going on?" she inquired patiently.

Joey pasted an innocent expression on his face and looked up at the ceiling. The little girl pointed her finger at him, giggling harder.

Five years of working for Mallory Merritt had honed Diana's ability to hide what she was truly thinking or feeling. Mallory's talent for pinpointing weaknesses and using them as a weapon made presenting a calm and serene mask a necessity of survival. That was the only reason Diana had been able to carry on a normal conversation with Joey Finch after waking up in his arms less than an hour ago. *In. His. Arms.* She didn't know how it had happened, but it had. Somehow. During the small hours of the morning. And the feeling was glorious—warm, safe, and wanted.

After soaking in as many sensations as possible, she slid out of bed without waking him. Her reasons for being so very careful were twofold. First, he looked exhausted in the morning light. *Exhausted,* she reminded herself, *but still incredibly attractive.* The shadow of his long lashes and the dark stubble on his pale cheeks had elevated "hot" to an entirely new level. Diana shivered just thinking about it.

The second reason, she had to admit, was a selfish one. She wasn't sure how he would react to waking up with her cuddled against him. She simply couldn't risk the chance that he might push her away. As things now stood, she had a lovely memory of a perfect moment. That fact, coupled with the knowledge—less than twenty-four hours old—that he was attracted to her, was turning her brain to mush.

People liked to talk about having butterflies in their stomachs. Ha. Butterflies were for amateurs. She had passed butterflies before the sun came up. Now, it seemed as if a whole family of frogs was hopping around in her stomach, careening off the walls in some kind of reptilian gymnastics competition. But no one would guess because of her relaxed, easy smile. She hated to be grateful to Mallory for anything, but hiding those feelings was a skill Diana could never have learned on her own.

As she watched Joey with the children, she couldn't help but find his antics charming. He would make a wonderful father. That thought popped into her mind unbidden. *Slow down, girl.* She gave herself a mental shake. Something about waking up in the arms of Joey Finch was wreaking havoc on her thought processes. They were as scrambled as the eggs on the buffet. Diana sighed. She knew a future with her heart's desire was a long shot. But, well…a girl could dream, couldn't she?

Reality—in the form of a server—interrupted her musings. The teenage girl smiled at the surprised look on Diana's face. "I didn't mean to startle you," she said. "Would you like some more coffee?"

Diana shook her head, ruefully. "No, thank you." The girl nodded and moved on to the next table. It was then that Diana realized that Joey, the lady in front of him, and two very excited children were staring at her. *Uh-oh.* She had seen that look before. She braced herself. The cat was out of the bag.

The little girl ran straight to Diana, followed closely by the boy. Joey and the children's mother came, too, but more sedately.

The little girl stopped a few feet from Diana. "Are you the *real* Nanny Di?" she asked, hopefully.

Her brother regarded Diana with the narrowed eyes of a ten-year-old skeptic.

Diana guessed that the little girl was about two years younger than her brother. She always tried to give her fans age-appropriate answers. "Now, both of you know that Nanny Di is a character in a book, right?" she asked, seriously, as she looked each child in the eye, in turn.

Both children nodded, equally grave.

Diana continued: "And you know that all of her adventures take place between the covers of a book?"

The children nodded again.

Diana smiled. "Well, *I'm* the person that puts Nanny Di and her adventures in those books," she confided. "I write them."

The little boy's skepticism disappeared instantly to be replaced by childish admiration.

The little girl's big eyes grew even wider. "You're a *famous* person," she whispered in awe.

Diana laughed. "Well, I don't know about that." Taking the little girl's hand, she pulled her into the circle of one arm. "Would you like to know a little bit more about me?"

Both children nodded eagerly. Their mother nodded, too. Even Joey found himself leaning forward a bit. They were spellbound, hanging on her every word.

"My name really is Diana—Di, for short—and I work as a nanny."

"So, you *are* the real Nanny Di," the boy said. He triumphantly came around Diana's chair to stand on her other side.

The excited little girl peppered Diana with questions. "And do you take care of a little girl named Mara Lee? And does she have a talking iguana? And is his name Ignacio? Iggy, for short?"

"The little girl I take care of is named Amalie," Diana said. "And she has a *stuffed* iguana named Ignacio. We call him Iggy, for short."

The little girl hopped up and down with excitement. "My name is Molly and my brother's name is Jacob. And we have a dog named Pepper. My favorite book is *Nanny Di and the Talking Iguana*," she confided.

"We have to read that one a lot," Jacob confided to Joey, man-to-man. "All. The. Time. She has it *memorized*."

His sister stuck out her tongue at Jacob before turning back to Diana. "Which book does Amalie like best?"

Diana thought a minute. "I think she likes *Nanny Di and the Practical Princess*. Amalie loves anything that has to do with princesses."

"Oooh, I do, too," Molly said, happily.

"This might be the best day of Molly's life," the children's mother informed Joey, under her breath. "Diana's wonderful with children."

"Yes, she is," Joey agreed.

"You're a lucky man," she continued in the same low voice.

"Yes, I…what?" Joey's voice cracked, unexpectedly.

Molly's mother laughed. "You two are adorable."

Joey latched onto the obvious in a desperate effort to change the subject. "What's your favorite *Nanny Di* book?" he asked Jacob, uncomfortably aware of Diana's amused expression. He wasn't sure if she was laughing at something that Molly was saying or if she was laughing at him. He chose not to think about it.

"I like *Nanny Di and the South American Surprise*," his young friend answered.

"That's the one with the penguins, isn't it?" Joey asked. When Jacob nodded, he added, "I think that's my favorite, too." He and the boy eyed each other with understanding. They were obviously on the same wavelength.

The children's mother ended their mutual admiration society. "We can't thank you enough for the wonderful stories you write, Miss Diana. Can we, children?"

"Thank you, Miss Diana," the children said in unison.

"I'm so glad that you enjoy them," Diana said, truly touched by their enthusiasm. "Would you like a new book to take with you?"

"Oh, yes!" Molly squealed. "Oh, Mama! Can we?"

"Please, Mama," Jacob begged.

"Of course," their mother replied, enjoying their excitement. "I love being able to say, 'yes.' " The smile she gave Diana was full of genuine gratitude.

Diana reached into her enormous tote bag and pulled out two books. "My new book is *Nanny Di and the Runaway School Bus*. It won't be on sale until September, but you two can get an early start on your reading."

She signed the title page of each book, writing a short note for each child. Molly and Jacob could hardly wait for her to finish.

Joey wanted to laugh. What else did she have in that bag? He wouldn't have been surprised if she pulled out a whole case of books. Or a live iguana. Or a tapdancing penguin. *Hmm*. Well…maybe that last one *would* surprise him, but not the other two. No wonder she had been able to escape her kidnapper *and* level Roman's doorman. That tote bag was a deadly weapon.

He watched Diana's face as she said goodbye to Molly, Jacob, and their grateful mother. Diana was glowing with delight, truly a woman who had found her calling. What she did made a difference in the lives of children every day. Diana's books made children *want* to read. Joey was both humbled by and fiercely proud of the woman who was, even now, digging in her magical tote bag.

Suddenly, Joey had a brilliant idea. "Nanny Di should have one," he said, as he dove into his second helping of breakfast.

Diana glanced up from her rummaging. "One what?" she asked, confused by the sheer randomness of his comment.

"A ginormous, magical tote bag," he said, with his mouth full. "Imagine the possibilities. Nanny Di could pull anything out of it that she needed."

Diana thought about his idea, gave it legitimate consideration. She really did. He quickly finished his breakfast as he waited for the verdict, enjoying the endless variety of expressions that flitted across her lovely face as she pondered his genius idea.

He particularly liked the way her freckles looked when she wrinkled her nose. He'd never thought much about freckles before. He supposed lots of women had them, but he doubted there was another woman whose freckles were as appealing as Diana's freckles. Did his sisters have freckles? His mother? Shirley or any of the women he had asked out on a date? For some strange reason, he didn't have the slightest idea.

Diana stood up. "Are you ready to go?" she asked, picking up her heavy tote bag and hoisting it—Joey lacked a better word—onto her shoulder.

He stood up, too. "Well?" he asked as they left the dining room.

She paused at the bottom of the stairs that led to their room. "Well, what?"

"Is Nanny Di going to have a ginormous, magical tote bag in her next book?" He couldn't wait for her answer.

"I don't think so," Diana said, starting up the stairs.

Joey couldn't believe it. He had been ready to receive her accolades for his great idea. "Why not?" he asked, as they climbed the stairs.

Diana shrugged. "A magical tote bag just isn't realistic."

"Realistic?" Joey huffed. "I can't believe you're worried about *realistic*. Nanny Di *has a tal-king i-gua-na*," he enunciated, carefully.

"*I* can't believe *you're* still worried about my tote bag," Diana said, more than a little amused.

"Not *your* tote bag. *Nanny Di's* gigantic, man-eating, magical tote bag," Joey said as they reached their room.

"Nanny Di doesn't need a gigantic, man-eating, magical tote bag." She made no move to get the key out of her own gigantic, man-eating tote bag. She just stood there, looking at him. He saw the spark of humor in her eyes.

Joey was enjoying himself, now. "Well, what about Genevieve?" he asked.

Diana crossed her arms and leaned against the wall. She raised her eyebrows, the perfect picture of a woman content to wait all day. "What about Genevieve?" she asked politely.

"Genevieve could use a magical, man-eating tote bag to protect herself from the earl."

"You mean the Earl of Ravenwood?" When Joey grimaced at the mention of the name, she continued, "She doesn't need protection from the earl. He's the good guy. Remember?" She smiled, patiently, glancing at the door.

Joey smiled back. "He's a *reformed* rake."

"Reformed rakes make the best husbands," Diana intoned. "It's one of the cornerstones of historical romance."

"Lady Genevieve will have to remember that." He leaned against the wall and waited, like Diana; but Diana made no move to find the key. With a sudden flash of insight, he realized what was going on. "Diana," he said, as gently as possible, "go ahead and look for the key. I promise I won't make a single joke about your ginormous, enormous, magical man-eating tote bag." He grinned, wickedly pleased with himself.

Her eyes danced. "Thanks, so much, for your kind consideration, but Joey...*you* have the key."

And so he did. He pulled it out of his pocket, unlocked and opened the door, all without saying a word. He couldn't, however, resist a formal bow. "After you, milady...and your magical man-eating tote bag."

He followed milady and her bag into the room, enjoying Diana's laughter "Reformed rakes make the best husbands." For some inexplicable reason, the phrase resonated with Joey. He would have to remember that. Grinning from the sheer exhilaration of sparring with Diana, he followed her into their room.

CHAPTER TWENTY-TWO

"*W*ake up, Joey," Diana said. "We're here." She turned off the main road and slowed onto a paved driveway, stopping at the closed gate. This was as far as she could go without the security code.

"What?" Joey struggled to escape the fog of sleep and to make sense of the approximate location of "here." He rubbed a weary hand over his eyes and studied his surroundings.

Diana laughed at her passenger's befuddled confusion. He was cute—*so* cute—right after waking up, something she now knew from personal experience. The last twenty-four hours had taught her a lot about Joey Finch. And none of it—not one thing—had in any way discouraged her interest in him. Or her attraction to him. If anything, their shared experiences had made Joey Finch even more irresistible than he had been before.

She liked Joey, genuinely liked him. He was smart and funny and easy to talk to. He was interested in her writing and, well…sometimes, he was just plain sweet. Her instincts had been right about him all along, she realized with a great deal of satisfaction. The overprotective male component of her family would be very displeased to discover *that* little tidbit of information.

"We're at the gate to Heart's Ease," Joey said in surprise. "How did we get here so fast?"

"We didn't get here *so fast*," Diana informed him. "You've been asleep for three hours."

"Three hours?" Joey was suddenly wide awake. "I've been asleep for three hours? Why didn't you wake me up?"

"Well..." Diana shrugged. "It was so peaceful and quiet that I just couldn't bring myself to do it." She grinned.

Joey put his hand over his heart. "Ouch," he said, in mock dismay. "Watch your mouth, Miss Merritt. Words *can* hurt."

She laughed at his dramatic flair. "Oh, stop. You know I'm only kidding. There was no way I was going to wake you up. You were exhausted."

"Hmph." This time Joey's disgruntlement was real. "You're just as exhausted as I am. The least I could have done was to stay awake and keep you company."

Diana waved her hand at him as if to say staying awake for days was perfectly normal. "Nannies never sleep, Joey. We're good at it." The shadows under her eyes were a direct contradiction to her bright smile. The genuine worry on his face prompted Diana to try a diversion. "What you really mean is that you wish you'd been awake so that you could monitor my driving skills," Diana said, satisfied to see Joey's worry change to amusement.

"If I was worried about your driving skills, I wouldn't have slept for three hours," Joey said, leaning his head back against the headrest. "My pass code is 0-8-0-6-8-8."

Diana punched in the numbers and watched as the gate swung slowly open. "Your birthday?" she asked.

"Yeah," Joey said. "Not very original, is it?" He raised his arms over his head and stretched his cramped muscles. "My neck may never recover." He moved it side to side, grimacing at the stiffness.

Diana laughed and drove the truck across the bridge. Honeysuckle Creek churned and bubbled over the rocks below before disappearing around a bend where a grove of tall pine trees temporarily hid it from view.

Like everything else about Diana's new home—including her companion—it was charming.

They passed the gatekeeper's cottage, renovated fewer than three years before. Until her marriage to Blane a year ago, Joey's sister, Grace—and her three-legged dog, Atticus—had been the sole occupants of the cottage. Now, Grace and Blane divided their time between the main house at Heart's Ease—Blane's childhood home—and his former bachelor apartment in Providence, Rhode Island. Blane's decision to move McCallum Industries' North American headquarters to nearby Winston-Salem, in November, would allow them to live in Honeysuckle Creek year-round.

Darcie lived in the cottage, now, although—in Joey's privately held opinion—his sister was a resident in name only. Her belongings lived there, yes, but when Devin was working in Rhode Island, Darcie stayed with his daughter at the main house. While in Honeysuckle Creek, Devin, of course, stayed at the main house with his daughter. Darcie was there, too...most of the time. Joey thought Darcie slept at the cottage on occasion so as not to confuse Amalie, but he didn't delve too closely. He was a firm believer that no big brother in his right mind really wanted to know all the details of his little sister's bedtime logistics.

For his own peace of mind, he quickly focused on Diana's driving abilities. "Where'd you learn to drive a truck, anyway? I can't imagine it was in downtown Alexandria." He found himself uncommonly eager for her answer. She was one of the few people—male or female—whose driving skills he actually admired.

"Not Alexandria." Diana shook her head. "Contrary to popular opinion, anyone with the last name of Merritt doesn't reside at the family law firm. You've probably been to Uncle Gary and Aunt Naomi's house in Alexandria." At Joey's nod, she continued: "That's where Connor and Lance grew up. But we—Roman and I—didn't grow up in Alexandria." She hesitated for a split second.

Joey jumped on that hesitation immediately. "So, where *did* you and Roman grow up?"

"Farther," she said, tonelessly.

Joey frowned at her cryptic answer. "Farther than Alexandria?"

Diana sighed the long-suffering sigh of a person who has given the same explanation one time too many. "No. Not farther than Alexandria. Just…Farther."

"Farther than what?" Joey asked, totally confused.

"Farther, Virginia. It's a little town about forty-five minutes from Alexandria. Mom and Dad built a house on the edge of the family farm after they got married, and that's where Roman and I grew up. Our extended family runs the farm. We always help out when we're home. That's where I learned to drive a truck. I can also drive a tractor and—if everyone else is incapacitated—the combine."

Diana waited, anxious to see on which side Joey would fall. Heaven knew she had listened to enough snide comments about *the farmer's daughter* and *the little milkmaid* from Mallory and her snobbish friends to last a lifetime. She slowed the truck to a crawl, giving Joey time to respond before they reached the main house.

"That's awesome," Joey said, sincerely, completely unaware of her turmoil. "I loved coming to visit Blane when we were growing up so I could hang out with the horses. We probably spent more time in the stables than in the house. It wasn't the same after he left, but I still came out here as much as I could, especially in high school, and when I was home on college breaks. Something about a lot of land and animals that clears a man's head, you know?" Joey gazed out at the lush green pastures. From a distance he could see several men working with one of the horses in the corral as two fat, little ponies munched on grass in the shade nearby.

Diana gazed at Joey. And fell a little bit in love. How could she not? His easy acceptance of her country roots and his sincere appreciation for the pastoral beauty all around them resonated with her soul. Maybe, she admitted to herself, she should have said that she fell a little *more* in love. She didn't have time to ponder the nuances, because their destination was right in front of them.

Heart's Ease.

Diana's haven, for now, and the inevitable end of their journey. She forced herself to face the reality she had studiously managed to avoid since waking up at the Acorn Knob Inn. It was time to say goodbye to Joey Finch. She couldn't help but wonder when—and if—she would see him again. He was moving back to his hometown, she reminded herself. He had plenty of friends and family in Honeysuckle Creek. Would he have time for one more? Especially if that *one more* was a troublesome nanny with long, red hair, a writing career, and a psychotic kidnapper/stalker on her tail? Diana grimaced. No chance Joey Finch would be able to forget about *her*. Oh, no, she thought, sarcastically. He would think of her every time he saw the small, brick-induced scar on his forehead.

"You can pull the truck around the drive, Diana," Joey said, pointing to the side of the house near the garage.

"All right," she said with a sunny smile. *Autopilot, Diana,* she instructed herself. *Don't think. Just keep moving.*

Before she could take the key out of the ignition, she saw the kitchen door of the main house burst open to reveal a very relieved Barry and Lucinda Merritt. Diana stared at them, uncomprehendingly. How could her parents possibly be here? Her worlds were colliding. She closed her eyes for a second to see if she was imagining things. But, when she opened them again, her parents were still there.

Barrett Merritt preferred to be called Barry, for obvious reasons. Like all the Merritt males, he was tall with an athletic build. He had, thus far, managed to avoid the "middle-age spread" that currently afflicted his brother, Gary. Barry had a thick head of auburn hair and dark gray eyes. *Like Diana,* Joey thought. Barry was even-tempered, reasonable, and very deliberate when making decisions. His desire to have all the facts in front of him before reaching a conclusion drove Gary and their younger brother, Robert, crazy. Both of them relied on their instincts. Joey, however, appreciated Barry's willingness to be a sounding board for a young attorney trying to get his bearings. Joey had an excellent relationship with Diana's father.

Lucinda Merritt's strawberry-blonde curls, brown eyes, and soft Southern accent gave her the allusion of genteel fragility. Joey knew from experience that nothing could be farther from the truth. Lucinda's good looks hid a spine of steel. She was equal parts sass and practicality. He had seen her bring all the Merritt men to heel at one time or another, to his everlasting amusement. Lucinda also had the distinction of being one of the few who could handle Gary's overbearing—but well-meaning—wife, Naomi. While Joey regarded Naomi with a kind of terrified awe, he was completely comfortable with Lucinda. Diana's mother had always treated him with kindness and motherly concern.

Diana's hair was a gorgeous combination of both parents while her eyes were an inheritance from her father. Those lovely eyes were currently wide with shock.

"Mom and Dad are here?" Diana's brain was having trouble processing what her eyes were telling her.

Joey could hear the strain in her voice.

"You see them, too…right?" she asked, a little desperately.

"See who?" asked Joey. The look she gave him was so full of confusion that he stopped teasing her immediately. "Yes, I see them, too. Your mom and dad are here."

"How did they…?" Her voice trailed away as she watched Devin, Blane, and Grace follow her parents out the door. Atticus trotted happily beside them.

Diana dropped the keys into Joey's outstretched palm, opened the door, and jumped to the ground on legs that were, suddenly, weak. Somebody caught her arm before those knees gave way entirely, and she looked up into her mother's face. "Oh, Mama," she whispered, throwing herself into Lucinda's comforting embrace. Diana tried not to cry. She really did. But one tear followed another down her cheeks in a steady stream. Lucinda's eyes were full, and even Barry's were suspiciously shiny. Their relief at seeing their only daughter safe and sound was obvious.

Devin, Blane, and Grace tactfully remained on Joey's side of the truck. Once Atticus caught a glimpse of Joey, the shaggy canine could barely contain himself. Vibrating with excitement, he sat down on Blane's foot to wait for one of his all-time favorite humans. As soon as his target's feet were firmly planted on the ground, the overly enthusiastic furball pounced. So intent was Joey on heading straight to Diana's side, he nearly fell over the ecstatic dog. Blane's quick reaction was the only thing that kept Joey from tumbling to the pavement. Blane steadied his friend until Atticus scrambled out of the way. The determined canine didn't give up, however. He merely backed up a few steps, biding his time.

After Joey regained his balance, it was Grace who halted his second attempt to join Diana. She placed a gentle hand on his arm. "Give them a minute, Joe," she said, softly. "Diana's parents drove half the night to get here. They were worried sick."

One look at his intuitive sister halted him in his tracks. She was studying him intently. And she was biting her lip. That meant she was thinking too hard. Making assumptions. Conjuring nonsense. Blane was no better. He was standing with his arms crossed, feigning nonchalance. That was always a sign of trouble. Devin stood beside Blane, staring straight at Joey, his single eye full of suspicion.

They don't understand, Joey rationalized. All he wanted to do was check on Diana. He simply wanted to make sure she wasn't crying again. If she was, well, somebody had to make those tears disappear. And that somebody was Joey Finch. After all, he had already proven himself quite adept at making Diana smile. However, if the arrested expressions on the faces of his audience were any indication, the trio was currently over-analyzing Joey's innocent intentions. He could tell. And that spelled T-R-O-U-B-L-E.

Self-preservation kicked in. Joey leaned back against the side of his truck, carefully schooling his expression to one of polite disinterest. "Of course, they need a minute," he agreed, scrambling in his head for something logical to say. "I just wanted to answer any questions they may have." There. That sounded reasonable, he thought, adding, "Two eye-witnesses are better than one," for good measure.

Fortunately for him, Atticus chose that moment to make his next move. He lunged for his target. Joey gave the ecstatic dog his complete attention, thereby avoiding the continued perusal of the trio in front of him. "Go check on Diana for me, Atticus," he whispered into the dog's single ear as he gave it a thorough scratch.

Atticus' intelligent eyes peered into Joey's intently as if he understood his mission. After enjoying a few more seconds of having his head scratched, the wily dog obediently trotted around to Diana's side of the truck.

As it turned out, Joey didn't need a canine diversion to draw attention away from himself. Blane and Devin easily accepted his words.

Blane gave Joey a friendly punch on the shoulder. "Can't wait to hear *your* version of this mess. We only got the bare minimum from Roman and that was secondhand. Rafe is fairly itching to hear the whole story from both of you."

"Looks like you're marked for life," Devin said, inspecting Joey's stitches. "I have it on good authority that women love intriguing scars." He motioned to the extensive markings on his own face and grinned. "You're not quite there yet, but you're off to a good start."

"Thanks a lot," Joey said, laughing ruefully. He forced himself not to turn his head in Diana's direction. No need to call further attention to himself. "Diana's bags are in the back," he said conversationally. "Do you need me to tell you which ones belong to her?" He walked around to the truck bed to loosen the bungee cords and move the blankets that covered Diana's suitcases.

Devin laughed. "Diana and I have been traveling together since we were babies—*and* she's Amalie's nanny. I'm pretty sure I can tell which ones belong to her."

Blane lifted a medium-sized suitcase in a multicolored floral pattern. "This one definitely belongs to Joey," he said, with a wide grin.

"Absolutely," Devin agreed. "And these have to be his, too." He pulled a large suitcase in the same floral pattern out of the truck bed, followed by a matching garment bag.

Damn, Joey thought. How had he forgotten about those flowers? He decided to play it off. "Oh, yeah," he responded. "Ha. Ha. Ha. Laugh it up, guys. It just so happens that Connor and Roman moved the suitcases from her car to my truck in the parking deck. I didn't even see them." That wasn't quite true, as he had seen Diana's luggage at the Acorn Knob Inn. He didn't think this was a good time to explain that he had been too busy looking at Diana to pay attention to her suitcases. He decided a little ridicule was a small price to pay for his privacy.

As he watched Blane and Devin carry Diana's luggage to the house, Joey was disappointed to discover that the object of his concern was already ahead of them, almost to the kitchen door. Barry's arm was set around her shoulders and Lucinda was holding her hand. Joey, it seemed, had been replaced. At least for the time being.

He was pleased to see Atticus trotting behind the trio, looking for all the world like a canine Secret Service agent. He was not pleased, however, to see Diana's parents apparently peppering her with questions. Joey didn't like that at all. Poor Diana. Couldn't they see she was exhausted? She should be resting instead of answering a lot of irrelevant questions. He would tell them so, he decided, as soon as he got into the house. Then he would whisk her away to a comfortable bed in Blane's guest wing. He would bring her chocolate twirls and hot tea in a bear mug. He would ask her questions about the Earl of Ravenwood until she fell asleep all warm and cozy, cuddled up against…

Grace waved her hand in front of his face. "Jo-ey Finch! Are you in there?"

"What?" he asked, impatiently, brushing her hand aside.

"I called your name three times already," Grace said, watching him closely. "I think your brain stayed in Virginia." She couldn't hide the knowing smile that appeared on her pretty face. "Or, maybe, it went into the house…with Diana."

Well, hell. Joey turned his back to her, checking under the seat for anything of Diana's that might have fallen out of her tote bag. It also gave him a moment away from the all-seeing eyes of his too clever sister. She was right, even though he wasn't about to admit it. His brain *had* gone into the house with Diana.

He reached into the console and grabbed the bag that held the last two packs of the chocolate twirls he had purchased at the convenience store. He placed them in her enormous tote bag, just beside the pink cover of her rose gold MacBook. She would smile when she found the chocolate delicacies. He was sure of it. A smiling Diana, he realized, had become imperative to his peace of mind. He picked up her ginormous, magical bag and hoisted it onto his shoulder. Before turning around, he pasted on a cocky expression. Only then did he acknowledge his sister's words.

"My brain is right where it always is, Brat." His voice held the slightly joking, slightly condescending tone that drove his sisters crazy.

Grace frowned in aggravation.

Good, he thought. An annoyed Grace was a distracted Grace. "And *your* brain, as usual, is full of romantic nonsense."

She opened her mouth, but he cut her off.

"Well-intentioned nonsense, but nonsense all the same." He put his arm around her shoulders as they started toward the kitchen.

"Hmph." Grace bumped his hip with her own. "I hear you were something of a hero yesterday," she said, softly.

"Who told you that?" Joey asked, unable to keep the surprise out of his voice.

"Rafe Montgomery," Grace answered, stopping as they reached the kitchen door.

Joey blinked. Rafe's good opinion meant something to him.

Grace raised up on her toes to kiss her brother's cheek. "I'm glad you were there, Joey."

"Me, too," he said, his throat suddenly tight. He opened the door and followed his sister inside.

CHAPTER TWENTY-THREE

*D*iana was starting to miss the man-eating strangers. She would honestly prefer a confrontation with them *and* their banjos to being held hostage by the well-meaning, but single-minded, Trio of Doom. And, if she survived their interrogation, she could only anticipate more questions, prying, and scolding from her know-it-all brother when he arrived the next morning. *Hurray*, she thought, dispiritedly, borrowing Amalie's favorite phrase.

The questions had begun before she sat down, alone, on one of three sofas in the grand foyer. Her parents sat on the adjacent sofa. Diana knew that her father was listening to every word but keeping his own counsel. Her mother made notes in the little sketchbook she carried everywhere. Her parents trusted Rafe Montgomery implicitly and had no problem letting him take the lead. Although Diana appreciated their presence and silent support, she knew Barry and Lucinda expected her to answer every question without flinching or making a fuss. When the situation demanded it, her mother was every bit as tough as her father. And so, too, was Diana. At least, that's what her mother implied. Diana was a *Merritt*, after all, and would, therefore, rise to the challenge.

The Trio of Doom sat on the sofa across from Diana. Devin's single eye was full of familial concern; for once, he seemed incapable of sitting still. Elbows on his knees one minute. Elbow on the armrest of the sofa the next. Ankle crossed over his knee the next. In between, he tapped his foot on the floor, bouncing his knee up and down. Blane tried to halt the incessant motion by smacking Devin's knee with his hand and holding it down, but a few seconds after removing his hand, Devin was at it again.

Blane, ever the consummate professional, managed to look bored by the whole interview. But his bland expression and relaxed demeanor weren't fooling anyone. He was as intent on Diana's every word as her agitated cousin.

Rafe, in Diana's opinion, was the only person present who seemed to be enjoying himself. He liked nothing better than the pursuit of justice. His eyes glittered with intensity. His questions came lightning fast. He brooked no resistance from Diana. Or interference from anyone else. Hesitation was not allowed. He was willing to push, press, and prod until he found the answers for which he was searching.

Diana felt like a bug under a magnifying glass. While the Trio of Doom hashed out some tiny nuance of some equally tiny detail, Diana let her mind wander. She assumed that the continued absence of Darcie and Amalie from their little gathering was not an accident. Amalie was prone to eavesdrop on adult conversations. The little girl often ended up repeating *her* version of what was overheard, usually with embarrassing results.

Yes, Diana thought, it was better that Amalie wasn't in the room. Diana wished with all her heart that she, herself, wasn't in the room, either. She wondered if there was anything she could possibly do to escape her present circumstances. She considered screaming at the top of her lungs and jumping on the furniture, but quickly dismissed the idea. Such an outburst would probably cause more problems than it would solve. Surreptitiously, she familiarized herself with the location of every exit. Just in case.

The only moment of hope she had experienced after the questions began died a quick—and tragic—death. Approximately ten minutes earlier, Joey opened the kitchen door and poked his head into the room. For a few seconds Diana thought he was going to save her. But after sizing up the situation, he retreated to the kitchen. She didn't blame him a bit. She did take some consolation from the fact that he didn't look happy about her situation. Of course, she was only *assuming* his irritation had something to do with her interrogation. Maybe, she informed herself, the scowl on Joey's face had absolutely nothing to do with her. Maybe he was simply hungry.

Lord knew that *she* was hungry. The spectacular breakfast buffet at the Acorn Knob Inn was only a distant memory. And even though she had eaten enough for a small army and probably shouldn't be hungry again until next week, she was. Grace had murmured something earlier about freshly baked banana bread and hot tea when they walked through the kitchen but, as of yet, none had appeared. *Another Finch sibling preoccupied with hot tea*, Diana mused…an irrelevant, but highly interesting, observation.

Joey, she decided, probably intercepted his sister in the kitchen. He was probably eating banana bread and drinking tea at this very moment.

Without her.

Without whom? she asked herself, sarcastically. Without Diana Merritt, that's whom. Diana Merritt? Diana who? She couldn't help but be a little annoyed. Joey's presumed defection was something of a surprise. She had assumed they were in this together. She really couldn't blame him for avoiding the interview with the Trio of Doom. Diana could think of a few other places she, herself, would prefer to be….

The dentist's office.

Or prison.

Or a stateroom on the sinking *Titanic*.

Or the surface of the sun.

Or the torture chamber of a medieval castle. *Oh, wait*, she thought sarcastically. *Not that one. I'm already there.*

And, she reminded herself, she was enduring the torture without Joey Finch. And without him, she was…what? Disappointed? Abandoned? All by herself in a room full of people? Diana was going to choose letter D—*All of the Above*—on that question. She was certain she would be handling this interview so much better if Joey was sitting beside her. He would hold her hand and make her laugh. He would tell jokes about the Earl of Ravenwood or Diana's ginormous magical tote bag. Diana sighed softly. If Joey was with her, she wouldn't feel so alone.

Well, he's not here. And he's not going to be here, damn it. Iggy says, "Suck it up, Nanny Di." Wow, Diana thought. Strong language for an imaginary iguana.

Nanny Di and the Foul-Mouthed Iguana.

Diana thought that title was pretty amusing, but she discarded it after remembering Molly and Jacob at the Acorn Knob Inn. She had a responsibility to her young fans; she wouldn't treat that lightly. Unless, she decided, she went stark raving mad during this interminable interview. That would probably excuse her from creating a multitude of inappropriate book titles.

She squared her shoulders, trying to focus on the Trio's discussion. It was a wasted effort. She didn't remember if her kidnapper had any distinctive markings—tattoos or whatnot. And, frankly, she was just too tired to care about the color of Cowboy Bill's eyes.

"I don't know what color his eyes are," she heard herself say. "I was trying to get away from him, not invite him to tea."

Tea. *Drat.* Tea made her think of banana bread. Banana bread made her think of the kitchen. The kitchen made her think of Joey Finch in the kitchen eating banana bread *and* drinking tea...*without her.*

Diana glanced toward the kitchen again, fully expecting the door to be closed. It wasn't. It was open, and Joey was propped against the doorframe, watching her with an indecipherable expression on his handsome face. Diana could see Grace hovering behind him, holding something in her hands. Joey winked. Once. But that was all it took for a spark of hope to take hold in Diana's heart.

Hang on, Diana.

Joey silently telegraphed the message to the red-haired woman on the couch. She was totally drained of energy, but still so very lovely. He wanted to stride across the room and rail at her tormentors, demanding they save their questions for later. That course of action, however, would only create other questions, which Joey was neither able nor willing to answer.

"Help is on the way!" he wanted to shout. He had to settle for a wink. He was pleased to note that Diana visibly relaxed after that wink. She trusted him. *Well,* he thought with satisfaction, *it won't be long now.*

As if on cue, a blur of shaggy fur flew around the corner of the hallway and sprinted into the grand foyer. A large—and to Diana, blessedly familiar—stuffed iguana was wedged tightly in Atticus' scruffy jaws. From his place in the doorway, Joey smiled. A pivotal plot point of his plan depended on the overly intuitive canine. And Joey was not disappointed. His clever co-conspirator was nothing, if not dependable.

Atticus moved faster on three legs than most dogs did on four, Joey thought, admiringly. The wily fellow leapt over the arm of the sofa where Diana sat, deposited the iguana in her lap, jumped to the floor, and planted his furry behind firmly on Blane's foot. The dog gazed at his master, innocently, as if he was not the catalyst of Joey's hastily thrown-together plan.

Part Two of that plan came racing around the corner, her blond ponytail streaming behind her. Amalie was wearing a pink cover-up over her matching pink swimsuit. Both were adorned with images from Sleeping Beauty—her favorite princess. Today.

"Atticus! Atticus!" she called in a high-pitched, childish voice.

The little girl slid to a halt when she reached the grand foyer. Her eyes briefly flew to Joey in the doorway. He nodded, encouragingly. Heartened by his approval, Amalie focused her attention on her next task. She tiptoed, very deliberately, toward the couch. "At-ti-cus!" she enunciated slowly… and tonelessly. "Where…are…you?"

Joey cringed, barely avoiding the suspicious glance Rafe sent his way. The child was as transparent as a piece of glass. The singsong quality of her voice instantly revealed that she was part of a wider conspiracy. When Amalie reached the side of the couch, however, she forgot the rest of the script. Her excitement at seeing Diana after so many weeks took over.

"Nanny Di!" Amalie squealed, throwing herself into Diana's arms.

Diana hugged the little girl close, despite Amalie's slightly damp swimsuit and the strong smell of sunscreen. Oh, how she had missed this lively bundle of joy.

Amalie could barely contain her excitement. "Oh, Nanny Di! I'm so glad to see you! I've missed you so much! Mama Darcie and I have been having the most fun! I don't have to call her Miss Darcie anymore because she and Daddy are going to get married! So, I can call her *Mama* Darcie or maybe just Mama!" She turned to Devin for confirmation. "Isn't that right, Daddy?"

Devin's lips turned up in a pleased smile. Clearly, the fact that his daughter adored the woman he was going to marry was one of the greatest blessings of his life.

From his place in the doorway, Joey saw Darcie walk into the grand foyer just in time to hear Amalie's words. Her smile, as her eyes flew to the face of her future spouse, was breathtaking. The glance they exchanged was filled with so much love, longing, and soul-deep understanding that Joey had to look away. *Those two are almost too much*, he thought, while—at the same time—wondering, ironically, if anyone would ever look at him like that.

Devin smiled at his daughter. "That's right, Amalie. Darcie and I are going to get married, but it's still a secret because we aren't *officially* engaged yet." He put a finger to his lips. "Shhhhh. We can't tell *anybody*."

Amalie grinned from the snug cocoon of Diana's arms. She looked at her rapt audience. "Y'all won't tell, will you?" Her earnest expression was priceless.

"Y'all?" Diana raised her eyebrows in amusement as the Southern phrase fell effortlessly from the little girl's mouth. Diana had used the word all her life courtesy of a Charleston-born mother and aunt and summers spent in South Carolina. She had nearly dropped it from her speech the past five years, however, to avoid Mallory's ridicule. The fact that Amalie had picked it up so fast was strangely satisfying.

Laughter filled the room as the tension was broken. That was when Part Three of Joey's plan jumped into action. Darcie moved to the couch, giving Diana a hug while pulling her to her feet. At the same time, Grace came in from the kitchen, carrying a tray with several pieces of banana bread, a cup of tea, and a glass of milk. They moved like clockwork. Darcie put her arm around Diana on one side, Amalie grabbed her hand on the other.

"Oh...look...Nan-ny Di!" Amalie said in the same singsong, overly rehearsed voice. "Aun-tie Grace...has...a...snack...for...us!" She lapsed into regular tones as she added, "Mama Darcie says I can call her *Auntie* Grace instead of *Miss* Grace because she's going to be my aunt when Mama Darcie marries my daddy."

Grace grinned as she moved toward the hallway that ran between the kitchen and several guest bedrooms. "That's right, Amalie. And look what I have! Yum-my ba-na-na bread!" She enunciated the last part in the same singsong manner Amalie had used earlier.

"What a surprise. We don't want to miss *that.*" Darcie's rich voice was full of laughter as she and Amalie propelled Diana out of reach of the Trio of Doom. They did not, however, manage to escape the barely contained excitement of Atticus, who smelled banana bread. He raced across the grand foyer, his nose in the air.

Darcie and Diana had nearly reached the hallway when Amalie suddenly stopped walking. She tugged, insistently on Diana's hand.

Diana leaned down in concern. "What's wrong, 'Malie?" she asked.

"Iggy," the little girl whispered. Her other hand came up to cover her mouth in horror as she realized her mistake. "I was supposed to get Iggy." Her eyes were full of longing as she pointed to her beloved stuffed iguana, lying belly-up on the couch.

Grace smiled kindly. "It's all right, Amalie. Go get him. I know how much Iggy *loves* banana bread." She winked at the worried little girl.

Amalie's face cleared instantly. She skipped to the couch, retrieved the hapless iguana by the tail, and turned around. That's when her eyes found Joey, still standing in the doorway of the kitchen.

 She ran to him, her face full of excitement. "We did it, didn't we, Mr...I mean, Uncle Joey?" She hopped on one foot in a semicircle until she was facing Diana's direction. "Mama Darcie says I can call him *Uncle* Joey because he's going to be my uncle when she marries my daddy!" Amalie kept hopping until she was, once again, facing Joey.

Unfortunately for *Uncle* Joey, the child started over: "We did it, didn't we, Uncle Joey? Your plan worked! We saved Nanny Di from the *terror-gation!*"

"In-ter-ro-ga-tion," Diana intoned, out of years of habit. The sudden smile that bloomed on her face, however, was all for Joey.

"In-ter-ro-ga-tion," Amalie repeated, happily, skipping back to Diana. Darcie grabbed the little girl by the hand and tugged her forward.

"Mama Darcie, what's a *terror-gation*?" her childish voice asked before she disappeared into the hallway.

Joey couldn't help but smile at Amalie's version of the situation the Trio of Doom had placed Diana in. Despite the lively curiosity inspired by his actions, Joey didn't regret a thing. How could he when his damsel-in-distress paused to mouth the words "thank you" before accompanying Grace down the hallway. And her smile...well, Joey would do just about anything for that smile. Feeling ridiculously light-hearted, under the circumstances, he watched Atticus' scraggly nose and the rest of the intrepid canine follow the fragrant smell of banana bread into the hallway.

And that was that.

Time to face the music, Joey thought, not surprised to find himself under the scrutiny of every remaining eye in the room. He casually strolled to the couch, so recently vacated by Diana, and settled himself to take her place. He nodded at Diana's parents on the adjacent couch. Barry nodded back, managing to convey his approval without an outward change of expression. Lucinda, however, was beaming. She looked as if Joey had just granted her heart's desire.

He wasn't sure what that was all about, so he focused his attention on the men seated across from him: his best friend and brother-in-law, Blane; his good friend and future brother-in-law, Devin; and secret-agent-special-forces-and-who-the-hell-knew-what-else Rafe Montgomery.

"Any word on the kidnapping cowboy?" Joey asked, casually. A question, he decided, was the best way to avoid other, more personal inquiries. The answer he received, however, was rather disheartening.

According to Rafe, the Alexandria police were still unable to find any trace of Diana's kidnapper. The "cowboy" had disappeared into the crowded street, never to be seen again. The police did manage to find his rental car. After tracing it back to the rental company, they discovered that the car was issued to a man calling himself Kenneth Wade.

Hearing the name of the dead man was unnerving. Joey couldn't help but wonder if the death of Wade, Devin's attack a year ago, Mallory's death in June, and Diana's attempted kidnapping were all related. He couldn't imagine how, but he had to wonder. He broached that question to the Trio of Doom.

Rafe readily admitted that, while they had wondered the same thing, they had yet to find the common denominator that would link all four occurrences together. "And," he added grimly, "it's not for lack of trying."

Silence descended as the small group digested this less-than-welcome news. A few seconds of contemplation was all it took before the attention of the three men returned to their newest victim...*Um, witness,* Joey corrected in his head. Sacrificial lamb was not a role he was accustomed to playing, but he was determined to give it a try for Diana's sake. Not, however, without making a statement first.

"Diana calls the three of you the Trio of Doom," he said. "Did you know that?" He was gratified to see the genuinely contrite expressions on the faces of Blane and Devin.

Blane's brow wrinkled with worry. "The Trio of Doom..." he said, slowly. "That's pretty awful." He ran his hand through his hair in agitation. "We didn't mean to make her feel pressured like that, Joey. We're only trying to help. I hope she knows that."

Devin was even more upset than Blane. "I am an ass," he said. "I knew answering our questions was hard on her, but I didn't realize she sees us as the bad guys."

Barry spoke up then. His observation was spot-on. "That's because Diana always *appears* to take everything in stride," he said. "She's good at pretending everything is fine, even when she's upset."

"*Especially* when she's upset," Lucinda chimed in. "It's a necessary survival skill for a girl growing up with a big brother and older cousins. But, Devin…" Lucinda's face was regretful. "She perfected the skill working for Mallory."

Devin nodded in agreement. "I know that now. But then…well, I had no idea how awful Mallory treated Diana until it was too late to do anything about it. I still feel guilty about what Mallory put her through." Devin looked miserable. "And now, this…"

Lucinda shook her head. "Diana would do it all over again, Devin… for Amalie. And for you. You know that." His aunt's voice rang with such confidence that Devin and Blane looked somewhat relieved.

Rafe, however, was inordinately pleased by the title. "The Trio of Doom," he intoned, nodding his head in satisfaction. "An excellent moniker. I like it. That means Diana knows the seriousness of the situation even if she pretends not to. Two kidnapping attempts, my friends, are not random accidents." His intent gaze raked Joey's face. "We aren't through with the questions, though. You understand that?"

Joey refused to back down. "Tomorrow, then," he said, looking Rafe in the eye. "When she's rested."

"When she's rested," Rafe agreed, vaguely. "But what about…"

"Tomorrow." Joey was adamant. Diana deserved that much consideration.

Rafe nodded his head, reluctantly. "Tomorrow, then. Right after breakfast." There was a glint of respect in the older man's eyes.

Joey grinned as he faced the Trio of Doom. "Cheer up, guys, you've still got me. I was at Chutley's the whole time. I looked the devil in the face and lived to tell about it."

The three men looked intrigued. Joey braced himself for the *terror-gation* to come. "Gentlemen," he said. "Do your worst."

CHAPTER TWENTY-FOUR

*J*oey Finch was the cool head under pressure. The guy who thought on his feet. The man whose patient silence often yielded rich rewards.

Calm.

Unflappable.

Rational.

Or maybe, Joey thought, that was the way he *used* to be. Before an encounter with an errant brick—or was it a collision with a red-haired woman?—turned his life upside down.

He berated himself for his carelessness as he eased his truck over to the shoulder of the road. He could see the entrance to Heart's Ease from his present location. Fewer than a hundred yards, if he guessed correctly. It may as well be a hundred miles because he could also see the words *"Honeysuckle Creek Police Department, 'Protect and Serve' "* on the car that had pulled up behind him. The car with the flashing blue light.

Joey watched the opposing figure of Theo Granger climb out of the car. He couldn't help the relief that washed over him as the officer walked toward the truck. He and Theo were friends. They drank beer together. They even sang karaoke on Saturday nights. Theo had an excellent voice. Surely this was one police officer who would go easy on Joey Finch.

"What the hell were you thinking?" the big man roared, obviously irate.

Or not.

Joey's shoulders slumped.

Theo glared at his friend. "I repeat. What were you thinking?"

Joey sighed. "I guess I wasn't." It was an admission of guilt even if it wasn't quite true. He *had* been thinking all right. He'd been thinking about Diana Merritt. He'd been thinking about how the highlights in her hair resembled the shades of the loveliest sunset he could imagine. He'd been thinking about her soft, very kissable peach-colored lips and her long, slender limbs. He'd been thinking about the graceful way she moved and how she smiled when he said something ridiculous…

Theo cleared his throat. His expression had changed from one of annoyance to one of concern. "Joe," he said. "Is everything all right? You haven't been drinking or anything, have you?"

"No way, Theo." Joey was extremely offended. "You know me better than that. It's only seven o'clock in the morning. Of course I haven't been drinking."

"I didn't think so." Theo looked relieved by Joey's response. "Just checking. You had a funny look on your face for a minute there." He studied his friend with curious eyes. "I didn't stop you because I thought you'd been drinking," the big man reiterated. "You weren't swerving or doing anything erratic like that, but you were going way too fast for this road. And, besides, it's pretty early for you to be out of bed, isn't it? Where are you headed?"

Joey pointed to the entrance to Heart's Ease.

Theo shook his head, trying to hide his grin. "I need to see your license and registration, please."

Joey opened his glove compartment. He handed the requested items to Theo and waited while the big man walked back to his car to access his computer. Joey sighed and shut off his engine. He checked his phone for messages. He didn't have any. Probably because nobody who texted him was awake at seven o'clock on a Saturday morning. The fact that he was up early enough to receive a warning ticket—at least he hoped it would be a warning ticket—was the direct result of an irresistible desire to see Diana again.

If not for his newly acquired obsession with the delectable Miss Merritt, he, too, would be in bed, enjoying the comforts of a soft, plush mattress. He would *not* have been abusing his accelerator in a desperate rush to see the woman he could not erase from his mind. Diana was like some powerful drug...Twenty-four hours and he was addicted.

Theo came back to the truck, paper in hand. He returned Joey's license and registration. Then he handed Joey the paper. "Sorry about the ticket, Joe, but my karaoke performances wouldn't be half as good without you. I'm just making sure that you think about your speed next time."

Well, hell. Joey glanced down at the *this-is-not-a-warning-ticket* ticket. "Fifty-four in a forty-five?" he asked, meeting Theo's *this-is-for-your-own-good* gaze. "Seriously?"

"That's right." Theo couldn't hold back his grin this time. "Don't worry, Joe. You can probably get it reduced to faulty equipment if you know a good lawyer."

Joey just sat there. For once in his life, he couldn't think of a single thing to say.

Theo patted the side of the F-150. "Let's be safe out there," he said, before heading back to his police car.

In a few seconds, the police car disappeared around the bend in the road. Theo's original question, however, lingered. The words echoed in Joey's head. What the hell *was* he thinking? The answer to that question, he decided, was a no-brainer. Literally. His brain appeared to have vanished, leaving behind nothing but a continuous litany of pleasing images of Diana Merritt. In his apartment. In his truck. In the emergency room. In their room at the Acorn Knob Inn. In his bed.

Well, hell. All his logical, well-ordered, and dependable thought processes were being held hostage by a red-haired siren who *didn't want a relationship*, he reminded himself. And that should make him—Joey Finch, quintessential bachelor—very happy because *he* certainly didn't want a relationship.

And he *was* happy, he told himself. So very happy. Happy. Happy. Happy. Joey glanced at his disgruntled reflection in his rearview mirror. He released a disgruntled breath. If he was so damn happy then why wasn't he smiling? Excellent question. He pondered that question as he watched one squirrel chase another squirrel around the trunk of a large maple tree. After considerable effort, he was able to supply a respectable answer. He would probably *feel* happier if it wasn't so early.

And, he rationalized, as for his ill-fated—and much too early—morning expedition…well, he just hadn't taken the time to think it through. Yes, he wanted to see for himself that Diana was safe and sound. Nothing wrong with that, he told himself, calmly. He was worried about her. That was all. He was worried about his *good friend*, Diana Merritt. He would have done the same for anyone—male or female—whom he considered a good friend.

But his present path was fraught with unforeseen problems. What if nobody was awake when he arrived at Heart's Ease? What was he going to do then? Break into the house? Would they find him lurking around the kitchen when they wandered in? Frying bacon? Making toast? Setting the table? Wouldn't that be unexpected? Or strange? Or, possibly, just a little bit creepy? Of course it would, he told himself disgustedly.

And what would Diana think? *She* didn't want a relationship, he reminded himself. He seemed to spend a lot of time reminding himself of that unsettling fact. She just wanted to "enjoy being friends." *Friends.* Ha. Maybe she wouldn't even want to see her good *friend*, Joey Finch, today. Maybe she was already sick to death of him. Or—even worse—maybe she would think he was stalking her…like Cowboy Bill. That idea was totally unacceptable.

Then there was the rest of the crowd staying at Heart's Ease. How would they react to his out-of-character, early-bird appearance? In particular, how would his nosy sisters deal with their brother showing up at—what they knew was to him—the ungodly hour of seven o'clock on a Saturday morning? Joey almost groaned aloud as he imagined their suspicion. Their knowing glances. Their subtlely unsubtle references to his romantic intentions. He grimaced at the thought. No good could come from that kind of speculation…for himself or for Diana.

Thanks to Theo Granger—and his *this-is-not-a-warning-ticket* ticket—Joey had gotten a reprieve from his own overzealous intentions. An expensive and highly inconvenient reprieve, but a reprieve all the same. He certainly had no wish to cause trouble for his lovely, red-haired siren… um…*good friend*. So, Joey did the only thing that made sense. He turned his truck around and headed back the way he had come. The wisest course, it seemed, was to put some distance between himself and Diana Merritt. For both their sakes.

More than likely, he decided, the attraction, admiration, and, particularly, his unusual feelings of protectiveness for the charming Miss Merritt were all the result of their tumultuous twenty-four hours together. It was also possible, he told himself firmly, that even the prophetic brick was nothing but…well, a brick. A plain, old brick.

A. Brick.

And, given his own history where women were concerned, it was altogether likely that the next time he saw Diana Merritt, he wouldn't feel a thing.

Joey's good intentions lasted a week. Exactly one week. Seven twenty-four-hour days. One hundred sixty-eight hours. Furthermore, he spent every single one of those one hundred sixty-eight hours trying *not* to think about Diana. He tried to distract himself with the myriad activities involved with moving into his new townhouse in Honeysuckle Creek, including a roundtrip to collect his belongings from his apartment in Alexandria.

Moving was exhausting. He should have collapsed into bed every night, falling asleep as soon as his head hit the pillow. *Yeah, right,* he thought, sarcastically. Instead, he had to expend a great deal of effort to banish the lovely Miss Merritt from his mind so he *could* fall asleep. His nocturnal efforts, however, were for naught as the delectable woman with the gorgeous red hair spent most of the nights haunting his dreams. In short, it was the longest week of his life.

Joey could barely remember the names of most of the women he had dated over the last few years. The fiasco with Shirley/Chrissy was a prime example. To a man like himself, the inability to stop thinking about *one woman* was a new and exhilarating phenomenon. Also, he was honest enough to admit, slightly terrifying. It was just as he had suspected, all those years ago. Diana was different. She was a go-for-broke, all-or-nothing, wholly-enthralling force that blanketed his life like a cloud—filling in every heretofore unnoticed crack and crevice. Sometimes she was as familiar as the bubbling waters of Honeysuckle Creek. Peaceful and serene and, well…comfortable. At other times, she was exotic as an uncharted sea. Alluring and intriguing, with hidden depths he craved to explore. She was smart *and* sassy, with an edge of challenge that called to Joey's solitary soul.

During the week he spent trying *not* to think about Diana, Joey found himself unable to ignore the glaring truth. He had, he realized, *chosen* to follow the Diana-is-hands-off guidelines laid out by her brother and cousins because it suited him. It was an easy excuse for refraining from contact with the one woman he could not resist. His senses knew it. His brain knew it. Hell, even his body knew it. He was as drawn to the lovely Diana Merritt as a moth to a flame—and all those other tired clichés. Now that he had allowed himself to sample the delights of her presence—for a mere twenty-four hours, no less—there was no going back. He missed her. And what, he had asked himself, was he going to do about *that*?

The answer was easy. After a week of internal deliberation, he decided he was going to show up for breakfast at Heart's Ease. On Saturday morning. At a reasonable hour, this time. And that's exactly what he did.

After his speeding ticket—in a fog of pitiful ignorance—Joey had assumed that the next time he saw Diana, he wouldn't feel a thing. That the brick would indeed prove to be just a brick. But he quickly realized that nothing could have been farther from the truth. The feelings that roared under, over, around, and through his body at his first sight of Diana in a week were impossible to deny.

Or ignore.

Or avoid.

Joey was as captivated by her on that Saturday morning in the kitchen at Heart's Ease as he was on the second floor of Merritt Brothers Law Firm nine years ago. He was captivated by Diana the next day, too, by the pool. And the day after that, under the shade of an ancient dogwood tree. As a matter of fact, he had been captivated by Diana Merritt every day for the past three weeks, which was exactly how often he had chosen to visit Heart's Ease. But, he asked himself, was he captivated by the thrill of the chase? Or the fact that she didn't want a relationship? Would he lose interest after they went out on a date? Did he *want* to lose interest?

He honestly didn't think so. Because in all his life he had *never* felt this way about a woman. After nine years of simmering attraction, he had finally allowed himself to succumb. He was—what word might Diana use to describe Ezekiel's feelings for Genevieve?—*smitten*. That was it. Joey was definitely *smitten*. *Besotted*. That was a good one, too. He was *smitten* and *besotted* with Diana Merritt. Also *enthralled, bewitched, beguiled, enamored*, and the other thirty or so synonyms he had discovered while trying *not* to think about her.

Did these feelings mean that Joey's stint as a "one and done" was finally, well...*done*? Yes, he decided, they did. A relationship with Diana Merritt opened a whole world of endless possibilities. And he was free to pursue those possibilities—and the delightful redhead—with noble intentions and a clear conscience. But...

What was he going to do if she still didn't want a relationship? The answer to that question was obvious. He would just have to convince her. And he would too, because failure—his life without Diana Merritt in it—was no longer an option. Besides, he could think of any number of very pleasurable ways to try and change her mind.

Joey was, however, determined to keep his feelings for Diana to himself. At this point, he did not need—or want—the assistance of his "helpful" siblings. Or Blane. Or anyone with the last name of Merritt. Considering that he and Diana were already being examined under a microscope at Heart's Ease, he would have to be very careful. Joey breathed a sigh of relief.

He had plotted his course—and now he was ready to begin his never-be-fore-experienced quest to change a woman's mind. He was ready, that is, until he realized that he had one very big problem.

He had absolutely no idea what to do.

Joey was still pondering his options on Friday morning...four weeks to the day since his unexpected collision with Diana Merritt—in the door-way of Chutley's Bar and Grille—changed everything. Well, he amended, maybe not *everything*. He was, after all, living in Honeysuckle Creek. And he was working at his father's law firm, just as planned. But Joey's focus had shifted. Or maybe, he admitted ruefully, his heart had shifted. He, Joey I-Used-To-Avoid-Relationships-At-All-Costs Finch, was intent on pur-suing a relationship with Diana I-Don't-Want-A-Relationship-Now-We-Can-Enjoy-Being-Friends Merritt. And if that wasn't the ultimate irony. Or karma. Or another example of God's unending sense of humor, then he didn't know what was.

His thoughts made him restless. His restlessness pulled him out of the comfortable chair behind the desk in his office. His feet propelled him across the hall to Darcie's office where his sister inadvertently put his new-found intentions to the test.

Joey leaned against Darcie's desk, regarding his sister with surprise. "What do you mean '*we're* going to Karaoke Night.? Who's *we*?"

Darcie didn't bother to look up. She continued flipping through the ancient law book on her desk, searching for who knew what.

"Grace, Blane, Devin, and I are going out to an early dinner at Celine's," she explained. "After that we're meeting Lou, Evander, Roger, and whoever else shows up for Karaoke Night. You're welcome to come along. You need to let me know pretty quick about dinner, though. I'll have to add you to our reservation."

"What about Diana?" Joey asked. Diana, he knew, was still heed-ing Rafe's request to remain sequestered at Heart's Ease for a month. One month. Four weeks...plus a couple of days. In exchange for her compliance,

Rafe had agreed that if there was no reappearance of Diana's kidnapper after the time was up she was free to resume a normal life. A more vigilant life, but a normal one.

Darcie had privately informed Joey that Diana negotiated those terms with the skill of a professional diplomat negotiating a peace treaty, impressing even Rafe. Diana blushed charmingly when Joey asked her about it. "I guess my Merritt was showing," was all she said, much to Joey's admiration.

And, now, the time was almost up. He figured they would gather at Heart's Ease for the last weekend of Diana's *Rafe-induced* quarantine. But it appeared Darcie had other plans. He waited in vain for his little sister to answer his query, but she was engrossed in her law book. "What about Diana?" he repeated, a little louder.

"She's keeping Amalie for us," his sister said, absently, surprised when Joey's hand covered the page she was reading. She glanced up, instantly intrigued by the irate expression on her brother's handsome face.

Darcie raised her eyebrows calmly. "Problem?"

Joey was suddenly angry on Diana's behalf. "Hell, yes, it's a problem," he stated. "Not only are you leaving Diana at Heart's Ease all by herself while y'all go out and have a good time without her; but you're dumping Amalie on her when Saturday is supposed to be her day off. It's especially cruel because you know Diana promised not to leave the property until Monday morning."

Darcie placed her arms flat on the desk in front of her and clasped her hands together. "Are you finished?" she asked, patiently.

Joey thought for a second. "No, I'm not. You are taking blatant advantage, Princess, and I won't have it."

"*You* won't have it," Darcie echoed.

"No," Joey said, putting his other hand on the desk, beside the book, and leaning closer to glare at his sister. "*I* won't have it."

"Are you finished now?" Darcie asked, studying him.

"Yes," he said, straightening to his full height. "I believe I am." He crossed his arms, clear challenge in his gaze.

Darcie launched into her defense. "First of all, brother dear, the whole thing was *Diana's* idea. *She* suggested we go out because she knows Devin, Blane, and Grace are going back to Providence tomorrow for a couple of weeks before Amalie and I meet them in Scotland. Secondly, *she* volunteered to keep Amalie so we could have some adult time together. She said she wanted to show us how much our support means to her. Thirdly, *we* offered to pay her since it's her day off and she refused. We'll pay her anyway." Darcie paused, regarding her brother with interest. "Any more questions?" she asked.

"No," Joey said, a little unnerved by the look in her eye. "That should do it."

Darcie propped her chin on her hand, studying Joey's subdued expression. "I'm glad to know that Diana has such a staunch defender. Now I know why you've been hanging around so much...." She smiled happily, as if she had just discovered all his secrets. "To make sure *we* aren't mistreating her."

Uh-oh. Joey had overplayed his hand. They both knew that Darcie's statement was laughable. No one could have treated Diana better than his remarkable family. Joey realized he'd better tread carefully. This was the first time anyone had referenced his daily presence at Heart's Ease. He had foolishly assumed that his family had more important things to do than notice his comings and goings. He should have known better.

"About that," he began, pinning what he hoped was a convincingly innocent expression on his face. "May I?" he asked, indicating the chair in front of Darcie's desk.

She nodded, suspiciously. "Please do." She once again clasped her hands together in front of her.

Joey sat, casually crossing his foot over his knee. "The last time I was in Alexandria, Connor asked me to check on Diana and to let him know how she was doing. That's why I've been spending so much time at Heart's Ease," he lied. There. That sounded convincing. Even Darcie couldn't find something wrong with that.

"I know," she responded. "Connor mentioned it when he called. He asked me to do the same thing."

Well, hell. Joey hadn't expected that.

His overly astute little sister continued. "You, know, Joe," she said, thoughtfully, "checking on Diana and choosing to spend every spare minute of your time with her are two completely different things. Mrs. Hofmann doesn't even ask if you're coming to dinner anymore; she just makes extra."

Joey laughed weakly, rising to his feet.

"So, have you decided yet?" Darcie asked, placing both hands flat on the desk. The sly smile on her face made her resemble some exotically beautiful cat. Waiting at a mouse hole.

"Decided what?" Joey responded, determined not to tug on his collar. It suddenly felt very tight.

"If you're coming to Celine's with us or not."

"Oh, that," he said, in relief. "No. I don't feel like being a fifth wheel tonight."

"You can bring a date," Darcie suggested, lightly. "I'm sure you can rustle one up. You've never had a problem with that before."

For the first time in his life, the idea held no appeal. "No, thanks. I'll find something else to do."

Darcie's lack of response—she nodded once before her eyes returned to the book in front of her—was disconcerting.

"Well, um...see you later, Darce." The open doorway beckoned, promising a temporary respite from this entirely unexpected inquisition.

"Joey," his sister said.

He had the strong urge to keep right on walking, as if he hadn't heard his name. If he stopped, he had a feeling he was going to regret it. But he didn't have it in him to walk away from his little sister.

He turned around in the doorway. "Yeah?" he asked, bracing himself for the unexpected.

Darcie shrugged, apologetically. "I don't want to pressure you or anything, but if you're going to ask Diana out, you better do it soon."

"And why is that, little sister?" Joey replied, blandly. "Not that it's any of your business." He tried to sound bored, but his heart sped up.

"Because right now she doesn't know anybody but us. On Monday, she'll be free to go places and meet new people and..." Darcie shrugged again. "Just don't wait too long. I mean...if you're interested." Her innocent eyes studied him for a moment before returning to the pages of the ancient book.

When Joey stepped into the relative safety of the hallway, he realized he was sweating.

CHAPTER TWENTY-FIVE

A little after five o'clock in the afternoon, Diana glanced out the kitchen window at the front of the main house. From there she had an unobstructed view of the long driveway that led back to the main road. The driveway was currently empty. For the first time in three weeks, it looked as though she would be spending an evening without the presence of Joey Finch. She wondered what he was doing. She assumed he was meeting his siblings and their significant others later for dinner and karaoke. It sounded like a lot of fun. Dinner and karaoke. Diana loved karaoke.

Two more days, she thought. Only two more days remained until she could, once again, take her place in the land of the living. Her exile hadn't been as difficult as she had anticipated. Actually, she admitted, it hadn't been difficult at all. Instead of feeling isolated and alone, she felt as though she had enjoyed an extended vacation in an especially beautiful resort. Everyone who worked on the grounds of Heart's Ease—from the stables to the gardens to the main house—had been very, very kind. Even Mrs. Hofmann had gotten into the spirit, offering her a few cooking lessons. Diana was well on her way to mastering a delicious apple strudel.

Blane and Grace were, of course, Southern hospitality personified. They treated her as a special guest and had gone out of their way—from one end of the beautiful estate to the other—to keep her entertained. Horseback riding. Hikes in the woods surrounding the pastures. Swimming in the gorgeous pool. Cookouts (they didn't call them barbeques in North Carolina). Movie nights. Billiards. Volleyball in the wide backyard. Spending time with Blane and Grace—and with Devin and Darcie—was a pleasure. And Diana loved being reunited with Amalie. The pale, frightened little girl she had left in Rhode Island in June was once again her happy, busy self.

And, of course, there was Joey Finch.

Diana sighed. Everything about the past month had been lovely, but the thing that she had enjoyed the most was spending time with the rascally Mr. Finch. After that first week—when he was distressingly absent— he had visited Heart's Ease every day.

Every. Single. Day.

Diana was still a little confused as to the motivation behind his daily appearances. At first, she assumed he was just dropping by to see Grace and Darcie or, maybe, Blane and Devin. She didn't even consider that he might be there because he wanted to see *her*. During that first interminable week, Diana couldn't help but wonder if Joey missed her. Heaven knew she missed him, despite the fact her parents and brother had stayed at Heart's Ease until Tuesday.

She didn't blame Joey one bit for avoiding her big brother, especially after the way Roman behaved the night of the second kidnapping attempt. Diana almost managed to keep her suspicious sibling from discovering the details of her night at the Acorn Knob Inn…until someone—probably her dad—filled him in. Roman had been seething when he burst into the guest wing's small sitting room….

"One bed?" Roman bellowed. "What do you mean there was only one bed?" He turned away from his sister just in time to miss the look she exchanged with their mother. But the serene figure sitting on the couch beside her daughter raised her eyebrows. "Sit down, Roman," she said. "You're being ridiculous."

"Ridiculous, Mother?" He continued to pace back and forth despite her gentle reprimand. "How is it ridiculous to be concerned for my sister's welfare?"

Lucinda shrugged her shoulders. "Your sister is perfectly well. Just look at her." She frowned at her son before focusing her attention back on the sketchbook in her lap.

"I'm not just talking about her health, Mother," Roman replied. "I'm talking about her—"

"Okay. That's enough," Diana interrupted in a tight voice before her brother could get really wound up. She had no intention of discussing the intimate details of her night with Joey Finch—or anything else about Joey Finch, for that matter—with her super-opinionated big brother. "How's that sketch coming, Mom?"

"It'll be ready in a bit," her mother said, studying the drawing in front of her.

Roman growled low in his throat. He actually growled. The sound caused both women to look at him with identical expressions of annoyance.

Lucinda put down her pencil to address her son again. "Your sister is twenty-eight-years old, Roman," she stated, patiently. "Or have you forgotten?" Her tone of voice implied that Roman was acting like an eight-year-old child.

Diana gave her brother a superior smirk. "Thank you, Mother."

Lucinda regally inclined her head. "You're welcome, Diana."

Diana's smirk quickly disappeared at her mother's next few sentences.

"Diana is twenty-eight years old," Lucinda repeated. "You, Roman, are thirty-one. Thir-ty-one. I'm fifty-six years old with no grandchild in sight."

"Mother!" Diana squeaked, glaring at Roman as if their mother's pronouncement was all his fault.

Lucinda started counting additional grievances, ticking each item off on her fingers. "No weddings. No engagement parties. Not even a Sunday dinner with a significant other." She shook her head sorrowfully, although neither one of her children missed the sparkle of mischief in her eyes. "In light of this unfortunate situation, my moral compass seems to have become a bit skewed. So, you will forgive me, Roman, if the thought of Diana sharing a room—and a bed—with Joey Finch does not bother me in the least. I happen to like him, you know. Quite a lot." She picked up her pencil and calmly resumed sketching.

Roman's exasperated gaze flew to his sister.

Diana sighed. Her brother would never stop badgering her if she didn't at least give him a little bit of information. "In addition to the bed, there was also a very comfortable leather chair in the corner of the room, Roman," she said. "Two of them, actually." I didn't sleep in them, she added to herself, but they were there.

Her brother was not impressed.

Diana tried again. This next point was designed to gain sympathy for the poor, unfortunate man with whom she had spent the night. "Joey closed his eyes the minute his head hit the pillow," she said. Of course, he opened them again right after I finished my shower and came out of the bathroom, she recalled, but they were closed for a little while.

Roman's dark gray eyes still held a trace of suspicion.

Diana forced herself to carry on. "The poor man had a head injury, remember?" she finished. That didn't stop me from spending the whole night curled up against him, though, did it now? She watched Roman, trying to gauge his reaction. She wouldn't blame him if he didn't believe her. Her story had more holes than a wheel of Swiss cheese.

From the look on Roman's face, he wasn't buying it. Usually, Diana would do anything for her brother's approval. This time, for some reason, his lack of faith in her judgment made her angry.

"All right, Roman," she said in a voice oozing with sarcasm. "You want the truth? Well, here it is: I spent the whole night having sex with Joey Finch in that huge king-sized bed. And that was despite his head injury, my attempted kidnapping, and the fact that both of us were completely exhausted. And, let me tell you, he was magnificent." She had risen from the couch to stand in front of her brother with her hands on her hips, daring him to say a word.

"Whoa, now, sis." Roman grinned. "Don't go all crazy on me."

Diana watched the tension drain from his body...the complete opposite of the reaction she expected.

"Calm down," he advised, flopping into the chair beside the couch. "It's all good." He stretched his legs out in front of him regarding her with amusement. Diana stared at him in complete confusion "Roman, I don't understand you at all. You get all worked up when I mention sleeping in a chair, but when I come right out and talk about having sex—"

"That's because, little sister, I'm one step ahead of you." Roman waggled his eyebrows at his perplexed sibling. "You would never have said the word sex *if anything really happened between you and Finch, especially not in front of Mom."*

Lucinda didn't move. She only glanced at her son for a moment before her eyes returned to her sketchpad.

Nobody said anything for a few seconds. Lucinda continued to sketch. Roman basked in the glow of his assumptions. And Diana breathed a silent sigh of relief for her narrow escape.

"All right," Lucinda said, turning the sketchpad around to show her work. "Here she is. What do you think?"

Her mother was, without a doubt, the most talented person Diana knew. Period. It had been nearly a decade since Lucinda received the prestigious Caldecott Medal as the artist of Split, Splat, Where's My Hat?*—one of the bestselling children's picture books of all time.*

Since then, the accolades had continued for her illustrations in such well-known works as: Fish, Wish, Ice Cream in a Dish; School is So Cool; *and Graham Spencer's beloved* Little Billy *series. Currently Lucinda was involved with Pandora Newgate's travel series,* Over the River and Down the Hill*—or, as Roman liked to call them, the* Where the Hell Are We Now? Books. *And, of course, the* Nanny Di *series.*

Diana and Roman studied the sketch their mother had just completed. The Jolly Judge sat behind her bench, gavel in hand, peering at them over her reading glasses. Her light-colored hair curled around her shoulders; the lacy collar of her robe was a decidedly elegant touch.

"I like the way she looks." Diana was pleased. "She's strong and feminine."

"Is that supposed to be Judge Eldridge?" Roman asked, purposely mentioning the least attractive member of Alexandria's legal community.

"Of course not." Lucinda laughed, giving her son a smart smack on the hand.

"Ow," Roman yelped, grinning.

For the first time since her brother had barged into the library that morning, Diana began to relax.

"I don't know if she looks jolly enough, though," Diana mused. "What do you think, Roman?"

"I think she looks constipated," her irrepressible brother replied.

Both Diana and her mother burst out laughing. Lucinda turned the sketchpad around and went to work. A few minutes later, her children gave their wholehearted approval to the final sketch of the jollier, decidedly unconstipated-looking judge.

"What's next after Nanny Di and the Jolly Judge?" Roman asked. "Nanny Di and the Ballsy Bailiff?"

" 'Ballsy'?" Diana asked. "Is that even a word?"

"It's a guy-word," Roman informed her smugly.

"Nanny Di and the Loveable Lawyer," Lucinda answered, giving her daughter an approving smile. She was quite proud of Diana's newest series.

" 'Nanny Di and the Loveable Lawyer,' " Roman repeated. "Finally, a book about me." He thoroughly enjoyed the commiserating look exchanged by his sister and his mother. "Let me know when you want me to pose for the cover, Mom," he joked, rising from his chair.

"Where are you going?" Diana asked, trying not to laugh at his antics.

"To work out, of course." Roman flexed his impressive biceps and gave his sister a wink. "I'm doing it for you, Diana. If I have to take my shirt off to pose for your book cover, I've got to look good."

Diana burst out laughing as her overconfident brother strutted out of the room.

"He's always had such low self-esteem, poor dear," Lucinda observed wryly. She carefully tore a page from her sketchbook and folded it before rising from the couch.

"Where are you going?" Diana asked.

"I'm going to call Lani and give her an update," Lucinda replied. She had called her best friend and sister-in-law Allana by her nickname "Lani" since they were little girls.

"But you just talked to Aunt Allana yesterday," Diana said. "And there isn't anything to update."

"Then I'll tell her there's no update to the update," Lucinda said, philosophically. She handed Diana the folded page she had torn from her sketchbook.

Diana took the paper without unfolding it. "What's this?" she asked.

"My preliminary sketch for the Loveable Lawyer," Lucinda said, heading for the door.

Diana was puzzled. "Why the secrecy, Mom? You could have shown me the sketch and taken Roman down a few notches at the same time."

Her mother laughed. "I don't think Roman is quite ready to see this sketch yet."

Diana wrinkled her forehead. "But, Mom, I don't understand."

Lucinda paused in the doorway. "You will," she said over her shoulder, before disappearing into the hallway. Her soft trill of laughter echoed behind her.

Wondering what her mother was up to, Diana unfolded the sketch. She gasped in surprise. The man staring back at her was an exact likeness of the most loveable lawyer she knew.

Diana realized Joey's presence at Heart's Ease would have added an awkward element to an already awkward situation...at least while Roman was stomping about. But that didn't make her miss the rascally Mr. Finch any less, especially after her family returned to Virginia. And it didn't make her stop wondering where Joey was and what he was doing. Or… with whom.

So, Diana tried to convince herself that Joey was very busy moving back to Honeysuckle Creek. Moving was hard work, she told herself. And exhausting. But more than that, moving was a legitimate reason for his absence. And before she had time to worry—the very next Saturday, in fact—he walked into the kitchen at Heart's Ease and helped himself to breakfast. To her delight, she found that nothing had changed. He was still overflowing with wisecracks, charm, and wicked smiles.

The attraction was still there, too. As the days passed, she could feel that attraction simmering between them, like a banked fire. Adding a few logs could make the glowing embers burst into flame. *Or a big bucket of water could extinguish the fire altogether,* she reminded herself soberly. Since Joey made no move either to fuel or to douse the embers, Diana was left to wonder. She had seen him every day for the last three weeks, she told herself. That had to mean something, didn't it? Or did it? She didn't have the slighted idea.

"Are you positive you don't want us to stay here?" Grace asked. She watched Diana's face, anxiously, for any sign that she had changed her mind about keeping Amalie while Grace and the others went out. "You know we wouldn't mind a bit."

Diana smiled at Grace's concern. "It was my idea, remember? And…" From the corner of her eye, Diana caught a flash of movement at the bend of the driveway. Joey's white F-150 came into view. She couldn't help the pleasant tingle of anticipation that rushed through her. It looked like Mr. Finch was going to make an appearance, after all.

Grace followed Diana's gaze. "What a surprise," she intoned in a voice that said she wasn't surprised at all.

Diana looked down, inquiringly, into Grace's sparkling green eyes. What must it be like, she wondered, to be so perfectly petite? "Is Joey meeting you here to go to dinner?" she asked.

"No, he isn't." Grace smiled. "Darcie said he wasn't going with us. It looks like he's here to see you."

Diana regarded Joey's sister uncertainly. Convincing herself that Joey probably wouldn't return the next day had become a nightly ritual.

Grace's eyes were full of mischief. "And, Diana, just so you know, I've never seen Joey make this kind of an effort for any woman. So"—Grace winked—"don't make it too easy for him," she said, before walking outside to join Blane, Devin, and Darcie.

Diana couldn't help the warm feeling that swept through her at Grace's confident assumption. If only it were true, she thought wistfully. But only for a moment. Allowing herself too much wishful thinking wasn't a good idea, so she hurried outside to join the others.

CHAPTER TWENTY-SIX

*J*oey quickly realized that heading to Heart's Ease—and Diana—after work was the right decision. He was glad he hadn't changed his mind after his conversation at the office with Darcie. A few feet away, Honeysuckle Creek burbled through myriad boulders and smaller rocks, creating a series of small waterfalls. The sound of falling water added to the happy cacophony of singing birds, crickets, and Amalie's giggles. The little girl was playing with Atticus—Blane and Grace's three-legged dog—on the lawn a few yards away. Joey was seated on a blanket. And beside him was the woman he couldn't stop thinking about.

Diana seemed delighted by the swift-moving water. And Joey, of course, was delighted by Diana. She sat with her legs stretched out in front of her. Pretty as a picture. Her gorgeous hair was pulled into a simple knot on top of her head. She was wearing a black tank top, woven, or crocheted or something—Joey wasn't sure—and white cut-off jean shorts. He was still enjoying the way those shorts made her long legs appear even longer, not to mention the way they molded to the rest of her tight, little assets. Thinking about those assets too much made Joey's own assets a little too tight....

All his thoughts centered around the woman beside him. Nothing unusual about that, he thought ruefully. He was a healthy male lusting after a female whose every breath was too damn inviting. Diana might not realize her own appeal, but Joey did. He realized her appeal every minute of every day. His brain wasn't whole anymore. Instead, his faulty cerebrum was unable to function without thoughts of a certain redhead running through it. That's why he was still here—two hours later—watching the sun slowly dip behind the distant mountains. The glowing orb, it seemed, was in no hurry to leave this glorious vista. And neither was he. At least, he wasn't in any hurry to leave Diana—a glorious vista in her own right. In fact, Joey didn't want to go to dinner or sing karaoke or do much of anything anymore that didn't involve Diana.

Except for his meticulously planned career path, Joey hadn't spent a lot of time thinking about the next fifty years. Now, he was surprised to feel a strong sense of anticipation regarding his own future. That statement alone—so completely out of character—was a clear indication of how far he had fallen. He felt turmoil in ever unfortunate part of his body. He glanced at Diana; he was unable not to.

Diana's pure profile met his hungry eyes. Porcelain skin with just a smattering of freckles. She had freckles on her shoulders, too. He would like to connect those freckles. With his lips. But…

Were he and Diana on the same page? For once in his life, Joey was afraid to find out. They had agreed that they shared an attraction. But he still remembered the shining happiness on Diana's face when he confirmed that he wasn't a *relationship kind of guy*. What had she said? That they could just be friends, then.

The more he thought about it, the more that simple remark annoyed him. Especially since he made the remarkable discovery that he *was* a relationship kind of guy. He always had been. He just hadn't found the *right* relationship. Or maybe he hadn't had enough courage to acknowledge the *right* relationship. It had taken a collision with a brick to open his eyes.

Would he have been as eager to embrace the prophecy of the brick if he felt no attraction whatsoever for the woman he was with? What if the brick had fallen on his head when he was talking to Shirley? He was honest enough to admit he would have laughed the whole thing off instead of considering it an act of God. But since it happened with Diana, he *wanted* it to be an act of God.

He stole another glance at the lady in question. She was as comfortable eating pizza out of a cardboard box as she would have been dining in a five-star restaurant. As content with her dinner companions—a lovesick lawyer, a five-year-old child, a stuffed iguana, and a damp three-legged dog—as she would have been with Newport's highest society. Currently, she was gazing at the sky, watching the puffy clouds reflect the beginnings of—what was certain to be—a spectacular sunset. At least, that's what Joey thought she was doing. That's what he would be doing if he was completely unaffected by her presence. And Diana appeared completely unaffected by...him. *Well, hell.*

How, he wondered, could she be so damn unaffected? Couldn't she feel the simmering heat that was building between them? The lightning strike when his skin accidentally bumped hers? His all-encompassing, unavoidable fascination with another person—namely herself? What if she *couldn't* feel it? Joey asked himself with a feeling of mild panic. What if it was all one-sided? What if he had finally met the right woman but she didn't think he was the right man?

Diana could look at the beautiful waters of Honeysuckle Creek all day. She could also look at Joey Finch all day. But that was an entirely different issue. She found herself equal parts flattered and confused that he had chosen to stay at Heart's Ease with her instead of going out to dinner. Was it possible he had decided to focus his attentions solely on her? While an appealing thought, it was also quite laughable. Joey Finch was a one and done, she reminded herself, firmly, a no-relationship kind of guy. She had to remember that all of this—the fun conversations, the shared laughter, the connection—would come to an end.

Eventually.

Joey was staring at the creek, miles away. Diana wondered what he was thinking about. She hoped he wasn't, even now, planning his escape. She sighed, lying back on the blanket to study the sky. The clouds were lightly tinged with the myriad hues of sunset. Yellow. Orange. Red. The colors were glorious. But what did Joey think? Was he as enthralled by nature's awe-inspiring display as she was? Probably not, she decided. Another quick glance confirmed the enigmatic Mr. Finch wasn't even looking at the clouds. He was still staring at the creek. Just...staring.

Drat. Joey was probably bored, she decided. What if he was bored? She wasn't one to chatter all the time. Joey *seemed* to enjoy the comfortable quiet that sometimes settled between them. But, what if he didn't? What if he regretted spending time with her when he could have been picking up girls in a karaoke bar? What if he was trying to come up with a polite way to leave without hurting her feelings? She knew he would never intentionally hurt her feelings. He was, after all, a really nice guy...just *not the relationship kind.* Blah, blah, blah. *Drat.*

Much to her relief, Joey surprised her. Instead of getting up and making some excuse to leave, he flopped back on the blanket beside her. Diana's heart beat a little faster. They hadn't been this close since the Acorn Knob Inn, except for one rather unfortunate collision during a volleyball game the previous week. And that was an accident, so it didn't count.

Hmm. Now that she thought about it, the past two hours made up the one and only time she had been alone with Joey Finch since she arrived at Heart's Ease. Well, she amended, alone if she didn't count Amalie playing nearby. How strange. She mulled it over in her mind.

Or was it strange? What if their lack of alone time wasn't by coincidence, but by design? But if so, whose design? Devin, her overprotective cousin? Joey's siblings? Or was it Mr. Finch himself who wished to keep her at arm's length? Whoever it was must have changed his—or her—mind. At present, the only thing separating her from Joey was a stuffed iguana whose plastic eyes regarded her with interest.

"What do you see?" asked the complicated man beside her. He was peering at the cloud formations intently.

"I think I see a horse," she said. "Galloping into the sunset."

Joey grinned. "Good effort. But, what about the castle? Do you see that?"

"Castle?" Diana asked. "Where?" She searched the vast space above her head.

He pointed to the far side of the sky. "Do you see it now?"

She shook her head.

Joey reached between them to move Iggy. Then he slid over until his hip touched hers. He took her hand and pointed in the direction of the castle.

"Oh," she whispered. "Now, I see it…." The heat of Joey's hand made Diana's skin tingle. The delicious, shivery feeling spread rapidly up her arm and beyond.

The brief contact of his hip against hers ran through Joey like a bolt of electricity. He lowered their arms to rest between them but didn't release her hand. Instead, he twined his fingers with hers. A perfect fit, he thought with satisfaction. Of course, that made him wonder if all of her would fit all of him just as perfectly. *Easy, Finch*, he admonished himself. He had decided, earlier, to go slowly—testing the waters, as it were—before jumping into the deep end. Holding hands was a good place to start.

Diana's breathy little gasp of awareness severed the threads of Joey's good intentions: they vanished like the rapidly changing cloud formations. He turned his head toward her only to find her watching him. The intensity in his eyes made Diana's heart pound. Every part of her body responded to his touch.

Amalie's squeal of laughter followed by a loud splash broke the moment as effectively as a dousing with creek water. Joey's heart started pounding for an entirely different reason. He cautiously propped himself on his elbows to survey the damage, releasing Diana's hand in the process.

Diana sat straight up, looking around frantically. How could she have forgotten her small charge so completely? To her everlasting relief, Amalie remained safe and dry on the bank of the creek. Unfortunately, the same could not be said for Atticus. The dog resembled a furry seal cavorting in the creek. He jumped from rock to rock then into the water, sometimes submerging his whole body. Amalie's claps and giggles only encouraged his antics.

With regret, Joey watched Diana's sensual fog fade away, even as he applauded her sense of duty.

"Amalie Rose Merritt!" Diana shouted. "You better not put one single toe in that water! Your daddy did *not* give you permission for a swim! And neither did Mama Darcie!"

"I won't, Nanny Di!" Amalie yelled back quickly. "I promise!"

Apparently, Joey realized, the triple-name threat still worked as well as it had when he was a little boy. Hearing *Joseph Ezekiel Finch* in that tone of voice would have made him promise Diana just about anything. He couldn't help but chuckle at her effortless transformation from red-haired siren to formidable nanny. Until her narrowed gaze focused on him.

Diana was barely able to think clearly—or breathe, for that matter—and Joey was laughing? *At* her? Or *with* her? She glanced at him again. No, definitely *at* her. *Drat.* "And what are you laughing at, Joey Finch?" she demanded.

Joey stretched back out on the blanket, trying not to grin. At least Diana only used *two* of his names. "Oh, nothing," he said, folding his hands behind his head. His eyes searched the sky. "Just checking out the clouds." Diana's horse, he decided, now resembled a dog seated on his hindquarters and begging for a treat. The castle had taken on the appearance of an elongated football stadium.

Diana huffed out an annoyed breath and lay back onto the blanket. She wasn't sure why she was so annoyed. Only that she was.

Joey tried to think of something to say to bring a smile back to his companion's lovely face. "So…how are things going for Ezekiel and Genevieve these days?"

Diana answered the question more honestly than she intended, distracted by her racing heart. "Ezekiel is trying to convince Genevieve that he's reformed, that he's not a rake anymore." Diana couldn't quite hide her rueful smile. "She wants to believe him, but she can't quite decide if she should trust him."

Her words lodged in Joey's brain. *Ouch.* A direct hit. Diana couldn't be talking about him, could she? Of course not, he told himself, because he—like his fictional counterpart, Ezekiel—wasn't a rake anymore. Or even a rascal. He was reformed. And the proof was right beside him. After seeing Diana every day for the last three weeks, he still couldn't get enough of her. Nothing one-and-done about that, he decided.

As a matter of fact, he wasn't sure that he would ever get enough of her. She was his siren. She fulfilled his every need, desire, and fantasy. She filled his heart and soul so completely there wasn't room for any other woman. And there never would be. *Well, hell,* he thought. Was he in love with her? What if he was in love with her? And what if he told her and she didn't believe him because she didn't think she could trust him? The idea that Diana might not trust him was alarming. He scrambled into a seated position.

"What can Ezekiel do, Diana? he asked somewhat at a loss. "What can the earl do so Genevieve will believe him?" What began as Joey's attempt at a lighthearted conversation suddenly had a life of its own.

"I don't know," she said, softly. And she didn't. There was no right answer to Joey's question. She had no idea what would tip the scales. She felt like she was hurtling toward the edge of a cliff. And she didn't know whether to hold onto the ledge or take the hand of the man beside her and jump. What she did know was that any immunity she had garnered against the charms of Joey Finch had faded away like morning mist.

He found himself desperate for a response. "There has to be something I…um, Ezekiel, can do."

Joey's urgency awakened some provocative little imp of whom Diana was, until now, unaware. She didn't recognize the voice that spoke up next. "He could kiss her," the sultry voice suggested.

Kiss her? Diana almost looked around for the owner of the mysterious voice. *Who said that?* she wondered until she realized the truth. *Good Lord. It was me.* Her mouth had just taken over, independent of her brain. Her question certainly got Joey's attention, though. His dark eyes got even darker, if that was possible. He was looking at her as if she was the last chocolate twirl in the box.

Kiss her.

The suggestion had come straight from the peach-colored lips that Joey had been fantasizing about for days. Weeks. Maybe years. He propped himself on one elbow. He leaned over and tucked a long curl behind Diana's sexy, little ear. He had never considered that ears could be sexy, but Diana's were. Along with the rest of her.

"And what will the lovely Lady Genevieve do if Ezekiel takes such a chance?" he asked, in a husky voice. Diana's eyes were glowing. What he saw in their depths called to him. She was entirely too tempting.

"Hmm...she might slap him," she teased, waiting to see what he would do. She hoped he couldn't hear her heart pounding.

He leaned closer. "I don't think I like that option," he said, his eyes boring into hers.

"Or..." the imp whispered, "...she might just kiss him back."

He could read the unconscious invitation in her dark, gray eyes. His own eyes fell to her lips—her soft, peach-colored lips. He studied them, noting the brief distance between her lips and his own. He placed his other hand on the opposite side of the blanket, so he was leaning over her. *Better*, his carnal self exulted. Yes, this was much better. His lips were scant inches from their destination....

"Uncle Joey!" Amalie's voice broke the spell. "Are you and Nanny Di playing *Sleeping Beauty*?" she asked.

"Amalie!" Diana sat straight up, smacking her forehead on Joey's chin. "Ow," she exclaimed, glaring at the offending chin.

"What?" he asked, in a disgruntled voice. "It wasn't *my* fault." He rubbed his chin, moving his jaw back and forth.

Amalie danced around them, happily oblivious to what she had interrupted. "Hurray! Sleeping Beauty is awake! That means you must be a magical prince, Uncle Joey, because she woke up *without* a kiss. I know you didn't want to kiss her because that would be nasty! *Real* kissing is nasty," she confided. "Daddy says so. Daddy says I shouldn't kiss a boy until I'm thirty-bejillion-something years old."

Atticus chose that moment to rejoin their party after a particularly deep foray into the creek. He jumped on the blanket, inserting himself between Diana and Joey. Without warning, he shook off every drop of water from every part of his scraggly fur. Water flew from his head, his three dirty paws, and everywhere in between. His ear flapped. His tail swung back and forth. When he was finished, he plopped down on the blanket, put his face on his paws, and sighed contentedly.

Amalie laughed delightedly. She might as well have been rolling in the creek *with* the troublemaking canine. Her clothes were soaking wet. Droplets of muddy water ran down her face and off the tip of her nose. "Oh, Atticus, you're so funny! Don't you think he's funny, Uncle Joey?"

"Oh, yeah," Joey said, drily. "He's hilarious."

Diana couldn't stop the tiny giggle that bubbled up in her throat. She wasn't sure if it was hilarity or hysteria—maybe a little bit of both—but she couldn't hold it back. Joey was a mess. His pristine blue polo shirt was covered with spots of muddy water. Apparently, Atticus had stepped on him when he jumped between them: two doggie-sized footprints stained his khaki shorts. His hair was dripping with water, and a purple bruise decorated the tip of his chin. Diana burst out laughing.

Joey grinned ruefully. He couldn't help it. Her laughter was contagious. He had to join in, even as he regretted the bright red spot on Diana's forehead, courtesy of his chin. Diana had fared little better than Joey. She too, was dripping with creek water. It ran down her cheeks and dripped from the little tendrils of auburn hair that had come loose from her topknot. Drops of water spotted her tank top and shorts, but she had been spared the muddy feet of the happily relaxed dog that currently lay between them.

Amalie stopped dancing and pointed toward the house. "Daddy and Mama Darcie are home," she squealed. "And Auntie Grace and Uncle Blane!"

Sure enough, the unwelcome foursome was heading across the lawn. Diana's startled eyes met Joey's before she quickly looked away.

"Sorry about your forehead," he whispered. Under the circumstances, they were the only words he could manage.

Diana could only nod. She leapt to her feet, overcome by the urgent need to gather Amalie's belongings. Was her nanny-like behavior prompted by the unexpected appearance of her employer? Or—as Joey suspected—was her impromptu exhibition of good citizenship the result of a desire to avoid the curious eyes of the intruders? Joey was betting on the latter. His appreciative gaze followed her to the water's edge. As Diana bent to retrieve a plastic ball and bat, he realized he had fallen under the scrutiny of the overly observant little girl beside him.

"Uncle Joey," Amalie asked, her big blue eyes full of hope. "Are you going to marry Nanny Di?"

"Am I going to...what?" Amalie had his full attention now. Joey glanced toward the house, thankful the nosy quartet was still too far away to hear this entirely unexpected conversation.

Amalie was completely serious. "Marry Nanny Di," she said. "You have to, Uncle Joey. If you don't marry her then somebody else will. And she'll move away. And we won't be together anymore."

Joey was speechless. Marriage? *Good Lord.* He was still reeling from the realization that he was, indeed, a *relationship kind of guy.* However, the idea that Amalie put into his head had never occurred to him. Diana? Married to someone else? *His* Diana? Yes, *his* Diana, he admitted to himself. She had been *his* Diana for quite a while now. At least in his head. And in his heart. What if *his* Diana married somebody else? What if she moved away? What if he couldn't talk with her? Or laugh with her? Or hold her hand? Or just look at her?

A cold, hard knot formed in Joey's stomach at the thought. Because, well...he could see it happening. Easily. Diana was practically irresistible. What single guy in his right mind *wouldn't* want her? The thought of Diana marrying anyone was completely unacceptable. Unless—his brain whispered automatically—the person she married was none other than Joey Finch.

That was it, he decided. That was the answer. The perfect solution to his dilemma. He almost smiled with relief. Was he going to sit back and let some other guy marry his siren? Hell no, he wasn't. Who was he to argue with a falling brick? He would marry her himself. What a brilliant idea, he congratulated himself. *Joey Finch, you are some kind of a freakin' genius.* He was going to marry Diana Merritt. But...

A terrible thought stopped him in mid-plan. He nearly growled with the frustration of it. What if his feelings were one-sided? What if Diana wasn't *interested* in marrying Joey Finch? What if she wouldn't even go out with him? What if she wanted a relationship, but not with him? What would he do then? Darcie's words came roaring back to haunt him once again: *"You just wait, Joey Finch, you're going to fall in love with some poor, unsuspecting woman eventually. It's only a matter of time. And when that momentous day comes, I hope with all my heart that the lady of your dreams doesn't give you the time of day."*

Joey glowered at Darcie as she approached. He couldn't help it. This was all, without a doubt, her fault.

Or, at least, quite possibly, her fault.

Or, at least, partially her fault.

Or not.

In reality, Joey knew he had no one to blame but his too-cool-pretend-to-be-a-player-one-and-done self. Yes, he acknowledged, grimly, he was one hundred percent to blame. *Damn it.*

Before Joey could move, he was surrounded by his siblings and their significant others. They were happily talking and laughing, obviously enjoying themselves. He envied them their ignorance of Amalie's earth-shattering revelation. He felt as if his very foundation had been ripped from beneath his feet.

"What happened to karaoke?" Diana asked, joining the group.

She looked calm, poised, and completely put-together, with none of the insecurities that were Joey's new companions. *Damn it again.*

"What happened?" Darcie repeated, her eyes brimming with laughter. "Oh, the drama."

Grace took up the story from there. "The newly hired assistant cook forgot to take a pizza out of the oven. The kitchen filled with smoke and the poor guy freaked out and pulled the fire alarm," she explained. "It was an accident. He's only seventeen."

"You mean the newly *fired* assistant cook," Devin added.

"I doubt it," Blane said. "According to Evander, the fire alarm puller is the owner's nephew. Poor kid had never cooked a pizza in his life. Except in the microwave."

Darcie grinned. "Maybe they should have started him out wiping tables until he got the hang of working in a restaurant."

"Anyway, we left after the fire department evacuated the building. So, what have y'all been up to?" Grace asked, innocently.

Diana's eyes met Joey's before darting away.

Amalie, blissfully unaware of the tension, offered her version of events. "We ate pizza, Auntie Grace, and it was *so* yummy! Then I played with Atticus, but he decided to swim in the creek. I didn't even put one toe in the water, Daddy, because you and Mama Darcie didn't say I could." Her angelic smile fooled no one.

Darcie took in Amalie's still soggy clothes and damp hair. She raised her eyebrows at the little girl. "And you are soaking wet because...?"

Diana held her breath. She knew from experience that Amalie could *oh-so-innocently* complicate a situation. *Blame Atticus, Amalie,* she silently encouraged the little girl. *Please blame Atticus.*

As if she could hear her nanny's plea, Amalie complied. "Atticus shook water all over me," she explained, earnestly. The little girl showed Darcie the water spots on the front and back of her T-shirt and shorts.

Diana started breathing again. She exchanged a conspiratorial glance with Joey. Perhaps, she hoped, what almost happened on the blanket would stay on the blanket.

Amalie hopped up and down with excitement. "Guess what?" she asked. "Nanny Di and Uncle Joey played *Sleeping Beauty.*"

Or perhaps not.

Diana nearly groaned aloud.

"Nanny Di was the princess!" Amalie continued, happily. "And Uncle Joey was the prince! But Nanny Di woke up before Uncle Joey had to kiss her. I bet Uncle Joey was glad he didn't have to kiss her. Kissing is nasty. Right, Daddy?" she asked, turning to her father for confirmation.

"That's right, 'Malie," Devin concurred. "Kissing *is* nasty. No kissing for you until you are forty-five." He pinned his single eye on Diana's guilty face.

"Now, Devin," Darcie said, laughing, but her own eyes were focused on her brother's flushed face. She smiled smugly. "Kissing isn't *that* nasty, is it, Uncle Joey?"

Joey wanted to throw her into the creek.

But Darcie wasn't finished. "So, what happened to your chin?" she asked. "It looks a little bruised."

Amalie graciously supplied the answer. "Nanny Di sat up too fast and bumped it with her head." She pointed at the red splotch on Diana's forehead. "See."

"Sat up?" Devin inquired suspiciously.

Diana ignored him. "Just a little accident," she said. "At least Joey didn't end up in the emergency room again." With that pitiful attempt to change the subject, she threw the proverbial ball into Joey's court.

But instead of dribbling down court, Joey just sat there. Waiting. And knowing, without question, that he was doomed. And, sure enough, it didn't take long.

"So, what fell off that scaffold and hit you in the head anyway?" Darcie asked her brother. "You never told us. Was it a hammer, or something?"

Diana opened her mouth, but Joey jumped in before she could answer. There was no way in hell he wanted the nosy quartet to hear the word *brick*. The members of said quartet referenced that prophetic conversation all the time as it was. They would never shut up if they knew the prophecy had been fulfilled.

"Oh, just some construction stuff," he improvised. "You know, stuff you'd find on any scaffold."

"What were you doing under a scaffold, anyway?" Devin asked, curiously.

Joey narrowed his eyes at Diana. *Don't say it,* he telegraphed silently. *They will never let me hear the end of it if you say it.*

Diana raised her eyebrows. *You deserve it,* she telegraphed back, her gray eyes full of merriment. *You know you deserve it.*

She was right. Joey knew it. She was going to throw him under the bus.

"He was dancing under it," Diana volunteered. "Trying to show me how safe scaffolds really are."

"Oh, ha, ha, ha, Diana," Joey said, watching the delighted reactions of his *loving* family. "You are *so* funny." He wrapped his arms around himself, pretending to shiver. "It sure is cold down here under this bus," he said.

"I have to admit, his moves were impressive," Diana explained to her rapt audience. "Right up until he ran into the scaffold."

"Oh, Joey…" Grace sighed, shaking her head.

Devin laughed, enjoying himself a little too much for Joey's liking. "Funny, but I never figured you for a dancer."

"He has an extensive skill set," Blane said, grinning at his long-time friend.

Everyone, it seemed, was enjoying his discomfort immensely.

Everyone, that is, except Darcie.

She merely looked annoyed. "You still haven't answered my question, Joey," she said. "What kind of construction stuff? What was it, exactly, that fell on your head? What's the big secret?"

"It was a brick." Diana innocently delivered the information that sealed his doom. "Thank goodness it was only the one. There were several that were really close to the edge of the scaffold."

Joey's sisters and their significant others could only stare.

Amalie chose that moment to resume her prattling. "It was *so* funny when Atticus jumped on the blanket and sprayed us all with water!" she said, blissfully unaware of the undercurrents swirling around her. "Uncle Joey said it was hi-larry-us. What's hi-larry-us?"

"Hilarious," Diana said, automatically. "He said it was hilarious."

"'Hilarious,'" Amalie repeated, dutifully. "Nanny Di, what's hilarious?"

Diana chose that moment to extricate herself from the situation before Amalie could say anything worse. "That means funny, 'Malie. And since we are covered with hilarious creek water, it's probably a good time for a bath." She took the little girl's hand and started across the lawn.

"With bubbles, Nanny Di? Amalie asked excitedly. "Can I have bubbles, please? The strawberry kind?"

Diana's answer died away on the light breeze.

Joey watched until Diana and Amalie disappeared into the house. Even though he knew what was coming he couldn't stop himself from enjoying the view. With a sigh, he turned his head, unsurprised to find himself under the intense scrutiny of the nosiest and most annoying human beings he had ever had the misfortune to know.

"What?" he asked irritably.

"Oh, nothing," Darcie replied, smugly. "We're just glad you and Diana had a good time." She hesitated only a fraction of a second before adding, "Prince Charming." She was smiling her cat-at-the-mouse-hole smile for the second time that day.

Grace's hands were clasped in front of her heart. She was regarding Joey as if he was the hero in one of the musicals she loved so much.

Blane's lips quirked up into a pleased grin.

As for Devin…well, the expression in his single eye was a little harder to read. Diana worked for him, yes, but she was also family. He reached out to put a firm hand on Joey's shoulder.

"Finch," he said. "You have my approval for now, but if you hurt her, I'll kick your ass." With a none-too-gentle squeeze, he released Joey's shoulder.

Darcie, of course, couldn't resist the opportunity to torment her brother a little longer. "Just tell me one thing," Joey's irrepressible sister implored. "Was it a *big* brick?"

Diana didn't allow herself to process the events of the past two hours until Amalie was up to her neck in strawberry-scented bubbles. The memory of Joey's burning gaze sent all kinds of possibilities through her mind. No one had ever looked at her the way he'd looked at her tonight. He would have kissed her if Amalie hadn't interrupted them. And, Diana admitted, she would have let him. Let him? Ha. She had practically begged him to kiss her—in the convenient guise of Lady Genevieve, of course. That fictitious lady had a lot more courage than Diana.

At least Genevieve was *trying* to give Ezekiel the benefit of the doubt, Diana thought. Maybe she should take notes. Maybe she should give Joey the chance to prove he, too, had reformed. Whatever he thought about relationships, he was obviously interested in pursuing *something* with her. For now, anyway. That meant he must feel *something* for her other than dratted friendship. Didn't it?

But, she worried, what if it was only lust? She hoped that what Joey felt for her was more than lust. Or maybe he was sticking around for the thrill of the chase. She really hoped it wasn't just the thrill of the chase. Diana flinched as a handful of bubbles hit her mouth, sliding down under her chin.

Amalie exploded into giggles. "Nanny Di has a beard!"

Diana shook her "beard" from side to side. Then she reached into the tub, scooping up bubbles with both hands. Grinning, she piled the sweet-smelling suds on top of the little girl's head. "Amalie has a pointy head," she said, enjoying the little girl's giggles.

The past two hours had brought one issue into clear focus. Regardless of the outcome, it was time to take a chance on the mutual attraction she shared with Joey Finch. Nine years was long enough to wait, she decided with the optimism of a lady who had, recently, almost been kissed. Besides...what did she have to lose? Only her heart, she chided herself. But it was too late to worry about that. There was no doubt in her mind... If Joey asked her out on a date, she was going to say yes.

CHAPTER TWENTY-SEVEN

*D*iana was going to say no. No to Joey Finch. No to any kind of outing, picnic, restaurant, movie, ballgame, or anything that could possibly be defined as a date. She had learned quite a lot about the rascally Mr. Finch during her first five days of freedom. Most of it unsolicited.

She didn't know why she was even the least bit disconcerted to discover that Honeysuckle Creek, North Carolina, wasn't a whole lot different than Farther, Virginia. Nor why she was at all surprised at the interest generated by her move to the small town. After all, where she grew up, sticking one's nose into other people's business was almost a divine right. The fact that nearly everyone Diana met already knew who she was meant that *she*, unfortunately, was the current topic of conversation.

And, of course, in typical, small-town fashion, each person had already formed some sort of opinion about her as well. Diana deemed her association with the Finch family fortunate, as was her own reputation as the author of the *Nanny Di* books. For the most part, she was received with genuine warmth and friendliness. But she didn't know whether to be amused or horrified at the overwhelming assumption that she was Joey Finch's latest objective. The horrifying part was her own secret wish to be just that. Diana, however, didn't want to be the latest. She wanted to be the *last*. Hence the problem.

Since their first-kiss-that-wasn't came to such an abrupt end nearly a week ago, she had noticed a subtle shift in the attentions of the unpredictable Mr. Finch. Oh, they still laughed and joked around; still talked about everything under the sun. That hadn't changed. But the intensity between them seemed to ramp up a little bit more every day. The banked heat in Joey's eyes was a little hotter, scorching wherever it touched. He sat a little closer to her, then went out of his way to brush her hand or arm. *Accidentally,* of course. And it seemed that whenever she glanced at him, he was watching her. Under the circumstances she was forced to discontinue her favorite hobby, namely, watching him. And his continued appearance at Heart's Ease every evening was very encouraging.

Less encouraging, however, were the offhand comments, jokes, and words of "advice" she received from her new acquaintances. Everyone, it seemed, had something to say about Joey Finch and *his current objective.* Something Diana—the aforementioned *objective*—quickly discovered on Monday after her first class at Broad's Yoga Studio.

After dropping Amalie at school, Diana had spent that first day of freedom exploring her new home. The downtown area of Honeysuckle Creek was loaded with charming shops, inviting restaurants, and a lovely park. What could be better? She thoroughly enjoyed herself.

The intermediate yoga class she had chosen was just difficult enough to be challenging. And the instructor and the participants of the class—all except three Mallory look-alikes in the back corner—were friendly and encouraging. Yes, everything was going well, right up to the minute she walked out of the studio.

As soon as Diana stepped through the door, the three Mallory look-alikes—who proved to be Mallory *act*-alikes as well—surrounded her on the sidewalk. Her guard went up immediately. No doubt in her mind, this was an ambush.

Each of the women introduced themselves with varying degrees of fake Southern hospitality.

The first one smirked. "I'm Leslie," she said. Her eyes raked Diana from head to toe.

The second one smiled but Diana recognized the contemptuous look in her eyes. "I'm Liz," she announced, fluttering her eyelashes

The third one possessed the strongest Southern accent. "I'm Ca-as-sidy," she drawled.

I'm outnumbered, Diana thought. She knew all about false overtures of friendship from women like these. She had excelled at dodging them when she worked for Mallory. One wrong move on Diana's part and she had no doubt one of the predatory women—perhaps all three—would pounce.

"You're Di-ana," the one called Liz said, in a singsong voice. She sounded just like Amalie when the little girl was trying to wheedle Devin into buying her something she didn't need.

Diana pasted a bright smile on her face. "That's right. It's nice to meet you."

The three exchanged a look of pure joy, each assuming that Diana was as naïve as she seemed.

"So, tell us, Di-ana…I like saying your name," Cassidy said. "Di-a-na. Di-a-na."

"I bet Joey Finch likes saying Di-ana, too," Liz observed, her smile never reaching her eyes.

Oh, so that's it, Diana thought with annoyance. She didn't enjoy this kind of game.

Leslie glared at Liz before pinning a fake smile on her lips. "So, Di-ana," she purred. "Looks like you're the fla-avor of the month."

"Da-aily spe-cial," Cassidy added.

"Woman of the ho-ur," Liz chimed in.

They laughed uproariously, enjoying their own humor. All the while, they watched Diana for any sign that they had hit a nerve, eager to insert their barbs and innuendos in any visible cracks they could find—or cre-ate—in her armor.

Diana laughed along with them instead of rolling her eyes…surely a more appropriate response to such spiteful nonsense. She—unbe-knownst to the catty little trio—had been trained to handle bitchy by

Lucinda Merritt…an undisputed expert in the field. Her mother would reduce these three to cinders in a matter of seconds. And, although Diana wasn't quite that skilled, she could hold her own. She had seen worse. Much worse. Compared to Mallory, this trio of venomous women were unskilled amateurs.

"The daily special?" Diana asked, innocently. "You mean like banana pudding?"

"Yes," Leslie snorted. "Just like…" She paused to exchange a look with her malevolent friends. "No. That doesn't even make sense."

"It makes sense for two of them," Cassidy argued. "Fla-avor of the month and da-aily special. It just doesn't work for the wo-man of the ho-ur."

"Shut up, Cassidy," Liz hissed.

Diana smiled at the genuine confusion on their faces. "Y'all are so funny," she said.

Liz's catlike eyes were full of spite. "Actually," she stated, finally getting to the point. "What we have to tell you isn't funny at all."

"That's right." Cassidy nodded, raising her overplucked eyebrows. "We just wa-ant to wa-arn you."

"Yeah." Leslie was quick to agree.

"Warn me about what?" Diana asked, clutching her yoga bag to her chest.

Leslie almost snarled, "We just wanted to tell you to enjoy it while you can."

Diana made her eyes wide and limpid. "Enjoy what?"

The three women paused dramatically, exchanging knowing glances before answering at the same time: "Joey Finch."

Diana gasped. "What do you mean?" She looked from one to the other in apparent dismay.

"Well…" Cassidy explained, "…whether you know it or not. He's a *one and done*."

"*A one and done*," Liz intoned, obviously enjoying Diana's distress.

Leslie delivered the coup de grâce. "After one date, honey, he's done."

"Believe me, Di-a-na." Liz's voice oozed with fake sympathy. "We've all been in your shoes at one time or another."

Leslie nodded.

"I ha-aven't," Cassidy admitted, looking a little perplexed.

"He doesn't like short hair," Leslie said, reaching over to flip Cassidy's short locks.

"Well, I ca-an't help I have short ha-air," Cassidy muttered, a disgruntled frown on her face. "He doesn't like re-ed ha-air either. Or ta-all girls." Cassidy gestured to Diana, in frustration. "But he-ere she is."

Before Diana could learn anything else about Joey's supposed preferences, a new participant joined the fray. "All right, ladies. That's enough. You're blocking the sidewalk, not to mention my new display." The slightly bored voice came from Lou Boggs, owner of Looks by Lou. Diana had enjoyed meeting the tall, cool blonde at Blane and Grace's wedding. Lou was Grace's best friend and the designer of her stunning wedding dress.

Diana's tormentors fell all over each other in their eagerness to be noticed by the beautiful woman.

"Lou A-ann!" Leslie screeched. "My fav-o-rite person."

"We never see you anymore, Lou Ann," Liz whined.

"We miss you sooo much," added Cassidy, sadly.

Lou studied the trio for a second, her blue eyes full of disdain... and, perhaps, a touch of pity. "Uh-huh," was all she deigned to reply. She brushed off the fawning ladies to pull Diana into a hug. Lou's smile for Diana was warm and genuine. "I'm so glad to see you, honey. And you're right on time."

"I am?" Diana asked, returning her acquaintance's embrace. She wasn't quite sure what Lou was talking about, but she was willing to go along with whatever the savvy woman was up to.

"Of course," Lou said, stepping back and pulling Diana with her. She put her arm protectively around Diana's shoulders. They faced the egotistical bullies together.

Liz refused to back down. "On time for what?" she demanded.

"For her appointment, of course," Lou said, her expression hinting that Liz was slightly dense.

"She has an appo-ointment?" Cassidy whined. "I've tried to get an appo-ointment for six mo-onths."

Lou's smile was a little feral. "Busy, busy, busy," she said.

Leslie pouted. "Why does *she* need an appointment?"

"*Diana*," Lou said, emphasizing that "*she*" had a name, "has an appointment. I don't believe the reason for that appointment is any of your business."

Liz smiled slyly. "It's because she has a date with Joey Finch, isn't it?"

"We told he-er he's a *one and done*," Cassidy added, eager for Lou's confirmation.

Leslie shook her head at Diana's apparent gullibility. "She's wasting her money if it's because of Joey Finch," she said.

"Since when did you three become the Honeysuckle Creek Hospitality Committee?" Lou asked, in disgust. "You certainly know how to make a newcomer feel welcome, don't you? Ble-ess your selfish, little hea-arts." She easily slipped into an accent that must have originated in deepest Georgia.

Diana was pleased to see her trio of tormentors looked a little embarrassed.

Lou continued to scold them. "I don't suppose I need to point out that Diana's a famous author. The *Nanny Di* series, remember?" She paused, her words dripping with sarcasm. "No, ladies, don't even think of asking for her autograph. She has better things to do just now. As for the reason for her appointment, well, Diana has plenty of opportunities to wear designer originals." Lou paused again for effect. "You three need to remember that Honeysuckle Creek isn't the *only* town in the world...and Joey Finch isn't the *only* man."

After making her point, Lou turned toward the door of her shop, tugging Diana with her. She opened the door and, giving Diana a little push, propelled her into the store.

"Run along, now," she called back to the envious trio. "We're busy." She made a shooing motion with her hand as if she was getting rid of a flock of biddies.

Maybe she was.

"Bye, Lou Ann." Leslie waved furiously.

Liz looked slightly worried. "See you soon…I hope."

Cassidy launched into an elaborate farewell speech. "You're the be-est—"

Lou closed the door and leaned back against it, effectively cutting her off. "They are a walking nightmare," she said, all traces of Georgia gone from her North Carolina accent.

Diana smiled as she gazed around the beautiful shop. "Thanks for the rescue," she said, sincerely. "I wasn't paying attention and then"—she snapped her fingers—"just like that, I was surrounded."

Lou nodded. "I feel I should apologize for them. Most people in Honeysuckle Creek are a bit more considerate, but those three…" She shook her head. "They're at the top of the bitch scale, for sure."

"No worries," Diana replied. "Unfortunately, I've seen worse. And, besides, you aren't responsible for them."

"Maybe not now," Lou said, frowning. "But a couple of years ago, I was *one* of them. You might even say I was the ringleader. I'm not proud of it, but there it is."

Diana shrugged. "We all make mistakes."

"True," Lou agreed, her warm smile making another appearance. "I lost my way for a little while. I call those the dark years." She shrugged, then motioned for Diana to follow her deeper into the shop. "Let me show you around."

"Thanks for coming outside when you did, Lou," Diana remarked. "Best. Intervention. Ever."

Lou looked at Diana shrewdly. "Actually, I told Darcie I was going to call you as soon as you got settled. If you've got a minute, I have a proposition for you."

Diana nodded, curious to see what Lou had in mind.

Lou smiled. "Come with me."

Diana followed her into the fitting room and through the door that led to the storeroom. Lou walked to the table closest to the door and picked up a piece of material in the most beautiful shade of blue Diana could imagine. It wasn't quite turquoise or teal, but somewhere in between.

"This color is made for you, Diana. I thought of you the minute it came in. I'd love to make a cocktail dress for you...." She reached behind her and picked up a piece of sheer mesh, embroidered with delicate flowers in shades of rose and pink. "I want to use this for the overskirt." When she placed the mesh on top of the turquoise–teal material, the effect was magical.

Diana was thrilled at the thought. "Are you sure, Lou? I mean, I would love for you to design a dress for me, but I don't want to be any trouble."

"Are you kidding?" Lou asked. "I can't think of anyone better suited to this material. And if you don't mind posing, I'd be thrilled to hang your photo right up in my shop."

Diana had noticed the large, framed photographs that decorated the walls. She gazed at the lovely material wistfully. "Well, if you really want a photo of me..."

Lou laughed. "Seriously? I *need* a photo of you. You have a different vibe than the rest...sort of elegant boho or something like that. I can't wait to make this dress. Once I get started, it will only take a couple of days."

"You don't make all of the dresses yourself, do you?" Diana asked as they returned to the fitting room so Lou could take her measurements.

"Oh, no." Lou shook her head. "I have a very talented crew to do most of the sewing. I only make the dresses I'm particularly excited about." Once they got started, Lou made short work of Diana's measurements. After typing them into her laptop, she walked with Diana to the front of the store.

"Oh, Lou," Diana said, after giving her talented friend a quick hug. "I can't believe you're designing a dress for me." She was bubbling with excitement. "Now I just have to find somewhere to wear it."

Lou gave an exaggerated wink. "You could always wear it on your date with Joey Finch."

Diana laughed, even as her pulse accelerated.

"I'm serious," Lou said. "Gracie says she has *never* seen Joey act this way before…not with any other woman. And Darcie swears you're the one. She mentioned something about a brick."

Diana smiled a little shakily. "Joey got hit in the head with a brick, but I don't see what that has to do with anything." She shrugged. "Oh, well…" she said wistfully. "I guess we'll see, won't we?"

Lou winked. "I guess we will. And it wouldn't be a bad idea to turn him down the first time he asks." She unconsciously echoed Grace's words from Friday night: "Don't make it too easy for him."

Diana was still pondering Lou's words when she walked into Jack's restaurant for a post-yoga reward.

The confident young man behind the to-go counter grinned. "Welcome to Jack's. What can I do for you today, Diana?" With his baseball cap turned around backwards, he looked altogether too cocky for his own good.

Diana grinned back. She remembered Zack Kimel, Blane's youngest groomsman. She was pleased that he remembered her, too. "I'd like a medium cinnamon whip latte, please."

"Darcie's favorite, huh?" he asked, taking her order.

Diana nodded. "She says it's the best coffee she's ever tasted."

Zack turned to put the order through the window behind him, clearly pleased by her words. He turned back around to face her, leaning comfortably on the counter. Curiosity glowed in his eyes. "So…" he asked, "…how's it going?"

Diana was puzzled for a second until it dawned on her what he meant. "Oh. I really like Honeysuckle Creek. I think I'm going to love living here."

Zack shook his head. "Naw, that's not what I meant. Everybody likes living here. It's a great town. I was talking about Joey."

"Joey?" she asked, innocently.

"Yeah." Zack waited patiently for Diana to speak. When she didn't, he continued. "Are you the one?"

Diana was taken aback by his overly forthright manner. "Excuse me?" was all she could manage.

"You know...his one true love and all that," Zack answered confidently. "'Cause I think you are. Wanna know why I think so?"

Diana could only nod. She knew she should probably tell the outrageous Zack to mind his own business, but truth be told, she wanted—no, needed—to hear what he had to say.

"It's on account of how he acted at Blane and Grace's wedding. You matter to him. I could tell. I remember how mad he got when Devin's bitchy wife yelled at you. I thought then that you might be the one. Since you came to town, Joey's gone M-I-A. I mean, we haven't seen him in weeks... not even for karaoke."

Apparently, Diana surmised, missing karaoke was a serious offense.

Zack shook his head sorrowfully. "I've had to sing his part a couple of times, and, well...I'm not a bass." He leaned closer as if to impart highly confidential information. "We have a bet about you and Joey," he confided, giving no indication as to the identity of "we." "My money's on you." He said the words as if he was bestowing a great gift.

"Um...thank you?" Diana squeaked.

"No problem," Zack said. "Just remember...with him, it's all about the chase. Joey likes the chase. Don't let him catch you too fast. You've got to let him think he's catching you when *you're* really catching *him.*" Zack winked.

"Hey, Zack, shut your trap and give the lady her coffee, already." Those words came from the man who had appeared at the window behind Zack. He had to be Zack's brother, Diana thought. The resemblance was striking.

Zack's grin faded. He turned around to pick up Diana's coffee from the window. He carefully placed it on the counter at her elbow. He motioned with his hand to the now empty window. "That was my brother, Newt." He looked a little embarrassed. "My *older* brother," he said.

Diana understood completely. She nodded, wanting to make him feel better. "I have an older brother." She took a sip of her coffee. As promised, it was to die for. "Darcie was right," she said. "This is amazing."

"Thanks." Zack's grin returned along with his nineteen-year-old confidence. "I bet your older brother doesn't have any use for Joey, does he?"

"Not a bit," Diana laughed. No point in denying her interest at this point. Zack wouldn't believe her anyway. She had a pretty good idea that young Mr. Kimel was going to be an ally. After all, he had bet on her.

The rest of Diana's week continued in much the same fashion. When she stopped by the Honeysuckle Creek Diner for a breakfast biscuit on Tuesday, she received some unwanted advice from a waitress named Della Mae.

"Now, honey, don't you get too wrapped up in Joey Finch," the waitress told her. "He's not the settling down kind. Don't you waste a minute worrying your pretty, red head about him. Plenty of nice young men in this town who are the marrying kind."

An oil change and tire rotation at Payne's Auto Repair resulted in an equally unpleasant warning.

"Joey's a heartbreaker, plain and simple," Buford Payne said, shaking his head. "Yep, it's true. I've known him since he was a young-un. You be careful, now," the mechanic advised. "I'd hate to see a pretty young lady like you with big ole tears in her pretty eyes."

Not the marrying kind? Heartbreaker? Big ole tears? *Ouch.* Diana decided she could do without that kind of advice.

On Wednesday, she stopped by the main office of Honeysuckle Creek Academy to drop off a permission slip that had fallen out of Amalie's bookbag. The cheerful secretary beamed at Diana through her thick glasses. With her enormous eyes and fluffy gray hair, she resembled a wise, old owl.

"My little Joey-bird's never been interested in a steady *anything*, Diana, but I've got high hopes for you," Ellen announced with a wink. "Just don't make it too easy for him."

Maggie Parker strolled into the office just in time to hear that part of the conversation. Diana remembered the vivacious Spanish teacher as the director of Blane and Grace's wedding. The combination of Maggie's hair—just a shade lighter than Diana's—and her beautiful, turquoise eyes made the lovely woman hard to forget.

"Ellen's right," Maggie agreed. "Don't make it too easy for him. The longer you hold his interest, the better chance you have of keeping it."

Their advice was worth thinking about. After all, Ellen had known her "little Joey-bird" since he was a baby Finch. And how could Diana not trust the words of Maggie Parker—a fellow redhead?

On Thursday, Diana visited Mabel's Unusual Antiquities in search of a birthday gift for her mother. Her quest was as unsuccessful as Mabel's advice was unfortunate.

"Joey Finch is the best-lookin' thing in this town," the antiques expert informed her. "You enjoy him while you can, darlin', before he gets tired of you and starts chasin' after the next girl."

Diana's appointment at the Snips 'n Clips Salon was equally discouraging.

"You should turn him down if he asks you out," Lolly Jones intoned as she trimmed Diana's hair. "That's the way to keep him around. Once you go out with him, it's goodbye Joey Finch."

Diana's decision to order her mother flowers from Honeysuckle Creek Flower and Gift resulted in a semi-encouraging conversation with the owners of the exquisite shop.

"A little birdie told us that somebody's been spending all his time with you since you came to town," Charlie Ray enthused. "And I can't say that I blame him. With your pretty, red hair and those gray eyes...well, honey, all I can say is that you are just stunning. It's no wonder Joey Finch can't get enough of you."

Diana's eyes grew round with surprise. She wasn't used to such florid compliments about her looks. She knew Charlie Ray didn't mean any harm. She could tell by the twinkle in his eye that his words were completely genuine. There was kindness there, too. As for what he implied about Joey, well...she wished with all her heart the words were true. But she couldn't say that. *Drat.*

"Um...thank you." She glanced at Evon, Charlie Ray's partner, not quite sure how to respond.

Evon just smiled.

Charlie Ray looked at Evon impatiently. "Don't you think so, Evon?" he prompted the much quieter man.

"Charlie Ray," Evon said, gently, "I'm sure that Joey is interested in Diana's mind, too."

"Well, of course he is, Evon." Charlie Ray's smile beamed. "Our Miss Diana is the whole package." He patted her hand where it lay on the counter, still clutching her debit card. "But..." He shook the finger of his other hand at Diana, playfully, "...don't you give in too quick like, darlin'. Make him earn the prize. Our Mr. Finch needs to appreciate what he's getting."

Why, oh why, Diana asked herself, did conversations about Joey Finch always have a "but"?

By Friday morning, Diana was certain Joey was on the verge of asking her out, thus requiring a decision on her part. Should she turn him down and prolong the lovely interlude between them? She was not at all ready for Joey to give up his pursuit and lose interest in her. But, thanks to a week's worth of "helpful advice," she was starting to believe that was exactly what was going to happen if she agreed to go out with him. Public opinion in the small town of Honeysuckle Creek clearly aligned with that of Diana's family and friends...Joey Finch was a one and done. And he probably always would be. But—and she wasn't at all surprised that there was a but...

What if they were wrong? Was it possible that one date with Diana Merritt wouldn't be enough for Joey Finch? That he, in fact, wouldn't be able to let her go? Should she take a chance? Trust her instincts? Trust the simmering desire that she could feel between them? But...

Drat. There it was again. *But...*

What if they were right? Diana knew *she* wasn't ready to move on. She didn't relish the prospect of becoming just another name on the long list of Joey's conquests. What if he didn't remember *her* name after a few months or a few years? What if he called her Delilah or Dolores instead of Diana? Or, worse than that, what if he didn't call her anything at all? After finally having Joey in her life, his absence would produce a crushing void... one she wasn't sure she could ever fill again.

In other words, if he asked her out on a date, she was going to say no.

Or was she?

Diana arrived at the Finch house a few minutes early on Friday. She was looking forward to attending what had been touted as the football game of the year. Honeysuckle Creek Academy was taking on Berkley

High School, the defending 1A state champions. Since parking would be at a premium, Diana, Darcie, and Joey were going to ride with Joe and Juli Finch. Amalie, who was not yet a football fan, was spending the evening with Joey's great-grandmother.

While they waited for the rest of their party to get home from work, Diana chatted with Juli and spent a few minutes getting reacquainted with the formidable Sofia Hanover. Grandma Sofi quizzed Amalie about kindergarten and her stuffed iguana—who had, of course, accompanied the little girl. She was charmed by Amalie's highly detailed answers to her questions, while the little girl beamed at being singled out for such special attention. It was clear the two were going to have a wonderful evening together.

Three seconds after announcing that her iguana was very hungry, Amalie skipped into the kitchen with Juli in search of cookies. Grandma Sofi immediately turned her intense perusal on the two remaining occupants in the room: Diana and the hungry iguana mysteriously left behind by his cookie-loving owner. The elderly lady's self-satisfied smile made Diana nervous.

Grandma Sofi nodded approvingly. "You have done well, Diana," she said in her distinctive accent, part Spanish, part Italian...and all Grandma Sofi. "You protected Amalie from the evil in her life. Your life....It is better now that the wicked witch is dead, no?" She regarded Diana serenely.

Despite being warned, Diana was surprised at the older woman's blunt speech. Although, she admitted to herself, she was also in complete agreement. Describing Amalie's deceased mother as a wicked witch was an apt comparison. "Um...yes, things are better, but...um, I'm sorry that Mallory had to die to make them better/" Diana struggled to explain her still complicated feelings on the matter. "I just wanted her to change."

Grandma Sofi nodded again. "Yes, Diana, a wasted life is a tragedy. You no longer live in Mallory's tragedy, nor does Amalie." She shrugged her elegant shoulders. "That is for the best." She paused, peering at Diana with her snapping dark eyes. "*You* want a husband, no? And children?"

Diana smiled. "Oh, yes. I definitely want a husband and children someday."

"You listen to your heart," Grandma Sofi said. "And your heart is big. The man who wins it will be a lucky one." As her accent deepened, so did her smile. It was as if she could see a future Diana only dreamed about.

"Joey's heart...it, too, is very big. Two big hearts. That is good. Joey has waited a long time for you. You will make beautiful babies," she announced in a confident voice.

Diana gasped in shock. "What?" She had walked right into Grandma Sofi's little trap.

"Joey wants you. I see it." The ancient lady motioned to the closed door to the kitchen. "We all see it. His father. His mother. His sisters. The truth is clear. He is different with you. It is in his eyes when he speaks of you. Always in the eyes." Her own dark eyes beamed with approval. She seemed totally oblivious to the fact that she had blindsided Diana.

Beautiful babies?

"Everything is too easy for Joey," Grandma Sofi continued. "He is a rascal, no? Yet he always comes out smelling like a daisy. Growing things takes work, you see? It is the same with love. Joey needs to work for what he wants, Diana."

At this point, Diana realized that Juli—Joey's *mother*—was standing in the now open kitchen door. She appeared torn between *saving* Diana from the bizarre conversation and *listening* to the rest of the bizarre conversation.

The elderly lady blithely continued. "You know what they say..."

Juli and Diana hung on Grandma Sofi's every word. The canny woman had already twisted the phrase "smelling like a rose." What memorable idiom would she next destroy to make her point?

Grandma Sofi raised her eyebrows, obviously expecting some sort of response from Diana.

"What do they say, Mrs. Hanover?" Diana asked slowly, not exactly sure who *they* were.

The old lady shook her head. " 'Mrs. Hanover'? Oh, no, Diana. *You* may call me Grandma Sofi." She waited patiently for Diana to do so.

"What do they say, Grandma Sofi?" Diana whispered, obediently.

"Abstinence makes the heart grow fonder," Grandma Sofi finished, with a flourish.

Diana went hot with embarrassment. "Oh, *no*, Mrs. Hanover...I mean, Grandma Sofi, no. You're mistaken. Joey and I haven't...I mean we aren't...I mean..." She couldn't find the words.

She glanced at Juli—Joey's *mother*—apologetically. Diana couldn't imagine anything more awkward for a mother than to hear someone else discussing her son's sex life. Even if the sex being discussed was imaginary. On second thought, Diana decided, it was slightly *more* awkward to *be* the unfortunate woman designated as the son's sex partner...albeit *imaginary* sex partner. And it was beyond awkward for *that* unfortunate woman to be standing less than ten feet from *that* mother during the discussion of that mother's son's sex life.

Drat.

Juli rushed into the room, an equally apologetic expression on her face. "Grandma Sofi," she corrected, gently, "I think you mean *absence*. Not abstinence. *Absence* makes the heart grow fonder."

Grandma Sofi's disapproval would have floored a lesser opponent. "No, Juliette," she rose to her feet, banging her cane on the floor. "*You* are wrong. Ab-sti-nence. The lack of satisfaction. It makes the man focus on what he really wants without all of the..." She waved her elegant hand—the one not holding the cane—in the air, searching for the right words.

"Physical perks?" Juli suggested, delicately, as she walked over to the sofa. She leaned over to pick up Amalie's very hungry iguana.

"Distractions," Grandma Sofi stated, carefully, her eyes shining with mischief. "In other words," she suggested to Diana, calmly, "don't make it too easy for him."

"Grandmama," Juli said, in a matter-of-fact voice. "Let's go into the kitchen before Amalie eats all of the cookies and this poor iguana starves to death." She gently took her unpredictable grandmother by the arm, urging her toward the door.

Diana's face was burning up. She had no doubt that her cheeks were flaming. She wanted the floor to open up and swallow her whole. She didn't know where to look; she certainly couldn't look at Joey's mother.

As soon as Grandma Sofi had disappeared into the kitchen, Juli turned back to the blushing young woman.

"Diana," she said, softly.

Diana reluctantly looked up, into eyes full of kindness and a world of understanding. To her admiring surprise, Juli smiled, her green eyes dancing.

"Don't make it too easy for him," she advised, with a wink.

CHAPTER TWENTY-EIGHT

*N*ine. Years.

Joey had kept his distance for nine years. In the end, it hadn't mattered in the least. From the minute Diana ran into him in the doorway of Chutley's he was a goner. He could admit that now; could admit that he wanted her. He wanted Diana Merritt in his life. Not because of her gorgeous hair. Or her long, lovely limbs. Or the smattering of freckles sprinkled across her nose and cheeks. And not because of her spirit. Or her courage. Or her ability to make the best of any situation. And not because she got his jokes. Or the amazing fact that she appreciated his corny sense of humor. It was all those things and so much more.

She was smart and witty and kind. She liked to laugh; she liked to be quiet. He had never known anyone who was as comfortable as he with quiet. She never felt the need to fill the void with chatter. She never *tried* to entertain him. She just did. And she shared his love of literature and good writing. Because of her family background, she understood his passion for the law. He had never considered how important that was to him, but it was.

And she was delectable. Sexy. Hot. (So hot!) Just thinking about her legs—her long, long legs—was enough to send waves of heat pulsing through Joey's body; he had to take a cold shower almost every night.

And she didn't even realize it. She was his perfect fit in every way. Every. Possible. Way. He needed her. Craved her. Couldn't, at this point, imagine his life without her.

Well, hell.

How had Joey Finch, quintessential bachelor, come to such a desperate point in a few short weeks? And how was it that while he was busy wrapping his head around the new vision of his future, he had never once considered that Diana—the other half of that imagined future—might have a different vision? He had expected—at least he had hoped—that, well... that Diana wanted him, too.

Might as well admit it, Finch, he admonished himself. *You assumed she wanted you because when it comes to women, you're an arrogant son of a bitch.* He lifted a silent apology for his word choice to his own sweet mother. His whole life, women had always fallen at his feet. They stood in line for his attentions. They vied for his notice. And why not? he had asked himself. Joey Finch was a hell of a guy. He was a catch. Any woman would consider herself lucky to go out with him.

Ha. Fool that he was, he had wrongly assumed that *all* women were the same. Quite a flawed way of thinking for someone with two independent sisters, a like-minded mother, a fierce great-grandmother, and an extremely perceptive father. He had been raised better than that, Joey reminded himself. He had a law degree, for crying out loud. Shouldn't that make him a bit more in tune with human nature? Apparently not.

Apparently—and he hated to admit it—he had become what he had sworn he would never be. He was, he realized with a good deal of self-loathing, shallow. And arrogant. He couldn't forget arrogant. Yes, that was him. That was Joey Finch, in a nutshell. Arrogant. Shallow. And... afraid. Afraid to take a chance. Afraid to put himself out there. Afraid of being hurt or humbled or embarrassed. He wasn't willing to risk the angst and drama and potential heartbreak. No reward could be worth the loss of his bachelorhood or his comfortable existence. No woman could be worth the trouble.

Until Diana Merritt collided with him in a doorway. Until he realized that he would do anything to protect her. Until... He absently rubbed the scar on his forehead. How was it possible the one woman he couldn't get out of his mind, the woman he was destined to marry—according to a very distinctive sign from God—wouldn't go out with him on a date?

Joey pulled his phone out of his pocket to check the time. Nearly midnight. He'd been sitting in his truck in his parents' driveway since she turned him down.

Turned. Him. Down.

No reason. No excuses. Nothing.

She just smiled and said, very politely, "I don't think so, but thank you for asking." Then she got into the car with Darcie and Amalie and rode away, leaving him staring at their taillights.

Her refusal was a puzzle he had yet to figure out. Fortunate that he liked puzzles, Joey mused. He liked them a lot. It was one of the reasons he had gone into law. He liked working through the nuances of a case. Sometimes the difference between a verdict of *guilty* or *not guilty* hinged on one tiny detail. He took tremendous satisfaction in sifting through facts and information to find the details that kept an innocent man out of prison. Now, *he* was on trial. And Diana Merritt was the only one who could set him free.

Joey started his truck. Before he pulled out of the driveway, he made his decision. He had never backed down from a challenge in his life, and he wasn't going to start now. He and Diana were meant to be together. And just like the fictional Ezekiel in Diana's work in progress, he would find a way to win his Genevieve. Failure, as was oft quoted, wasn't an option.

On Saturday morning, Joey found himself comfortably ensconced on one end of the couch in his father's home office. His present location wasn't surprising. Whenever he found himself in need of advice, he almost always ended up in this exact location. What was surprising, this time, was the reason he was here. He had rarely asked his father for advice about women. And he had *never* asked his mother. Yet, here they both were, at his request. Joe's expression was unreadable, but Juli regarded him with motherly concern. Joey needed help. *Serious, because-it's-for-the-rest-of-my-life help.* So, here he was.

Joe propped his elbows on his desk and clasped his hands together. He studied his son without saying anything.

Joey didn't know where to start. He merely sat there, awkwardly, looking from his dad to his mother, who was seated on the other end of the sofa. He felt like a pendulum.

Juli finally took pity on her speechless husband and son. "Your father and I assume that you want to talk about Diana," she said, gently.

"That's right," Joey agreed, nodding his head in relief.

More silence.

Juli raised her eyebrows at Joe, who was, apparently, deep in thought. She sighed. No help there, she thought. If father and son were discussing anything else—a ballgame, for example, or legal news—she would have difficulty getting a word in. On matters of the heart, however, she would have to take the lead. "You like Diana?" she asked Joey.

"That's right," Joey said, again. It seemed the only words he was currently able to produce.

"We like her, too," Juli said. She looked at Joe inquiringly. When he continued to remain silent, she prodded him a little. "Don't we, Joe?"

"Hmm?" he asked, shaking himself out of his thoughts.

Juli gave him an exasperated glare. "We like Diana, too, don't we?"

"Oh, yes, yes," Joe agreed. "Of course, we do." He nodded his head, zoning in on an issue he was comfortable discussing. "Is there some problem with Diana we need to know about? The kidnapper hasn't contacted her, has he?"

Joey ran his hand through his hair in agitation. "No, no, Dad. It's nothing like that. She hasn't heard a thing from the kidnapper. Hopefully, the bast...um, sorry, Mom." *Damn,* Joey thought. He usually had more finesse. He tried again. "Hopefully the sorry no-good—"

"—bastard?" Juli asked, pertly.

Joe snorted in appreciation.

Joey grinned. He had somehow forgotten that—when she deemed it necessary—his mother could be as fierce as Grandma Sofi. "Yes," he said. "Bastard. Hopefully the sorry, no-good bastard is gone for good."

"Glad to hear it," Joe said. He glanced at Juli, figuratively throwing back the conversational ball.

"Is there some other problem with Diana, then?" Juli asked, delicately. "Something we can help you with?"

Joey blurted out the words he never expected to say. "She won't go out with me."

"Really?" Juli said. "Hmm."

Joey watched his mother as she leaned back against the cushions of the couch and tucked her legs under her. *Uh-oh,* he thought with resignation. She was getting comfortable, which meant that she had something to say. Maybe quite a lot to say. And while she appeared sympathetic, she was not a bit surprised, he realized, that the girl of her only son's dreams had turned him down.

Joey glanced at his father. Joe didn't look surprised, either, but he did look intrigued. Still, he said nothing. For the time being, it seemed Joe was quite willing for Juli to take the lead. Joey wondered how long his articulate and ever astute father would be able to hold his tongue.

At that point, Joey recognized one indisputable fact: he was the *only* person in the room blindsided by Diana's negative response to his offer. Just more proof that he was an idiot, he surmised, sighing heavily. He may as well get on with it.

"Diana turned me down," he admitted. "She turned me down flat. No explanations. No excuses. Nothing but"—he mimicked Diana's reply in a high voice—" 'I don't think so but thank you for asking.' " Oh, how he hated saying the words out loud. Her casual refusal still stung.

Joe's brief silence didn't last. "Why don't you just kiss her?" he asked with a glint of relief in his eyes. He had seen the way Diana gazed at his son. To him, Joey's problem seemed very easy to solve.

"Joe," Juli scolded. "Kissing isn't the solution to *every* problem."

Joe raised his eyebrows. "It made you stop dating Will, didn't it?"

Joey choked down the unexpected urge to laugh.

Juli looked at her son, shaking her head. "Your father brings up the most inappropriate topics at the most inappropriate times."

"It's part of my charm," Joe said, with a satisfied grin. Not only had he broken the ice with his son, but his words had caused a rosy blush to appear on his wife's pretty face.

Joey could tell his mother was trying not to smile at her incorrigible husband. "I still can't believe you dated Will," he said, suddenly able to speak.

"I wouldn't really call it dating," Juli explained. "We went out a few times, but only for a summer. I was a college senior and Will was getting ready to start law school. We were bored and…"—she crossed her arms and shot the accused a sassy glare—"…your father was busy being *difficult*. And pigheaded," she added as an afterthought.

"Ouch," said Joe, shaking his head. He turned back to his son again. "I don't know, Joey. Diana might just be doing you a favor by turning you down."

Joey laughed. "No, she's not doing me any favors. She and I, well… we're really close, Dad. Really compatible. We can talk about anything. I mean anything. She's funny and sweet and…well, she's just *right*, you know? She even laughs at my jokes." He shrugged his shoulders. "I just don't understand why she won't go out with me."

Juli tilted her head to the side, studying her son. "Are you sure about that?" his mother inquired, patiently.

Joey looked puzzled. "Of course, I'm sure," he said. "It's a complete mystery to me."

Rather than immediately taking his side, as he expected, his mother simply looked at him. "Joey Finch, do you mean to tell me that you have no clue under the sun why a woman who obviously enjoys spending time with you is unwilling to take the next step?"

"Well, no," he responded, furrowing his brow. "Unless it has something to do with..."

Juli briefly raised her eyes to the ceiling as if asking for divine intervention. Then she just sat, waiting for her lovestruck son to figure it out. She glanced at Joe, who seemed equally confused. *Men,* she thought with a mental eye roll.

For some unknown reason, Joey's mind focused on Ezekiel. The Earl of Ravenwood. The poor, pathetic, son-of-a-bitch rake—*reformed* rake, he corrected himself—who couldn't convince the woman he wanted that he had genuinely changed. What had Diana said about Genevieve? *"She wants to believe him, but she can't quite decide if she should trust him...."*

And there was Joey's answer...it was staring him in the face. Diana didn't trust him. *Well, hell.* He felt like hiding under a rock. His earlier confusion fell away, leaving a large, gaping hole full of his own failings.

Every time he had taken a girl on a date and never called her again. Each one of those dates was in that hole.

Every time he used the phrase, *I don't want a relationship.* In the hole.

Every time he justified being a selfish, pompous jackass by explaining everything to the girl *before* they went out. Up front. No false expectations. Oh, yeah. Each time was in the damn hole.

It was full of his empty, self-serving words; he had dug that hole all by himself. Crafted it by hand. Filled it over the years. And now, it was standing between him and the woman with whom he wanted to spend the rest of his life. His Diana. His strong, brave Diana didn't trust him. That realization scared the hell out of him. He couldn't lose her. He had to convince her that *she* was different.

He wanted to take one of the pillows he was leaning against and pound it into dust. Instead, he took a deep breath and prepared to confess all. He was going to have to tell his beloved mother that her only son was a poor, pathetic son of a...Well, maybe not that. A poor, pathetic loser. Yeah, he thought. Loser was the right word.

Juli dared to break the silence. "I can tell by the expression on your face that you might have come up with a reason for Diana's refusal. Yes?"

Joey nodded soberly. "Mom, I think it might have something to do with..." He paused, turning to face her. It was past time for him to take responsibility for his own behavior. "So, it's like this, Mom. In Alexandria, I have a reputation of sorts."

She nodded, calmly. "As a *one and done*."

Joey looked at her in horror. "How did you...? Who told you...?" His eyes flew to his dad, who was watching the exchange with interest.

Joe held up both hands as if to ward off the accusation. "Oh, no, Joey," he said. "Don't look at me. I didn't tell her. You should have realized by now that your mother just...knows things." He motioned to Juli with his head, widening his eyes to indicate that she possessed some supernatural cognitive ability.

"Oh, hush, Joe Finch," Juli said, ignoring her grinning spouse. "You didn't need to tell me anything. It's not exactly a secret." She turned back to her astonished son.

"What do you mean it's not exactly a secret?" Joey asked despite feeling that he would regret hearing the answer.

Juli's gaze softened at his distress. "Sweetie," she said gently. "You're known as a *one and done* around here, too. But not in a bad way," she added, trying to soften the blow.

"Since when?" he sputtered.

"Since high school," she replied.

"High school?"

"Think about it, Joey," Juli said. "Except for the prom and a few school dances, you never went out with girls one-on-one. Your group of friends got together at somebody's house instead. Or went out together."

"That's true," Joe interjected. "I certainly paid for enough pizza and wings to prove it," he added. "Not to mention chips, burgers, hot dogs..." He ticked the items off on his fingers. "And cases and cases of drinks, especially after games."

Juli laughed. "And you loved every minute of it, Joe Finch. You loved hanging out with those kids and hearing them talk about trick plays and touchdowns and what the coach said in the locker room."

Joe smiled fondly at his son. "I wouldn't give anything for those days," he said, before pulling the conversation back to the original topic. "But, Joey, I honestly don't remember a single time you went out with the same girl twice while you were in high school. What about college?"

Joey shook his head. He had never really thought it, but his dating habits were rather telling.

Juli answered in his stead. "You were that friend a girl could count on when she didn't have a boyfriend, weren't you? I swear, Joey, you went to so many cocktail parties and formals your freshman year that we finally just bought you your own tux because rentals were costing us a fortune." As if sensing his bewilderment, Juli managed to be positive. "But you always sent pictures. That was nice."

"There was a different girl in every picture," Joe added, helpfully.

"Thanks, Dad." Joey grimaced. "Yeah, I guess I was the go-to guy all through college. And law school, too, although not as often. Studying, you know." Interesting that he had never thought about his habits long enough to see the pattern. Cocktails and formals were fun. And he had never minded being some girl's last-minute date, as long as *everybody* was on the same no-commitment page. He shook his head at his own foibles before continuing. "After I went to work for Merritt Brothers, well...I guess I got the reputation as something of a player, but it was just more of the same."

Joe looked serious. "Opposed to commitment, hmm?"

"Not at all," Joey said, thoughtfully. "I was having too much fun with my high school buddies and my college fraternity brothers to date one girl. Romantic entanglements seemed too time-consuming and a lot of trouble back then. After I met Diana—nine years ago—I was in denial. I wasn't ready, even though I was drawn to her. I guess I just didn't want to admit that I had already met the right girl. But I also didn't want to waste any time on the *wrong* girl, so I played it cool." Now that he thought about it, his actions made perfect sense. Perfect sense, that is, for a cowardly and pathetic loser who was afraid of commitment, he added to himself.

"At least you didn't leave a trail of broken hearts behind you." Juli always managed to put a positive spin on things. "From what I understand, the girls you dated still think well of you. For the most part."

Joey had no idea how his sweet mother could possibly have attained such accurate information about his life. And he flatly refused to explore what she meant when she had said *"for the most part."* He absolutely did *not* want to know.

"So," Julie continued, choosing her words carefully. "If *I* was Diana and *I* was privy to the details of your dating history, *I* wouldn't expect you to call me again after one date, either. And if *I* enjoyed spending time with you, *I* wouldn't want that time to end. Therefore, the only way to prolong *our* time together would be to refuse to go out with you."

"There's your answer, Joey." His father nodded. "Listen to your mother. She's never wrong."

Juli scoffed in disbelief. "Except when *you* can't find *your* keys or *your* socks or *your* favorite T-shirt," Juli responded. "Then, it's all *my* fault and *I* am always wrong."

"Yep," Joe agreed. "That's how it works." He relaxed back in his chair, enjoying himself immensely.

Joey blew out a frustrated breath. "That means the bottom line is that Diana doesn't trust me."

"Can you blame her?" his mother asked, softly.

Joey shook his head, soberly. "So, what do I do now?" he asked, looking from one parent to another. He was back to being a pendulum.

"That's up to you," Juli said gently. "We can help you pinpoint the problem, Joey, but you're the one who has to figure out how to solve it. You have to find some way to win her trust."

"Or you could just kiss her." His irrepressible father offered the suggestion with a devilish gleam in his eye.

Joey had a feeling it wasn't going to be that easy.

While Diana spent her weekend visiting her family, Joey spent *his* weekend preparing, researching, and planning. It was intensive, exhausting work. But by Monday morning, he was confident, determined, and ready to put all that he had learned into practice. Very soon, he told himself, his efforts would come to fruition. And some day, he would tell Diana that he—like Ezekiel, his fictional counterpart—found the way to his lady's heart through the pages of a romance novel.

Four romance novels, to be exact. He spent the weekend reading four romance novels. And not just any kind of romance novels. No, he had specifically chosen four romance novels about reformed rakes: *For the Sake of a Rake, Always Take the Rake, What to Make of the Rake,* and—his favorite by far—*Ravishing the Rake.* Roland, the main character in that fourth page-turner, was the one with whom he most identified.

Through his efforts, Joey had learned that the most difficult problem for a reformed rake—especially a newly reformed rake—was convincing the world that he was truly reformed. In other words, the love interest of a reformed rake did not initially believe that she was anything other than the next conquest in a long line. Since Joey refused to consider the possibility that Diana did not return his feelings—such an option was completely unacceptable—he was more than willing to settle on her disbelief in his sincerity as the most logical reason for her refusal.

Now, all he had to do was to convince her that he could be trusted with her heart. Easier said than done, if what he read was any indication, he thought soberly. But, be that as it may, every single one of the reformed rakes he had read about managed to find his happily ever after by the end of his respective novel. Joey intended to devote every ounce of his reformed rakishness to convince Diana that he was for real. His tenacity would be his secret weapon. He was prepared to woo and win his lady with the prowess of the craftiest—and most reformed—rake.

He glanced with satisfaction at the surprise that was presently lying on his desk. He had purchased the lovely bouquet of flowers earlier that morning from Evon at Honeysuckle Creek Flower and Gift. Charlie Ray's signature glitter highlighted the single violet lily surrounded by peach-colored dahlias and cream-colored roses. A few sprigs of greenery and a lovely cream-colored ribbon made entirely of lace bound the bouquet together. Joey smiled in anticipation. Each of the reformed rakes in the novels he had read used flowers to convince his lady of his sincerity.

He planned to present the lovely bouquet to the equally lovely Miss Merritt at the end of her yoga class. He had been imagining her delight all morning...from the first hint of a sparkle in her dark, gray eyes to the blinding smile that was sure to follow. Flowers were an excellent way to start his first—and last—attempt at courtship. *First*, because he had never before had to try to garner the attention of a female, and *last*, because Diana was the only woman he wanted. Or would ever want. Period. That suspicion, hovering for years in his subconscious, had solidified into indisputable fact since Friday night...a night which would forever live in his mind as *The Night She Turned Me Down.*

CHAPTER TWENTY-NINE

*D*iana nearly groaned aloud when she walked into Jack's restaurant on Monday morning. The email only mentioned that one of her book company's representatives was in the area and wanted to discuss a few details. Diana tried to make it plain when answering said email that the meeting wasn't convenient. She suggested a face-to-face meeting was neither necessary nor desirable at this time. She did *not* receive a reply. Now she knew why, she thought regretfully.

Nigel Barclay.

Why did it have to be Nigel Barclay?

To his credit, Nigel was a fantastic editor. He really was. The best in the business at adjusting the subtle nuances of an American children's book so it would appeal to British children, and vice versa. He had a spectacular track record of success.

Diana knew she should have expected that Nigel would show up eventually. Somewhere. But not…here. Not in Honeysuckle Creek. And not this morning. Or any morning, for that matter. She glanced across the restaurant. Nigel was chatting on his phone. Probably with his "mum," she thought, uncharitably. His back was to her; he hadn't seen her yet. She was tempted to escape to the sunny sidewalk while she still had the chance.

Part of her wish to avoid a face-to-face meeting with the annoying Brit was because, since their introduction several years ago, Nigel had developed what Diana could only term an adolescent-like crush on her. According to Nigel's aunt, Tracy Whittington—head of the children's division of Vandermere Publishing—Diana and Nigel were perfect for each other. The proverbial "match made in heaven."

Diana begged to differ. Imagining a relationship with Nigel made her thoughts run a little farther south than heaven.

Nigel was tall and thin; he was as unathletic as anyone Diana had ever met. She was fairly certain the man had never seen the inside of a gym. Or lifted weights. Or lifted *one* five-pound weight. Or a large can of soup. Or a pencil. And while there was nothing wrong with being unathletic, it proved beyond a shadow of a doubt that Nigel Barclay was *not* Diana's perfect match.

A vision of Joey's muscular physique crossed her mind. Yes, she thought, even as she pasted a polite, and very professional, smile on her face. Joey's physique was so much more to her liking. She hadn't seen the attractive Mr. Finch since turning him down on Friday night. She had no idea whether her refusal to go on a date had piqued Joey's interest or permanently squelched it. Diana sighed, edging one foot backwards toward the door.

Nigel turned just then. An annoyingly smug smile crossed his face. Diana glanced longingly at the door. *Drat.* She had missed her chance. Nigel held up a slender hand, a silent communication requesting she let him finish his phone call before she…what? Ran to him from across the restaurant? Threw herself in his arms? Tackled him to the ground in uncontrollable joy? *Please.* The man's ego knew no bounds.

That was the thing about Nigel, she decided. She didn't mind that he probably couldn't fight his way out of a paper bag. Or even *find* his way out of one. She didn't mind his pasty complexion, too soft hands, Harry Potter glasses—the stems were the colors of Gryffindor—or his limp fish handshake. Well, that wasn't exactly true, she admitted. She *did* mind his handshake…quite a lot, actually. But she would have been able to tolerate Nigel's less than pleasant characteristics *if* he was a nice person.

Unfortunately, he wasn't. Nigel wasn't nice at all. The thought of being kind or considerate never entered his mind. He was arrogant, conceited, and condescending. He considered the majority of humanity beneath him. He was quick to point out flaws in those around him while refusing to acknowledge his own. And, to top it all off, he considered himself God's gift to all women. But specifically, God's *extra-special gift* to Diana Merritt. She forced herself to maintain a pleasant expression.

Nigel shut off his phone and returned it to the clip at his belt. He walked toward Diana, soft hands outstretched. She had no choice but to put her hands in his. He pulled her toward him, leaning in to plant a kiss on her lips.

Arrogant jerk.

She deliberately turned her head, so his lips barely grazed her cheek. "Nigel," she heard herself saying in an unenthusiastic monotone. "What a surprise."

"I know," Nigel grinned slyly. "Isn't it?" He spread her arms wide as he looked her over with a critical eye. "Yes, yes," he said, almost to himself. "Lovely, as always."

Diana felt like a horse on the auction block. She half expected him to hold her mouth open so he could inspect her teeth. *"Lovely"* was an extreme exaggeration, in her opinion. She was dressed for yoga class, for goodness' sake. Leggings covered with small, pastel flowers in varying shades of lilac and purple. A scoop-neck tank top in lilac over a purple sports bra. A thin, lilac jacket, perfect for the slight chill that had finally appeared in the morning air. No-tie fabric sneakers covered in an off-white eyelet material. High ponytail. *And* devoid of makeup and jewelry. *"Lovely"?* Ha.

Nigel released her, placing his hand at the small of her back to propel her toward a booth against the interior wall of the restaurant. Diana gritted her teeth at the man's proprietary air but allowed him to direct her.

She wanted to punch him.

Out of the corner of her eye, she saw Zack Kimel cleaning off tables in the main dining room. He studied Nigel with a speculative air before pulling his phone out of his apron pocket.

Joey's phone rang, interrupting his musings. Zack Kimel was on the other end of the line. Joey figured his young friend was probably calling to find out why he hadn't shown up for karaoke in a month. Unfortunately, Joey was wrong.

"Hey, Zack," he said. "What's up?"

Zack's voice drawled back: "So...your girlfriend's having breakfast with some British dude and I just thought you ought to know."

"My what is...*what*?" Joey sputtered.

He heard Zack snort and imagined the annoyed expression that must be on the face of the overconfident young man.

"Don't try to deny it, Joey. We all know she's your girlfriend, even if *you* haven't figured it out yet. We—your friends and I—haven't seen you in weeks. Not even for karaoke. That's serious. Hell, for you, that's unheard of. So, you might as well just ask her out and get on with it."

Now why didn't I think of that? Joey asked himself sarcastically. No one would ever accuse Zack Kimel of being subtle. But Joey managed a smooth reply. "Thanks for the advice, Zack."

"You better take my advice quick," Zack continued impatiently. "Because I think you might have some competition."

"What are you talking about?"

"Diana's having breakfast with some British dude," Zack repeated. "He's the real deal, too. Got the fancy accent and everything. Slid right into the booth beside her, too."

Well hell. Joey's heart began to beat faster. What now?

"Do you want me to make him uncomfortable?" Zack asked, eagerly. "Spill some pancake syrup on him or something? Or I could accidentally tip a whole pot of coffee on his—"

"No, no, that's okay, Zack," Joey interrupted. "I'm on my way." He ended the call, pausing only to grab the bouquet off his desk. As he headed out of his office, he nearly collided with Darcie at the top of the stairs.

"Whoa, there, sis," he said, taking hold of her arm to steady her.

"Where are you headed in such a hurry?" she asked. "And why do you have those flowers?" His sister was nothing if not observant.

"Don't worry about it, Darce," Joey said easily. "I'll see you later." He released her arm and hurried down the stairs.

"I can't wait 'til you have some work to do," Darcie called to the empty air. "Hmph." She walked into her office pondering the odd exchange with her brother. Prodded by instinct, she looked out the front window just in time to see Joey—flowers in hand—hurrying up the street toward the town's main intersection. Darcie smiled. She didn't know what her brother was up to, but she would bet her last dollar it had something to do with Diana Merritt.

Diana strategically placed her overlarge gym bag between herself and the wall. Then she sat down at the farthest outside edge of the booth, making sure there wasn't room for anyone else to join her. Not even a scrawny fellow like Nigel.

But that scrawny—and annoyingly bossy—fellow would not be deterred. "Slide over, please," he directed. "We need to be on the same side so you can see my computer."

Drat. He had a point. Placing her gym bag in the space between them, Diana slid over until her left shoulder touched the wall. Nigel, ever resourceful, used his too-soft hands to whisk the barrier out of the way. He tossed her bag into the opposite seat before she realized his intention. With a self-satisfied smile, he slid into the booth beside her. Diana could feel the pressure of his nonmuscular thigh against hers as he leaned over to pull his laptop from his briefcase. When he resumed his previous position, his skinny shoulder bumped against her.

He opened his laptop, carefully. She repositioned herself under pretense of seeking a better angle to see the computer. Turning slightly, so that her back was against the wall, she thrust her elbow sharply into Nigel's side. He grunted in pain.

"Oh, I'm sorry," Diana said, cheerfully. "Did I hurt you?"

Nigel looked down his superior nose at her for a moment, but finally gave up a little space between them. Diana heard a snort of laughter and glanced back to find her young friend, Zack, wiping down the perfectly clean surface of the booth behind her.

"You, there." Nigel glared at Zack. "You don't look overly occupied. Take our order."

Zack grinned good-naturedly. "Yes, sir," he said, taking a pencil from behind his ear and digging his order pad out of his apron pocket. He stepped close to the edge of their table.

"Welcome to Jack's, the home of stacks, snacks, and—" He paused as Nigel held up a pale, soft hand.

"Would it be too much trouble for you to dispense with this excruciating nonsense in favor of simply taking our order?" The smile on Nigel's face stood in direct contrast to his words.

"Nigel," Diana said, sharply, in her nanny voice. "Shame on you. *I*, for one, would like to hear what this industrious young man has to say."

Nigel backed down in the face of his companion's displeasure. "Yes, yes, well…whatever pleases you, my lady."

Diana smiled at Zack, mischief glittering in her eyes. Zack returned her smile, his own eyes full of devilment. *Good,* she thought. *We're on the same page.*

Zack cleared his throat and resumed: "Welcome to Jack's, the home of stacks, snacks, and packs. I'm Zack…"

The young man handed them two menus. He then proceeded to go through every item on the menu. In excruciating detail. He discussed the merits of each of the many savory combinations. Pancakes and sausage. Pancakes and bacon. Pancakes and eggs. Pancakes and sausage *and* eggs. The combinations were *endless.* Then he explained various combinations of combinations. Pancake platter with fruit and oatmeal. Pancake platter with omelet. Pancake platter with gravy and a biscuit. And on and on and on. After this enlightening information, he launched into a memorable account of the "stack" specials of the week: apple or pumpkin spice. He ended with his own personal recommendation of a large pumpkin spice stack with nutmeg whipped cream and bacon on the side.

Diana was impressed. Zack should be on the stage. His delivery was flawless. He was sincere enough to be above reproach, but full of an over-abundance of information designed to drive the impatient Nigel crazy. Diana wanted to applaud.

When the young man finally finished, she glanced at Nigel's face. His cheeks. His temples. Even his throat was bright red. She decided the color was something of an improvement. His normally washed-out complexion was remarkably corpselike. Nigel's skinny chest moved up and down with his aggravated breathing. His hands were balled into tight fists.

Good work, Zack. Diana was pleased. Nigel looked like a man ready to upend the booth in frustration. Or at least ready to *try*, she mused. In all actuality, the solid booth was probably too heavy for him.

"So...what'll it be?" Zack asked, his hand poised to write down their order.

"I'll just have coffee," Diana said, pleasantly.

"What?" Nigel sputtered. "After listening to the interminable words pouring out of the mouth of this...this..."

"Server?" Zack asked, politely.

Nigel waved his hand in the air as if he could make Zack disappear. He glared at Diana. "After all of that ridiculous nonsense, you want coffee? No stacks? No stacks on top of stacks? No nutmeg whipped cream?"

Diana shrugged. "I already had breakfast this morning with Amalie."

"How *is* Amalie?" Zack asked, conversationally. "Still excited about kindergarten?"

Diana nodded. "Oh, yes. To hear her talk, you would think she was the only little girl who ever went to kindergarten. She loves her teacher."

"I loved my kindergarten teacher, too," Zack said. "Mrs. Newsome was the best. I remember this one time when—"

"Enough," Nigel bellowed, rudely. "Kindly take our order and leave."

Diana raised her eyebrows at Nigel's imperious tone.

"But," Zack objected. "I haven't gone over the coffee menu."

Diana almost giggled at Nigel's expression. She was tempted to let Zack's performance continue, but she was afraid the irate man's head was going to explode.

"That's okay," she told Zack. "Just bring me black coffee with cream and sugar, please."

Zack shook his head sadly, as if thoroughly disappointed in her choice. "No cinnamon whip latte?" he asked hopefully.

Diana smiled. "Not today." She turned to Nigel. "Go ahead, Nigel."

"Toast," Nigel said, in his most condescending tone.

"Toast?" Diana and Zack spoke at the same time.

"What kind of toast?" Zack asked. "We have white toast, wheat toast, sour dough"

"White," Nigel ground out through gritted teeth.

"Would you like that with honey, cinnamon—"

"No," said Nigel.

"No?" asked Zack. "You mean you want plain toast?"

"Yes," Nigel said. "Plain. Toast."

"Okay."

"And tea," Nigel continued. "Just plain tea." He paused for a second. "In a cup," he added, as an afterthought.

Zack's eyes lit up. "Hot or cold?"

"What kind of idiotic question is that?" The fact that Nigel was a first-time visitor to the South was glaringly obvious. Southerners prided themselves on sweetened iced tea. "I want regular tea. Normal tea. Like every other sane member of the human race, you idiotic boy."

"All righty then." Zack exchanged a veiled glance with Diana, a question in his eyes.

Diana nodded, all traces of humor gone. Nigel was an ass, she thought, plain and simple. And he deserved exactly what he was going to get.

Zack left to fill their orders.

"I can't believe you're subjecting yourself to life in such an unpleasant, little town, Diana, darling," Nigel said, all smiles as he fiddled with his laptop. He looked around the nearly empty restaurant. "This trashy hovel is obviously on the way to bankruptcy."

Diana didn't point out that Jack's was legendary in this part of the state. Nor did she mention that the outside portion of the restaurant was almost always full, especially in the fall of the year. And she didn't volunteer the information that nine-thirty on a Monday morning wasn't a high-volume time of day for the hardworking locals. She didn't say a word.

Nigel got down to business. "The first thing I think we should change about your books is the appearance of Nanny Di." He showed Diana some preliminary sketches in which Nanny Di took on the appearance of a stereo-typical British nanny. Older. Plumper. Less attractive.

Diana crossed both arms over her stomach. "No," she said.

Nigel blinked, apparently intrigued by Diana's response. "Do tell me why."

She was happy to enlighten him. "Part of the appeal of the *Nanny Di* series is the relationship between Nanny Di and Mara Lee...sort of a big sister–little sister thing. If you make Nanny Di older, you'll take that away. Not to mention that Nanny Di must be exceptionally physically fit for the series to be believable. The adventures are pretty strenuous." Diana had already discussed the possibility of changing the physical appearance of the character with her illustrator–mother. Both agreed that the illustrations must *not* be changed. Diana was adamant about this point.

Nigel listened carefully, weighing her words. He finally nodded his agreement. "I see exactly what you are saying, Diana. We won't touch the illustrations."

Diana relaxed. When focused on his work, Nigel was the consummate professional. Too bad he was such a presumptuous jerk every other hour of the day.

"Any other changes will be minor, along the lines of *scones* instead of *crackers and cheese, lift* instead of *elevator*...you understand the concept?" He closed his computer. "I'll send you the edits for your approval."

"That's it?" Diana couldn't believe it. "*That's* why you wanted a face-to-face meeting? We could have accomplished that in an email."

Nigel smiled smugly. "Of course not, you silly goose." He tapped her nose with his long, thin finger. "A face-to-face meeting was my excuse to spend the day with you. And now, I'm all yours."

He was obviously proud of his genius plan. He was so high and mighty, excruciatingly proud that he reminded her of a peacock...only not as appealing. No, she decided, not appealing at all. Seriously unappealing. And exasperating. And incredibly annoying.

Diana really wanted to punch him.

"Look, Nigel..." she began, but she stopped abruptly. For some unknown reason, Joey Finch had just barreled through the front door of Jack's. He was carrying a bouquet of flowers, and he appeared to be looking for someone.

Zack came out of the kitchen at that exact moment. Joey stomped over to the young man and started giving him an earful. She wondered what Zack had done, surprised when the young man laughed off Joey's apparent upset. He put his hand on Joey's arm and shook his head. He made a gesture of grabbing something with his hand and twisting. Joey's eyes widened in disbelief.

At that moment, Nigel made the unfortunate decision to take hold of Diana's chin with his skinny fingers and direct her attention back to himself.

"I'm right here, Diana," he said, silkily.

She leaned back to escape his grasping fingers, but he chose not to let go. It was a choice he would soon regret.

"False alarm, Joey," Zack said, confidently. "Diana's totally in control of the situation. In fact, I'd say she's got him by the balls."

Joey scanned the restaurant for proof. His eyes zoned in on the booth by the wall. He didn't like what he saw. No, he didn't like it at all.

"Like hell she does," he muttered under his breath before tossing the bouquet onto the counter.

Zack put out a hand to stop him, but Joey pushed it off. He stalked across the room, coming to the edge of Diana's booth just as Diana attempted to wrest her chin from Nigel's determined grasp.

"Get your hands off her!" Joey snarled in a voice Diana had never heard him use.

Nigel squealed.

At least that was the only description Diana had for the high-pitched sound that emerged from his lips. The startled peacock—or was that *chicken?*—dropped his hand from her chin, nearly falling out of the booth in his haste to put distance between them. Joey caught him under the arms before he could hit the floor. He hauled Nigel up and set him none too gently on his feet.

Diana was stunned. Nigel was at least five inches taller than Joey's five-foot, ten-inch frame. Yet, she could swear that at one point Nigel was completely airborne.

"Wha-wha-what are you doing, you adolescent cretin?" Nigel finally managed to stutter.

"Adolescent cretin?" Joey asked, somehow managing to stare down the taller man.

Diana slid gracefully out of the booth to stand between them. "Joey, this is Nigel Barclay, my British book editor. And Nigel, this is Joey Finch, my..." Diana hesitated for a fraction of a second, searching for the proper words. *Dream lover?* No, she cautioned herself. Too much information. *Ideal man?* No, unnecessarily embarrassing. *Future spouse and father of my children?* Absolutely not. Too pathetically unbelievable. "My, um…very good friend," she finished, lamely.

Diana's answer pleased Nigel immensely. He puffed out his skinny chest and preened like some overly proud rooster.

Not so, Mr. Finch. He was extremely displeased with Diana *and* her word choice.

Diana pasted a tight smile on her face as she waited for one of them to say something. Anything.

"Delighted to meet you, Finch," Nigel gloated. "Any *very good friend* of Lady Diana is a friend of mine." He held out his soft, pasty hand.

"Barclay," Joey managed to grunt. He flinched at Nigel's limp, fish-like handshake.

Diana couldn't blame him. She skillfully dodged Nigel's attempt to put his arm around her waist by reaching for her gym bag.

"Lady Diana and I have been friends for three amazing years," Nigel explained, quickly hiding his frown at Diana's defection.

"*Di-ana* and I have been *very good friends* for nine years," Joey said, smugly, moving a step closer to her.

Diana slung her gym bag over her arm, putting a barrier between herself and this new version of Joey Finch. She still wasn't quite sure what had caused his sudden appearance, but she had a strong suspicion Zack Kimel had something to do with it.

Nigel smirked. "I was just getting ready to tell this lovely lady that *I* will be totally at her disposal when she comes to London for her official book launch. *I'll* be her personal tour guide every single minute. Night and day." Nigel delivered the last few words with stinging precision.

"*We'll* enjoy that," Joey said, smoothly. "Won't we, Diana?" He eyed her confidently, waiting for her to confirm his words.

Diana had no idea what he expected her to say. This posturing was getting old fast. "I'm not sure, Joey," she replied. "What exactly will *we* be enjoying?"

"*We'll* enjoy Nigel showing *us* around London," he explained.

"I'm certain that *we* will," Diana agreed with only a tiny bit of sarcasm. "Since *we've* talked about going to London together *so* many times." She smiled, pleased to notice a dull flush had appeared on the lower part of Joey's face. At least he realized she wasn't buying his impromptu speech.

She heard another snort of laughter from Zack, who had appeared at Joey's elbow. She narrowed her eyes at him, calling him out as the catalyst of the whole debacle. Zack ducked his head, eyeing her hopefully. Diana made a drinking motion with her hand and mouthed the words *"to-go cup."* He turned back around and headed toward the kitchen.

Nigel and Joey were glaring at each other, reminding Diana of a staring match between a sleek Bengal tiger and an irate ostrich. *Hmm,* she mused. Her bird imagery was certainly in top form today. She ticked them off on her fingers: peacock, chicken, rooster. And now she was comparing Nigel to an ostrich. Funny how much she was enjoying the comparison, even while experiencing the strong urge to apologize to her feathered friends for the unintentional insult.

"Well," Nigel finally announced. "It's been lovely, but Lady Diana and I have a full day ahead of us." He reached out to take her arm, but she pulled it out of his reach.

"Nigel," Diana began, speaking slowly in an attempt to make him understand. "I told you in the email—the one you didn't bother to read—that today wasn't a good day for a meeting. I have a yoga class in"—she checked the cookie clock on the wall at the front of the restaurant—"fifteen minutes. And after that, I'm picking Amalie up for a dentist appointment. I work, Nigel. I am a *full-time* nanny in addition to writing books. I have responsibilities."

Nigel fluttered his hands in distress. "I don't know why you insist on taking care of that little brat. Surely you have enough fodder for your stories by now."

Joey opened his mouth, but Diana took over. "For your information, Nigel, Amalie *isn't* a little brat. And I *don't* take care of her to get ideas for stories. She's a sweet, little girl and I love her. That's reason enough for me." She glanced at Joey, who was regarding her with approval, as if she had performed well. She had seen that look before. On the face of her brother, her cousins, her father...

She suddenly understood exactly why Joey was there. It was crystal clear. He had come to rescue her. To swoop in and save the day. He obviously thought her too weak and fragile to handle the situation all by herself. He was treating her like a child.

And she hated it.

Where, she asked herself, was the man who stood *beside* her as she confronted Roman and Connor? Where was the man who placed himself on *equal* footing with her? The one who *supported* her as she fought her own battles? She was torn between a crushing sense of disappointment and a strong desire to punch Joey Finch. Where, she asked herself, were these violent urges coming from?

Zack reappeared just then, bearing a tray with a to-go cup, a Styrofoam cup with a straw, and a plate containing one lonely piece of toast. He stepped into the fray, moving between Diana and Nigel to place the Styrofoam cup and toast on the table. He handed Diana her to-go cup with an endearing grin that said, *I'm sorry. You can fuss at me later.*

"Thank you, Zack," Diana said, with a slight smile. It was obvious that he regretted calling Joey.

"Wha-wha-what is this?" Nigel was irate. He was holding the Styrofoam cup, an expression of true horror on his peaked face. His lips were screwed up as if he had just tasted the pure juice of a strong lemon.

Zack shrugged his shoulders. "You ordered tea and toast."

"This swill isn't tea," Nigel argued. "It doesn't even resemble tea."

"Oh, lighten up, Nigel," Diana instructed. "You got exactly what you asked for." She took a sip of her coffee.

Joey, she noticed, was trying not to laugh at Nigel's childish display.

Nigel, however, refused to let it go. "I demand to see the manager."

Zack shrugged again. "Okay. Let me see if he's here." He turned slightly to speak to the man behind the to-go counter. "Hey, Eli, is Dad here yet?"

"Not 'til eleven-thirty today, little bro," Eli hollered back.

"Dad's not here until eleven-thirty today," Zack said, politely. "Would you like to wait?"

"No, thank you," Nigel said, his beady eyes narrowed to slits on his pasty face.

"If you decide to wait, I'll give you a free refill on that tea," Zack added, pleasantly.

"No, thank you," Nigel said through gritted teeth. He grabbed the toast, barely managing to unclench his jaw long enough to bite into it.

Zack started to place the check on the table, but Diana intercepted it. "I've got this." She handed her credit card to the mischievous young man. He dutifully took it and headed to the cash register.

Nigel chewed in silence as he and Joey continued their nonverbal sparring.

Diana was finished with both of them. "Well, thank you, Nigel. Please email me the edits. I hope you have a pleasant trip back across the pond."

"But I thought we were going to spend the day together," Nigel whined, looking for all the world like a little boy whose ice cream had just melted.

Diana tossed her head. "Spend it with Joey. He doesn't seem to have anything else to do today."

The incredulous looks they both turned on her made her earlier discomfort almost worth it.

Almost.

She collected her credit card from Zack on the way out. "You and I are going to talk about this," she said right before she walked out the door.

344

Zack watched her go with admiration on his face. He liked Diana Merritt.

Nigel watched her go with unrequited longing. He was going to tell his mum all about this. And his Aunt Tracy, too.

Joey watched her go with the uneasy feeling that he had done something wrong. He just wasn't sure what it was. He was relieved that Diana's relationship with Nigel wasn't a stumbling block on the road to his happily ever after. *Their* happily ever after, he corrected himself. Zack's phone call had thrown him. He had never cared if a woman he asked out had other romantic interests. Sometimes he preferred that she did because it kept her from getting hung up on him. But hearing that Diana was having breakfast with another man…well, he didn't like how that felt. It was a new and very unpleasant feeling, one with which he was unfamiliar. Only when he experienced Nigel's limp fish handshake did he know he didn't have to worry.

"Listen, Joy," Nigel sneered. "By the way, isn't Joy a woman's name?"

Joey turned back to his nemesis. "It isn't Joy. It's Jo-ey. *Two* syllables."

Nigel waved his pale hand in the air, completely disregarding Joey's explanation. "All right, Joy…"

"Jo-ey."

"Jooy." Nigel deliberately lengthened the one syllable.

What an insufferable bastard, Joey thought. "Joe-ee," he said.

"Joooy," Nigel said, obviously enjoying himself.

"Joseph," Joey said, firmly. "My first name is Joseph. My *friends* call me Joey. *You* can call me Joseph."

"Are you dating Lady Diana, *Joseph*?" Nigel asked, superiority oozing from every syllable.

Joey wanted to lie, but he couldn't do it. It wasn't fair to Diana. "Not yet." It was all he could think of to say.

Nigel nodded in superior satisfaction. "That's what I thought." He continued in his most condescending tone. "Listen, *Joseph*, I have even less interest in spending one more minute in your presence than you do in mine."

"I doubt that," Joey muttered to himself.

"Pardon?" Nigel asked, expectantly.

"Nothing," Joey said.

Nigel grabbed his laptop and shoved it into his briefcase. "Then, I'll bid you good day...Joy." He hesitated just a second before grabbing his Styrofoam cup and heading out the door.

Joey walked to the front window and watched him go, pleased to note that he stomped off in the opposite direction from the one Diana had taken. Zack joined Joey at the window. Neither one of them said a word.

After a few seconds, Zack gave in. "I told you she had him by the balls," he crowed.

"You were wrong, Zack," Joey replied. He shook his head at the puzzled expression that formed on the young man's face. "Nigel doesn't have any balls."

Zack guffawed in appreciation. He had little time to enjoy Joey's putdown.

"Zack, table six!" Eli shouted.

"On it!" Zack yelled back. He left Joey gazing out the window, but he paused as he passed the counter. "Hey, Joey," he called back, laughter in his voice.

Joey turned his head. "Yeah?"

Zack indicated the forgotten bouquet lying on the counter. "Thanks for the flowers," he said with a chuckle before heading back to work.

Joey groaned. Diana wasn't happy with him. He was sure of that. He hadn't even given her the flowers and he had already messed up. He was terrible at this courtship thing. Being a reformed rake, he sadly realized, wasn't easy. He wasn't giving up, though. Diana was worth any amount of effort.

When he picked up the bouquet, the squashed lily and a few bits of ragged greenery were left behind on the counter. Apparently, he had been a bit careless when he dropped the flowers earlier. He smashed the remaining flowers together to cover up the gaping hole, frowning as a few of the dahlia petals and one of the roses fell off and joined the lily. After tossing the evidence of his floral abuse in the trashcan and brushing some glitter off the counter Joey headed out into the fall sunshine.

The air was already heating up, indicating another warm day was on its way. Summer hadn't relinquished her grip on the South, even though the mornings were starting to cool off nicely. Not unusual weather for the end of September. Joey figured he should probably check in at Parker and Finch but decided that another half hour wouldn't make that much difference. After this week, he wouldn't have as much free time at work. Hell, he wouldn't have *any* free time. But for now, he figured a casual stroll by Broad's Yoga Studio was a good idea. And if he happened to run into a certain irate woman with glorious red hair, well, so be it.

CHAPTER THIRTY

$\mathcal{S}$tanding on her yoga mat by the large front window of the studio, Diana tried to concentrate on her breathing. She really did. She tried to relax and stretch her tense muscles. But she never quite succeeded in releasing the pent-up stress that had invaded her body.

She arched her back into half camel.

As irritated as she was with Nigel, he had nothing to do with the keen disappointment she felt at the discovery that Joey Finch was *not* the perfect man. He was, it seemed, as overprotective and doubtful of her ability to handle herself as her brother and all the rest of her family.

Diana resumed a kneeling position to switch sides.

She should have figured that Joey's willingness to step back and let her handle herself in Alexandria was a fluke. A rare, atypical, and probably not to be repeated fluke. Well, Joey had shown his true colors today. Good thing she found him out when she did because this changed…absolutely nothing.

Drat.

Who was she kidding? She was *still* crazy about Joey Finch. He was *still* the epitome of everything she had ever wanted. She was just annoyed.

That's all. And she wanted to make sure Joey knew exactly how much his behavior had annoyed her.

She leaned forward into child's pose.

"Diana."

Diana turned her head. Aria, one of the women who had befriended her during her first class, had hissed her name. Child's pose made it easier for the two women to communicate. "What?" Diana whispered.

"Don't look now," Aria whispered in reply, "but I think Joey Finch is watching us through the window...."

Diana's head popped up. Sure enough, Joey was grinning at her on the other side of the glass. Grinning and waving.

"I told you not to look," Aria said, trying not to laugh at the horrified expression on her friend's face.

Diana quickly touched her forehead back to the mat. *Drat, drat, drat, and double dratting damn.*

After a few seconds, Aria cheerfully modified her statement. "I was wrong, Diana. He's only watching *you.*"

Diana's whole face felt like it was on fire. "I want the best-looking man I know to watch me doing yoga, said *no one ever,*" she muttered, pressing up into downward dog.

On her other side, Aria's younger sister, Elise, joined their whispered conversation. "Amen to that," she said in agreement.

Diana could almost feel Joey's eyes boring into her. How mortifying. She felt about as graceful doing yoga as an elephant attempting ballet.

Diana was the most graceful woman Joey had ever seen. Every sweeping movement of her long, supple limbs was elegant and lovely. The arch of her spine. The curve of her neck. Even the adorable way she pointed her dainty toes. She called to him like a flower attracting a particularly thirsty bee. He found himself unable to look away even after she caught him in the act. He felt like an idiot, smiling and waving in the face of her obvious displeasure.

Strike two, you idiot, he admonished himself. Not only had something about his encounter with the ridiculous Nigel Barclay made Diana angry, but the expression on her face when she caught him watching her wasn't exactly filled with joy. Since their initial eye contact, she steadfastly refused to meet his gaze again. To make matters worse, his presence outside the yoga studio was starting to attract the attention of passersby.

"Shopping for your next Friday night, Finch?" his longtime friend Roger Carrington asked, punching Joey in the arm as he walked by.

"Thinking of taking a yoga class, eh, Finch?" was the comment from Dr. Long, his dentist.

When a couple of ladies from the church choir walked by, Joey decided to wait for Diana inside. At least there he could escape public scrutiny.

"I think he's leaving, Diana," Elise hissed as they moved through a vinyasa.

"Good," Diana said, tentatively checking the window when she pushed up into cobra. Sure enough, there was no sign of the redoubtable Mr. Finch. He must have gotten the message and moved on. *Good,* she told herself again. It was exactly what he should have done. Moved on. On down the sidewalk. Back to his job. But…how was he going to see her displeasure if he couldn't *see* her displeasure?

"You spoke too soon, Elise," Aria said, gesturing to the front door with her head. "Look."

Diana glanced at the door and nearly lost her balance. Once again, Joey Finch had surprised her.

Joey felt the eyes of every member of the class when he walked in the door. He realized, just too late, that he was still holding the flowers for Diana. The slightly abused bouquet was like a beacon, calling even more attention to his unexplained—and possibly unwanted—presence. *Oh yeah,* he thought sarcastically. *Nobody's going to notice me here.* All of the women were frozen into the same deliberate pose: one foot set flat against the side of their thigh while standing on one leg. They looked like a flock of giant flamingos.

He scanned the group, realizing that he knew most of the women in the room. Too late, he glanced at the instructor—only to realize that he knew her, too. He had pursued Brianna Broad for a couple of months after his sophomore year of college. After their one and only date, he promptly lost interest. *Great,* he thought. Another reminder that he really was an ass.

Brianna obviously wasn't one to hold a grudge because she was currently grinning at him from the front of the room. The other women regarded him with varying degrees of surprise, interest, or—in the case of the three maintenance-intensive women in the back—desperation. Waving their arms in a bid to attract his attention, the trio resembled three deranged chickens trying to take flight.

Only one woman in the room appeared oblivious to his presence. Diana flatly refused to make eye contact, choosing instead to focus on the large front window. Joey had to make a quick decision. He could run for his life while his dignity was still more or less intact. Or he could do what he did best and charm that room full of women from the top of their messy buns and ponytails to the bottom of their yoga pants. At this point he would do almost anything to make his red-haired siren notice him.

You were an ass, Finch, he encouraged himself. *Now you are a reformed ass...rake...rascal.* Yeah. Reformed *rascal* sounded better. He tossed the bouquet on a chair by the door. Then he raised his leg and bent his knee, pressing the bottom of his shoe to the side of his calf, doing his best to mimic the flamingo pose. He raised his arms over his head like

351

a ballet dancer. Several of the ladies giggled. Aria and Elise exchanged a knowing glance behind Diana's back. Joey knew them, too: he had taken Ari to a church picnic a couple of summers ago. *Damn, damn, damn.* He never thought he would live to regret any of those innocent outings. He did, though. He regretted anything that made his current pursuit of the delectable redhead in yoga pants more difficult.

Diana remained perfectly still, determined not to react to Joey's performance. *Don't look at him,* she instructed herself. *Do. Not. Look.*

The class returned to mountain pose. Joey looked rather proud of himself...until Brianna gave the instructions for tree pose on the other foot. Joey wobbled a bit, but he finally managed to stick his foot to his calf. This time he raised his arms straight into the air in a touchdown motion. The women who could maintain their balance gave him an enthusiastic round of applause. The others cheered.

All but one.

Do. Not. Look. Diana tried to firm her resolve but felt herself weakening. *He's so adorable,* she argued with herself. *Adorable,* she added the next moment, *but overprotective. Do. Not. Look.*

Brianna took control of the situation. "Great work, Joey, but I don't think the seams of your pants will survive the rest of the class. You may want to have a seat by the door to wait."

He good-naturedly complied, picking up his bruised bouquet. He had to brush a stack of rose petals and dahlia parts out of his chair before taking a seat. He studied the drooping bouquet. For some reason, there seemed to be fewer blooms than he remembered. And the flowers that remained intact didn't look quite right. He tried to push the surviving flowers together to hide the missing ones but decided to stop when the last dahlia popped off. He kicked it under the chair. The lacy ribbon that held the bouquet together hung drunkenly from the flower stems. One side of the ribbon was smeared with something that looked like chocolate syrup, probably from the counter at Jack's. He lifted what remained of the bouquet to his nose and took a big whiff. At least it still smelled nice.

He glanced up, then…Diana had finally lost her battle not to look at him. She quickly looked away, but he saw the tiny smile that appeared on her lips before she managed to hide it. He must look like a complete moron sitting there with his nose smashed into his flowers. He didn't know if she was laughing *at* him or laughing *with* him. He was afraid it was the former. He dropped the floral mess on the floor, pulled out his phone, and pretended to check his messages.

As Brianna instructed the class to lie back into corpse pose, Diana struggled to keep her face straight. She closed her eyes. The situation was getting more ridiculous by the minute. Her inability to resist Joey Finch's charm was maddening. It was becoming harder and harder to remember why she was unhappy with the man. How could she remain angry with someone who would go to such lengths to get her attention? He was *so* cute sitting in his chair, smelling his scraggly, little bouquet. And waiting… for her?

She wondered if he had picked the flowers himself. They had to be for her. Didn't they? *Of course,* she chided herself. *Don't be silly, Diana.* Those flowers *must* be for her. He'd been dragging the bouquet around since he burst into Jack's to…

Her eyes flew open at the memory, freeing her from her lovesick haze. Wait just a minute, she thought. Hold everything. He'd been dragging that dratted bouquet around since he burst into Jack's to infuriate her with his overbearing and overprotective behavior. Now she remembered why she was so angry with the charming Mr. Finch. Diana sat up with the rest of the class, her gray eyes narrowed into slits.

Joey Finch might look harmless enough, she fumed. Pretending to do yoga in his khaki pants and button-down shirt. With his sleeves rolled up to reveal his muscular forearms. And a lock of his dark hair brushing the scar on his forehead. He might look sweet and goofy smelling his homemade bouquet while his dark eyes watched her every move. But… Harmless, sweet, and goofy could turn into bossy, patronizing, and opinionated in an instant. She had watched that happen with her own family too many times to count. No, she decided. She would not let Mr. Finch off the hook so easily. He needed to learn his lesson, and who better to teach him than Nanny Di herself?

The yoga class ended. Finally. Joey couldn't wait to apologize for upsetting Diana. He still wasn't sure what he had done to make her angry, but he didn't care. He would apologize anyway. He would say anything she wanted. His personal dignity didn't matter in the least. But Diana did. She mattered a lot. She had almost smiled while he was smelling the bouquet. He would present the remains to her, along with a heartfelt "I'm sorry."

He was determined to put a sunny smile back on her beautiful face. Then he would ask her out again. And surely, this time, her luscious peach-colored lips—her *as-of-yet-unkissed-by-Joey-Finch* luscious peach-colored lips—would say yes. He'd spent quite a bit of time lately thinking about those lips. He planned to remedy that unkissed problem as soon as he possibly could.

His lovely daydream evaporated immediately amid the chaos of one class ending and the other beginning. Without warning, he was surrounded by women. Big ones. Small ones. Old ones. Young ones. Some sporting fake tans and botoxed lips. Others with a more natural look. Natural blondes. Bleached blondes. Brunettes. Even a couple of carrottops. But no long red curls glowing with gorgeous highlights of auburn and a thousand other shades. Where was Diana?

He glanced at the throng milling around him. So many women, all talking at once.

Talk, talk, talk.

Blah, blah, blah.

The noise made his head swim. He felt like the only rooster in a crowded chicken coop. To make matters worse, most of the chickens were eager to talk to the rooster…namely him. Joey maintained a polite façade from sheer force of will. He answered questions—about his family, his job, how he liked being back in Honeysuckle Creek—while keeping his eyes peeled for the one woman in the yoga studio who was trying to avoid him.

Aria caught his eye and pointed to the front window. Joey saw the redhead hurrying down the sidewalk, her big gym bag slung over her shoulder. He gave Ari a quick thumbs-up—he had always liked her—and started inching backwards toward the door. His heel caught on something, nearly tripping him. The forgotten bouquet. Or what was left of it. It had been trampled more than once. He reached down and snagged it, anyway, before anyone else could step on it. He backed out the door, breathing a sigh of relief when he made it to the sidewalk…until he turned around.

Liz Grubbs, Leslie Cline, and Cassidy Meadows stood in front of him, purposely blocking his way. They were the proverbial mean girls in his high school graduating class. Almost all his female friends had been victimized by the trio at one time or another. Joey had never pursued Cassidy. She wasn't his type. But—he hated to admit it, even now—he had once gone to a birthday party with Liz during freshman year, and he had taken Leslie to the spring dance when he was a sophomore. That was before he matured sufficiently to realize that their sweet, Southern belle masks hid selfish, grasping personalities.

The three witches would stop at nothing—no matter how cruel or dishonest—to get their own way. He still couldn't forget how they had treated his sweet sister, Grace, while she was estranged from her best friend, Lou Boggs. He neither liked nor wanted anything to do with the bitchy, little trio.

Yet, here they were, smiling their fake, syrupy smiles as if they expected Joey Finch to fall all over himself in his efforts to please.

"Jo-ey," cooed Cassidy. "Did you pick tha-at pitiful, little ole bouquet all by yo-our lonesome?"

"I'd be happy to help you find some more flowers, sug-ah." Leslie struck an awkward pose. Joey assumed she was trying to look sexy. He thought she looked like a department store mannequin.

"Um…that's okay," Joey said, craning his head to keep Diana in sight.

"You're not chasing after Little Miss Redhead, are you?" Liz asked, a slight edge in her voice. "I certainly hope not. She's not at all your type... so washed-out and boring and no personality to speak of. You're way too good for her."

Joey's pleasant expression didn't falter. *Yep, you're still the Queen Bitch, Liz,* he thought.

Cassidy pointed at the pitiful bouquet, with a sad smile on her face. "I thi-ink it's a go-od choice if it's for *her*. It lo-oks just li-ike *her*."

The three demons squealed with laughter as Joey studied the stems in his hand. The ribbon had disappeared and so had most of the glitter. There were only three roses left...well, one of them had half its petals and the other was squashed on one side. There was only one perfect rose left, he decided. But so what? The flowers—*flower*—wasn't for the critical women in front of him, anyway. The condition of that perfect rose wasn't any of their business. He was wasting his time with the venomous trio while Diana was getting away.

Leslie twirled a finger in her own brown locks. "Redheads aren't your style, Joey. I remember you as more of a brunette kind of guy."

After scarcely a moment in their presence, Joey already was heartily sick of their comments. He opened his mouth to tell them exactly what he thought of their tactics when something Liz had said gave him pause. She— and her minions—were acquainted with Diana, it seemed. Which meant...

"The three of you talked to Diana, didn't you?" he asked, carefully.

Liz couldn't wait to enlighten him. "Oh, yes. We told her *all* about you last week."

"Oh, really?" Joey mused, without cracking a smile. "And just what did you say?"

Cassidy giggled. "You kno-ow...how you're a one and done."

Joey's heart started to thud heavily. What exactly had they told Diana? And more importantly, how much did their malicious words have to do with her refusal to go out with him?

"A one and done," he said, tonelessly. "Am I?"

"Silly," Leslie giggled, batting her fake eyelashes. "You know you are."

"Everybody knows tha-at," Cassidy agreed.

Joey laughed weakly. He was trying not to let his sudden anxiety show. "I mean, how did you explain my…um…one-and-doneness to Diana?"

"After one date with Joey Fi-inch, he's done," Cassidy recited, gleefully.

The spiteful three burst into delighted laughter.

Well, hell. Joey almost groaned aloud. No wonder Diana wouldn't go out with him. He wasn't even sure he wanted to go out with himself.

"You should thank us, Joey," Liz purred.

"For what?" he asked, brusquely. *For ruining my life? For discouraging the only woman I've ever wanted?*

The catty woman's confident smile slipped. "For protecting you. She's *obviously* not your type, Joey. That red hair…" Liz shivered as if having red hair was a terrible disease.

"And she's *too* tall…" Leslie added.

"*And* her hair is too long and thick and curly," Cassidy said.

Liz and Leslie looked at her like she was an imbecile.

"What's wrong with that?" Joey asked. He was out of patience with their immaturity and snide remarks. "Wouldn't you like to have long, thick, curly hair?"

Cassidy thought about it for a second. "Yes." She nodded soberly. "Yes, I would. I wonder if Diana would have any tips about that. She really does have gorgeous hair…."

"Shut up, Cassidy," Liz and Leslie intoned together.

Joey almost grinned. Maybe he hadn't given Cassidy enough credit. She was bitchy, but maybe she wasn't quite as bitchy as the other two. Be that as it may, Joey could see the long, thick, curly red hair of the woman he wanted, preparing to cross the street. He needed to catch up with her before she disappeared into the park. Or drove away. He realized he had no idea where she had parked her car.

"Ladies, if you'll excuse me, I have somewhere I need to be." Joey stepped neatly around the three witches.

The hateful trio appeared shocked that he dared to take his leave before they were finished with him.

"Where are you going?" Cassidy demanded, hands on hips.

Leslie pursed her lips into a pretty pout. "You're not chasing after *her*, are you?"

"You can't be serious," Liz said. "She's so…so…"

"Accomplished? Beautiful? Charming and kind?" Joey asked, turning back with a wink. "Yes, she is." His words provoked outraged gasps from the petty trio. He left them standing on the sidewalk; he couldn't help but feel somewhat vindicated. As he started off in pursuit of his ideal woman, his pace accelerated along with his heartbeat.

CHAPTER THIRTY-ONE

$\mathcal{D}$iana couldn't get far enough away from Broad's Yoga Studio. Joey's unexpected appearance had been bad enough...but watching half of the women fawn all over him? Well, it was just too much. She didn't have any trouble sneaking by him because he was surrounded by his...She hesitated, searching for the right term. Surrounded by his *fan club*. Yes, that was it, she thought, uncharitably.

His. Fan. Club.

Of which, she assured herself, she was *not* a member. Nor was she going to be a member. *Ever.*

Diana crossed the street, intending to cut through Honeysuckle Creek Park. Walking through the well-kept park was a pleasure she reserved for herself after every yoga class. The sheer beauty of the place raised her spirits. The bright blue sky was free of clouds. The sun shone warmly, determined to keep the seasons guessing as long as possible. The grass was carefully tended, still green and thick. The trees were just beginning to turn, promising a glorious autumn spectacle yet to come. And, best of all, mums were everywhere she looked. Most of them were beginning to bloom, hinting of their future red, yellow, lavender, white, pink, and bronze splendor. A few around the gazebo in the middle of the park were already in full flower.

Unbidden, her mind drifted to Joey's face when she had caught him smelling his bouquet. She felt some empathy for his poor flowers. They hadn't had an easy day, either. She remembered how lovely the bouquet was when he tossed it on the counter at Jack's. Perfect blooms. Just the right touch of greenery. And tied with a lovely, lacy ribbon. Of course, she reminded herself, that was right before he rushed to her rescue, even though she didn't *need* to be rescued.

The whole scenario was confusing. How had she misread Joey so completely? Until this morning, she was certain he understood how important his support was to her. His support. Not his interference. She didn't want someone to fight her battles *for* her. She needed someone to stand *beside* her. And, Diana sighed, wistfully, perhaps sometimes she needed someone to hold her hand and tell her everything was going to be all right. But...

Those flowers were for her. She knew they were for her. And, despite everything, she wanted them. She wanted them desperately.

Drat. She wanted Joey Finch desperately, too.

Joey finally caught sight of her on the other side of the gazebo. "Di-a-na," he called. "Di-a-na, wait!" He sprinted the last few yards, stopping about three feet away from her. His pitiful smattering of greenery—it didn't resemble a bouquet anymore—dangled from his left hand.

She turned around when he called her name, her ponytail gleaming in the sunshine. She crossed her arms over her chest and waited. Her dark gray eyes were full of disappointment. And mistrust.

Good Lord, he thought. *What did I do?* She had never looked at him like that before. He would do anything to make her stop.

"Diana." He took a cautious step forward. "Diana, I'm so sorry."

She narrowed her eyes but held her ground. "Why, Joey?" she asked, evenly. "Why are you sorry?"

He hesitated about a second too long. "Um…I'm sorry that you're upset…that I upset you." There. That was broad enough to cover a multitude of sins. He smiled, anxiously.

Wrong answer. Diana's chin came up. "You don't have any idea why I'm upset, do you?" She stood there looking at him. Waiting.

With a sudden flash of insight, he realized that she was using his own tactic on him. And Joey didn't like it. No, he didn't like it at all. But, he had to admit, her silence worked like a charm. He found himself babbling, merely to fill the empty air between them.

"I know that I upset you and I'm very sorry for that. You don't know how sorry I am. I didn't mean to interrupt your meeting." He paused, hopefully. "Is that it? Are you angry because you didn't get to finish your meeting? Because if that's what it is, I can promise you that I will never interrupt another meeting again."

She shook her head. Her disappointment deepened.

Damn. He tried again. "Or is it because of Nigel? I didn't intend to be so rough on him. You have to admit, though, he asked for it. I mean, who does he think he is anyway? But, if he's a good friend of yours—although I don't see how that's possible—I'm sorry that I didn't treat him with the utmost—"

"Oh, please." Diana groaned. "Nigel is an ass."

Joey couldn't believe the feeling of relief that flowed through him at her words. He was secretly harboring the impossible idea that Diana was somehow involved with the pompously arrogant Brit.

She was eyeing him with disbelief now. "You don't know, do you? You, Joey Finch, are one of the smartest men I've ever met, and you don't have a clue what you did." She turned around and started walking again.

The pleasure he felt at being one of the smartest men Diana had ever met dimmed under her spot-on accusation. She was right. He had absolutely no idea what he had done.

He trotted after her. "You're right, Diana," he admitted. "I have no idea why you're upset with me." There. He'd told the truth. He looked like a jerk, but he told the truth. He waited, almost holding his breath, to see what she would say.

She hesitated, but in the end she couldn't resist the genuine concern in his eyes. She stopped walking.

"You acted like *them*," she said, softly. "I thought you were different, but you acted just like *they* do."

Joey stopped beside her. "I don't understand. Who are *they*?"

She wasn't looking at him. "Roman and Connor and Lance and the Trio of Doom and every other male in my life. They act like I'm weak and incapable of handling a situation by myself. They want to swoop in and take over. They treat me like a child who needs to be rescued…like I'm too helpless or too stupid to take care of myself." She kept her eyes on the gravel walk at her feet.

Would he apologize now? She doubted it. He would probably tell her she was being a drama queen. Roman had done that more times than she could count. What if Joey decided she wasn't worth the trouble? She peeked at him through her eyelashes. And she couldn't have been more surprised by what she saw.

Joey was staring at her as if she had lost her mind. "What are you talking about, Diana? You are one of the most capable people I know. And one of the bravest." He ran the fingers of his flowerless hand through his thick, dark hair in obvious agitation. "That's *not* why I came to Jack's this morning. That's not the reason at all."

And Diana believed him. She couldn't help it. His distress was real. A wave of hope swept through her. Maybe, just maybe, she had misunderstood his motives. But if he wasn't being overprotective… "Then, why, Joey?" she demanded. "Why did you come barreling into Jack's like a knight determined to slay my dragons *for* me?" Her hands were on her hips and she appeared ready for battle herself if Joey failed to explain himself to her satisfaction. One of her long curls had come loose from her ponytail. She shoved it behind her ear impatiently.

Damn. Joey was fairly certain he knew the answer to her question. *Admit it, Finch,* he informed his, apparently, fragile ego. *You were jealous as hell.*

Jealousy was an unfamiliar emotion; one he hadn't experienced since Ana Martin chose Blane instead of Joey as her dance partner on the first day of sixth grade cotillion. Though Joey had quickly recovered from Ana's supposed slight, he still remembered the all-encompassing feeling. But way back in the sixth grade he had never had to admit he was jealous.

This time, he realized, was going to be different. And tricky. It was one thing for him to identify his own feelings of jealousy. It was entirely another matter to admit those feelings to Diana. He would have to phrase his explanation very carefully. But, as had happened before in her presence, he opened his mouth and the truth fell out.

"When Zack called, he told me you were having breakfast with some 'British dude' so I guess I just wanted to check out the competition. Then, when I saw him touching your chin..." Joey paused as anger swept through him again at the thought of Nigel's hands on Diana's delectable face. Nigel didn't deserve the privilege of thinking about Diana, much less touching her. Joey should have thrown the pompous bastard to the ground when he had the chance.

He tried to shake off that feeling—envy...fear...possession—but the Green Monster dug in its claws and hung on. Maybe Diana wouldn't notice, he thought. One glance at her, however, confirmed that wasn't going to happen. Diana looked stunned. *Damn.* How transparent could he be? Joey felt like the word *jealous* was stamped across his forehead. In giant capital letters. In neon green.

"Joey?" Diana asked in disbelief. "You were jealous?" Her lips turned up in a tiny smile.

Way to go, Captain Obvious, he berated himself. So much for hiding his emotions. He tried to backpedal. "Um...jealous? I might use another word besides jealous." He tried to sound casual. "Maybe concerned. Or um...uneasy. I didn't know the guy and I just wanted to make sure..." He blew out a breath. "It's really hot out here, isn't it?" he finished lamely.

Diana's radiant smile was his undoing. The sparkle in her eyes sent him tumbling over the brink. He would admit anything if she would keep looking at him just like that.

"Jealous of *Nigel*?" she asked, her gray eyes dancing.

Joey shrugged his shoulders ruefully. He reached out and took her hand, pleased when she didn't pull away. "Well, you see," he said, "after one look at old Nigel, I could tell that he has a lot going for him."

"Oh, really?" she mused. "I hadn't noticed."

They strolled down the gravel path hand in hand.

Joey grinned, happy with her response. "Yeah, well, I'm a detail guy. I notice things like that. He's tall, for one thing. Probably able to reach anything on the top shelf at the grocery store, even if it's way in the back."

"Hmm," Diana said. "That's a good point. And a very useful skill. But I think Nigel's more likely to say something condescending and walk away than to use his height to actually *help* someone."

Joey scrunched his face, as if deep in thought. "True. But he has charming table manners. Did you see the way he bit into his toast?"

"Yes, I noticed that." Diana nodded, placidly. "And he was so *kind* to Zack, too."

They shared a smile of complete understanding.

"Nigel is an ass," she said. "He deserved everything he got—up to and including his sweetened iced tea."

"He took it with him, by the way," Joey added, grinning.

"What?" Diana gasped. "I can't believe it." She started giggling then, from the sheer relief that she had misjudged him. Or was it from shock that Joey-He-Really-Is-The-Perfect-Man-Finch was jealous? And jealous of Nigel, no less, which naturally made Joey even more perfect. Maybe she was giggling—all right, practically giddy—because her *perfect man* was holding her hand. Or maybe it was a combination of all three.

The sound of Diana's laughter soothed Joey's soul, somehow. All was suddenly right with the world. He would have been content to spend the rest of the day walking around Honeysuckle Creek Park with his charming companion, until he realized she had suddenly stopped walking.

"What's wrong?" he asked, reluctant to relinquish her hand.

She pointed to the neat, little convertible parked on the other side of Broad Street. "My car," she said. "I have to pick up Amalie for the dentist." She squeezed his hand before letting it go. He let their grasp release slowly, allowing his palm to slide against hers. He immediately missed the contact.

She gave him a shy, little smile. "Um, Joey, can I ask you a question?"

"Of course." Had she asked for the moon at this point, he couldn't have denied her.

"Is that flower for me?" She pointed to the pitiful remains of the bouquet he still held in his hand.

Joey glanced at what was left of his first effort at courtship...one perfect bloom and a bunch of drooping greenery. He was a little embarrassed. "Yeah, but it looked a lot better when I bought it. I should probably just throw it away."

"Oh, no," she said, quickly, holding out her hand. "Please don't. I want it."

Joey shook his head. "That's okay, Diana. You don't have to..."

"No, really, Joey." She was completely serious.

He shrugged and handed her the scraggly mess. Uncertainty had replaced his usually confident expression. Diana experienced a strange sense of having lived this moment before. Not déjà vu, exactly, but...suddenly the passage she had written—just the night before—popped into her head....

"Are those for me?" Genevieve asked, sweetly. Ezekiel looked a little shy. She had never seen him look that way before. The flowers he clutched in his hand were obviously plucked from the borders of the garden on his way out of the castle. The earl must have rushed outside as soon as he saw her walk

by the window of his study, she realized. And he felt the need to bring flowers. Genevieve's soft heart melted at the thought. She tried to remind herself that Ezekiel probably gave flowers to all his paramours—of which she, most certainly, was not—but the thought just wouldn't stick this time. So, she let it go. This time Genevieve was going to give Ezekiel the benefit of the doubt.

And she, Diana decided, would follow Genevieve's lead. This time Diana Merritt was going to give Joey Finch the benefit of the doubt. She was going to trust her instincts. If—when—he asked her out again she was going to say yes.

Joey couldn't tell what Diana was thinking. Her eyes held a faraway expression, as if she was gazing at some happily ever after that only she could see. Her lovely face was slightly flushed. Her delectable, peach-colored lips tipped up at the corners in the barest hint of a smile. Joey felt dazed and unfocused and very, very warm. He desired nothing more than to close the distance between them to touch her kissable lips with his own. He was standing in a park beside the woman of his dreams surrounded by nature's gorgeous vista. It was the perfect opportunity to ask her out on a date...the moment that would take their relationship to the next level. Then he could kiss her. Not a lover's kiss, he scolded himself. Not yet. A small kiss. A kiss that hinted of kisses to come. But he hesitated....What if she didn't kiss him back? What if she turned her head? What if he asked her out and she said no? Again. The doubts and insecurities he had managed to suppress since The Night She Turned Him Down roared to the surface. He opened his mouth to speak but closed it immediately when his usually glib tongue refused to cooperate. He opened his mouth again. Nothing came out. He closed it quickly. He tried once more. Still nothing. He imagined he looked like some sort of demented fish. Aimlessly floundering. Gasping for breath. Mouth hanging open. Not a pretty picture.

He glanced around, desperate for inspiration, as two older gentlemen walked by. The two men, deep in discussion, ignored Joey and Diana completely. Joey heard only a fragment of their conversation. "...Such a second-half team," the first man grumbled, shaking his head in frustration. "We're never going to win any games at this rate." The second man nodded in agreement. "Too bad we can't skip the first half of the game and go straight to the second. At least, then, we..." Their voices trailed away as they walked on with no clue of the impact of their words.

For Joey, it was as if the heavens had opened, shining down on him the light of divine inspiration. And in that moment, he knew exactly what to say. He opened his mouth to share his brilliance with the most important woman in the world.

"Diana, would you..."

"Yes," she answered instantly. Her eyes flew to his in surprise. Joey looked torn between amusement and concern. *Oh, drat, drat, drat.* He hadn't even finished asking the question, had he? *Way to not look too eager, Diana,* she berated herself. *Or too pathetic.*

Joey was filled with hope for the first time since The Night She Turned Him Down. Today, he decided, was going to be different. Today would be The Day She Said Yes. He was certain, now, his idea would work.

"Diana, would you like to go out with me on a second date?" He watched the frown appear on her pretty face.

"A second date?" she asked, tilting her head to study him in confusion. "But..."

Joey grinned, confidently. "Well, we already had our first date," he said. "Remember? We ran into each other at Chutley's and went back to my apartment for tea."

Diana's confusion melted away as a blinding smile took its place. "I do remember," she agreed.

The smile was nearly his undoing, but Joey somehow managed a reply. "Then, we drove to Alexandria. And on the way we stopped for coffee..."

"And chocolate twirls," Diana added, getting into the spirit of things. "After that, we tried to eat at McDonald's, but ended up in the emergency room." Her smile turned mischievous.

"Hmph," Joey grunted. But he was too happy she was playing his game to object to her teasing.

Diana continued, enthusiastically: "We took the *scenic* route to the beautiful Acorn Knob Inn..."

"Where we shared a bed with two zip codes..." Joey added, wickedly pleased with the way her eyes flared at the mention of their night together. Not to mention her soft intake of breath. "And a fabulous breakfast buffet," he finished with a flourish.

His mention of food allowed Diana to recover her equilibrium. To a degree. She could still hear the breathless quality in her voice as she ended their story. "And then you took me to my new home...well, I guess I took you," she said, apologetically. "Wow."

"Wow," Joey nodded in agreement. "Quite a first date, don't you agree?"

Diana's eyes were glowing. "I have *never* heard of another first date quite like ours," she answered honestly. She lifted the rose to her pert, little nose, inhaling the lovely fragrance.

Joey couldn't have been more surprised by the look of genuine pleasure that lit her lovely face...until she leaned over and kissed him on the cheek.

"Thank you for the rose, Joey. You're so sweet."

Before he could recover from the soft brush of her peach-colored lips, she was crossing the street, heading to her car. If he reacted this strongly to the feel of those lips on his cheek, touching those kissable lips with his own would probably kill him. He decided immediately that he was willing to take that chance. He watched as she opened her trunk and placed her gym bag inside. She walked to the driver's side and opened her door. It dawned on him, then, that he was blowing his golden opportunity.

"Diana," he yelled, across the street, not caring who heard.

She turned her head inquiringly, still clutching the remains of his bouquet.

"Will you go out with me on Friday night? he yelled across the street.

She flashed him a smile that warmed him where he stood. And, suddenly, he knew exactly what was going to happen. She was going to go out with him. He was going to take her to the nicest restaurant in town. They were going to have a wonderful time at dinner. That was a given, he thought. He *always* had a wonderful time with Diana.

After dinner, he would take her home. And then, he was going to kiss her. He was going to put his hands in all that gorgeous hair and kiss those peach-colored lips the way he had dreamed about every night since the Acorn Knob Inn. He had dreamed about more than kisses, he reminded himself, but it was only their first—um…*second*—date. There would be many more dates to come. Many more kisses. And touches. And long, hot nights…

"Yes!" she yelled back. "I would love to go out with you, Joey Finch. Text me the details." After blowing him a kiss, she got into the car and closed the door. A few seconds later, she started the motor and backed out of the space.

Joey watched her drive away with—what he assumed was—the most smitten, besotted, head-over-freakin'-heels lovesick expression that ever graced the face of a mortal man. She *wanted* to go out with him, he rejoiced. She thought he was sweet. She loved his bouquet—what was left of his bouquet—even though it was a mess. Maybe Diana Merritt loved him, too…just a little.

CHAPTER THIRTY-TWO

"*H*onestly, Lou. How many bobby pins do you have to stick into her head?" Darcie grumbled, glancing at her watch.

"I'll be finished in a couple of minutes," Lou mumbled, her mouth full of pins.

More pins? Diana privately thought her hair could already withstand hurricane force winds, but she kept that opinion to herself.

"Amalie and I would like to see the finished product *before* we go to the airport. Wouldn't we, Amalie?" Darcie winked at the excited, little girl.

Lou stuck her tongue out at Darcie. "You can't rush perfection," she said.

Darcie wrinkled her nose. "Hmph."

Diana chuckled at the exchange. She was happy for their support, even if her head had become a giant pin cushion. She was enjoying her new housing situation immensely. In addition to being easy to live with—a lovely quality in a roommate—Darcie was also vastly entertaining. And, an added bonus, the stunning brunette told the most interesting stories about her brother. Yes, Diana thought, she had learned quite a lot about the esteemed Mr. Finch since moving into the gatekeeper's cottage.

Although the lovely cottage was on the grounds of Blane's well-protected estate, its proximity to the highway was initially deemed too risky by Diana's self-appointed bodyguards. The minute her "safety restrictions" were lifted, however, she packed her bags and moved in. More often than not, Diana had the place to herself as Darcie spent so much time at the main house. She admired the careful way Darcie and Devin handled their relationship, the bulk of which occurred under the watchful eyes of an inquisitive five-year-old girl.

"Nanny Di looks like a princess!" that five-year-old squealed, excitedly. "Can she wear a tiara? Oh, Miss Lou, can she? Can she borrow one of your tiaras?" Amalie bounced on Diana's bed in excitement.

Lou, who spent years on the pageant circuit, had acquired an impressive collection of tiaras. The lovely blonde laughed at that thought, sticking in the last pin. "There. All finished."

Amalie, however, refused to give up. She was beside herself with excitement at her own brilliant idea. "Nanny Di, do you want *me* to ask Miss Lou if you can borrow one of her tiaras?" She tried to whisper, but she didn't have much success. "Miss Lou and I are great friends. I'm sure she won't mind."

"Now, Amalie…" Diana began. She was extremely grateful to Lou for offering to do her hair and makeup. On her own, she would have ended up with mascara in her eyebrows and lipstick up her nose because her hands were shaking so badly. But, Diana decided, she drew the line at tiaras, regardless of what the stylish blonde had to say.

Lou winked at Amalie. "You and I will always be great friends, Amalie. But since this is Nanny Di's very first date with Uncle Joey—even though they've already spent enough time together to count as fifty first dates—…" Lou shot Darcie a knowing glance before continuing, "…we should probably let Nanny Di decide."

Darcie snorted with suppressed laughter, but Lou managed to keep a straight face. Diana's expression was a charming combination of irritation and resignation.

"Diana," Lou continued. "Do *you* want to borrow a tiara?"

"No, thank you," Diana said, politely. "I don't need any more metal in my hair. I already feel like a human lightning rod."

Lou was delighted by Diana's unexpected comeback. "That's the spirit," she praised. "I had to use all of these pins because I'm not going to spray your hair. You'll thank me for that when you take it down." She arched her eyebrows, glancing again at Darcie. "Or when *somebody else* helps you take it down."

Darcie chuckled at that, but Amalie looked puzzled. "Who's going to help her take it down, Miss Lou? Mama Darcie and I will be in Scotland when she gets home so we can't help her."

"We'll be on the *plane* to Scotland," Darcie gently corrected her.

But Amalie was genuinely concerned. "Will you come back to help Nanny Di take her hair down, Miss Lou?" she asked.

"No, sweetie," Lou explained. "Zack and I are taking Mr. Evander out for his birthday after the game."

"Poor Nanny Di," Amalie said, sadly. As she watched Diana sip from her water bottle, Amalie's little face was downcast. She pondered the problem. Two seconds later, the little girl was all smiles. "I know who can help!" she announced, innocently. "Don't worry, Nanny Di! Uncle Joey can help!"

Diana choked, nearly spitting out her water.

Darcie patted her on the back, grinning from ear to ear. "That's a wonderful idea, Amalie," she said, agreeably. "Uncle Joey is the perfect choice."

Diana narrowed her eyes at her friends, who were having entirely too much fun at her expense. "You two are incorrigible," she declared.

"Spoken like a true nanny," Lou said, grinning back innocently.

"Nanny Di *is* a true nanny," Amalie observed. "She's *my* true nanny." She smiled at her true nanny. "Nanny Di, what does in-cur-age-abel mean?

Is it like courage? I know what that means. It means Mama Darcie and Miss Lou are very brave."

"They certainly are," Diana remarked to no one in particular.

Lou helped Diana off the stool that she had placed in the bedroom and turned her around to face the mirror. "A star is born."

Diana couldn't help but smile as she studied herself in the mirror. Lou was a master of subtlety. She managed to bring out the best of Diana's features—her dark, gray eyes and her peach-colored lips—while downplaying the rest. Her pale skin had a natural glow. *And*, for once, she actually had cheekbones.

She turned her face from side to side. "Will you come over and do my makeup every day?" she asked, ruefully.

Lou shook her head. "Silly girl! What are you talking about? You don't even need makeup. You're what we in the business call a natural beauty."

Diana made a little sound of disbelief. "That's what *you* are, Lou. Not me."

"Save the mutual admiration society meeting for later." Darcie could always be depended upon to be practical. "Uncle Joey won't be late! I'll get the dress," she said, her head disappearing into Diana's closet.

"I'll go and wait for Uncle Joey," Amalie announced, jumping off her perch on the bed.

Uncle Joey was currently driving to Heart's Ease while deep in the throes of a serious bout of date nerves. His first-ever bout with date nerves, if he were being honest. If he harbored any doubts that what he felt for Diana Merritt was the real deal—and he had absolutely no doubts about that—the disturbing feelings in his stomach would have convinced him. It was as if he had swallowed an entire box of the bouncy balls he used to get out of the machine at the Honeysuckle Creek Diner when he was a kid. The overly active orbs were currently out of control and would probably bounce in perpetuity until his anxiety was assuaged. In other words, until his date with Diana was finally underway.

He still wouldn't blame her if she changed her mind, he admitted. His history revealed him to be a flight risk. Under the circumstances, Diana was putting enormous trust in him. He was both heartened by her trust and scared to death he was going to screw up.

He turned into the drive that led to Heart's Ease, pausing to punch in his code. He could hear his heartbeat in his ears; he could feel the bouncing balls in his stomach. He took a deep breath, blowing the air out slowly as he drove across the bridge. Three cars stood silently in the driveway of the gatekeeper's cottage: Diana's convertible, Darcie's Jeep, and Lou's light gray Mercedes. Three cars.

Great. Just great, he thought. It was bad enough that he had to pick Diana up under the overly interested, never-miss-a-detail eyes of his baby sister. But now he had to deal with Lou, too.

Relax, Finch, he told himself, as he got out of the car. *You finally got the date, now go get the girl.* He hoped he looked calm, cool, and completely in control. He couldn't help but glance in the window of his car to make sure. It was an old habit. He ran his hand through his hair to fluff it up. Then he walked toward the house, heart pounding, stomach churning. Just as he reached the bottom of the steps leading up to the porch, the front door flew open.

"Uncle Joey!" Amalie shrieked, completely undone with excitement. She rushed down the steps, jumping into his outstretched arms. "Nanny Di looks like a princess! She's *beautiful*! Miss Lou made her dress and *it's* beautiful, too! She fixed Nanny Di's hair and makeup!"

"I'll bet she looks beautiful," Joey said, settling the little girl on the side of his hip.

"Oh, yes! She really does! Nanny Di said she wants Miss Lou to fix her hair and makeup every day, but Miss Lou said Nanny Di is beautiful without makeup," she confided. "Do *you* think Nanny Di is beautiful without makeup?" She didn't wait for an answer. "I do. I think Nanny Di is the most beautiful nanny in the whole world! Don't you? Don't you, Uncle

Joey? Don't you think that Nanny Di is the most beautiful nanny in the whole world?" Amalie looked at him earnestly, her blue eyes demanding nothing less than complete honesty.

So distracted was Joey by Amalie's chatter that he barely noticed Darcie standing in the open front door. He walked up the steps to the porch. His sister spoke first. "Take a breath, Amalie," she said, her rich voice filled with laughter. "Let Uncle Joey get a word in edgewise.

Lou joined her in the doorway, holding out her arms for the excited little girl.

Amalie went to the attractive blonde willingly, winding her little arms around Lou's neck. But, typical of the loquacious five-year-old, she refused to be silent. "Don't you think Nanny Di is the nicest, bestest, most beautiful nanny in the whole world, Uncle Joey?"

"Best." Joey could hear Diana's amused voice, even though Lou and Darcie were currently obstructing his view. "Not bestest," Diana's voice instructed. "Best. And thank you for the lovely compliment, Miss Amalie Merritt."

"Not bestest. Best," Amalie said, mimicking her nanny agreeably. "And you're welcome, Miss Nanny Di." She turned to Joey, determined to get an answer. "Don't you think Nanny Di is the nicest, bestest—best"—she glanced behind her to see if she had said it right that time, grinning with pride at Diana's affirmative nod—"most beautiful nanny in the world?"

Darcie and Lou were trying not to laugh at the exchange; both were thoroughly enjoying their bird's-eye view. Joey wouldn't have been a bit surprised if either one—or both—tried to tag along. He could almost picture the nosy pair climbing into the back of the BMW he had borrowed from his father. And he could only imagine what kind of texts they would send to Grace, already in Scotland, the minute he and Diana backed out of the driveway.

"Uncle Joey! Uncle Joey!" Amalie demanded, impatiently. "Don't you think so? Don't you think Nanny Di looks beautiful for your date?"

Despite the *thump-thump-thump* of his heart and the *ping-ping-ping* of the hundred or so bouncy balls in his stomach, Joey managed to answer.

"Diana always looks beautiful, Amalie," he said. He ignored the nods of approval from his unwanted audience. "I'm absolutely positive that she looks beautiful now, but unfortunately," Joey informed them, politely, "I can't see her."

Darcie and Lou had the good grace to look a little embarrassed. They quickly stepped out of the way, giving Joey and Diana their first glimpse of each other.

Honestly, Joey Finch, Diana thought, a little breathless, *you look good enough to eat.* His dark hair was flawless, as always. His blue blazer fit his broad shoulders like a dream. The sudden memory of waking up draped over that muscled chest at the Acorn Knob Inn popped into her head uninvited. That delicious moment had become a recurring dream from which she often awakened tangled in the blankets and uncomfortably warm. A frisson of heat rushed through her, despite her efforts to appear calm and poised.

Her eyes continued sweeping over Joey of their own accord. His khaki pants were smartly tailored. His white shirt crisply starched. His shoes the picture of masculine style. He was the epitome of masculine elegance. Effortlessly. As comfortable in dress clothes as he was in running shorts and a T-shirt. The man had style. She would give him that. Classic style. And a whole lot more.

Diana realized she was staring a second too late to do anything about it. She felt a little better when she realized that he was staring, too. And he wasn't saying anything. Well, she admitted, *she* wasn't saying anything either, but why wasn't *he* saying anything? She felt her anxiety level inexorably start to rise. *Drat. Drat. Drat.* What was going on inside his head?

Unbeknownst to Diana, there was quite a lot going on inside Joey's head. Although his gilded tongue's well-honed abilities had, for once, failed him, his mind was in overdrive. The images of his beautiful Diana came fast and furious: Diana typing on her rose gold computer in the passenger seat of his truck. Diana playing hopscotch with Amalie. Diana cheering for the Virginia Cavaliers, even though—in his opinion—she was cheering for the wrong team. Diana eating pizza and singing karaoke. Diana running from her damn kidnapper, her gorgeous hair spread out behind her as she raced across the street against the light. And—as if he would ever forget—Diana waking up in his arms at the Acorn Knob Inn.

When he told Amalie that Diana always looked beautiful, Joey was telling the truth. But *beautiful* didn't do justice to the vision standing on the porch of the gatekeeper's cottage. This version of Diana was…His fixated brain struggled to find the words. He finally settled on one.

Stunning.

Just…*stunning.* His mind emptied itself of every other thought. The word *stunning* reverberated in his head, timing itself with perfect harmony to each beat of his heart.

Lou had outdone herself, yet again. Diana's dress was sheer elegance, the lovely blue color a perfect foil for her delicate, peach-tinted complexion. The material draped across one soft shoulder before falling in five graceful tiers from her waist to end just below her knees. The wide band of blue that cinched her slender waist accentuated the quiet curve of her hips, drawing Joey's eye to the rest of her enticingly hidden features. The intricate embroidery on the mesh overlay gave the impression of an exquisite garden…a magical place where a man would gladly lose himself forever. Her elegant feet were encased in neutral-colored block heel shoes. The shoes' braided straps wound across the top of each foot and around her slim ankles. Her glorious hair, upswept into an elaborate twist, looked soft and inviting. A few loose strands curled around her face, making Joey's hands itch to tuck a single strand of that glorious bundle behind her ear. She was the epitome of the statue of a beautiful Greek goddess come to life.

Joey could only stare.

The blatant admiration on his face, coupled with the burning heat in his eyes, told Diana all she wanted to know. Joey Finch liked what he saw, she decided. She released the breath she hadn't realized she was holding before quickly reminding herself to take another. Then, she smiled.

Diana's smile steadied Joey. All the way to his soul. His heart stopped pounding and resumed a normal beat. The bouncy balls in his stomach finally stopped bouncing. The rightness of the moment resonated through his consciousness. He had no reason to be nervous, he realized. He didn't need to focus all his efforts on being the charming—but forever unattainable—Joey Finch...*one and done*. He could just be, well...himself. No, he thought, not himself. A *better* version of himself. Diana did that for him.

Joey's frozen vocal cords loosened. "Not beautiful, Amalie," he said. "Stunning."

Diana felt every syllable. His words rained down on her like a lovely spring shower, watering small seeds of hope until they blossomed into something that almost resembled confidence.

"Thank you," she said. "I had a little help." She hugged Darcie first, before turning to hug Lou, who was still holding Amalie. Somewhere in that exchange, the clever child managed to attach herself to her nanny. Diana gave the little girl her own hug before planting her on her feet. She leaned over to brush one blond curl off Amalie's forehead. "Have fun in Scotland, Amalie," she instructed. "Be very good and listen to Daddy and Mama Darcie."

"And Iggy," Amalie added, planting a kiss on Diana's cheek.

"Well..." Diana hesitated, raising her eyebrows at Darcie in silent warning. "Maybe not Iggy."..."Listening" to the mischief-making iguana was always a precursor to trouble for the angelic-looking child.

Joey smothered a chuckle while holding out his arm to his dream date. "Shall we?" he asked.

"I'd be delighted," Diana said.

Twining her arm through his, Diana allowed Joey Finch to escort her to the waiting BMW. Joey opened the passenger side door of the black M3.

"No truck?" she asked, her eyebrows arching delicately.

Joey grinned at her question. "For our *second* date? Are you kidding? I'm trying to impress you, woman."

Diana patted his arm. "Too late for that," she said, her eyes dancing. "I've known you for quite a while, remember?"

"Ouch," Joey said, with complete good humor. "Wait a sec," he said before she could slide onto the soft, leather seat. He leaned in, reaching toward the driver's seat.

Diana tried not to notice the pleasing view. She pinned her mind, instead, on what he could possibly be up to. The mystery was quickly solved when he reappeared bearing three peach-colored roses—petals intact. The little bouquet was tied with lace and wrapped in glittery paper that screamed Honeysuckle Creek Flower and Gift.

Joey handed the roses to a delighted Diana. "Impressed?" he asked, basking in her breathtaking smile.

"Oh, Joey," she sighed, happily, "it's gorgeous, but you didn't have to—" "But I wanted to," he explained, waving her words away with a casual hand. "I figure it was the least I could do after my last floral failure."

She brought the roses to her adorable nose and inhaled. "They're heavenly, Joey. And, besides, I blame Nigel for every squashed flower in that other bouquet."

Joey nodded, enjoying her response…especially the part about blaming Nigel. "Ready to go?"

"Of course." Diana slid into the seat, clutching her bouquet as if it was her most treasured possession.

Joey closed the door and strolled to the other side of the car, feeling like a king. The last *first* date of his life—oops, the last *second* date of his life—was off to a perfect start. How could three flowers make Diana smile like that? he asked himself, silently tipping his hat to reformed rakes every-where. He would always be grateful for their wisdom and spot-on advice. He slid into his seat and started the motor, filled with keen anticipation of the night ahead.

"I don't think I've ever seen roses this shade of peach before. It's my very favorite color," Diana remarked, still studying his floral offering.

"Mine, too," Joey agreed, almost bashfully. "It's the exact color of your lips."

"Oh." Diana made a breathy, little sound of surprise, raising one hand unconsciously to touch those very kissable lips. That sound and Diana's gesture made Joey's own lips tingle. His heart began to beat a little faster. Suddenly, the air was thick with…something. He struggled to speak casu-ally. "Charlie Ray can do anything. He and Evon are crazy talented."

"They're wonderful, aren't they?" Diana agreed, allowing the delicious tension between them to return to its perpetual simmer.

CHAPTER THIRTY-THREE

*T*he Dogwood Hills Vineyard was the best venue London County had to offer. Not only was the scenery gorgeous—rolling hills, endless grapevines, picturesque waterfalls—but the vineyard's restaurant was divine.

Il Ristorante Della Collina was elegance without end. The white tablecloths were pristine. The candlelight was soft. The flowers still held the freshness of the morning dew. Every aspect of the establishment was a delight for the senses. And the food was spectacular.

Joey and Diana started out with an appetizer of bruschetta, followed by a salad with grilled portobello mushrooms, tomatoes, and goat cheese topped with a homemade balsamic vinaigrette. Simple, but delectable. Their entrée, osso buco, was the most stimulating preparation of the dish Diana had ever tasted, including the portions she had sampled while vacationing in Italy. The addition of saffron risotto and grilled asparagus to her plate was photo-worthy. She didn't dare snap a picture of her plate in such an elegant venue, but she wanted to. All the accompanying wine choices were carefully selected to heighten their culinary experience.

Joey leaned back in his chair. He had laughed more in the last several hours than, well...than the last time he was with Diana Merritt. He watched her wipe a tear of laughter from her gray eyes.

"Oh, my," she said. "You must have been a handful when you were little. I bet your parents were terrified every time somebody handed you a microphone."

Joey grinned. "Slightly terrifying but oozing with charm. That was me."

"Ha. Still is you," Diana said, with a smirk.

Their waiter approached, then, to remove their plates. "Dessert?" he asked politely. At Joey's nod, he handed them the dessert menu.

"Dessert, too?" Diana asked. "Are you kidding me? I'm not going to fit into this dress ever again."

It was Joey's turn to smirk. Her figure was perfect, in his opinion. Dessert wasn't going to change that. If he was honest, he would have to admit he was far more interested in getting her out of that dress than worrying about whether she would be able to get back into it again. He quickly quashed that thought, smashed it under his feet; stomped it into submission.

He was thankful Diana believed his days of being a one and done were...done. At least, he thought that's what she believed. If she didn't, he rationalized, she wouldn't be sitting across from him reading the dessert menu. He would not risk losing her trust by allowing his carnal urges to run amok. No, he promised himself, this time he was going to do everything the right way. Winning his dream girl left no margin for error. And—even though his urges arose from the honest desires of his heart—that meant subduing his overeager libido.

"Sir." Their server interrupted his thoughts. "Have you decided?"

"Diana?"

She shook her head. "You decide. You know what I like."

The server cleared his throat, glancing at Joey. His face was completely devoid of expression.

Joey wanted to laugh at the server's interpretation of Diana's innocent remark. Joey decided the man deserved a bigger tip. "We'll have the mousse—and two spoons," he said, decisively.

"Very good, sir." The server disappeared into the kitchen.

"Mousse is the perfect choice for a date dessert." Diana nodded decisively. "It's easy to eat and not dangerous."

"Dangerous?" Joey asked, intrigued. He had never thought of dessert as dangerous. If mousse is the perfect choice, then what's the worst choice, the most "dangerous" dessert?

"Something that's on fire," Diana said. "Like cherries jubilee. That's the worst date dessert. Kevin Tavist burned his eyebrows off on our first date."

Joey laughed in surprise. "Are you serious? How did he do that?"

Diana frowned in thought. "I'm not sure. I guess he stuck his face in it or something. I wasn't really paying attention. There's a picture of him on my Instagram somewhere…the day after he got home from the emergency room."

"Wow," Joey said, impressed. "I was thinking of something with caramel syrup. You know, something stringy and sticky and potentially embarrassing. But fire is definitely worse than caramel. What about the worst date food other than dessert?"

"Spaghetti," Diana responded. "Too many messy possibilities. All that sauce. It stains, you know. And those noodles flying everywhere. It's a disaster waiting to happen. What do you think is the worst?"

"Kabobs," Joey said, confidently. "Some girl I took out—Lisa or Linley…no, I think it was Linda—ordered kabobs and rice. She was trying to get the chicken off the skewer, and her fork slipped. Rice went everywhere—all over the floor, and even in her hair—and the chicken went flying across to the table beside us. It landed in a very snobby-looking lady's wine glass. The glass tipped over and spilled red wine all over the lady's white dress."

Diana looked horrified. "Is that really true?"

"Yeah," Joey said, shaking his head in mock sorrow. "Linda burst into tears and the manager came and asked us to leave."

"Poor Linda." Diana couldn't help but laugh at the picture Joey painted.

"It was good for her," Joey said. "Linda thought a little too well of herself. She needed to be brought down a notch or two. She wasn't like you.

You would have laughed and made the best of it. You always make the best of everything." He took a sip of his wine.

"Why, thank you." Diana was touched by the compliment he had stated so matter-of-factly.

The server reappeared with the crowning glory of their meal: torta de cioccolatino, a glorious combination of mascarpone mousse, dark chocolate ganache, and Chantilly cream. The large, delicious-looking mousse was topped with…could it be?

"Are those chocolate twirls?" Diana squealed exuberantly, garnering the attention of the patrons at three nearby tables.

Joey grinned, proudly, obviously pleased by her reaction to his surprise. "Of course, they are, Diana. I told you we were dining in a five-star restaurant."

"Now this is the perfect date dessert." Diana grabbed one of the spoons, scooped the largest piece of twirl, and popped it into her mouth. She closed her eyes in bliss.

Joey wondered if anything else would make her look as blissful as she looked now. He stomped on that thought, too. Grabbing the second spoon, he dug into the dessert before Diana could scoop another piece of twirl. But when Diana's tongue flicked out to swipe a bit of mousse off the corner of her lips, Joey's heated reaction forced him to continue the Worst Date game. Anything to get his mind off those delicious lips.

"Worst place for a date?" he asked, quickly.

"Hrss stbls," Diana answered, her mouth full of mousse. She answered as fast as she could. The banked desire in his eyes when he looked at her lips was making her desperately in need of a distraction.

"What?" Joey asked, clearly amused.

Diana swallowed. "Sorry. Horse stables. Derrick Blumfield took me to his horse farm on a date. He showed me the stables and handed me a shovel. I handed it back. He never seemed to understand why I wouldn't go out with him again."

"Country boy, huh?"

"More like entitled redneck," Diana said. "Mucking the stables was his punishment for wrecking his dad's truck. He thought I was cheap labor. What's your worst place for a date?"

"An extended family reunion." Joey made a disgusted face. "I must have been hugged and kissed by every great-aunt and elderly cousin that could catch me. They all kept asking when Suzanne and I were going to tie the knot. Over and over and over. It was the most awkward experience of my life."

"The *most* awkward?" Diana asked.

"Well, maybe not the *most* awkward." Joey sighed. "Maybe I was exaggerating a bit."

"No way," Diana teased. "Not you."

They shared a smile as they finished the last two bites of chocolate mousse in tandem.

"Perfect place for a date?" Joey asked.

"That's an easy one." Diana smiled, looking around the beautiful room. "I can't imagine a more perfect place than this."

She was still trying to figure out how Joey had arranged for them to have a dessert topped with chocolate twirls. It seemed highly unlikely that a five-star restaurant would serve anything that wasn't made on the premises. And, delightful as they were, chocolate twirls were not quite worthy of the elegant room in which they were dining.

Her question was answered when the owner of Il Ristorante approached the table after the straight-faced server dealt with the check. Carlo shook Joey's hand and smiled at Diana.

"How was your meal, my friends?" he asked, in his lilting Italian accent.

"It was perfect, as always, Carlo," Joey said. "Thanks for the extra effort."

"It was absolutely delicious," Diana enthused.

Carlo's smile widened. "So, this is the lady who loves her chocolate twirls?" When Diana nodded, Carlo continued: "Joey had quite a challenge convincing my pastry chef to add them to the mousse. Armando swore they would 'ruin the spirit of his divine creation.' " Carlo laughed. "You must be very important to Joey."

"She is, Carlo," Joey said, softly. "She's very important."

Diana felt a tingle run down her spine. Was this really happening or was it some amazing dream? If it was a dream, she was in no hurry to wake up. When Diana realized that Carlo was still talking, she struggled to focus on his words.

"Have you been on the balcony to view the falls yet? They are beautiful at night...and"—he waggled his eyebrows suggestively—"very romantic."

Joey stood, holding out his hand to Diana. "That's just where we were heading, Carlo." Diana let him help her to her feet, enjoying the way he kept her hand in his.

"Um, Carlo..." Joey hesitated, looking a little embarrassed. "Um, would you mind taking our picture?" When Diana glanced at him in surprise, Joey shrugged his shoulders. "Darcie," he explained. "She made me promise to send her a picture. She'll probably kill me if I don't...." He ran his finger around his collar as if it was too tight. "And throw my body over the falls."

Diana couldn't help but laugh at that. She noticed that Carlo was laughing, too. He was, apparently, familiar with Joey's fiery sibling.

"Of course." Carlo nodded. "I would not want to be on your sister's bad side, either. Follow me."

He led them around the corner of the restaurant and through a door labeled *"Employees Only."* They followed him down a hallway and through another door that read *"Private."*

"This is my office," Carlo said, welcoming them into the elegantly appointed room. "It has a view over the falls. My wife says this is the perfect photo spot."

Five minutes later, the picture was on its way to Darcie and Joey was off the hook. They left Carlo on the phone in his office and retraced their steps toward the dining room. Joey paused in the hallway at another door labeled *"Service Stairs, Employees Only."*

He tugged Diana toward the door.

"What are you doing?" she asked. "It says *'Employees Only.'* " She pointed to the sign. " *'Em-ploy-ees On-ly,'* Jo-ey," she reiterated, enunciating clearly as if he was illiterate. "And, in case you haven't notice," she continued, "neither of us works here."

Joey brushed off her words, determination in his eyes. "I have a great idea." He tugged her hand again.

Diana glared at him, refusing to budge. "The last time you had a great idea, you ended up with a brick on your head. Remember?"

"That was different. I know what I'm doing this time." At her still doubtful expression, he tried to explain. "We'll get a better view of the falls from the second-floor balcony."

She eyed him suspiciously.

"Waterfall. Lights. Romance." He waggled his eyebrows in a perfect imitation of Carlo.

"Blood. Concussion. Emergency Room," she stated, pertly. She did not, however, pull her hand away.

Joey sensed that she was wavering. He was close to victory. "Acorn Knob Inn," he said, confidently. "Breakfast buffet."

She gave in. "Oh, all right. You win," she said, but she didn't look happy about it.

When he opened the door, she allowed him to lead her through it. They started up the stairs, her hand still in his.

"Hmm, well, at least no alarms went off," Diana mused. "I guess that's something."

"Diana," Joey said, as they entered the darkened banquet room at the top of the stairs. "You're going to have to trust me." She followed him across the large room, the site of Blane and Grace's rehearsal dinner.

"I remember meeting the date you took to the rehearsal dinner," Diana said. Even in the dark, Joey could see her smirk. "What was her name again? Sugar? Maple Syrup? Artificial Sweetener?"

"Honey," Joey stated, tonelessly. "Her name was Honey." He grimaced. Honey had not been one of his better date choices.

"Hmph. Funny you remember the name of that one," Diana observed. She sounded almost jealous.

Joey latched onto the revelation with gusto. "And why shouldn't I remember Honey?" Joey asked. "She was a lovely girl."

"If you say so," Diana said, disbelief evident in her voice. "She wasn't exactly a Rhodes Scholar or anything. I had to show her how to use the automatic hand dryer in the ladies' room. You know, the one that's paperless. She just kept standing there, waiting for the paper towel to pop out." Diana shook her head, her eyes twinkling with mischief. "But, if that's the kind of girl who attracts you…"

"Diana," Joey said, cheerfully. "Shut up. And look."

They had passed through a set of glass doors and reached the edge of the balcony. Diana gasped at the incandescent beauty in front of her. Three waterfalls made up Dogwood Falls. The second waterfall stood directly across from them, tumbling over the rocks before churning downstream a few hundred feet for the final drop. The careful placement of colored lights enhanced the lovely vista. It was magical.

Or maybe it was magical because she was standing beside Joey Finch. Diana considered that possibility. Or maybe she was dreaming. She was leaning toward the dreaming scenario. The other one—the one where she finally won Joey's heart—still seemed too unlikely to believe.

"The falls are beautiful, Joey. I understand why you wanted to come up here," she said. She shivered, as much from the heat in Joey Finch's eyes as the chill in the air.

Joey, ever the gentleman, took off his jacket. After turning her so she was facing him, he spent a few seconds draping and adjusting the jacket so that she was snugly covered. Diana was enveloped in his warmth and his scent. It was delicious. She wanted to close her eyes and breathe him in….

When the jacket was arranged to his satisfaction, Joey paused, his hands still holding the lapels. He studied her face. Her sparkling eyes reflected the colored lights in the water. He found himself so caught up in the vision in front of him that he almost forgot his real reason for bringing her up here.

Almost.

"Diana, Diana," he chided. "I'm surprised that anyone as well-acquainted with the habits of rakes and rascals as you could be so naïve." He wasn't quite sure how he managed to sound so casual. His teasing tone belied the primal need that had taken hold of every cell in his body.

Diana's eyes were wide and questioning. What was he up to? she wondered. She didn't like being called naïve. She tried to take a step back, but he tightened his hands on his jacket to keep her where she was. His eyes held a wicked light, intriguing enough to hold her in place.

When Joey continued, his voice sounded a little strained, even to himself. "How could you believe that a rascal—even a fine, upstanding *reformed* rascal like myself—would bring a gorgeous lady to a deserted, moonlit terrace for the simple purpose of viewing a waterfall?"

Diana was mesmerized by the husky undertones in his voice. She couldn't pull her eyes from his….He thought she was gorgeous? She effortlessly fell in with his game, batting her eyelashes in make-believe innocence. Sometimes, her ability to fake the low-country accent of her Charleston-born mother was an invaluable skill. "Why, Joey Finch, wha-a-tevah do you mean?" she drawled. "Wha-at othah reason could you po-ssibly ha-ave for bringin' me he-re?"

His eyes lit with pleasure at her response. He tugged her forward until her mouth was inches from his. "Just…this." His lips brushed hers softly. As light at a butterfly. Those peach-colored lips were soft. So very soft. As soft as he had imagined….

Once. Twice. Three times, he lightly touched her delicious lips with his own. Then…nothing.

Her eyes flew open in surprise. The silent reproach in their depths brought a slow smile to Joey's lips. Raising his hand to her cheek, he brushed his finger slowly down her silky skin. Her soft intake of breath urged him on. He tipped her chin up with that hypnotizing finger. His thumb lightly traced the delicate contours of her bottom lip.

Back and forth.

Back and forth.

"What's wrong, sweetheart?" he asked, obviously enjoying having the upper hand for the moment.

The self-satisfied way he asked the question pulled her from the seductive spell he was weaving around her. If not for the fact that Joey's gaze was fixed on Diana's mouth, he would have noticed the narrowing of her eyes.

The provocative little imp—the one that Joey, alone, had the ability to conjure—reared her head. It was time to teach the rascally Mr. Finch a lesson. Diana's teeth clamped down firmly on Joey's hapless digit.

"Ow!" he yelled, trying unsuccessfully to tug his thumb away. "You bit me!" The contact ran through his body like a white-hot bolt of lightning. He had *never* felt anything like it. Diana's gray eyes gazed into his as she parted those lovely lips to release her prisoner. He pulled back, half in shock, half in disbelief. Every good and noble intention he possessed fled along with any semblance of rational thought. The lovely lips of his siren beckoned his primitive self to take, to seize what was his. What, he finally realized, had *always* been his. He cupped the sides of her face. His fingers plunged into the silky hair of his goddess, dislodging several of her endless number of pins.

Hairdo forgotten; Diana allowed him to pull her closer. Why, she asked her impatient self, was he purposely drawing out every single second? She wanted more than the gentle press of his lips against hers. Why was he taking so long to kiss her? To really kiss her? Either time had slowed to a crawl or Joey Finch was trying to drive her mad. Her frustration was almost unbearable. *If he teases me like last time,* she thought, *I swear I'll… Oh…*

His lips had melded to hers. Finally. His tongue demanded entry, seeking not to tease or charm, but to possess. She opened for him instantly, sliding her arms around his neck. He felt the press of her lithesome body. His jacket slid from her shoulders, unheeded, to join the forgotten hairpins. He pulled her closer, the better to explore the soft, warm curves of her back, before returning his hands to her glorious hair. He angled her head for better access.

The kiss became hotter.

The sheer force of Joey's desire took Diana's breath…what little breath she had left. But Diana was not complaining. Breathing was optional, she realized, and decidedly overrated. Instead, she welcomed the onslaught, her arms clinging to his strong shoulders. She was drowning in his heated touch. She pressed her body into his muscular frame. Closer. And closer still. She craved this man as if she lay dying of thirst in the desert and he was the last glass of water.

He kissed her greedily, assuaging the hunger that had assailed him for so long. He had wanted this since he saw her standing on the front porch of the gatekeeper's cottage several hours ago. No, one portion of his overheated brain decided to argue, that wasn't right. Before that. Since the Acorn Knob Inn. No, that wasn't right either. Before that. Since she ran into him at Chutley's. Or maybe since the first time he laid eyes on her. Nine long years ago. *Well, hell.* Joey wasn't sure. He only knew he had wanted her for a long time. Too damn long. And now, he wanted more. He couldn't get enough of her intoxicating scent. Her incredibly delicious lips. The sweet haven of her mouth. The warmth of her in his arms. The way she returned his ardor as if she, too, hadn't truly lived until this moment.

A shout of laughter from some unseen restaurant patron on the balcony below made him pause. He struggled to surface from their raging sea of desire. So enthralled was he with the woman in his arms that he had forgotten where they were. Not only that, he realized in surprise, he had also forgotten that they weren't alone.

Joey struggled to calm his racing heart. *Get a grip, Finch,* he reprimanded himself. *Have a little class.* He forced himself to pull back. To take a deep breath. To think for them both. He might have been successful if her bare shoulder—formerly hidden by his wayward jacket—hadn't attracted his gaze. Her delicate collarbone beckoned. The provocative, little spot where her neck met her shoulder called for his lips. His quest for sanity vanished as quickly as their little puffs of breath in the chilly autumn night.

To hell with class....

Raucous laughter and a squeal of delight shocked them both back to the present again. Diana could barely focus on anything but the man in front of her. The man who kissed like a dream. Fascinated her. Intrigued her. Captivated her. The man she desired above all others. He was watching her, she realized. What did he see when he looked at her?

Had there ever existed a more breathtaking woman? Joey couldn't imagine how. Diana's eyes were dazed. Her pupils, slightly dilated. Her cheeks, flushed. Her hair, in gorgeous disarray. A few loose curls had escaped her elegant coiffure, spilling over her shoulders and down her back. Her lips—her soft, peach-colored lips—were slightly swollen from *his* kisses. She was gloriously rumpled, her consistently put-together appearance all but forgotten. And if he couldn't help exulting that he had been the one to rumple her, well...he was only human, wasn't he? He reached out to tuck one of her curls behind her ear, as some vestiges of a previous conversation flashed through his mind.

"Diana...?" he whispered.

"Hmm?" she asked, her eyes never leaving his face.

"You never told me what happened when Ezekiel kissed Genevieve," he answered, his fingers softly stroking her cheek.

"What?" she asked, adorably confused by his question. Didn't he know she couldn't think straight when he was touching her like that? *Ezekiel? Genevieve? Who were they? And why was Joey talking about them instead of kissing her?* She struggled to make sense of his words.

Joey chuckled softly as his hand moved to her neck. He couldn't seem to stop touching her. Her face suffused with color. She was trying so hard, but she was obviously flustered. He saw the exact moment when she comprehended his words.

"When Ezekiel kissed Genevieve?" she repeated, desperately striving for composure. "Did he?" For the life of her she couldn't remember.

Joey smiled. "She gave him two options, Diana. Two options of what would happen if he kissed her," he explained patiently. When Diana still looked confused, he added, "Did she slap him? Or did she kiss him back?" His lips trailed from her temple, drifting down to her soft cheek. He couldn't resist nibbling on her tempting, little ear. *Sensitive little ear*, he noted in the Catalogue of Diana's Preferences he was logging for future use. He nibbled again, just to be sure. *Yes...exquisitely sensitive.*

Diana shivered. He was killing her, she thought, and all because... Suddenly, she remembered exactly what Genevieve did. "She kissed him back, Joey," she said, her voice a sultry whisper. "Because she couldn't resist him...."

Joey's whole body tightened at her response. He found himself, once again, in complete empathy...or sympathy...or *something* with the reformed—and apparently, quite noble—Ezekiel. How did the poor earl remain reformed when he and his Genevieve were living in the same house? In other words, how the hell did he stay out of Genevieve's bed? Joey couldn't even keep his hands to himself on the darkened balcony of a very crowded restaurant. Still, he couldn't resist pursuing this dangerous line of questioning. "And what about you, Diana?" he asked, hoarsely. "Are you going to slap me?"

"Only if you stop," she said, surprising a bark of laughter from him.

"Diana..." Joey said in a voice he barely recognized. "...I have no intention of stopping...."

"Hey!" The voice cut through the air with all the force of someone firing a gun. "Hey, you two!"

Joey and Diana exchanged a startled glance. They were no longer alone.

"Hey!" The voice was louder and a little closer.

Diana unwound her arms from around Joey's neck. Joey leaned down to pick up his wrinkled jacket. He placed it back around Diana's shoulders.

They leaned on the railing, gazing casually at the waterfall, as if they hadn't been in each other's arms a few seconds before.

The owner of the voice—a distinguished, older gentleman with an abundance of white hair—stepped out of the shadows. He was, unfortunately, wearing a uniform.

Drat. Diana almost groaned. She could only hope the security guard hadn't been on the balcony very long. She felt heat flooding her cheeks.

Joey straightened to his full height as he turned to address the uniformed man. Funny how Joey's style and confidence gave him the illusion of being much taller than he was. Diana was always amazed at the way he managed to hold his own—and, sometimes, dominate a conversation—with much larger men by sheer force of personality. No one would ever be able to look down on Joey Finch, even if he or she could, well…look down on him.

"Is there a problem, officer?" Joey asked, calmly.

The security guard's intelligent gaze swept the guilty couple. Joey's jacket, wrinkled. His shirt, untucked. Diana's hair, tumbling from its pins. Her lips, swollen and well-kissed. The older man's serious expression relaxed into a smile. Diana was surprised—and relieved—by the mischief in his eyes.

"Nothing to worry about, folks," he said, benignly. "I have it on good authority that a couple of teenagers were having a little bit too much fun up here on this balcony just a few minutes ago." He allowed his words to sink in before he continued: "Since you two have been up here for a while, I figured you might have seen those lovesick teenagers.

Joey nodded his head gravely. "Yes, sir," he agreed. "We have seen them." He pointed to the far end of the darkened balcony. "I believe they went that way." He turned to Diana, eyes brimming with glee. "Didn't they go that way, Genevieve?"

Diana immediately followed his lead. "Why, yes, Ezekiel," she said, trying desperately not to giggle. She pointed to the darkened balcony. "They went that way."

The security guard nodded. "That's what I thought," he said. "Thank you, folks." His knowing eyes held a world of understanding. "And since I'm sure the two of you will be gone when I come back," he said, gently, "I hope you enjoy the rest of your night."

"Yes, sir," Joey said, respectfully. "We will."

The security guard tipped his hat to Diana—and winked—before disappearing into the darkness.

"Come on," Joey whispered, tugging Diana toward the glass doors that led to the banquet room. He reached for the handle of the door, before pulling them both into the darkened room. He grabbed her hand and, together, they fled, skirting between the close-fitting tables until they reached the main staircase. They wanted to put as much distance as possible between themselves and the security guard just in case he changed his mind. Joey held out his arm to Diana, noting, even in the dim light, the lovely flush their flight had lent to her cheeks.

"Shall we?" he inquired, solemnly.

Diana wrapped her hand around his arm. "Of course," she said with equal gravity.

They strolled down the main staircase as if they were guests-of-honor at the grandest society ball ever held in Honeysuckle Creek. When they reached the bottom, Diana leaned over to release the hook on the velvet rope that was supposed to keep people from climbing the stairs. After they walked around it, she carefully refastened it.

No one present—servers, patrons, hostesses—paid them the slightest bit of attention. They walked out of the restaurant and emerged into the chilly air, Diana still holding onto Joey's arm. He escorted her to the BMW, opening her door and making sure she was settled before heading to his side of the car. Only when he was seated behind the steering wheel did he chance a look at the woman beside him.

The expression on her face reminded him of a guilty child sneaking a peek at her Christmas presents. He imagined that his own face wore exactly the same expression. They shared a delighted grin.

"Best. Date. Ever," they said in perfect unison.

CHAPTER THIRTY-FOUR

$\mathcal{T}$heir initial glee upon reaching the car unscathed quickly turned into a less manageable emotion. One minute Joey and Diana were laughing and congratulating themselves. Perfectly at ease. Completely comfortable. But the next minute…

Out of nowhere, a sultry silence enveloped them like a cocoon, stealing their ability to speak. And with that simmering silence came heat. A discernable rise in temperature that was impossible to ignore.

Joey stole a glance at Diana. She was watching him. Watching a slow flush burn its way up the side of his face. He could feel the heat crawling up his chin, flushing his skin all the way to his forehead. Worse than that was the knowing, little smile that flitted around her lips. She looked like she knew every thought flying around in his head. *That* realization made his current condition even worse.

"Are you hot?" he blurted out.

She gaped at him. Her gray eyes wary. "Excuse me?" she asked.

Moron. Idiot. Imbecile. Jackass.

Joey's internal harangue was swift and thorough. "Do you think it's hot in here?" he asked politely, not at all surprised when his voice cracked a little.

"Oh," she replied, faintly. She looked a little embarrassed. "Not particularly. I'm, um…perfectly comfortable."

Another wave of heat threatened to swamp Joey. He could feel a tiny sheen of perspiration on his upper lip. He hoped she didn't notice. If he got any hotter, he was pretty sure he would burst into flame. He focused on the seemingly endless road ahead. He had driven this stretch of highway countless times, could do it with his eyes closed. But right now, it was taking forever.

Stupid. Naïve. Unsophisticated. Ignorant.

Diana was drowning in a sea of embarrassment. *Excuse me?* She wanted to groan at her simpleminded response. Why did her brain immediately take the word "hot" and go *there? You know why*, she scolded herself. *Because you were in Land of Lust again.* Her fevered imaginings ranged anywhere from a simple kiss to elaborate scenarios that involved…heated things. And thinking about those things made her feel, well…hot. The fact that Joey Finch had kissed her senseless a few minutes before wasn't helping. She fanned herself with her hand.

"Now that you mention it," she said, carefully. "I am a little hot." *Drat. Drat. Drat.* She cringed in horror at her own witless words.

Rephrase. Reword. Rewind.

Joey shot her a speculative glance. "You are?" he asked. *Well, hell.* That was it. He was burning up. He was going to spontaneously combust right there in the seat of his truck.

"No, I mean…yes." She let out a breath of frustration. "I am a little warm." There. That sounded respectable. And innocent. And innocuous. And…lame. She fanned herself again weakly.

"Oh, yeah. Right, right," Joey said, turning on the air conditioning. To maximum high. The sweltering silence was grating on his last nerve. Why couldn't he and the lovely lady in the passenger seat fall back into their usual relaxed banter? At this point he would settle for *unrelaxed* banter. Or any banter at all. He tried, unsuccessfully, to think of something else to talk about. Instead, he just sat there, like a speechless clod.

The whole situation, he surmised, was because of the kiss. Or, as his astounded nervous system dubbed it: *The Kiss That Changed Everything.* What he felt for Diana exceeded any other attraction he had ever felt for any other woman. That was old news. But he had *never* imagined, even in his wildest dreams, the impact of a single kiss. He and Diana, Joey decided, were like two sparks on dry tinder. Combustible and hot. Even now, he wondered if her initial reluctance to go out with him really was—as his mother intimated—because Diana was afraid that Joey would lose interest after one date. He almost laughed at such an impossible scenario. Like hell he would ever lose interest in Diana Merritt. He would *never* get enough of her, not until the day he died. And, maybe, he admitted to himself, not even then. A surreptitious glance at the woman beside him showed her as deeply in thought as he.

Out of the corner of her eye, Diana caught Joey looking at her. She waited for him to speak—an activity she, herself, seemed unable to accomplish at present. But she was doomed for disappointment. Joey's eyes quickly returned to the road, leaving Diana to wonder what he could possibly be thinking. By now, she decided, her bright red face was probably glowing in the dark. Like Rudolph the Red-Nosed Reindeer's famous nose. She hoped Joey hadn't noticed.

For safety's sake, Joey forced his eyes to remain on the road. If he continued to focus on the irresistible woman beside him, they—and his dad's BMW—would probably end up in a ditch. He wished he could think of something clever to say, but nothing came to him. Clever had clearly deserted him several miles back, along with Brilliant, Fascinating, and Charming. Since he was fairly certain Lame and Inappropriate were still hanging around, he decided not to risk it. He concentrated on driving, keeping his mouth firmly closed.

Diana's dithering increased. Had Joey noticed her luminous face? she asked herself irritably. *Drat.* She didn't blame him for looking away. The blinding crimson glow was probably making it difficult for him to see the road. She wouldn't be surprised if Joey put on sunglasses. She touched her palm to her burning cheek. Her face, she decided, had to be the same color as her hair. What a hideous thought that was. She nearly squirmed in embarrassment. Would the car ride never end? Would they *never* get to Heart's Ease?

A few seconds later, she risked a peek at Joey. No sunglasses, she mused. That was a good sign. She nearly sighed aloud as her eyes focused on his lips. Kissing Joey Finch was magical. She couldn't begin to catalogue the myriad sensations that were still running through her body. Euphoria was at the top of the list because he had *finally* kissed her. Ecstasy wasn't far behind because the kiss was, well…incredible. Delight was obviously on the list. And passion. Passion like she had only imagined. Her body still thrummed with it. Yearning was on the list, too—even though that one was slightly pathetic—because Diana wanted more. Oh, did she ever. She wanted more of Joey Finch…more of everything. But…

What she *really* wanted—more than anything—was Joey's heart. His *entire* heart. Simply put, she wanted him to love her the way she loved him. Was it even possible for him to love her? Or was she completely crazy and—as previously suggested—slightly pathetic? A horrible thought dug its cruel tentacles deeply into her wistful imaginings. What if Joey kissed *every* girl the same way? What if his ability to kiss a girl senseless didn't apply solely to Diana Merritt? What if his extremely skillful lips were the reason he was so fondly remembered by all the girls he had dated?

She dismissed that unacceptable notion as quickly as it came. Joey, she reminded herself, seemed as shaken by what had occurred on that darkened balcony as she was. Actually, she decided, his uncharacteristic silence during the interminable ride to Heart's Ease was somewhat reassuring. And who knew what would happen when they finally reached the gatekeeper's cottage?

Joey ruminated on his plan as he parked the BMW in the driveway of the gatekeeper's cottage. He reminded himself of his plan as he helped Diana out of the car. He reiterated his plan to himself as he took Diana's hand and strolled up the sidewalk. He reiterated the reiteration of his plan to himself again—in very forceful terms—as he walked up the front porch steps with Diana. And he made his lust-clouded brain repeat the words of his plan one more time as he followed Diana around the corner of the porch to the kitchen door:

I cannot, will not, and must not—under any circumstances—allow myself to accompany Diana inside the gatekeeper's cottage. No matter what she says, how she says it, or what she doesn't *say, I will not—cannot—change my mind.*

The words had become something of a litany in his mind. A vow, of sorts. And the necessity of keeping that vow, of sticking to his plan, was simple. There was no way—*absolutely no way*—he would ever be able to keep his hands to himself if he went inside that cottage with Diana Merritt. And he was not—*absolutely was not*—going to sleep with the lovely Miss Merritt on their very first *official* date. No way. Zero way. He wanted her to trust him. To believe that he had changed. That he was truly reformed. He wanted her to understand that she was different, not just some one-night stand. So—per his preexisting plan—there would be *no* prelude to lovemaking, *no* lovemaking, and absolutely *nothing* that involved the removal of so much as one item of clothing. Not even an earring. And Joey Recently-Reformed-Rascal Finch was totally fine with that decision.

Wasn't he?

Yes, he reminded himself. Again. He absolutely was. He was. Seriously. That was why he would bid farewell to Miss Merritt outside the cottage. At the door. *Without* going into the cottage with her. He would leave her outside that door. *Alone.* And he would go back to his townhouse by himself. *Alone.* He was adamant, determined to stick to his plan. So, why, then did the vast majority—all right, every single one—of his blasted body parts have other ideas?

Just look at her, his mind whispered. *How can you walk away from that?* Her hair was loosely held up by the pins that had, thus far, survived his eager hands. The glorious strands of red reflected the porch light, begging for release from their metal prison. Even though his jacket was still draped around her shoulders, hiding her soft curves from view, Joey's mind continued to imagine Diana's warm, inviting body without it. And without other things…like every other damn article of clothing she was wearing.

Get a grip, Finch, he demanded. *You're better than this.* He desperately reminded himself of The Number One, Never To Be Ignored For Any Reason, Cardinal Rule of Joey Finch: no sex on the first date with a woman who, in any way, wanted a relationship. Period. He had lived by that rule for years. He had always been able to turn around and walk away. Always. Why, then, was this time so hard? The answer was easy. Because this time was with *her.*

Diana successfully disarmed the door then hesitated, her hand on the doorknob. As she turned to Joey, he knew beyond a shadow of a doubt, exactly what she was going to say.

"Would you like to come in?" she asked, unconscious invitation in her eyes.

Hell, yes, I'd like to come in, his rowdy libido screamed. With extreme effort, he tamped it down. The struggle was real. "I better not," he managed to say, determination making his reply a bit too abrupt.

"Oh," she said, softly. Her eyes were puzzled, almost hurt.

Well, hell, he thought, in frustration. Now he had hurt her feelings. *Way to go, Finch.* This was not going according to his marvelous plan. Diana was supposed to be impressed by his iron-clad self-control, amazing self-restraint, and maturity. Instead, she looked as though she wanted to cry. He was really screwing up this courtship thing. And, at that moment, he swore he felt the disapproval of every reformed rake that had ever come before him.

Diana tried to smile. "I guess I'll say goodnight, then…" she said, turning her back to him as she slowly opened the door.

"Not yet," he said, unable to help himself. He took two steps, removing her hand from the knob then pulling the door closed, bringing her with it until her back was flush against his chest.

Diana's palms lay flat against the door as Joey's body pressed against hers. He was solid and warm. And even though she was still wearing his jacket, she felt a shiver run down her spine. Joey's breath blew lightly against her ear, sending her heart soaring into overdrive. His voice was dreamy, mesmerizing in its intensity.

"Do you know why I can't go inside with you, Diana?" he whispered as his hands rose to rest lightly on her jacket-clad shoulders.

"Why?" she managed to ask, barely able to reply as his lips grazed the soft skin of her cheek.

He grasped the jacket, slipped it off her shoulders, and tossed it on top of an enormous mum in a planter beside the door. His body resumed its former position, pressing her against the sturdy wooden door. "Do you have any idea what I want to do to you?" he breathed, his lips moving to her neck.

"What?" she gasped as his lips paused at the juncture between her neck and her bare shoulder.

Joey's overheated imagination took over as the words poured heedlessly from his lips. "I want to unzip this dress and watch it slide down your body until it pools at your feet. I want to find out what it is you're wearing underneath. I want to take your hair down pin by pin and watch it fall around your bare shoulders." He paused as his lips leisurely traced a velvet path from her neck to the tip of her shoulder.

Diana was thankful for the heavy door frame in front of her. Without its solid support she would surely fall into a boneless heap at his feet. The blood in her veins was molten with desire, and Joey showed no sign of letting up. On the contrary, he put his hands on her waist and turned her around. Her back was pressed to the door.

"Do you want to know what I would do next?" he asked, hoarsely.

She nodded her head, unable to verbalize her wanton thoughts.

"I would ask you to take off the rest of what you're wearing under that dress. Every stitch. For me. While I watch." He was driving himself crazy with his own words, but he couldn't seem to stop.

The potent desire in her eyes was his undoing. He moved his hands to her hair, plucking out each remaining pin slowly, almost sensually. There must have been at least thirty. They scattered down to the porch. He threaded his fingers through the thick red mass, massaging her scalp until she moaned with pleasure. He trailed one finger down the side of her face, down her neck and to the shoulder of her dress. Diana's breath came in short, brief puffs. She was falling deeper and deeper into the sensuous web he was weaving around them.

Joey tucked the tip of his finger under the material of the dress. She could feel his burning gaze as he traced a path, ever so slowly, down to the middle of her neckline. He could feel her heart beating like a rabbit. Joey hesitated for a second; he was poised at the very limits of his control. She deserved more than this, he reminded himself. *So* much more…. He forced himself to stop, trailing his finger upward to rest under her chin. He tipped up her chin and looked deeply into her eyes.

"I'm falling in love with you, Diana."

He pressed a single kiss to her lips, aching in its sweetness. Then, he picked up his jacket, turned, and walked away.

Diana stood where she was, leaning back against the door. She had never been so overcome with passion, so completely lost in another person. Her instinctual response to his every touch, every whisper, every desire was overwhelming. She had no control over the way he made her feel…no wish to resist him at all. Thank heavens that he did. She had watched him reach for that control. Seen the muscles tighten in his jaw. Watched the tendons stand out in his neck. She saw him take control of himself. If he hadn't…

She watched him drive away. The taillights of the BMW disappeared quietly across the bridge and winked out of sight.

"I'm falling in love with you, Diana…."

Laughing softly, she began the arduous task of finding and collecting the pins Joey had scattered all over the side of the porch. She had to find every last one, at least before Darcie returned. And Amalie. The sighting of a single pin would have them asking too many questions. Diana wanted to keep this moment between herself and Mr. Finch.

"I'm falling in love with you, Diana…."

She bent down to pick up the last pin. It was at the very back corner, where the side porch blended seamlessly into the back deck. A dreamy smile drifted across her face. How careless he had been, tossing pins

403

everywhere! And she loved it. She loved the fact that she could make him lose control like that. It was only fair, she decided, since he could disarm her with a touch. She couldn't help but play the scene over and over in her head. Joey made her feel special. Like a rare and precious treasure. She hoped he felt even half of what she was feeling but…

How could he when she hadn't told him how *she* really felt about *him*? Diana frowned at the pins in her hands. True, she rationalized, her feelings were written all over her face—and every other part of her body— but maybe he hadn't noticed. *Drat.* And she hadn't said anything out loud after he spoke the words that melted her heart…

"I'm falling in love with you, Diana…."

Joey had bared his soul to her, trusted her that much. The least she could do was to bare hers. She had to tell him how she felt; she wasn't going to wait another minute. She would tell him right now. She would call him and say…what? What was she going to say? She had absolutely no idea, but she was certain that she would think of something.

Suddenly exhilarated, Diana opened the door—not an easy task with full hands—and placed the pins on the kitchen counter. She came back for her clutch purse, which had fallen beside the welcome mat when Joey pressed her into the door. She opened the snap on her purse, locating her phone immediately. Finding things was so much easier in a tiny purse, she mused. She located Joey in her directory and pressed his number. Humming a happy, little tune, she turned to go into the cottage. She was just about to shut the door behind her when she heard a phone ring.

Twice.

She pulled her phone away from her ear and listened to the echo outside the door. Her heart jumped in her chest. Memories of hearing Mallory's ringing phone right before finding her dead body flashed through Diana's mind. She quickly shoved such horrible thoughts into the farthest, darkest corner of her mind. This was *Joey's* phone, she reminded herself. Not Mallory's. And besides, Diana reasoned, nothing bad could possibly happen on the best night of her life. *Nobody* was that unlucky.

She followed the sound of Joey's phone to the large mum beside the welcome mat. Reaching behind the lovely blooms, she easily located the wayward device. The overwhelming relief that swept through her was, even in her own estimation, a bit excessive. *See,* she scolded herself, *no need to worry.* No worries. And no drama. The explanation was obvious. The phone must have fallen out of Joey's pocket when he tossed his jacket onto the plant.

After careful inspection, Diana was relieved to find that Joey's brand-new phone had escaped unscathed. She would hate to be responsible, even inadvertently, for another cracked screen. Although Joey insisted that Diana wasn't at fault—and, truth be told, *she* wasn't the one dancing under a scaffold—he wouldn't have been anywhere near that scaffold if it wasn't for her. Diana sighed dreamily. She had never imagined then that a few, short weeks later she would hear him say *"I'm falling in love with you, Diana…."*

Which brought her back to her present conundrum. How was she supposed to tell Joey she was falling in love with him when she was standing on her own porch with *his* phone in her hand?

Be brave, Nanny Di.

Maybe that dratted iguana was right, for once, she decided. She would be brave. She would take Joey his phone tonight. She would walk right up to his townhouse and knock on his door and tell him she was falling in love with him. And he would…

Diana shivered. She didn't know what he would do, but she was certain that she would enjoy it.

Joey had all the windows open and the air conditioner running full blast even though the coolness of the October night should have been sufficient. He was always overheated after spending time with Diana. *Always.* And tonight was no exception. Tonight, the heat between them had nearly melted his reformed-rake good intentions.

He had *almost* gone too far. He had *almost* taken complete advantage of Diana Merritt's pliant, more-than-willing, endlessly enthralling body. In other words, he thought in disgust, he had almost behaved like a completely *unreformed* rake. It made no difference that she was willing. Actually, he reasoned, Diana had seemed *more* than willing. He couldn't help but be pleased by that. She had looked so disappointed when he refused to go inside the cottage with her....

Maybe he should have changed his mind. Maybe he should have stayed at the gatekeeper's cottage. With her. That thought was so powerful that Joey almost turned the car around. Almost. He forced himself to keep driving. He was a dirty dog for even considering a return to the cottage. He really was. And, he informed himself, a dirty dog with good intentions was still a dirty dog.

On the bright side, he *hadn't* taken advantage of her willingness. Or her enthusiasm. Or the way she responded to his every touch. He was rather proud of himself for that. *And* he had given her a date to remember.

Joey harbored only one regret. One single regret. If he was completely honest with himself, he would have to admit that when he told Diana Merritt he was falling in love with her, he was lying.

CHAPTER THIRTY-FIVE

*J*oey Finch was a liar. He had been lying all along.

Every kiss. A lie.

Every touch. A lie.

"I'm falling in love with you, Diana...." The biggest and most painful lie of all.

Diana stood in the shadows of a giant magnolia tree at the edge of the parking lot near Joey's townhouse. She stood there, trying to make sense of what she had witnessed. Trying to keep breathing. Trying not to cry.

She would never have believed what had just happened—was it only five minutes ago?—if she hadn't seen it with her own eyes. She would never have believed that Joey Finch—*her* Joey Finch—would betray her.

But she had seen it. With her own eyes.

And he did. Betray her.

With—of all things—a petite, perfectly proportioned blonde who barely came up to his shoulder.

If, she hypothesized, he hadn't tossed his dratted, damned jacket onto the porch, and if his dratted, damned phone hadn't fallen out of his dratted, damned pocket, she would never have found out.

Diana sighed. Yes, she would have. She would have found out tomor-row. Or the next day. Or the next week. Or she would have figured it out when the longed-for next date never materialized. *Hellfire and damnation.* Her grandfather's favorite oath seemed appropriate for what she was feeling.

Five minutes ago, she had pulled into the parking lot still giddy from the evening. Since it was nearly midnight, most of the spaces were full. She pulled into the last available one in the first row. It was two spaces down from the streetlight, completely hidden in the shadows. She took a deep breath to calm herself. She felt all bubbly inside, like a glass of champagne. She got out of the car and tucked her clutch bag securely under her arm. She held Joey's phone tightly in her other hand. As she prepared to step out of the shadows, she heard a car door shut, followed by the sound of running feet. She paused, instinctively, to see who was joining her in the deserted parking lot.

To her surprise, the figure of a petite woman darted by. The woman made a beeline for Joey's townhouse, disappearing into the darkness of his tiny front porch. Before Diana could move, the porchlight came on, the door opened—and Joey stepped onto the porch. Diana was too far away to hear their brief conversation, but she was close enough to see what hap-pened next.

Joey reached out his hand and gently touched the blonde's chin, studying her face for a few seconds. Then, he held out his arms—and the blonde threw herself into them.

Diana's purse slid noiselessly from beneath her arm. The soft leather barely made a sound as it hit the asphalt. Joey's phone met a similar fate, dropping unnoticed from her nerveless fingers. She watched the scene unfold in horrified disbelief.

Joey tucked the tiny blonde close and pressed a kiss to the top of her curly head. They remained like that for what was probably less than a minute. To Diana, it felt like hours. Joey turned and, with the blonde still cradled in his arms, withdrew into the townhouse. Someone turned off the light, throwing the porch into darkness once more, and Diana's soul with it.

Five minutes.

Three hundred seconds.

And her dreams had been snuffed out as effectively as flipping the switch had extinguished Joey's porch light. She slumped against her car, stunned into immobility. She wanted to get into that car and drive straight to Farther, Virginia. She wanted to throw herself in her mother's arms and cry until she couldn't cry anymore. She wanted her father to give her a hug and tell her everything was going to be all right. She wanted to tell Roman and Connor and Lance and Devin what had happened so that they would...what? Swear and stomp around? Call Joey Finch horrible names? Find him and beat the crap out of him? Tell her that *they* had been right all along while *she* had been wrong?

The last thought hit her hard because it was nothing short of the truth. She had been warned for years—nine years, to be exact—that Joey Finch wasn't the right guy for her. As the locals in Farther would say, "He ain't the marryin' kind." Well, she had gambled; had bet all she had. And she had lost. She had no business being surprised. None, at all. She should have expected it. She *had* expected it, but Joey Finch had wormed his way into her heart. So, now what?

She straightened her shoulders. She was a Merritt, wasn't she? Of course, she was. And Merritts didn't give up...even when the odds were against them. She was twenty-eight years old. She was a successful author. And she was a damn good nanny. She liked living in Honeysuckle Creek. She would find a way to go on, she decided, without the part of her heart that would always belong to Joey Finch.

As Diana bent down to pick up her clutch purse, she suddenly remembered why she was standing under the magnolia tree in the first place. Joey's forgotten phone lay facedown in the parking lot, beside her purse. She gingerly turned it over, reprimanding herself for the first thought that crossed her mind—the petty hope that the screen was cracked. It wasn't. *Drat.* She picked up the phone and her purse, unsure of her next move.

The selfish part of her wanted to throw the phone into the thick vegetation or, better yet, into the parking lot. That way it could be crushed under the tires of a car as effectively as her heart had been crushed by Joey Finch.

The Lying Lawyer and the Vindictive Nanny.

She chuckled grimly at that.

The better part of Diana—the one that recognized she had no one to blame for her current predicament but herself—knew what she had to do. She couldn't avoid the lights, so she forced herself to stroll through the parking lot until she reached the sidewalk that led to Joey's townhouse. She walked confidently up the two steps that led to the tiny front porch, as if she was supposed to be there. She placed the phone on the small, wooden bench beside the front door. She turned around, just as casually, to return to the blessed shadows and her car. She slid into the seat and closed the door.

Only then did she allow herself to relax. As she waited for her hands to stop shaking, she made a decision. She would have closure. Joey Finch might be a one and done, but this time, he was going to learn a lesson.

The Lying Lawyer and the Nanny He Would Never Forget.

Diana knew exactly what she was going to do.

Joey headed toward the entrance of Honeysuckle Creek Pizza and Karaoke, fighting the disturbing feeling that had been following him around all day.

Something. Was. Wrong.

The niggling, little whisper started in the back of his mind first thing in the morning when Diana didn't answer her phone. He wanted to hear her voice as soon as he woke up; wanted to reassure her that his days as a one and done were over and, well…done. He wanted to tell her that he was a one-woman man now and *she* was that woman.

Unfortunately, Diana didn't answer her phone.

He made an unsuccessful effort to ignore the unpleasant feeling in the pit of his stomach each time—five in all—he got her voicemail. His

410

stomach felt a little worse when he tried texting her. Eight times. She failed to answer any of his texts except the very last one.

When she finally replied to his question—*What time do you want me to pick you up?*—she simply said, *I'll see you there.* He couldn't help but think there was something slightly off about that. Why was she going to "see him there"? Why didn't she *want* him to pick her up?

Because something was wrong, that's why.

Joey sighed. Didn't he already have enough to deal with? Trying to keep Ana's situation quiet would not be easy. Especially in a small town like Honeysuckle Creek. One little bit of gossip and—*boom!*—the whole sordid story would blow up in their faces. If that happened, poor Ana would be devastated. She was counting on Joey, and he would *not* let her down.

And how was he supposed to think straight, anyway? he asked himself. His brain kept lapsing into a sensual fog; his entire body reeling from his passionate interlude with Diana the previous evening. Of course, he reminded himself, grimly, something was wrong with Diana now. Or maybe not. He wasn't sure anymore.

Talk about bad timing, Joey grumbled to himself. How could he explain Ana's presence in his apartment to Diana *without* breaking his promise to the curly-haired blonde? There was, he finally concluded, only one option: he would have to make sure Diana didn't find out about his very attractive houseguest. The knots in Joey's stomach stretched a little tighter. Why did everything have to be so complicated?

Roger Carrington was easily the best-looking man in the room. Diana had been sitting alone, waiting for Aria and Elise—her friends from yoga—when Roger unexpectedly planted himself in the chair beside her. With his thick head of curly hair, intelligent eyes, and swoon-worthy physique, he was almost *too* handsome. His winning smile and witty personality made him a charming companion.

She remembered Roger as one of the groomsmen from Blane and Grace's wedding. She had to admit her wounded ego was quite flattered that *he* remembered *her*. She was enjoying their chat until the tingling at the back of her neck alerted her to the presence of the man who—less than twenty-four hours ago—had broken her heart.

Joey was standing behind her. *Drat.* Diana hated being so physically aware of a man who didn't want her. On the plus side, she was able to brace herself for their encounter. After their date, she reminded herself, it had taken Joey less than half an hour to find her replacement. She forced herself to focus on her hurt and humiliation. She didn't even glance in Joey's direction but pretended to listen to whatever her handsome companion was saying.

Roger paused midsentence, looking beyond her shoulder. "Well, look who's finally here," he said, a mischievous grin on his face. "What took you so long, Finch?"

"Carrington," Joey responded, pinning a friendly smile on his face. He had been less than pleased—all right, extremely *dis*pleased—to discover Diana chatting with the currently single and—according to every female Joey knew—extremely attractive man.

"I've been keeping Diana company until her friends get here," Roger added, conversationally.

The appreciative glance Roger gave to the woman sitting beside him didn't escape Joey's notice. Nor did the fact that Diana had yet to acknowledge his own presence. It was also clear that Roger had no idea Diana wasn't waiting for "friends." She was waiting for Joey Finch. Wasn't she?

The unpleasant knots in Joey's stomach tied themselves into larger, *extremely* unpleasant knots. The fact that Diana looked unbelievably lovely wasn't helping the situation. She sported a long, gauzy shirt; skinny, black jeans; and high-heeled ankle boots. The dark gray color of her shirt was the same shade as her eyes. She had draped two long necklaces around her neck. Her hair was pulled back from her face, her glorious curls cascading down her back. The gorgeous display reminded him of how she had looked standing on the porch of the gatekeeper's cottage last night. *After* he removed the pins from her hair.

What the hell was going on?

"Hello, Diana," he said, trying not to sound as if his heart was in his throat.

"Hello, Joey Finch," she replied with a breezy smile.

He waited for her to get up and join him. She didn't move. He looked at her, raising his eyebrows slightly. She looked back, wearing that damn innocuous smile.

Roger glanced from one to the other, an arrested expression on his face. He and Joey were good friends. There was no doubt about that. He did, however, enjoy making Joey feel as uncomfortable as possible whenever he could.

"So, you two are, um…together?" he asked. "A couple?" His pleasantly worded question did not hide his avid interest.

"Yes," Joey said immediately, relieved that Roger understood.

"No," Diana objected, shaking her head. Her smile had disappeared.

Roger's fascinated gaze flicked between Joey's expression of genuine disbelief and Diana's calm demeanor.

Joey almost swore aloud. The waves of tension rolling between himself and the beautiful redhead were practically visible to the naked eye. What was wrong with Roger anyway? Could it be any more obvious that Joey needed to talk to Diana? Alone? Even an idiot with half a brain—and Joey gave Roger credit for much more—would tactfully walk away. One glance at his friend's smirking face, however, dashed any hope of that. Roger had no intention of leaving. He was thoroughly enjoying the chance to torment his old buddy, Joey Finch.

Roger happily poked around for more information. "Let me get this straight. The two of you are going out, aren't you? he asked. "You know… dating?"

"Yes," Joey said decisively, glaring at Diana.

"No," Diana replied, glaring at Joey.

Joey ran his hand through his dark locks in complete frustration. What was he supposed to do now? "How can you say that after last night?" he asked, not thinking of what his question sounded like.

"Whoa." Roger stood up, raising both of his hands as if to ward off Joey's words. "Too much information for me. I'm out." He quickly removed himself from the standoff.

Diana crossed her arms and threw Joey a look of unfettered disgust. "Great. Now he thinks we're sleeping together."

"We could be." Joey regarded her hopefully. "I thought we were headed that way last night...toward a relationship, I mean. *Way to go, Finch. Just what every woman wants to hear.* He nearly laughed at his own ineptness. *Who's the idiot now?*

His words played right into Diana's hands. She had carefully rehearsed this moment during a long and sleepless night. It was time for the big finish. "One date does *not* constitute a relationship, Joey Finch," she snapped. "You, of all people, should be aware of that. I've always known that you're not a 'relationship kind of guy.' Well, guess what?" She paused, narrowing her eyes. "Maybe I'm not a 'relationship kind of girl.' "

Joey's shocked expression as she threw his own words back in his face told her victory was within her grasp. There was no doubt in Diana's mind that she was going to feel awful later. She knew it; accepted it. But she was determined to have the last word. Afterwards, she would deal with her broken heart—not to mention a tangled-up mess of hurt feelings, unanswered questions, and unrequited longing—with as much dignity as she could manage.

Joey couldn't believe what he was hearing. "Diana," he croaked out. "I don't understand...I mean...last night we...I thought we..." His voice died away as she rose to face him.

In a calm, composed voice, Diana delivered the final blow. "Maybe I'm just like you, Joey Finch. Maybe I'm a one and done." She stepped neatly around him and walked away without a backward glance.

To Diana, it was a hollow victory at best.

To Joey, it was total annihilation.

He sat down at the deserted table, feeling like he had been kicked in the teeth. Until this moment, he had never believed mere words could cause physical pain. But they could. And they did. The knots in his stomach turned into one big knot, roughly the size of a large boulder. A *very* large boulder that was currently pressing against his heart.

For about two minutes, he allowed himself to feel like a fool for the way Diana had played him. For two more minutes, he allowed himself to be angry at her callous disregard for his feelings. He glanced across the restaurant to find her talking with Aria and Elise, a serene smile firmly on her face. How could she be so happy when she had just ripped his heart out and stomped on it with her dainty high-heeled ankle boots?

A flash of memory brought his heretofore absent intuition into sharp focus. He had seen that same expression on Diana's face, he realized, when she was on the receiving end of the venom spewed by her heinous employer, Mallory. According to Darcie, Mallory had berated and belittled Diana at every opportunity. But the face that Diana presented to the world was serene and unshakeable. Diana, Darcie added, was a master of concealing her hurt. With Mallory, Diana's ability had been a survival skill. A necessity. But with Joey Finch?

He watched her longingly from across the room. Her expression was calm, like a painting of the Madonna. Although he was too far away to check, Joey was confident that her eyes lacked their usual sparkle. He was willing to bet the smile plastered across her face didn't have the warmth he was used to. The more he thought about it, the more certain he became that his assessment was accurate. His brave Diana was in protective mode now because—and it was hard to admit—she had been hurt. By Joey Finch, who was currently at a loss to explain why. What had he done wrong? Or even worse...what did she *think* he had done? Joey frowned. It was almost as if she knew about Ana. But how could she? Only Joey and Dr. Stafford knew the real story. And Joey hadn't told anyone that Ana was staying with him. Still...

Seventies Night karaoke was in full swing. Various soloists, duets, and groups took to the small stage to attempt songs by, among others, the Bee Gees, Abba, James Taylor, and Lynyrd Skynyrd. *Attempted* being the key word. Some of the singers *attempted*—and some of them *succeeded*. Joey barely refrained from covering his ears during a particularly awful version of Queen's "Bohemian Rhapsody."

That song really needed to be taken off the list, he decided. "Bohemian Rhapsody" was simply too painful for karaoke. He clapped along with everybody else, though…Karaoke was supposed to be fun, wasn't it? He usually had a great deal of fun, didn't he? But not tonight, he thought. Tonight, he was sitting by himself, refusing any invitation to sing, as well as the overtures of his friends to join them. He was sitting all by himself, watching Diana ignore him.

His heart beat a little faster when she stood up and looked his way, challenge in her gaze. What was she doing? he asked himself, hopefully. Was she coming over to talk to him? Was she going to demand the explanation he couldn't give her? Was she…walking to the microphone instead? *Damn.* No wonder he had avoided relationships before now. Too complicated. What would she sing? A romantic ballad by Barry Manilow? Maybe a bouncy disco hit by Donna Summer? How about Dolly Parton's "Jolene." Diana could pull it off. Any of them. Joey leaned forward expectantly, both elbows on the table in front of him.

"You're So Vain."

The woman he loved was singing Carly Simon's "You're So Vain." About…him. The words were spot on…the first two verses anyway. And he deserved every one of them. She painted a perfect picture of her opinion of…him. That made it even worse.

And she was killing it. Even though it hurt, he couldn't help but be proud of her. Her voice was pitch-perfect. She had real talent. And she had stage presence. She smiled, playfully; every gesture and nod sharpening the impact of the words of the song. She looked like she was having a wonderful time; like she didn't have a care in the world. Only Joey Finch knew that she was, in fact, deadly serious.

His phone vibrated in his pocket, just as his own personal musical rebuke was receiving the biggest applause of the night. He pulled his phone out and grimaced. Darcie. Again. His little sister was obviously displeased at his monosyllabic text messages. She wanted information and she wanted it *now*.

Sorry, Darce, he thought, putting the phone back into his pocket. He had no desire to discuss the present state of his love life with anyone, especially his nosy, little sister. If he continued to ignore her, she would, eventually, stop calling…Wouldn't she?

He laughed, grimly. Of course not. This was Darcie he was talking about. When *she* wanted information, she was relentless. She would drive him and everyone else crazy until she got what she wanted. How many times had she called, anyway?

He reluctantly pulled his phone out again to look through his back-log of recent calls. Six calls from his intrepid sibling since last night. And one call from…Diana? His heart did a little jump in his chest. How had he missed a call from Diana? He checked the time of the call: eleven thirty-eight p.m. She must have called him while he was driving home from their date. That was odd. Granted, he was in a lust-filled haze at the time, but he should have heard his phone ring.

Joey felt a cold chill, as if something truly awful was about to happen. He thought back to last night. It had taken nearly an hour to convince Ana that she needed to see a doctor. She might be tiny, but Ana was stubborn as hell. When they finally left for the emergency room, Joey saw his phone lying on the bench outside his door. He grabbed it on the way to his truck. He hadn't thought about it again until just now, but why had his phone been on that bench? He didn't remember putting it there. He knew he had it at dinner when Carlo took the picture for Darcie. He had carried his phone in his jacket pocket the whole time. Diana was wearing his jacket when he took her home and then…

With a sinking heart, Joey realized what must have happened. The timing was too perfect. Diana's bare shoulder. Soft, smooth skin. Hot, hot kisses. He remembered tossing the jacket onto a plant. His phone must have fallen from his pocket outside of Diana's door. She found it and was returning it to him when she saw…

Joey mumbled every swear word he had ever heard in his life. He even made up a few colorful phrases à la Connor Merritt. Diana had seen *everything.* And now he knew exactly what she was thinking: he was a lying bastard who had already moved on to his next victim, less than an hour after leaving her. It didn't matter that Ana would laugh herself silly at the thought of herself being in a romantic liaison with Joey Finch. What mattered was what Diana believed.

He found himself halfway across the room before he gave the slightest thought to what he was going to say. He glanced toward Diana's friends, realizing that the woman he wanted wasn't there: Diana's triumphant karaoke performance had ended without Joey noticing. Aria pointed toward the exit while tossing Joey a wink and a knowing smile. Obviously, Diana had yet to inform her friends of Joey's betrayal. He nodded his thanks and headed to the door. A hand with perfectly manicured red fingernails shot out from the last table before the exit, attaching itself to his arm. He looked down into the suspicious eyes of Lou Boggs. She was sitting with Zack and Evander.

"Oh, Joey," Lou said, the worry evident in her tone. "What did you do?"

He paused to gently unhook himself from Lou's grip. "Diana and I have, um…had a little misunderstanding. That's all. I just need to talk to her."

Zack shook his head sadly. "Must be a pretty big *little* misunderstanding," he added. "She was glaring right at you while she sang…Dude, she slayed you with that song." Zack's filter was, as always, noticeably absent.

"Diana and I need to talk," Joey repeated. "That's all."

Evander's eyes were full of sympathy. "You better hurry, then, Joe. She just left."

Joey hurried to the parking lot, glancing around a bit frantically before spotting Diana headed toward her Mustang a couple of parking spots away. "Diana. Wait," he called as her hand closed around the car's door handle. He saw her hesitate; could almost feel her desire to flee. Then, he watched her square her shoulders and take a deep breath. When she turned around, her serene smile was firmly in place. She was magnificent.

"Diana," he began, but stopped. He still didn't know what to say.

"Yes," she asked, pleasantly.

The words poured from his mouth in abject desperation. "Look, Diana, I know what you *think* you saw, but that's not what you *really* saw. I mean, it is, but it isn't."

A tiny frown marred her forehead, as she tried to understand.

"I mean. It's all very easy to explain," he said, trying to sound confident.

She spoke. "Is it?"

"Yes," he said, surprised that he was out of breath.

"Easy to explain?" she asked, doubtfully.

"Yes. Very easy. So easy, in fact, that you're going to laugh. At how easy it is. Not at me. At the easiness of the explanation." He sounded like an idiot.

"Well?"

"Well, what?" He hadn't thought this through. Now she was going to ask him to explain. He was well and truly screwed. *No, no, no. Please don't ask. Please don't...*

For some reason, his idiocy seemed to amuse her. "I cannot wait for this easy explanation that is apparently going to send me into gales of laughter. Please, explain."

His shoulders dropped dejectedly. "I can't."

Frustrated, Diana threw her hands in the air. "Joey, I don't have time for this."

His gaze held hers. "I can't explain because it isn't my story to tell." Something flickered in her gaze, giving him a bit of hope. "You'll just have to—"

"Trust you?" she interrupted, sadly. "I did."

He opened his mouth, but nothing came out. What could he possibly say to that?

She waited a few seconds, before whispering, "Goodbye, Joey."

His hope died along with his ability to speak. He watched her drive away. His heart pounded with a helpless sense of regret and…fear. She was gone. What the hell was he going to do about that?

CHAPTER THIRTY-SIX

*J*oey was still searching for an answer on Wednesday afternoon. It had been the longest four days of his life. Four days were an eternity without Diana. And, for the first time, his dependable rakes—reformed and otherwise—didn't have answers. That's because even his fictitious counterparts didn't get themselves into a situation as asinine as the one he had gotten himself into. It was too unbelievable to be fact *or* fiction.

Diana *didn't* trust him because he *couldn't* explain Ana's situation. He couldn't explain Ana's situation because *Ana* trusted him. If he broke Ana's trust, he wouldn't be trustworthy. Therefore, he wouldn't be a man Diana could trust, would he? But Diana didn't trust him anyway. And it was his own fault. *Damn.*

He called in an order at Jack's in time to pick it up during court recess. When he arrived, Zack was on duty. The young man regarded him solemnly from behind the to-go counter, his friendly smile noticeably absent. Something was up.

"Hello, Zack," Joey said, casually. "I need to pick up a coffee order."

"That'll be three dollars and seventy-two cents." Zack pushed one of two cups of coffee toward Joey. He had yet to crack a smile.

Joey handed Zack his debit card, watching as the young man completed the transaction.

"Sign here," Zack said.

Joey could feel Zack's eyes appraising him while he signed his name. He braced himself, but nothing could have prepared him for the blunt young man's next words.

"Are you sleeping with Ana Martin?" Zack asked, leaning on the counter. He was watching Joey's every move.

Joey nearly dropped his coffee in surprise. "Hell no," he answered, emphatically. "Why would you ask me such a stupid question, you asshole?"

Zack relaxed, grinning. He was obviously pleased with Joey's reaction. "I didn't really think you were sleeping with her, but I had to make sure." He motioned toward the coffee in Joey's hand. "I wouldn't drink that if I were you," he advised.

"Why not?" Joey asked suspiciously.

"It's half coffee and half hot sauce...the kind with habanero peppers." Zack picked up the other coffee cup on the counter. "Here's yours."

Joey narrowed his eyes. "Trying to poison me, huh?" he asked, switching coffee cups. He took a tentative sip and nodded in approval. As usual, Zack knew something. It was up to Joey to discover how much. Joey leaned against the counter to begin his interrogation.

"So, tell me, Zack," he began. "If I had answered in the affirmative—in other words..."

Zack was offended. "If you were sleeping with Miss Martin. I know what *affirmative* means, Joey. I'm majoring in criminal justice."

"Sorry." Joey studied the disgruntled young man. "If I was sleeping with Miss Martin—which I most assuredly am not—would you really have let me drink that coffee?"

Zack considered the question. "Yes." He crossed his arms decisively.

"Why?" Joey asked.

Zack shrugged. "Because of Diana. I like her."

Joey sighed. "I like her, too, Zack. As a matter of fact, I am one hundred percent let's-buy-the-ring-and-plan-the-honeymoon in love with her. But then, you probably already knew that." He might as well just spit it out. He felt sure Zack was way ahead of him.

"Yep," the young man replied. "I figured that out…"

"When I almost punched old Nigel in the face?" Joey asked.

"Nope," came the surprising answer. "When you stared down Devin's bitchy wife when she was trying to embarrass Diana before the wedding. I've never seen you look at a girl the way you looked at Diana that day. It was like you couldn't believe she was real."

"Hmph," Joey said. Zack was quite a student of human nature. "Congratulations, Zack. You knew before I did."

"I knew before you were ready to admit it," Zack countered.

Joey took a sip of his coffee. The kid's observations were always spot-on. Joey didn't know how he did it.

"So…" Zack leaned on the counter. "Why is Ana Martin staying at your townhouse?" And just like that, the interrogator became the interrogated.

"How do you know she's staying with me?"

"Newt lives two doors down from you, Joey," Zack explained. "He saw her."

Well, hell, Joey thought. He and Ana had tried to be so careful, too. Were all the Kimels as observant as Zack? The implications of the apparent answer to that question were terrifying.

"Newt won't tell," Zack promised.

"And why is that?" Joey asked.

"He likes Ana. And Diana," Zack said. "And you, of course," the young man added as an afterthought. It was true. Joey and Newt had known each other since kindergarten. They had always gotten along.

Zack continued: "Miss Martin's staying with you because of her brother, isn't she? Earl's a mean son of a bitch. I don't blame Miss Martin for wanting to stay somewhere else while he's in town, especially with all the losers he brings home with him. I hope he leaves or goes back to jail soon. We don't need his kind in Honeysuckle Creek."

Joey relaxed, nodding his agreement. Ana's secret was still, well…a secret.

"I'm guessing you and Diana had some sort of falling out about it or something. Anyway, I have some information for you. And you have to swear you'll forget that I'm the one who told you." Zack leaned over the counter, looking from side to side as if he was about to impart state secrets. At that moment, the waiting area was blessedly devoid of patrons.

"I swear," Joey agreed. What was Zack going to tell him now?

"Diana's got a date," Zack said.

"What?" The word was ripped from Joey's throat before he could stop it. "With who? Don't tell me Nigel's back causing trouble."

"You might wish it was *only* Nigel when I tell you," Zack said.

Joey forced himself to be calm. "If it's not Nigel, then who?" What was the deal? Did Diana have a plethora of British suitors whom she hadn't told him about?

"She's going out with Roger. He's taking her to Celine's on Friday night. Their reservation is at seven thirty." Zack enunciated the time deliberately, giving Joey a look brimming with unspoken advice. He stood up to his full height, grabbed a rag, and started wiping the counter.

"Roger?" *Well, hell.* Zack was right. Joey would have preferred Nigel. Or someone *like* Nigel. Or a perfect stranger. Or anyone else but the good-looking and charmingly confident Roger Carrington, who was also his friend.

Several customers wandered into the to-go area before Joey could question Zack further. "Good luck, Joey," Zack said, with appropriate gravity. "And remember, you didn't hear it from me."

Joey had the sudden feeling he was playing a bit part in some old spy movie, receiving his assignment from his handler. *This is your mission if you choose to accept it. Good luck. This message will self-destruct in five seconds.* He waved his farewell and walked out of Jack's, emerging onto the sidewalk.

Finally admitting aloud that he was in love with Diana Merritt made Joey feel lighter as he strolled back to the courthouse. Or was it, he wondered, just the caffeine? Either way, the strategic portion of his brain—lying dormant since Diana left him in the parking lot on Saturday night—roared to life. If he couldn't *tell* Diana the truth, maybe he could *show* her.

A short time later, he had devised a plan.

"Ana Banana," Joey called, cheerfully, barreling through the door to his townhouse on Friday afternoon. "Where are you?"

"In your chair," she replied. "And I'm not moving."

Ana was curled up in Joey's big recliner, looking like an adorable waif. What a difference a week had made. The bruises around her eye and on her forehead were fading nicely. The swelling was gone completely. The contraption on her left hand—holding her broken fingers in place—should have made use of her hand difficult, if not impossible. Typical of Ana, she had slipped off her shoulder harness and was typing away on her MacBook.

Joey was glad to see the sparkle return to her eyes, along with a large portion of her sass. He sat down on the sofa, debating the best course of action.

Ana paused, her eyes narrowing slightly. "I know that look." She sighed in resignation. "Spit it out, Joey. What do you want?"

"Ana, I need a favor," he said, an exaggerated wheedling note in his voice.

"Oh Lord." Her eyes narrowed even further. "What kind of favor?"

"Just dinner," Joey said, casually.

She looked puzzled. "You want me to make dinner? Okay. I can do that." She grinned, reaching for her phone. "I can order pizza with the best of them."

"Um, that's not exactly what I have in mind," Joey admitted. "I want you to *go* out to dinner with me."

Ana's reaction was exactly what he expected. "Out to dinner? Looking like this? You can't be serious."

"Oh, but I am serious, Ana." Joey pleaded. "Look. I need your help." He tried to look pitiful and desperate enough to appeal to Ana's soft heart.

Ana wrinkled her nose. "Oh, all right. I'll wear dark glasses and a hat. You know I'll never say no, Joey Finch, not after all that you've done for me." She leaned toward him, her pretty face alight with curiosity. "Who am I pretending to be this time? she asked. "Your imaginary girlfriend again? Is that it? You want me to scare some crazy stalker away?" When Joey did not immediately reply, she continued in the same vein. "What do you want me to tell her? That you were the one who beat me up?"

"No," Joey said, firmly. "Definitely not that. I need you to go to dinner and act like you're *not* my girlfriend. I need you to be exactly what you are…one of my oldest friends. I need you to make it clear that you and I are *just friends*."

Ana eyed him suspiciously. "Why?" she asked.

"Let's just say that I'm trying to prove a point and leave it at that," Joey said, smoothly.

"Do I have to climb in or out of a window this time?" Ana raised her left hand, waving the contraption for her injury around. "Because I don't think that's an option."

"No, you do not have to climb in or out of a window this time. All you have to do is go to dinner with me. At Celine's." He braced himself. "In two hours."

"*Two hours?*" Ana shrieked.

"Now, Ana…" Joey began.

"Good Lord," said a familiar voice. "What is that ungodly noise?" Lou Boggs strolled into the room, a huge smile on her face. "Sounds like a long-tail cat in a room full of rocking chairs." She delivered the old saying in her best Southern drawl.

Ana tried to bolt from the room, but her hand had become stuck in her blanket, effectively trapping her in the big chair. She lifted her chin defiantly. The effect was spoiled by the trembling of her lower lip.

Lou continued with the same no-nonsense attitude she used to barge into Joey's townhouse: "Anastasia Martin, Joey said you lost a fight with the stairs again." She carried a large basket, which she placed on Joey's kitchen table, along with her purse.

Ana was relieved by Lou's words. The tiny blonde loved her job as a teacher at Honeysuckle Creek Academy. After years of concentrated effort, Ana had managed to rise above her family's trashy reputation. She could, finally, hold up her head in her hometown. Her worst nightmare was that someone would discover her shame. Having a brother like Earl was humiliating enough. If anyone found out that he, occasionally, took out his violent urges on his sister, Ana would once again find herself the target of vicious gossip. Or, worse than that, pity. She had already lived through that once. She refused to do it again. She had worked too hard at making something out of her life to find herself at the mercy of gossiping busybodies.

Lou approached her friend with her usual assurance. She gently placed her hand under Ana's chin, tilting her face from side to side. "Ana, honey," she said in a soft voice, "if I could get my hands on your sorry excuse for a brother, I'd kick his ass."

"Get in line," Joey growled.

"What do you mean, Lou?" Ana stammered. "I hit my head when I fell down the—"

"Oh, stop, honey," Lou said, firmly. "I *dated* Earl for three months after David and I broke up, remember?" She spoke of Ana's violent brother with icy disdain.

"Oh, that's right…" Ana said, some of the stiffness disappearing from her spine. "I forgot about that." Lou had experienced first-hand the violence hiding behind the attractive face of Earl Martin.

Lou leaned over to enfold her friend in a tight hug. "You had to do my makeup for me a couple of times, if I remember correctly. I'm just returning the favor. Don't worry, I'm the soul of discretion." She stood up, efficiently wiping away a few stray tears. "And, Anastasia, my door is always open. I have an extra bedroom and…" She gave a quick glance around Joey's apartment. "My bathrooms are always clean."

"My bathrooms are clean," Joey remarked to no one in particular.

Lou looked amused. "Not *male* clean, Joey," she said, as if that explained everything. "*Female* clean." She turned her attention back to Ana. "As a matter of fact, why don't you move in with me until Earl leaves town again? I would love it, and it might be easier to explain than your current arrangement." She glanced at Joey before resuming her suggestion. "You can tell everyone that your *dear* brother is in town with his *charming* friends. And there isn't enough room in your house for everyone, so you decided to stay with me. End of story."

Ana's eyes filled with tears of sheer gratitude. "I would like that, Lou."

Lou smiled. "Consider it done. I'll take your bags with me when I leave. That way, Joey can drop you off at my house after dinner. I'll give you the extra key and you can make yourself at home. And, Ana," Lou said, reaching out for Ana's good hand, "please remember that you don't have to deal with Earl alone. You have friends."

Ana gripped Lou's hand as if it was a lifeline, allowing her friend to tug her out of the big chair. "Lou," she began, "I can't thank you and Joey enough for—"

"Hush, honey. We don't have time for that now," Lou said, gently. "Go take a shower and wash that curly head. We have work to do."

Ana gave a watery chuckle. "Yes, ma'am." She headed toward the guestroom.

"What do you think, Lou?" Joey asked as Ana disappeared down the hall.

"I think there is a special place in hell for Earl Martin and all the people like him," she said, swiping angrily at a leftover tear. Her gaze was far away as she wrestled with demons of her own.

"What about Ana? Can you hide her bruises?" Joey finally asked, breaking the fraught silence. It was the only thing he could think to say.

"Piece of cake," Lou said, with satisfaction, snapping out of her reverie. "No one will ever know."

"That's great," Joey replied. But he couldn't help hoping that Lou's makeup skills weren't quite as good as she thought they were.

CHAPTER THIRTY-SEVEN

*D*iana should never have agreed to go out with Roger Carrington. She should have turned him down the minute he asked. She should not be walking with him now—wearing her purple midi dress, with the V-neck and triple flounces—to a table at the restaurant called Celine's. The dress wasn't her favorite, but it would do for a date with Roger Carrington.

He wasn't her favorite, either. Not at the moment, anyway. Hindsight was most assuredly twenty-twenty, she decided. At the time Carrington had asked her out, though, she had been so upset with Joey Finch that she would probably have agreed to go out with Satan himself. Anything to prove a point.

And even though Roger Carrington wasn't Satan, he wasn't any kind of a saint, either. According to Aria, Roger's past was littered with a string of broken hearts as long as Honeysuckle Creek. He was, at one time—in romance novel terms—a living, breathing *rake*. But no longer did the elusive Mr. Carrington play the role of heartbreaker. And why was that? Oh, of course. Because Roger had changed.

He was a rake who had reformed.

He was a reformed rake.

Diana received Aria's words with about as much enthusiasm as she would have received a summons to jury duty. A *reformed* rake? Ha. The term didn't apply outside of fiction. Once a rake, always a rake. *Oh, goody,* she thought, with biting sarcasm. *I'm going out with another reformed rake. That's just terrific, because things worked out so well the first time.* So well, in fact, that she had no desire to repeat the experience. Still, she was stuck, so she may as well make the best of the situation.

Diana glanced around as the server seated them at their table. The restaurant was nice and—although she hated to admit it—her companion was nice. So far. She tried not to be suspicious. She tried to give Mr. Rake—er…Mr. Roger—Carrington the benefit of the doubt. To his credit, Roger was all that was polite. He was interesting and witty and, well…nice. She was sure the food would be nice, too. As a matter of fact, the whole evening was shaping up to be nice. A nice first date. Wasn't that just…nice?

She eyed her date skeptically, armed with the secret knowledge that if Roger turned into an *un*reformed rake at the end of the night, she would take her cousin Connor's advice and kick the attractive Mr. Carrington in the balls.

Roger continued talking—something about playing football—oblivious to the fact that the male portions of his anatomy were in jeopardy. Diana wasn't really listening anyway. She had clicked on autopilot the minute Roger had picked her up. So far, he hadn't noticed.

"Well, look who's here," Roger said, as if he wasn't the least bit surprised.

Something in his tone, some underlying sense of anticipation, had Diana turning her head toward the entrance of the restaurant. What she saw there—or rather, *who* she saw—had her senses fully engaged once more. Her senses were, in fact, *so* engaged that she didn't know whether to run screaming into the parking lot…or throw up. Because Joey Finch had just walked into Celine's.

Diana nearly panicked. What was Joey doing here? Her overwrought brain struggled to make sense of his unexpected appearance. Was Joey following her? And if so, why? Because he missed her? Because he was jealous of Roger Carrington? Because he was desperately in love with her? Or was he just…hungry? That was the reason, she decided, dispiritedly. Joey Finch was hungry. He was here for dinner. And she was pathetic. But seriously, she asked herself, how could she possibly have such terrible luck?

Nanny Di and the Most Unreformed Reformed Rake in the Exalted History of Rake-dom.

Joey stood there in khaki pants and a button-down shirt, looking handsome and desirable and, oh-so-sexy. *Drat. Double drat. Damn double drat. Damn damn, double double…Shut up, Diana.*

She studied him, surreptitiously. No need to call attention to herself, she rationalized. He hadn't seen her yet, anyway. *That's because he's not looking for you, Diana. He's here for dinner, you idiot,* she reminded herself. *D-I-N-N-E-R. Dinner. Not D-I-A-N-A.*

D-I-A-N-A watched Joey nod at something the hostess said. Then he turned to the woman beside him. The blond woman. The tiny, blond woman. The adorable, tiny blond woman with curly hair. The adorable, tiny blond woman with curly hair she had seen on Joey's porch last Friday night. Diana closed her eyes for a moment. This could *not* be happening to her. This *wasn't* happening to her. It was some kind of horrible nightmare that…

"Diana," Roger said, causing her eyes to pop open. He regarded her with amusement. "I don't know if you remember Ana Martin or not, but she's trying to get your attention. If you don't wave back, I'm afraid her arm will fall off."

Sure enough, the blonde was waving her hand almost frantically in Diana's direction. Diana raised her hand to acknowledge the woman she now remembered as one of Grace's bridesmaids. As soon as Ana realized that Diana saw her, she beamed with pleasure. She pulled on Joey's arm, pointing to Diana and Roger.

If, Diana thought, sarcastically, she had known that every other person she was going to run into in Honeysuckle Creek was a member of Blane and Grace's wedding party, she would have taken better notes. Or *some* notes. Or written *something* down. Honestly. Why were the lives of these people so intertwined? It was completely ridiculous.

432

"Let's invite them to join us," Roger said, motioning to Joey and Ana. His eyes were brimming with suppressed laughter.

Diana's mouth fell open in surprise. What was the matter with Roger Carrington? Was he insane? Had he been drinking heavily before picking her up? Had he had one concussion too many when he played football? Or was he just too stupid to realize that inviting Joey—Diana's we-didn't-date-long-enough-to-say-*ex*-but-he-might-as-well-be-ex-boyfriend—and Ana to join them for dinner was a bad idea? Ana was Diana's replacement, after all. Perhaps Roger just liked to stir things up? Did he make a habit of poking his nose where it didn't belong? Did he enjoy the misery of others? She narrowed her eyes and glared at her reformed rake of a date.

Roger laughed outright at the expression on her face. "Oh, come on, Diana," he said. "It'll be fun." His eyes gleamed with a wicked light.

Yes, she decided, there was something *very* wrong with Roger Carrington. *Drat.* She managed to arrange her mouth into a serene, Madonna-like smile. "That is a fabulous idea, Roger," she said, evenly. "I was just thinking how much fun it would be to invite Joey and Ana to join us for dinner. You read my mind."

He saluted her with his water glass but didn't have time to reply before being partially covered by Ana's shawl as she engulfed him in an enthusiastic hug. She gave a similar hug to Diana, which would have been incredibly awkward but for Ana's genuine excitement.

"Oh, Diana," she said. "I don't know if you remember me or not, but I remember you. I'm so glad to see you again." She grinned at Roger and Diana, her eyes glowing with happiness. "This is going to be so much fun."

Diana automatically smiled back. This was definitely going to be fun, she thought. Like having-a-tooth-pulled-without-anesthesia fun. Or having-the-piano-lid-fall-on-your-fingers fun. Or almost-choking-to-death-on-a-chicken-bone fun. Yes, this was going to be *FUN*.

The chair on Diana's left brushed her leg as Joey pulled it out. She glanced up and met his hooded gaze. "Sorry," he said, as he sat down. He was immediately pulled into the animated conversation between Roger and Ana.

Diana was having an animated conversation of her own. In her head. Why were she and Roger sitting at a table for four instead of for two, anyway? And why were these chairs so close together? What was wrong with this restaurant? Or maybe Roger the Rake was to blame. Shouldn't he have requested a table for two? Wasn't this supposed to be a date? At least Roger was seated on her right and not across the table from her, but still. And why was Roger so eager for Joey and Ana to join them? It was almost as if he enjoyed putting Joey in awkward situations. Was that why he asked Diana out? To mess with Joey Finch? Despite the circumstances, Diana felt her protective instincts rise. This was clearly a disaster waiting to happen.

Joey needed to leave.

Now.

Diana moved her hand, suddenly, knocking her napkin on the floor. Joey, ever the gentleman, leaned over to pick it up for her. She leaned over at the same time.

"Leave!" she hissed.

Luckily, she and Joey had the seats against the wall, so their exchange went unnoticed.

"Beg pardon?" he asked, reaching for the napkin.

"You. Need. To. Leave." There. That was easy to understand.

"No," he said, handing her the napkin and returning to an upright position.

Joey was pleased with the way his plan was progressing. Stopping by Celine's for lunch yesterday had paid off. Not only had he been able to convince the hostess—Joey's date for a Halloween carnival in middle school—to seat Diana and Roger at a table for four, but Roger played right into his hands by inviting Ana and him to join them. Yes, his plan was working well so far. Diana's reaction told him that she hadn't written him off entirely. She was seething but hiding it well behind a serene smile. Damn, but he wanted to kiss that smile off her lips.

The server, a young man with *"Stan"* on his nametag, brought menus and took drink orders. He also brought Diana another napkin at Joey's request. Joey grinned at the chilly thanks he received from the ever-polite nanny seated on his right. The conversation turned to dinner as they perused the menus for their choices. All except Ana.

"I don't even have to look," she said. "I'm ordering spaghetti. Celine's spaghetti is the best I've ever tasted." She smiled at Diana. "If you're not sure what to order, I'd recommend the spaghetti. It's really delicious."

"What do you think of the spaghetti, Ana?" Roger asked, drily.

Ana wrinkled her nose at him. Her adorable nose. She was adorable in every way, Diana reluctantly admitted. Perfectly proportioned. Lovely complexion. Beautiful smile…with dimples. And those golden curls. Ana was like a porcelain doll come to life. And she was full of personality. She was also sweet. *Drat.* She was the perfect woman for Joey Finch. *I always wanted dimples*, Diana thought, wistfully. Unfortunately, the only dimples she had were on her thighs. She really needed to start swimming again. Soon.

But not tonight. "I'm getting the spaghetti, too, Ana," Diana said, closing her menu. "It's the perfect date food, don't you think?" She couldn't resist throwing that pointed barb at Joey Finch.

Joey smirked. *Challenge accepted.* "Maybe we can order cherries jubilee for dessert."

"What an original idea, Joey," Diana said, politely. *Touché, Joey Finch.*

"Date food?" Ana asked, genuinely surprised. "This isn't a *date*. I could *never* go out with Joey. Dating Joey would be like dating my brother." She wrinkled her adorable, little nose just thinking about it. "Of course, I would *never* date my brother, either, even if he wasn't my brother. Earl is to be avoided at all costs. You should never go out with my brother, either, Diana, if he ever asks." She continued talking, seemingly oblivious to the fact that no one else was joining in. She taught freshmen English. She was used to talking to herself.

Diana was watching Ana, a puzzled expression on her face. Joey was watching Diana, hoping she was paying close attention to Ana's revelations. Roger's eyes flitted from one to the other. He seemed to be enjoying himself immensely.

Stan returned, bringing their drinks and a basket of breadsticks to the table. Ana picked up a breadstick with her right hand. She bit into it, closing her eyes in enjoyment. "Mmm. The real reason that Joey and I came to dinner is because he's tired of eating pizza." She smiled at Diana. "My culinary skills are nonexistent. I've been staying at Joey's place this week while my brother is in town. There just isn't enough room at our house for me with Earl and all of his friends."

Roger finally spoke up. "My good friend, Earl." The way he said it made it clear that Earl was neither good nor any kind of friend. Roger grimaced. "You can stay at The Castle any time, Ana. You can have your own wing." It was true. Roger's mansion was enormous.

Ana's sweet smile lit her whole face. "Aww, Raj. That's so nice of you, but I'll be staying with Lou starting tonight. She said I can move in with her until Earl leaves." She took another bite of her breadstick, beaming at Roger.

Diana's napkin once again went flying off the table with a neat flick of her wrist. At the same time, her foot connected sharply with Joey's ankle.

"Oh, dear, my napkin," she said, glaring at him.

"Ow!" he said, surprised at how hard she had kicked him.

They leaned over at the same time.

"What is this about, Joey?" she whispered, urgently, reaching for the errant napkin. "What are you trying to prove? I was there. I know what I saw. Why can't you just tell me what's going on?"

"It's *not* my story to tell." His whisper was equally urgent. He covered the hand holding the napkin with his own. "I can't tell you, but I'm trying to *show* you."

Diana tried to pull her hand away, but Joey refused to let go. "Please, Diana." His eyes implored her. "Please, try to understand."

She nodded, once.

Satisfied, he released her hand. They resumed their seats at exactly the same time. Ana and Roger were regarding them with undisguised interest.

Diana waved her napkin in the air. "Got it." She felt like an idiot.

The appearance of Stan with an enormous bowl of salad saved her from calling further attention to her idiocy. He graciously served each person's plate with a delicious assortment of greens. He even managed not to look surprised when Joey asked him for another napkin.

For the first time, Ana raised her left hand to rest on the table.

"Good Lord, Ana," Roger said, in surprise. "What have you done *now*?"

Ana's eyes widened. Her good hand flew to the curls artfully arranged on the right side of her forehead. She fluffed them anxiously. "I fell down the steps again. I hit my head on the bannister when I fell."

"Is the bannister okay?" Roger quipped. "You have a pretty hard head."

Ana poked out her tongue in response.

If Diana hadn't been paying close attention, she would have missed the carefully concealed bruising of Ana's forehead. She also noticed that the bruising continued down the right side and around Ana's eye. Whoever had done her makeup had done a stellar job. Diana's forehead wrinkled into a tiny frown. She glanced at Joey, who was watching her intensely.

Roger laughed at Ana's response. "What about that thing?" he asked, pointing to the contraption on her left hand.

"When I landed, my hand was behind me and I broke two fingers," she explained.

"Ouch," Roger said, digging into his salad. "Stuff like that happens to you all the time."

"Yes, it does," Ana laughed. "I am *so* clumsy...." She picked up her fork and attacked her salad hungrily.

Diana didn't move. She knew exactly what had happened to Ana Martin last Friday night. And she was horrified. She had lived through the same scenario with her cousin, Lydia. The words were very familiar.

I fell down the steps again....

Diana seriously doubted that Ana was acrobatic enough to fall forward into the bannister, hit her head, turn around, and fall backwards to

437

land on her hand. She just couldn't get it to make sense. She found the word *again* to be significant.

What have you done now?...

Stuff like that happens to you all the time....

Roger's words were telling. They painted a picture of repetition. This kind of thing had happened to Ana before.

I am so clumsy....

How many times had Lydia brushed off this bruise or that sprain with that exact phrase?

And, finally...

It's not my story to tell.

Joey had said those words twice. Diana had said them, herself, many times, sworn by Lydia not to reveal the truth that was so painful to her cousin. There was no doubt in Diana's mind. Last Friday night, Ana Martin had been beaten.

For Diana, the reality was devastating. Her eyes flew to Joey's awaiting gaze. Her napkin hit the floor. They leaned down at the same time.

"Her brother...?" Diana whispered, grimly.

Joey nodded. "Yes."

Their gazes held.

"I am so sorry," she said. She grabbed the napkin. Before Joey could sit up, she was on her feet, napkin in hand.

"I have to get another napkin," she gasped, turning away from the fascinated gazes of Ana and Roger. But, instead of heading toward the server's station, she made a beeline for the small hallway that led to the closed outdoor patio.

Joey righted himself in his own chair. He couldn't believe the sweet relief that flooded through him. Diana understood. He was exonerated of all wrongdoing. Now, he could get back to the business of wooing his lady love. Except...his lady love was nowhere to be seen.

"Well?" Ana asked, expectantly, irritation in her eyes.

He slowly realized that he was under the extreme scrutiny of his dinner companions.

"Well, what?" he asked, again glancing around for Diana.

Roger made a disgusted sound. "Go after her, genius." He pointed toward the outdoor patio.

Joey leaped to his feet. A few seconds later, he disappeared into the hallway.

Roger shook his head. "I guess all those lawyer brains don't leave a whole lot of room for common sense." He raised his wine glass and grinned at Ana.

Ana smiled as she clinked her glass against his. "Do you think they'll come back?" she asked, curiously.

"Of course," Roger said, laughing. "They're both too polite not to finish dinner. I have a feeling that I'm the one taking you home, though."

"To Lou's," Ana said. "And I have a feeling you're right." She studied her dinner companion for a moment with new eyes. "You've become quite the matchmaker the past couple of years, haven't you, Raj?"

"Yeah." Roger shrugged. "I guess I have at that." He shook his head, ruefully. "But this time it's going to cost me fifty dollars." In deference to Ana's confusion, Roger reluctantly elaborated. "I lost a bet."

"A bet?" Ana was clearly delighted. "Seriously?"

Roger nodded, then waited for the inevitable. He didn't have to wait long.

"With whom did you bet, Mr. Carrington?"

Roger grinned at his companion, as amused by her textbook grammar—she *was* an English teacher, he reminded himself—as by her genuine enjoyment of his predicament.

"I bet Zack Kimel fifty dollars that Joey would lose interest in Diana after one date," he admitted.

"Zack Kimel?" Ana burst into a peal of infectious giggles. She was well-acquainted with the enterprising Mr. Kimel. "You lost fifty dollars to Zack Kimel? Oh, I can't believe it!"

Watching Ana's eyes, alight with laughter, Roger couldn't help but feel his ill-fated bet was worth every penny.

Joey found Diana standing alone on the patio, gazing at nothing. He approached her carefully.

"Diana, honey," he said, softly. "Are you all right?"

She turned to face him, using the back of her hand to wipe away a telltale tear. "I'm glad you helped Ana. I'm so glad she knew you were there for her, that she could trust you." Her words were soft but fierce.

Joey waited, watching the emotions play across her face. Whatever she was working through was intense. He just wasn't quite sure what it was.

"Lydia didn't ask for help, Joey. She didn't ask any of us. Kyle got in her head. He made her think she deserved to be his punching bag." The tears were running down her cheeks now. "She almost *died*, Joey, because she didn't think she could trust us. She tried to deal with an abusive husband on her own."

In two strides Joey had wrapped Diana in his arms. He didn't say anything at all. He simply held her until she gained control of the rampant emotions running roughshod over her composure. He marveled at her unselfish compassion for Ana, a woman she barely knew. Diana hadn't, once, thought of herself or the personal implications of the last few minutes. All her concern was for Ana. How could he not love a woman like that?

"I want to help her," Diana said, taking a deep breath. "What can I do? Do you think she would be willing to talk to me about it?"

Joey shook his head, still holding her close. "Just be her friend, Diana. When she learns to trust you, she may open up. Trust, for someone like Ana, takes time."

Diana leaned back so she could look into his eyes. "And for someone like me, apparently. I'm so sorry I didn't trust you, Joey. Last Friday night… it was like my worst fears were coming true. Can you ever forgive me?"

"How can I not?" Joey asked, completely serious, for once. "It looked bad…even I can see that. You know my history. You've been warned about me for years. How could I expect you to think anything else?"

Diana studied him, a small smile teasing the corners of her mouth. "Maybe because I know you." She placed her hand over his heart. "Here." She patted his chest. "I should have known better."

"Do you, Diana?" Joey whispered. "Do you know better now?"

She kissed him, then. She just couldn't help it. Had there ever been a better man than Joey Finch? Not for her.

He wasn't prepared for his body's reaction to the gentle brush of her lips. The softest, sweetest kiss in human history—he was certain of that— was over far too soon.

As the initial shock Diana felt at discovering Ana's situation dimmed, the truth hit home. Joey *hadn't* been lying. He *hadn't* found a replacement for her. Their relationship *hadn't* changed at all. Diana nearly melted into a puddle of relief. But only for a moment. Her warm, happy thoughts disintegrated when it dawned on her what she had said last Saturday night after Joey's fictitious betrayal. Not to mention what she had done.

Her eyes widened in horror. "Joey, I…I lied," she said. "At karaoke. I said I—"

"—wasn't a relationship kind of girl," Joey finished for her, trying to hide his grin.

"But I said that I—"

"—was a one and done," he intoned, solemnly. "Just. Like. Me." His eyes were twinkling now.

Her head dropped forward, onto his shoulder. "And I…oh, Joey…I sang…" She couldn't bring herself to say it.

" 'You're So Vain,' " he proclaimed, with satisfaction. "And you dedicated it to me." He waited a beat before adding. "I could tell."

Diana realized, then, that he was laughing. She could feel the deep rumble in his chest. She couldn't bring herself to look at him, though.

Couldn't bear to see even the smallest hint of disappointment in his eyes. But, maybe, she thought, hopefully, since he was laughing...

"Diana," he said.

She cautiously raised her head, surprised to find his face alight with a wicked grin. He looked absolutely delighted. What was wrong with him? He should be furious.

"I deserved it," Joey said. "All of it. Consider your musical tribute a payback on behalf of all the girls I ever told I wasn't a 'relationship kind of guy.' And your performance? Well, according to Zack, you killed it."

"Good old Zack," Diana said, softly.

"Yeah," Joey agreed. "Good old Zack. He told me about your *date* with good old Roger."

Diana's face filled with remorse. "I regretted it the minute I said, yes, but..." She shrugged. "What could I do except see it through?" She tilted her head to one side. "My *date* didn't bother you, did it?" she asked, innocently, batting her long eyelashes.

Joey growled. "Hell, yes, it bothered me." He tugged her closer. "Seeing you with anybody but me is totally unacceptable, Miss Merritt."

Her body tingled at his possessive tone. "I'll try to remember that, Mr. Finch," she said, saucily.

He held her tightly, suddenly overcome with emotion. Him. Joey Finch. Overcome with emotion. How, he asked himself, had he managed to live without Diana Merritt for thirty years? Holding her securely, he couldn't imagine what life would be like without her for thirty *seconds*.

"I was so afraid," he whispered in her ear. "I thought I might lose you...."

"I was afraid, too," she said, her hold fierce and unyielding. "Afraid that you were never really mine to lose."

They shared a moment of indelible sweetness, standing there in the dark on the deserted patio, their breathing in perfect accord. Joey sent a quick word of thanks heavenward for the woman in his arms. She made him a better man, the man he wanted to be.

Joey's phone vibrated, interrupting their epiphany. He sighed in irritation. "If that's Darcie, I swear…"

Diana laughed softly. "Go ahead and answer it. I'll say hi and that should satisfy her. For the moment."

Joey's arms slid from her reluctantly. He reached into his pocket to pull out his phone. "Hello," he said. "Ana…?" As he listened, a guilty grin spread across his face. "Yes," he said. "Everything's just fine." He winked at Diana. "What? Oh, okay, Ana. We'll be right there." He replaced his phone, holding out his hand to his—dare he say it?—girlfriend. "Ana says our spaghetti is ready."

Diana bit her lip. "Uh-oh. We've been summoned." She put her hand in his, a small thrill running through her veins at the thought that she could hold his hand now. Any time she wanted. As they approached the dining room, she stopped abruptly, pulling Joey up short.

"What about Roger?" she asked. "I feel sort of funny facing him, now." She glanced down at their clasped hands. "It's sort of awkward."

Joey squeezed her hand encouragingly. "Don't worry about Raj. He seemed to be enjoying himself."

Diana realized Joey spoke the truth. "You're right. He didn't seem surprised to see you when you showed up. As a matter of fact, he couldn't wait to invite you and Ana to join us. Is there something wrong with him?"

Joey burst out laughing. "No, there's nothing wrong with him. He's actually a good friend. But he does like to stir things up, especially where I'm concerned. We knocked heads occasionally when he dated Gracie. You know how older brothers are."

"Do I ever," Diana agreed. "Can't wait 'til Roman hears about us." Her smile was wide and cheeky.

He leaned in to plant a quick kiss on her cheek. "You, my dear, are worth any amount of trouble. Big brother or otherwise."

Hand in hand, they walked into the busy, main dining room.

As it turned out, Diana had nothing to worry about. Roger welcomed them back to the table with good humor. There was none of the awkwardness she anticipated. She was also quite amused to find three additional napkins waiting for her. Clearly, Stan wasn't taking any chances.

Joey got straight to the point. "Diana and I are a couple."

"That's so wonderful!" Ana squealed, jumping out of her chair to hug Diana. She almost took the tablecloth with her when her finger contraption got stuck in the fold. Roger made a grab for the tablecloth, barely saving their dinner. Half of the dining room patrons applauded. Roger—who possessed great stage presence—gave their audience a deftly executed bow followed by a smart salute.

Ana sat down after hugging Joey. She beamed at the new couple as they settled into their own chairs.

Roger studied Joey and Diana. "So, let me get this straight. We"— Roger indicated himself and Joey—"are swapping dates." He grinned. "How intriguing. I had no idea you were *into* date swapping, Joey."

Diana frowned. "I don't think *date swapping* is a thing," she said, politely while her eyes danced with laughter.

"I'm *not* his date," Ana stated, pointing to Joey.

Roger looked at Joey in mock outrage. "So, *you* get my date, but I don't get yours."

"I'm *not* Joey's date," Ana said, adamantly.

Roger ignored her. "That doesn't seem quite fair." He seemed to consider the implications for a second. "Sorry, Joey, I changed my mind. I'm out."

"I'm afraid *our* minds are made up," Diana said, gently. "Thank you for being so nice about it, though." Her words were accompanied by a hopeful smile.

Joey twirled his fork in the delicious-looking saucy noodles. He pointed his loaded utensil at the man across from him. "Cheer up, Raj. You don't get the girl this time, but you do get spaghetti."

"Well, when you put it that way..." Roger gazed happily at his plate. "I guess that's fair."

Diana shared a wry glance with Ana. "And now I've been traded for a plate of spaghetti."

Ana patted her hand. "It happens," she said, sympathetically. "At least it's going to be the best spaghetti you've ever tasted...."

"Just remember one thing, Carrington," Joey said, pointing his dripping fork toward Roger again. "If you keep flirting with my girl, I'll tell our good buddy, Stan, to give the check to *you*."

To emphasize his words, Joey popped his huge bite of spaghetti into his mouth. His table companions watched as one, lone strand of spaghetti separated itself from the rest. The strand landed squarely in Joey's napkin, but it left behind a trail of tomato sauce on the left side of his shirt.

Diana gestured to the mess. "See? Worst date food ever."

"I thought you said it was the best," Ana remarked.

"I lied," Diana said, serenely, struggling with her own pile of noodles.

Ana snorted with appreciation.

"You three are pathetic," Roger observed. He, then, proceeded to demonstrate the fine art of eating spaghetti correctly.

A sort of contest ensued, filled with good-natured insults and laughter all around.

"I need another napkin," Ana announced, when they were mopping up after their feast. She was barely able to speak for laughing. She raised her hand to wave at their expressionless server. He nodded, disappearing into the kitchen. He returned with a large roll of paper towels, which he placed squarely in front of Ana.

"This table has exhausted its designated supply of linens," he said, without cracking a smile. "Does anyone need a to-go box?"

"Just for Ana and me," Diana volunteered. "Roger ate everything in sight, and Joey decided to wear the rest of his." She smiled, prettily, at Stan, who did *not* smile back.

Joey motioned their server closer. "You do know that you're going to get one hell of a good tip, don't you, Stan?"

"I expect nothing less," Stan said, calmly. "Would you like to see the dessert menu?"

"Of course we would," Ana said enthusiastically. She held up her hand as if she was telling Stan a secret. "The guys are paying, so we *have* to get dessert. Right, Diana?" she asked, hopefully.

Diana nodded enthusiastically.

Stan cleared the table without comment, disappearing through the kitchen's swinging doors.

"Poor Stan," Roger lamented. "He doesn't have much of a sense of humor, does he?"

"Oh, I don't know," Joey said. "I thought the paper towels showed great potential."

Diana shook her head, echoing Roger's words. "Poor Stan. It's probably been the longest night of his life. He seemed awfully eager to give us the to-go boxes. I bet he never wants to see us again."

"I, for one, can't wait to see him again," Ana put in. "I think he likes me."

Roger looked at her as though he thought she was crazy. "How can you tell?"

She smiled confidently. "I can tell."

Roger snorted his disbelief as Diana and Joey exchanged a smile.

Ana clapped her hands with excitement when Stan returned with the menus. "I don't even have to look," she said. "I'm ordering tiramisu. Celine's tiramisu is—"

"The best you've ever tasted?" Roger asked with a smirk.

Ana wrinkled her nose at him. "As a matter of fact, it is."

"Four tiramisus," Roger said, confidently.

"*Two* tiramisus," Ana amended, quickly. "With *four* spoons."

Stan nodded, disappearing once more.

Roger crossed his arms on the table, watching Ana inquiringly.

Ana shrugged. "They're enormous. You just wait and see."

CHAPTER THIRTY-EIGHT

"*T*hat tiramisu was bigger than my head," Joey said as he and Diana—hand in hand—strolled to his truck a short while later. He carried the bag of to-go boxes in his other hand.

"I can't believe Stan got Ana's number," Diana giggled. "He *was* a pretty good-looking guy."

"Hmm," Joey said. "I'm not sure I like you checking out other guys."

Diana shrugged. "Oh, really?" She glanced at Joey through her lashes. She suddenly felt daring, and just a little bit naughty. "Would you rather I check *you* out?"

"Oh, please do," Joey said, confidently, dropping her hand. "I want to see how I stack up against *Stan*."

Diana stopped walking to give Joey a thorough perusal. Letting her eyes sweep upward, she noted khaki pants covering muscular calves and thighs. She had seen those legs in shorts, so she knew. His trim waist. His broad-shouldered frame—to-die-for arms and shoulders—topped with a handsome face. Dark, mysterious eyes. And thick, soft, hair. She had run her hands through that hair, so she knew that, too. *Devastating.* By the time she finished, her heart was beating madly.

Joey found himself in unfamiliar territory. His request had been made in jest. He was only trying to mess with Diana a little bit, maybe shake *her* composure. Just for fun. But her frank appraisal had the opposite effect. Now, *he* was the one getting overheated.

But Joey wasn't the only one in over his head. Despite the chilly air, Diana felt a fiery blush blossom on her cheeks. To hide her reaction from her too-perceptive escort, she patted him on the chest with her hand.

"You'll do," she said, calmly, turning in the direction of the truck.

"What does that mean?" he asked, grabbing her hand. He pulled, turning her around to face him.

She pointedly surveyed the tomato sauce stain on the front of his shirt. Her lips tipped up in a sassy grin. "Well, you *are* wearing your dinner."

"At least I still have my eyebrows." He waggled his still intact eyebrows comically. "That has to count for something."

Diana laughed. "That's only because there's no such thing as flaming tiramisu." She attempted to turn again.

"Oh, no, you don't." He tugged her toward his chest. Suddenly they were close. So close, he noted with pleasure, that he could see the flush coloring her cheeks as well as her rapid breathing. She was as affected as he.

"The shirt is easy to fix." Joey grinned wickedly. "All I have to do is take it off."

Diana gasped softly at the image of a shirtless Joey Finch in the parking lot of Celine's. For some reason, her eyes focused on his lips. She simply couldn't help it. His lips were masculine, but soft to the touch. And very skilled. Those lips had kissed hers, so she knew. Yes, she thought, his lips were *quite* skilled. Suddenly, she wanted to feel those lips on hers.

"Do you know how much I want to kiss you right now?" he rasped.

What is he? Diana marveled. *A mind-reader?* Her eyes met his. "Why don't you?" she whispered, impressed with her own daring.

Joey would like nothing better. After a week of dreaming of Diana's delicious lips, his appetite had not been assuaged by their single kiss on the deserted patio. He was desperate to sample those peach-colored delicacies again. But as his lips approached their target, a high-pitched, childish giggle pierced the air.

He forced himself to survey the parking lot. Children. Parents. Couples. Friends. Senior Citizens. *Well, hell,* he fumed. A few seconds ago, Joey would have sworn the parking lot was empty. His gaze met Diana's.

"Too many eyes for what I have in mind," he said, succinctly.

Oh, my, Diana thought, dreamily. *That sounds promising.*

"Look, Mommy," a childish voice observed. "Those people are dancing."

Joey's eyes lit up with mischief. Quick as a flash, he put his left hand—the one holding the to-go bag—around Diana's waist. He raised their clasped hands to shoulder level, assuming a dancing stance. She scarcely had a second to catch her breath before he swept her into an abbreviated version of a waltz.

The skirt of her purple dress billowed around her as they whirled in the direction of his truck. Her tiny purse, with its long, silver chain, flew out from her shoulder in a giant arc. She could feel the rhythmic *tap-tap-tap* of the to-go bag against her hip. When they arrived at the passenger side of the truck, Joey ended their impromptu performance by lowering Diana into an elegant dip. Their audience burst into spontaneous applause. When she was once again standing upright beside him, he caught her eye and nodded. Understanding his unspoken message, she executed a flawless curtsey to go along with Joey's flawless bow.

He couldn't take his eyes off Diana. Her cheeks were a delicate shade of peach. Her lovely lips were slightly parted. Her hair was in spectacular disarray. If he didn't get to kiss her soon, he was going to expire.

Joey flung open her door then practically tossed her—and the to-go bag—into the passenger seat. In a flash, he was seated behind the wheel, shoving the key into the ignition. Glimpsing his own determined gaze in the rearview mirror, he took a deep breath, making a concentrated effort to slow down. He still had to drive to the cottage, he reminded himself. And he didn't need to get another speeding ticket from his good friend Theo Granger. Besides, he certainly couldn't make love to Diana in the front seat of his truck, could he? Hmm…he pondered the logistics of that appealing idea a few seconds before jerking himself back to reality. Of course, he couldn't.

Get a grip, Finch, he scolded himself. The erotic images that filled his head had him gripping the steering wheel with white knuckles. Try as he might, he couldn't unthink them. Instead, he attempted to concentrate on backing out of the parking space. The reflection of his headlights on the car parked in front of him. The Luke Combs song playing on the radio. Anything but the girl sitting beside him. What would *she* say if she knew what he was thinking?

Diana could barely breathe from giggling. She felt giddy, almost drunk with happiness. She gazed at her dancing partner as he pulled into traffic. He was the Fred Astaire to her Ginger Rogers. Her perfect match.

"You," she managed to gasp. "You. Are. So. Much. Fun." She was clearly delighted with their performance.

"Seriously?" he asked. "You think I'm fun?" Mercifully, his attention focused on something besides sex in a truck.

Joey was the first to admit he had the tendency for impromptu whimsy. There was no other way to describe it. Falling into the role of a bartender or a ballroom dancer as the situation warranted was as natural to him as breathing. This was who he was. And Diana got it. She got him. She didn't think he was immature or ridiculous. She wasn't embarrassed by his shenanigans—as his family liked to call them. Diana thought he was *fun.* Joey knew he was grinning like an idiot.

Diana fanned her flushed face. "I always have fun with you," she said.

"Even when we're dodging bricks?" he asked.

"Of course," she replied, teasingly. "But you aren't very good at dodging."

"True," he agreed. She had a point. He had the scar to prove it. "Even when we're running from man-eating strangers?"

"Yes," she said. "Or security guards."

Joey chuckled at the memory. "That man was one step ahead of us," he admitted, ruefully.

Diana laughed out loud. She couldn't help it. Being with Joey was like that. "See, even talking about the fun I have with you is fun."

They rode in contented silence for a few minutes. How had he survived the last week without Diana? Joey asked himself. It felt like a year since he had felt this good.

"Say," Joey said, before his mind could return to the erotic delights that were possible in an F-150. "What's going on with Ezekiel and Genevieve? I haven't had an update in a while."

Diana cleared her throat. She crossed her legs, shifting uncomfortably in her seat. The next moment she uncrossed her legs and sighed.

Joey almost laughed at her discomfort. "Better tell me the bad news, Diana." He had a pretty good idea of what she was going to say.

"Ezekiel and Genevieve are currently…estranged," she announced.

"What a surprise," Joey said, wryly. "I thought they were perfect for each other. What happened?"

Diana narrowed her eyes. "He kissed her."

"He kissed her. What's the matter with that?" Joey asked. He was taking this very seriously. On Ezekiel's behalf, he told himself. "Didn't she like his kisses?"

"Of course she liked them," Diana replied, as if Joey was the most clueless person who ever lived. "They were the best kisses ever. They were magical. But…"

Gratified as Joey was by the fact that Ezekiel's kisses were the best ever, he was starting to feel a bit uneasy. "But…" he asked, carefully.

Diana paused, watching his face. "Do you know what a cravat pin is?" she asked.

"I suppose it's a pin for a cravat, whatever a cravat is," Joey answered.

"It's a piece of fabric worn like a necktie, sort of like a scarf. Men wore them in the eighteen hundreds. A cravat pin was like a tie pin. It held the

452

folds of the cravat together. Sometimes the pins were very fancy, decorated with jewels and precious metals."

"I suppose Ezekiel has a fancy one...."

"He does. It's pure gold with a real sapphire in it. The Sapphire of Ravenwood."

"Ravenwood...hmph!" Joey grimaced at the mention of the good doctor.

Diana ignored him. "So, after Ezekiel kisses Genevieve and leaves her room..."

"He was in *her* room?" Joey was impressed. Ezekiel was doing better than his twenty-first century counterpart. "Nice job, Ezekiel."

Diana let out an impatient breath. "Oh, good grief. She's his governess. He was meeting with his governess about his wards."

Joey was skeptical. "Sure, he was," he said, doubtfully. He obviously understood Ezekiel better than Diana did.

She continued her defense of the situation. "It was completely innocent."

"Completely innocent. Until he kissed her."

"Until he kissed her." Diana's face felt hot, but she continued her explanation. "But, even then, he leaves her room before things get out of hand."

"I knew he was a good guy." Joey was pleased with his alter ego. "Those must have been some kisses."

"Oh, they were. They were." She unconsciously fanned her flushed face again, remembering their own kisses.

In that moment, the easy atmosphere between them disappeared, replaced by a strong awareness that they weren't merely discussing Ezekiel and Genevieve anymore.

"So, what happens after he leaves?" Joey asked, his voice a little strained.

"After he's gone, she finds his cravat pin lying on the floor. She doesn't want him to worry about the Sapphire of Ravenwood, so she decides to take the pin downstairs and put it on his desk."

"Uh-oh," Joey said. He had a bad feeling about what was coming.

"Uh-oh is right." Diana sighed. "When Genevieve gets to the end of the hall, she looks over the balcony railing to see Ezekiel wrapped in the passionate embrace of a beautiful, blond woman."

"What?" Joey hissed, angry on Genevieve's behalf. "Who is *she*?"

"His ex-fiancée," Diana announced, solemnly. "The widow of his dead brother."

"No!" Joey gasped, horrified.

"Yes," Diana said, nodding her head.

"I bet the blonde threw herself at Ezekiel and it only *looks* like a passionate embrace, right? I bet Ezekiel doesn't *know* Genevieve saw them and he has no idea why Genevieve's so upset. I bet he comes up with a plan to make Genevieve realize that *she's* the only one for him."

Diana hesitated. "I'm not sure what's going to happen yet. That's as far as I got before—"

"—tonight." Joey's smile was smug. "Because at dinner, you found out that *your* rascal really is reformed. That's when you decided that you were madly in love with him. With me. That you are madly in love with me." *Well done, Finch. Not awkward at all,* he praised himself, sarcastically. Why did he even bother to open his mouth?

His words triggered a powerful memory in Diana's brain.

I'm falling in love with you, Diana….

Had it only been a week since Joey whispered those words in her ear? She had tried not to think of them since the night everything fell apart. Now, she couldn't seem to think of anything else.

Joey turned onto the road that led to Heart's Ease and stopped at the gate. He punched in his code. He hoped Diana didn't notice that his hands were shaking slightly. His whole body—arms, legs, even his neck and throat—felt like a tightly coiled spring. The only thing that could unwind the emotional tension inside him was kissing Diana. Long, hot, slow kisses. Yes, that was definitely the answer. As the gate swung open, he hit the accelerator a little faster than he intended. He glanced at Diana. She didn't seem to notice.

I'm falling in love with you, Diana....

Joey said that *after* he kissed her, Diana reminded herself. Was he going to kiss her again? Of course he was. He had almost kissed her in the parking lot of Celine's. Another kiss was inevitable. But before that could happen, Joey needed to hurry up and park the dratted truck. And Diana didn't care where he parked. She didn't even care if he parked in the middle of the bridge.

I'm falling in love with you, Diana....

If Joey didn't kiss her soon, Diana decided, she was going to die. Plain and simple. *Drat.* She didn't particularly want to die in the passenger seat of an F-150. Not when the night was so full of lovely possibilities. And kisses. Lovely kisses. Her eyes flew open as the import of Joey's teasing words suddenly made sense.

He had said *she* was madly in love with *him*, she remembered. Diana already knew she was in love with Joey, but...*madly*? The very phrase implied that she had no control over her feelings. No ability to resist. No choice in the matter. None at all. She mulled that over for a few seconds, considering the implications of the phrase. Was she madly in love with him? she asked herself. Yes, she decided. She rather thought she was. Or maybe she was just mad. Mentally off-balance. Crazy. In fact, she could barely keep her feet from pressing an imaginary accelerator on her side of the car. If she wasn't already going mad, she soon would be if she had to wait much longer for a kiss from Mr. Joseph Ezekiel Finch.

The truck stopped in the driveway of the gatekeeper's cottage.

"Thank God," Joey said, leaping from the vehicle. At that moment, kissing Diana was more important than taking his next breath.

Before Diana could draw *her* next breath, he opened her door. He was breathing hard, as if he had run a long way. Her befuddled brain noted that it wasn't a long way from the driver's side of the truck to the passenger side. He must be breathing that way because…

He placed his hands on her waist. The heat in his eyes made her gasp aloud.

"Oh, my."

Before she could spout any more profundities, he hauled her out of the truck, letting her slide slowly along the front of his body as he brought her down. The contact was delicious, igniting the desire for more. His lips were on hers before her feet touched the ground. Greedy, this time, and impatient. His tongue easily breached the useless barrier of her lips to delve into her warm mouth. She slipped her arms around his neck, her hands plunging into the silky strands at the base of his hairline. Her starving senses rejoiced, loving the feel of his mouth on hers. She was plunged into a passionate whirlwind of burning lips, tangled tongues, and the heat of his possession. She couldn't breathe—and she didn't care. She could only respond to the feelings raging through her, clinging to Joey as the only solid thing in the sensual cloud that had enveloped her.

Joey exulted in Diana's impassioned response. In the way she clung to him. In the frenzied quality of her kisses. He wanted to devour her. To possess her. To stake his claim so completely that it could never be revoked. He wanted her. Now.

A battle raged between his primitive self—the ancestor of every caveman who had dragged his woman back to his cave—and his enlightened self—the man who knew Diana's decision-making abilities were currently incapacitated. Swallowed up in the flames of desire, she would do anything he wanted. He could tell. She was pliant in his arms, completely tuned to his every move. She would be that way in bed, too. That realization nearly sent him over the edge.

He fought the urge to make love to her against the passenger seat of his truck, right there in the front yard of the gatekeeper's cottage. He barely restrained himself from picking her up, carrying her into the house and finding a convenient bed. Or couch. Or kitchen chair. Or countertop. She made a small sound, somewhere between abject surrender and utter contentment, as if kissing Joey Finch beside his truck was the epitome of all her dreams. That little sound made him pause.

This was Diana. His Diana. And he could do better. He would do better. He tore his mouth from hers, cuddling her against his chest, her head tucked against his shoulder. He listened to her ragged breathing. It rivaled his own. He would allow the chilly air to cool their passion, until he, for one, obtained some level of control.

She didn't know how long she stood there, listening to the slowing of Joey Finch's frantic heartbeat. She could feel the tension in him, the deliberate effort he made to cool the unbridled flames that burned between them. He wasn't trying to snuff them out, she realized, but to contain them. To bank them into a simmering warmth that, when prompted, would once again rage. And she was grateful. Grateful that one of them had retained a little self-control. She reluctantly admitted to herself that a few minutes earlier, she would happily have tossed up her skirts for him. Right there in the driveway.

"Drat." Her own self-control was appallingly absent.

"Hmm?" he asked softly.

She glanced up, regarding him curiously.

"You said 'drat,'" he explained, patiently. Her confusion was adorable.

Her eyes widened. "I said it out loud?" she squeaked.

He nodded, fighting the desire to kiss the perplexed expression on her face.

"Did I say anything else?" she asked, anxiously.

"No," he said. "Just drat."

"That's good." She was visibly relieved.

"Why is that?"

"Because I don't want you to know what I'm thinking."

Her cheeks reddened in front his eyes, making him intensely curious about the clearly naughty thoughts running through her head. Her eyes were wide and bright. Her lips were moist and a little puffy from his kisses. They reminded him of twin peaches...ripe for the plucking. The nearly overpowering urge to pull her back into his arms caught him off guard. He forced his hands into his pockets instead.

"Don't forget the to-go boxes," he said, trying for nonchalance.

"Oh," she breathed. "The tiramisu. We *don't* want to forget *that.*" She turned back for the bag and her forgotten purse.

"No, we don't," Joey said, attempting to distract himself from thoughts of sharing the delectable dessert with the delectable Diana tomorrow. At breakfast. In bed. His attempt at distraction was unsuccessful. As was his effort to keep his eyes from enjoying the way the purple cloth of Diana's dress draped over her lovely backside as she reached for the tiny purse. He jumped on that item like a lifeline as she turned back around.

"Where is your ginormous, enormous, magical man-eating tote bag? I can't believe you went somewhere without it." To his delight, her eyes narrowed at his teasing.

"*Duh*, Mr. High Fashion," she said, with a toss of her lovely red head. "The big one doesn't coordinate with my dress. And for your information, I do have other bags." She dangled the silver chain of the small multicolored purse in front of his face, for emphasis.

He made a grab for her purse, but she swung it out of the way just in time. "Oh, no," she said, with satisfaction. "I can't let you learn all of my secrets at once." She handed him the to-go bag and hooked her arm through his.

"That purse isn't big enough to hold *half* a secret," he quipped, reaching around to shut the door of his truck. By unspoken agreement, they strolled toward the front steps of the gatekeeper's cottage, both conscious of the decision waiting at the kitchen door. An uneasy silence descended as they climbed the front steps. Diana struggled to come up with a way to invite Joey in that made her sound savvy and sophisticated. She had never asked a man to spend the night before.

What do you want for breakfast?

Want to try out my new mattress?

I sleep on the right side of the bed, how about you?

She dismissed them all. She could *never* ask those questions with a straight face anyway. She finally settled on *Would you like to come in?* It was safe. It kept all options open. And it didn't make her look either desperate or pathetic.

While Diana was creating and discarding phrases, Joey was struggling with his basest desires. He knew he could kiss his way past any roadblocks Diana could muster. He had already proven that. He couldn't help but interpret that to mean she was all in. But there was no way he would risk her waking up the next morning with so much as a hint of regret. He wanted no more misunderstandings between them. He *never* wanted to spend another week like the last one.

The moment was upon them before either was ready. Diana spoke first.

"Joey, would you like..."

But she never got to finish her carefully planned question.

"Diana," Joey said, interrupting her, "I can't keep my hands off you." He surprised both of them with his lack of delicacy or tact. He would have been slightly ashamed of himself if he hadn't seen her lips tip up into a shy, little smile. He couldn't help but smile back. He waited for her to speak, to say something...anything.

Her shy smile turned sultry, but she remained silent.

His own tactic.

Why was she always so successful using his own tactic against him? It was a rhetorical question, only. At present, Joey couldn't deal with the suspense long enough to answer. Instead, he found himself, once again, compelled to fill the silence. And the minute he opened his mouth, he couldn't stop talking.

"I don't mean that I'm *incapable* of keeping my hands off you, Diana," he explained. "Of course I *can* keep them off you. I just mean that I don't want to. Keep my hands off you, I mean. I just want to..." *Well, hell.* He was babbling. He never, ever babbled. Where was the calm, level-headed attorney that usually inhabited his body? Joey had no idea, but it was glaringly apparent that controlled and sophisticated fellow had completely disappeared.

"Joey," Diana said, watching him pace back and forth across the porch.

He raked his hand through his hair in frustration at his own inability to explain himself. "But I wouldn't *keep* them—my hands—on you if you didn't want me to. I mean, if you told me to stop kissing you or touching you or whatever we were doing, I would stop. Immediately. You know me well enough to know that I'm telling the truth. Even if I had to take a cold shower—or two—later. Or maybe two cold showers every two hours or..." He growled in frustration. "I sound like an idiot. I can't believe I'm..."

"Joey." She was touched by his sincerity and the toll it was taking on his usual aplomb. She found his lack of finesse terribly sweet. It went straight to her heart. The best part was he had absolutely nothing to worry about. He just didn't know it yet.

She watched him take a few more steps, mumbling to himself, before taking matters into her own hands. He wasn't paying attention anyway. After disarming the security system, she opened the door. Joey walked right by her to continue his one-sided conversation in the kitchen. She was rather pleased with that as it negated the need for her to invite him in. She managed to take the to-go bag out of his unresisting hand as he passed her. She placed it in the refrigerator. Now that she had taken care of the tiramisu, all she had to do was tell him to stop worrying. She was going to ask him to stay. All night. With her. A tiny thrill shot straight through her at the thought. She was so intent on her plans that his question startled her.

"You believe that, don't you, Diana?"

"Believe, um...what?" she asked. His eyes bored into hers. He was definitely paying attention now. Too bad she hadn't been.

Joey was standing right in front of her. He raised his hand to tuck a stray curl behind her ear. The intensity of his words sent a shiver down her spine. "You believe that I'll stop, don't you?" His hand settled gently on the nape of her neck.

The warmth of his hand was making it difficult to focus. "Stop?" It was all she could manage.

He leaned forward. His lips brushed hers in the softest, sexiest kiss imaginable. "You know I'll stop if you want me to, don't you?" He whispered the words into her very sensitive ear.

The delicious shivers started up again. She couldn't help it. Nevertheless, she met his gaze with absolute conviction. "I know," she whispered, echoing Joey's words a week earlier. "But I have no intention of asking you to stop."

CHAPTER THIRTY-NINE

"*I have no intention of asking you to stop.*"

Were sweeter words ever spoken? Joey didn't think so. The banked heat simmering in his eyes flared to life. His other hand came up to cradle Diana's face as he took her mouth in a scorching kiss. It was all-encompassing, all-consuming. She closed the distance between them, plastering herself against him as her hands frantically searched for a place to alight. Her mind was completely blank save for one word.

More.

His hands moved from her face to skim lightly over her shoulders and down her arms. He found her hands, linking his fingers with hers. He broke their kiss to look into gray eyes, the color of a stormy sky. Her lips were wet and lush. Her hair was tumbling from its pins. She drew in great gulps of air, as if she had just finished a marathon. She was irresistible.

"Do you want me to stop?" he rasped, determined to stay in control.

"More." It was a cross between a whisper and a moan, but he understood his siren's call.

Grinning wickedly, he released her hands. She squeaked when he grasped her waist and lifted her to sit on the kitchen counter. Her hands gripped the counter's edge. He stepped between her thighs, wishing her dress would simply disappear. Of course, that would speed things up, and he had no desire to hurry through the first of an endless number of steamy encounters.

His arms snaked around her waist as his lips drew a course from her delicate ear lobe—blocked by a dangling silver earring—to the soft place where her neck met her shoulder. He didn't make it much farther before he was intercepted by two long necklaces and the material of her dress. He took a step back, planting one hand on the counter beside her hip. He raised the other one to her chin.

"You, my love, are wearing *entirely* too many clothes," he rasped, his voice filled with ironic humor.

Diana regarded him with wide eyes as her brain homed in on two words: *my love.*

He released her chin, allowing one finger to trace a path to the lowest point of the V-neckline that her dress left exposed. He tucked his finger underneath the neckline, pulling it out a little before letting it go. His knuckles brushed softly up the center of her chest then returned to her chin. His thumb brushed her bottom lip. Back and forth...back and forth. Like a pendulum. Joey's touch was hypnotizing, making it difficult for Diana to focus on anything else. And it was making her stupid.

Diana could tell he had a plan. The deliberately slow, almost teasing pace of his lovemaking was following a preordained path she could not see. Suddenly, she wanted to throw *him* off-balance. She wanted to make *him* lose control. There was nothing to fear if he did. She trusted him, even as he tried to hide the naked hunger she glimpsed in his dark eyes. She felt a surge of womanly confidence that overpowered her first-time-with-Joey-Finch jitters.

Her lips turned up into a teasing smile. She, too, relinquished her death grip on the counter, surprised to feel the sting as her blood returned to her fingers. She raised her hands, very deliberately, to one of her necklaces. She slowly drew the long chain over her head. Her eyes never left the eyes of the man in front of her as she placed the necklace on the counter. She could almost feel Joey's heightened intensity. Yes, she thought, rather proudly, she had certainly ratcheted things up a notch.

Joey was caught firmly in her spell. With one simple act, she had turned the tables on him. She was most definitely in control, now. Amazing how a little thing like removing a necklace became an invitation in the presence of his siren. He could barely keep from reaching for her. His hands fisted at his side as he waited to see what she was going to do next.

She removed the second necklace, followed by her earrings. One. At. A. Time. She pulled out the remaining pins holding back her hair. She ran her fingers through the crown of her head, fluffing out the portion that had been pinned. She shook out the auburn locks until her curls swirled around her in all their unruly glory.

Joey felt a tightening in every muscle in his body as he imagined Diana's hair as being the only ornament gracing her delicious figure. He was growing harder by the second. He had to get her out of her dress, but how? There weren't any buttons. No hooks. No snaps. Not a single zipper was in sight. The damn purple dress was ruining his life…How did it come off? One glance at Diana confirmed she had no intention of making this easy for him. Her eyes were filled with determination. Determination? What was she trying to do? Kill him?

"Did Roman pick out this dress for you?" he asked desperately. "Did he buy you those necklaces to drive me crazy?"

She opened her lovely, peach-colored lips: "For your information, Mr. Finch," she said, as she hopped off the counter, "my brother has nothing to do with my wardrobe choices." She took him by the hand and led him, unresisting, into the living area. She stopped in front of the fireplace. Turning her back to him, she gathered her shimmering hair to one side. That's when he saw it.

The. Zipper.

Joey's eyes glued themselves to the back of Diana's dress. The nearly invisible zipper had been there all along, hiding under all that gorgeous hair. Who would have thought Joey would be so very glad to see a zipper?

But, he realized, it wasn't just any zipper. Oh, no. It was a pathway to the pot of gold at the end of the rainbow. The place where his dreams and heated imaginings finally met the glorious reality that was Diana Merritt.

Joey tried to raise his hand, but now that the moment was upon him, he couldn't seem to move. What was wrong with him? Now was not the time for prepubescent nerves to kick in. He'd been fantasizing about seeing Diana naked since listening to her take a shower at the Acorn Knob Inn. Or was it since dancing with her at Grace and Blane's wedding? Or maybe since he first laid eyes on her nine years ago? *Well, hell.*

What if he'd been in love with Diana Merritt since he walked out of Connor's office and saw her sitting at the admin's desk? The truth hit him with the shock of an explosion. Joey had been in love with Diana since the moment he first laid eyes on her. And it had taken him only nine years to figure it out. He wanted to hit himself in the head with a brick. A much softer, gentler brick than the prophetic one that had fallen on him from the scaffold at McDonald's…but a brick, nonetheless. He was an idiot.

Diana glanced over her shoulder and cleared her throat. "Problem?"

"What?" Joey asked, momentarily shaken by the realization of the latent state of his heart.

"It's a zipper, Joey," she said, impatiently.

"What do you mean?" he asked, struggling to focus.

Seriously? Diana was clearly going about this all wrong. Joey's reaction irritated her as much as her own obvious incompetence vis-à-vis the art of seduction.

"If you pull the little tab, my dress will fall off," she said, sarcastically.

Joey couldn't help but smile at her sass. His temporary paralysis faded, replaced with the heady knowledge of what was to come.

"Oh, will it now?" he asked, an unmistakable note of teasing in his voice. He was finished with slow. He wanted Diana—and he wanted her *now*. He grasped the zipper and pulled. Just as promised, the dress slithered gracefully along the warm, beguiling length of her body, landing in a silent heap at her feet.

Nobody moved.

Nobody said a word.

Joey could only stare, transfixed by the elegant shape of Diana's back, the curve of her spine, her slim waist, her tempting hips, her long legs. He admired the way her tapered ankles disappeared into the billowing dress at her feet....

Diana was horrified by the realization that she wasn't wearing the lacy turquoise bra and panty set she had worn on their first date. In her mind's eye, Joey Finch and sexy lingerie went hand in hand. She was wearing a light blue T-shirt bra and a pair of dark green cheeky boy shorts covered with yellow daisies. She had worn the mismatched pair for her date with Roger Carrington because, well...it was a date with Roger Carrington. She had known beyond a shadow of a doubt that *Roger* wasn't going to see what was under her dress. But now...

"Turn around, Diana." Joey's voice was husky.

Diana shook her head.

Joey closed his eyes. His heart sank to the floor. She wasn't ready. She was going to tell him to stop. And he was going to explode and burn to cinders that would subsequently blow away, never to be seen again. Yep. A fate he had earned. Regardless, he resolved that, for her, he would stop right here. Right now. Even if...no, even *when* it killed him.

"Diana, do you want me to stop?" He somehow managed *not* to sound like he was preparing to die.

She surprised him by spinning around and throwing herself into his arms. She pressed herself tightly against him. Her lips sought his. His sensual self rejoiced. She obviously didn't want him to stop. Yes, he decided, Diana clearly wanted to continue. And Joey was more than happy to oblige.

A myriad of thoughts flitted through Diana's head as if they were the wings of a butterfly. If Joey was kissing her, then his eyes were closed. If his eyes were closed, then he couldn't see that she wasn't wearing sexy underwear. It made total sense. Sort of. So much for her grand attempt at seduction. Weak, but there it was.

She hadn't counted on the ability of Joey's lips to remove every thought from her head. Her thought butterfly flew away, apparently in search of someone with more brain cells. In a few seconds, she was all but melting in Joey's arms, her unfortunate lack of lingerie forgotten. Her hands slid up Joey's chest to anchor themselves on his shoulders, kneading his taunt muscles like a cat flexing her claws.

Joey's hands roamed her back, finally reaching down to squeeze the firm muscles of her buttocks. He pulled her toward him until she could feel his arousal pressing against her.

She couldn't help but mold herself to him, enjoying the erotic feel of him through her green cheeky boy shorts with daisies. They were suddenly her favorite pair.

He squeezed her behind once more before his hands travelled to the sides of her hips. He slid them slowly upward, grazing her waist, before stopping right below her breasts. He tore his lips away from hers, turning his face into her neck. He was fighting for control again, but she was too far gone to notice.

"Front or back?" he asked, in a gritty whisper.

She tried to focus on his words, but she was hot and feverish and very, very uncomfortable in her own skin. She wanted...no, she *needed* his touch. Why was he stopping? Why didn't he...? Suddenly, understanding dawned on her. *Oh...front or back.*

"Back," she panted, already starting to turn.

He stopped her, reaching around to unclasp the hook of the bra with one flick of his fingers. *Of course, he did.*

She tried to catalogue that little maneuver for a future reformed-rake reference, but then he touched her. And she nearly stopped breathing. Whatever she had imagined hadn't come close to this. His hand moved upward to cup her breasts, gently, almost reverently. He studied each one, taking his time to note the shape, the silken feel of her skin, the way her heart sped up when he stroked the tender undersides. He bent his lips to taste the peach-colored—why was he not surprised—tips, lolling his tongue around each, playing and teasing until he had surmised what pleased her.

As soon as he was certain, he redoubled his efforts. Diana's world spun and shook, filled with the sensation of his hands on her breasts. She clung to him, barely able to hold herself upright. Her sighs and the way she clutched his shoulders told Joey she was enjoying the fruits of his efforts. He was more than enjoying them. But he was, he realized with wicked satisfaction, neglecting other enjoyable efforts…and other enjoyable fruits. To explore those delights, however, he had to stop caressing her luscious breasts. Easier said than done. He forced his hands lower, away from the tempting morsels. The lower his hands went, the greater the temptation to touch her in other delicious places. He slid his hands into the back of her cheeky boy shorts, squeezing the silken skin of her buttocks before returning to the supple muscles of her back. She moaned and rubbed herself against him. Her knees nearly buckled from the pleasure of Joey's caresses…she would have fallen if not for his quick reflexes. He caught her then carefully lowered her to the furry rug in front of the fireplace.

She sank gracefully into the softness, sitting back on her knees. He reached across her naked body and flipped a switch on the wall: the gas logs blazed to life. It was an afterthought, but a very good one. He almost gasped at the reflection of the firelight on the exquisite vision in front of him. Her hair was aglow with color. She made him think of Botticelli's *The Birth of Venus*. She was a goddess, beyond alluring, even with most of her erotic parts covered. She was fire come to life. He burned for her.

He unbuttoned his shirt. Diana watched his every move. He could see the admiration in her eyes. She made him feel like a king. Every minute he had ever spent in the gym. Every drop of sweat. Every aching, sore muscle had been worth it. He dropped his shirt to the floor. He kicked off his shoes, glad he didn't have to deal with socks. He unfastened his belt. His pants quickly joined the rest of his clothes in a heap on the floor. He didn't remove his boxers—not just yet—a measure that would, hopefully, keep him focused.

He knelt on the fluffy rug in front of Diana, placing one hand on either side of her hips. With a quick tug, her cheeky boy shorts slid down to her knees. He helped her wiggle the rest of the way out of them. She kicked them to the side, trying not to feel self-conscious as he gazed at her.

His hands moved to her hair, patiently rearranging the silky strands until her breasts—and her triangle of auburn curls—were uncovered. He wasn't about to let her hide behind her hair. He wanted all of her. All that she could give. All that she was. Somehow, Diana resisted the urge to cover herself, but she couldn't meet his eyes. She felt her cheeks glowing with heat. She couldn't help but wonder if he was disappointed.

"Diana," he said, in a gravelly voice. "Look at me."

Slowly, she raised her chin to look at him. Her gray eyes were full of uncertainty, as if she feared she didn't measure up to his exacting standards. What he saw there humbled him. The truth was she was so much more. In every way. So much more than he deserved.

"Diana," he continued, "you are *so* beautiful. You're everything a man could want. Inside and out." He reached for her hand, bringing it to his lips, as if she was a princess. "And no one could *ever* want you the way I do."

Some of the tension left her shoulders. She let him tug her down to lie on the rug beside him. His kisses were long and thoroughly arousing. His hands roamed her soft skin until she was pliant and relaxed in his arms. They sank deeper into the soft rug, luxuriating in the feel of skin on skin. Almost. Her hands dipped beneath the waistband of his boxers.

"Not yet," he whispered between fevered kisses. "You, first."

His hand brushed gently through her triangle of auburn curls, seeking her heat. He grunted in satisfaction as his search yielded the moisture he was looking for. He stroked her, circling the tight, little bud, slowly exploring her soft folds. He pressed into her with one finger, delighted by her breathy moans and the way she pushed against his hand. She was tuned to his every touch, no matter how slight. He continued his gentle massage until she writhed against him, demanding more. He urged her on until she arched her back and gave in. He would never forget the beauty of his Diana's passionate release amid the firelight. What had he done to deserve such a woman? The answer was easy. Nothing. She was a gift from God.

When her final spasms faded, she smiled with pure amazement. She had never experienced anything as wonderful in all her life. She stretched her arms overhead. "Mmmm..." was all she could manage. She felt like a contented kitten in the warm sunshine, basking in Joey Finch's possessively smug grin. He certainly looked proud of himself. Well, she was proud of him, too. She had never imagined feeling this way.

Before this moment, Joey assumed he couldn't be more smitten, enamored, besotted, head over heels, and "plumb whupped," as the old men at the Honeysuckle Creek Barber Shop would say. But Joey was wrong. Gazing into Diana's glowing eyes before the firelight, he fell even deeper in love with his red-haired siren. That she was experiencing a similar fate was obvious. If any woman had ever looked at him with her heart in her eyes, it was Diana. For some miraculous reason, she loved him. And he couldn't wait another minute to make her his.

Joey crawled, rather inelegantly, to his pants, extracting a condom from the pocket. He stripped out of his boxers and turned around to find Diana's amused gaze.

"Confident, weren't you?" She had propped herself on one elbow, relaxed, now, and full of sass.

"Lucky for you," he said, opening the packet with his teeth. His wicked eyes gleamed in the firelight.

"Lucky for *you*," she responded, once again lying back on the soft fur.

He moved quickly, until he was looming over her, all humor absent for the moment.

"Diana, I have a confession to make," he said, seriously. "Last week, when I told you that I was falling in love with you, I lied."

She raised her eyebrows, waiting. A week ago—an hour ago—she would have been terrified of that comment. But now...

"The truth is I wasn't *falling* in love. I had *already* fallen. I don't even know when it happened. Maybe weeks ago. Months ago. Maybe, it was nine years ago. I'm just sorry that it took me so long to realize it."

She reached up and stroked his cheek. "You're worth the wait," she said, softly. "I always knew you would be."

He turned his head to kiss her palm. "Thank you for waiting." They shared a moment of silent understanding, knowing it was only the calm

470

before the storm. Joey kissed his captivating lover's sweet lips, eager to possess the only woman he would ever love. She welcomed his hot, hard weight as he covered her. She could see the tension in his arms as he tried to hold himself back, but she would have none of it.

"I want you, Joey Finch," she whispered, fiercely. "Now and always."

He watched her face as he slowly pressed into her, willing to stop at any sign of discomfort on her part. Discomfort was the very least of what he was feeling as he slowly inched into her warmth. They hadn't talked about experience. He assumed he was not her first lover, but something about the way her eyes widened made him wonder if he was wrong. She was suddenly very tense. He could feel it. And not in a good way. Gone was his confident siren of minutes ago and in her place...

"Diana?" he rasped, forcing himself to hold still.

"Hmm?" She swallowed. Her eyes still incredibly wide.

"Have you ever done this before?" he asked. Her uncertainty had helped cool his need to possess. Somewhat.

She gave a weak chuckle. "Oh, yes. Of course, I have. It's just been a long time."

He raised his eyebrows in disbelief. He hadn't ridden a bicycle in a long time, but that didn't mean he had forgotten how.

She exhaled a little breath. "I've *sort* of done this," she confessed. "More or less. I mean, I've done things...just not exactly *this* particular thing." She closed her eyes in embarrassment. *Drat.* This was not the way she would write a love scene. "There isn't any obstruction."

"What?" he asked, confused now. This was, by far, the most bizarre conversation he had ever had in the midst of lovemaking, particularly because his body parts—that is, *one* part in particular—had never been quite so ready to finish the job.

She shrugged, miserably. "The doctor said there's no obstruction because of horseback riding or heavy exercise or something. My mother was the same way. I assumed that meant it would be easy for you to...But you're so large..." She trailed off.

Talk about an ego booster. Diana's observation was, by far, the best "problem" Joey ever had to solve. Not only was he to be her first lover—a precious and unexpected gift—but she thought he was well-endowed. Joey's masculine pride swelled, along with his eager member. He leaned in to press a gentle kiss on her worried lips. He was also going to be her *only* lover, he promised himself. It was a responsibility he would gladly shoulder for the rest of his life. He gazed into those wide, gray eyes.

"You," he whispered, "are perfect...Trust me, Diana."

She nodded as he took her lips in a kiss designed to distract. When he felt her relax, he withdrew and pressed in again, a little farther than before, giving her time to get used to him. He could feel the sweat beading on his brow from his own efforts of restraint. He vowed to make this first experience good for her if it killed him...something that was becoming a distinct possibility. He withdrew and slid in again. Her body welcomed him this time, all resistance gone.

"Yes..." she gasped. "Oh, yes, Joey...Just like that...Again."

Sweeter words were never spoken. Or gasped. Or squealed. Diana was not a quiet lover. And Joey couldn't have been more delighted. He surged forward, filling her with his hard length. He felt the pressure building at the base of his spine, but he held on, determined the two of them would go over the edge together. As her frantic movements increased, he knew she was close. Her back bowed upward as the spasms began again and he let go, joining her in a firestorm of pleasure...the most intense pleasure of his life. His ironclad control was a distant memory, the woman in his arms a revelation. He collapsed onto his side, holding her close for a few sweet moments that needed no words.

Diana broke the silence. "I think I'm dead," she said. "You killed me." She kissed his chin, cuddling in his embrace. "To die of pleasure," she breathed. "Do you think it's possible?"

Joey laughed at her nonsense. "If it is, then I must be dead, too."

She grinned. "You were definitely worth the wait."

"Um...about that." He had to know how he had gotten so lucky. "How is it possible that someone like you hasn't ever..."

Diana propped up on one elbow to explain. "Well, I dated a few guys in college, but never seriously. I was never one for sleeping around, anyway. I only had one real boyfriend and that was in high school."

Joey forced himself to focus on her words, not on the erotic picture she embraced simply by lying on a fur rug in front of the fire. He was marginally successful.

He ran his fingers up and down the soft skin of her arm. "Tell me about him."

"There's not much to tell. I dated Terrell Fletcher for three years in high school. I honestly thought we would get married. I wasn't madly in love with him or anything, but our families were friends. He was a nice guy." Diana shrugged. "We had a lot of fun together."

Joey looked at her in disbelief. "And he *never* tried anything with you in three years?" Although grateful for Terrell Fletcher's lack of initiative, Joey had to assume that Diana's high school Romeo was three bricks shy of a load.

"Of course Terrell tried a few things, here and there, but never anything with consequences. You, of all people, should be able to understand why." She giggled, waiting for him to figure it out.

Suddenly, the reason for poor Terrell's admirable self-restraint was crystal clear. "The Boys," Joey said, using the Merritt family's name for the fearsomely protective foursome.

"Exactly," Diana nodded. "Right after we started dating, Roman invited Terrell to go fishing with The Boys. All of them showed up. Even Devin. I think they scared Terrell to death, especially Connor. Anyway, after spending the day with them, he was almost afraid to kiss me."

"I can understand that," Joey said. "Dating a Merritt is not for the faint of heart. So, whatever happened to poor, old Terrell?"

Diana raised her eyebrows. "*Poor, old Terrell* decided *he* didn't want me to go to U-V-A. *He* decided I should live at home and go to community college with him."

"And you were unable to resist the call of Charlottesville and the Virginia Cavaliers, so it was goodbye, Terrell." Joey was proud of Diana for giving old Terrell the boot. "How did he take it?"

Diana shook her head in disappointment. "He didn't take it well. He left me standing in the parking lot of a Dunkin' Donuts. Just drove away without a backward glance."

"How did The Boys deal with that?" Joey couldn't help but be a little curious about the fate of Terrell Fletcher.

"They took him fishing the next week," Diana said, solemnly. "And…" Her voice dropped to a whisper, becoming low and mysterious. "Nobody ever saw Terrell Fletcher again."

Joey chuckled at her teasing. "No, really. What did The Boys do?"

Diana shrugged. "They didn't do anything. They were relieved. They thought he was too wimpy to be a part of the family, anyway. No balls, as Connor would say."

Joey laughed. It was exactly what he would expect from the male facet of Diana's family. "Wonder how they'll feel about *me* becoming part of the family?" he asked.

A little thrill ran through Diana at Joey's pointed reference to their future. "I guess you'll find out soon, won't you?" she asked, with a delighted grin at Joey's apparent confusion. "You'll be in Alexandria all next week, remember?"

For once, Joey was caught off guard. And utterly nonplused.

"Don't worry," Diana said, patting his muscular chest. "You'll be fine. But…" Her eyes sparkled in anticipation. "If they ask you to go fishing with them, you should probably say no."

CHAPTER FORTY

$\mathcal{B}$acon. Was there anything as wonderful as the smell of bacon first thing in the morning? Joey didn't think so. As a matter of fact, he decided bacon just might be the best smell in the universe. Diana had already found the way to his heart. Apparently, she knew the way to his stomach, too.

He was nearly in the hallway before he realized that he was completely naked. He quickly decided his unclothed state was probably not ideal for greeting his lady love after their first night together. Joey paused in the doorway of Diana's bedroom to mull it over. Unless she was naked, too, he thought, delighted by the possibility. Was she? Was she, even now, frying bacon without a stitch of clothing covering her delectable body?

Or even better...was she waiting for him to try out the unused counter from the night before? That counter had serious potential, he admitted. *Down, boy,* he scolded himself, shaking his head at his own erotic thoughts. Frying bacon in the buff would be painful, if not outright impossible. Besides, he figured Diana needed a respite from his amorous attentions. He had given her very little rest during the previous twelve hours. Even irresistible sirens needed a break now and then, didn't they?

He turned around and headed to the dresser beside Diana's desk. Sometimes, when he came home to visit while on vacation from Merritt Brothers, doing yardwork or other little jobs for his sisters got messy. So, he always kept shorts, sweatpants, a couple of T-shirts, and two or three pair of boxers in the dresser's bottom drawer. There were also several flannel shirts in the back of the closet.

He pulled open the drawer, pleased to find his emergency stash untouched. He pulled on a pair of shorts and a long-sleeve T-shirt. He planned to work out later, even though he had already had quite a workout last night. He grinned at the thought. Life with Diana was good.

Joey's eyes scanned the perfectly organized surface of Diana's desk. It reminded him of Darcie's perfectly organized office. How do organized people ever find anything? he wondered. He would be lost without the numerous stacks of paper and books that occupied his desk at Parker and Finch. He understood clutter. Clutter worked for him. His eyes landed on the paperweight neatly placed in the center of the desk.

He studied the uneven object with interest. What was it supposed to be? Some kind of modern art? That was a surprise. He figured Diana would prefer art with flowers and plants, not this unrecognizable thing in the shape of a…A what? A glob of clay? He picked it up curiously. Maybe it was upside down, he decided. He turned it over.

Ah, so that was it. Someone had written *"To Nanny Di. Love, Amalie"* in permanent marker on the bottom of the thing. His heart got all warm and mushy. Diana would be a wonderful mother, there was no doubt in his mind. And she was going to be the mother of *his* children, he told himself. *His* children. Would they have a little girl with red hair and freckles like her mother? Or, perhaps, a little boy with Joey's dark eyes and penchant for trouble? He couldn't help but chuckle at that terrifying thought.

As he started to replace the paperweight, he got a good look at the paper underneath. The man in the drawing looked exactly like…him. His grin widened. Yes, that was definitely Joey Finch seated behind a desk. Except for a few, um…artistic additions, that is. Someone—a rather angry someone, it seemed—made the adjustments with a red pen. There were horns poking out of the top of his head. A devil tail peeking from behind his desk. And a nicely rendered pitchfork propped against it. The flames billowing around the sides of the desk were also done in red. The words *"Nanny Di and The Loveable Lawyer"* were penned over the drawing. Someone—perhaps the vengeful owner of the red pen—had marked out the pleasing word *"Loveable"* and replaced it with the darker word, *"Lying."*

Diana's methods of revenge tickled Joey. He chuckled, remembering her rendition of "You're So Vain" at Honeysuckle Creek Pizza and Karaoke. She must love him a lot, he decided, to react so strongly to his imaginary betrayal. She was fierce, but sweet. Strong, but soft. Passionate, but, well... *really* passionate. Was it any wonder he had fallen in love with her?

Joey replaced the paperweight carefully. Whistling, he headed in the direction of the kitchen to find his girl. And, hopefully, some bacon.

Diana nearly dropped the tongs she was holding when Joey strolled into the kitchen. It should be illegal, she decided, for anyone to look so divinely delicious at ten o'clock in the morning. Especially since he wasn't even trying.

He was wearing workout clothes, and old ones at that. His feet were bare. His perfect hair, rumpled. His usually smooth face, unshaven. But despite those minor imperfections—or maybe because of them—he was still an eleven out of ten. And he was *hers*. A happy little thrill rushed through her at the realization that the man she adored was finally hers.

"Good morning, Miss Merritt," he said, a wicked gleam in his dark eyes. He propped his shoulder against the refrigerator.

"Mr. Finch," she said, inclining her head regally while a smile flitted around the corners of her mouth.

She felt him studying her. Peach-colored toenails. Long legs. Short, cream-colored robe—the one with the lace-trimmed sleeves and the pink roses. Her hair was presently twisted on top of her head, having flatly refused to cooperate after the strenuous activities of the night. She glanced in his direction. If his hot gaze was any indication, he didn't seem to mind her messy bun.

He watched her remove the last piece of bacon from the pan. She placed it on the paper towel–covered plate to drain before switching off the burner and moving the pan to the back of the stove. He prowled toward her like some jungle cat stalking its prey. When he was close enough, he placed his hand on the side of her neck, tugging gently, bringing her face close until his lips were flush against hers.

It was a lazy, seductive kiss. A kiss between lovers. A promise of what was to come.

"Mmmm," Diana purred, as he pulled back an inch. "More."

Joey's grin was pure masculine satisfaction. "Your new favorite word, I presume?" he asked.

"Mm-hm," she sighed, as he nibbled the side of her neck. "After breakfast, I'll show you what I'm wearing under this robe."

"One of those green cheeky things, I hope," he added between kisses.

"Better," she promised, dreamily.

"Sounds like breakfast can wait." His hands moved to the belt of her robe. "More," he said, playfully.

Joey's prophetic *"more"* quickly turned into *more* than either he or Diana bargained for.

Much more.

Joey had barely made progress with the knot on Diana's robe when the doggie door flew open. They watched Atticus wriggle through the small space in stunned silence. A silence that did not last. The scruffy canine rushed into the kitchen of his former home barking with joy. And all they could do was stare at the happy fellow in sheer disbelief. If Atticus had arrived that meant...

The glance Joey and Diana exchanged was filled with mutual horror. They were well and truly caught, with no escape in sight. Extra horror for Joey because of the identity of those doing the "catching." He mentally ticked off the illustrious group on his fingers.

First there was Grace, his hopeful, idealistic, I'm-in-love-so-everyone-else-should-be-in-love-too-isn't-life-wonderful little sister. She would probably burst into a musical number from some Broadway show, then call Lou immediately and tell her to start designing Diana's wedding dress.

Then there was Darcie, the nosiest, never-let-up-until-she-knows-every-last-detail-even-if-it's-none-of-her-business baby sister ever to plague a big brother. She would hound him for days until she was satisfied with his explanation. And when she was finished, she would hound him some more.

Then he would have to deal with Blane, his I-can't-wait-to-repay-you-for-all-the-crap-you-gave-me-when-I-fell-in-love-with-your-sister best friend and brother-in-law. Whether he gave Joey hell—all in good fun, of course—or sat back to watch the fireworks, Blane would enjoy Joey's predicament immensely.

And the last—but unfortunately for Joey, not least—member of the party: Devin I'd-be-happy-to-kick-your-ass Merritt, Diana's overprotective cousin/boss. Devin was the wildcard of the bunch, seeming to encourage Joey's relationship with Diana and discourage it at the same time. Joey had no idea what Devin would do once he realized Joey had spent the night.

And along with Devin came Amalie I-may-be-super-cute-but-it's-only-a-matter-of-time-until-I-say-the-wrong-thing Merritt. How had Joey forgotten about the ever-observant little girl? She would join the mayhem at some point. He could only imagine her innocently embarrassing comments.

As Joey pondered his fate, Diana accepted hers. She recognized the inevitability of their discovery because, well...they were lovesick idiots and should have spent the night at *Joey's* townhouse. What were they thinking, anyway? Of course, she rationalized, there hadn't been a great deal of actual thinking going on after she and Joey left the restaurant.

Still, how could they have forgotten that Darcie lived in the gate-keeper's cottage, too? The answer to that was almost too easy. Because after walking into the cottage with Joey last night, Diana had forgotten anyone else existed. And so, apparently, had Joey. That pleasing realization and memories of their night together—still fresh in her mind—brought a smile to her lips, despite their dire circumstances. She just couldn't help it.

Joey returned her smile, tempted to kiss her again, regardless of their impending doom. Instead, he regretfully stepped back, putting a respectable distance between himself and his lovely lady. "Sunday got here awfully fast," he said, ruefully.

Diana frowned. "It isn't Sunday, Joey," she said, following his line of thought. "It's Saturday." Her eyes widened. "Wait a minute. They aren't supposed to be back until *tomorrow*."

Joey rubbed a hand through his rumpled hair, rumpling it a little more. "Well, unless Atticus swam across the ocean by himself, they're back. And that means they came home—"

"Early," they said in unison as the kitchen door swung open.

The travelers had returned.

One. Day. Early.

Wordlessly, Joey pulled another pack of bacon from the refrigerator. He placed it on the counter. Diana nodded in agreement. Perhaps if their uninvited guests' mouths were full of food, they couldn't ask embarrassing questions. Not his most brilliant plan, Joey admitted to himself, but it was all they had. At least until Amalie raced across the kitchen. Then they had absolutely nothing.

"Nanny Di! We're back," Amalie squealed the next moment. The little girl threw her arms around her nanny, putting a temporary halt to Joey's fabulously pathetic plan of distraction-by-bacon. Diana picked up the excited little girl, spinning her in circles, as overjoyed by the reunion as Amalie. She planted her small charge on the end of the counter, peppering her with questions.

Joey couldn't help but smile at their enthusiasm, even while he privately mourned the possibility of finding out what Diana was wearing under her robe. He listened as Amalie busily gave her nanny every detail of the past week. Every single one. No tiny bit of information, it appeared, was too insignificant to share.

Diana's attention never wavered. Was she really that absorbed in the one-sided conversation? Joey wondered. Or was she trying to distract Amalie? To keep the little girl talking about something besides whether— or not—Uncle Joey was sleeping with her nanny.

Or maybe it was a convenient way to delay the inevitable reckoning with her large—and currently scowling—cousin, who had just appeared in the doorway. Devin looked fairly intimidating from where Joey was standing. Distraction or avoidance? Joey wondered. Either way, he decided, Diana's method was brilliant.

After assuring himself that she was, momentarily, safe from scrutiny, Joey chanced another glance at Devin to find he—not Diana—was the focus of the fierce-looking man's single eye. Joey watched Devin stomp toward him, pulling Darcie's enormous suitcase. He stopped about two feet away, his expression unreadable. Joey returned Devin's glare, flatly refusing to flinch under his unblinking perusal.

On the outside.

On the inside he was nothing but one big flinch. And lots of little flinches. He was a Finch flinching. He was a flinching Finch. Any other time, his clever wordplay would have been amusing. He was certain Diana would appreciate it. Unfortunately, this was *not* any other time. This time was, well…Joey wasn't really sure what this time was.

So, he waited. For Devin to say the first word. Or throw the first punch. Or do whatever he thought he needed to do to defend the Merritt family honor. But Devin didn't move. He just stood there: a pirate thirsting for vengeance. Joey could feel Devin's blazing hostility. He wasn't foolish enough to think the irate man would just turn and walk away. Nevertheless, Joey latched onto the feeble hope—even as he berated himself for his own stupidity—that Devin was waiting for an opening to begin a mature and rational discussion.

Or not.

As the standoff lengthened, Joey reluctantly discarded that benign idea in favor of a more painful one. Devin wasn't waiting for conversation, Joey realized. Diana's leonine protector was waiting for Joey to say something stupid, thus providing Devin with a solid excuse to punch the guilty party in the mouth.

Or break his nose. Both prospects were extremely unappealing. He was, Joey realized belatedly, rather fond of his nose. As a matter of fact, he was fond of his whole face. He sighed, even as he refused to look away from Devin's single burning eye. He didn't blame the man. Considering the way Joey had initially reacted when he discovered Devin's interest in Darcie, it was only fair for Devin to return the favor. Joey just hoped the favor didn't involve broken bones. Or missing teeth. Or—God forbid—blood.

Blane's arrival provided a momentary break in the action. Or lack of action, as it were. He entered the kitchen carrying two smaller versions of the bag Devin had been pulling. His appearance gave Joey a welcome excuse to break eye contact with Devin.

"How did I get stuck with the bags *without* wheels?" Blane grumbled. "What did Darcie pack in these suitcases anyway? Feels like they're stuffed with bricks. Better watch out, Joey," he grinned. "I know how your head attracts 'em."

Nobody laughed.

After Blane's little joke fell flat, his eyes swept the room. There was no mistaking the significance of Diana's robe, Joey's disheveled state, or the one-sided staring contest underway in the middle of the kitchen. Blane— always cool under pressure—kept his easy grin firmly in place. Joey, however, was not at all deceived by his best friend's casual expression. He could tell the man was ready to intervene, if necessary. Unfortunately, at this point, Joey couldn't ascertain on whose behalf Blane would intercede.

That was new. And a bit disconcerting.

To avoid Devin's burning gaze, Joey turned his attention to Atticus. He idly watched the industrious dog conclude his sniffing inspection of his former quarters. After his canine nose was satisfied, the scruffy beast made a beeline for his favorite uncle. He planted his furry behind firmly on Joey's foot, leaning against his leg in a strong show of solidarity. *Good, old Atticus.* At least Joey had one ally. He scratched the dog behind his only whole ear.

Blane, however, didn't waste time choosing sides. He walked straight to Devin, nudging him with one of the heavy suitcases. "I take it we're supposed to take these bricks to Darcie's room?" he asked, easily.

"What?" Devin finally took his eye off his nemesis to glance at Blane.

Blane held up one of the bags. "The bricks? Do we take them upstairs or"—Blane motioned to Joey—"drop them on his head right now?"

Devin's lips, unexpectedly, turned up in amusement. "Upstairs," he answered, after taking a few overly long seconds to ponder his options. "I'll enjoy it more if he's not expecting it." He headed for the stairs. Blane followed, chuckling at the expression on Joey's face.

Before Joey could relax, a scuffle in the doorway caught his attention. He braced himself for the drama to come as both of his sisters made their expected entrance. Grace paused inside the doorway, already biting her lip in indecision.

"I told you it was too early to come bursting into the cottage," she hissed, attempting to grab Darcie's elbow.

But Darcie barreled right past her. "Oh, I don't know," she said, smiling her cat-with-the-cream smile. "Looks to me like we got here just in time."

With an apologetic glance in Joey's direction, Grace followed Darcie into the cottage.

Darcie slid close enough to bump Joey's hip with her own. "What do you think, brother dear," she asked. "Didn't we get here just in time?"

Grace, thankfully, didn't give him a chance to reply.

"Hi, Joey. Hi Diana," she said quickly, trying valiantly for normalcy.

"Hello," Diana said, politely, as Amalie peered around her shoulder.

Joey glared at his sisters. Darcie's grin widened, but at least she didn't say anything else. Grace—who had never met a silence she couldn't fill—started babbling. "We decided to come back early," she began. "It was a mutual decision. Decided by all of us. I guess that's kind of what *mutual* means, isn't it?" She laughed weakly.

No one joined in.

Undeterred, Grace's eyes fell on the scraggly dog sitting on Joey's foot. "Except for Atticus. Our decision was mutual except for Atticus. He didn't get a vote. He's a dog," she explained unnecessarily. "And dogs don't vote." She bit her lip. "We didn't actually vote. We just sort of talked about coming back. And then agreed." She continued chewing on her lip, studying her audience.

Joey privately hoped that was the end of Grace's successful quest to make an awkward situation more awkward, but she struggled on.

"So, that's why we're here a day early. We probably should have called. Or texted. Or told you in some way that we were going to appear a day early. To avoid any, well…you know…unfortunate surprises. But…well…" She looked, hopefully, from Joey to Darcie to Diana and back to Blane and Devin, who had rejoined the group after getting rid of Darcie's bags.

No one, it seemed, had anything helpful to say.

"Here we are," Grace finished brightly.

Still nothing, not even a cough or a timely sneeze.

"Your robe is lovely, Diana," Grace added, a bit desperately.

Amalie, unwittingly, broke the impasse. "Nanny Di," she asked excitedly. "Does your nightgown match your robe?"

"Um…no." Diana managed to gasp. She wasn't wearing a nightgown. Or pajamas. Just very sexy—and, apparently, never to be seen by Joey Finch—lingerie.

Amalie, thankfully, didn't pursue that line of questioning. She instead chose something worse. "Uncle Joey," she squealed, peeking around Diana's shoulder. Her shrill, childish voice echoed in the kitchen. "Did you and Nanny Di have a sleepover last night?"

Oh, drat. Diana mentally wrung her hands. She should have known that it was only a matter of time until Amalie pointed out the obvious. Of course, she rationalized, it wasn't like the obvious wasn't, well…obvious.

Diana—in her short, flirty robe—and Joey—looking oh-so-rumpled—were the epitome of "caught in the act."

No, she corrected herself, not caught *in* the act. Maybe caught *after* the act. Yes. That was better. But not much better, she decided. Because no one—save Amalie—had any illusions regarding the nature of Diana and Joey's *sleepover*. There was clearly no other explanation—rational or otherwise—for his presence in her kitchen. Fortunately, Blane, Grace, and even the outspoken Darcie were just a little too polite to address the issue head on.

Unfortunately, Diana was certain that one member of the group—whose last name just happened to be Merritt—would have no qualms about broaching the subject. She had, thus far, managed to avoid interacting with Devin. And she would like to continue to do so for as long as possible, thank you very much. She had absolutely no idea what her overprotective cousin was going to say—or do—on behalf of the rest of her overprotective family.

Diana's eyes flew expectantly to Joey's, seeking assistance. He was—she knew from experience—wonderful at diffusing awkward situations. Joey would save them. *Say something*, she telegraphed him urgently. *Anything*. She watched him open his mouth. She waited for him to say something clever.

He didn't.

He didn't say anything at all. She watched him close his mouth in defeat. For once, Joey's creativity had failed him. Them. *Drat*.

The timer on the oven chose that moment to beep.

"Oh," Diana gasped. "My biscuits!"

To her astonished surprise, Devin himself came to the rescue. In two steps, he whisked his talkative daughter off the counter and planted the little girl firmly on his hip. Diana grabbed a pair of potholders and opened the oven. She pulled out a pan of beautifully formed, perfectly browned biscuits.

Devin poked his nose into the air and gave a big sniff. "Smell that, Amalie?" he asked with a grin.

She stuck her nose in the air and sniffed, mimicking her father. "Biscuits!" she squealed, clapping her hands. "Nanny Di made biscuits!"

"That's right, 'Malie," Devin agreed, easily. "I have a feeling Uncle Joey's here for the biscuits." He raised his eyebrows in Joey's direction. "Isn't that right, Uncle Joey?" *Truce*, his eye seemed to say.

"Your dad is right, Amalie," Joey agreed. "I am definitely here for the biscuits. And the bacon," he added, hastily. "Don't forget the bacon."

That explanation apparently satisfied the little girl. Devin set Amalie's feet on the floor with instructions to wash her hands in the bathroom. Atticus trailed after her, freeing Joey's foot from his surprisingly heavy bulk. Joey stomped his numb toes on the floor to get the blood moving again. Atticus really needed to lose a few pounds, he decided.

Devin leaned over to plant a kiss on Diana's cheek, receiving a pleased smile in return. He grinned at Joey. "It's about time you two figured things out," he said, holding out his hand.

Joey shook it gratefully before turning his attention back to the girl of his dreams. And her culinary skills. He breathed in the enticing aroma of baked deliciousness. "I didn't know you could make biscuits," he said to Diana, with something like awe.

Diana shrugged her shoulders, struggling to contain her pleasure at the expression on Joey's face. "You can thank Grandma Merritt for that," she said briskly, placing the biscuits into a breadbasket lined with a towel. "Somebody probably needs to set the table, and..." She looked around to find that Grace and Blane were already pulling dishes and coffee mugs from the cabinet.

Darcie grabbed a bowl and started cracking eggs. "Hope everybody wants scrambled." She grinned at Diana before giving her an encouraging wink.

"Scrambled sounds perfect to me," Diana said, with a happy smile, opening the package of desperation bacon. She seemed as relieved as Joey by Devin's unexpected approval.

Joey's own relief was tempered by uncertainty. How would the rest of the Merritt family react when he showed up in Alexandria? He wasn't worried about Diana's parents. She had already spoken to them and received their enthusiastic approval. The real hurdle would be convincing The Boys—eyewitnesses to Joey's regrettable history as a one and done— that his intentions were sincere. He hoped Roman, Connor, and Lance would be as accepting and supportive of his relationship with Diana as Devin. But, under the circumstances, Joey had his doubts. It was just as likely that he—like poor Terrell Fletcher before him—would get his own invitation to go fishing.

CHAPTER FORTY-ONE

$\mathcal{J}$oey couldn't arrange a meeting with the rest of The Boys until the following Friday. Connor and Roman were out of the office, working in Charleston, South Carolina, the first part of the week. They returned on Wednesday night, and both had full calendars on Thursday.

Joey was busy in court with Lance every day until the jury's verdict in the case he was working came back late on Thursday afternoon. Lance's client was acquitted, as they had known he would be. It wasn't a complicated case, but it was still nice to be on the winning side this time.

Per Joey's request, he and The Boys met in Connor's office on Friday morning at eleven thirty. Joey was unaccountably nervous but determined to be honest with the men whose family he one day hoped to join. He walked into the room carrying four cups of coffee and a box of assorted pastries from their favorite bakery. He knew from his days as Connor's intern that the big man favored the Boston cream eclairs, so Joey had ordered two.

The Boys were already waiting for him, even though Joey was five minutes early. That, he observed, was enough to mess with a man's courage. Connor was sitting behind his large desk, looking even more irritable than usual. Roman was looking out the window. He glanced back when Joey came in, a scowl on his face. Lance was standing by Connor's big bookcase, flipping through a large volume of a law textbook. His back was to the door. When he turned around, the expression he wore was carefully neutral.

Their reaction was entirely unexpected. Devin's easy acceptance of his relationship with Diana had allowed Joey to let down his guard. His subsequent conversations with Diana's parents, in addition to her uncle Gary, left him feeling hopeful. Even Diana's aunt Naomi gave Joey and Diana's relationship one hundred percent approval. By the time Joey had spoken with that formidable woman, he was feeling confident he could handle Diana's brother and her cousins. He assumed he would get the same treatment from the redoubtable trio. Apparently, that was not to be the case. *Well, hell.* Joey was used to being part of the solution in this particular room, not the problem.

He fought down the unexpected urge to turn around and run. Where had that thought come from? Joey Finch was no coward. But then, he realized, he'd never attempted something like this before. He had counted on his friendship with these men overriding what they knew of his one-and-done reputation. But how well did they *really* know him? The *real* Joey Finch? Would they trust him with their beloved sister and cousin?

He placed the box of pastries on the corner of the desk, opening the lid. After handing around coffee, he sat down in one of the chairs directly across from Connor.

"Boston cream eclairs are mine," the gruff-looking man growled after perusing the selection in silence.

"I call the apple fritter," Roman said. He grabbed the confection, grimly saluting Joey with his coffee, before planting himself in the chair to Joey's right.

Lance was a little more appreciative. He seated himself in the chair against the wall. "Thanks, Joe," he said, in response to Joey's questioning glance. "Just coffee for me." But he changed his mind almost instantly after watching his cousins devour their pastries. "Well, maybe I will have a cinnamon roll." He stood and moved his chair closer to the desk, effectively penning Joey in.

Joey was surrounded, a quick exit no longer an option. He couldn't help but see the situation for what it was…a carefully planned strategy on their part. The silence stretched uncomfortably. These men were his friends, Joey kept reminding himself. He took a sip of coffee. He had never thought much about it before, but Connor, Lance, and Roman were quite a fearsome trio. He began to doubt the wisdom of meeting with them all together. Maybe he should have…

"Well?" Connor barked with his mouth full of Boston cream eclair. "Why have you called this little meeting?"

Connor's hands were huge, Joey noticed. He could knock a man's head off with one swipe of his giant paw. That observation was not encouraging.

"And why did you feel the need to bring a bribe?" Roman asked, gesturing to the remaining pastries in the box. "This better not have anything to do with Diana." He almost growled the words.

Roman was no less forbidding than Connor. His business suit hid a muscular physique. That, along with the fact that Joey was sleeping with his sister, was a little unnerving.

Joey cleared his throat. "As a matter of fact, Roman, it *does* have to do with Diana, but in a good way." His voice sounded nervous, even to him.

Roman's intense stare turned downright hostile.

Joey glanced at Connor, who continued to chew in silence. He obviously wasn't getting any help from the big man. Joey's eyes moved to Lance, who was watching him thoughtfully.

"Go ahead, Joe," Lance said. "What do you want to tell us?"

Joey felt a little better. It seemed that Lance, at least, was willing to listen to what he had to say. "I just wanted to tell the three of you that Diana and I—"

"Hellfire and damnation, Finch. You're messing around with my sister, aren't you?" Roman stood up so quickly that his coffee sloshed onto his pants, leaving a large, wet stain on his left thigh. "Damn it," he said, glaring at the man beside him. He grabbed several napkins off Connor's desk and mopped at his leg.

Joey took advantage of the opening. "Diana and I are...together," he said, baldly. His announcement was decidedly lacking in verbal finesse. He braced himself for their reaction.

"Together," Connor said, crossing his substantial arms across his substantial chest.

"Together how?" Roman asked, politely. Too politely. If possible, his glare intensified. He had given up on his stain to focus his hostility on Joey.

Joey swallowed. "You know. *Together* together."

Connor and Roman didn't react. They just sat there staring at him. Joey glanced hopefully at Lance.

"*Together* together," Lance said, with unexpected sarcasm. "That certainly clears everything up, doesn't it?"

Joey felt a surge of irritation. They certainly weren't making this easy on him. It wasn't like he had done anything wrong. On the contrary, he was trying to do the *right* thing by making them aware of his relationship with Diana.

"*Together* together," Connor repeated. "What kind of a lazy-ass, inarticulate, sorry use of syntax is that, Finch? And what the hell does it mean? Are you taking her to a ballgame, marrying her, or just sleeping with her?"

Roman growled at his cousin's words but remained silent.

"*Together* together," Connor said, for the second time, shaking his big head, in disgust. "If that's the best you can do for our Diana then you can get the hell out of her life." He paused to glare at Joey. "Kindly remove your sorry ass from my office."

"Now hold on just one damn minute." Joey rose to his feet, shoving back his chair. It hit the wood floor with a loud crash. "Let's get one thing straight right now. I'm in love with Diana and she's in love with me. We are together. *Together* together. We're a couple. And, as far as I'm concerned, we will continue to be a couple as long as I have breath in my inarticulate body. I'm talking the whole nine yards, here, gentlemen. Engagement. Wedding. Honeymoon. Kids. Grandkids. Hell, great-grandkids are not an impossibility. So, you three better get it through your stubborn, arrogant heads that I'm not going anywhere. You might as well accept the fact that you, gentlemen, are stuck with me." Joey stood there, breathing hard. He was so agitated that it took him a few seconds to note the change that had taken place in his adversaries. His *former* adversaries, that is.

Connor's serious expression had turned into a satisfied grin. Lance was smiling and nodding his head in approval. Even Roman had an amused expression on his face. The truth dawned on Joey. They had played him and played him well. And they looked extremely pleased with themselves.

"Well, it's about damn time." Connor leaned across his desk, shaking Joey's hand with genuine enthusiasm.

Lance stood up. "Glad to hear it, Joe," he said. He, too, shook Joey's hand.

Joey turned to Roman, still, thankfully, his friend. "Well, Roman," he said, gingerly. "What do *you* think?"

Roman grinned. "If you ever hurt her, I'll kick your ass."

Joey couldn't help but laugh at that. The Merritt family, it seemed, was all about kicking ass. He knew *exactly* where Roman was coming from. "If I ever hurt her, I'll kick my own ass," he said, firmly, relieved beyond words that the ordeal was over.

"That's all I needed to know. Welcome to the family, brother." Roman grabbed him in a bear hug, pounding him on the back.

The next few minutes were filled with the kind of joking camaraderie Joey had enjoyed while working at Merritt Brothers. When he returned his chair to its pre-outburst position, he sank into it. He was finally able to relax for the first time since he entered Connor's office. "You three are a tough crowd," he admitted, ruefully.

"You look a lot better than you did a few minutes ago," Connor observed with a deep chuckle. He looked better, too, but Joey did not remark on it.

"You didn't *really* think we'd go easy on you, did you?" Roman asked, appearing quite pleased with himself.

Joey grimaced. "No, of course not. But for a minute there..." He paused for effect.

"What?" Lance asked, curiously. "What did you think we were going to do to you?"

Joey kept his expression as serious as possible. "For a minute there, I was afraid you were going to ask me to go fishing."

Lance and Roman burst out laughing. Connor looked from one to the other, a confused expression on his face. "What's wrong with fishing?"

"He's talking about that Fletcher kid Diana dated in high school," Lance said. "Don't you remember, Connor? You know...the wimpy one. What was his name?" He directed the question to Roman, who was closer in age to the unfortunate Fletcher kid.

"Terrell Fletcher," Roman said. "You remember, Connor, we took him fishing. All three of us *and* Devin." He turned to Joey. "Diana told you about that, did she?"

Joey chuckled. "She did. I think she meant it as some sort of a warning. Hence, the pastries."

Roman glanced, admiringly, at his cousin across the desk. "Connor, you scared the hell out of poor, old Terrell. It was a thing of beauty."

"Yeah," Lance added, a big grin on his face. "I bet he was afraid to shake hands with Diana after that." He paused, thoughtfully, before adding, "But, looking back, you probably shouldn't have held him under so long."

"I only held him under for a few seconds," Connor said, looking quite proud of himself, if a little embarrassed by the familial praise. "Just long enough to teach him a little bit about respecting women." He eyed Joey thoughtfully. "How good are you at holding your breath, Finch?"

"Probably better than you," Joey answered, much to Roman and Lance's amusement.

"He has you there, brother," Lance said, and even Connor laughed at that.

Mission accomplished, Joey thought, standing to make his goodbyes. "Well, time for me to hit the road." He was more than eager to get back to Honeysuckle Creek. He had never missed anyone in his life the way he had missed Diana during the last five interminable days.

"Oh, no you don't," Lance said. "No way you're leaving without lunch."

Joey hesitated. "Thanks, but I was really planning to get something on the way home."

"A fast-food drive-thru?" Roman asked. "Bad plan, Finch."

"Especially since we already made reservations at the Old Town Tavern," Connor added, smugly. "Take your pick, Finch: lunch at the Tavern or fishing."

"You already made reservations?" Joey laughed, but their faith in him warmed his heart. He couldn't let them know that, of course. "How can I turn down a free meal at the Tavern?" He shrugged his shoulders like he was doing them a favor.

Roman cuffed him on the back of the head. "Who said it was a *free* meal?"

"Yeah," Lance added. "What about the unwritten rule that says the newest member of the Merritt family pays the check?"

Joey shook his head. "I'll need to see that *unwritten* rule in writing."

Lance chuckled. "Don't worry, Joe. Connor will pay. He always does."

"The firm will pay," Connor said, decisively. "This is a working lunch. Poor old Finch has had to put up with *you* all week." He looked pointedly at Lance. "He needs some kind of compensation for that."

As Joey and Roman headed toward the door of Connor's office, the big man tossed a large box to Joey, who caught it easily.

"Nice hands, Finch," Connor said, approvingly. "Receiver?"

"Yeah," Joey confirmed. "Slot receiver. What's this?"

"Your costume for tonight," Connor said. "Diana asked me to pick one up for you."

Joey had been too busy missing Diana to think about getting a costume for the annual Honeysuckle Creek Fall Festival. The box was taped up and wrapped in plastic, making it impossible to open without a great deal of effort. Joey shrugged. "Thanks," he said. "I'll check it out later." He followed Roman down the hallway.

Lance, however, hung back to wait for his troublemaking brother. "Okay, Connor," he demanded as soon as the big man caught up with him. "What's in that box?"

"It's a costume for our future cousin-in-law to wear to the Honeysuckle Creek Fall Festival," Connor said, innocently. "Weren't you paying attention?"

Lance wasn't buying it. He eyed his brother suspiciously. "I know you too well, Connor Merritt. You're up to something. Don't even try to deny it." Connor's history of practical jokes was legendary.

"Why, little brother, what are you talking about?" Connor tried to keep a straight face, failing miserably. "I did exactly what Diana asked me to do. I picked up a costume for our dear friend, Joey Finch."

Lance couldn't help but grin at Connor's careful phrasing. "What *kind* of costume is in that box?" Lance asked.

"What kind of costume do you *think* is in that box?" Connor replied.

Lance laughed out loud. Connor's success at answering a question with a question was unmatched. "I don't know. I'm guessing it's something like a giant chicken or a cow with udders." He studied his brother, but Connor's face gave nothing away. "Hm, it has to be some kind of animal. Something hairy. Very hairy and embarrassing. A giant skunk, maybe?"

Connor's refusal to speak was telling.

Lance shook his head. *Poor Joey Finch.* "Anyway, Connor, I might not know what kind of obnoxious costume you picked out, but I do know one thing." Lance grinned. "Payback is hell. You better watch your back."

"Why, little brother," Connor said, matter-of-factly, "I thought that was *your* job."

As they walked out of his office, Connor's loud guffaw echoed in the hallway.

CHAPTER FORTY-TWO

*J*oey studied himself in the mirror. He did *not* see Superman looking good in his blue tights and cape with a big, red *S* on his chest. He did *not* see a devil-may-care Zorro, flashy with his cape and sword. He did *not* see Indiana Jones with his whip and spiffy fedora; Maverick, from *Top Gun*, cool and confident in his flight suit; or Captain Morgan, the cocky pirate from the brand of rum. Hell, he didn't even see Captain Crunch. That would have been an improvement over the hideous thing that stared back at him from the mirror.

Joey should have had his head examined for trusting Connor The-King-of-Practical-Jokes Merritt to take care of his Halloween costume. Hindsight was certainly twenty-twenty. And right now, his hind sight was, literally, huge. The sight of his behind, that is, was huge. In other words, his rear end was *huge*. He grimaced at his reflection. When Joey was six years old, he played a sheep in the children's Christmas program at church. He still remembered crying because the big, round, fluffy costume he had to wear made his behind look twice as big as it really was. He couldn't do anything about it then; he wasn't able to do anything about it now.

He was already several hours later than he originally planned, courtesy of lunch at the Old Town Tavern. He couldn't show up without a costume, not when he had promised Diana...his lovely Red Riding Hood. At least, he assumed that she was Red Riding Hood, the logical companion to his Big, Bad Wolf. He couldn't imagine his long-legged lady dressed as one of the Three Little Pigs. No, his lovely Red Riding Hood was waiting for a rendezvous with her Wolf. And that Wolf had no intention of disappointing her. Revenge would simply have to wait. He was, he decided, going to punch Connor Merritt squarely in the jaw the next time he laid eyes on the big, grinning jackass. That thought cheered Joey considerably...until his eyes returned to the mirror.

The hideous costume covered him with fur from head to toe, except for the round hole where his face poked through. The costume was made like a jumpsuit—or those footed pajamas he had worn as a toddler—with a cleverly concealed zipper on the side. Granted, he had strained muscles he didn't know he possessed getting into the furry monstrosity. *And* he was probably going to have to cut himself out of it. But he would give kudos to the designer for the costume's extreme creativity. He had to admit that, from the front, at least, the costume had possibilities. There was even a detached nose with elastic that went around his head. Not too bad. And if that was the extent of it, he was reasonably confident that he could have pulled it off. Furry wolf ears and all.

But that *wasn't* the extent of it. Because firmly attached atop those wolf ears was a frilly, white cap. The kind of cap an old-fashioned grandma might wear. The cap drooped drunkenly to the side of his left ear, as if the Wolf had had one too many. Yep, Joey decided, from the looks of things, the Wolf had been tippling in the blackberry brandy again.

To make matters worse, the damn cap wouldn't come off. After a few tugs, he realized that the ridiculous accessory was *sewn* in place. With *wire*. And not just any wire. Unbreakable wire. Impossible-to-cut wire. Wire from the very depths of hell. He had tried scissors, three knives, even a pair of wire clippers, but the cap remained firmly in place.

Cap—One. Pathetic-looking wolf—Nothing.

He turned sideways, peering into the mirror over his fur-covered shoulder to revisit the scruffy, sorry, limp excuse for a tail hanging off his much-lamented behind. Unfortunately, it was also sewn with the same uncuttable wire. Joey was quite certain there was absolutely no way that any-one—*anyone*—in his right mind would ever willingly request this costume.

Herein lay the issue with the label on the box. Clearly written in oversized letters were the words *"Big, Bad Wolf."* No explanation. No description. No warning. Just...*"Big, Bad Wolf."* The wolf looking back at Joey in the mirror was neither big nor bad. He was overweight and unkept with a penchant for wearing women's hats. *And* he apparently had a drinking problem.

This was *not* the wolf Red Riding Hood met in the forest, Joey fumed. Oh, no. That wolf was a predator—diabolically charming, in his own way—tempting Little Red to stray from the path of her good intentions. Suave and maybe a little bit sexy. Joey could have worked with that sort of *before* picture.

Instead, he got the *after* picture. *After* the wolf ate Little Red's grandma, that is. And Joey had already surmised that Grandma was a stout, healthy woman. The wolf's stomach poked out a good foot and a half in front of him. Joey couldn't even see his furry, oversized feet. It was like being pregnant, he thought, feeling a pang of sympathy for expectant mothers everywhere. Good thing the stuffing—and there was a lot of it— was soft, or else there would have been no way he could manage to wedge himself in the driver's seat of his truck.

He studied his reflection again, squaring his shoulders. He saw an enormous pregnant wolf wearing a stupid-looking hat. What was the best thing he could do, facing what he was sure would be complete and total humiliation? Should he pretend he had chosen the costume on purpose? He rolled the idea around in his mind for a few seconds. Yes, that was exactly what he should do. He was going to walk into Parker and Finch as if the ridiculous costume was all his idea. Could he pull it off?

Of course he could.

His natural ability for extricating himself from his own shenanigans had given him the necessary skillset. He *could* make the whole situation seem plausible. He would find his Red Riding Hood. Charm her luscious self. And take her back to his lair, where he would have his wolfish way with her.

With a feral grin, Joey took two steps toward his dresser to grab the keys to his truck. Or, rather, he attempted to take two steps. He actually ended up in a furry heap on the floor. Walking with his damn, oversized wolf feet was like navigating a balance beam wearing water skis. Not to be outdone, he regained his footing with a low growl. He was, he realized, becoming more wolflike by the minute.

Concentrating intensely, he managed to make his way to his truck. He heaved himself into the driver's seat. His tail, however, decided not to come along. It took three tries to get the blasted thing into the truck with the rest of him. When he pulled out of the parking lot of his townhouse, it was nearly nine o'clock. The pointy end of his sorry tail was sticking in his left ear. The quicker his wolf made an appearance, the quicker he—and his Red Riding Hood—could disappear.

When she was seven years old, Diana found a beautiful princess costume while shopping with Devin's sister, Lydia. Diana didn't ask for it, but her beloved aunt Allana bought it for her anyway. Since then, she had missed being a princess for Halloween only twice: once, when she was sick in bed with strep throat and once when she was pledging her sorority. She and her fellow pledges had dressed as Smurfs that year. Diana was, of course, Princess Smurf, but that time didn't count. The blue body paint spoiled the overall effect.

She gave herself a thorough once-over in the mirror of the small powder room on the second floor of Parker and Finch. Although she loved her previous princess costumes, this one—a medieval princess—had to be her favorite. She had purchased the beautiful ensemble on sale nearly a year ago. She couldn't wait to wear it.

Her long, flowing dress was made of rich, burgundy velvet with dramatic bell sleeves. Intricately-embroidered flowers—in elegant golden thread—graced the square neckline. Edging of the same flower design wrapped around the sleeves and the bottom of the dress. The elaborate embroidery also embellished the long slit down the side of the skirt. The slit was a sexy, little twist…one Diana hoped Joey would appreciate. A heavily embroidered sash of burgundy velvet encircled her waist. A delicate head-piece of golden leaves completed the ensemble. A length of burgandy chif-fon— attached to the back of the headpiece—flowed down her back, past her hips. Black, mid-calf boots with laces and block heels gave the outfit a sassy flare. She felt sassy. And provocative. And ready to see Joey Finch.

Diana had ordered his costume—the male counterpoint to hers—from Masquerades and More in Alexandria. The store had quite a follow-ing among local theater groups and had even supplied costumes for several Broadway shows. Thinking about Joey's dark good looks clothed in medi-eval armor had nearly given Diana heart palpitations. Thank goodness Connor agreed to pick up the costume for her. She shivered in anticipation as she turned off the light. It was almost time for her appointed rendezvous with her very own knight in shining armor.

The official end of trick-or-treating in the Honeysuckle Creek busi-ness district was nine o'clock. By eight-thirty, Parker and Finch had almost run out of treats. All that remained were two cookies, four caramel apples, and enough regular apples for Darcie to make a single pie. By mutual agreement, Diana, Darcie, and Grace decided to cut off the outside lights, thereby signaling to late arrivals that they had missed their chance.

Diana had thoroughly enjoyed the last several hours. She loved handing out treats to the excited, little trick-or-treaters. She had never seen so many adorable costumes in her life. Or so many hilarious adults. At least, not since she was a student at the University of Virginia. She had long believed that no one was more creative than a college student on Halloween, especially after a couple of drinks. But the costumes she had seen tonight made her rethink that assumption.

No group had worked harder on their costumes than Will and Maggie Parker and Joe and Juli Finch. Will, although considerably more fit than Fred Flintstone, managed to look sufficiently caveman-like to fill his role. Red-haired Maggie was the perfect Wilma Flintstone, while Joe and Juli made an adorable Barney and Betty Rubble. The creative foursome left Parker and Finch around eight-fifteen to get ready for the adult costume contest at nine o'clock.

As Diana joined Darcie and Grace in Darcie's office, she had to smile at the sight that greeted her. Cat Woman was sitting in one of the chairs in front of Darcie's desk. Her feet—stylishly clad in low-heel, black ankle boots—were propped on the edge of the desk. With her big, green eyes and her cat ears tilting crazily to one side, Grace looked more like an adorable kitten than Batman's on-again, off-again nemesis.

Darcie—kicked back in the chair behind her desk—was absolutely stunning as a Pirate Queen. No surprise there, Diana thought. She was wearing skin-tight black pants and a long, off-the-shoulder white shirt with huge, billowing sleeves. The neckline and cuffs were adorned with white lace. Her shiny plastic cutlass was securely tucked into the bright, red sash that cinched her waist. She wore thigh-high black boots with high heels. Her black pirate hat—trimmed with gold braid and decorated with black lace and a single, large, black feather—was lying on her desk.

Grace indicated the chair beside her. "I hear Joey sent you another rose this morning," she remarked as Diana sat down for the first time in hours. They had been so busy handing out treats there hadn't been time to chat.

"He did," Diana said, with a smile. "And this time, I got a note, too." She pulled the note that accompanied the rose out of her pocket and tossed it on the desk. Grace picked it up eagerly and opened it

Darcie leaned forward in anticipation. "And what did our *terribly creative* brother say in his *terribly creative* note?" she asked.

Grace frowned at her sister's sarcastic tone. "Joey wants Diana to meet him at the playground at the Academy at nine o'clock tonight."

Darcie sat back in her chair. "Hmph," was her only comment.

Diana wrinkled her forehead. "What does 'Hmph,' mean?" she asked.

Darcie shrugged. "Nothing, really. I guess I'm still disappointed with our *unoriginal* brother's *unoriginal* ideas. A flower every day. It's the same thing Blane did for you, Gracie."

"Not exactly." Diana was quick to defend her absent boyfriend, even though she privately agreed with Darcie. Borrowing ideas from his brother-in-law was uncharacteristic of the usually inventive Mr. Finch. Still, she rationalized, it was sweet of him to send anything at all. She knew he had been very busy in Alexandria all week.

"Blane increased the number of flowers he sent every day," Grace reminded Darcie. "And he sent yellow roses. Not red."

"True." Darcie still didn't look pleased.

"And…" Diana added, "…he was trying to win Grace back. Joey doesn't have to worry about that. He's already won me." She and Grace exchanged a smile.

"Also, true," Darcie agreed. "The flowers are sweet, Diana, don't get me wrong. I just expected better of our usually *very* creative brother."

"But sometimes Joey is a bit too creative," Grace countered. "Maybe Diana should count herself lucky to get flowers instead of something like… oh, I don't know…jars of pickles. Or tubes of toothpaste. Or puppies."

Diana chuckled at the thought.

"You're probably right." Even Darcie was grinning at Diana now. "I guess you're pretty lucky at that." The Pirate Queen got up to walk to the front window, clearly on the lookout for Devin and Amalie to return from trick-or-treating. They had taken Blane with them for—what Devin called—practice for the future. Blane laughed at that, saying he was only in it for the candy, but it was obvious he was pleased to be invited. That was more than two hours ago.

"I swear," Darcie lamented, "Amalie is going to be so full of sugar that she'll be bouncing off the walls."

Diana chuckled at that comment. Dealing with Amalie on sugar-overload would fall to someone else tonight.

"Oh, laugh it up, Your Highness," Darcie smirked. "You're going to be bouncing off the walls, too…the walls of Joey's townhouse."

"Or maybe bouncing *on* Joey's bed," Grace said, suggestively.

"Gracie Marie!" Darcie shrieked with a grin.

The trio dissolved into laughter. The fact that Joey's sisters already acted like Diana was a member of the family warmed her heart.

"I can't wait to see how Blane likes trick-or-treating with Amalie," Diana remarked. "He seemed a little stunned after eating breakfast with her the other day."

"Blane's eaten breakfast with her plenty of times before," Darcie observed. "Maybe he's thinking about having his own talkative little one soon. Hmm?" She raised her eyebrows at her sister, but Grace refused to take the bait.

"I keep telling him that little boys can talk as much as little girls, but he doesn't believe me," she remarked, stretching her arms over her head.

"Aunt Naomi says when Connor was little, the only time he *stopped* talking was when he was eating," Diana remarked. "She swears that's why he still has such a gigantic appetite. She just kept giving him food to shut him up."

Darcie and Grace laughed.

"Joey was quite a talker, too, wasn't he, Gracie?" Darcie asked.

"Until *you* came along," Grace teased. "After that, *nobody* could get a word in edgewise."

Darcie stuck out her tongue at her mischievous sibling. "Hmph."

"And speaking of Joey..." Diana said, glancing at the clock on the wall. "I better get going." Even though her destination was down the hill behind Parker and Finch, the ground dropped off abruptly at the edge of the parking lot. The rough, rocky terrain covering the steep slope made an easy descent almost impossible. So, Diana was going to walk down Main Street to the Academy. The playground was on the other side of the court-yard between the elementary and middle schools.

Grace looked a little concerned. "Diana, honey, are you sure you want to walk all the way down to the Academy by yourself?" She glanced toward the window in the corner of Darcie's office. From that vantage point, the playground was visible, although parts of it were covered in deep shadows.

"I don't mind going with you, Diana," Darcie volunteered, a little too sweetly. She walked back to her desk to pick up her hat.

"Of course, you don't mind," Diana grinned, shaking her head. "*You* want to find out what kind of surprise your brother has planned." She crossed her arms, pinning Darcie with her tell-the-truth-nanny look. "Am I right?"

"Of course," Darcie agreed easily, placing the hat securely on her head. She nodded, making the feather on her hat bounce up and down. "What kind of a sister would I be if I *didn't* want to know what my charming brother was up to?" She thought about it for a minute. "How about if I *drive* you down to the courtyard?" she offered. "I'll wait outside, of course."

Grace rolled her eyes at her determined sibling.

Diana smiled. "No, Darcie. I'll be fine. It's really not that far."

Darcie sat down in her chair, looking disappointed. "What if I promise not to peek?" she asked.

Grace spoke up, quickly. "*I'm* going to peek. At least until you wave at me from the playground to tell me everything is okay." She chewed on her lip before adding, "And be sure to take your phone."

Feeling like a teenager again, Diana pulled her phone out of the pocket of her dress. "Yes, ma'am," she said, politely.

Grace nodded, somewhat mollified.

Diana returned the phone to her pocket. "I'll be fine," she reiterated, giving each sister a quick hug. "And I won't forget to wave."

A few minutes later, however, Diana was starting to second-guess herself. She had disregarded Grace's concern and Darcie's offer to accompany her for one simple reason. She trusted Joey Finch. He would *never* ask her to meet him on the playground if there was the slightest possibility of danger. She knew him well enough to be certain that her welfare was—and always would be—a priority for him. Nevertheless, her trek so far had done nothing to inspire confidence.

Contrary to what Diana expected, the streets were practically deserted. She could hear the faint echo of the loudspeaker from the costume contest when she started walking, but even that comforting sound was fading with every step. The distance between the streetlights lengthened as she walked down the hill and around the curve, leaving her unexpectedly anxious when she could no longer see Parker and Finch.

She tried to distract herself as she walked past the lovely Victorian structures—now home to businesses—by trying to imagine what the street had been like when it was new. Did those early residents of Honeysuckle Creek spend time with family and friends on their porches? Did courting couples—dressed to impress—promenade beneath gaslights? Did they sneak a quick kiss in the shadows? Was this street full of life? She hoped so. Because, unfortunately for her, it was completely deserted right now. And dark. And creepy.

The last business on Main Street—before Main Street became Academy Street—was Dr. Winehart's dental practice. The building, of course, was dark and deserted. No surprise there. No legitimate dentist passed out candy for Halloween. Too self-serving. And who wanted a toothbrush or dental floss as a treat? Absolutely no one. No children, anyway. Still, Diana decided, a friendly light in the window would be most appreciated.

When she reached the bottom of the hill, the trees were much thicker and closer together. The edge of the grassy front yard of the Academy's elementary school beckoned. Getting there, however, involved passing half a football field's worth of dark, shadowy trees. Why was it so dark down here, anyway? Didn't anybody in this town care about well-lighted pedestrian walkways? What about nighttime programs at the Academy's elementary school? Did little children and their parents have to traverse these dark, deserted sidewalks getting to and from their cars? And were they as creeped out by the shadows as she was?

"Be brave, Nanny Di."

Drat. The voice of that damned iguana echoed in her head, giving unsolicited advice as always. The glorified lizard's pet phrase ran through

505

her head at the most annoying moments. Still, she thought philosophically, annoyed was better than scared.

Snap!

Diana nearly jumped out of her skin at the sharp crack of an acorn hitting the sidewalk. She looked up automatically, narrowing her eyes as she spied the culprit. The squirrel, perched on a low-hanging branch, seemed to be laughing at her. After a few seconds, her furry tormentor disappeared into the upper bows of the tree. She could hear him chattering as she forced her feet to move. For some reason, the squirrel's unprovoked attack was unsettling; and not merely because death by acorn was extremely unappealing. Her mind latched onto several unpleasant scenarios....

What if Joey was running late? What if he was stuck in traffic? What if his phone died and he couldn't call her? An affirmative answer to any of these questions would leave Diana waiting alone in a dark, creepy, deserted playground. She shivered at the thought. At least she had her own phone. And Grace, she reminded herself. Grace was watching to make sure she was safe. That thought made her feel slightly better. But…

What if Joey was intentionally luring her to the playground so *he* could scare her? It *was* Halloween night, wasn't it? Ghosts. Ghouls. Slasher movies. Diana considered the unpleasant possibility. What if he was staging an elaborate practical joke? She felt a flash of anger. She hated practical jokes. Despised them. Such a tactic would be a huge mistake on the part of the fun-loving Mr. Finch. As a matter of fact, she fumed, a practical joke of such magnitude would be a game-changing mistake, especially if Joey had any desire to find out what she was wearing under her medieval costume.

She glanced up, surprised to see that her grumbling had led her straight to the bright streetlights in the front yard of the elementary school. Light was a wonderful phenomenon, she decided. Now all she had to do was walk through the courtyard between the elementary and the middle schools; then she would have access to the playground. That was easy enough. She could do this, she told herself. She walked confidently toward the space between the buildings, stopping to peek around the corner.

The space was dark. And creepy. And deserted. *Drat.* How many times had she used the words *dark, creepy,* and *deserted* in the last ten minutes? Her writer's mind rejected the overuse of these three adjectives. Synonyms. What she needed were a few, good synonyms. Or a thesaurus. But wouldn't she look silly carrying around a thesaurus?

She could use her phone to search for synonyms, but she needed to conserve her battery. She had snapped quite a few pictures earlier tonight, not to mention the adorable videos she had taken of Amalie. She must have sent those to at least ten people. She couldn't resist sharing the cuteness. No, a thesaurus would be better, she rationalized. She could always use it as a weapon, if necessary. Or to whack Joey Finch over the head for dragging her down here so he could scare her to death.

She took a deep breath before entering the dark, creepy, deserted courtyard. She walked as fast as she could toward the wrought iron gate. If it was locked, she was going to run all the way back to Parker and Finch.

Without stopping.

Or breathing.

She pushed the gate. It swung open easily. *Drat.* She stepped into the empty—synonym for *deserted*—playground, jumping several feet into the air as the stupid, unlocked gate clanged shut behind her. That gate was the last straw, she thought. Game over. No lingerie sightings for Joey Finch tonight.

The playground was completely enclosed by the short, wrought iron fence, which connected it to the elementary school building. Three smaller gates, which matched the detestable main gate, were placed in the middle of the fence on each side. One side of the fence separated the elementary playground from the middle school sports complex. The other was beside the too-steep-to-climb hill behind Parker and Finch. The back fence was a preventive barrier to the thick wooded area located behind the playground. A child could easily become lost in those trees in a matter of minutes.

She glanced around the *uninhabited* playground, taking note of the *vacant* swings, the *forlorn* sand boxes, the *lonely* basketball court, and the *solitary* climbing wall. When she had finished, Diana congratulated herself on the extensive variety of synonyms she had used for *deserted*.

Stretching across the entire back of the space, completely bereft of the happy children that filled the playground by day, was its crowning glory: a jungle gym to end all jungle gyms. Navigating the complicated combination of slides—at least four—and twisted tunnels—Diana counted five—was a heady experience for even the most jaded playground aficionado. In addition to those challenges, there were enough spires, turrets, bridges, and connecting walkways to please any child.

Amalie, who would have been satisfied with a single slide, called it the Playground Kingdom. According to her teacher, she said it so often, most of the children in her kindergarten class had started using the nickname.

Perhaps Diana's next book—*Nanny Di and the Dark, Creepy, Deserted Playground*—would be about the Playground Kingdom's missing synonyms.

Or maybe she would call it *Nanny Di and the Lawyer Who Never Saw Her Lingerie.* Maybe that would teach Mr. Joey I'm-Waiting-For-You-In-A-Dark-Creepy-Deserted-Playground-Where-The-Hell-Are-You! Finch a lesson.

Diana sighed. She pulled her phone out of her pocket to check the time. Five minutes to nine. She would wait for her simply hilarious boyfriend exactly five more minutes. No more. No less. She sank down onto one of the colorful benches in front of the giant jungle gym. If Joey was planning to scare her to death, she may as well be comfortable. Only then did she remember her promise to wave at Grace. She glanced up and up and up to the top of the steep hill. It was easy to see Grace's silhouette in the window. Diana waved her hand. Grace waved back immediately but remained where she was.

Apparently, Joey's sister planned to keep vigil until she saw her brother arrive. A small gesture...but it made Diana feel a lot better. The distance between them couldn't be more than a couple of hundred feet... straight up. Well, almost straight up. If Grace opened the window, she could probably hear Diana if she talked very loudly.

Or if she screamed.

CHAPTER FORTY-THREE

*J*oey turned into the driveway beside Parker and Finch. He pulled into the back parking lot the firm shared with Honeysuckle Creek Optometry. He parked in his assigned space, one of the few that could be seen from the street. He jumped out of his truck, with impressive agility, planting both of his furry feet squarely onto the ground. At least, that was what happened in his head.

In reality, one of his furry feet got stuck in the steering wheel, leaving him dangling headfirst over the pavement. On the plus side, his enormous, swollen I-ate-Grandma wolf belly saved him from smashing his face into the concrete. On the negative side, his overstuffed stomach pinned his arms underneath him, effectively immobilizing them.

At least he wasn't wearing his stupid-looking wolf snout, he thought, trying to be thankful for small favors. The repulsive thing was still lying on the console between the seats.

He hung upside down for a few seconds, pondering his options.

He couldn't move his arms so he couldn't reach his phone.

He couldn't tear his way out of the costume because he couldn't move his arms. And even if he could take hold of part of it with his hands, he wouldn't be able to rip the fur. It was quite thick in addition to being sewn with indestructible wire.

And he couldn't chew off his foot. That idea wasn't out of the question, but from his current angle, he couldn't reach his foot with his teeth. So, where did that leave him?

He tried to imagine the picture he made, hanging by one gargantuan furry foot from the steering wheel of his F-150 in a hideous wolf costume, his arms pinned by the aforementioned costume and his head dangling inches from the ground. The mental picture he was trying to create wasn't quite complete, he realized. How had he forgotten his enormous wolf rear end? And his raggedy wolf tail? Probably because, in his current position, all the blood in his body was rushing straight to his head.

Joey tried to be positive. He didn't think anyone had witnessed his graceless exit. But he had to acknowledge the unfortunate fact that, regardless of witnesses, it seemed he was well and truly stuck.

The best-case scenario, Joey decided, was that someone would come by, extricate him from his dilemma, and leave. But who? Ideally it would be someone who didn't know him. Maintaining anonymity, if possible, was a must. It was the perfect solution. All he needed was to find a foreign tourist who was just passing through with no intention of returning. Ever. He tried to turn his head to look for a convenient non-English speaking tourist. This plan was only partially successful. His head moved but his costume didn't.

After several oxygen-deprived moments, Joey returned his head to its original position. He was out of options, he realized, reluctantly discarding his brilliant idea. He would just have to wait for someone to find him. All the vehicles belonging to his family and friends were still in the parking lot. They would be back eventually. And, if he wasn't dead from a stroke by then—he already had a slight headache—they would rescue him.

There would be no rescuing his dignity, however. This latest shenanigan was sure to go down in the annals of Finch family history. He sincerely hoped Diana found him first. Or his parents. Or Grace. Or, maybe, even Will. Any of those five would help him first and ask questions later.

He would *never* hear the end of it if his furry body was discovered by Maggie, or, worse, Darcie. Those two would immediately alert anyone within a five-mile radius. Joey shuddered at the thought. The only thing worse than discovery by Maggie or Darcie would be...

The sound of a dog barking interrupted his musing. *Great.* He was probably about to be attacked by somebody's wolf-hating hound. Or by some dog who couldn't wait to relieve himself on a ridiculous wolf costume instead of a handy bush. Joey couldn't decide which would be worse.

As the barking grew louder, he braced himself for the worst. He was both surprised and relieved when Atticus' furry nose gently poked him in the face. The scruffy dog regarded him curiously for a second before giving Joey's fur-covered self a thorough sniff. Atticus barked again...a puzzled, questioning sound. It dawned on Joey, just then, that Atticus probably wasn't out here by himself.

"Well, well, well. And what do we have here?" said a deep, slightly amused voice.

Joey grimaced. It was Devin. And he wasn't talking to himself, which meant he wasn't alone. But who was with him? Joey figured it wasn't Darcie, because she would already be screeching at the top of her lungs. There was no doubt about that.

"I'm not sure what that big, furry thing is, but it's hideous," Blane's voice observed, cheerfully.

Blane. It just had to be Blane, didn't it? Joey almost groaned. Nobody enjoyed finding Joey in awkward situations more than his oldest and best friend, something Joey understood completely. If the situation was reversed, well...he would be enjoying himself tremendously. At this moment, however, the only thing preventing him from banging his head on the concrete in frustration was his enormous, bloated wolf belly.

Blane continued, his voice laced with amusement: "Why do you think it's hanging there like that?"

"Maybe it's sleeping," Devin speculated, getting into the spirit of things.

"I think it's dead," Blane disagreed. "It smells terrible."

"Now wait just a minute," Joey growled. He could deal with the teasing about his horrendous costume, but now things were getting personal. He was quite sure he did *not* smell terrible. Well, he was pretty sure. *Damn. Did* he smell terrible?

He didn't have time to find out, because the next thing he knew, Amalie had squatted down beside Joey, leaning in so that her sweet, little face and big, blue eyes were almost level with his face. "Hey, Uncle Joey."

"Hey, Amalie." Joey had to grin at the little girl's courage. She wasn't at all afraid of the big, hairy thing hanging from his steering wheel.

"What are you doing?" she asked, curiously.

"Oh, I don't know," Joey replied. "Just hanging around, I guess."

Amalie's childish giggles rang out in the empty parking lot. "Oh, Uncle Joey, you're so funny!"

"Smile, Amalie," Devin said as a bright light flashed.

Amalie quickly disappeared from Joey's view. "Ooh, Daddy! Let me see!"

Joey almost groaned. "Did you just take a picture of me?"

"Uh-huh," Devin answered, matter-of-factly. "Connor asked me to send him a picture of you in your costume."

"Connor is a dead man," Joey growled.

"Yeah, I have to admit that this is a little over-the-top...even for Connor," Devin admitted. "Hold it steady, Amalie. That's right."

Joey heard Devin and Blane draw closer. Four boots appeared in his line of sight. One pair on either side of his head. He felt a hard tug on his foot.

"Ouch!" he yelled. "My foot isn't supposed to bend that way."

"Sorry," Blane said. "What do you think, Devin?"

Joey waited, impatiently, as they studied his unfortunate foot.

"Why don't you push this part and I'll pull here," Devin suggested.

"Yeah, that might work. Then you can grab him under the arms and lift while I—"

"Break his foot," Joey interjected.

"Easy, Yogi," Blane said. "You got into this all by yourself."

"I. Am. Not. A. Bear." Joey informed his terribly clever brother-in-law through gritted teeth. "I am a—"

Without warning, Blane freed his furry foot. Joey's world tilted as Devin lifted him, setting him on his feet as if he weighed no more than Amalie.

"Wolf," Joey wheezed, trying to get his bearings. He leaned over, fur-covered hands on his equally furry knees. He was, admittedly, a little bit dizzy. "I...am...the...Big...Bad...Wolf." He managed to gasp.

Blane and Devin burst out laughing.

"I think you need to drop the 'Big and Bad' part." Devin struggled to speak through his laughter. "You are, without a doubt, the sorriest-looking wolf I've ever seen."

"Ditto that," Blane added with a hearty chuckle.

Joey listened to them laugh for a few seconds. He was glad they were enjoying themselves. Not really. He *really* wanted to punch both of their laughing faces. He changed his mind, however, when he finally regained his equilibrium and got a good look at the two of them. Joey rarely thought about his own height. Five-ten wasn't exactly tiny, but he did constantly seem to find himself in the presence of excessively tall men. No big deal. Until now. Or maybe it was their costumes that made them such a formidable pair.

Blane towered over him as Batman, complete with mask, cape, and full body armor. Only a compete fool would make fun of *him* for wearing tights. He looked cool, confident, and capable. Three things that Joey had not felt since donning his ridiculous costume.

Dressed as a pirate, Devin was even more intimidating than usual. His blousy white shirt was belted over black pants that disappeared into knee-high black boots. The buckle on his belt matched the buckles on his boots...obviously Darcie's doing. On his head, he wore a black tricorn hat. Devin's scarred face and the eye patch he wore every day gave the costume a sinister realism.

Standing between the two of them made Joey feel as out of place as a donkey between two thoroughbred stallions. There would be no doubt in anyone's mind which one was the ass.

Devin spoke up. "That's enough, Amalie. You can push the red button in the middle now."

"Okay, Daddy," she said, carefully following his instructions. She skipped over to hand the phone back to Devin.

Joey looked at the big pirate in horror. "You...you videoed this fiasco?" he choked out in disbelief. "For Connor?"

Devin shrugged. "Not for Connor," he corrected. "For us. For posterity. I mean, how often do you get to see Batman..."

"Uncle Blane!" Amalie squealed, enthusiastically.

Devin nodded approvingly at his daughter. "And an incredibly handsome pirate..." He looked at Amalie expectantly.

"Daddy!" she yelled, clapping her hands and giggling.

"Rescue the sorriest-looking wolf..."

"I get it," Joey said, holding up his paw. "That would be me."

Amalie tugged on his fur-covered hand. "Uncle Joey?"

"Yes, Amalie," Joey answered.

"I like your hat." Amalie smiled up at him so sincerely that Joey couldn't help but grin back. She was adorable in her blue Elsa costume, her blond hair in a long braid down her back.

"Thank you, Amalie," he said, feeling slightly better. At least somebody liked his pathetic excuse for a costume.

Devin chose that moment to take a selfie of the raggedy wolf and his intrepid rescuers. "Okay, Batman, Grandma...smile."

Joey snarled instead.

The next moment, Darcie stepped out the front door of Parker and Finch, closing it behind her. "What's taking so long?" she asked, coming down the front steps. "I've been waiting for y'all to come in. I saw you from the window. What are you doing out here?" She stopped short at the sight of the furry thing with her brother's face. "Joey? Is that you?" She stepped closer, studying him intently. "Are you supposed to be some kind of bear? A bear with a hat? Are you Mama Bear from *Goldilocks*?"

Joey squared his shoulders. "I am the Big Bad Wolf," he said with as much dignity as he could muster.

Darcie burst out laughing. "Oh, Joey, honey, was that the last costume in the store? It had to be the last costume in the store."

"I'm wearing it for Red Riding Hood," Joey informed her. "And I would appreciate it if you could tell me where I can find her."

"It looks like you ate her," Darcie quipped, much to the enjoyment of Blane and Devin. Amalie couldn't seem to stop giggling.

"Oh, never mind," Joey said, irritably. "I'll find her myself." He started for the door, nearly tripping over his useless wolf feet. Blane grabbed his arm to prevent him from going down.

Joey sighed. "Maybe it would be better if I waited here. Darce, would you please go inside and tell her I'm here?"

Darcie looked at him, blankly.

"Di-a-na," Joey enunciated, patiently. "Where is Di-a-na?"

Darcie blew out an annoyed breath. "Di-a-na is waiting for you on the playground."

"Why is Diana—?" Joey started to ask when the front door of Parker and Finch flew open again.

Grace stepped onto the porch. "What are y'all doing out here?"

Joey closed his eyes, wondering what he could possibly have done to deserve not one but two nosy sisters?

"We're just hanging out with Paddington Bear here," Blane answered.

"Uncle Blane, you're silly!" Amalie objected. "He doesn't look like Paddington Bear."

"That's true, *Uncle Blane*," Devin said. "Paddington dresses better. I would say Uncle Joey looks more like Fozzie Bear."

"But..." Amalie started to object again.

"Without the tie and hat," Devin explained.

Satisfied by his answer, Amalie skipped to the porch. Grabbing Grace's hand, she tugged her onto the sidewalk, chattering all the while.

"Fozzie Bear with a hangover," Devin added so only Joey and Blane could hear.

"Or a really down-on-his-luck Winnie the Pooh," Blane suggested.

Joey growled.

"Say," Devin remarked, "that was pretty convincing. Maybe you could..."

Grace and Amalie reached the end of the sidewalk.

"Joey? It *is* you," Grace said, her green eyes widening. "Why are you wearing a bear costume?" she asked.

Joey sighed. He was going to find his wolf snout and glue the damn thing to his face.

Grace's lovely eyes narrowed. "And why are you still standing here when poor Diana is waiting for you on the playground?" she asked. "All by herself. In the dark."

They all looked at him expectantly.

"Why is Diana waiting for me on the playground?" Joey asked. "In the dark?" he added to satisfy Grace.

"Because of your note," Grace said. She exchanged a worried glance with Darcie.

"What note?" Joey had no idea what she was talking about. He noticed that Blane and Devin were watching him closely.

"The note you sent her this morning, with the flower," Darcie explained. She was looking at him strangely. "Joey," she said, with concern. "Are you feeling all right?"

"Amalie said you fell out of your truck," Grace added. "Did you, by chance, fall on your head?"

"No, I did *not* fall on my head." He brushed off their concern. "And I did *not* send Diana a note. Or a flower." *Well hell*, he thought. Somebody was making a move on his girlfriend. If it was Roger Carrington, he was going to kill him.

"She got a flower every day this week, Joey," Grace said. "We just assumed you were the one who sent them."

Joey frowned. "Give me a little credit for originality. A flower a day is Blane's gig, not mine." He didn't like this. No, he didn't like it at all.

"I knew it," Darcie said, triumphantly. "I knew that you were more creative than that. But, if it isn't you, then *who* is Diana meeting on the playground?"

Joey was suddenly gripped by a strong feeling of dread. "What did the note say? Does anybody know?" he asked urgently.

"I do," Grace volunteered. "She let me read it. It said, '*Meet me at the elementary school playground tonight at nine o'clock. It's been a long time.*'"

The back of Joey's neck began to tingle as he remembered a beard and a cowboy hat and pair of cold, cold eyes. Suddenly, the scenario made perfect sense. "It's him," Joey said, unable to keep the fear out of his voice.

"Who?" Grace asked, biting her lip. Her green eyes were full of apprehension.

"Joey, what are you talking about?" Darcie demanded.

"Texas Pete," he said, struggling to reach the phone in his furry pocket. At least his fingers were free. The fact that the fur covered only the backs of his hands was the one positive thing about his heinous costume. "Cowboy Bill." At their blank looks, he tried again. "It's the psycho, damn it—sorry, Amalie—the one who tried to kidnap her."

For about two seconds nobody moved. Then...

"Grace," Blane said, calmly, "call 9-1-1." His voice was strong and encouraging, the voice of a man used to being in charge in a crisis. "We're going to the playground."

Grace nodded. "I'll call you after I talk to them. I'll stay at the window upstairs so I can see what's going on and..." She glanced at Joey's pale face. "...I'll tell you if I see them leave the playground." She ran toward the porch.

In other words, she would let them know if the psycho forced Diana into the woods behind the playground. Joey knew exactly what his sister *wasn't* saying.

"Where are your keys?" Darcie demanded. No chance she was staying behind.

"Somewhere around the front seat." Joey grimaced as his fur-covered fingers finally grasped his phone in his pocket. "I dropped them when I fell." He could hear Darcie mumbling under her breath as she searched for the missing truck keys.

Devin smiled gently at his daughter. "Amalie, go inside with Auntie Grace." He put his hands on her shoulders and turned her toward the porch.

Amalie resisted, planting her little feet on the sidewalk. "No, Daddy," she said. "I want to go with you. I want to help Nanny Di."

Devin crouched down to look into her blue eyes. She stared stubbornly back. "Amalie," he said. "Somebody has to stay here and help Auntie Grace. Can you do that for us? And for Nanny Di?"

She nodded, reluctantly. "Yes, Daddy." She took off toward the porch, turning around to yell behind her: "Tell Nanny Di that Iggy says to be brave." She ran up the stairs and disappeared through the front door.

Devin blew out a breath of relief. He turned to Blane expectantly, used to following his lead. "Okay, Boss-man, what's the plan?"

Darcie held up the keys. "Found them!" she yelled, triumphantly.

Joey finally managed to pull his phone out of his pocket, uncomfortably aware that his hands were shaking as he tried to find Diana's number.

Darcie grabbed the phone from his furry grasp. She pressed Diana's number before handing it back. Then, she took charge.

"Fuzzy Wuzzy isn't going to fit inside with the rest of us. Throw him in the truck bed," she instructed. When all three men looked at her in surprise, she continued: "Don't look at me like I'm not doing anything. I'm driving." She hopped into the driver's seat.

Blane raised his eyebrows at Devin. "There's your plan," he said. "Unless, of course, you disagree."

Devin couldn't help but grin. "Do you really think I'm that big of an idiot? Do *you* want to disagree with the Pirate Queen?"

"Hell, no," Blane said. "Even Batman has his limits."

Darcie poked her head out of the window. "Hurry up!" she yelled. "Diana is waiting."

CHAPTER FORTY-FOUR

*D*iana was tired of waiting. As a matter of fact, she was fed up with waiting. And she was pretty fed up with Mr. Joey Finch, too. On principle, she flatly refused to call or text him. *He* should have called *her* if he wasn't going to be waiting when she got here. *He* should have texted *her*. *Drat*.

The playground was growing darker and creepier by the minute. Thus far, it was still deserted unless she counted herself—one extremely irate princess. Diana tried to think about the flowers Joey had sent. And the note. Although the flowers and note were sweet, she couldn't help but feel that something was off about his gesture. In addition to his uncharacteristic—and frankly disappointing—lack of originality, she wondered why he hadn't at least hinted about the flowers when she had talked to him on the phone. Especially since *she* hadn't mentioned them. Was it possible he had gotten distracted by his work in Alexandria? Had he forgotten the flowers? And the note? And about meeting her on a dark, creepy, deserted playground?

Diana blew out a frustrated breath. She was tired of sitting on the increasingly uncomfortable bench. She was cold. And she was hungry. She should have grabbed one of the last caramel apples, but for some reason she assumed that this little rendezvous would involve food. She also assumed it would involve the presence of Joey Finch, but, obviously, she was mistaken.

She stood up, ready to remove her princess self from this unpleasant scenario when she heard the loud clank as the gate closed behind someone. Well, it was about time.

She stomped toward the main gate, prepared to give her handsome knight an earful. But the figure that stepped out of the shadowy corridor wasn't a knight. *Seriously?* Diana couldn't believe it. When Joey finally decided to show up in this ridiculous meeting place, he wasn't even wearing the costume she had so carefully chosen. Instead, he was attired in a costume based on Edvard Munch's painting *The Scream*.

He was covered from head to toe with a long, hooded black robe that was tied around his waist with a dark sash. The jagged hem of the robe mirrored the jagged hem at the ends of the draped sleeves that covered his arms. He also wore black gloves. Diana could see the tips of his boots poking out from the bottom of the robe.

The most unnerving part of the costume, however, was the mask. A skull had replaced Joey's head. And the hideous thing appeared to be melting. Black, sunken eyeholes, nose, and mouth, all running down the pasty, white surface. Where was her handsome knight in shining armor? She hadn't had such a disappointing Halloween since Roman decided he was too old for trick-or-treating. She had gone without him, after that, but Halloween was never the same. Determined that tonight would *not* set a precedent, she walked straight up to Scream Joey and let him have it.

"So, this is your big surprise? The flowers? The note? This is the reason that I was supposed to meet you here? So you could play a nasty practical joke?" she asked, planting her hands on her hips. "Ooooh, I am *sooooo* scared." Scream Joey didn't say a word. He merely stood there with his melting face and his tacky black robe as Diana continued to vent her frustration. "I can't believe that this is the best Halloween prank you could come up with. And you didn't even wear the costume that I picked out for you. How do you think *that* makes me feel?"

Nanny Di and the Loveable Lawyer's Pathetic Prank.

The title had potential. And Joey was *still* loveable, even though, at this moment, Diana wanted to break him in half. She huffed in frustration.

Scream Joey didn't move. His refusal to speak was making everything worse.

"Well," Diana prodded. "Don't you have *anything* to say for yourself?"

Blane grabbed Joey's arms as Devin took his legs. They hoisted him, unceremoniously, off his furry feet. Joey struggled to hold onto his phone. "Sorry, Joe," Blane said, as they rolled his scruffy bulk into the truck bed. Atticus jumped in beside him, determined not to be left behind.

"Better hold on," Devin warned. "Darcie won't go slow."

Rid of their fur-covered burden they ran to the passenger side of the truck and jumped in. Devin in the middle beside Darcie. Blane riding shotgun.

Joey crouched on his fluffy knees, holding onto the side of the truck with one fur-covered hand and holding onto his phone with the other. Atticus' comforting weight snuggled at his side. The wind rippled through their fur as Darcie backed out of the parking space. Joey gripped his phone, wondering why it was taking Diana forever to pick up. He could only pray they weren't too late.

Scream Joey might as well be made of wood, Diana decided. Or plastic. *Recycled* plastic, hopefully. He flatly refused to speak no matter how many times Diana asked the same question.

"Don't you have *anything* to say for yourself?"

Scream Joey refused to say a word. He simply stood there, breathing. At least she *thought* he was breathing. What he needed was a taste of his own medicine. Diana stood completely still, hands on her hips. She deliberately pressed her lips together to keep from making a sound. It was

Joey's tactic. Using it on him had worked before. She would just have to wait him out.

Then, she heard her phone.

She fished in her pocket...Grace was probably wondering what was going on. Diana had stepped out of her line of sight when she walked back to the main gate. The least she could do was to let Grace know that Joey had arrived.

She glanced at her phone.

The call was from Joey.

JOEY?

She looked at the phone again.

JOEY!

How could the call be from Joey? Diana struggled to understand what was happening. Joey was standing in front of her wearing a stupid Scream costume. He was playing an adolescent prank on her. He was trying to scare her.

Or was he?

A terrible feeling of foreboding stole through Diana's body. Her heart started pounding as she slowly raised her eyes once again to Scream Joey. Or, rather, Scream *Not* Joey. Why hadn't she noticed his height before? He was too tall to be Joey, even with thick heels. He was too thin through the shoulders. And Joey did *not* own a pair of biker boots. At least, she didn't think he did.

Drat.

"Who are you?" she asked, refusing to show her fear. Her earlier tirade had kept the hooded nightmare from doing anything so far. Maybe she could talk her way out of this until...what? Even if Joey was on his way, he might not arrive in time. Diana was on her own. Scream Not Joey was making her skin crawl, just like...

"Who are you?" she demanded again, although there was no doubt in her mind as to the identity of her attacker. She should have realized Joey wasn't the one sending the flowers. Not because he wouldn't send her flowers, but because he wouldn't have been able to resist teasing her about them. But, she realized, regretfully, it was too late to do anything about that now.

As that knowledge sank in, she battled an overwhelming wave of fear. She was immobilized, rooted to the ground under her feet. She felt hot all over. Flushed, but with little prickles of cold stabbing her skin. Like little, tiny pinpricks. She checked to make sure the hideous specter in front of her wasn't holding a voodoo doll.

He wasn't.

Time slowed to a crawl. Even the wind drifting through the trees was silent. And although Diana was as still as a statue, her mind was working at warp speed.

"Be brave, Nanny Di."

Well, it's about time, she thought. She knew that busybody iguana would show up sooner or later. And even though she hated to admit it, the words gave her the courage she needed. An icy calm swept through her, replacing her fear.

She imagined the smug smile Bill Watkins was wearing under his mask. *Smug* because he finally had the upper hand. Or so he thought. Because, really, Diana didn't like *smug*. She had no use for *smug* at all.

"Be brave, Nanny Di."

Facing her nemesis, she watched him watching her. At least, she was fairly certain he was watching her. It was very hard to tell because of his melting eyes. She paused, struck with a dilemma. It suddenly became very important to have an appropriate name for her opponent. That's what he was anyway. Her opponent. And a proper opponent had to have a proper name.

Scream Not Joey?

Scream Bill?

Scream Psycho?

Psycho Bill?

Yes, she told herself, calmly. *Psycho Bill* was the best choice. Simple, yet descriptive. So now she knew the name of her opponent and of their battlefield…Amalie's beloved Playground Kingdom. Now she needed a plan.

The previous week, Amalie's kindergarten class participated in the Academy's active shooter drill, an unfortunate sign of the times. Instead of being frightened, however, Amalie was proud of the fact that she knew what to do if the unthinkable ever happened. The little girl spent the rest of the week making sure all the important people in her life knew what to do, too. Diana could almost hear her chant the words: *"Run. Hide. Fight."*

Diana would never be certain if time deliberately leapt into overdrive or if Psycho Bill just got tired of waiting. He made the first move, stepping toward her very deliberately. She countered by taking a very deliberate step back. *Drat, drat, drat.* This was bad. Her mind raced to come up with an escape plan. She scanned the area, noting that the gate that led to the middle school fields was the closest. Could she reach that gate before Psycho Bill? Maybe.

Maybe not.

Psycho Bill walked slowly toward her. She backed up until her hip bumped into the corner of the swings. Her survival instincts kicked in, followed closely by her adrenaline.

Run.

She made a quick dash toward the middle school gate. Psycho Bill, easily anticipating her sudden move, got there first. She changed direction at the last minute, heading back to the main gate. He picked up his pace and beat her there too. She knew now that he was just playing with her. Like a cat with a mouse. He could catch her any time he wanted. He just didn't want to. Yet. She really should have remembered that running was Psycho Bill's specialty.

Nanny Di and the Physically Fit Psycho.

So, she reasoned, if outrunning him wasn't an option, what was next? Oh, yes…

Hide.

She started to the middle school gate again, changing her direction when Psycho Bill took the bait. Turning sharply, she ran to the enormous jungle gym at the back of the playground. There were enough tunnels, twists, and turns to hide her from the most determined psychotic kidnapper. All she had to do to gain the advantage was crawl inside a tunnel.

She knew she shouldn't look back—the number one rule in competitive swimming—but she needed to know Psycho Bill's location. She started up the ladder, climbing to the tallest turret on the very end of the fabulous jungle gym. When she reached the top, she glanced back just in time to see Psycho Bill trip over a sandbox. He sprawled face-first into the soft sand. *Yes, yes, yes,* she thought.

Nanny Di and the Clumsy Psycho.

Psycho Bill's mask must be obscuring his vision, she realized. Good to know. Too bad the sand was so soft, she thought, uncharitably.

His clumsy fall bought Diana more time to hide. Hiding in the tunnel was a great plan. If he followed her in, she could go down a ladder or slide and run to the main gate. Or any gate. At this point, she couldn't afford to be choosy. If he didn't follow her, she could safely hide until help arrived. She might even be able to dial 911 from the tunnel.

She stepped into the turret, dropping to her knees at the entrance to the tunnel. It really was the perfect hiding place, she thought, if she was five years old like Amalie or petite like Grace. Unfortunately, she wasn't. Her legs were too long. Even if she could force her body into the tunnel, she might get stuck. She would be a sitting duck. A sitting duck who was stuck. A stuck sitting duck. *Drat, drat, drat.* She discarded hiding as an option, leaving only…

Fight.

Diana didn't have much time. She turned around, surveying her current situation. The too-small opening to the too-small tunnel was behind her. To each side was a plastic wall with a clear, round window, also made of plastic. In front of her were two handles, one attached to each side of the ladder. An idea formed in her mind. It was a little risky, but at this point, she was out of options.

Grabbing the handles, she positioned herself as she used to for the backstroke at those long-ago high school swim meets. Saying a little prayer for courage, she leaned back, pulling her knees to her chest. Her timing had to be impeccable. She would have one chance to make contact. She forced herself to breathe.

In and out.

In and out.

She strained her ears for any sound that might indicate Psycho Bill was about to make his move. She heard only silence. So...

She waited.

Handles grasped in a death grip.

Legs poised to strike.

Muscles straining.

Arms shaking.

She resisted the almost unbearable temptation to peek out of the turret. Just one little peek. Just to see what he was...

"Hello, Diana."

Diana gasped as Psycho Bill's hideous melting face popped up right in front of her. It startled her so much that she almost lost her grip. She recovered, hanging on as she smashed her boots into his face with all the force she could muster. She heard a horrible cracking sound when her feet made contact with his melting nose. Psycho Bill fell backwards, screaming in pain.

Diana wasted no time. She poked her head out to check her options. Her attacker was lying on the ground, hunched on one side, holding his head. She could hear him moaning and mumbling, rather incoherently.

As stealthily as possible, she climbed down the ladder. Giving the prostrate Psycho Bill one fleeting glance, she ran toward the main gate— and freedom. She made it only ten feet before he grabbed her from behind. Before she could make a sound, she was flat on the ground, her mouth full of dust.

He flipped her over, pinning her with his body. His hands pressed her wrists into the hard ground. He leaned over her, his melting face shutting out the stars shining in the October sky.

"You bitch," he snarled. "You broke my nose." The blood from his injury had already stained part of his melting nose and mouth.

Diana struggled to fight back, but he was stronger. And angry. He was very, very angry. She was as helpless as a butterfly pinned to a piece of foam board.

"Don't you understand?" he yelled. "You. Broke. My. Nose." As he raised his hand to strike, she closed her eyes, anticipating an explosion of pain.

Joey mumbled a prayer of thanksgiving as Darcie pulled into the Academy's elementary school parking lot. He didn't care that she probably took half the tread off his tires when she squealed to a stop. He was simply thankful to be alive and in one piece. Of course, it was just his luck that his hideous costume was completely intact. He had to admit, though, that the stupid, furry hood was probably the only reason his head was still attached to his body.

Darcie had driven down the hill like a bat out of hell. There was no other way to describe it. All Joey could do was hold onto the side of the truck bed and try not to die. He figured he would probably bounce if he was thrown from the truck and hit the ground, because his overstuffed costume would cushion him, but he didn't want to test his theory. Atticus had hunkered down beside him, trying desperately not to slide every which way in the bed of the truck. Joey put his furry arm around the intrepid canine for morale support. He had no idea what had happened to his phone or whether Diana had ever answered it.

When Darcie cut the engine, Joey poked his furry head up just in time to see his sister leap out of the truck. Devin and Blane were already halfway to the main playground gate. None of them had given a thought to the raggedy wolf stuck in the truck bed. Even Atticus deserted him. The scruffy canine barely paused to throw him a sympathetic glance before leaping out of the truck to follow his master.

Well, hell. How was Joey supposed to get out by himself?

Joey heard an enraged male scream from the direction of the playground. The anger in the man's voice gave him hope that Diana was fighting back. His Diana was brave and resourceful, but Cowboy Bill was a professional. She needed help. She needed Joey Finch. He tried to throw his fur-covered leg over the side of the truck. His fluffy stomach forced him backwards. Losing his balance, he rolled into the tailgate, growling in sheer frustration.

What was happening on the playground? He had to get to Diana. He crouched on his knees, with his enormous stuffed stomach pressed tightly against the tailgate. He found the latch and pressed. The tailgate popped open, propelling him forward. He caught himself on the edge, managing to regain his footing without further mishap.

But, what now? Running in his oversized wolf feet was an impossibility. He focused his attention on the shadowy courtyard, lifting one foot straight up off the ground—almost knee level—before planting it in front of him. He lifted his other furry foot, mimicking the same high step. Once he got the hang of his new gait, he increased his pace, his scraggly tail bobbing along behind him.

Instead of the sharp slap she was expecting, Diana heard her assailant's sharp intake of breath as he mumbled, "What the—?"

She cautiously opened one eye. Something had distracted Psycho Bill. He was gazing toward the main gate. His hand was still ready to strike, leaving one of her arms free. She reached up to grab his mask. It took only a moment for her fingers to clasp the flimsy material. Before Psycho Bill realized what was happening, she held the blood-soaked garment in her hand.

Bill Watkins—or whatever his real name was—let out a scream of anger. His nose was a bloody mess, the skin under his eyes already turning a dark purple. Diana got a good look at his wild-eyed, maniacal expression right before she heard the gate clang shut. Instead of slapping her, Bill's hand went to her throat.

The next few seconds were a blur. The scruffy form of Atticus—moving faster than any three-legged dog had a right to—soared through the air, snarling like a hungry lion deprived of his prey. He plowed straight into Diana's attacker, giving him no chance to react. Bill and the growling dog rolled over, battling to gain the advantage. Fighting like a demon, Bill managed to regain his footing despite Atticus' efforts to sink his teeth into every available part of his opponent's body. Bill ran toward the back fence, the snarling dog nipping at his heels. Somehow, he made it over the wrought iron posts and ran off into the woods. Atticus, unable to make the leap, paced back and forth in front of the fence, barking menacingly.

Diana was momentarily stunned by the appearance of the canine. She never expected the loyal three-legged dog to be the one to come to her aid. As she struggled to stand, she heard voices shouting her name. When she turned toward them, she couldn't quite believe her eyes. No one could ever imagine a more bizarre rescue party.

The fearsome pirate reached her first, wrapping her in his secure embrace. He was breathing hard from his exertions. She could feel his heart pounding as he held her to his chest.

"Thank God you're all right," he said, an unusual tremor in his voice.

When she looked up into Devin's face, her eyes filled with tears. She simply couldn't help it. So much emotion shone in his single eye. He was truly the very best of cousins.

Batman ran by then, pausing only long enough to receive Devin's nod, indicating he should continue. Blane's cape flew out behind him as he jumped the back fence. He disappeared into the woods, rushing in the direction Bill had taken. Atticus hopped up and down, howling his frustration at his inability to follow.

Diana read the concern on Devin's face. "Go ahead," she urged. "I'm fine." After a glimpse of his doubtful expression, she reiterated firmly, "I. Am. Fine. Go with Blane." She would never forgive herself if something happened to him.

"Go, Dev." The urgent voice of the Pirate Queen reached her ears. "He might need your help." Darcie put her arm around Diana's waist, steering her to a nearby bench.

With each step, Diana's knees became a little wobblier. She sank onto the hard bench gratefully. Only then did she realize she was shaking uncontrollably.

"Oh, honey," Darcie said, kindly. "I know you're freezing. I should have grabbed Joey's stadium blanket out of the truck."

"Wh-wh-ere...i-is...J-Joey?" Diana asked through chattering teeth, because, surely, he should have been there by now.

"Good Lord," Darcie said, in horror. "We left him in the truck bed."

Diana could have sworn Darcie said something that sounded like *truck bed*. But that couldn't be right. She must be hearing things. "Y-you... l-left...h-him...wh-where?" she asked.

"In the truck bed," Darcie explained. "Now, don't you worry, Diana, honey..." she said in response to Diana's confused expression. "There's nothing *wrong* with him." She thought that over as only a sister can. "Well, aside from the stuff that's always wrong with him. This time it's..." Darcie pointed to a furry blob that was struggling to fit its bulk through the main gate. "Well..." She shrugged. "I guess you can see for yourself."

Diana wasn't exactly sure what she was watching as the furry bearlike creature wriggled its swollen stomach back and forth in a valiant attempt to push its way through the gate. The bear-thingy's little white hat bobbed up and down with every wiggle of the creature's extra-wide hips. When the bloated ball of fur was finally able to force itself through the gate, it nearly overbalanced. After a herculean effort, requiring much flailing of each of its furry appendages, the creature managed to stay on its feet.

"Should we clap?" Diana whispered to Darcie

"I don't think so," Darcie said in her rich tones. She had never quite mastered the fine art of whispering. "He seems a little bitter about the whole situation."

Diana could certainly understand that. The fur-covered creature—Diana's brain refused to acknowledge that it was Joey—waddled toward them. After a few seconds, Diana decided *waddle* was a bit of a stretch to describe the way the furball moved. The fuzzy fellow utilized more of a hopping motion. Fur-Ball hopped on one foot while kicking out the other foot high in front of him. But he did it all without bending his knees. It was like some bizarre new dance step. The closer he came, the easier it was for Diana to accept the fact that the fur ball was, indeed, Joey Finch. And, she decided, figuring out what had happened was simple. While she was fighting off a psychotic kidnapper, her handsome boyfriend had, tragically, been swallowed by a bear.

Whole.

"You see it, too, right?" she asked Darcie, just to make sure.

"Uh-huh." Darcie nodded. "It's like I can't look away. I want to," she added, "but I can't."

Diana glanced at the lady pirate, who sat beside her totally unaffected by the strangeness of it all. Darcie's calm acceptance of the situation made Diana question her own sanity.

Was she dreaming?

Had the stress of her third failed kidnapping attempt sent her over the edge?

Had she hit her head when Psycho Bill tackled her? She had to admit she felt a little woozy....

Or maybe there was a logical explanation for whatever this was.

Diana watched the furry-bear-that-ate-her-boyfriend hop toward her. She tried to ignore the way he seemed to list to the right, almost as if the ground was tilting. She sat perfectly still. *Wait a minute,* she thought. *The ground* is *tilting.*

As a matter of fact, the whole world was tilting.

Very slowly.

And Diana was getting warm, too.

Very, very warm.

Diana felt herself tipping inexorably to the right. Fur-Ball deserved a lot of credit, she mused. He had excellent balance. She didn't quite understand how he was still able to walk: it must be difficult with the ground pitching back and forth. If her vision would clear up—the wavy lines were getting in the way—she would have a better idea how he was doing it.

Perhaps she was in the middle of an earthquake. That was a logical explanation for what she was currently feeling. She grabbed the bench, holding on with both hands. She tried to turn her head to see if Darcie was still there, but that was when Fur-Ball started spinning. Around and around and around.

She couldn't take her eyes off him.

Diana closed her eyes, but it didn't help. Now, she was the one who was spinning.

She could hear Darcie's voice coming from a distance. Darcie must have fallen off the bench. Now, Darcie was talking. To her. No, not to her.

Darcie was talking to herself. No, that wasn't right, either.

Darcie was talking to someone. No, two someones.

Some-Two, Diana thought. She would have chuckled if she wasn't so tired. Sometimes she was downright hilarious.

The Hilarious Nanny and Some-Two.

Sounded like a promising start to a new series. Or the title of some long-lost Dr. Seuss book.

Devin's deep voice blended with Darcie's. She heard another deeper voice. Blane? Whoever it was, she could hear them talking. She just couldn't see them. She couldn't see anything....

Diana slumped onto her side.

"Di-a-na!" Joey dove toward the bench, making it just in time to cushion Diana's fall with his enormous belly as she slid, silently, to the ground.

CHAPTER FORTY-FIVE

*N*o one could ever accuse Joey Finch of being a morning person. He did *not* have the ability to be charming the minute he got out of bed, unlike his sister Grace. Nor did he possess the early morning vitality of his sister Darcie.

He was the *other* Finch sibling. The one who groaned when the alarm went off at seven o'clock in the morning. The one who spoke in monosyllabic grunts until after his coffee, workout, and shower. In that order.

The fact that he was currently lying in bed at the crack of dawn with a goofy, lovesick smile on his face was wholly attributed to the gorgeous redhead lying next to him. Well, not next to him, exactly. As far as proximities went, he decided, she was sort of draped over him, a detail that made his grin widen.

Watching Diana slide from the bench and onto the ground a few hours earlier had taken a year off his life. He had never felt so helpless. Until that moment, he hadn't allowed himself to consider the possibility that Diana might be hurt. He didn't know what he would do if something happened to her. But—and he had thanked God many times since she opened her eyes—she had escaped with only a few scratches.

She was, however, exhausted by the attack. The subsequent interview with the police hadn't helped, either. Although necessary, their questions required her to relive the entire unnerving experience again. Diana was amazing, Joey thought. She never faltered. Never cried. Never gave any sign of the terror she must have felt. She had, however, kept a tight grip on his furry hand the whole time.

His ridiculous costume had come in handy, providing the levity so desperately needed. Getting him back to Heart's Ease—deemed the safest place for Diana—had been hilarious enough. The efforts to extract him from the furry death trap were hysterical. In the end, Rafe took pity on him, producing a pair of his own "special" pliers. The wily fellow cut him out of the costume from neck to belly. Joey's relief at stepping out of the pile of fur surpassed even the good-natured barbs from his audience. He chuckled quietly as he lay there in bed, remembering their suggestions of stuffing the carcass to display it on the porch of Parker and Finch or turning the furry mass into a rug.

The sound of Diana's small, breathy sigh brought his thoughts back to the present. She was currently tucked against his side, her right leg tossed over both of his, her head lying on his shoulder. Her glorious hair spread out over his chest. He studied her lovely face, glad she was sleeping peacefully. The alarming specter of Psycho Bill had apparently refrained from haunting her dreams. Or, perhaps, those dreams had been all about Joey Finch.

Joey hoped so, anyway. In the aftermath of another attack, he had done his best to distract her. Hell, who was he kidding? *He* was the one who had been distracted. He was completely spellbound. Making love to Diana was an all-encompassing experience full of sensations he didn't know were possible and emotions he hadn't known he had.

Maybe it was the feelings she inspired or maybe it was the overwhelming realization that he could have lost her. Joey wasn't sure, but after Diana drifted off to sleep—exhausted and sated—he found himself in the grip of fear. Not a casual fear, like when the lights went out unexpectedly, but an all-encompassing, annihilating, sickening terror. He found himself sweating, shaking, completely incapable of drawing a deep breath. The *what-ifs* crowded his mind, devouring his ability to reason.

He silently climbed out of bed, searching desperately for a distraction. That's when he saw Diana's computer. Spending a little time with Ezekiel and Genevieve forced him to focus on something else. As his fear dissipated, however, he was left with a few questions. Questions that could be answered only by the sleeping woman he quietly rejoined in the bed.

He studied her face in the pale light. Her long eyelashes fanned out below her eyelids. A slight sprinkling of freckles stood out against the delicate flush of her cheeks. She was beautiful, yes, but she was so much more. He admired her bravery and her resourcefulness. She had, apparently, done a number on Psycho Bill, kicking him in the face like that. It made Joey incredibly proud and, at the same time, nearly sick with the supposition of what could have happened if her aim had failed.

Diana was, without a doubt, the love of his life. Anyone previously acquainted with Joey Finch—*one and done*—would be astounded at the ease with which the former bachelor embraced his fate. But to Joey the process had been effortless, as automatic as breathing. And now she was his. The most important thing in his world. To cherish. To protect. The woman he wanted for all time. The knowledge both humbled and empowered him. It also caused him to question his own mental capacity. What kind of an idiot was he for waiting nine years to be with someone like Diana?

"I can hear you thinking," Diana said, softly, without opening her eyes.

"Diana, love," Joey began, enjoying the sweet smile that appeared on her face at his words. She took his breath. She really did. That's why his question was so important. "Diana, love," he repeated. "Am I stalwart?" He wasn't surprised when her eyelids popped open.

She frowned in sleepy confusion. "Are you...? What?"

"Stalwart. Lionhearted. You know, a warrior. A knight in shining armor." Joey paused for clarification. "*Your* knight in shining armor."

"My knight in...?" Her sweet smile disappeared as the reason for his question dawned on her. "Joey Finch, have you been reading my novel?" Sitting up, she took stock of her surroundings. Her rose gold computer was open on the desk in the corner. She looked at him questioningly. "How did you...?"

He couldn't help but grin at her response. "You *gave* me your password, remember?"

She frowned, sleepily. "Yes, but that doesn't mean you can just read my novel without asking." She crossed her arms, huffing out a frustrated breath. She was adorable.

"*Our* novel," Joey corrected.

Diana's eyebrows went up. "And how do you figure that?"

"Well, it's about *us*," Joey said. "Duh."

"It is *not* about us."

"Of course it is." Joey relaxed back against the pillows, preparing to defend his case.

Diana pointed her finger at him accusingly. "You, Joey Finch, are not an earl. Nor are you an injured war veteran." She considered him a moment. "Although you are something of a rake."

"A reformed rake," he corrected her, with an unrepentant grin.

"A reformed rake." Diana conceded that point, much to his satisfaction. "However, Mr. Finch, Genevieve is a governess, not a nanny."

"Governess...nanny..." Joey shrugged. "Same thing."

"No, Joey, it's not. A governess is primarily a live-in teacher and a nanny is..." Diana started to explain but gave up at the confident smirk on Joey's face. "Anyway, Genevieve teaches Ezekiel's wards. *You* don't have any wards."

But Joey was prepared with his counterpoints. He had been awake for quite a while. "*Genevieve* takes care of Ezekiel's brother's children. *You* take care of my future brother-in-law's child."

"Oh, whatever." Diana fell back against the pillows in defeat, closing her eyes. She waited for Joey to gloat over his victory. Instead, he gently shook her shoulder.

"Diana," he said. "Diana."

She cracked open one eye. She was mentally exhausted—thanks to another fun-filled encounter with a psychotic kidnapper. She was physically exhausted—thanks to the amorous attentions of the man beside her. And she was just a little irritated that Joey had read her novel without asking. "*I* think you need to stop reading so much into *my* novel. And maybe you can start by *asking* before you open *my* computer."

"Hush, Diana," Joey said, urgently. "You can give me my boundaries later. Just, answer my question. Am I stalwart...like Ezekiel?" A strange tension had replaced his smile.

Diana opened her other eye, propping herself up on her elbows to regard him curiously. "Joey, what are you really talking about?" She could tell that he was worried about something, that her answer was important. He looked exhausted. Dark shadows loomed under his eyes. An unusual frown lurked on his face. She reached out a hand to touch his cheek, intensely aware of the prickly feel of his overnight growth of beard. "Of course you're stalwart, Joey," she began soothingly. "You're the most..."

But Joey didn't want to be placated. He brushed off her hand and got out of the bed. Once his feet hit the floor, he started pacing the room. "No, Diana," he disagreed. "I'm not. I'm not stalwart. I'm not lionhearted. I'm not a warrior. And I'm certainly nobody's knight in shining armor. As a matter of fact, I'm about as far away as I can be from any of those things."

Diana watched him pace with growing concern. It was unlike Joey to doubt himself. "I don't understand," she whispered. What had gotten into him?

He returned to the bed. "Don't you?" He sat down on the mattress, taking both of her hands in his. "I didn't save you," he said.

Diana's lovely brow clouded with worry. "But, Joey, it doesn't matter who..."

"Ezekiel fought off Genevieve's attacker with a sword. A *sword*, Diana. *He* saved her, but I didn't save you."

She squeezed his hands. Hard. "But Joey..."

"I. Didn't. Save. You," he reiterated. He leaned forward to place his forehead on her hands. "You needed me," he mumbled. "And I showed up in a damn bear suit."

"It wasn't a bear suit, Joey," Diana was quick to point out. "It was a wolf costume. And you were wearing it…" Her voice trailed away as Joey raised his head, his eyes burning into hers.

"I love you more than…more than…Damn it, Diana. I would do anything for you. *Anything*."

"I know," she said, softly. "I would do anything for you, too."

"But when you needed me most, I was tripping over my own feet."

"They weren't *your* feet," Diana said, kindly. "They were…"

Joey continued as if she hadn't spoken. "Yeah, the wolf's feet. And you were fighting for your life. Alone. That isn't very warrior-like. Ezekiel would have…"

"But Joey, you wore that wolf suit for *me*." Diana placed her hands on either side of his face. "And you wore it because you thought *I* wanted you to wear it. Even though you looked ridiculous."

"Yeah," Joey grimaced.

"And even though Devin and Blane are going to make fun of you for the rest of your life," she pointed out helpfully.

"Yeah, and even though I felt like a fool," Joey added; but looking into Diana's glowing eyes, he realized he *didn't* feel like a fool anymore. He felt like a hero. Her stalwart, lionhearted hero. Her warrior. Maybe, even, her knight in shining armor.

"Don't you see, Joey?" Diana asked. "Wearing that bear suit…"

"Wolf suit," Joey corrected with great dignity.

"Wolf suit," Diana agreed, smiling. "It's easy to say the words—*I'll do anything for you*—but it's harder to live them, Joey." She shrugged. "You did." Diana's smile turned mischievous. "Besides, the thought of you with a sword is terrifying."

Joey put his arm around her and pulled her snugly to his side. "Diana, why aren't *you* terrified?" It was a legitimate question. Every time

Joey thought about how close he had come to losing her, *he* was terrified out of his mind. He broke out in a cold sweat just thinking about it.

"But I was, Joey," Diana admitted quickly. "When I realized you weren't under that mask, I was—"

"But why aren't you terrified now?" Joey interrupted. "Lord knows I am. In the aftermath. Why aren't you afraid in the aftermath? I don't understand how you do it."

Her words couldn't have surprised him more. "It's because of you, Joey," she said, simply.

"But I obviously can't protect you, so why...?"

"Now you hush." Diana took a deep breath. "I've thought about it a lot, because the first time—after I jumped out of the boat—I was so frightened that I couldn't even think about what had happened. I tried to block it from my mind, the same way I did after finding Mallory's body. But the second time, I ran into you." She paused, ducking her head, as if a little embarrassed. "This is going to sound *exactly* like a romance novel, but— even when things look the worst—I can only picture one ending for you and me. A happy one. You, Joey Finch, are my happily ever after."

Joey was made speechless by her unconscious declaration. His heart was so full, he feared it would explode.

Diana waited anxiously, hoping he would understand what she was trying to say. Far from looking askance at her words, his smile nearly melted her heart.

"You mean breakfast-together-every-morning happily ever after?" he asked.

Diana nodded. "Uh-huh. With biscuits and bacon."

"And unmade-beds-and-dirty-socks-on-the-floor happily ever after?" Joey asked, getting into the spirit of things. "And dogs-and-kids-and-rocking-on-the-front-porch-when-we're-happily-ever-after old?"

Diana smiled, trying to ignore the prickling at the corners of her eyes.

"And white-dress-toss-the-bouquet-honeymoon happily ever after?" he asked gently.

"Joey," Diana squealed, "we've only been dating two weeks! Officially," she added as an afterthought.

"Two weeks?" Joey asked, feigning shock. "Woman, you've been in my head for nine years. I just didn't realize, until recently, that you were in my heart, too."

They were the sweetest words Diana could ever imagine. And that was saying a lot for someone who was writing a romance novel.

Joey sighed, tugging her a little closer. "We'll have to wait a little while, though."

"To give everyone a chance to get used to the idea," Diana agreed.

"Nope," Joey said. "To give your cousin and my sister a chance to get married. After everything Darcie and Devin have been through, she would kill me if I beat her to the altar." Joey shuddered in mock terror.

Diana couldn't help but laugh. She wasn't in any kind of hurry. She was just...happy.

"I can see it now," Joey said, with great satisfaction. "Mr. and Mrs. Joseph Ezekiel Finch, Sr., request the honor of your presence at the marriage of their son, Joseph Ezekiel Finch, Jr., to..."

Diana was quick to correct her future husband's breech of etiquette "The bride's parents do the inviting, Joey, or the bride and groom do it together. But even then, the bride's name comes first." The words were out of her mouth before she considered the consequences.

"All right then, Miss Proper." Joey grinned, clearing his throat. "Mr. and Mrs. Barrett Merritt request the honor of your presence at the marriage of their lovely, charming, multi-talented daughter, Diana..." He paused, waiting for her to fill in the middle name.

"Merritt," Diana said. *Drat.* How was she going to get out of this? Her face felt hot; she knew her cheeks were flushed. She hoped Joey wouldn't notice in the pale light of dawn.

Joey glanced at the lovely, charming, multi-talented—and slightly flushed—woman in his bed. "Diana...?" he said, again, raising his eyebrows.

Diana raised her eyebrows in reply. "Mer-ritt," she finished firmly.

Joey was intrigued. It appeared that the lovely, charming, multi-tal-ented—and *extremely* flushed—Miss Merritt was unwilling to reveal her middle name. His curiosity was roused at her reluctance to share some-thing so mundane. Or maybe not so mundane.

He decided to be straightforward. "What's your middle name, Diana?"

"Maybe I don't have one," she replied pertly.

"Hmm," Joey said, studying her. "Oh, you have one, all right," he said, smugly. "I can tell. And it must be awful." He appeared genuinely pleased by that.

Diana refused to yield. "Maybe you're wrong. And anyway, why do you seem so happy that I might possibly—and I said *possibly*, mind you— have an awful middle name?"

Joey put one hand over his heart. "It makes you more human, my dear Diana, in the face of your sheer perfection."

Diana rolled her eyes. "Good heavens."

"Olga?" he guessed.

"No."

"Helga?"

"No."

"Wilhelmina?"

"No, and why do you think it's German, anyway?" she asked indig-nantly. "My ancestors were English."

"Ah-ha," Joey crowed, triumphantly. "So, you *do* have a middle name. I knew it." He looked so pleased with himself that Diana had to laugh. It was only a matter of time until he found out, anyway, she decided, so she might as well let him have a little fun.

His guesses came fast and furiously. "Ermengarde? Ethel? Gladys? Agnes?"

She regarded him in mock dismay. "Seriously?"

"Fanny, Matilda, Eunice, Hephzibah?"

"Hephzibah? Really, Joey? You don't think much of my parents, do you?"

"How about Gertrude?"

Diana simply looked at him.

"That's it, isn't it?" Joey grinned in triumph. "Diana Gertrude Merritt. We can name our first daughter Gertrude and call her Gertie for short."

"Poor thing," Diana commiserated with her unknown future daughter. She took advantage of Joey's distraction to climb on top of him, straddling him with her thighs. He groaned his approval, bringing a temporary halt to their game. Hmm, Diana thought. Perhaps she was on to something. Some games were more fun than others. She bent forward slowly, her lips nearly touching the muscled expanse of Joey's chest.

But, as Diana failed to remember, anyone who underestimated Joey Finch did so at his or her peril. Before Diana's lips could reach their target, she found herself flat on her back, their positions reversed. Now, Joey leaned over, his own lips tantalizingly close to the warm, tempting spot where Diana's neck met her shoulder. He pressed an open-mouthed kiss to her skin, then blew lightly. Diana shivered, her body melting at his touch. Joey kissed his way up her neck, slowly ascending to her ear. His hands closed gently on her wrists, effectively pinning her to the mattress. Diana closed her eyes, luxuriating in the sensations he provoked.

"And now, my love," he breathed, punctuating each of his words with a kiss. "What. Is. Your. Middle. Name?"

Diana's eyes flew open. She was trapped. She knew it. And Joey knew it, too. And he was enjoying himself tremendously, if the expression on his face was any indication. They would both enjoy themselves tremendously in just a few minutes anyway. She could tell from his shift in position. But she couldn't resist teasing him one more time.

"My middle name is"—she turned her face into her pillow—"Jinuumbean." At the same time, she rubbed her hips against his.

"Oh, no," he said, wickedly. "Behave yourself, my lady. And you shall be richly rewarded for your endeavors." He waggled his eyebrows up and down, making Diana laugh aloud.

"Genevieve," she said, simply.

He looked at her in surprise. "What?"

"My middle name is Genevieve," she said, ruefully. "Diana Genevieve Merritt."

"Of course, it is," Joey nodded, a slow smile suffusing his features. He didn't know why he hadn't seen it before. Diana Genevieve Merritt fit her perfectly. Just like she fit him. Diana and Joey. Genevieve and Ezekiel. She was his match in every way. And he couldn't wait to get started, reminding her precisely how perfectly they fit together.

"I love you, Joey Finch," she said, gazing at him with her heart in her dark, gray eyes. "I knew all along you were more than just a one and done. And I was right. Now, you're my one and *never* done."

He rolled the phrase around in his mind for a few seconds. "Your one and *never* done, hmm? I think I like that." His grin turned surprisingly wolfish, causing Diana to giggle. "What's so funny?" he asked, waggling his eyebrows wickedly.

"Because..." she explained, "...when you look at me like that, you look exactly like the Big Bad Wolf." Diana laughed at his shocked expression. "*Before* Grandma," she hurried to add.

"No stupid little cap?" he asked.

"No stupid little cap," she confirmed.

"C'mere, Red Riding Hood," Joey growled, determined that this time, the Wolf would have his own happily ever after.

After Diana drifted off to sleep, Joey stared wide-eyed at the ceiling. Psycho Bill was still on the loose. Diana's attacker had vanished into the woods despite Blane and Devin's best efforts to catch him. Vanished, Joey fumed. Literally. Like some demonic spirit returning to the depths of hell. Until the next time. And Joey had no doubt there would be a next time.

He released a pent-up, frustrated breath. Maybe the aftermath of Psycho Bill's third attack was messing with his head, but Joey couldn't seem to shake the bone-deep certainty that the future of his and Diana's happily ever after rested entirely with him. He didn't know what would happen— the how's or the when's—but he somehow knew that his actions and his actions alone would decide the outcome. He could only pray that when the time came, he would be ready.

And not dressed as a damn bear.

CHAPTER FORTY-SIX

*J*oey watched Diana's face as the echo of the last shot floated away on the crisp, morning breeze. He almost laughed at her incredulous expression.

"I still can't believe it," she said, handing him the binoculars. "Even though it happened right in front of me."

Joey grinned in satisfaction. "Told you so," he said, smugly. His plan to distract Diana from the trauma of the night before was working.

Her eyes shone with enthusiasm. "Some of my cousins shoot skeet. And I've always been impressed with their skill. Until now," she added. "Alina is amazing. I have *never* seen such accurate shooting in my life."

Joey hoisted himself up from the blanket they had occupied for the last half hour. "You've heard Blane and Devin talk about how Ian and Alina worked for the "government"—the UK, I'm assuming—and how they think Rafe did, too?" He extended his hand to help Diana up. At her nod, he continued: "Well, after watching Alina's crazy ability with firearms I'm convinced she was an assassin."

"She prefers the term 'sharpshooter.' "

The words came out of nowhere. Joey startled, turning his head in the direction the voice had come from. Diana, too, had flinched at the words; she would have fallen to the ground if Joey hadn't maintained his grip on her hand. There was no mistaking the amusement lighting up Rafe Montgomery's face as he stepped out of the trees. Joey scowled in return, trying to slow his beating heart. The unpredictable man moved like a wraith, always appearing—and disappearing—without warning. Joey turned his attention back to Diana, who looked equally flustered.

"Easy, now," he said as Diana regained her footing. He didn't blame her for being on edge. He was jumpy himself. " 'Sharpshooter,' then," Joey said to Rafe, slightly embarrassed for calling the man's daughter an assassin. And for being caught.

But Rafe wasn't remotely bothered by Joey's faux pas. Instead, he smiled at Diana. "Did you enjoy Alina's target practice, Diana?"

"Oh, yes," Diana said, her enthusiasm returning. "She's amazing."

Rafe looked across the clearing toward his daughter, his eyes full of fatherly pride. "I may be slightly biased, but I agree." When he turned back to Diana, however, he was all business. "Diana, we would like to talk with you when you return to the house."

Uh-oh, Diana thought, with a sinking heart. *We.* She knew exactly to whom Rafe was referring. When her eyes met Joey's, she could tell he was thinking the same thing.

"And who exactly *is* 'we,' Rafe?" Joey asked politely.

The lines around Rafe's eyes crinkled with humor. "Why, I'm talking about the Trio of Doom, of course," he said, clapping a hand on Joey's shoulder. With a wink for Diana, he turned around and disappeared into the trees.

Diana put her hands on her hips, studying the face of her innocent-looking boyfriend. "I wonder how Rafe found out I call his little band of inquisitors the Trio of Doom," she remarked. "You don't happen to know anything about that, now do you, Joey Finch?"

"Oh, look," Joey said, quickly. "Here come Ian and Alina." The appearance of Blane's aunt and uncle put a halt to Joey's own personal inquisition.

The conversation wasn't over, though, if the expression on Diana's face was any indication.

"Good morning," Joey called out to the approaching pair. They had arrived from Scotland the day before to attend the ribbon-cutting and other events connected to the opening of McCallum Industries' new North American headquarters the following week. Blane's grandfather had also accompanied them.

There was no doubt that Ian and Alina were a striking couple. Ian possessed the same broad shoulders and impressive build as Blane—his nephew—and Douglas—his half brother. The resemblance was striking, except for Ian's red hair, which he must have inherited from his mother. His accent—with that lovely Scottish burr—was charming. At least in Diana's opinion.

Alina, in contrast, was tiny. The top of her head didn't reach her husband's shoulder. Perfectly proportioned and delicate, she was an exquisite beauty with her dark hair and large, liquid eyes. Alina, however, possessed hidden depths, if the bits and pieces of conversation Diana had, inadvertently, overheard could be trusted. She had always assumed Devin and Blane were exaggerating Alina's "special skills and abilities." But after watching Alina hit target after target, Diana was starting to wonder. Alina's prowess with firearms, coupled with the fact that she was the daughter of the ever-mysterious Rafe Montgomery, made her seem quite formidable indeed. She would make the perfect heroine of a romance novel.

The Heart of a Spy. Something like that.

Diana knew for a fact that Ian and Alina had worked for the "government" before Blane went to live with them. But which government? No one seemed to know. She had listened to Devin and Blane speculate about Rafe's former employer(s) many times. MI6? CIA? Or some other secret government agency? Was Rafe involved in espionage? Were Ian and Alina? The details were simply too hazy and obscure. Blane and Devin had never come to a satisfactory conclusion regarding Rafe's mysterious past.

Ian and Alina didn't look like spies, Diana decided as the couple drew closer. Sporting Barbour field jackets and boots, they were the epitome of outdoor chic. Even Alina's hat—a fedora with tartan trim—was stylish and sophisticated. But Diana was quick to acknowledge that something about the attractive pair, some undefinable quality—a focus to their eyes that conveyed a hyperawareness of their surroundings, perhaps—gave the impression they were more than they appeared to be.

"I wasn't expecting an audience," Alina said in her funny, little accent...rather like Spanish with a soft Scottish burr.

Diana smiled. "Thank you for letting us watch your target practice. You are amazing."

Ian grinned proudly. "She never misses. Do you, love?"

"Not since I was seventeen," Alina agreed easily. The way she said the words didn't sound like a boast.

Diana couldn't help but speculate. Was Alina, in fact, telling the truth? A quick glance at Joey told her he was wondering the same thing.

As though to acknowledge their suspicions, Ian furrowed his brow, giving his wife a searching look. "I don't know about that, love," he said. "You missed *me* when you were quite a bit older than seventeen."

A tiny smile teased the corner of Alina's elegant lips. "That is because I *meant* to miss you, Ian" she said, giving Diana a conspiratorial wink. "I missed you on purpose."

"On purpose?" Ian asked in genuine surprise. "That's the first time I've ever heard you say you missed me on purpose." He mulled Alina's revelation over in his mind for a few seconds before a wide grin split his face. "And I know exactly why you missed."

"Oh, really?" Alina asked, fluttering her eyelashes at her husband. "Then, please enlighten us, Ian." She gestured to Joey and Diana, including them in this bizarre conversation. "We all want to know. Why didn't I shoot you when the opportunity presented itself? Hmm?"

Ian smiled triumphantly. "Simple. You deliberately missed me because you were in love with me." He shook a playful finger at his wife. "Don't you dare try to deny it."

Alina shook her head, her eyes sparkling with laughter. "No, my love," she said. "You—are wrong. I missed you because I felt sorry for you."

She addressed Joey and Diana, who were regarding her with something like awe. "Ian is a terrible shot," she informed them.

" 'Terrible' is rather harsh, Alina." Ian looked a little affronted. "Shall we say, instead, that my skill level doesn't quite measure up to yours?"

Alina's smile widened. She was thoroughly enjoying teasing her husband. Or was she teasing? Diana couldn't quite decide.

"Why were you shooting at Ian?" Joey asked Alina, unable to contain his curiosity any longer.

"Jo-ey!" Diana scolded, nudging him with her elbow. "That might be private."

Alina's laughter pealed like bells in the quiet morning. "No, no. It is fine. Ian had done nothing wrong. My shooting at him was an accident of ignorance, you see?"

"Um…" Diana clearly did not see. Joey appeared equally flummoxed by Alina's cryptic statement.

"Try again, love," Ian encouraged, amusement in his eyes.

"An accident of ignorance on *my* part," Alina continued. "Not his. I tried to shoot him *before* we discovered that we were on the same side."

"Oh," Diana said, breathlessly. Another glance at Joey revealed that he was just as fascinated at the glimpse into Ian and Alina's past as she was.

Alina smiled at their reaction. "And now, you see?" At their nods of affirmation, she turned to Ian. "We should get back, don't you think?"

Ian offered his arm in a courtly gesture. "Whatever you say, love." Before Alina joined him, he winked at Joey and Diana. "I'm afraid not to agree with her," he said in an overly loud whisper. "She might try to shoot me again." Alina popped him smartly on the shoulder before linking her arm with his.

Diana tried not to giggle as she and Joey followed the intriguing pair onto the path that led back to the house. They couldn't help but overhear the rest of their conversation. "Admit it, Alina," Ian encouraged. "You didn't shoot me because you were in love with me."

Alina raised up on her toes to kiss his cheek. "Maybe a little," she admitted, a smile in her voice.

Joey and Diana dropped back, letting their distance from the other couple widen. "What about you, Diana?" Joey asked. "Are you in love with me?"

"Hmm," she murmured, coyly. "Maybe a little."

Joey's response to her words kept them under cover of the trees just a bit longer.

CHAPTER FORTY-SEVEN

*B*y the time Joey and Diana joined the others in the grand foyer of Heart's Ease, the Trio of Doom had swelled its numbers. The original three—Rafe, Blane, and Devin—were seated on the sofa in the northern part of the foyer; their backs turned to the ballroom. Ian, Alina, and Grace occupied the sofa directly across from them, their backs to the large windows at the front of the house. Darcie was already seated on the sofa placed at a right angle to the other two. It was opposite the large, stone fireplace on the western end of the foyer. She smiled when they entered the room, patting the cushion in invitation. Diana sank down beside Darcie. Joey sat on Diana's other side.

The new additions made the title "Trio of Doom" a misnomer, Diana realized, trying to ignore the crawling anxiety threatening to take over her heart and lungs. She latched onto the suddenly urgent need to find a new name for the group. The Suspicious Seven, perhaps? That was a pretty good one. Or what about the Seven Spies? Probably not a good idea, she realized, when three of them actually were spies in real life. What about the Snooping Seven? Or even better…the Seven Snoops.

Nanny Di and the Seven Little Snoops.

She almost giggled, thinking it over before discarding the charming title. While a delightful idea for a future children's book, the words did not reflect the severity of her current situation. She finally settled on the Septet of Supposition. She was aware some might argue there were eight people in the room besides her, but she refused to count Joey. He was on *her* side.

However, a quick glance at the concerned faces around the room confirmed what Diana already knew. The rest of them were on her side, too, she conceded. She was finally able to acknowledge the truth, even if part of her rebelled against the necessity of answering their questions. Joey bumped her shoulder with his own. For moral support, she supposed. His presence gave her the courage for the ordeal ahead.

"Shall we begin?" she asked the inquisitors.

Rafe nodded, pleased with her initiative. "Diana, I would like for you to tell us exactly what happened, starting with..."

As it turned out, Diana's third interrogation at the hands of the Trio of Doom—or, rather, the recently upgraded Septet of Supposition—was very different than the previous two. Or, she was willing to admit, perhaps *she* was what was different. The first time she had stubbornly refused to *listen*. The second time, she had stubbornly refused to *talk*. But with Joey sitting beside her, the words poured out. She related every detail from the past week, beginning with when she received the first rose and ending when Psycho Bill disappeared into the thick woods behind the playground.

Rafe studied Diana hopefully. "Is there any way you came into contact with your attacker's blood? On your costume, perhaps?"

Diana hesitated. "I don't know...I mean, I guess it's possible but... Wait a minute," she gasped, remembering. "When I pulled off the mask 'Bill' was wearing, half of it was soaked with blood from his nose. Then..." She struggled to remember what happened after that. "I must have dropped it," she said, regretfully.

"You did," Darcie said, excitedly. "You dropped it when you passed out. I didn't know whether or not it was part of your costume, so I stuffed it in your pocket."

Rafe's face suffused with excitement. "Where is your costume now, Diana?"

"On the floor of my bathroom," Diana said, already standing.

She rushed up the stairs, Darcie on her heels. A ripple of anticipation swept through those who remained. When the pair returned a few minutes later, Diana was waving the stained mask victoriously in the air. She handed the bloody mask to Rafe, who received it almost reverently.

"Great work, Diana," Rafe said. He rose to his feet, barely able to tamp down his excitement. "You, too, Darcie."

Diana grimaced. "Thanks, but it was a happy accident. I wasn't exactly thinking clearly at the time. Just an instinctive response, I guess."

"Great instincts, Diana," Joey grinned, proud of her contribution. He patted her seat on the sofa beside him. Diana sat back down, but Darcie waited, hands on hips, for her brother's praise. When none was forthcoming, she stuck out her tongue before resuming her former spot on the sofa.

"So, what happens now?" she asked, anticipation on her face.

When Rafe hesitated, Alina answered for him. "Now our associates will find out if Bill is in our data bank. He's bound to be, given what we know about him."

"And...?" Darcie prompted.

Alina smiled at her persistence. "And, if so, we will know his true identity and how he fits into the puzzle."

Darcie frowned. "Puzzle? What puzzle?"

The rest of the company exchanged curious glances. Clearly, nobody—with the exception of Rafe and Ian—had the slightest idea what Alina was talking about. Diana's writer's mind was running amuck with options. Was it possible that Rafe, Ian, and Alina were *still* working for the government? *A* government? *Some* government *somewhere*? Were they, even now, involved in an undercover operation? She was inclined to believe almost anything after seeing Alina's "target practice" earlier. Not to mention listening to Ian and Alina's tantalizing conversation. Besides, *our associates* and *data bank* sounded official and mysterious. Or maybe that was because of Alina's funny accent. Still, Diana felt as if she had fallen asleep and awakened in the middle of a James Bond movie.

Alina regarded her father—who was looking at the ceiling—questioningly. "Papi…" she scolded, "…why is it that only Ian and I seem to know what I'm talking about? Hmm?"

Rafe blew out an impatient breath. He waved the bloody mask at his daughter. "We have crucial evidence in our hands, Alina. I don't have time to explain every nuance of the puzzle.'"

Ian snorted with laughter. "Give it up, Rafe," he advised. "You've seen that look on Alina's face before. You might as well sit down and start explaining." He nodded sagely at his father-in-law…the voice of experience.

Sighing heavily, Rafe resumed his seat even though it was patently obvious he would rather be elsewhere.

"And now, the puzzle…" Darcie said, eagerly.

The air in the grand foyer thickened with anticipation. And dread. Diana could feel it. Perhaps it was the result of her most recent brush with danger. Or maybe it was her reluctance to reveal the small and—she hoped—insignificant detail she still hadn't told anyone: Bill was standing in the hallway after she found Mallory's corpse. Whatever the cause, the details of that awful day exploded in Diana's brain. She closed her eyes, waiting for the crushing guilt that always followed the horrible memory—guilt that Mallory's death was somehow her fault.

"Diana." Joey's whispered word pierced her consciousness. His hand clasped hers securely, warm and comforting. He was safety amid a swirling storm of uncertainty. She opened her eyes. "Are you okay?" he asked, watching her closely.

She nodded, squeezing his hand. She smiled weakly.

Joey was relieved even though Diana's smile was a shadow of its usual self. He would whisk her away, he decided, as soon as possible. "Go ahead, Rafe," he said, aware that the group was regarding Diana with concern… the last thing she needed.

Rafe nodded in resignation. "A year and a half ago, Kenneth Wade, an employee of McCallum Industries, accidentally stumbled upon information implicating another McCallum employee in an illegal—and quite extensive—drug operation. One that had nothing whatsoever to do with McCallum Industries, I might add." He glanced at McCallum Industries' CEO.

"Thank God for that," Blane said, ruefully.

Rafe nodded once, then continued. "Anyway, Wade decided to blackmail the guilty employee. He threatened to tell McCallum Industries' head of Legal everything he had discovered. He made an urgent appointment with Devin. Under the circumstances it's not surprising that the guilty employee—let's call him the Mastermind—decided Wade had to be eliminated."

"But Wade never kept that appointment," Devin added. "He went on a cruise instead."

Rafe confirmed the point. "When the ship docked in Belize, he went zip-lining and died in a freak accident. We, of course, now know that Wade's death was, in fact, no accident. A few days later, you, Devin, nearly died when a car plowed into you. Which brings us to the question—"

"Were Wade's death and Devin's attack connected?" Darcie supplied. She paused a minute for Rafe to answer. When he didn't, she continued. "Well...were they?"

"Yes," Rafe said. "We now have an informant who is in possession of quite a few pieces of the puzzle, if you will. Yesterday, this woman—a former colleague gone bad, actually—waltzed right into the offices of our associates desperate to make a deal. Ian," Rafe said, "I'll let you tell this part."

Ian smoothly took over. "The woman, who now goes by the name Calliope, confirmed our suspicions about Wade's death. She claims she was paid by the Mastermind's second-in-command to lure Kenneth Wade to the top of the zipline platform from which he plummeted to his death. I'm sure you all remember that the official report from Belize determined a faulty harness was to blame. Calliope has identified the man who paid for—and was present during—the tampering of the harness and Wade's death."

"Was it Bill?" Blane asked. "Was Bill the man who arranged Wade's murder? Is he Second-in-Command?"

Rafe shook his head. "No, Blane. Bill didn't go to Belize. At the time of Wade's murder Bill was in Newport trying to—"

"—Get rid of me," Devin interrupted. "Just in case Wade had already spilled the beans to me about the Mastermind's illegal operation."

Rafe nodded. "Calliope confirmed what we have suspected all along, Devin. Your vehicular attack was not supposed to happen. It was the direct result of misinformation. Bill assumed that Wade had revealed certain details to you before going on his cruise. Details that made you a liability."

Devin nodded. "So, he tried to kill me to keep me quiet. That makes sense. I guess."

"I can't believe it." Diana spoke into the silence that followed Devin's words. How could her cousin be so calm when she was completely horrified? "Bill was driving the car that hit Devin," Diana breathed. "And that was months before he approached me in the park. I see what you mean about connections, Rafe," she said. "All those months, and I had no idea." She turned her troubled eyes to Joey.

Somehow, Joey managed to meet Diana's gaze with an encouraging smile, but inside he was reeling. Devin had nearly died because of the man called Bill. And, now, the same man was trying to kidnap Diana. The same dirty, rotten son of a bitch.

"So, now we know the players," Grace said. "The Mastermind, the Second-in-Command, and Bill. And we know how and why Kenneth Wade was killed, and why Devin was attacked. But how is all this connected to Mallory's murder?"

Ian continued, "According to Calliope, Bill dropped the Mastermind off at your townhouse, Devin, so he could murder Mallory. Then, Bill picked him up afterward."

"So, Bill—the minion—drove the getaway car." Blane said. "Making him an accessory to murder."

"Getaway boat," Ian corrected. "Apparently the Mastermind likes to do things in style."

"But the docks are always under security surveillance," Devin added. "Isn't there a way to check the cameras…" His voice trailed away at Rafe's shake of the head. "Oh, I guess you already thought of that."

"We don't know who we're looking for," Alina said. "We didn't recognize anyone on that dock in the video. Perhaps he's wearing a disguise. Or perhaps the Mastermind used a less visible area for access to and from the boat." She shook her head in frustration. "Believe me, the information from those cameras has been carefully culled. To no avail."

Darcie's expression turned calculating. "So, Bill is the common denominator." She began ticking off the facts on her fingers. "He attacked Devin *because* of Kenneth Wade. He drove the getaway boat. And…"

"…Bill came back to the townhouse," Diana said slowly, aware of the surprised eyes turned her way. "After he drove the getaway boat. He showed up right after I found Mallory's body. He was just…there." Until that moment, she had been unwilling—unable, really—to make herself relive the exact sequence of events that occurred the day she found Mallory's body. She still struggled with the guilt she felt for being late for work that day, as if she, single-handedly, could have prevented Mallory's murder. She hadn't been able to say that out loud, so she hadn't said anything. Until now.

Diana wasn't sure how Rafe would respond now that he knew she had withheld information. Would he be disappointed? Angry? Suspicious of her motives? She met his eyes reluctantly, only to discover she had worried for nothing. Rafe already knew about Bill's post-murder appearance at the townhouse. She could see it on his face. So, it seemed, did Ian and Alina. The others, however, looked at Diana with varying degrees of surprise.

Ian smiled with satisfaction. "Apparently our informant *can* be trusted."

Alina agreed. "Another point in Calliope's favor."

Diana's apology burst through her lips. "I'm sorry, Rafe. I'm so sorry I didn't tell you. I just…couldn't. I couldn't talk about it. I didn't want to think about that day. Or Mallory. Or Bill." Her voice wobbled despite her best efforts to control it. "I was completely hysterical after I found Mallory's body. And Bill just appeared. He helped me. Well, sort of. I mean, now I know he had an ulterior motive, but it felt like he was helping me. He found my phone. He dialed 9-1-1. He even told me what to say at the beginning of the call. I was…grateful. That's why I didn't listen to your advice, Rafe. Or to Blane and Devin when they told me not to go to Newport. That's why I went to meet him anyway. I…I wanted to thank him for helping me."

"And, instead, he tried to kidnap you," Joey said, trying to keep the fear out of his voice. He wished he was lionhearted at that moment, like Ezekiel. He wished he was brave. But he wasn't. At least, not when it came to Diana. Because the mere thought of losing her turned him into a sniveling coward who wanted nothing more than to run away with his lovely lady and hide under a rock until the danger had passed. Some knight in shining armor he was turning out to be, he thought in disgust.

Diana, unaware of Joey's internal struggle, was busy bracing herself for Rafe's reaction. But instead of a reprimand, she received something else entirely.

"We understand, Diana." Rafe's eyes were, indeed, filled with a wealth of understanding. "Sometimes it's easier to pretend the trauma didn't happen or that it happened to someone else."

Diana managed a shaky smile. If Rafe understood, maybe…

"And now, Diana?" Ian asked, gently. "Are you ready to talk about what happened that day?"

Alina smiled. "I know you can do it, Diana," she encouraged.

"Yes," Diana said. "Yes, I think I can." Buoyed by their kindness and the way Joey squeezed her hand encouragingly, Diana took a deep breath. "When I walked into the townhouse…"

CHAPTER FORTY-EIGHT

*H*er audience listened as Diana revealed every heretofore hidden detail of the horrible day Mallory was murdered. She had never been able to talk about it before…even with the therapist her parents had insisted upon hiring. But sitting in the middle of the sofa, clutching Joey's hand, she explained exactly what happened up to and including the bizarre "coincidence" of Bill Watkins' unexpected appearance in the foyer of Devin and Mallory's townhouse.

Her listeners sat in tense silence when she finished. Diana studied the patterns in the Oriental rug beneath her feet, refusing to meet anyone's eyes. Whether or not it was true, she had the uncomfortable feeling everyone in the room was passing judgment. Under the circumstances, she could only pray she was not found wanting.

Rafe finally spoke. "Diana."

Those three syllables, spoken so softly, forced her to raise her head. But instead of looking at Rafe, Diana's eyes flew first to her cousin. "Oh, Dev," she gasped. "I am so sorry I was late that day. If I hadn't been none of this…"

"Stop it, Diana." Her cousin furrowed his brow in distress. "You are *not* going to start blaming yourself—again—for something that was completely out of your control. There was no way you could have known…"

But Rafe didn't let him finish, either. "Diana," he said, again softly. "Look at *me*."

She reluctantly complied. To her surprise, the expression on his face was completely lacking in judgment. Instead, his eyes were filled with empathy. And compassion.

"Diana," Rafe said, again. "Mallory's death was *not* your fault."

His words stunned her. "But, Rafe, if I had been there I could have…"

He shook his head. "I know what you're thinking, Diana. If only you hadn't been late for work, nothing would have happened to Mallory. You could, somehow, have prevented the murder. But I'm telling you that you're wrong. Mallory's murder was *not your fault*.

She gazed at him in disbelief. "But Rafe, I…"

"You couldn't save Mallory," he said, his intense gaze fixed on Diana's face, almost as if he could force her to accept his words as fact. Rafe leaned forward, intently. "Her desire for money and status—her own greed—was to blame for her death. Mallory had an affair with the Mastermind. But she wanted more. She became a liability. He was going to kill her one way or another. If not that day, then some other day. There was nothing you could have done to prevent her murder."

"Oh, Rafe, do you really believe that?"

"I do," Rafe confirmed, briskly.

And, just like that, so did Diana. She believed him. Rafe would *never* make such a statement if it wasn't true.

Joey relaxed his protective vigilance for a moment, pleased by the genuine relief blooming on Diana's face. "I've been telling her that for weeks," he confided.

"Try *months*," Devin added with a grin in his cousin's direction. "I guess she needed the opinion of an expert." He indicated Rafe with a respectful dip of his head.

Maybe Diana did need absolution from an expert. Or maybe just talking honestly about her trauma was cathartic. She didn't really care because at that moment she felt lighter, as though she could take a deep breath again. She hadn't realized the weight of her burden until it was gone. To be free of the guilt she had battled for months was an incredible gift. Her spirits rose even higher at the encouraging nods and smiles directed her way. Mallory's death *wasn't* her fault. It wasn't her fault at all. She silently thanked God for clarity.

While Diana adjusted to her welcome epiphany, the conversation continued around her. She did, however, intercept the I-have-important-things-to-do-so-let's-move-this-along glare Rafe threw to Alina. The petite woman smiled, giving her father an almost imperceptible nod, before she took the lead.

Alina's lilting accent caressed each syllable as she addressed the group. "I think all of you are probably wondering why the Second-in-Command hasn't been arrested yet, especially since we know his identity."

Darcie regarded her with wide-eyed respect. "Yes," she breathed. "That's exactly what I want to know. How do you do that?"

Alina laughed, delighted with Darcie's response. "It was the question I would have asked, too," she explained. "No one has been arrested because the Mastermind is indeed a mastermind. Every clue we follow, every trail, every smattering of information leads straight back to the Second-in-Command. If our associates arrest *him*, the Mastermind could walk away right now and suffer no consequences. Mina—I mean, Calliope—is the only viable link we have. And while she has been marvelously accommodating when it comes to information about the Second-in-Command and Bill, she won't give us the Mastermind's name.

"But why?" Grace asked.

Ian volunteered the unsatisfactory information: "The name is Calliope's bargaining chip. And her safety net. The only information she will provide is that the murderer works for McCallum Industries and that he will be present for the Board of Directors' reception at the new headquarters."

Surprise rippled through the room at Ian's words. Blane hung his head, one hand rubbing his forehead. He blew out a breath of frustration. "It's Douglas, isn't it, Rafe?" he asked, bleakly. "The Mastermind—the murderer—is my damn uncle Douglas."

Rafe didn't say a word. He waited patiently for Blane to continue.

"Well," Blane asked, watching Rafe carefully. "Do *you* think Uncle Douglas is the Mastermind?"

"Do *you*?" Rafe responded in kind.

Blane rose from his chair and began to pace.

Rafe restated his question. "In other words, Blane, do you think your uncle is *capable* of murder?"

Blane shook his head. "Hell, Rafe, I don't know. He's been the villain in my life since I was twelve years old. Can I see him as the kingpin of some illegal drug operation? Sure. He has *zero* scruples when it pertains to business. He'd sell his soul for money. But murder?" Blane flopped back in his chair.

Rafe raised his eyebrows. "You're forgetting one thing, Blane. Douglas will attend the Board of Directors' reception," he said. "But so will the members of the board. Any one of them could be the Mastermind."

Alina watched her father carefully. "You're certain, then?" she asked, anxiously. "You think the Mastermind will make his move during the reception?"

"The reception is the eye of the storm." Rafe shrugged. "All the players will converge to assess the threat and, if necessary—"

"Eliminate the target," Alina said. She glanced—one by one—at the members of their rapt audience.

When Alina's eyes met hers, Diana was struck by their sadness. Had Blane's aunt lived through a similar scenario? One with tragic consequences for the target? Diana sat perfectly still, stunned by the implications. Were they talking about *her*? Was *she* the target that might be eliminated?

Joey, simultaneously, reached the same conclusion. He spoke up immediately, drawing the focus of all eyes. "Wait just a minute," he began. "Are the three of you implying that *Diana* is someone's target?"

She clung to his hand, trying not to show how unsettling she found Alina's words. Was she now the target of a murderer as well as a kidnapper? Or were the two threats one in the same?

Alina turned puzzled eyes to Joey. "We're not talking about Diana," she said. "The target to whom we're referring is…" She stopped, looking to Ian for help.

"Amalie," her husband finished, softly. "The target is Amalie."

Complete silence met Ian's words.

Grace spoke first. "But why?" she asked. "Why is Amalie someone's target?"

A stab of fear struck Diana in the heart. The only reason the little girl could be a target was…

"Because of what she saw." Devin spoke the words Diana was thinking. "Isn't that right, Rafe?" At the older man's nod, Devin continued, with a tortured sigh. "I was a fool to assume whoever murdered Mallory wouldn't want to make sure he covered his trail. Amalie saw the Mastermind, didn't she? My daughter saw the man who murdered her mother." To his credit, Devin remained outwardly calm. Other than the unnatural pallor of his skin and the way his knuckles turned white where he gripped the arm of the sofa, he received the upsetting news with stoic resignation.

Rafe sighed. "In order to answer your question, Devin, let me give you a little background information. Calliope, it seems, has enjoyed a lengthy liaison with the Mastermind. During that time, she has accomplished numerous 'tasks' for her lover, per his request."

"Murder?" Joey asked.

Rafe nodded again. "Possibly, although we don't expect her to admit to that. According to her, she's the lure…the one who draws the victim to the designated murder site. This time, however, when the murderer asked her to do a job for him, she signed her own death warrant. In other words, she said, 'No.' " Rafe paused to let that sink in.

"But why did she refuse?" Grace asked. "Did she suddenly develop a conscience?"

"Simple," Rafe said. "Calliope is adamant on one point. She doesn't kill children. She also told me, in no uncertain terms, that she won't assist with any murder unless the world will be better off without the victim. She used Kenneth Wade as an example." Rafe raised his voice, mimicking a thick Eastern European accent. " 'The man was a pig. A blight on the world. He deserved everything he got.' "

"Talk about a God-complex," Darcie observed.

"So, the Mastermind asked Calliope to help him kill Amalie," Devin said, returning to the subject uppermost in his mind.

"And Calliope refused," Darcie said encouragingly. "Even though her refusal made her a target."

"Imagine that," Blane mused. "An assassin with scruples."

"Some assassins have scruples," Alina said, matter-of-factly.

"It's no wonder Calliope turned herself in," Grace said. "She'll probably be safer in prison."

Rafe smiled at her naïveté. "Calliope offered herself as a witness against the Mastermind, Grace. To put him and his colleagues in prison. In return, she wants all potential charges against her dropped. *And* a new identity."

"Wow," Joey breathed. "She must know some serious—"

"She knows enough to shut down one of the most successful and long-running drug operations on the East Coast," Ian interrupted. "Not a bad trade."

Devin's mind, however, was understandably occupied by the threat to his daughter. "But, Rafe, it's been months since Mallory was killed. Why hasn't the Mastermind—the murderer—tried to 'eliminate the target,' as you say, before now?" Although Devin delivered the question in a calm voice, he seemed unable to sit still. He left the sofa and wandered to the fireplace, staring into the cheerful flames.

Rafe sighed. "According to Calliope, the Mastermind isn't sure if Amalie remembers him. He plans to use her reaction to him during the reception to gauge her memory."

"Like hell he will," Devin snarled, turning around. "Amalie will be as far away from that reception as I can take her!"

Rafe seemed to expect Devin's answer. "In that case, the game will continue."

"What do you mean 'the game will continue'?" Devin's single eye regarded Rafe coldly.

Rafe shook his head sadly. "The Mastermind will wait for another day to assess Amalie's memory. He's already been waiting a long time. Months. If Calliope's confession forces his hand, he may not take the time to assess. He may just…"

Devin advanced on Rafe menacingly. "I don't care what I have to do to protect Amalie. I *will* find a way to keep my daughter safe."

Rafe waited, studying the irate father for a few seconds. "We *have* been keeping your daughter safe for months, Devin," he said, mild reproach in his voice. "We're not going to stop now when we're so close to the end."

Devin frowned at Rafe's words. "I hope I'm wrong, Rafe, but it sounds like Amalie has been in danger since her mother's death." When Rafe failed to reply, Devin continued: "And you didn't even bother to tell me, did you? What about school? We've been sending her to school all this time *unprotected*. And you never told me?" Devin was almost shouting now.

Rafe stood firm. "Not exactly 'unprotected,' Devin," he said, almost apologetically.

"What are you talking about?" Devin demanded. "Explain. Now."

"Very well," Rafe said calmly. "You see, Devin, Amalie's teacher, Miss Everly…she's a member of McCallum Industries' security team. In addition to being a damn fine kindergarten teacher," he added.

Rafe's words stopped the frustrated man in his tracks. Completely disarmed by the surprising revelation, Devin's bravado fell away. "Oh," was all he managed to say. His struggle to be calm in the face of Rafe's logic was painfully obvious. "Well, um…thank you for that. Thank you for taking care of her. But I"—he glanced at his family and friends—"and I feel sure I speak for the rest of us, would like to have known what was going on. I don't understand why you didn't tell us."

Alina spoke softly: "He was protecting you, Devin. All of you." She regarded her father fondly. "He didn't want Amalie's life—or any of your lives—disrupted by fear. Not when he could take steps to protect you. Because you are *family* to him. And to us," she added, swiping away a quick tear.

"We are a family," Devin said, simply. "But I've just realized that my daughter is the target of a murderer. And I don't know what to do with that kind of information. I want to take her away and hide her somewhere she'll be safe. Why can't you understand that?"

Joey understood completely.

Rafe nodded. "I understand your feelings, Devin, admire them, even. But the hard truth is that Amalie will *never* be safe until we catch her mother's murderer."

Devin sighed. "So, are we going to show Amalie some photos to see if she can identify him, or what?"

Rafe shook his head. "Not exactly."

Devin paused as the full import of the situation dawned on him. "No." His response was quick and final. "No, Rafe. Amalie will *not* be the bait to catch a killer." His hands curled into fists.

"I understand exactly how you feel, Devin," Rafe reiterated. "But—"

"Like hell you understand how I feel, Rafe." Devin looked at the elegant man in disbelief.

"Amalie needs to be present during the reception so the murderer can see her reaction," Rafe continued before Devin could object. "Or lack thereof. If she doesn't identify the man who murdered her mother, Amalie ceases to be a target. This could work in your favor; however, I under-stand your—"

"How can you sit there and tell me you *understand*?" Devin began to prowl the room aimlessly. "You can't possibly *understand*," he said. "None of you can."

From her seat on the sofa Darcie watched Devin helplessly; for once, she was unsure what to do. Joey put a sympathetic arm around his sister. She leaned against him gratefully.

Rafe sighed. "But I do." He stood up and approached his distraught friend, looking him in the eye. "I understand, Devin, because I was you once...a father faced with an impossible choice." Rafe's voice rang with truth. "My daughter was only a few years older than Amalie when she, too, saw something she wasn't supposed to see. She became the target of a crime syndicate. My associates offered to help end the threat—something of which they were quite capable—but I refused. So, we ran. For ten years, Devin. We ran. And in the end..."

Alina left her seat to make her way to Devin's side. "I lost my mother and my brother," Alina said. "And I almost lost my father." She put a soft hand on Devin's arm. "I was that little girl, Devin. I don't want Amalie to go through what I endured. Please let us help. Together, we can end this once and for all."

Rafe gripped Devin's shoulder firmly as their audience waited for his decision. The two men regarded each other a moment longer as an unspo-ken agreement passed between them. Devin's acceptance came in the form of an abrupt nod. As he stepped back from Rafe, he seemed resigned to the necessity of his choice. His watchers relaxed and the somber mood in the room lifted.

Satisfied, Rafe returned to his seat.

"But what about Diana?" Darcie asked, a frown marring her lovely face. "Why is Bill trying to kidnap Diana?"

"Did Calliope say anything about me?" Diana asked. "Anything at all?"

Rafe smiled apologetically at Diana. "Calliope seems to think that Bill…likes you."

"He *likes* me?" Diana asked. "He wants to kidnap me because he *likes* me?"

"Well," Alina volunteered. "It's more like he's *obsessed* with you."

"Obsessed? With me?" Diana couldn't hide her disbelief. "But why?"

Joey mulled the question around inside his head for a moment. "I get it," he said. "I mean, well…I'm kind of obsessed with you."

"But *you* don't want to kidnap me," Diana burst out. When Joey didn't immediately answer, she punched him in the shoulder.

"Ow!" Joey said. "I was only kidding." He grinned for the first time since the interview began. "Well, sort of." He winked at Diana, who wrinkled her nose at him.

Darcie punched him in the other arm. "Ow!" he said again, rubbing his arm. "I said I was only kidding," he reiterated.

"Hmph," Darcie said.

Rafe smiled, obviously amused by their nonsense. "Diana," he asked briskly. "Where is your iPhone?"

Joey looked at Rafe curiously. "Why do you need Diana's iPhone?" he asked.

The intrepid man smiled his approval at Joey's protectiveness. "Diana needs to share her location with us…" Rafe indicated each person in the room "…in case we need to find her."

"You mean if—no, *when*—Bill tries again," Diana said, bravely. At least, she tried to say it bravely. She thought her voice wobbled a little, but no one seemed to notice.

"Your phone, Diana…?" Rafe asked again.

Diana grimaced. "An iguana ate my phone," she said, truthfully.

Darcie grinned. "Again."

"Again," Diana said. She couldn't help but smile at the varying degrees of confusion in the room. "Last week, the fabric ripped in the back of Iggy Iguana's throat. Since then, some of my things—my hairbrush, my lipstick, my phone—have mysteriously disappeared. When I ask Amalie if she's seen them, she gives the same answer:"

" 'Iggy ate it,' " Diana and Darcie said together.

Their response brought laughter all around, a relief after the fraught tone of the past half hour.

Rafe gave Diana a commiserating smile. "So, Iggy ate your phone, hmm? Well, if you can compel him to cough it up, I'd like to make sure the settings are conducive for our purposes."

Diana stood up, unaccountably relieved the ordeal was over. As she turned to go in search of the insatiable iguana, Rafe's voice stopped her.

"One more thing, Diana...I'm afraid you're quarantined again. Please don't leave the estate until you hear otherwise. You will be staying with Blane and Grace instead of at the cottage. Ian and Alina will be here, too. They are quite capable of handling any situation that might arise."

Even though the edge in Rafe's voice let Diana know his instructions were not suggestions, she didn't feel constrained by her lack of freedom. Instead, she was grateful for the layers of protection. Not only for herself, but for Amalie.

CHAPTER FORTY-NINE

*A*lthough the new North America headquarters of McCallum Industries was impressive, Diana quickly decided that the reception for the Board of Directors and their guests had little to recommend itself. Unless, she hypothesized, one enjoyed waiting around to see if a five-year-old little girl could identify her mother's murderer. Because that was exactly what Diana was doing...what they were all doing per Rafe's instructions. Per Rafe's *plan*.

The plan—Operation Board of Directors, as Joey called it—was brilliant in its simplicity. Instead of allowing the murderer to assess Amalie, Amalie would assess the murderer. In a controlled environment. With multiple—*multiple*—layers of protection. It was easy and safe. Well, Diana surmised, as safe as it could possibly be for a little girl who had witnessed a murder.

Amalie would have the opportunity to meet each of the board members individually. Her reaction to them—and their reaction to her—would, hopefully tell the watchers all they needed to know. The murderer was almost certainly male. *If*, that is, they could trust their combined knowledge of Mallory's preferences and the information from Calliope, the enigmatic informant. But Amalie would meet the three female members of the board anyway so as not to tip their hand. And because, according to Rafe, they were taking no chances.

But where was Rafe? Diana hadn't seen any sign of the elusive man anywhere. And, to Diana, that was a bit disconcerting. Questioning Alina yielded zero information.

"Papi has been *detained*," Rafe's daughter explained, shrugging her shoulders, as if her father's absence was of no consequence whatsoever.

One word. *Detained*. Spoken with a sparkling smile.

Maybe it was the way Alina *pronounced* the word, her unusual accent heightening the mystery of her simple reply. Or maybe, Diana decided, it was the work of her own overly active imagination. Regardless of the reason, she couldn't help but feel there was more to Rafe's absence than any of them were supposed to know. After all, one would expect the *planner* of the *plan* to be present to assure the proper execution of said *plan*. Wouldn't one? Diana sighed, telling herself not to worry. Nothing was going to happen until after the board meeting ended, anyway, and perhaps Rafe would appear by then. Other than Rafe, the only person who had yet to arrive was Blane's uncle Douglas.

Diana glanced at the small group holding vigil in the lobby. Everyone, it seemed, was feeling the strain. And each one dealt with the tension in his or her own way. Joey planted himself by the refreshment table near the lobby's eastern back corner. Diana studied him for a moment, wondering how she had ended up with such a handsome boyfriend. The man was casual perfection. His blue blazer emphasized his broad shoulders and trim waist. His dark dress pants hinted at the muscular thighs underneath. His dress shirt, sans tie, revealed a tantalizing bit of skin. Even his shoes struck just the right balance between relaxed style and effortless cool. His short, dark hair, cooperating as usual, made her wish she could drag him into a closet to run her fingers through the silky strands. Apart from a few cookie crumbs at the corner of his mouth, he could have stepped out of a magazine ad. For some reason, the crumbs made her smile.

Grace stared out the enormous front windows, her teeth absently worrying her bottom lip. She looked lovely in a simple black midi dress. High heel black pumps with pointy toes and small, silver earrings completed her understated, professional ensemble. At least that's what Diana assumed Grace was thinking. The attempt was spoiled by the colorful embroidered flowers embellishing the bodice and long sleeves. With that cheerful pop of color and her sparkling green eyes, she looked anything but businesslike. Diana thought Grace was adorable.

Darcie, always the most restless of the group, paced the perimeter of the room in her three-inch black stilettos. Diana, who almost never wore heels, felt a pang of sympathy for Darcie's elegant feet. She was, as always, beautiful. Sheer sleeves added to the elegance of her form-fitting sheath. The deep crimson color was a perfect foil for Darcie's dark eyes and hair. But then what color wasn't? Diana mused. She had to admit that meeting Darcie for the first time—years ago—had been intimidating. She hadn't realized then that she was meeting someone destined to become one of her dearest friends. And, hopefully, her future sister-in-law, she added to herself.

Diana considered her own reflection in the front window. Since she was the nanny, her attire was a bit more relaxed. Her dark blue peasant dress with the sweeping skirt and ruffled hem was her new favorite. The long sleeves ended in delicate ruffles at her wrists. A haphazard sprinkling of autumn leaves added a touch of flare. She was wearing her favorite boots, too…a lovely low-heel pair in light brown suede. Her red curls were cooperating—for the moment—pulled into a loose ponytail with a few strands left long to frame her face. She tried, consciously, to soften the tense expression on her face, but finally gave up when she realized she looked like everybody else in the room.

Almost.

Only Amalie and Alina seemed unaffected by the coming storm. Amalie was cuteness overload in a green jumper with a white long-sleeve shirt. She played hide-and-seek with Iggy by closing her eyes and throwing the iguana across the lobby floor. It soon became clear that Iggy wasn't terribly creative, as far as hiding places went. Amalie found him every time, but at least she was entertained. The knees of her white tights were in danger of getting dirty, but since the floors were new and relatively clean, Diana didn't say anything.

Alina, always exquisite, wore a black knee-length knitted dress. The portrait neckline and cuffs of her long sleeves were edged in black satin. A single strand of pearls adorned her neck, a cluster of tiny pearls on her tiny earlobes. Even in her black heels, she barely reached Ian's shoulder. Anyone who knew Alina—or had seen her shoot a gun, Diana added—realized the woman's delicate, fragile appearance was thoroughly misleading. She sat with her feet tucked under her on one of the sofas in the lobby, seemingly engrossed in a book. The fact that she was reading a spy novel hadn't gone unnoticed by Diana. A quick peek over Alina's shoulder revealed the title: *The Scorpion.* A fierce-looking scorpion curled around the words *Chapter Seven.* So, Diana mused, spies read books about spies in their spare time. That fact struck her as odd. After all, *she* didn't read books about nannies in *her* spare time.

But even the fascinating Alina couldn't keep Diana's mind from her worries for long. Knowing that Amalie might identify Mallory's murderer in the next hour was unsettling enough. But for Diana, the possibility that Bill might also be lurking nearby was even worse. He had already proven himself adept with disguises. He could easily hide himself as a nondescript member of the catering staff with no one the wiser. *One problem at a time,* Diana thought. She found herself in need of a worthy distraction. And that's how she ended up at the refreshment table with Joey Finch. The delicious array of local delicacies, she decided, was certainly the bright spot of the interminable reception.

Diana silently reprimanded herself even as her fork delivered another bite of sugary perfection to her mouth. Sugar cake was too simple a name for such deliciousness. Melted sugar pooled on the top of the buttery, yeasty bread. Diana silently vowed to visit Winkler's Bakery in nearby Old Salem very soon. She and Amalie would enjoy learning about the historic eighteenth-century Moravian settlement. And wasn't it Diana's duty as Amalie's nanny to take advantage of local educational opportunities? Of course it was. Learning was important, she told herself, and…oh, who was she kidding? Diana was just inventing reasons to eat more sugar cake.

Amalie, however, hadn't shown the slightest interest in the sugar cake. Instead, she had fallen in love with Dewey's lemonade cake from the nearby bakery of the same name. The little girl grabbed Grace's hand and pulled her clear across the lobby to show her the heaping tray of pretty, pink cake squares with yellow icing. After being told to "wait until the reception starts" by both her nanny and her future stepmother, the little girl had finally found an ally. Darcie trailed behind the co-conspirators.

"Please, Auntie Grace," Amalie begged. "May I have a pretty, pink cake square?"

"Well, of course you can, sweetie," Grace replied, her green eyes sparkling with mischief. She picked up a plate and carefully placed a cake square in the center. She tried to give the plate to Amalie, but the little girl stopped her.

"Please, Auntie Grace, may Iggy have one, too?" Amalie asked, her big, blue eyes shining with innocence.

Diana exchanged an amused glance with Darcie, who had developed her own immunity to Amalie's wiles. By mutual agreement they were keeping an eye on their little cake square con artist.

"Please, Auntie Grace," Amalie intoned pitifully. "Poor Iggy is very, very hungry."

Grace grinned at that. "Well, of course, Iggy needs a cake square of his own," she agreed, much to Amalie's delight. "What was I thinking?" She placed another cake square on the plate, handing it—along with two plastic forks and two napkins—to the little girl. Then she watched until the child seated herself, without incident, against the wall beside her poor, starving iguana. Only then did Grace meet the identical expressions of disapproval on Diana's and Darcie's faces.

"What?" Grace asked, mimicking Amalie's wide-eyed innocence. "I'm the *fun* aunt," she said.

Diana couldn't help but laugh at Grace's admission. Darcie merely rolled her eyes.

Joey chuckled. "Well played, Gracie," he praised, enjoying his sister's sass. He had spent quite a bit of time devoting himself to two large trays labeled Moravian Cookies. The spice cookies, although incredibly thin, packed quite a flavorful punch. He was standing in front of the table with one cookie from the Dewey's tray in his left hand and one cookie from the Mrs. Hanes' Moravian Cookies tray in the right hand. He bit into the left cookie, chewed, and swallowed. Then he repeated the process with the cookie in his right hand. Darcie and Grace watched him curiously, clearly trying to figure out what he was doing. If Diana hadn't been so involved with her sugar cake, she would have already asked.

Grace didn't hesitate. "What are you doing, Joey?"

His reply was unintelligible. "Mm sdemn shwmnen iz betrmp."

Darcie shook her head in sibling-disgust. "You're such a pig."

Diana couldn't help laughing as Joey narrowed his eyes at his sister. He finished chewing his cookie, swallowed, and said, with as much dignity as possible, "I'm trying to decide which cookies taste better: the ones from Dewey's or the ones from Mrs. Hanes' Moravian Cookies."

"By eating all of them?" Darcie asked.

"Yes," Joey answered, solemnly. "I am more than ready to sacrifice myself for the sake of research. I plan to eat all of them." To demonstrate his point, he took another bite of the cookie in his right hand.

"You've eaten both kinds before," Darcie grumbled. "I don't know why you can't figure it out without cleaning off both trays. How can you eat so many cookies at one time, anyway?" she added, surveying the rest of the food.

"I'm too nervous to eat anything," Grace added. "Aren't you, Diana?"

"Mm-hm," Diana mumbled, trying desperately to swallow the sugar cake already in her mouth. She surreptitiously placed her plate with the uneaten half of her second piece on the table behind her. Joey chuckled appreciatively at her subterfuge. She wrinkled her nose at him.

Darcie glanced toward the second-floor balcony that led to the new McCallum Industries' boardroom. "I don't know why it's taking so long," she fretted. "Poor Gracie is going to chew her lip off if they don't come out soon."

Grace appeared surprised to discover she was, indeed, chewing her lip. "Is my lipstick gone?" she asked.

"Long gone," Darcie said.

"Why don't you go help Gracie fix her lip?" Joey suggested.

Darcie raised her eyebrows at her brother. "So you can eat your cookies in peace?" she asked.

Joey shrugged. "Something like that," he said, dryly.

Grace pointed to her mouth. "Lips," she said, indignantly. "I have two." She puckered her lips and made a kissy noise before going to find her purse.

Darcie patted Diana's arm sympathetically. "How *do* you stand him?" she asked. Without waiting for an answer, she followed her sister.

"She's gone," Joey pointed out unnecessarily. "You can finish your sugar cake."

Diana reached behind her for her plate only to find that an over-zealous member of the catering crew had already taken possession of her remains. "Drat," she said aloud.

Joey picked up the cake server and proceeded to plop another piece of sugar cake onto another plate. "It's not a chocolate twirl," Joey grinned. "But it'll have to do."

And that, Diana thought, was why she loved him.

But, alas, before Joey could hand her the plate, Amalie bounded over, empty plate in hand. "Oooh, Nanny Di," the little girl squealed. "That's your third piece of that sugar thing. And I only had two pieces of lemonade cake. Can I have another piece of lemonade cake? Can I? Can I, Nanny Di? Please?"

Diana almost gave in to the plea in the little girl's big, blue eyes. Almost. But *almost* was the same as *no* in nannyspeak. Reluctantly, she handed her plate back to Joey. Amalie's angelic face scrunched into a frown. "Neither one of us needs more sugar, 'Malie," she said.

"But I'm hungry. And Iggy's hungry, too. We've been waiting forever and ever. I don't think Daddy and Uncle Blane are ever going to come out of the *boring* room," Amalie sighed dramatically.

"Board," Diana said. "Not boring. Board room."

"*Bored* room," Amalie repeated. "That's what I meant. They're having their *boring* meeting in the *bored* room."

Diana shook her head. "Board meeting," she began, "Not—" But one look at Amalie's confused face—and the amusement on Joey's—told her she was fighting a losing battle. "Oh, whatever," she finished.

Joey, however, couldn't let it go. "Hey, Amalie, do you think we should call this room the *really bored* room?"

Amalie pointed at Joey with her iguana. "See," she said triumphantly as Darcie and Grace—lipstick intact—joined them. "Uncle Joey's bored, too. That's why he's trying to eat all the cookies."

Joey waggled his eyebrows at the little girl. "*I* am conducting a scientific experiment," he stated, biting into another cookie.

"I want to conduce a 'sperience, too," Amalie squealed. "I want to be like Uncle Joey..."

"Good Lord," Darcie said out of the side of her mouth, causing Diana and Grace to giggle.

"I want to conduce a 'sperience with lemonade cake," Amalie continued. "And Iggy wants to conduce a 'sperience, too. Can we, Nanny Di? Can we conduce a 'sperience?" She smiled happily. "You like it when I learn new things," she added with the skill of a tiny diplomat.

Diana nodded. "I *do* like it when you learn new things, Amalie. But I *don't* like it when you have too much sugar."

Amalie quickly changed tactics. And targets. "Can we, Auntie Grace?" Her voice took on an I'm-pitiful-and-you're-the-only-one-who-can-save-me tone.

"Well..." Grace was torn between her desire to be the *fun* aunt and her wish to keep the peace. "Only if Mama Darcie and Nanny Di say it's okay."

Amalie turned to Darcie, who was busy frowning at her sister. "Can we, Mama Darcie?"

"No, you may not. And neither can Iggy." Darcie didn't mince words, but she did supply an explanation. "Uncle Joey is conducing his 'sperience using the same type of cookie made in two different places. Unfortunately for you—and for Iggy—the cake squares were made in the same place by the same people. So, you see, Amalie"—She glanced at the hungry iguana—"and Iggy, there is no reason for you to conduce a 'sperience. Do you understand?"

Amalie nodded earnestly. "I understand, Mama Darcie, but Iggy is having trouble."

"Then you need to explain it to him again," Darcie suggested. She watched her soon-to-be stepdaughter sit on the floor at her feet to give the stubborn iguana a lecture on the necessary requirements for conducing a 'sperience. When she looked up, the other three adults were regarding her with something like awe.

"What?" she asked.

Grace smiled. "Aw, Darce," she said. "You're going to be such a wonderful mother."

"I told you she was a natural," Diana said, approvingly.

"Mn argaren," Joey agreed with his mouth, once again, full of cookies.

"Hmph," was Darcie's characteristic reply, but she looked pleased by their words.

"I want to be magic like Cinderella's fairy godmother," Amalie announced about half an hour later. She pondered her own words for a moment before focusing her attention on her uncle Joey. He had joined Alina on the sofa after announcing his cookie experiment had ended in a tie. He was, he said, open to performing further research at a later date.

"Uncle Joey," the little girl said, "do you know what?"

"What, Amalie?" Joey asked. The *really* boring room had gotten *really, really* boring, in his opinion, so he welcomed the distraction.

"I want to be magic, like Cinderella's fairy godmother," she repeated, eagerly.

Joey found himself at a bit of a loss. "And...?" he asked, not certain what the little girl wanted.

"I want to be magic like Cinderella's fairy godmother," Amalie repeated, leaning both elbows on Joey's knees.

"Okay," Joey said, feeling out of his element.

"Ask her what she would do if she was a fairy godmother," Alina advised in an amused whisper.

Why not? Joey asked himself. Maybe if he did, Amalie would remove her tiny—and sharp—little elbows from his knees. "What would you do, Amalie, if you were a fairy godmother?"

The little girl beamed with joy. "I would wave my magic wand and make the boring meeting be over." She waved Iggy's tail in the air to demonstrate.

Diana's voice floated to his ears from behind the sofa. "What else would you do, Amalie?" Her hand closed softly on Joey's shoulder. He reached up to cover it with his own, glad his reinforcements had returned from the ladies' room. Darcie and Grace leaned on the back of the sofa, one on either side of Diana. Joey winked at Diana, basking in the warmth of her smile. He knew he had a lot to learn about children, but he was eagerly looking forward to filling their house with redheaded girls one day. And, maybe, if he was honest, a boy or two.

The pint-sized fairy godmother waved her iguana back and forth, indicating the back of the lobby area. A curving staircase with wrought iron balusters connected the lobby to the second-floor balcony. Amalie waved Iggy's tail toward the balcony. "I would make Daddy and Uncle Blane and Uncle Ian come down the steps. And, then..."—she waved the acrobatic iguana's tail toward the elevator near the bottom steps—"...I would make Grandad Fergus and his new friends come out of the elevator."

No sooner were the words out of Amalie's mouth than the sound of voices wafted down from the balcony. A few moments later, Devin and Blane appeared at the top of the staircase. They started down the stairs, followed by Ian and the other eleven board members. Before the last board member reached the lobby floor, the elevator doors slid open to reveal Fergus and the members' guests who had just finished their tour of the facility.

"Good job, Iggy!" Amalie squealed, excitedly.

Diana gave Joey a smug smile. "See," she said, proving her long-contested point. "Why would Nanny Di need a ginormous, magical tote bag when she has Iggy?"

Joey couldn't help but agree. "You were right," he admitted. "That iguana has skills."

"You have no idea," Darcie agreed, stepping around the sofa to take Amalie's hand. "There's Daddy, Amalie. Let's go meet the board."

"The *bored* what, Mama Darcie?" the little girl asked with a puzzled frown.

"Never mind," Darcie said. She led Amalie across the floor, bringing her over to where Devin and Blane were waiting. With an amused wink in Diana's direction, Grace followed the pair to assume her hostess duties as wife of the CEO.

Diana watched Ian casually make his way across the room to join his wife. Alina, too, casually stowed her novel in her purse, then rose, casually, from the sofa. But Diana wasn't fooled. A quick glance over Alina's shoulder had confirmed that she was still on the same page—Chapter Seven, with the scorpion—that she had been reading over an hour ago. Diana felt vindicated. It was just as she suspected. Real spies didn't read spy novels. They only used them as a cover. Quite an impressive observation for an amateur, she congratulated herself. With abilities like that, maybe she, herself, had potential as a spy.

Or maybe not. After pondering Alina's special skills with firearms for a few seconds, Diana changed her mind. Maybe she could *write* a good spy novel. Yes, she decided, that was better.

Nanny Di and the Spy.

No, she thought, too simple. And it didn't tug at the imagination.

Nanny Di Was a Spy.

Better, she told herself, but still not exactly right. Maybe...

Nanny Spy and the Bad Guy.

Now, that one was clever, although she really didn't want to write a spy story for children. She finally settled on a more intriguing title:

The Nanny Had an Alias.

Joey's voice interrupted her flight of whimsy. "How're you holding up?" he asked, joining her behind the sofa.

Diana couldn't help the chill that ran through her at hearing Joey's words. The wait was over. It was time to unmask a murderer. "I'm fine," she lied, determined to ignore her racing heart. "I'm…we're all going to be fine."

Joey took her hand in his, wishing he was half as brave as the red-haired warrior beside him. She was trying so hard to appear strong and unaffected by the coming ordeal. Only the death grip she currently had on his hand gave away her inner turmoil. Together, they watched Devin, Darcie, and Amalie approach the first board member.

"Here we go," he said, surveying the possible suspects. "Anybody look like a murderer to you?"

Diana shook her head. "Frankly, no." None of the people in the well-dressed, professional group met her preconceived notion of what Mallory's murderer would appear like. "They're not very threatening, are they?" she asked glumly.

Joey grimaced in agreement. "Maybe we're approaching this the wrong way, Diana," he suggested. "According to Calliope, Mallory was having an affair with the man who murdered her. So…which one would Mallory choose as a lover?" he inquired. His speculative gaze perused the crowd.

Diana took her time answering. She studied each possible suspect at length before letting out a frustrated little sigh. "None of them look like anyone Mallory would find sufficiently attractive. Or sufficiently wealthy. So, I honestly have no idea."

"Well, I do." Joey's voice oozed with confidence.

"You do?" Diana asked, hopefully. "Which one?" She waited breathlessly for Joey to solve the puzzle.

"The little, old man over there with the pointy ears. He's talking to Fergus. I think he's a leprechaun so he's exactly Mallory's type. You know… pot of gold and all that."

Diana let out a bark of laughter that caused several heads to turn in their direction. She bumped her hip against her ridiculous boyfriend. "Hush," she said. "He's not a leprechaun." She tried to stop giggling. She really did. But her emotions had run the gamut the past few minutes. In truth, it felt good to laugh, as much from Joey's nonsense as from relief that they *weren't* in the same room as the murderer. She didn't know why she was so relieved. The failure of Rafe's operation only prolonged the ordeal for everyone, but there it was.

And silly or not, Joey was right. The little board member did look like he had stepped out of a very old box of Lucky Charms. He was adorable, right down to his tiny, and slightly pointed, ears. There was absolutely no way the cute little man had murdered Mallory.

Joey grinned, pleased with the success of his silliness. Some of the color had returned to Diana's face. And, although she was still squeezing his hand, it no longer felt like she was trying to break every single bone in it. A definite improvement, he decided. The best way he could help Diana was by keeping her spirits up. He latched onto the task, glad to have something to do. When it came to injecting levity into a situation, he was the man for the job.

CHAPTER FIFTY

"Three more to go," Joey said out of the corner of his mouth as they watched Devin and Darcie introduce Amalie to another board member.

"Two more to go," Diana corrected him. "Ian doesn't count."

Joey nodded in agreement. "Oh yeah. I forgot he was on the board." He caught Diana's eyes before grinning wickedly. "My money's still on the leprechaun."

"He's *not* a leprechaun," Diana reiterated, trying not to giggle. At this point, the mere mention of the word *leprechaun* was hilarious. Honestly, she was having far too much fun considering the seriousness of the situation. She tried to contain her mirth as Fergus led the leprechaun and a heretofore unnoticed diminutive woman to meet Devin, Darcie, and Amalie, who were walking toward them.

Joey choked on a chuckle. "Uh-oh. Looks like there's a Mrs. Leprechaun."

"And they're both wearing green," Diana gasped as the hilarity threatened to consume her again. Both parties had stopped a few feet away, close enough for Diana and Joey to hear their conversation...and close enough for the man and woman to hear any inappropriate giggles aimed their way. Diana couldn't bear to hurt the couple's feelings, not when they had such delighted smiles on their cute faces. There was absolutely no way, she reiterated, the adorable leprechaun had murdered Mallory. No way at all. But...

"I remember you!" Amalie squealed the minute she saw him.

"And I remember *you*," the man said without hesitation.

Diana gasped. Was it possible? Could it be? Was a heartless, murderous leprechaun standing five feet away? Diana grabbed Joey's arm as he turned to her. The surprise on his face mirrored her own.

For about two seconds.

"You're Mr. O-something," Amalie said. "Mr. O..."

"O'Malley," the leprechaun said, his smile even wider than before. "And you're Amalie. Devin's daughter."

"That's right!" Amalie said, nearly vibrating with excitement. "You were at Uncle Blane and Auntie Grace's wedding. Nanny Di wouldn't let me have two pieces of cake and you gave me yours."

The leprechaun—Mr. O'Malley—looked a little embarrassed. "Actually," he admitted. "I gave you my wife's piece of cake."

The tiny woman—obviously Mrs. O'Malley—put her tiny hands on her tiny hips. "You what?" she demanded in mock outrage.

Amalie laughed at their nonsense. She motioned for them to come closer, as if she wanted to tell them a secret. "We have lemonade cake for the 'ception," Amalie confided. "It's pink, Mr. O'Malley. With yellow icing, Mrs. O'Malley. And it is *so* yummy!"

"Is that so?" Mr. O'Malley said, seriously.

"Maybe Mrs. O'Malley won't be mad about the wedding cake if you get her some lemonade cake, Mr. O'Malley," Amalie advised, politely.

"Thank you, Amalie, for such sound advice," the little man said gravely. He offered his arm to his wife.

She took it with a puzzled look on her face. "But, Mr. O'Malley," she said. "We don't know which way to go."

"You're right, Mrs. O'Malley," her husband said. "Whatever will we do?" They both looked at Amalie expectantly.

The little girl grinned with delight. "The lemonade cake is over there," she said, pointing to the refreshment table.

With a twinkle in his eye, the courtly old man offered his other arm. "Lead the way, young lady," he said. Amalie took his arm and did just that.

Darcie spoke first when the little girl was out of earshot. "Well," she said, "that's it. The murderer is *not* a member of McCallum Industries' Board of Directors."

"No real surprise there," Devin observed, as Blane and Grace joined their group, followed almost immediately by Ian and Alina. Their sober demeanors reminded everyone that the ordeal was far from over.

Blane glanced at his uncle, then at his grandfather. "Grandad, you must be hungry, too...I'll bet Amalie would love to share some—"

"It's all right, Blane." Fergus gently interrupted his grandson. "I know what's going on. I've known for some time. Douglas is a criminal...and a murderer."

Blane placed a bracing arm around the older man's shoulders.

"An *accused* murderer," Ian said. "We have to have more proof, Dad. We need someone to corroborate our informant's story."

"So, Calliope finally gave you a name?" Blane asked.

Ian sighed. "Yes. And the name is, of course, Douglas McCallum. But until we get more proof, we have only her word against his."

Devin sighed. "You need my five-year-old daughter, the eyewitness," he said, resigned. "You need Amalie."

Alina put a gentle hand on his arm. "It's always possible that we're wrong, Devin. Calliope could be lying. She could be one of Douglas' scorned lovers, trying to get revenge."

"But you don't think that's the case," Darcie said.

"We don't think that's the case," Alina agreed, evenly. "Papi has spoken with her. He trusts her."

"Where is Rafe, anyway?" Blane asked. "I keep expecting him to walk in."

Alina smiled a calm, soothing smile. "Papi has been—"

"*Detained*," a multitude of voices chimed in.

"Detained," Alina echoed. "I'm glad all of you are such excellent listeners." Her smile turned charming.

Diana was surprised—or maybe not so surprised—to discover that she wasn't alone in her curiosity about Rafe's whereabouts.

"So, I guess the next step is for Amalie to see Douglas," Joey said, thinking ahead. "When do you think that will happen?"

"Any minute now," Ian said, ruefully. "Douglas landed at the airport fifteen minutes ago. He's on his way."

Douglas McCallum settled himself in the comfortable backseat of the Lincoln Town Car that would take him to the reception for the McCallum Board of Directors. The courtesy car, he had to admit, was something of a surprise. Since discovering his uncle's embezzlement—and removing him as president of the North American branch of the company—Blane had been less than accommodating in the courtesy department. Douglas still couldn't believe his idiot nephew hadn't fired him out right, a fact he continued to view with disdain rather than gratitude.

Still, Douglas couldn't help the self-satisfied smile that bloomed on his lips. He was, he thought admiringly, something of a genius. He still marveled at the ease with which he had convinced Max—Rafe Montgomery's loyal assistant—to switch sides. Although Douglas regarded such disloyalty with distaste, he was delighted to use Max's insatiable greed to his own advantage. In a matter of hours, Rafe would be dead. And the constant threat to Douglas' double life would die with him.

Eventually, Max, too, would be a liability, Douglas decided. But that was a project for another day. For now, it was enough to know that—thanks to the evidence Max had carefully planted—Rafe would take the fall for the death of Mallory Merritt. End of story.

Or was it?

Douglas grimaced. He still had to deal with one small problem. Literally. One small, blond, eyewitness to the murder...Mallory's daughter. Killing a child was not a task to which Douglas aspired. He had already decided, rather magnanimously, he thought, to give Mallory's spawn a chance to grow up...if the little brat didn't recognize him today. But if she did...

Douglas took a deep, cleansing breath. He had a contingency plan in place for that, too, he reminded himself. Either way, the fate of the Merritt child was in no way tied to the fate of Douglas McCallum. So, there was nothing to worry about.

And if the unthinkable happened and the whole thing blew up in his face, there was always his doomsday scenario to turn to. That plan—in place from day one—traced every illegal activity in Douglas' past straight back to Calli. Yes, he admitted to himself, he wasn't proud of that scenario. Or even happy about it. But, if necessary, he was ready and willing to sacrifice his long-time lover to save himself.

As for Billix...well, the little bastard would be okay as long as he followed orders. And kept his idiot mouth shut. Douglas laughed mirthlessly at that unlikely scenario. Perhaps a short prison stretch would teach Bill not to be such a smart-ass, he thought philosophically.

Douglas sighed, refusing to dwell on the negative possibilities of the next few hours. Instead, he forced himself to focus on the endless possibilities of a world without Rafe Montgomery.

"Where is Amalie?" Darcie asked, glancing toward the refreshment table.

Every head turned at her words. Every eye skimmed the area before moving outward. The level of tension ratcheted up a notch. Maybe a notch and a half.

"There she is," Joey said, pointing toward the front windows.

Sure enough, the little girl was skipping happily back and forth between the windows and the side wall where Iggy waited. The savvy iguana seemed to be guarding several plates holding several cake squares. The watchers relaxed, a few chuckles rising among themselves....

Diana shook her head in mock sympathy. "I hate to tell you this, Devin, but you're in for a long night." At the confusion on his face, she explained: "Amalie is going to be in sugar overdrive. She won't sleep well, and when she does sleep, she'll have sugar-induced nightmares. That's exactly what happened after she ate too much cake at Grace and Blane's wedding."

Devin grinned. "Good thing you'll be in the room right beside her, isn't it?"

Drat, Diana said to herself, she hadn't thought of that little detail. She grimaced at her cousin's smug expression.

"What happened after our wedding?" Grace asked, obviously seeking a diversion.

"Well..." Diana frowned, trying to organize her story. She hadn't thought much about that night with regard to Amalie. She had been too busy pondering the significance—or lack thereof—of her single dance with Joey Finch at the reception. "I had already gone to bed when Amalie came flying into my room. She closed the door behind her and begged me not to open it, even though Iggy's tail was caught. She insisted the Grim Reaper was in the hallway."

"The Grim Reaper?" Devin asked. "Where did that come from?"

Darcie frowned. "That seems a bit macabre for our little girl. She usually talks about butterflies and princesses."

"With an occasional reference to Santa or the Tooth Fairy thrown in the mix." Diana agreed completely. "At the time I just chalked it up to too much sugar and excitement. Or maybe something she saw on tv. Anyway, she kept telling me the Grim Reaper was in the hallway. When I finally convinced her to let me open the door, we went into the hallway and did a little dance to scare the Grim Reaper away."

"Is that when Amalie stopped going upstairs?" Grace asked, furrowing her brow.

Diana looked at Grace in surprise. "I guess so," she said. Grace was right, she realized. Amalie hadn't been upstairs at Heart's Ease since that night. She flatly refused to go.

"How strange," Darcie said.

"It is strange, isn't it?" Diana concurred. "I've never really thought about why she didn't want to go upstairs. I just figured it had something to do with Mallory."

Alina's heightened interest was obvious. "Has anyone asked Amalie why she doesn't want to go upstairs?"

"No," Darcie said. "If you remember, Amalie wouldn't say a word for weeks after Mallory died. It was only after she came to Heart's Ease that she started talking again. Her therapist told us it was better not to ask questions. She said Amalie would tell us about the trauma eventually."

"Maybe it's time," Alina suggested gently, surveying the faces around her. "Are there any objections?" she asked. "Devin? Darcie? Diana? You three know her best. May I try?"

Devin spoke first. "I have no objections, if Darcie and Diana don't." When neither expressed concern, he continued: "But I want all of us to hear your questions." His eye met Alina's in unspoken communication. "And I expect you to stop if she becomes upset."

"Of course," Alina agreed, easily. She quickly turned, wending her way through the chattering groups to find the blue-eyed little girl who had all the answers.

"She's very good at it, you know," Ian said to Devin, conversationally.

"At what? Interrogation?" Devin asked, wryly.

Blane grinned, having been on the receiving end of Alina's interrogations many times during his teenage years. "You say that like it's a bad thing."

Devin glared at his friend.

Ian laughed at their exchange. "Not *interrogation*, in a threatening sense, Devin," he explained. "She's good at finding things out. Obtaining information. Acquiring—"

"She knows how to make you spill your guts. Plain and simple," Blane said, interrupting. "One minute she's talking to you and the next, well… you're telling her everything you've ever done." He shook his head in mock defeat.

"And I suppose you're speaking from experience?" Devin asked, amused in spite of himself.

"Yeah," Blane said. "No sixteen-year-old alive can withstand Alina's tactics."

Ian agreed. "No adult male, either. Alina is a force of nature."

The watchers were quite entertained when the "force of nature" walked up behind her husband just in time to hear his description of her. She held Amalie by the hand.

"Why, thank you, Ian," Alina's voice said, sweetly. "What a lovely thing to say."

"See what I mean?" Ian couldn't help but laugh at her subterfuge.

Diana glanced at Amalie. The little girl had a streak of yellow icing across her nose and pink crumbs down the front of her jumper. She was hopping from foot to foot, clearly full of energy. Iggy's tail bobbed up and down with each hop. Diana studied her small charge for a moment. "A-mal-ie," she said. "How many cake squares have you eaten?"

Amalie counted on her fingers twice and looked up into the air, as if performing some complicated mathematical problem. "Maybe…nine?"

Diana's mouth fell open in dismay. Amalie had never eaten nine of anything in her life. "*Nine*?" Diana repeated in horror, pinning her with a disapproving glare.

"Or seven?" The little girl hedged. "Or, maybe, six?" When nobody commented on that number, Amalie smiled. "Yes, I had six."

"Gonna be a long night," Devin murmured to Diana, under his breath. They exchanged a commiserating glance.

"Amalie," Alina began. "I like cake squares, too." She waited until she had the little girl's full attention. "But do you know what I *really* like?"

"What, Aunt Alina?" Amalie could barely stand still. She kept swinging her arms back and forth. Iggy swayed drunkenly.

"I like wedding cake," Alina announced.

"Ooh," Amalie squealed, hopping up and down. "I love wedding cake."

Alina leaned closer. "Can I tell you a secret?"

"Ooh," Amalie repeated. "I love secrets."

"Me, too," Alina confided. She covered her mouth with her hand as if she had done something very naughty. "I ate *three* pieces of wedding cake at Uncle Blane and Aunt Grace's wedding."

Amalie laughed delightedly. "I ate *five*," she said, mimicking Alina's gesture.

Diana raised her eyebrows at Devin. "See?"

Devin grimaced.

"*Five* pieces of wedding cake?" Alina asked. "Oh, my goodness." She grinned at Amalie like they were old friends. Amalie grinned back. "Did you like my secret?"

Amalie nodded. "Oh, yes, Aunt Alina! I loved your secret!"

"Will you tell *me* a secret, Amalie?" she asked. She waited for Amalie's nod before asking the question. "Why won't you go upstairs at Uncle Blane and Aunt Grace's house?"

Diana held her breath. What would Amalie do?

The little girl stood there calmly, swinging Iggy back and forth. "Because of the pictures."

Diana relaxed.

Alina glanced at Devin, who nodded, giving his permission for her to continue. "What pictures are you talking about, Amalie?" Alina asked.

The little girl didn't hesitate. "The pictures of the Grin Ripper."

Diana spoke out of habit. "The *Grim* Reaper."

"Oh, Nanny Di," Amalie giggled. "You're so silly. The Grim Reaper is pretend. Like the one in your book. The Grin Ripper is real. He's in the pictures with Uncle Blane's mommy."

Every eye focused on the child whose innocent revelation had just ignited a firestorm of reaction.

"I have another secret for you, Amalie," Alina continued, still in the same soothing tone of voice. "And it's a good secret. Would you like to hear it?"

Amalie nodded eagerly.

"The man in the pictures with Uncle Blane's mommy isn't the Grin Ripper."

"Yes, he is," Amalie objected. "I saw him coming out of Mommy's room after the wedding and he *told* me he was the Grin Ripper." She looked to Diana for support. "And then I told Nanny Di."

Diana knew exactly what to say to make Amalie understand. "'Malie, do you remember when we read *Nanny Di and the Terrible Twosome*?"

"The book about the two brothers who looked alike?" the little girl asked.

"That's right," Diana praised. "Those brothers were twins, weren't they?"

Amalie nodded.

"Well, Uncle Blane's daddy—the man in those pictures—was a good man. He was very kind and he loved Uncle Blane very much. He died a long time ago, so he can't be the Grin Ripper."

"But…" Amalie began, her little face twisted into a big frown.

"But…" Diana said, heartened by Alina's approving nod, "…Uncle Blane's daddy had a twin brother. They looked exactly alike. And…" She hesitated, not wanting to be the one to put the terrible truth into words.

"My daddy's twin brother—my uncle Douglas—is the Grin Ripper," Blane said in a clear, emotionless monotone. "He's the man who scared you in the hallway."

The confusion disappeared from Amalie's face. "I'm glad the Grin Ripper isn't your daddy, Uncle Blane," she said, smiling at Blane. She spoke to Iggy just as happily. "We can go upstairs again, Iggy! Hurray!"

Alina silently motioned for everyone to stay where they were. Apparently, her interrogation wasn't over yet. "Did you ever see the Grin Ripper again, Amalie?"

"Uh-huh," the little girl admitted. "He came to our old house…the one where I lived with Daddy and Mommy."

Diana let out a shaky breath. Her worst fears were coming true.

"I saw him from behind the curtains. After Mommy went to sleep, he chased me up the stairs to my room. The man from the park—the one who liked to talk to Nanny Di—chased me, too. But I was too fast. I shut the door and locked it. Then I hid under the bed."

"What a smart thing to do," Alina praised. "I'm so proud of you."

Alina's eyes swept Diana's face. She was obviously assessing whether a reaction to the news that Bill was involved yet again was forthcoming. Diana's steady gaze must have reassured her. When Alina looked away, Diana congratulated herself for passing the woman's you're-not-going-to-do-or-say-something-stupid-are-you? test. She then congratulated herself again for not revealing her own I-may-look-calm-on-the-outside-but-inside-I-am-a-mess mental state. The penetrating glance she received from Joey told her that he, at least, didn't share Alina's opinion. She chose to ignore him.

"And what did the Grin Ripper do after you hid under the bed?" Alina would have all of it out in the open, whether the rest of them wanted to know what really happened or not. She was lancing the boil, Diana thought, and it hurt far more than she had ever anticipated.

"The Grin Ripper knocked on the door until the man from the park told him it was time for Nanny Di to come home. Then the Grin Ripper yelled at me just like he did in the hallway after the wedding. He said if I told anyone about him, he would hurt somebody. That's why I stopped talking," Amalie explained, in her childish voice. Her honesty was heartbreaking. "Because the first time I told Nanny Di about the Grin Ripper, he hurt my mommy. I didn't tell anybody the second time because I didn't want him to hurt Daddy or Nanny Di or Mama Darcie. But now..." The little girl's eyes widened with fear. "I just told everybody—and, oh, Aunt Alina! The Grin Ripper is going to come back!" Her words were, unfortunately, prophetic. A few moments later, Douglas McCallum walked through the door.

Joey had applied the phrase *perfect timing* to many situations. But he had *never* seen a more perfectly timed entrance than the one Douglas McCallum made into the lobby of the new headquarters of McCallum Industries. The detestable man carried the whole thing off like he was the star of a movie. A particularly unnerving horror movie, in Joey's opinion.

The son of a bitch waltzed through the glass doors as if he owned the building. He was the image of the Grim Reaper—or Grin Ripper, as the situation warranted—dressed in black from his shiny shoes to his very expensive trench coat. Joey experienced an almost dizzying sense of déjà vu, having lived through an equally disturbing appearance from "Uncle Douglas" eighteen years earlier. One that nearly destroyed Blane's life. A glance at his siblings—and Blane—told Joey they were struggling with similar memories.

Douglas had no such qualms. He walked toward Blane, greeting various board members along the way with an airy confidence. Despite the board's knowledge of his embezzlement scheme, Douglas remained popular with several of the older members. Those misguided souls placed the blame for the younger man's "errors of judgment" at the feet of Fergus, the "neglectful father of poor Douglas." Joey was sure the responsibility for planting those seeds of mistrust against Fergus could be attributed solely to "poor Douglas."

To an outside observer, however, Douglas McCallum was the picture of a man with a clear conscious. To those who knew him, he was the devil incarnate. Waving his arms for silence, Douglas cleared his throat. With an oily smile, he addressed the crowd in the lobby.

"I would like to congratulate my nephew, Blane, for creating such an impressive work environment and for continuing to advance our company in spectacular fashion." He began a slow round of applause and was instantly joined by the majority of those not holding a plate. Several raised their glasses in Blane's direction.

No one in their group, save Ian or Alina, seemed able to react. Blane regarded his uncle as if he had grown two heads. Joey, Grace, and Darcie were visibly hostile. And Diana had absolutely no idea what to do. Her eyes followed the progress of Ian and Alina, moving so slowly and casually that no one would guess their final destination.

As the duo flanked Douglas—one on either side—Diana wondered, admiringly, how they were able to maintain their focus under such extreme duress. She, herself, was wobbly, as if someone had pulled the rug from under her feet. Ian was Douglas' half brother, after all. Someone like Diana—who adored her own brother—couldn't imagine what it must feel like to abhor a sibling.

A quick glance at Amalie showed her surprisingly unintimidated by the appearance of her nemesis…the Grin Ripper. Instead of the passivity Diana expected, Amalie looked ready to burst. With words. *Drat.* Diana saw the freight train of trouble coming down the track too late to do anything about it. From where she stood, she could only watch the explosion.

The little girl, her loyal iguana by her side, pointed her finger at the overconfident man who murdered her mother. "You're the Grin Ripper!" she shouted. "You put the powder in my mommy's drink that made her sleep forever! You," she continued, "are a bad, bad man!" Her words filled the void left by the earlier applause. Nobody moved. Her shrill voice rang through the lobby like Gabriel's trumpet on Judgement Day. The eyes of everyone in the crowd gazed first at Amalie and then at Douglas McCallum. Diana knew the exact moment Amalie realized what she had done. Her bottom lip began to tremble. Her eyes were fixed on the evil in their midst. Diana could almost see the wheels turning in the little girl's mind.

Run. Hide. Fight.

Diana took a step toward Amalie, but she couldn't make it in time.

"*Run!*" the little girl screamed, encouraging herself. She headed straight for the front doors. She bumped into the glass, but the doors didn't budge. They were too heavy for a five-year-old, no matter how frightened.

Diana glanced at Devin. "I'll get her," she offered, sparing him a choice. As she hurried toward the panicked child, now pounding on the door, an irritated bystander—either completely deaf or totally oblivious to what had just occurred—opened the door wide. Amalie made her escape, Iggy's tail bouncing under her arm. Without looking back, Diana pushed her way through the chattering groups of people. When she finally stepped onto the sidewalk, she was horrified to find that Amalie, spurred by fright, was halfway down the block.

Diana didn't hesitate. She ran. Her sweet little girl—the one she had helped to raise from a baby—was in trouble. She was prepared to chase Amalie for miles. But to her everlasting gratitude, a doorman—probably from a nearby hotel—appeared out of thin air. He caught the frightened child before she reached the busy intersection, holding onto her despite her struggles. Diana waved frantically to get his attention, letting him know help was on the way. The doorman waved back with one hand, never losing his grip on Amalie. *He must have children*, Diana thought, approvingly. Effectively controlling a wiggling little octopus, she knew, took practice.

She could see the relief in the child's eyes as she came closer. With thoughts only for Amalie, she knelt on the sidewalk to envelope the little girl in her arms. Amalie leaned against her willingly, but when Diana tried to pull her forward, the doorman refused to relinquish his grip.

"It's okay," Diana said, easily. "I've got her now. You can let go." She looked up, then, into eyes as cold as ice.

"Hello, Diana."

CHAPTER FIFTY-ONE

*A*s soon as the shocked voices rolling through the lobby of McCallum Industries' new headquarters quieted to a dull murmur, Douglas raised his own voice "Poor little girl," he said, pityingly. "I knew she had struggled to accept her mother's tragic death, but I had no idea she was delusional."

"My daughter is *not* delusional," Devin objected. Only Darcie's firm grip on his arm kept him from taking an intimidating step toward the man they now knew represented a genuine threat to Amalie.

But Douglas refused to back down. "Now, Devin," he continued, managing to sound both sympathetic and condescending at the same time. "We all understand why you've been too *distracted* "—he raked Darcie with an insolent glance—"to pay close attention to your unfortunate child."

Darcie let go of Devin's arm. "Go ahead and hit him," she murmured. "He deserves it."

Ian smoothly intervened before Devin could take advantage of Darcie's uncharacteristic penchant for violence. "Douglas," he said, clearly, "it's time to go." His words were *not* a suggestion.

"But brother," Douglas said, the picture of innocent confusion, "I just got here."

Alina smiled sweetly. "Nevertheless, you're leaving."

Douglas dramatically put both hands over his heart, his distress obvious for all to see. "Surely..." he whispered—still loud enough to be heard—"...surely you don't believe that I...that...I..."

"Spit it out, Douglas. Before it chokes you," Ian said, settling back to watch his half brother's performance.

Douglas took several deep breaths. "Surely you don't believe that I—your own flesh and blood, your *brother*—am capable of murder?"

Alina tilted her head to one side, studying her brother-in-law. "Most people are capable of murder, Douglas, given the right circumstances."

Alina's casual words—though chilling—were true. At least in Joey's opinion. Such a disturbing assessment of human nature made him uncomfortable. He wondered what Diana would have to say about Alina's frank observation. He glanced toward the front doors. Again. *How fast can Amalie run anyway?* he asked himself. *And why is it taking so long for Diana to catch her?*

Ian shrugged casually. "The real question, *brother*, seems to be whether or not you are the murderous Grin Ripper we've heard so much about."

Douglas exploded with righteous indignation. "I am genuinely shocked, wounded to my very soul by your suspicions!" His voice cracked a little, giving credence to his facade of innocence. Several board members regarded Ian with disapproval. "The Grin Ripper? Clearly an imaginary figment of a disturbed mind. I can't fathom how you can attribute a shred of credence to the twisted hallucinations of a three-year-old."

Devin growled, low in his throat.

"Actually, Mr. McCallum," Darcie volunteered, evenly, "Amalie is five."

Joey glanced at his sister, but her fiery glare was fixed on the demon in front of her. If her boyfriend went for Douglas' throat, it was obvious she wouldn't raise a finger to stop him. Joey understood completely. He had no intention of offering assistance, either.

Douglas glanced around, making sure the eyes of anyone in the crowd he could claim as a potential ally were turned his way. "Five?" he gasped, once again facing his half brother. "The word of a five-year-old is enough to make you assume that your brother is a murderer?"

"Of course not," Alina said, shaking her head.

Everyone who heard her words turned toward her in surprise.

A smile of arrogance swept Douglas' features. He looked like a poker player holding all the aces. But only until Alina played her final card. Unfortunately for Douglas, it completed a royal flush. "We aren't *assuming* anything, Douglas," she explained. "Your guilt isn't even the issue. We *know* you killed Mallory Merritt."

Douglas' smug smile vanished. "You clearly don't know what you're talking about," he blustered, loudly, before lowering his voice to address his half sibling and sister-in-law. "And you clearly do not know who you're dealing with. You can't force me to go anywhere with you," Douglas snarled.

"Of course we can," Ian said, cheerfully.

"*Force.*" Alina lowered her voice until it was only audible to their small group. "*Force* is your favorite word, isn't it Douglas? I noticed that about you right away...right after we met. *Force* gives you all the power, doesn't it? At least in your experience." She studied the man in front of her, not bothering to hide her loathing. Joey could have sworn he saw a glimmer of unease cross Douglas' face.

Alina continued in a soft voice: "Do you remember, Douglas, when you *forced* me against the wall in the castle's library and tried to rape me? Ian and I had only been married two days. Two days, Douglas. And you couldn't wait to betray your brother by taking advantage of your poor, fragile sister-in-law."

The same way you tried to take advantage of my mother, Joey thought, savagely. A flash of rage roared through him, followed quickly by gritty satisfaction as he studied Douglas' slightly crooked nose. The predator had chosen the wrong prey in Juliette Hanover. As a result, he remained permanently marked by the righteous fury of Joe Finch. And by Joe's proficient right hook.

Grace's hand curled around Joey's in unspoken understanding. Darcie's soft gasp told him that his usually astute sister had only now put the pieces together. He watched the color leach from her face, wishing neither of his sisters had to know the ugliness of which Douglas was capable.

"If your little tirade is over, Alina, I would like to put an end to this ridiculous standoff." Douglas' voice was cold, but his eyes glowed ominously.

Unfortunately for him, Alina *wasn't* finished. On the contrary, Joey realized, she was just getting started.

"Do you remember what happened next, Douglas, after you forced me against the wall? Hmm? Do you remember how you ended up flat on your back with my knife against your throat?" Her words were even more powerful for being spoken in a calm, almost soothing voice.

Douglas remained perfectly still. Only the increased frequency of his breathing gave away his agitation.

"Guess what, Douglas?" Alina leaned closer to whisper. "Today, I'm carrying a bigger knife."

Devin glanced at Blane and Joey in wonder. *Where?* he seemed to ask. *Where is she concealing a knife?* Alina's elegant attire seemed devoid of convenient hiding places. Blane shook his head. *Don't ask*, he seemed to say.

Douglas' eyes never left Alina. From where Joey stood, they seemed to glitter with hatred. Or was it lust? He tried to ignore the sick feeling in his stomach. There was, he decided, something very, very wrong with Douglas McCallum.

"And now it's time to go," Alina announced. "We need to clear up a few more issues before we turn you over to"—Alina hesitated an instant before finishing her sentence—"the authorities."

"You're talking about the police, I presume?" Douglas asked tonelessly.

"Not exactly," she said, picking up her purse from the edge of the sofa.

"Trust me, *brother*," Ian added, "you *don't* want to know." With those disquieting words, Ian put a firm hand on Douglas' shoulder, urging him forward.

Douglas' eyes settled on the faces of the Finch siblings as he passed them. "Give my regards to your mother," he sneered.

"When hell freezes over, Uncle Douglas," Grace said, returning his burning gaze.

At Douglas' surprised expression, Darcie chimed in. "Don't worry about it, Mr. McCallum. Mama wouldn't accept the regards of a depraved son of a bitch, anyway."

Joey contemplated his sisters respectfully. Darcie was invariably protective of those she loved, but he had forgotten how fierce Grace could be if the situation warranted. His usually glib tongue failed him, however, as he tried to deliver his own set down. "Hey, Douglas," he called. "Take care of that nose." Not one of his better efforts, but under the circumstances, it was the best he could do.

The crowd parted for Ian and Alina, with Douglas walking between them. Joey watched as they disappeared through the front doors. The same doors through which Diana and Amalie should have long since returned....

What were the child and her nanny doing? Strolling on the sidewalk? Buying ice cream? Shoes? Toys? Or perhaps Amalie was so upset by her encounter with the Grin Ripper that she refused to come back inside. Yes, he decided, that's probably what was happening. And, if that was the case, Diana needed his help.

He took a step toward the doors only to trip over a large object. His heart dropped as he reached down to untangle his foot from the straps of a familiar, ginormous—possibly magical—tote bag.

Diana couldn't have gone far without her bag, he decided. He hurried to the front doors and stepped onto the sidewalk, looking left and right. No sign of the lovely, auburn-haired woman or the adorable little blonde. No sign of Douglas and his escorts, either. Joey huffed out a breath of pure frustration. Where the hell was Diana?

Diana was, at that moment, slightly less concerned about *where* she was—in the vehicle of a kidnapper—than about where she was going—to her own demise? And Amalie's? She sincerely hoped not, for obvious reasons. So, she tried to be logical. To start from the beginning.

How did Bill manage to be in the exact location at the exact time Amalie ran down the sidewalk? No way that was an accident, she decided. Was it possible, then, that the psycho was psychic?

Nanny Di and the Psychic Psycho.

Diana thought not. She wasn't sure she believed in all that stuff anyway. And, besides, if Bill was psychic, he would never have allowed her to break his nose on the playground.

What about the appearance of the Grin Ripper? she asked herself. Was it a coincidence? Or was it the culmination of a plot to kidnap a five-year-old little girl who could identify a murderer? She assumed the latter, because, well…it made sense. That led to her last and hardest-to-answer question:

If this was all part of a plot to kidnap Amalie, why had Bill grabbed the nanny, too? Even though she was terrified, Diana was strangely gratified that Bill had taken her along for the ride. Literally. She couldn't have borne knowing Amalie was alone. And Diana was confident she would come up with a plan to save them both.

Any minute now.

She was *pretty* sure she would think of something.

Anything.

Think. Think. Think.

Diana waited for the plan to materialize.

Nothing happened.

Drat. Drat. Drat.

Questions bounced off the walls of her paralyzed brain with the force of baseballs, the impact making her more than a little dizzy. Somewhere in the foggy, hazy, pitiful remains of her shell-shocked brain was the realization that survival might depend on her ability to think. Coherently. How else was she to come up with a brilliant plan? She didn't have her ginormous tote bag, which had already proven itself an effective weapon. Worse than that, she didn't have her phone.

Diana glanced down at the child huddled against her in the back seat of a nondescript Honda Accord. The car was black, she noted. As black as Bill's heart. His response to her pleas to let Amalie go had been troubling: "*Don't worry about her, bitch. I need the little brat for now, but we'll get rid of her soon enough. And then...*" The last part of his sentence was swallowed by the blaring radio, which started up when he started the car.

Diana recoiled from being any part of a "we" that involved Psycho Bill. And she didn't want to know what he said after "*And then...*" She really *did not* want to know. An involuntary chill ran through her, settling somewhere around her stomach.

"*Be brave, Nanny Di.*"

Diana fumed for a few seconds at the sound of the familiar—albeit imaginary—voice ringing in her brain. She should have known it was only a matter of time before the know-it-all iguana showed up. The arrogant reptile's habit of appearing in her head when she was at her weakest was more than a little disturbing.

Thanks, Iggy, she said sarcastically—in her head, of course—*that's super great advice. But I need you to be a bit more specific. In case you haven't noticed, I'm riding in a car with a psycho. And the psycho has a gun.*

What was wrong with her? she wondered. She was fairly certain that sane people did *not* have mental conversations with imaginary animals.

Or did they? she mused. Was talking to imaginary animals a sign not only of sanity, but profound sensitivity and giftedness? Were there others whose imaginary animals doled out sage advice and words of encouragement when their stress levels boiled over?

Or were they—like her—unfortunate beings who had a loud-mouthed, irritating animal in their heads delivering a string of unwelcome commentary and repetitive advice? No, she decided, reluctantly, they did not. She, alone, had created Iggy. And she, alone, had to live with the consequences… *"Said the woman who takes advice from a talking iguana."* The memory of Joey's teasing words on their way to the Acorn Knob Inn brought tears to her eyes. Joey. Oh, how she loved him. But would she ever see him again?

"Be brave, Nanny Di. He's your happily ever after, remember?"

Yes, Diana decided. The smart-ass iguana was right. Joey was her happily ever after, which meant that she *would* see him again. And she *would* save Amalie, too, she resolved. And herself. But to do those things, she would have to follow the dratted iguana's advice. She would have to be brave.

A quick glance revealed that Iggy was watching her, even now, with something of a challenge in his plastic eyes. She stuck out her tongue in response. But somewhere, in the murky wilderness that was her brain, the fog began to clear.

All right, you snarky reptile, she conceded reluctantly. *You win. I will do my utmost to be brave. But not because you said so,* she added quickly, lest the cocky fellow get the wrong idea. She would be brave, she determined, for the tiny blonde snuggled against her side. And for Joey, because, well…he already thought she was brave. So, she couldn't let him down. And because Psycho Bill was evil and any romance writer worth her salt knew that evil couldn't win. Yes, Diana decided, she would be brave just as soon as she figured out what exactly that entailed.

"Nanny Di?"

Diana looked into wide, blue eyes.

"Nanny Di," Amalie repeated, "Iggy says to be brave."

Diana responded to the child as she had a hundred times before. "Then, we must do what Iggy says."

Amalie smiled for the first time since Psycho Bill forced them into the car. "Nanny Di, Iggy wants to sit on your lap."

"Of course he does," Diana mumbled under her breath, still a bit put out with Amalie's fluffy sidekick. "Climb on over, Iggy." Amalie settled the iguana in her nanny's lap.

Diana's eyes widened and her heart skipped a beat as she stared into the calm, plastic eyes of the wisest, bravest, most daring iguana ever to bless her with advice. She would never—*never*—berate the fabulous fellow again. Because, in that moment, she realized there was much more to the stuffed iguana than, well…stuffing. So much more. And all because at some point, in the last few hours, Iggy Iguana—surely a gift from God in heaven above—had eaten Diana's phone.

CHAPTER FIFTY-TWO

"*A*ny sign of them yet?" Devin asked as he joined Joey on the sidewalk.

Joey blew out a frustrated breath. "No, and I think they've had plenty of time to get back by now."

"So do I," Devin agreed. "Damn it."

Blane was the next one to push through the glass doors. His face held the same uneasiness Joey and Devin shared. "Not back yet?" he asked.

Devin shook his head.

"Then we go after them," Blane said, trying for nonchalance. "That means we have to get organized." But before they could do anything, Grace burst through the doors, Darcie at her heels. "You aren't going to like this," she announced, holding out her phone. "Diana's in a car, headed out of town."

Three faces sporting identical shocked expressions stared back at her for a split second before they all started talking at once.

"Damn it," Devin said, again. "Is Amalie with her?"

"What the hell," Joey snarled. "We have to go after—"

"In a car?" Blane asked. "But how did you—?"

Darcie's velvet tones broke in, answering the easiest question first. "Grace is tracking her," she explained, urgently. "Just like Rafe said."

"That means Diana still has her phone," Grace added encouragingly. "That's positive."

Darcie nodded in agreement before deferring to Devin. "What do you want to do?"

Devin rubbed a hand through his hair, caught in a father's worst nightmare. "If Amalie's with her, we go after them. If not, we start a search here."

Darcie nodded, watching Joey. "I'm going after Diana," Joey said, holding out his hand for Grace's phone.

Grace nodded. She and Blane exchanged a meaningful glance. "We're going with you," she announced, surprising no one.

Darcie looked into Devin's single eye. "What's your gut feeling?" she demanded.

"Amalie's with Diana," Devin stated.

Darcie nodded. "Then we're going, too," she announced confidently. "We can call Fergus from Blane's Range Rover and tell him to organize a search of the nearby area. Just in case."

"I'll get our purses," Grace offered. "And Diana's bag," she called over her shoulder as she ran back into the building.

"You navigate," Darcie told her brother-in-law, removing Blane's keys from his motionless hand. "I'll drive."

"*No!*" The three men replied as one. They had already experienced Darcie's questionable driving-under-duress skills and had no desire to live through them again.

Grace burst through the doors, nearly dragging Diana's enormous bag. "Good Lord," she said to Joey. "What's in this thing?"

A ghost of a smile crossed Joey's lips. "What's *not* in that thing?"

Grace neatly whisked the dangling keys from Darcie's hand, returning them to her husband. "Blane will drive," she told her sister, briskly. "From what I gather, you nearly scared your passengers to death last week. And we don't have time for that."

"Hmph," was Darcie's only reply as they raced to the Range Rover.

Thanks partly to the comforting weight of the iguana-covered phone on her lap and partly—she was somewhat reluctant to admit—to the iguana's encouraging words, Diana was imbued with new courage. Shortly after Bill turned off the highway onto a two-lane road, she exchanged her fear for anger, the preferred emotion in this particular situation. Her fear gave Bill all the power and she would not—*refused*, as a matter of fact—give the deranged monster any more control than he already had.

By the time he stopped the car at the end of another deserted dirt road, she had come up with a plan to save Amalie. Granted, it was a risky plan—relying on fortuitous circumstances as well as the complete cooperation of a five-year-old—but it was a plan all the same.

Unfortunately, for the plan to succeed, Diana needed to relate the five-year-old's responsibilities to the five-year-old. Bill had ruined her opportunity by turning the radio off when he turned onto the dirt road. Diana supposed he didn't want loud music to call attention to their presence.

Whose attention could he possibly be worried about attracting? The trees? The sky? The leaf-covered ground? Or, she thought, sarcastically, maybe he was afraid the large stick by the side of the road would see them and alert the authorities. She peered out the car window at a landscape the very definition of the "middle of nowhere." She could probably scream her head off and no one would hear...a disturbing realization.

Bill turned to his passengers. His cold eyes were unnerving, so Diana resolved not to look directly into them. That was part of her brilliant plan. Instead, she fixed her eyes on his mouth. He made a great show of waving his gun around, an obvious reminder that he had one. As if she could forget about that.

"I'm going to get out of the car," he announced, still waving his gun in the air.

"Congratulations," Diana said. Bill did a doubletake, which pleased her immensely. What was he expecting her to do? Cry and beg for mercy? That was *not* going to happen...also a part of the plan.

"Shut up, bitch," Bill snarled. "I'm getting out of the car. And you're not."

Amalie's little voice spoke up. "Mr. Bill," she asked. "Why are you so mad?"

Bill's mouth fell open in amazement. Diana wanted to laugh. She couldn't have planned this conversation better herself.

"Maybe he's hungry," Diana said, matter-of-factly.

Amalie thought about that for a second. "Oh," she said. "Like Iggy. Iggy gets mad when he's hungry. Mr. Bill, maybe you should have a snack."

"I'm not going to have a damn snack," Bill burst out. "I am getting out of this car and you two are not." He was waving the gun again as he tried to regain control of the conversation. "If you get out of the car, I'll kill you."

"Aren't you going to kill us anyway?" Diana asked, chancing a glance at Bill's eyes. She was rewarded with the lovely sight of sublime irritation.

He spoke through gritted teeth. "It's not time yet," he volunteered. "I have to follow the plan."

Well, Diana thought. She certainly knew what that was like. And if she could only be rid of Bill's heinous presence for a few precious minutes, she would be able to fill Amalie in on all the details of *her* plan.

He opened his car door, pointing his gun at them as he turned to exit the vehicle. But before he could get out of the car, Amalie spoke up.

"Nanny Di, is Mr. Bill really going to kill us?"

Diana shook her head, aware that Bill had paused momentarily to listen. "No, Amalie," she said, calmly. "He's just bluffing."

Amalie looked puzzled. "What's *bluffing*?"

"That's when you're *not really* going to do what you say you are going to do," Diana answered. "Like when you say you're going to finish your vegetables after you eat your dessert."

Bill slammed the door.

Good, thought Diana. Even though he was still pointing his gun through the window, he couldn't hear her conversation with Amalie. In a clear and concise voice, Diana began the instructions she had already prepared in her head.

"Amalie, there is something wrong with Mr. Bill."

"Is he sick?" the little girl asked.

"Yes," Diana said, pleased with the question. "Mr. Bill is sick. There's something wrong with his brain."

"Is that why he wants to nannynap you?" Amalie asked.

Diana had no idea what the child was talking about. "Why he wants to *what*?"

"*Nannynap,*" Amalie repeated. "He can't *kid*nap you because you're not a kid."

"Oh, no, sweetie," Diana explained, glancing at the window. Good Lord. They didn't have time for a vocabulary lesson. "We say *kidnap* for everybody, no matter how old he or she is."

"Oh," Amalie said, satisfied with the answer. "Is that why he's trying to *kidnap* you?"

"Yes," Diana said. "We don't know what he's going to do next so we need to get away from him as soon as we can."

"Okay," Amalie said, happily, hugging her iguana. "Iggy says okay, too."

"Thank you, Iggy." *Stay close to Amalie,* she told the iguana, *and don't you dare spit out that phone.*

"I don't like Mr. Bill," Amalie elaborated. "And Iggy doesn't like him. He's mean. And he uses bad words."

"I know," Diana agreed. "I don't like him, either." With a gentle hand, she tipped up Amalie's chin to make sure she was listening. "Do you remember what your teacher told you to do if a bad person comes into your school?"

"Run. Hide. Fight," chanted Amalie.

"That's right," Diana praised. "Now, listen carefully."

The little girl nodded; her big, blue eyes were full of trust. Diana's heart twisted. "In a little while, I'm going to tell you to run. When I do, I want you to hug Iggy tight, holding him just like you're holding him now. Head up. Tail down." *So my phone won't fall out of his belly,* Diana added to herself. As long as Amalie had that phone, someone would find her.

"Head up. Tail down," Amalie repeated. "Head up. Tail down."

"Good," Diana praised. "When I say, 'Run,' you're going to hug Iggy tight—"

"Head up. Tail down."

Diana continued: "—and run into the woods. Then I want you and Iggy to hide."

"Just like hide-and-seek?" Amalie asked.

"Just like hide-and-seek," Diana affirmed. "But…I don't want you to hide like Daddy or Mama Darcie is looking for you. That's too easy. I want you to hide like *Uncle Joey* is looking for you."

"Ooh," Amalie said, her eyes dancing. "Uncle Joey's good at hide-and-seek. Iggy and I will have to find a very good hiding place."

"That's right," Diana agreed. "Good enough so that Uncle Joey would have a hard time finding you. And, Amalie, I don't want you to come out until Daddy or Mama Darcie or—"

"Uncle Joey!"

"—finds you." Diana looked into those little girl eyes she loved so much. "Promise me," she said. "Promise me you won't come out until someone finds you. Pinky swear." Diana held up her right hand, wiggling her pinky finger.

"Pinky swear?" Amalie asked seriously.

Diana nodded. "Pinky swear." They linked pinky fingers and repeated the words together. Diana breathed a sigh of relief, sure now that Amalie knew her part in the plan.

"Nanny Di," the little girl asked. "What will *you* do?"

"What?" Diana asked, somewhat at a loss.

"What will you do when I run?" Amalie asked. "Will you run, too? And hide like me and Iggy?"

Diana took a deep breath. She looked into those trusting eyes. And lied. "I'll be right behind you. And, 'Malie?"

"Uh-huh?"

"When you run, don't look back. Do you understand? Don't look back, no matter what you hear happening behind you. Can you do that for me?"

Amalie nodded. Only then did Diana release the breath she had been holding. What would she do when Amalie ran? She would do what Amalie's teacher told her to do.

Run. Hide. *Fight.*

Diana was going to fight.

CHAPTER FIFTY-THREE

*J*oey kept his eyes glued to screen of the phone in his hand—Grace's phone—watching the small, blue dot that somehow, horribly, represented the love of his life moving steadily away from him. "Can't you go any faster?" he asked Blane, irritably.

"See," Darcie said, triumphantly. "I told you I should have driven."

"Both of you need to hush," Grace said in an exasperated tone.

Joey glared at Grace.

"The turnoff is coming up," she explained. "We can't be more than a minute or two behind them."

Joey glared at her again.

"Can't get too close," Blane added. "Or he'll know we're back here."

Joey sighed. "You're right. And I'm sorry. I just want to…"

"We get it, Joey," Devin interrupted grimly. "We get it."

Darcie piped up impatiently. "So, what's the plan?" she asked leaning forward.

The others regarded her blankly.

"Great," she said, flopping back in her seat. "We're so all-fired impatient to catch up to them but we have no idea what we're going to do when we *actually* catch up to them."

Joey glared at Darcie. He couldn't remember the last time he *willingly* sat in the backseat between his sisters. Maybe never. But Devin had given him no choice by planting himself in the passenger seat of the Range Rover while Joey was watching the phone.

Joey glared at Devin.

"Turn right!" Grace yelled. Unfortunately, she yelled into Joey's ear. "Then stop!" she yelled again.

Joey glared at Grace. Again.

Blane swerved sharply onto a dirt road, sending Darcie sliding into Joey, who slid into Grace. He felt like the peanut butter in the middle of some long-forgotten sandwich from childhood. Damn but he hated the backseat. But, as he and his sisters tussled with each other to resume their original position, they exchanged a rueful smile. Joey's irritation melted away.

His siblings, he realized, were only trying to help. The same went for Blane. And Devin—stealer of the passenger seat—who was worried about his own daughter. So far, Joey hadn't been the least bit stalwart or lionhearted. Or, he admitted, even remotely helpful.

At least Grace was watching the phone, he thought, instead of wasting her time glaring at people. "Good job, Gracie," he murmured as the car came to a halt. Once again, he focused his eyes on the screen.

"What's going on?" Blane asked, foot on the brake.

"They've stopped up ahead," Joey said, taking up the reins of responsibility once more.

"How far?" Devin asked.

Joey studied the screen. "Maybe a quarter of a mile."

Blane pulled off the road and parked. "I think we need to go the rest of the way on foot," he said. "The element of surprise and all that stuff."

Darcie leaned forward again. "We need a plan," she said, evenly.

"We could rush the kidnapper," Devin suggested. "He can't fight all of us."

Joey shook his head. "Not a good idea. In Alexandria, Bill had a gun. He's bound to have one today. Too risky."

Devin nodded. "Why don't we assess the situation before we decide?"

The others murmured their agreement.

"Just remember," Darcie said. "Before anyone makes a move, we all need to agree." She sighed. "I'm not trying to be melodramatic, but no one has the right to make a decision that might endanger Amalie and Diana without running it by the rest of us."

Grace glanced at each of the men, in turn. "That means no crazy heroics, guys." She waited until each man gave his assent.

"Let's go," Blane said, opening his car door.

The smug expression on Bill's face as Diana stepped out of the car made her want to punch his recently broken nose. She turned her back on him to help Amalie, holding the little girl's hand until she scrambled out to stand beside her nanny on the rutted dirt road. Diana carefully placed Iggy—head up, tail down—in Amalie's arms, uncomfortably aware that Bill's gun was pointing straight at the little girl the whole time.

Drat, she thought, as they left the dirt road—per Bill's direction—and waded into the weeds alongside it. How was she supposed to put her brilliant plan in motion if Bill refused to cooperate? Diana fumed. The least he could do was point the gun at *her* for a while. Hopefully the next few minutes would give her the opportunity she needed.

After a few yards they traded the weeds for a thicket of trees before stepping into a small clearing. Falling leaves joined their brethren, creating a crunchy carpet beneath their feet. On the northern edge of the clearing the burned-out shell of an abandoned farmhouse stood in danger of being taken over by the encroaching foliage. The remains of the house, brooding and silent, would one day disappear completely. A small barn and silo, nearly reclaimed by tangled vines and tree growth, loomed on the western side of the clearing. The late afternoon light trickled through the tree limbs, casting the branches in flickering shadows. The entire area shrieked of neglect and decay. A forgotten place in time, Diana thought, and a perfect place to commit murder.

Her eyes searched the clearing, looking for anything that could be used to distract the man who continued to point his gun at the innocent child beside her. A small movement at the western corner of the house caught her attention. A deer, perhaps? Or turkeys? Maybe a bear? Diana didn't care if it was an entire pride of man-eating lions. If she could convince Bill to turn his gun in that direction, Amalie would have a chance to get away.

"What was that?" she squealed, pointing to the corner of the house. "I saw something move."

Instead of looking startled, Bill laughed. "That's just Calli," he said. "Come on out, Calli. We're here. And we're right on time."

Calli? Who—or what—was *Calli?* Diana had no idea what she was expecting, but it wasn't the middle-aged man who walked around the corner. His features, though pleasant enough, weren't particularly striking. Or, in Diana's opinion, memorable. He was wearing a bright blue sweatshirt, jeans, a pair of worn tennis shoes, and a baseball cap sporting the words "*Disneyworld MVP.*" He looked like any "average Joe" out for an afternoon stroll…with one very important exception. He was carrying a pistol.

Diana's heart sank. Two men. Two pistols. Unless she could somehow get them to point the pistols at each other, her plan was in serious jeopardy.

Calli's pleasant expression disappeared the moment he saw Diana. He closed his eyes briefly, taking a deep, cleansing breath. Clearly, he was trying to calm himself. When he spoke to Bill, Diana recognized the same controlled tones she used when Amalie was being difficult. In other words, Callie used his nanny voice.

"Your instructions were simple," he stated. "Grab the child. Three words. Three little words. Short and to the point. Grab. The. Child. And never—at any time while I was giving you those simple instructions—did I say, 'Grab the child *and...*' " He glanced at Diana as if he expected her sympathy. *Incompetent workers,* he seemed to say. *What can I do?* He was actually rather polite when he inquired, "Miss...?"

"Merritt," she supplied.

"Are you serious?" Calli asked in disbelief. "*You're* Diana Merritt. *You're* the nanny." He turned his attention back to Bill. "I can't believe this. I told you to forget about her after that debacle in Alexandria. *Douglas* told you to leave her alone." Calli blew out an angry breath. "Damn it, Billix," he snarled, his control slipping a bit. "Can't you do anything without screwing it up?"

Billix.

Diana had heard that name before. But where? She felt it was somehow important.

Billix. Billix. Billix.

The unusual name whirled through Diana's mind. Suddenly the memory was crystal clear. She was in Blane's office. The Trio of Doom didn't want her to go to Newport to meet her "friend" Bill Watkins. She remembered their questions....

"You said your friend's name is Bill. Do you know if Bill is the short form of something else? William, perhaps? Or Billix?

"Are you sure he said Watkins and not Watson? You're sure he didn't say Billix Watson?"

And Diana remembered Rafe's chilling words to Blane: "*Billix Watson was the psychotic thug who nearly beat you to death, Blane.*"

Nanny Di and the Psychotic Thug.

Psychotic. Thug.

Diana glanced at Billix Watson. Yes, she could see that. He was still a psychotic thug, she decided. And unless she was wrong, he was enjoying his confrontation with the mysterious Calli.

"Don't worry about her, Calli," Bill smirked, indicating Diana with his head. "She's with me."

Disbelief filled Calli's nondescript face. "With *you*?"

"With *me*," Bill said.

"You came here with *him*?" Calli asked Diana, amazement written on his face.

Diana was slightly insulted. Did this Calli person really think she was here with Billix Watson, Psychotic Thug, of her own free will? The situation was getting ridiculous. Her irritation increased, keeping her fear at bay. "I came here with him," she agreed, indicating Billix with her head. "At gunpoint."

Calli laughed at the annoyance on Bill's face. "This is unfortunate," Calli said, almost to himself. He looked at Diana guiltily. "And you're so pretty, too." He sighed heavily. "Such a shame for your family, especially after the way Billix ruined your handsome cousin's face. Something he also did—I might add—when he wasn't following instructions." He shrugged his shoulders, clear annoyance in his gaze. "There's no way around it, Billix. We're going to have to kill her, too."

"No, we aren't," Bill objected. He looked at Diana over Amalie's head. "Don't worry. I won't let Rafe kill you," he said.

"Um…thank you?" Diana didn't quite know what to say. Rafe? What was Billix talking about?

"I'm going to kill you myself," he announced.

Great. Diana was losing patience with this inane conversation. She turned to Billix with a pointed stare. "And why are *you* going to kill me, *Billix*?" She crossed her arms and waited.

He pointed to his crooked nose on his bruised face. "You *broke* my nose," he said, as if he was talking about the weather.

Calli looked on with interest.

"But *you* lured me to a deserted playground and attacked me," Diana said. "What was I supposed to do?"

"You *broke* my nose," Billix said as if that settled the matter.

Diana gave up, wishing she could break his nose again.

"Nanny Di?" Amalie leaned against Diana's leg.

Drat. Diana had almost forgotten that the child was listening to all this.

"Nanny Di? Is Mr. Bill going to kill you?"

"No," Diana said, scowling at Mr. Bill. "Mr. Bill is not going to kill anyone."

But Amalie wasn't finished. "Is Mr. Rafe going to kill us?" the little girl asked calmly.

"Of course not, Amalie," Diana said with conviction, wishing Amalie wasn't such a good listener. At least Diana wasn't hearing things. Amalie had heard Rafe's name, too. That, she decided, was proof she wasn't losing her mind. Yet.

She squeezed Amalie's hand. "No one is going to kill us." *Because I'm going to figure out how to make these two idiots shoot each other first.*

"Are they bluffing?" she asked.

Diana glared at Mr. Disneyworld MVP and then at the heinous Billix Watkins before turning back to Amalie. "Yes, Amalie," she said. "They're bluffing."

"I thought so," the little girl said.

The man called Calli laughed again. "I like your style," he said to Diana. "I can see why Billix brought you with him, even if he had to do it at gunpoint," he added, slyly.

"Looks like it's time for you to take a trip, Calli," Bill snarled. "Your tan is fading."

"At least I don't look like a corpse," Calli fired back.

Diana wondered how the two men managed to accomplish anything. They stood where they were, glowering at each other. Obviously, there was no love lost between them. Diana wracked her brain for a clever way to encourage their discord. She needn't have bothered, because at that moment, the bushes near the vine-covered barn began to move.

What now? Diana asked herself. Were they about to be joined by another gun-wielding fiend? Or was a psychotic thug-eating bear lurking in the bushes? She held her breath, praying for the latter, until Rafe

Montgomery stepped out of the brush near the silo. Her heart filled with relief. Her phone! Rafe had tracked her. She and Amalie were saved. She couldn't help but smile as he stepped into the clearing.

But Diana's smile faded quickly. Rafe wasn't alone. She focused on the man walking behind him in disbelief. She hadn't thought their situation could get worse until she watched Rafe Montgomery—savvy ex-spy, protector of those he loved, leader of the fabled Trio of Doom—being forced into the clearing at gunpoint.

CHAPTER FIFTY-FOUR

"Can't you two keep it down?" Joey asked, tired of the shuffling and muttered complaints emerging from the mouths of his sisters.

"No," Darcie quipped. "We can't."

"Have *you* ever walked on a dirt road covered with crunchy leaves while wearing heels and trying not to make a sound?" Grace asked, a trace of exasperation in her usually sweet voice.

Joey didn't reply. He was back to glaring.

Devin chuckled as he caught up to the siblings, erasing the strain from his face for a few seconds. But the worry returned as he studied the bend in the road. The sharp curve limited their vision of what lay ahead. Blane had volunteered to continue ahead on a short reconnaissance mission, leaving the rest of them to wait.

Darcie rubbed her hands up and down her arms, encased in sheer sleeves. "I couldn't have chosen a more inconvenient outfit if I tried," she admitted morosely. "It's a lot chillier out here than I thought. Poor 'Malie must be half-frozen by now."

Joey's sharp retort died in his throat. His sister was genuinely upset, not for herself, but for her future stepdaughter.

Grace put her arm around her sister's shoulders. "Amalie will be all right, Darce," she encouraged. "She's a tough little girl."

Once again, Joey's vexation melted away. His sisters were great. They really were. "She's also full of sugar," he added, helpfully. "Eating all those cake squares will keep her blood flowing."

"Poor Diana," Devin murmured.

Joey, who was trying *not* to think too much about what was happening with poor Diana, was relieved when Blane reappeared.

"They're in a clearing in front of some burned-out old house. Around the curve and up a small rise," he explained in a low voice. "There are some large rocks and a couple of boulders we can hide behind. But"—his severe gaze touched on each one of his accomplices—"we have to be quiet. All of us. At the same time."

They nodded their agreement, silently following in his wake. Joey would be the first to admit the going wasn't easy. Darcie slipped off her heels, tossing them unceremoniously to the ground. Grace's heels quickly joined her sister's. They finally reached the rocks after practically crawling up the small rise.

Joey poked his head up from behind the largest boulder. The others did the same. The tangled brush and tree limbs gave them ample protection to remain standing while allowing them to see and hear what was happening. At first glimpse, Joey's emotions split in half, joy and fear waging a fierce battle for control. Joy that Diana and Amalie appeared unharmed; fear of what was to come.

Amalie was sandwiched between Bill and Diana, their backs to their observers. By Joey's estimate, they couldn't be more than twenty-five feet away. His eyes scanned Diana's lithe form. She stood strong, the spackled sunlight striking sparks in her red hair. She held Amalie's hand in her own. So very close but impossibly out of reach. What he wouldn't give to switch places with her.

Every impulse in Joey's body was screaming for action. Only the pistol currently pointing at Amalie kept him from obeying. He sensed that Blane and Devin were battling their own urge to attack. Darcie and Grace were struggling, too. Joey would be the first to admit that his sisters, in protective mode, were not to be trifled with. God help Bill if those two ever got hold of him, he thought with approval.

"What the hell?" Blane said, under his breath.

For the first time, Joey looked beyond his heart's desire to the far side of the clearing. He didn't recognize two of the men, but a chill ran down his spine at the sight of the unflappable Rafe Montgomery standing with a pistol pointed at his back.

Rafe spoke first. "Norman Callahan, former headmaster of the Herbert M. Ward School for Adolescent Boys."

Calli smiled, smugly. "Rafe Montgomery, former stablemaster of the same institution. And the only man I know who ages backwards." Calli's eyes swept Rafe's lean, elegant form. "Damn, but you look good."

"I wish I could say the same for you, Calli," Rafe replied easily, enjoying the man's sudden frown.

Diana was amazed at Rafe's nonchalant poise. The barrel of a gun was being held against his back, for heaven's sake, yet he appeared completely relaxed. Almost amused. She struggled to make sense of the conversation.

"I'm only the *former* headmaster because of you, Montgomery," Calli said, a hint of accusation in his voice. "You made sure I lost my job."

Rafe shook his head. "Now, now, Calli. Recruiting troubled teenage boys into a life of crime is bad form. You shouldn't have expected *that* to go unnoticed."

Calli laughed. "You certainly dried up our supply. I'll have to say that for you. Lucky for our organization, we found other avenues."

"I see you kept one of the recruits from the old days," Rafe observed, switching his keen gaze to Billix Watson, Psychotic Thug. "Hello, Billix."

"Mr. Rafe," Billix replied. "Long time. No see."

Calli rolled his eyes. "Still as articulate as ever," he observed.

Rafe chuckled appreciatively. "Looks like you've been very busy, Billix, since you left the school."

Billix shrugged, almost proudly. "Yeah," he said. "I guess you could say I'm—"

"Head Thug?" Rafe asked, raising his eyebrows.

Billix laughed. "Yeah. I'm Head Thug," he proclaimed. "I'm in charge of all kinds of important jobs like—"

"Hitting innocent men with cars?" Rafe interrupted.

Billix scowled. "Now, that was a mistake, Mr. Rafe. I shouldn't have done that," he admitted. He looked at Diana. "You can tell your cousin I messed up the next time you see him. Oh"—he seemed to remember what he was planning—"never mind. You won't see your cousin again. My bad."

Diana looked at Billix in amazement. How could such a callous reptile of a man exist? she asked herself, with apologies to Iggy Iguana, uncallous reptile.

Calli cleared his throat, obviously eager to move things along. "And, now, Rafe, we have a little job for you," he announced.

"I assumed as much," Rafe replied, calmly.

Calli motioned to the man who remained behind Rafe. The unnamed criminal shoved the gun's barrel harder into Rafe's back, pushing him forward. Diana nearly gasped when she saw the man's face. She knew that man. His name was Max. He was the man charged with protecting Mallory after Devin's accident. He worked for McCallum Industries.

Had Max started an affair with Mallory while Devin was recovering from his horrible accident? Had they all been wrong about Douglas McCallum? Was Blane's uncle innocent? Was Max the man who murdered Mallory? Diana was irate. And terrified. And very, very confused. As if sensing her stare, Max glanced her way.

And winked.

At least Diana thought he winked. Maybe he just had something in his eye. The wind had picked up a bit, and leaves were falling like rain. No, she decided, as Max quickly turned his head away; she knew a wink when she saw one. Some of the tension left her body. Apparently, Rafe had a plan of his own. She just wished she knew what role she was supposed to play in it.

"That's Max," Grace hissed. "That's *our* Max. I've invited him to dinner. I've baked him banana bread." Her green eyes filled with tears. "And now he's holding Rafe at gunpoint. Max is a *traitor*."

Blane shook his head. "I don't believe it. Max is Rafe's righthand man."

"But the gun..." Darcie added, soberly.

Blane refused to listen. "This must be a part of Rafe's plan. Max would never betray him."

"Or us," Devin agreed, easily. "You all right, Boss-man?"

Joey pulled his eyes from Diana for a second to study his best friend. Blane's face was unnaturally pale. Probably from the shock of seeing Billix Watson, the dangerous boy—now a dangerous man—who had almost killed him all those years ago. Not to mention his former headmaster turned criminal. And now Max...trusted employee turned traitor. How many shocks, Joey wondered, could one man stand?

Aware of their perusal, Blane managed a brief smile. "I'm fine." He turned his head back to Rafe's voice and the unfolding tableau in the clearing.

"This is quite a reunion, Calli," Rafe said. "You. Me. Billix."

Calli narrowed his eyes. "If you want to call it that."

"Nothing like old friends, is there? I met another old friend of yours the other day. Her name is Calliope."

The cocky smile on Calli's face slipped a little. "*Calliope?*"

Rafe nodded. "You remember Calliope, don't you Calli? She's the one who was standing beside you on the scaffold in Belize when Kenneth Wade fell to his death."

Calli's expression remained neutral. "Shame about that faulty harness. Wasn't it?"

Rafe shook his head. "No good, Calli. She told me *everything*…how you came up with the plan, lured the man to Belize, paid off the zip line company. *Everything.*"

"And you believe her?" Calli scoffed.

Rafe smiled, perfectly relaxed. "Of course."

"I see," Calli said.

"Do you?" Rafe asked.

Calli sighed. "The thing is, Montgomery, it really doesn't matter what you know about me. After you kill the child and her nanny—because you're insane, you see—you're going to turn the gun on yourself. Murder–suicide. And then your efforts to frame Douglas McCallum for your own crimes will come to light. Such a shame what greed can do to a person, isn't it?"

Diana was horrified by Calli's plan, but Rafe didn't even blink.

"Good effort, Calli," he said. "Very impressive. And I do have to give you points for your loyalty to Douglas McCallum. *Blind* loyalty, but loyalty all the same."

"What do you mean *blind* loyalty?" Calli looked rather affronted by Rafe's words.

Rafe shook his head sadly. "Do you even know *why* Douglas wants you to kill the little girl?" he asked.

"Of course I do," Calli said. "She saw Douglas murder her mother."

Rafe nodded. "Very good. But do you know *why* Douglas murdered her mother?"

When Calli hesitated, Billix jumped in. "Because he was having an affair with her," he announced gleefully. "For months, Calli. It started at Blane's wedding and lasted until Douglas killed her." He counted to himself. "Eight months. More or less."

The man called Calli was visibly shaken. "That's not true," he objected. "Douglas and I have been together since boarding school. His one-night stands are just for show. So the press won't delve too deeply into his personal life. We've had that arrangement for years."

Billix snorted at that. "For show?" he asked. "Is that what he tells you, Calli? Eight months is a lot of 'one-night stands' to have with the same woman." He shook his head in mock dismay, enjoying every moment of his great reveal. "Douglas screwed Mallory Merritt for eight months, Calli, until she decided she wanted to tell the world about their relationship. Then he killed her. And guess what else?"

"Shut up." Calli's hand—the one not holding the gun—curled into a fist at his side.

Diana watched the men intently. She had never heard Billix string so many words together at one time. His obvious delight in causing Calli pain confirmed the deep animosity she had sensed between the two men. And now that the dam had burst, Billix couldn't seem to stop talking.

"There was another woman before Mallory," he chortled. "Her name was Sheila Preston. Douglas killed her, too, to keep her quiet. Same way. By making it look like an opioid overdose. And guess what else, Calli?"

Calli's face was drawn and wan, almost waxy under his tan. Diana thought he might be sick. Or faint.

"Shut up," Calli snarled. "You're finished."

Billix grinned in satisfaction. "Not quite. Got one more for you." He paused before digging his verbal blade deeper into the wound. "Douglas has been screwing Calliope, too. Right under your stupid, trusting nose. And those are only the women I know about. Looks like Douglas has been cheating on you for years, Calli. What do you think of your lover now?"

"I don't believe you," Calli said, a desperate quality in his voice. "You have no proof, Billix. Just words. If Douglas was here, he would—"

Throw you under the bus," Billix finished. "Way under the bus. And then he would spin his tires on your poor, trusting body. And after he was finished, he would walk away. Just like you never existed."

Calli shook his head. "That will never happen," he said, trying to regain some semblance of control. "And since Douglas isn't here—"

"But I am," came a voice from the eastern side of the clearing.

Grace grabbed Joey's arm, tugging frantically to get his attention. He ignored her, waiting to see Douglas McCallum step out from the trees. "*Joey!*" Grace whispered. She wasn't going to leave him alone.

He turned to her in abject irritation. "*What?*" he mouthed, noting her green eyes looked unnaturally large in her face. She motioned for him to crouch down behind the rocks. He complied. The movement attracted the attention of the others. Darcie dropped down beside them, leaving Blane and Devin on watch.

His sister was clearly frightened. "What's wrong, Gracie?" Joey asked, gentling his tone.

She pointed down the rise and toward the dirt road at their backs. "Someone's down there," she hissed.

Well, hell. Joey's eyes searched the trees carefully.

Nothing moved.

"I saw somebody down there. On the road," Grace insisted. "I swear."

Darcie's worried gaze met Joey's. "Gracie," she said. "I believe you saw something, but maybe it was an animal."

Grace shook her head. "It wasn't an animal. It was a person...a person dressed in black." She pointed toward the road.

Darcie and Joey scanned the area again, but to no avail.

"I just don't see anything, Gracie," Darcie whispered. "And I don't know what we can do about it. Not right now."

Grace nodded, doubt clouding her eyes. "Maybe you're right." She chanced a glance at the empty road again. "Maybe it was a deer. Whatever it was, it's gone now, anyway." She stood up, turning her attention back to the clearing.

Darcie and Joey followed suit. But as they waited for a seemingly reluctant Douglas McCallum to appear, Joey had to wonder…what had Gracie seen? A hunter? A hiker? A UPS man? Or, possibly, a man-eating stranger? The dirt road did remind him of the back road to the Acorn Knob Inn. He strained his ears but failed to hear the requisite banjo music. He was certain Diana would appreciate his effort. He shook his head in disgust. How the hell could he stand there making jokes in his head when His Future Everything was in danger? Fuming at his own useless stupidity, Joey focused on the promised appearance of the Grin Ripper.

Douglas McCallum finally stepped out of the trees, followed closely by Ian. He appeared surprised by those who were gathered. After a quick glance around the clearing, to make sure he was the focal point of attention, he began what Joey was sure would be an Academy Award winning performance. Grace's earlier sighting of *somebody* niggled at his brain. He glanced back at the deserted dirt road just to make sure it was still deserted.

It was.

"Rafe," Douglas said. "Thank God you're here. And Max."

He managed to hide the satisfaction in his gaze when he saw the gun Max was holding. But not quickly enough. Those keeping vigil behind the rock exchanged a worried glance.

Douglas wasted no time. He immediately directed his ire toward Calli. "Norman Callahan," he sneered. "I might have known." Turning to his half brother, he pointed an accusing finger in Calli's direction. "Whatever this is, it begins and ends with him. This man has been blackmailing me for years," he announced. "And all because of a minor indiscretion we committed in boarding school."

"*Minor* indiscretion?" Calli gasped, oblivious to anything but the enormity of Douglas' betrayal. "You said you loved—"

"He threatened to go to the press," Douglas interrupted as if Calli's devastated whisper was an annoying, buzzing insect he intended to swat. "And, well…I couldn't let that happen." The pain on Douglas' face was stunningly believable.

Joey realized that he would honestly have fallen for Douglas' innocent act…if he didn't already know that the man was a demon from hell.

Douglas' voice cracked convincingly. "I would never—*never*—willingly hurt our family, brother, or the company our father and grandfather worked so hard to build. So, I sacrificed my peace of mind and my personal assets to satisfy *his* demands." He took a deep, dramatic breath, as if deeply ashamed of his admission. "That's why I stole money from our father and from Blane's trust fund, Ian. I couldn't keep up with Norman's requests." He paused, giving his half brother a chance to speak.

But Ian didn't dignify Douglas with a reply. He remained unmoving and expressionless. Only the intensity in his eyes bore witness to his deeply personal reaction.

Calli, clearly devastated, was staring at Douglas as if he had never seen him before.

Billix, however, was enjoying himself immensely. "Hey, Calli." He waved until Calli glanced his way. "Under. The. Bus." He immediately made a growling noise intended to sound like the aforementioned bus.

Amalie, in Diana's opinion, had often done a much better imitation.

Calli straightened his shoulders, eyes blazing in the face of Douglas' nonchalance. "You lied," Calli gasped. "You said I was the only one. You said—"

"I said nothing of the sort," Douglas snapped. "You're sick, Norman. Your obsession with me is totally irrational." He dismissed Calli with a shrug. Once again, he spoke to Ian: "Callahan is a head case. He needs help."

"And you're a dead man," Calli stated clearly as he pointed his pistol at his faithless lover.

Diana crouched down beside Amalie, trying to shield the little girl's innocent eyes. Billix was so enthralled by the confrontation between the two men, he let his arm—the one holding the pistol pointing at Amalie— relax. The second Billix's gun moved away from his target, Diana saw her chance. She turned Amalie around, facing the direction farthest from the mayhem.

"Run," she whispered. "Run, Amalie!"

And Amalie—the most precocious, ask-a-million-questions-be-fore-following-directions five-year-old on the face of the planet—did exactly what her nanny asked her to do. For once. She ran, hugging her iguana—head up, tail down—until she disappeared behind some boulders in the trees. And she never looked back. And, for that, Diana was grateful. So very grateful. Because the little girl *didn't* see Billix grab her nanny's arm in a punishing grip as she, too, tried to run. And she *didn't* watch him jerk her nanny roughly against his side. Or wave his pistol in her face. Or hear his softly spoken words: "Not his time, bitch. You're not getting away this time."

Joey, however, saw everything. Including the way Blane and Devin moved to block his path as Amalie ran straight toward them. "Damn it!" he swore under his breath.

"Nobody makes a move without the rest of us," Blane said. "Remember?"

Joey gave a terse nod.

Devin reached out a long arm to grab Amalie mid-run and pull her behind the shielding rocks.

"Daddy! Mama Darcie! Uncle Joey! Auntie Grace and Uncle Blane!" Amalie's shrill voice rang through the trees before anyone could do anything to stop her.

"Well," Blane said, ruefully. "I guess they know we're here, now. So much for the element of surprise. But, thank God, Amalie is safe."

"And thanks to Diana," Grace murmured softly.

Joey's heart swelled with pride, even as he battled the overwhelming urge to do...what? What could he do that would possibly help Diana? *Something*, his heart told him. *Nothing*, said his head. And he had to agree with his head. His Diana was smart and selfless and so very, very brave. So far, she had managed to hold her own. Any protective impulse he allowed himself to follow might endanger the woman he loved. He forced himself to tamp down his impatience.

Joey leaned down behind the boulder to give the little girl a hug while her daddy resumed his position. Looking up, Joey saw Devin's eyes widen with surprise. "Holy..."

"What the..?" Blane sounded off at the same time.

Grace pointed to the clearing, tears shining in her eyes again, but this time for an entirely different reason. Darcie smiled at Joey, taking Amalie's hand so he could take a look.

He stood up to check the scene for himself. He blinked his eyes twice to make sure he really saw what he thought he saw. Calli was lying on the ground, held at gunpoint by Max—the traitor—who was, apparently, not a traitor at all.

"What...? How...?" Joey stuttered.

"Max," Devin said, amazement coloring his tone. "How did the man move so fast?"

"What did he do?" Joey looked from one to the other, desperate for information.

Grace put her brother out of his misery. "He kicked the gun out of Callahan's hand and took him to the ground. Then he tossed the gun to Rafe."

Blane snapped his fingers under Joey's nose. "Just like that." His relief was obvious.

Amalie, who had no idea what was going on, looked around their now not-so-hidden spot in the trees.

"Where's Nanny Di?" she asked, her little face drawn with worry. "I want Nanny Di!"

Darcie embraced her, rocking the little girl gently. "Hush," she crooned. "Nanny Di will be here in a little while."

For the first time since the ordeal began, Amalie burst into tears.

Well, Diana thought, she had finally gotten what she wanted. Billix Watson was pointing his gun at her instead of at Amalie. Diana's brilliant plan had worked. Too bad she didn't have the slightest idea what to do now. A loud moan brought her attention back to Calli, who was writhing on the ground, holding his arm.

"My arm," he wailed. "I think you broke my arm."

Max was leaning over him, the expression on his face more aggravation than concern. "Quit whining," he said. "You're not going to die."

But Calli only moaned louder.

"What a wimp," Billix said conversationally to Diana.

She didn't deign a reply. A strange calm had overtaken her body, fueled by the relief that Amalie was safe—thank God—and strengthened by the fact that Joey Finch wasn't very far away. She even managed a small smile when Max looked her way and winked.

"Ha," Billix laughed. "Cool twist, Rafe." He grinned at Diana. "I thought Max was Team Douglas for sure. The surprises just keep coming, don't they?"

Diana looked at him in amazement. Billix Watson had said more words in the last half hour than he had said the whole time Diana had known him. She thought about mentioning that but decided not to. The man was insane, she reminded herself. His emotions changed so quickly that any unsolicited comment might cause his deranged mind to become more unhinged than it already was, a risk she wasn't willing to take.

Max's unexpected move had come as a surprise. Even Douglas looked nonplussed. He glanced at Ian's unblinking visage, the first hint of worry clouding his eyes.

"I have a message for you, Douglas." Rafe's smile was brittle.

Douglas' eyes flew to his longtime nemesis. "And what would that be?" he asked, woodenly.

"*Calliope* told me to tell you hello," Rafe said. "In addition to all the other things she told me, some of them quite interesting."

"It's over, Douglas," Ian said, softly. "You may as well give up."

Douglas ignored those words, settling his attention on Max. "Curious," he said. "I thought you worked for me."

"I work for McCallum Industries," Max said, eyes—and gun—fixed on Calli.

"You know, Max," Douglas said, thoughtfully. "McCallum Industries doesn't have nearly the *incentive* plan that I do." He studied Max, searching for any sign the man was willing to turn to the dark side. "The perks, Max. So many perks…."

"I work for McCallum Industries," Max reiterated.

"Oh, give it up, Dad." Billix's words echoed through the trees.

CHAPTER FIFTY-FIVE

*D*iana gasped in shock. *"Dad?"* she whispered. "Douglas McCallum is your *dad*?" Was she the only person in the clearing who was surprised by the unexpected revelation? Apparently so, she thought, until she looked at Calli. Douglas' scorned lover was clearly shocked to the core.

"Yeah," Billix replied. "Douglas is my dad. My dear, old dad. Surprised?" He addressed the question to Diana.

She watched the rage overtake his visage the way a flood swallows a small town.

"He doesn't tell anybody he has a son. Not Douglas McCallum," Billix snarled. "Nope, he never talks about Billix Watson. He never even gave me his last name." His hands curled into fists, then uncurled. Only to repeat the process. "And do you know why?" he growled.

"Um...no," Diana whispered, afraid to move.

"Because I'm his *bastard*. His mistake. That's why. His dirty, little secret. If the world finds out about *me*, it will ruin his playboy image." Billix pointed to Ian across the clearing. "My uncle Ian...he's a bastard, too. And he's on the board of directors for the whole damn company. But not me. Not Billix Watson. All I get to be is—"

"Head Thug?" Rafe asked, helpfully.

"Yeah," Billix agreed. "I'm Head Thug, because I'm not good enough for him." His eyes narrowed into slits when he addressed Douglas. "But guess what, Dad? All that is going to change. Because *this* time I win. *You're* the one going to prison. Did you hear, Dad? Looks like Calliope turned herself into the feds. I wonder what she told them, don't you?" Billix glanced at Calli, who had raised himself to a sitting position. "And I bet ole Calli will have a lot to tell them, too. Won't you, Calli?"

"I'll tell them everything," Calli snarled, furiously, still cradling his useless arm in his lap. His hate-filled eyes turned on Douglas. "Everything you've ever done, Douglas. And I mean *everything*."

"I think he's going to tell them *everything*," Billix said to Diana, good humor restored. His triumphant gaze swept the clearing. "As for me, I'm going to Mexico. And Diana's coming with me," he added. "Now, I need somebody to get me a plane."

Nobody moved.

Billix waved his gun in Diana's face. "If I don't get a plane, I'll kill her."

"You're going to kill me, anyway," Diana said dispassionately. "Remember? I broke your nose."

Billix grinned. "Yeah, I'm going to kill you, but not before we have a little fun."

Diana's skin crawled at the thought.

"Billix." Douglas' voice rang through the clearing. "Stop this nonsense immediately." He started walking slowly toward his unbalanced son.

"Don't come any closer," Billix choked, poking the gun into Diana's side. "I'll kill her."

"No, you won't," Douglas said. "You're not going to kill this lovely, young lady."

Diana felt the gun against her side start to shake. What was Douglas doing? Shaky gun, shaky trigger finger. Was he *trying* to get her killed?

Billix's voice rose to a shrill wail as his shaking intensified. "I *will* kill her," he shouted. "And then I'll kill you, too."

"No, you won't," Douglas said, moving closer with each step. "That would be patricide, Billix. And killing your own father is no way to earn his respect."

To Diana's surprise, Billix accepted Douglas' words. He even appeared to ponder them. Douglas stopped about a foot away from his volatile son… and Diana. He reached out his right hand, motioning for Diana to come toward him. She shook her head, slightly. The gun was still poking in her side. She wasn't going anywhere.

Douglas sighed. "Billix, stop pointing the gun at Miss Merritt."

Billix looked confused. "But, Dad, without her I won't get to go to Mexico."

Douglas spoke plainly. "Son, you're not going to Mexico. With or without Miss Merritt. So, you may as well stop pointing the gun at her."

"But, Dad," Billix whined, his demeanor that of a ten-year-old, "I don't want to."

"Do it anyway," Douglas said in a voice that demanded compliance.

Billix's transformation from hardened criminal to sullen child was a change Diana had witnessed before. Nevertheless, she still couldn't believe it when the volatile man complied. The arm holding the gun dropped to Billix's side. When Douglas held out his right hand to Diana, she didn't hesitate to place hers in his cool grip. At that moment, she would have taken anyone's proffered hand, even a murderer's. She allowed Douglas to pull her behind him only vaguely aware of the efficient way his left hand gripped her arm as his right hand released her. She was too grateful for his timely intervention to wonder why.

With Diana stowed securely behind him, Douglas held out his free hand, palm up, to his pouting offspring. "Billix, give me the gun," he said, evenly.

Diana held her breath. What would Billix do?

Billix stomped his foot. "Oh, all right." He handed the gun to his father.

Diana didn't start breathing again until Douglas' fingers closed around the gun. Billix's eyes were oddly vacant as he waited for instructions.

"Now, go sit with Calli," Douglas said.

"But I don't like Calli," Billix whined.

"Calli doesn't like you, either, Billix," Douglas said. "Go ahead."

Billix kicked the dirt all the way across the clearing before throwing himself on the ground beside Calli. Rafe immediately turned his gun on Billix.

"He's never been…normal," Douglas said, close to Diana's ear. "Mood swings. Violent tendencies. Confusion. He's mentally unstable."

"And you exploited that," she accused with outrage. "Exploited his mental illness, instead of getting him the help he needed." She couldn't discern many physical similarities between father and son, other than slightly crooked noses—one for which she took credit. Only the aura of pure evil linked them forever in her mind. Because, like his son, Douglas McCallum made her skin crawl.

Douglas sighed again, his hot breath uncomfortably close to Diana's ear. "Yes," he said. "I suppose you're right. I have exploited him. And, now, Miss Merritt, I am afraid I must exploit you, as well."

With a vicious tug, he pulled Diana in front of him. Wrapping his arm securely around her waist, he pointed the gun at her head.

Diana was stunned. She couldn't move. Couldn't breathe. Couldn't think. No Nanny Di titles popped into her head. No annoying iguana offered advice. For the first time in her life, she was—for all intents and purposes—out of ideas. Her mind a vacuous chamber. A vast, frozen wasteland. Zero brain activity.

She had used every ounce of tenacity she possessed—and all her ready reserve—to make sure Amalie was safe. And now that the little girl was out of harm's way, it appeared that Diana's deep well of courage had run dry. Dry as dust. She couldn't even find one tiny drop of bravery to see a way forward.

Douglas' oily voice spoke in her ear, "Miss Merritt. It appears you and I are going on a little trip."

Diana wrinkled her nose. What was that smell? She knew that smell. Cigars? Motor oil? Molasses? Root beer? No, she decided. It was licorice. Douglas McCallum smelled like licorice. Diana hated licorice.

Douglas glanced at Rafe who was still pointing his gun at Billix. "Unless you want to watch the lovely Miss Merritt meet a tragic fate, you will call the airport and tell Hawkins to ready the plane for Mexico." He turned to Ian. "You can find someone to drive me to the airport, *brother*. No games or I'll blow her head off. Do it now. And remember, Rafe, Ian," he added, "I have nothing to lose."

Douglas' arm held Diana in a punishing grip. He whispered a licorice-scented litany of the depraved things he intended to do to her in her ear. But Diana ignored him. Her brain was busy describing Douglas with a *D. Detestable. Despicable. Devious. Disgusting. Diabolical. Distasteful. Dastardly. Dreadful.* The title came effortlessly, as easy as A, B, C, D.

Nanny Di and the Devil.

Douglas the Devil's endless—and endlessly disgusting—suggestions of how he would "entertain" her on their "little trip" showed no signs of abating. Since imagining herself at the Devil's mercy was not an option, Diana decided to think about Joey Finch.

Closing her eyes, she imagined him in her mind. His beautiful smile. His wickedly charming eyes. His style. His sense of humor. His wonderful laugh. And his voice. She wished she could hear him say *I love you* just one more time.

"Hey McCallum! Take me instead!"

Joey's voice? Well, Diana decided, it wasn't *I love you* but it was better than nothing. Or was it Joey's voice? Maybe she was hearing things.

She supposed she could always open her eyes to find out, but she decided against it. Douglas pulled her tighter against him. She felt the tension coiling in his nasty, licorice-smelling body.

"McCallum! Take me instead!"

Diana heard Joey's voice again. It was him, she decided. She was certain. Her imagination was good, but not *that* good. She opened one eye. Then the other. Joey was standing at the edge of the clearing, arms outstretched to show an absence of weapons. "Take me," he said. "Let Diana go."

"Joey, no!" Diana cried.

Douglas scoffed, his eyes burning with hatred. "Young Finch."

"McCallum," Joey replied. "Let Diana go."

Douglas loosened his arm, putting a little distance between himself and his captive. His insolent gaze swept Diana from head to toe. "I don't think so, Finch. I've been looking forward to getting to *know* your Diana. And I will *know* her. Every delectable inch."

Diana couldn't prevent a shiver of disgust at his words. The way Douglas said *know* left nothing to the imagination. Joey growled, low in his throat. His hands fisted at his side.

Douglas smiled, obviously pleased with the power he held over Joey. "You're just like your father, Finch. Rushing to the rescue. Such righteousness. Such noble intentions. Why should I want a paragon like you when I can have this tempting morsel?"

Joey struggled against the revulsion pulsing through him. "Because you hate my father and my mother," he said, steadily. "What better revenge than to take their only son?"

"Joey, no!" Diana gasped again as Douglas' fingers dug into her upper arm. She struggled against his side until he jerked her against him, his arm like iron.

Douglas considered Joey's request for a moment. "It's true that I hate your father," he said. "But your mother?" He shook his head, his eyes full of hunger. "No. Your mother is an—as yet—untried delicacy." He laughed, enjoying the expression of pure fury on Joey's face. "Miss Merritt is going with me," he purred. "Alone. But I like your idea of revenge, young Finch. So much, in fact, that I think I'll just kill you now."

He swung the pistol in Joey's direction.

Two shots rang out.

CHAPTER FIFTY-SIX

*D*iana was falling. Her hands—grasping at air. Her arms—flailing for purchase. Her balance—hopelessly lost. She hit the ground—*hard*—smacking the side of her head in the process. She lurched to her feet only to fall again as her knees refused to support her. She tried to crawl forward. Time came to a halt. Her mind focused on one goal. She had to get to Joey so she could stop the blood before he saw it. Because if he did, he would pass out. And if he passed out, she might not get to tell him goodbye.

A sob ripped from her throat as the clearing exploded with movement. Black-clad men and women poured from the trees like ants at a picnic. Diana was surrounded, people rushing by her on all sides. Her desperation grew. The people in black...they were blocking her view. She couldn't see. *Stand up*, she told herself. She had to stand up. She had to find Joey.

Strong arms grabbed her waist from behind, pulling her to her feet. "No!" she screamed. "Let me go!" She didn't have time to be a prisoner again. She had to get to Joey. But her screams only blended into the giant wave of sound that began immediately after the final gunshot and continued to swell over the clearing.

Plastered against what might as well be a brick wall, she could finally see over the antlike people swarming around Douglas the Devil, who was—for some reason—lying on the ground. Perhaps the ants had tackled him while she wasn't watching...after he shot Joey. She braced herself for the sight of the love of her life collapsed on the dirt, bleeding from double gunshot wounds. But he wasn't there. Completely panicked, her eyes scanned the ground in the area where she last saw Joey. Where was he? Where had they taken him?

Joey didn't remember crossing the space that separated him from Diana, so intent was he on reaching her. He wasn't in time to stop her fall, the first or the second one. But he did manage to steady her waist and pull her to her feet. His arms encircled her in a fierce embrace. He could feel her shaking and hear her sobs. But at that moment, he was incapable of speech. Incapable of action. Incapable of anything except savoring the feel of her body in his arms.

The clearing quickly filled with DEA and FBI agents, a healthy contingent of local law enforcement, and numerous EMTs. Joey noted five individuals speaking with Rafe. They seemed to be in deep conversation with him though their uniforms did not display any identifying insignia. The distinguished man had to stop talking several times to shake hands with numerous agents as they approached, all of whom seemed eager to congratulate him. Max was still standing watch over Calli as the EMTs worked to stabilize Douglas' now ex-lover's broken arm. Billix Watson was already cuffed, apparently waiting to be taken into custody. His eyes traveled between the agents surrounding Douglas and those gathered around Calli. The expression on his face could only be called triumphant. Joey assumed Billix was celebrating victory somewhere in his dark and twisted mind.

Joey tightened his arms around Diana a little more, surprised to feel her struggle. He forced himself to relax his hold, unwilling to let her go just yet. Her struggles only increased. That's when he realized something was wrong. She was fighting in earnest. And she was fighting *him*. He grabbed her from the back, he remembered. She hadn't seen his face. And he hadn't spoken. He thought she was weeping with joy and relief, but he was wrong.

Diana wasn't emotional. She was terrified.

She fought—twisting and turning—to break free from the unwelcome embrace. But to no avail. Tears of frustration ran down her face unheeded.

"Let me go," she begged. "I have to find him…Let me go."

"Diana, hush," said Joey, struggling to make his voice soothing and calm. "It's me, love. I've got you. I'm right here."

The arms wrapping around Diana tightened, but not cruelly. She felt…cherished. Treasured. Loved. And only one man had ever made her feel that way. She spun in his arms to face him. "Joey," she squealed. "Oh, thank God!" She was crying and laughing at the same time.

Diana threw her arms around his neck, holding him every bit as tightly as he had been holding her. She wanted to twine herself around him like a vine and never let go. She felt his heartbeat, strong and regular. Felt his abdomen expand and contract with his breathing. He was warm—even though the outside temperature was steadily dropping—and flushed. Her mind spun to a halt. Flushed? Why was he flushed? Was he injured? Had no one thought to ask? How was it possible for both bullets to miss him at such close range? Was he, even now, slowly bleeding to death?

Diana shoved herself out of his arms. She frantically ran her hands over his shoulders and arms. "Diana," he asked, bemused. "What are you doing?"

She didn't answer, only continued her exploration. When she ran her hands over his chest, he captured them with his own. "Diana," he said, gently. "What are you doing?"

"I'm checking to make sure you weren't shot," she said, eyes full of worry. She tried to tug her hands away.

Joey's eyes widened. She didn't know what had happened. She thought...

"Diana," he said. "Douglas didn't shoot me. He didn't shoot at all."

Her face clouded with confusion. "But I heard the shots."

Before he could explain an EMT placed a blanket around Diana's shoulders, urging her to sit on the ground. She complied, with Joey's assistance. Another, much younger EMT joined them and examined Diana briefly. Apart from a few bruises and a small goose egg on the side of her head, Diana was pronounced no worse for her ordeal. She was advised to take Tylenol for her headache and get lots of rest.

As Joey helped Diana to her feet, movement on the other side of the burned-out house caught her eye. Several figures—dressed in dark colors and lacking insignias—emerged from the eastern side of the house. *Spies,* Diana thought. *Real spies.* They looked just like she assumed they would. Low-key. Subdued. Almost invisible, even in the late afternoon light.

A few seconds later, Alina walked out of the trees, her appearance anything but subdued. Diana looked at Blane's aunt in amazement. Her lovely dress was pristine. She may as well be stepping out of McCallum Industries' new headquarters instead of a thicket of trees in the middle of nowhere. Her high-heel pumps were undamaged. Her elegant coiffure boasted no strands of hair out of place. Not even one.

Diana glanced down at her own sorry-looking attire. Her dress was torn in several places, including a sleeve that was barely hanging on by a thread. Her boots were scuffed beyond repair. She raised a hand to her hair, unsurprised to find that it had escaped most of her hairpins. She imagined she resembled some unhinged escapee from a horror movie. "How?" Diana demanded. "How can Alina look like that?"

Joey laughed at her expression. "Oh, Diana," he teased. "You look fine, too, except for a little dirt right here…." He brushed a hand down the side of her face. "But don't worry about that," he continued, helpfully. "It matches the dirt on your—"

"There she is," came the excited voice of the younger EMT, who was standing behind them. "That's the assassin."

The older EMT chided her partner, "Calm down, CJ, and don't point."

"But she's beau-ti-ful," the young man said in awe. "And, besides, I've never seen an assassin before."

"She prefers the term 'sharpshooter.' " The words popped out of Joey's mouth unbidden. He glanced at Diana, who struggled not to laugh.

"Sharpshooter, then," CJ amended. He was, apparently, an agreeable fellow. "But, Sue, she missed," he said. "I didn't think assass…I mean sharp-shooters ever missed."

Diana's eyes widened as everything came into focus. She mouthed the name, *Alina* to Joey, who nodded.

"She didn't miss, CJ," Sue replied. "She shot the gun out of McCallum's hand with the first shot and removed the top part of his ear with the second. Neither of those shots was a miss."

"Oh." CJ was obviously impressed.

Sue's sigh was audible. "The captain is waving us over. Come on. And try to stop staring."

"But, Sue," CJ protested. "Why didn't she kill him when she had the chance?"

The young man's voice died away with his question still unanswered.

"Nanny Di! Nanny Di!"

Amalie rushed into the clearing, throwing herself into her nanny's arms. Diana hugged the little girl, shedding a few grateful tears. Blane and

Devin appeared next, helping Grace and Darcie navigate the prickly pine-cones and sharp sticks in the clearing: strangely enough, the sisters were shoeless. Both were wearing what looked like men's socks.

Devin's arms surrounded Diana and Amalie. "Thank you, Diana," he said, gruffly. "Thank you for saving my daughter."

Diana could only nod as she hugged him back, her throat tight with emotion. She briefly laid her head on the shoulder of the man she had known all her life. He was so much more than her boss. Or just her cousin. Devin was her dear, dear friend and she loved him like a brother.

Joey was having similar trouble keeping his feelings in check under the emotional onslaught of sisters. It wasn't often he indulged in sentiment with his siblings. Usually, he joked and teased his way out of poignant moments. But Grace and Darcie's touching display left him no recourse but to hold them tightly for a few moments. His uncharacteristic silence spoke volumes.

A few moments later, Diana and Amalie were enveloped in a double embrace by Grace and Darcie while Joey exchanged bear hugs with Blane and Devin. With much laughing and a few tears, the group stepped apart to survey each other. Diana was somewhat gratified to see that Darcie and Grace looked as dirty and rumpled as she did. Of course, she decided, a dirty and rumpled Darcie was still more beautiful than a regular un-dirty—clean?—and unrumpled ordinary person. Diana glanced again at the sisters' feet. "Why are you wearing—"

"Our heels were too noisy," Grace volunteered. "And the pine needles hurt our feet."

Darcie grinned. "So, Blane and Devin selflessly donated their socks before we walked over here. We're starting a new trend." She studied her foot, lifting it and turning it from side to side. "What do you think?"

Joey pretended to consider it. "Hmm. I don't think it'll catch on."

Darcie tossed her head. "You're just jealous."

"Ha," he said, grinning. "I am definitely *not* jealous." He was, how-ever, enjoying the banter running through the group. It felt...normal. And he was ready for that.

"Nanny Di," Amalie squealed. "Auntie Grace says we're having cake for dinner!"

Diana settled the little girl on her hip. "Cake?" she repeated. "For dinner?"

Amalie nodded happily. "Uh-huh! She said we could eat *anything* I want. And I want cake!"

Darcie glared at her sister. "So says the 'fun' aunt."

Grace simply shrugged, her green eyes dancing with mischief.

Joey saw his chance to be a hero. "*Anything* you want?" he asked Amalie in exaggerated surprise. "I can't believe you didn't suggest pizza."

The little girl's mouth fell open. "Pizza?" she squealed. "Oh, Auntie Grace, Mama Darcie, can I change my choice?"

Devin sighed, shaking his head sadly. "And we"—indicating Blane along with himself—"are irrelevant to this momentous decision," he said, mournfully.

Grace replied to Amalie before Darcie could open her mouth. "If you want pizza, 'Malie, then pizza it is."

Darcie grinned, approvingly. "A much better choice. Thank you, Uncle Joey. And, you, too, Auntie *Fun*."

"Hurray!" Amalie yelled. "I love pizza. And Iggy loves..." She looked around, obviously expecting to find the wayward iguana somewhere in sight. She gasped dramatically. "Oh, no! I buried Iggy under the leaves, and I don't remember where." Her lower lip started to tremble.

Now, it was Diana's turn to save the day. "Track my phone," she said. "When you find it, you'll find Iggy."

"Are you telling me that ridiculous iguana swallowed your phone again?" Blane asked, amusement lighting his features.

Joey raised his eyebrows. "That's *Mr.* Ridiculous Iguana to you," he said. "Iggy's genius plan led us to Diana and Amalie."

Blane nodded thoughtfully. "True. Iggy is pretty clever. Maybe I should offer him a position at McCallum Industries."

Amalie giggled. "You're silly, Uncle Blane. Iggy doesn't need a job."

"Yeah," Devin added. "He's independently wealthy. Believe me."

"Maybe you can offer him Douglas' job," Joey suggested.

"Now that's a great idea." Blane clapped his best friend on the back enthusiastically.

"Da-ddy!" Amalie wailed. "Iggy's getting cold. And hungry." The little girl hopped up and down impatiently. "Track him, Daddy," she urged Devin. "Track Iggy so we can find him and get pizza!"

"Please," Darcie and Diana said at the same time.

"Please, track Iggy, Daddy," the little girl begged.

Devin grinned at Blane. "And suddenly I'm important again." He pulled out his phone. "Come on, 'Malie. Let's go find him." He held out his hand to Amalie. Darcie quickly took the little girl's hand on the other side.

"Hurray!" Amalie yelled, skipping between her father and her future stepmother.

Diana envied the little girl. The mention of pizza and a phone-eating iguana had erased all evidence of the afternoon's trauma. At least, on the outside. She could only pray there were no permanent scars on the inside.

From across the clearing, Rafe motioned for Blane to join him. He complied, putting an arm around Grace. "And now for the questions," he sighed. "You better get ready, too, Diana."

"I know." She sighed. "Don't tell Rafe, but I think I'd prefer my questions from the Trio of Doom."

The light was fading by the time the questioning ended. Calli and Billix had already been removed from the clearing, leaving only a defiant and belligerent Douglas McCallum awaiting transport. He was propped—handcuffed and shackled—against the corner of the ruined farmhouse a few yards from the path leading to Max's car. Rafe had arranged for Blane to drive the car back to Heart's Ease since he and Max would be riding with Ian and Alina. The mysterious foursome had to attend to "other obligations," according to Rafe. Joey and Diana would ride back to Heart's Ease with Blane and Grace. Devin, Darcie, and Amalie had already left in Blane's Range Rover. They were in charge of the pizza.

The local law enforcement and EMTs vacated the clearing first, followed by the DEA and FBI agents. Then all but six of the darkly clad individuals Joey dubbed "Nanny Di's spies" made their exit.

"Looks like Blane and Grace are finished," Joey pointed out. "It must be time to go."

Diana sighed. She had hoped that Douglas would be removed from the area before she had to face the horrible man again. *Drat.* Joey was right. Blane and Grace were crossing the clearing with Ian and Alina. It was time for them to leave. And since no one had seen fit to move the heinous devil beside the path, Diana was going to have to walk right by him. Her lungs seized with fear. The longer she was in Douglas' presence, the more repulsed she was by his aura of evil. And Douglas thought Billix wasn't normal? Ha, Diana thought, look who's talking. There was nothing normal about Douglas McCallum either.

Try as she might, Diana couldn't stop dwelling on the day she discovered Mallory's body. She had always thought Mallory cold, narcissistic, and shallow. But those traits paled when compared to the callous disregard for life that emanated from Douglas. He wore a mantle of cruelty like the ruthless tyrant that he was. Unrepentantly, and without mercy. Why had Mallory been so enamored of the man? Diana wondered for the hundredth time.

Blane spoke first, drawing her from her reverie. "We're finished with questions for now," he said, relief evident in his voice. "Are you two ready to go home?"

Joey nodded. "Absolutely. Diana needs to warm up."

"And you need pizza," Grace said, smiling at her always-hungry brother. She hugged Diana. "How are you holding up, honey?"

Before Diana could answer the kind inquiry, Douglas' arrogant voice rang out, demanding a response. "Alina!"

Alina approached her brother-in-law, stopping about two feet in front of him. "Yes?" she asked, politely.

Douglas smiled. His white teeth and the white bandage around the top part of his head contrasted eerily with his flushed face. "Why didn't you kill me?" he asked. "I know you didn't miss. You're too damn skilled for that. Can it be that you have"—he glanced at his half brother, standing about five feet away—"feelings for me?"

"*I* have feelings for you, *brother*," Ian said, his pose casual and relaxed despite his deliberate sarcasm. "All bad."

Douglas' eyes glittered. "Touché, *brother*." His eyes swept Alina's slim form hungrily. "Perhaps *she* desires me. Perhaps she's *always* desired me...." Douglas all but purred the words. "Why didn't you kill me, *Alina*?" He seemed to savor her name on his tongue. Diana shivered in disgust, wrapping the blanket closer around her.

"Don't flatter yourself, Douglas." Alina's voice oozed with disdain. "Fergus is the only reason I didn't kill you," she said.

Douglas couldn't hide his surprise. "My father?"

She smiled then. "I suspect it will be easier for Fergus to think of you rotting in jail than burning in hell." Her strange accent was particularly strong. "But don't worry, Douglas," she continued, "I know you'll get there eventually." With those parting words she turned her back to rejoin Rafe and his "friends."

Douglas' lust-filled gaze followed her until Ian spoke. "Don't even think about it, *brother*."

Douglas' eyes flew to his half brother's. What he saw in their depths quickly cooled his ardor. He paled slightly, averting his gaze. After a few seconds, Ian walked away without another word.

Blane took Grace's hand in his, tugging her behind him. His brisk pace revealed his intent to walk right by his uncle until Douglas spoke. The burning mania—what Diana felt sure was insanity—had disappeared from the man's eyes. For the time being.

Douglas' words were rational; his tone businesslike. "Go ahead and notify our lawyers, Blane," he said, acting as if such a request was perfectly reasonable. "I need to get my defense preparations underway as soon as possible. Before this debacle affects our stock prices."

Blane stopped so abruptly that Grace almost plowed into his back. He reached out his other hand to steady her before facing his uncle. "I'm sorry. Did you say something about lawyers?" He spoke slowly, the way he would address a small child. A small child who wasn't very smart.

Douglas' lip curled in irritation. "It's in my contract, Blane. You know that as well as I do," he almost snarled. "As an executive of McCallum Industries, I have full access to our legal department. So, tell your one-eyed head of legal to get his head out of his ass and start working on my defense immediately. And, Blane..." he added harshly. "Stop being such a sniveling son of a bitch."

Grace's eyes widened, whether from amazement or outrage was difficult to tell. But Blane didn't even flinch. Douglas had long since lost the ability to hurt his nephew. "I'm sorry, *Uncle*," he said with great dignity. "I'm afraid that isn't possible."

Douglas' restraint slipped a bit further. "What the hell are you talking about? My contract clearly states that as long as I am employed by—"

"But that's the problem." Blane was quick to interrupt what was sure to be an unnecessary tirade. He sighed, pityingly. "*You* don't understand, do you, *Uncle*? Well, let me make it easy for you. *You* don't get any legal help from McCallum Industries because *you*, Douglas McCallum, are no longer employed by McCallum Industries."

Douglas frowned in confusion. "What do you mean I'm no longer employed by McCallum Industries? What the hell are you talking about?"

"Haven't you figured it out yet? It's over, *Uncle*." Blane paused before delivering the words he had waited years to say. "*You. Are. Fired.*"

Without waiting for a reply, Blane—with Grace at his side—walked down the path and away from the hatred that contorted the visage of Douglas McCallum, former executive of McCallum Industries. The enraged man watched his last chance for salvation disappear into the trees before turning his venom on the nearest possible victims: Diana and Joey.

"I harbor one regret where you're concerned, Miss Merritt," he taunted. "Well, maybe two. Number one: I'm sorry I didn't shoot young Finch sooner."

Joey didn't react. He met the man's eyes with unconcealed loathing.

Douglas continued, his own eyes glittering with lust. "And number two: I'm sorry, Miss Merritt, that I didn't get to make your last moments... memorable."

Diana refused to look at his face. If eyes were truly the windows to the soul, she didn't want to delve too closely for fear of what she would see. How appropriate for the pitiless demon to spend his last moments of freedom propped against the burned-out wreckage of a long-ago fire. He had taken the life of Mallory—and who knew how many others—as surely as the flames had snuffed the life's blood from the house. And Diana knew—with a certainty that defied logic—he would have killed her, too, if not for the man standing beside her.

She was suddenly as cold as ice. "I don't think I can walk by him," she whispered to Joey, keeping her focus on the ground at her feet.

"Be brave, Nanny Di," Joey said, softly.

Her eyes flew to the face of her stalwart, lionhearted knight in shining armor. He had risked everything to save her. The warmth of the love shining in his eyes melted every frozen shard of fear that remained.

The smile that illuminated her lovely face was all for Joey. And it nearly took his breath. His heart settled into a comfortable rhythm for the first time since Diana disappeared through the doors of McCallum Industries. For reasons he still couldn't fathom this strong, resilient woman loved him back. And he intended to spend the rest of his life making her very glad she did.

Ignoring the ceaseless taunts coming from the despicable mouth of Mallory's killer, Diana and Joey made their escape. She never even glanced at the fiend-formerly-known-as-Douglas-McCallum as she and Joey left the clearing behind. Instead, she kept her hand securely clasped in the hand of the man who also held her heart.

EPILOGUE

Honeysuckle Creek
Six months later

*V*ienna Lambert flipped the sign on the door to *"Closed."* She turned around, a beaming smile on her face. "I simply can't thank you enough, Diana," she said. "Having your book launch at Scribbler's is the best thing that has ever happened to this bookstore."

Diana laughed. "Oh, I don't know about that." Privately, however, she was amazed at the turnout. The two one-hour sessions originally planned had become three. And every copy of *Reforming the Rascally Rake* had been sold. She looked around the bookstore's rows of well-stocked shelves. "Your bookstore is wonderful, Vienna. Scribbler's is such a welcoming place for independent authors trying to get started."

A quick knock put an end to their mutual admiration society. Blane's face peered behind the glass in the door, just visible behind Vienna's shoulder. Devin and Amalie peeked through the bookstore's large front window.

"Sorry about the fingerprints," Darcie said after Vienna unlocked the door to let the voyeurs in.

Vienna laughed good-naturedly. "Don't worry about Amalie. I have to clean little fingerprints off the glass multiple times a day."

"I was talking about Devin," Darcie quipped as Blane and the guilty party breezed through the door. They were followed by Amalie, her stuffed iguana tucked securely under her arm. Without a word, the giggling little girl headed straight to the children's section, her personal idea of heaven.

"I'm going to run out and get some lunch," Vienna said. "Stay as long as you like. Just make sure the door locks behind you when you leave. Thanks again, Diana." With a smile and a wave, she was gone.

"Did I hear my lovely wife say my name?" Devin asked, giving Darcie a quick kiss. The newlyweds had exchanged vows a few days before Christmas.

The new Mrs. Merritt batted her eyes flirtatiously. "Wouldn't *you* like to know?"

Joey wandered out of the store's Current Events section just in time to witness Devin and Darcie's display.

"Disgusting, aren't they?" Blane asked, indicating the pair with his head.

Joey slid his arm around Diana's waist, bumping his hip against hers. "Yep," Joey agreed. "But I guess it's understandable. You know how newlyweds are."

"Oh yeah." Darcie rolled her eyes. "Devin and I are just completely out of control. Any minute now we might try to do something really wild, like hold hands."

The men laughed, appreciating her sarcasm.

"How's Gracie doing?" Blane asked. "Any better?"

Darcie motioned to a long sofa near the magazines. Grace was reclining on the cushions, her complexion almost as green as the pillows behind her head. She waved weakly with one hand. Darcie gestured to the bag in Blane's hand. "I hope you got the biggest box. I think you're going to need it."

Blane triumphantly held up a giant box of YoHoHo Yogurt Bars, the only remedy they had found to ease Grace's first trimester morning sickness. "Don't worry, Gracie," Blane said, encouragingly. "This was the last box at the market, but I'll buy the company if I have to."

It was Devin's turn to raise his eyes to the ceiling. "You *already* bought the company," he pointed out helpfully. "Last quarter. Now, who's out of control?"

Blane ignored him, totally focused on caring for his pregnant wife. In less than a minute, she held a yogurt bar in each hand. Within five minutes, her complexion had returned to normal. She blew out a relieved breath, sitting up on the sofa. "I don't know why these yogurt bars help, but they do." She put the wooden sticks from the bars inside their wrappers. "I'm glad you bought the company," she said to Blane before sticking her tongue out at Devin. She stood up, carefully toddling over to her husband.

Blane smiled. "I bought a cooler, too, and some ice, so we can take them with us."

"Where are you going?" Diana asked with interest.

Well, hell. Joey almost said the words aloud. He had worked so hard to keep his plan a secret from Diana. They all had. He would have been supremely annoyed at Blane's slip if his friend hadn't looked so apologetic. He obviously regretted his words.

But Grace—the queen of handling awkward situations with, well... *grace*—effortlessly covered for her husband. "Everywhere," she said, dramatically. "We will take that cooler everywhere. I refuse to get into the car without it until after the baby is born." Her response didn't exactly answer Diana's question, but it had the desired effect.

Diana laughed delightedly at her theatrical prattle. The others quickly joined in. And if their laughter was a little strained, Joey's lovely authoress didn't seem to notice. Perhaps, he surmised, the excitement of a very successful book launch kept the usually perceptive redhead from feeling the undercurrents of secrecy swirling around her. Whatever the reason, he was thankful. Diana knew about their trip to the Acorn Knob Inn, of course. Her bags were already stowed alongside his in the back of his truck. But, he thought, with great satisfaction, Diana didn't know *everything* about the trip.

She *didn't* know that, for sentimental reasons, he intended to take the dreaded access road up to the inn. And she *didn't* know that most of her family and his family would arrive at the inn a few hours ahead of them to get everything ready for his surprise. She *didn't* know that Blane, Grace, Devin, Darcie, and Amalie would be headed to the inn as soon as they left the bookstore, hence Blane's need for the cooler. And she also *didn't* know that Joey had an engagement ring currently burning a hole in his pocket. But best of all, Diana *didn't* know that, in a few hours, Joey Finch—former one and done—was going to drop to one knee and ask Diana Merritt to be his wife.

Keeping his secret from the woman who knew him best had been an enormous undertaking. Thanks to his friends and family, he was very close to success. And he had no intention of spoiling his surprise now.

"Maybe Gracie should be the new spokesperson for YoHoHo Yogurt Bars," Joey suggested, hoping for a change of subject.

Devin jumped on that suggestion. "Arr-guably, the best idea of the day. Don't you think so, Darr-cie Finch?" His pirate-speak produced more laughter all around.

"Don't you mean Darr-cie Merritt?" his sassy bride asked.

"Arr-gh, Darr-cie Merritt," Devin groaned in mock defeat. "Arr-e you going to run me through?" he asked as Amalie popped out from behind the nearest bookcase.

"Oh, Daddy!" she giggled. "You're so funny." She turned to Darcie. "Mama, don't you think Daddy is funny?" She started calling Darcie "Mama," as soon as the pastor announced that Devin and Darcie were husband and wife. And Amalie's new mama loved it.

Darcie winked at the little girl. "You're right, Amalie. Your daddy is so funny that sometimes even I can't believe it." She blew a kiss to her hilarious spouse.

Devin grinned back good-naturedly. "I'll take that as a compliment."

"You only have two more weeks until your second trimester, Gracie," Diana said, encouragingly. "I'm sure you'll feel much better soon."

Joey piped in with his own words of wisdom. "I bet you're having a girl, Gracie. Everybody knows girls make you sick."

Darcie punched her brother in the arm.

"See?" Joey said, rubbing his stinging appendage. "Case in point."

Amalie hopped up and down, Iggy's tail bouncing along with her. "Girls don't make you sick, Uncle Joey!" she squealed. "Boys do! Boys are nasty! Except for Daddy!"

"Good girl," Devin muttered approvingly, much to Joey's amusement.

Grace leaned on Blane's arm. "I'm ready to go, if you are," she said, before smiling at Diana. "We're so happy for you, Diana. And I cannot wait to read *Reforming the Rascally Rake*."

"Me either," Darcie chimed in. "I'm going to start reading *tonight*." Her eyes gleamed with mischief as she glanced at her brother. "Does the story happen to be based on fact, by chance?"

Joey's eyes met Diana's. A delicate flush of peach was already climbing toward her temples.

"Of course it's based on fact," Joey said. "The main character is a fencing expert. You're all aware of my impressive fencing skills, aren't you?"

Blane burst out laughing. "You, with a sword?"

"God help us all," Devin added, waving his arm in imitation of Joey's supposed prowess.

Grace and Darcie giggled while Amalie pretended to fight her daddy with her own imaginary sword.

Diana sent Joey a wink of appreciation for his clever diversion. What was fact and what was fiction in her novel? Diana knew, but she had no intention of telling.

A few minutes later, Blane and Grace said their goodbyes; they were followed by Devin, Darcie, and Amalie. Joey watched them go, pleased that his secret was still intact. He pulled Diana into his arms for a slow, hot kiss. "Mmm," Diana sighed, her complexion deepening to a lovely shade of peach.

Joey took a leisurely minute to nibble on the sensitive spot under Diana's earlobe. "Gonna be a long, hot night at the Acorn Knob Inn," he murmured, pleased when Diana shivered in his arms.

She pulled back to look into his eyes, a secretive smile floating on her lips. "Let me get my tote bag," she said.

"Your ginormous, magical tote bag?" Joey asked, enjoying that smile.

"Of course," she said. "We have to take along some protection against the man-eating strangers, don't we?" With a flirtatious wink, she headed to the back of the store.

Joey made sure the door of Scribbler's was securely locked behind them before broaching his question. "So, what are we going to call our next book?" he asked. They strolled leisurely across Honeysuckle Creek Park. Joey intended to take his time with every part of their journey, beginning with a circuitous route to his truck.

Diana glanced at him in surprise. "*Our* next book?" she asked in pretend outrage, her dark gray eyes shooting sparks.

"*Our* next book," Joey agreed. "That's what I said."

To his delight, Diana stopped walking. "Seriously?"

Joey pretended to misunderstand. "Seriously. That's exactly what I said. Our next book."

Planting her hands on her hips, she regarded him in mock dismay. "I don't recall, Mr. Finch, that we have jointly written *our* first book.

Joey smiled, agreeably. "Well, I wasn't referring to the *writing* part," he said. "That part, Miss Merritt, is up to you. Duh."

"For your information, Mr. Finch, the book *is* the writing part. What else is there?" she asked.

Joey's smile stretched into a grin. "The *living* part," he explained. "If you're going to continue writing these autobiographical novels, you're going to have to have someone to autobiography with. That's me."

"Oh, that's you, is it?" Diana's eyes sparkled, even as she laughed at his nonsense.

"Uh-huh," Joey said, giving her a quick kiss on the cheek. The less than satisfying show of affection was a far cry from tumbling her onto the grass and ravishing her, the way he wanted. *Damn,* Joey thought, as every muscle in his body tightened. They were in the middle of Honeysuckle Creek Park. *And* Diana would probably kill him.

Maybe.

Or maybe not.

She knew better than anyone the indisputable fact that reformed rakes—in addition to making the best husbands—reverted to their rascally tendencies from time to time. But only with their own lovely ladies. Ezekiel would attest to that. Besides, it would make a great addition to Diana's next novel.

She was watching him. A bemused expression on her face. A dreamy smile on her lips. Who knew what she was imagining?

Oh, what the hell. Unable to resist the call of his siren, Joey pulled her into his arms and kissed her. In the middle of Honeysuckle Creek Park. He kissed her until the sound of whistling and clapping cut into their consciousness. Breathless and flustered, they raised their heads to discover some of the geriatric crowd from the Honeysuckle Creek Retirement Community applauding enthusiastically. Several of the fine old gentlemen were giving them a thumbs-up.

Joey and Diana continued their stroll as if nothing untoward had occurred. Neither, however, seemed able—or willing—to wipe the blissful smiles from their faces. Joey knew exactly what the title of their next book would be. And he was going to spend the rest of his life helping Diana write the story:

Nanny Di and the Happily Ever After.

THE END

ABOUT THE AUTHOR

*M*acee McNeill is a retired high school teacher who happily traded grading papers for writing novels. She lives on a large lake in North Carolina with her husband and two overly enthusiastic poodles. She adores spending time with her husband, their two grown sons, and their families. When she isn't writing, Macee sings harmony, bakes pound cakes and pies, runs, and cheers for the University of North Carolina at Chapel Hill, her alma mater.